more . . .

ALSO BY C.J. CHERRYH

CYTEEN*
RIMRUNNERS
HEAVY TIME
HELLBURNER
TRIPOINT
RIDER AT THE GATE
CLOUD'S RIDER

Published by
Warner Books

*Winner of the Hugo Award for Best Novel

FINITY'S END

C.J.CHERRYH

FINITY'S END

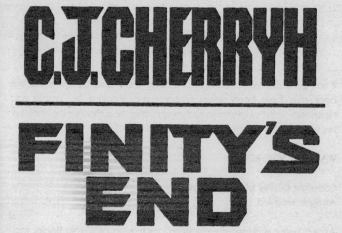

ASPECT®

WARNER BOOKS

A Time Warner Company

WARNER BOOKS EDITION

Aspect name and logo are registered trademarks of Warner Books, Inc.

Cover design by Don Puckey
Cover illustration by Steve Youll

Warner Books, Inc.
1271 Avenue of the Americas
New York, NY 10020

Visit our Web site at
http://warnerbooks.com

A Time Warner Company

Printed in the United States of America

Originally published in hardcover by Warner Books.
First Printed in Paperback: August, 1998

10 9 8 7 6 5 4 3 2 1

Chapter

I

A system traffic monitor screen showed a blip where none had existed in this solar system. The wavefront of presence which had begun far, far out above the star spoke a series of numbers to a computer in Pell Central and a name flashed to displays throughout the room.

The master display, hanging two meters wide above the rows of traffic control workstations, simultaneously flashed up the same name in glowing green.

Finity's End had come back to Pell.

"Alert the stationmaster," the master tech said, and the message flashed through Pell Station's central paging system.

By that time the signal, coming in from the jump range buoy at the speed of light, was four hours old. The Pell Central computers generated a predicted course based on data changing by the split second, a path outlined in ordinary green. The first projection supposed an abrupt drop in velocity well out from Pell's Star.

Suddenly the huge display changed, bloomed with colors from red to blue, based on the last three courses and velocities that ship had used coming into Pell on that vector . . . and projected into the sun.

It made a bright, broad display across the ordinarily routine, direct-path listings. It alarmed the newest technicians and sent hands reaching toward reset toggles. Merchanters didn't dive that close, that fast, toward the sun.

That ship had. Once. Years ago. That fact was still in the computer record and no one had purged it from files.

But the War was in the past. The navigational buoy, in its lonely position above the star, noted all arrivals in the entry range, and the information it sent to Pell Station showed no other blips attending the ship. *Finity's End* came alone, this time, and the master tech calmly informed the junior technicians that the pattern they saw was no malfunction, but no reason for alarm, either.

The buoy's information, incoming in those few seconds, was now a little further advanced. It had already excluded some predictions, and the automated computer displays continued to change as the buoy tracked that presence toward the sun—four hours ago.

By now, in realtime and realspace, the oldest of all working merchanters had either blown off excess V and set its general course for Pell, or something was direly wrong. Only the robot observer was in a position to have seen the ship's entry, and second by second the brightly colored fan of possibility on the boards dimmed as more and more of that remote-observer data came in. The fan of projection shrank, and eventually excluded the sun.

The screen was far less colorful and the technicians were far less anxious ten minutes further on, when the stationmaster walked in to survey the situation.

By now a message would be on its way from the ship to the station, granted that the tamer projections on the displays were true.

The captain of the oldest merchanter ship still operating would be, predictably, saluting the Pell stationmaster who, with his help, had founded the Alliance. The powers that dominated a third of human presence in the universe were about to meet.

But stationmaster Elene Quen, also predictably, strode to a com-tech's workstation and took up a microphone before any such lightspeed message could reach her.

"*Finity's End,* this is Quen at Pell. Welcome in. What brings us the honor?"

As far as the eye could see, Old River ran.

As far as the eye could see, thickets stood gray-green and blooming with white flowers beneath a perpetually clouded heaven.

Just beyond those thickets, huge log frames lay in squares on the earth, waiting for the floods to come—and downers were at work intermittent with play.

Hisa was the name they called themselves. Brown-furred and naked but for the strings of ornament and fur about necks and waists, they splashed cheerfully through the dozen log-bounded paddies that were already flooded. In broad, generous casts, they strewed the heavy, sinking grain.

Humans had watched this activity year upon year upon year of human residency at Pell's Star.

And Fletcher Neihart could only watch, *in* the downers' world but not quite *of* it, limited by the breather-mask that limited every human on the world. He'd never been limited by such a mask in his youthful dreams of being here, a part of the human staff on Downbelow: Pell's World, the same world that had swung below Pell Station's observation window for all his life, tantalizing, clouded, and forbidden to visitors.

But this was real, not photographs and training tape that only simulated the world. Here the clouds were overhead, not underfoot.

Here, the hisa workers, free of masks and moving lightly, toiled the little remaining time their easy world required them to work. Once the frames were built and once the world spun giddily toward spring and renewal, the hisa and the fields alike waited only for the rains.

Plants whose cycles were likewise timed to the monsoon were budded and ready. In the forests that bordered the log-framed fields, swollen at the slight encouragement of yesterday's showers, the sun-ripened puffers turned the air gold with pollen. You touched a puffer-ball and it went pop. On this day of warm weather and gusty breezes puffer-balls went pop for no apparent reason, and the pollen streamed out in skeins. Pollen rode the surface of the frame-bound ponds as a golden film. It made dim gold streamers on the face of Old River.

Pop. Pop. Pop.

Two hisa, also truant from work, made a game of the puffers at woods' edge, skipping down a high bank of puffer-plants and exploding the white, gray-mottled globes in rapid succession until their coats were gold.

Then they shook themselves and pollen flew in clouds.

"Gold, gold, gold for spring," Melody crowed at Fletcher, and scampered up to the top of the bank above the river, as her co-truant Patch, whose human-name came of a white mark on his flank, chased after her. Melody dived down again. And up, in an explosion of puffer-balls. "Silly Fetcher! Come, come, come!"

Fetcher was what they called him. They wanted him to chase them. But the staff wasn't supposed to run. Or climb. The safety of the breather-masks was too important.

"Gold for us!" Patch cried and, under his playful attack, pollen burst from the puffer-balls, pop, pop, pop-pop, in a chain of pixy dust explosions that caught the fading light.

Fletcher, watching this game up and down the little rise next a stand of old trees, exploded some of his own. That little hummock on which hisa played chase was a just-out-of-reach paradise for a teen-aged boy: things to break that only brought life and laughter—and created puffer-balls for next spring.

He was seventeen and he was, like the hisa, just slightly truant from the work of the Base.

But down here no one truly cared about a little break in the schedule, least of all the downers, who would all go walkabout when the springtime called, as it was beginning to do.

A last few days to seed the frames. A last few days for pranks and games. Then the monsoon rains would come, then the land would break out in blooms and mating, and no one could hold the hisa to something so foolish as work.

A teen-aged boy could understand a system like that. He'd worked so hard to be here, to be in the junior-staff program, and here was the payoff, a delirious moment that more than matched his dreams.

The hisa shrieked and ran and, abandoning rules, he chased, into the thicket along the river shore. They dived over the crest of another puffer-ball ridge. They laid ambushes on the fly and caught him in a puff of pollen.

And after they'd chased up and down, and broken enough speckled puffer globes to have the surface of the water, the rocks, and the very air among the tired old trees absolutely gold with pollen, they cast themselves down by the noisy edge of the water to watch the forever-clouded sky.

Fletcher sprawled beside them, flat on the bank. The breather-mask, its faceplate thickly dotted with pollen now, was the barrier between him and the world, and the need to draw air through the filtered cylinders of his mask left him giddy and short of breath.

Breathe, breathe, breathe as fast as possible at the rate the mask gave him oxygen. Downers when they worked Upabove, in the service passages of Pell, lived in those passages at the high CO_2 level that downers found tolerable. When they exited those passages into the human corridors of the Upabove, they were the ones to go masked.

On Pell's World, on Downbelow, the necessities were reversed, and humans were the strangers, unmasked inside their domes and masked out of doors.

On Downbelow, humans always remembered they were guests—worked their own huge fields and mills on the river plain south of here and tended their own vast orchards at the forest edge to grow grain and fruit in quantities great enough for trade with other starstations.

For more than they themselves needed, downers simply would not work. And what they thought of so much hard work and such huge warehouses, one had to wonder. It wasn't the hisa way, to deal in food. They shared it. One wondered if they knew Pell Station didn't eat all the grain Pell operations grew on Downbelow. There were wide gulfs of understanding between hisa and humans.

Risk yourself sometimes. Never risk a downer. Those were the first and last rules you learned. Kill yourself if you were a fool, and some staffers had done that: the air of Downbelow was more than high in CO_2, it was heavy with biologicals that liked human lungs too well. If your breathing cylinders and your filters gave out, you could stay alive breathing the air of Downbelow—but you were in deep, deep trouble.

Kill yourself if you were a fool. Run your mask cylinders out if you were a total fool. But never harm a downer, never ask for downer possessions, never admire what a downer owned. They didn't react as humans reacted. Bribes and gifts of food or trinkets won points with them.

So, happily, did humans who'd play games. After all the theorizing and the scientific studies, it came down to that: downers worked so they could live to play. So the staff, to gain influence and good will with downers, played games. Trainees brought up to the stringent, humorless discipline of the wartime Upabove learned different rules down here—at least the ones in direct contact with downers.

It made perfect, glorious sense to Fletcher.

Humans had learned, first of all lessons, not to be distressed when spring came full and downers went wandering, leaving their work to the mercy of the floods. The frames would hold the grain from scattering too far. The floods might lift and drift a frame or two, losing an entire paddy, but there was no need to worry. The hisa made enough such frames.

One year of legend the frames would all have gone downriver and the harvest would have failed entirely, but humans had held the land with dikes to save the hisa, as they thought. A wonderful idea, the downers thought when they came back from springtime wandering, and they were very glad and grateful that kind humans had saved their harvest, which they had been sure was lost.

But surely such disasters had happened before, and hisa had survived—by moving downriver to other bands, most likely. And all the human anguish over whether providing the dikes might change hisa ways had come to naught. A few free spirits now experimented with dikes, like old Greynose and her downriver brood, but the Greynose band worked fields where River ran far more chancily than here.

Improve the downer agricultural methods? Import Earth crops, or bioengineer downer grain with higher yields? Control Old River? Hisa crops needed the floods. Humans farmed crops from old Earth only in the Upabove, in orbiting facilities, to protect the world ecosystem, and those were luxuries, and scarce. Crops native to Downbelow were the abundance that fed the tanks that fed the merchant ships.

Processing could turn downer grain into bread and surplus could feed the fish tanks that supplied colonies from Pell to Cyteen. The agricultural plantations launched cargo up and received things sent down, sometimes by shuttle and not infrequently by the old, old method of the hard-shell parachute drop through Downbelow's seething and violent clouds.

The port and the launch site were busy, human places Fletcher had been glad to leave in favor of this study outpost along Old River. Here, in fields on the edge of deep, broad forest, things didn't move at any rapid pace and nothing fell from the sky. Here a hisa population not that great in the world met humans who monitored the effects of the vast operation to the south on hisa life, looking for any signs of stress and growing a little grain as hisa grew it, cataloging, observing—

And each spring for reasons linked to love and burrows and babies, downers would forget their fields, follow their instincts and go walking—females walking far, far across the hills and through the woods and down the river, with desirous males tagging after.

Fletcher hadn't been down here long enough to have seen the migrations. He'd come last year at harvest, and the monsoon was yet to come. He knew that there were tragedies in the spring: death along with rebirth. There were falls, and drownings . . . the old hands warned the young staffers of that fact: the oldest hisa went walking, too, and deaths in spring were epidemic—spirit tokens, those waist-cords and necklaces brought back by others to hang on sticks in the burying-place. Every spring was risky, with the rains coming down and River running high—and he worried about these two, Melody and Patch, *his* hisa, with increasing concern.

You were supposed to be trained just to speak with downers on Pell Station.

But he'd met Melody illicitly on the station—oh, years ago, when he was eight, a human runaway, a boy in desperate need of something magical to intervene—and Melody, squatting down to peer at him in his hiding-place, had said, "You sad?" in that strange, mask-muffled voice of hers.

How did you give a surly answer to a magical creature?

He'd been locked in his own shell, hating everything he saw, hiding in the girders of the dock, moving from one to another cold and dangerous place to evade station authorities who might be looking for a runaway.

His foster-family—his *third* foster-family—had been scum that day. All adults were scum that day.

But you couldn't quite say that about an odd and alien creature who crouched down near him in the cold, metal-tinged air and asked, "*Why* you sad?"

Why was he sad? He'd not even identified what he felt until she put her finger on it. He'd thought he was mad. He was angry at most everything. But Melody had asked what the psychs had skirted around for years, just put her finger right on the center of things and made him wonder why he was sad.

A mother that committed suicide?

Foster-families that thought *he* was scum?

He'd survived those. No, that wasn't it.

He was sad because he hadn't anyone or anywhere or anything and nobody wanted him the way he was. Not even his mother had.

He'd said, "My mother's dead," though it had happened three years ago. And Melody had patted his arm gently, as about that time Patch had shown up and squatted down, too.

"Sad young human," Melody had explained to Patch. "Gone, gone he mama."

It made him feel as if he was three years old. Or five. As he'd been when his mother had done the deed and left him for good and all. And he'd begun to feel embarrassed, and caught in a lie that was just going to get wider.

"Long time ago," he'd said, in a surly tone.

"Long time you sad," Melody had said, and put her finger on it again, in a way the psychs had never been able to.

And somehow then—maybe it had been Patch's idea— they'd gotten him up on his feet and talked to him about things that just didn't make any sense to him.

He knew he wasn't supposed to talk to them. The fact he was breaking a rule made him inclined to go with them and get in *real* trouble, challenging the authorities to take him out of the foster-family he'd been trying to escape.

He'd walked about with them for an hour in the open, uncaught, unreprimanded, and he'd seen the amazing details about the station that downers knew. And then one of Melody's mask cylinders had run out. They'd had to go to a locker within the service tunnels to get another, and he'd discovered a secret world, a world only licensed supervisors got to see— legally, among creatures only licensed supervisors got to deal with—legally.

He'd gone home to his foster-family and apologized, lying through his teeth about being very, very sorry. He'd stayed with that foster-family and followed their rules for another three whole years because their residence was near the access he knew to the maintenance tunnels. And the tunnels became his route to various places about the station, and his refuge from anger. He used masks that were for human maintenance workers, always in a locker by the access doors. He did no harm. For the first time he had a Place that was always his. For the first time in his life he had something to lose if he got caught. And for the first time in his life he'd reformed his bad-boy ways, gotten out of the crowd he was in and reformed so well the social workers thought his foster-family—his worst family of the lot—had worked a miracle.

He'd stayed reformed: he'd improved in school, which brought rewards of another kind. And even when, after the four-year rotation station workers were allowed, Melody and Patch had gone back down to their world, he hadn't collapsed and relapsed into his juvenile life of crime.

No. He'd already confessed at least part of his story (not the part about actually going into the tunnels) to his guidance counselor and made a solemn career choice: working with the downers on Downbelow.

Tough standards, tough program, tough academic work. But he'd made the program. He'd gotten his chance.

And, not surprisingly, because former station workers lived and worked around the human establishments on Downbelow, he'd met Melody and Patch inside an hour after reaching the forest Base last fall. She was grayer. Patch wasn't as big as he'd recalled. He'd grown that much in the nearly ten years since he'd seen them, and he'd not known how old his Downers had been.

It might be her last fertile season, and Patch her last mate. No other male pursued her that he knew of, and she would not, he understood, lead Patch all that long a chase when her spring was on her—but then Patch couldn't walk so far these days, either.

He wanted them back safely. But he knew, now, soberly, that ultimately he'd lose them, too. So days were precious to him. And this day—this was the best day of his life, this game of puffer-balls and pollen.

A hard downer finger poked him hard below the ribs, and he curled in self-defense. Melody and Patch were in a prankish mood and, lying on his back on the bank, he jabbed Patch back, which sent Patch screaming for the nearest tree-limb. In the trees downers could climb like crazy, and a human in heavy boots and clean-suit was not going to catch Patch.

Patch flung leaves at him. "Wicked, wicked," Melody cried, and flung a puffer-ball, which disintegrated on impact. Pollen was everywhere. Patch dropped, shrieking, from the tree.

Then it was pollen wars until the air was thick and gold again.

And until the restricted breathing had Fletcher leaning against a low-hanging limb gasping for air and sweating in the suit.

The light was dimmer now.

"Sun goes walk," he said. One couldn't say to downers that Great Sun set, or went down, or any such thing. The rules said so. Great Sun walked over the hills. These two downers knew Great Sun's unguarded face, having been up in the Upabove themselves, but it didn't change how they reverenced the star. He used the downer expression: "The clock-words say humans go inside."

They looked, Melody and Patch did, at gray, cloud-veiled Sun above a shadowing River. They slid arms about each other as they set out walking up the trail toward the Base, being old mates, and comfortable and affectionate. Where the trail widened, Melody put an arm about Fletcher, too, and they walked with him back down the river path until, past three large paddy-frames, they came within sight of the domes where humans lived, in filtered, oxygen-supplied safety above the flood zone.

"You fine?" Patch asked. "You got bellyache?"

"No," he said, and laughed. Downers didn't brood on things. If you didn't want a dozen questions, you laughed. They wouldn't let him be sad, and wouldn't leave him in distress.

They were absolutely adamant in that.

So he laughed, and poked Patch in the ribs, and Patch poked him and ducked around Melody.

Games.

"Late, late, late," he said. And then the alarm on his watch beeped, as all across the fields quitting time announced itself on the 'link everyone wore.

"Oh, you make music, time go!"

Not that they grasped in the least what time really meant. On days when a lot of the staff was out in the fields, the downers would gather to watch close to quitting time, and exclaim in amazement at the hour every human in the fields simultaneously quit work and headed back to Base, carrying whatever they'd been using, gathering up whatever they'd brought with them. The downers understood there was a signal and that it came with music. It was not the beep itself, the Director said, it was the *why* that puzzled the downers. The old hands like Melody and Patch, who'd seen the station change shift, and who'd worked by the clock, could tell the younger downers that humans set great store by time and doing things together.

("But Great Sun he come again," was Melody's protest against any such notion of pressing schedule. "Always he come.")

On Downbelow, in downer minds, there were always new chances, new tomorrows.

And one never had to do anything *that* pressing, that it

couldn't wait one more hour or one more day. You wanted to
know when to go to your burrow? Look to Great Sun, and go
before dark. Or after, if you were in a mood to risk the blindness of the nights.

One was never in too big a hurry. One could take the time
to walk, oh, *way* off the direct track home, in this still-strange
notion (to a station-born human) of being able to look across
a wide open space to see what other people were doing on
other routes. Upabove, it would have been corridors and walls.

Here, on this happiest of all days, he found his path intersecting Bianca Velasquez's route on *her* way home. They were
in the same biochem seminar. They mixed before discussion-
session. She'd always hung around with Marshall Willett and
the Dees. Who didn't hang around with him.

She was going to snub him. He could pretend to drop
something and let her go by while he rummaged in the gravel
of the path. Like a fool. He could save himself the sour end to
a good day.

But it ought to be easy to look at Bianca. It ought to be
easy to talk to her. Hi, just a simple hi, and put the onus of
politeness on her. Hi. Ready for the biochem quiz? What job
are you on? He had it straight. Civilized amenities were very
clear in his head until she almost looked at him and he almost
looked at her and by an accident of converging trails they were
walking together.

Not just any girl. *The* girl. Bianca Velasquez, who'd drawn
his eye ever since he'd first seen her. Suddenly his brain was
vacant. He couldn't look at her when he couldn't think and his
body temperature was rising in what he knew was a glow-in-
the-dark blush.

God, he was a fool. He must have inhaled puffer-pollen. He
didn't know why he'd chosen today to cross her path, just—
there she'd been; and he'd done it.

"Where *were* you?" she asked.

"Over there." He waved his hand at River. That sounded
stupid. And she'd noticed he was gone? God, if the supervisor
had seen him . . .

"So where were you?"

"Oh, beyond the trees. Down by the River."

"Doing what?"

"This downer I work with—Melody—she wanted to show me something." *I work with.* As if he was a senior supervisor. That sounded like a fool. She'd rattled him just by existing. He was already in a tangle and he'd only just opened his mouth.

"You're all over stuff."

He brushed his clean-suit. "Puffer-balls." Thank God, he had his inspiration for something to say. "It was all over. And the sun and everything. It was real pretty. That's why I went."

"Where?"

Fast thinking. Panic. Decision. "I'll show you."

"Sure."

Oh, God. She said yes. He didn't expect her to say yes.

"When?" she asked.

"Can you get away tomorrow?"

"How long?"

"No longer than I was today. About the same time. Right before sunset. When the light's right."

"I don't know. We're not supposed to be alone down there."

She thought he was trouble. And he wasn't. He had maybe one sentence to change her mind.

"Melody and Patch will be there. They used to work near my rez on the station. I've known them for years before I came down. We'll be safe." He blurted that out and then wished he hadn't been quite so forthcoming. She was a nice, decent girl from a solid, rule-following family. He'd just told her something the supervisors might not know from his records, and if they got to asking too close questions of Melody and Patch, *they* in hisa honesty could accidentally say something to get him canned from the program.

"All right," she said. "Sure. All right."

He could hardly believe it. She was from Family with a capital F, and he was from a non-resident household with an f only for fouled-up. She wasn't somebody who'd normally even talk to him on the Station. But she seemed to invite him to hold her hand, brushing close as they walked, and when he did slip his hand around hers, her fingers were chaste and cold and listless, making him ask himself was this the way Stationer Family girls were, or had he just made a wrong, unwelcome move?

"Got to watch your hands when you go through decon," he said. "I'm all over pollen."

"Yeah," she said, and gave a little squeeze of the fingers that made him suddenly lightheaded. He wasn't mistaken. She *did* want to talk to him. He hadn't imagined she was looking back at him in biochem.

He didn't expect this. He really didn't. "I thought you were, kind of, hanging with Marshall Willett."

"Oh, *Marshall*." Her disgust dismissed the very name and being of Marshall Willett, one of *the* Willetts, who'd been in close orbit around her for three months, acting as if he owned the Base and the senior staff, besides.

He didn't know what to say. He had a dream, and quite honestly that dream wasn't remotely Bianca Velasquez. It was being *in* this world and *on* this world on days like today.

It was lasting to be a senior in the Program on Downbelow. Getting involved with someone like Bianca wasn't a help: it was a hindrance he'd never sought.

But—here she was. Interested—at least in holding hands. And what did he do?

She was smart. She was far more serious-minded than Marshall Willett, whose reason for being down here he privately suspected was a family trying to make him do *something* for a career. Bianca was bright, she was pretty, she seemed to *care* about the work, and that—in addition to being able to stay down here amid the wonders of the planet for the rest of his life—that was just too much to ask of luck.

No. Back to level: permanent duty on the world was all he wanted, and he wouldn't risk that by making a wrong move on Bianca and her powerful Family, not even if she was standing stark naked in the pollen-gold and the sun of that bank.

God, he *liked* that image. She'd be so pretty. She had dark hair and olive skin. She'd be all gold with the sun and the pollen coming down in streamers . . . well, repaint that picture with breather-masks and the clean-suits. They'd plod about in clumsy isolation while Melody and Patch scampered and threw puffer-balls at them. And how much trouble could you get into with a girl, when neither of you could take off the breather-masks and all you could touch was fingertips?

They walked along hand in hand toward the domes, which now were ghostly pale against the rapidly advancing twilight. The white yard lights were on. Other workers were coming home, too, walking much faster than they were.

Their paths split apart again where the path reached what they called the Quadrangle, and the dorm-domes were very strict, male in one direction, female in the other, if you were junior staff . . .

As if they didn't have good sense until their twentieth birthday and then mature wisdom automatically happened; but in essence, he'd been glad to have the peace the no-females rules brought to the guys' side, and tonight he was glad of it because he didn't have to think of a dozen more clever things to say. He'd had maybe five minutes walking with her, avoiding making a total fool of himself. He had all night and tomorrow to get his thoughts together before he had to talk to her again.

Oh, my *God*, he had a *date* with Bianca Velasquez.

It was impossible. He'd never gone with a girl. And having a Family girl like Bianca actually make a date with him was . . . impossible. Bianca was so Family her feet didn't touch the floor, so virginal and proper her knees locked when she slept at night. He was disposed on one side of the equation to think it was some kind of setup: he'd met numerous setups in his life, for no other reason than he *was* nobody.

But over the weeks he had seen that she was smarter than that crowd, and maybe bored with them, and, the thought came to him, maybe she was lonely, too. Marshall seemed to think the Sun and all the planets sort of naturally swung round *him* because he was a Willett; Bianca was the only human being on the Base—including the supervisors—who didn't have to give a damn that Marshall was a Willett, because *she* was a Velasquez. Velasquezes didn't have to give a damn about Willetts, Siddons, Somervilles, or Kielers, which was the big clique down here.

So what did she do? She held hands with *him*?

He didn't have a family at all. He was non-resident scum.

He also stood six feet, had learned self-defense on Pell's rough-and-tumble White Dock, the bottom end of where he'd lived, at worst, with his fourth family, and he could beat shit out of Marshall Willett. So maybe that was her idea, her way of thumbing her nose at the lot of them. She'd been sort of a loner, too, in the center of a cloud of admirers.

And Marshall—Marshall would want one thing from her first off, which Fletcher had no intention of asking of her, not because he didn't think of it, but because, bottom line, his motive, unlike Marshall's, wasn't to get himself kicked out of the program.

She acted shy. He squeezed her hand when they parted company. Senior staff members habitually sat watch at the doors. They counted everybody in for the night, for safety's sake, to be sure nobody was left out with a broken leg or a dead breather-cylinder or something.

Nobody got a minute alone, if you were under twenty.

You were safe holding hands. If you couldn't manage the no sex rule till your majority, the Director had told them plainly, there was no shortage of applicants, ten for every slot they filled.

Tomorrow, Bianca Velasquez had promised him, and Fletcher Neihart walked on down the path to the men's dorms, past the monitors and into decontamination with a preoccupation so thorough the monitor had to ask him twice to sign in.

Chapter

II

The restaurant was old enough to have gone from glamour to a look of hard use and back to glamour again. Now it was beyond trends. Now it was a Pell Station tradition: Pell's finest restaurant, with its lighted floor, its display of the very real stars beyond the tables, features both of which were its hallmark, copied elsewhere but never the same.

The new touch was the holo display that set those stars loose among the tables, a piece of engineering Elene Quen had seen with the overhead lights on. The sight destroyed the illusion, but the magic was such when the dark came back that the senses were always dazzled, no matter what the reasoning mind knew of the technology behind the illusion.

The waiters settled their distinguished party at the best table, reserved from the hour *Finity's End* had returned her call. It was herself, her husband Damon Konstantin, Captain James Robert Neihart and his brother captains, Madison, Francie, and Alan. At this hour, the meal was breakfast for Francie and Alan, supper for James Robert and Madison; and with all four of *Finity's* captains away from the ship, business that had the ill grace to hit *Finity's* deck this close after docking would fall into the hands of *Finity's* more junior staff.

Cocktails arrived, glasses clinked, faces marked by years of war broke into honest smiles. Rejuv and time-dilation stretched out a life, but years on rejuv left marks, too, on all of them. Captain James Robert Neihart in particular, a hundred forty-nine years old as stations counted time, was fortyish in build, but he was gray-haired and papery-skinned close-up, his face crossed with all the hairline traces of the anger and laughter of a long, long life.

Seeing how the years had worn even on spacers, who played fast and loose with time, and counted the years on ships' clocks separate from station reckonings, Elene looked anxiously at her husband Damon, nearly two decades after the War, and for a fleeting, fearful second she accounted of the fact that they were none of them immortal. The years passed faster for her and for Damon than they did for any spacer.

And she'd been a spacer herself until she'd elected what should have been a one-year shore tour with a man she'd loved, a spacer's vacation on this shore of a sea of stars, a deliberate dynastic tie with the Konstantins of Pell.

Fateful decision, that. Her ship, *Estelle*, hadn't survived its next run: *Estelle* had become a casualty of the War years and the Quen name, once distinguished among merchanters, had all but died in that disaster. No ship, no Name was left of all she'd been. And so, so much had conspired to bind her here ashore. She'd fought her War in the corridors of Pell.

And had she aged to their eyes? Had Damon, in the seven years since *Finity's End* had last seen this port?

Were the captains of *Finity's End* all thinking, looking at her, How sad, this last of the Quens growing old on station-time?

Last of the Quens would be the spacer view. But thanks to Damon she *wasn't* the last of her Name. She'd borne two children, hers, and Damon's, for two equally old, equally threatened lines. The Neiharts of *Finity's End* might not yet have acknowledged the fact, but she'd more than given the heir of the Konstantins a son, Angelo Konstantin, stationer, born and bred in his father's heritage: more relevant to any *spacer's* hopes, she had a daughter, Alicia Quen. The Quens had no ship, but they *had* a succession.

Cocktails, and small talk. Catching up on the business of seven years with a thin, colorless: how have you been, how's trade, what's ever became of . . . ?

They ordered supper, extravagantly. They were spacers in from the deep, cold Beyond, on the start of a two-week dock-side liberty . . . the first truly wide-open liberty since before the War. And that in itself was news that set the dock abuzz.

"What's changed?" Damon echoed a question from Madison. "A lot of new facilities, a lot of improvements all up and down the dock. There's a number of new sleepovers, a couple of quality accommodations—"

"The garden," Elene said.

"The garden," Damon said. "You'll want to see that."

"Garden?" Francie asked. To a spacer, a garden produced greens: you grew them aboard your own ship if you had leisure and room. A garden was a lot of lights and timed water.

Pell's didn't grow just lettuce and radishes.

"Take it from me," Elene said. "You'll be amazed." But she had a curious feeling when she said it—*listen* to me, she thought. Here she was, praising Pell's advantages to spacers, and she tested the queasy feeling she had as she caught the words coming out of her mouth.

The mirror every morning showed her a stranger enmeshed in station business, and lately her eyes looked back at her, bewildered and pained at the change in her own face. Could she, going back all those years, still *choose* this exile and want this rapid passage of years?

Supper arrived with the help of several waiters. "Very good," James Robert said after his initial sampling, and the company agreed it was indeed a seven-year meal.

Rumors necessarily attended *Finity's* dealings on the docks, more than Madison's odd statement they were on a *true* liberty. Rumors preceding this dinner had reached her office, her breakfast table, even her bed—the latter straight from Pell's Legal Affairs office, Damon's domain.

What was certain was that before she ever docked at Pell, *Finity's End* had made a large draw on the Alliance Bank, a draw of 74.8 million against both principal and interest on the sum it had left on account for safekeeping in the War. Listing her latest port of departure as Sol 1, Earth, she'd logged goods for sale and made a modest trade of luxury goods on the futures market even before docking, a procedure legal here at Pell.

The market had reacted. If *Finity* came in selling cargo, then *Finity* was buying. Speculators had surmised from the instant she showed on the boards that, if she bought, she'd buy staples like flour and dry sugar, cheap at Pell, or lower mass cargo like pharmaceuticals, either one a reasonable kind of cargo for a ship in *Finity*'s kind of operation. Mallory of *Norway*, Pell's defense against the pirates, could always use such commodities. *Finity* served *Norway* as supply; such commodities rose in price. But since most direct shippers, even the most patriotic and forgiving, would rather see their shipments actually reach the destination they intended instead of being diverted to some lonely port out on the fringes of civilization, the bids for hired-haul goods and mail stayed stable.

Then, confounding all estimations, *Finity*'s futures buy had turned out to be goods for the luxury market, goods like downer wine.

Curious. The immediate speculation was that *Finity* meant simply to play the futures market during a couple of weeks at dock, create a little uncertainty, then dump those items on the market at the last moment, having made a one- to two-week runup in price on speculation—not legal everywhere, but legal on Pell. The market was jittery. Some political analysts, taking appearances as fact, said that if *Finity* was buying high-quality cargo on her own tab, the pirate-chasing business must be near an end, as some forecast it must be—and needed to be. The expenditure of public funds for continued operations was a burden on the economy.

The other opinion, completely opposite, was that some really big pirate action was in the offing, some operation that needed deep cover, so *Finity* was buying high-value (therefore low-mass) cargo with what only looked like her own funds so as to *look* as if pirate-catching was no longer on her agenda.

The tally of ships of the former Fleet caught and dealt with varied with accounts, even official ones. In the vast and deep dark of the Beyond, the negative couldn't be proven, and a destroyed ship, given the legendary canniness of the Fleet captains, was a wait-see, almost never a certainty. They thought they'd accounted for certain carriers. But the Fleet captains were canny and hard to nail. One Mazianni carrier with its rider ships was more than a lightspeed firing platform: it was also a traveling, self-contained world, deadly in its power and long-term in its staying power. A carrier, badly damaged, could repair itself, given time. Even if Pell declared a victory, surviving ships of the Fleet might pull off to the long-alleged secret base for a generation or so and then return, making the rebel captain Mazian again a major player in the affairs of the human species.

Elene inclined to a mix of those beliefs, convinced, first, that Mazian was a threat diminishing rather than rising; second, that the end of the pirate wars would be a wind-down and never a provable victory; and third, that the critical danger to the human species was *not* in a Fleet mostly driven in retreat, secret base or no secret base. The Fleet had been the demon in the dark for so long that it had taken on a quality of myth, so potent a myth that Alliance and Union administrators alike need only say the dire word *Mazian*, and a funding bill passed.

But the downside of that preoccupation with the Mazianni was an Alliance Council refusing to take their eyes off the Fleet and look instead to their primary competition: Union, the enemy the Fleet had fought before it turned to piracy.

Her own councillors said she was out of date, obsessed with history, unable to forgive the *Estelle* disaster. She should become more progressive in her thinking and give up the bitterness of a War grown inconvenient in modern politics.

Like hell.

"Seven years," Elene said, stalking her topic as the waiters carried off the empty salad plates. She knew who was at surrounding tables, two of her loyal aides and the policy chairman. She knew this area of the restaurant, she knew the noise levels, precisely how far voices carried, which was not far at all. She'd have skinned the maître d' if he'd settled anyone in her vicinity who didn't have a top clearance—since anyone who'd worked at all on the docks could lip-read, a skill which defeated the device she had also seen with the lights on, the one that also guaranteed the privacy of this table. "Seven years is too long to wait for a good supper, *Finity*. What are our chances we'll see you more often in the future?"

James Robert's expression was a parchment mask. The eyes, darting to hers, were immediately lively and calculating.

"Fairly good," James Robert said, an answer the commodities dealers would be very interested to hear. "Granted Union behaves itself." The inevitable stinger. Yea and nay in two breaths. James Robert to the core.

"We're turning full-time to honest trade," Francie said. "At least that's our ambition."

"Peaceful trade," Madison added, lifting his glass. "Confusion to Cyteen *and* to Mother Earth."

"To peace," Damon said, more politic, and Francie and Alan emptied glasses to the bottom.

Then the main course arrived, a flurry of carts and waiters, during which *Finity* passed around the bottle and did their own wine-pouring, to the consternation of the wait-staff—they were spacers to the bone, and if the waiters couldn't handle empty glasses fast enough, then they did for themselves, ignoring station protocols and etiquette as blithely as they'd done for decades. They were nothing if not self-sufficient and reckless of external protocols.

As the Quens had once been, on their own deck, Elene could not but reflect. And now the almost-last of the Quens finagled and hoped and connived for that right again, cursing the waiters dithering in and out at the wrong moment.

She could sway the internal government of Pell. That was half the Alliance. The approval of the Alliance Council of Captains—that was the sticking point in her plans. And that meant, significantly, the leadership of James Robert Neihart.

"A brave new world of peace," she reprised, as the waiters and the cart went away, and before the conversation could drift. "*Finity*, I have a proposal. Let me assure you we're sound-secured here at this table, for a start. I think you know that."

James Robert lifted his chin, looked at her through half-lidded eyes.

"A proposal for which I need funds and backing in Council."

Her husband Damon knew exactly what she was up to the minute she made the opening: she was sure he did, and she knew he was holding all his arguments resolutely behind his teeth. Two decades was time enough to say everything there possibly was to say on the subject between them, and he couldn't deter her now, make or break. If *Finity's End* was here to declare the War was entering a new phase, if there was a change in the offing, *she* had her agenda.

"For what?" Madison asked. "A crisis? A proposition?"

"Both," she said. *Finity* was *not* that far out of the current of things, at any time. *Finity*'s votes in the Alliance Council were regular, received on the network of ship contacts that didn't rely on hyperspace, just regular ship traffic at any station dock. "Peace with Union, yes, peace and trade, and *ships*, Alliance ships. *Built at Pell.*"

"We need another bottle," Madison said, "for this one."

James Robert, senior captain, hadn't given his reaction to the topic.

She signaled a waiter, hand signal, for three bottles. The maître d' was in line of sight. The wine arrived. There was the ancient etiquette of the bottle, the glasses. The universe teetered on a mood, a small-talk graciousness that still prevailed. The waiter filled glasses and withdrew.

She was acutely aware in the interim of a stationer husband at her side, a patient man, a saint of a man, who slept alongside a shiplost spacer's heartache and knew his home never was home to her. After two children and eighteen years, what was between them was no longer the blind love they'd started with. They'd seen and done too much, too desperately. But it was a lifelong commitment now, a partnership she'd never altogether betray because it had held the same interests too long. She reached, beneath the table, for his hand, and held it, a promise strong as an oath, keen as a cry.

"It's a serious business," James Robert said when the waiters were gone.

She knew all the objections. One rebuilt ship, as they'd debated time and again, opened up the question of what *other* War casualty ships might be resurrected, and where those ships would fit in the trade routes of the Alliance, in an age when merchanters, with a vastly changed set of routes, were doing well, but not *that* well.

Never mind Pell's internal debates in such a decision: merchanters, members of the Alliance Council of Captains, had suballiances within their ranks; and if *Finity* did her a favor on that scale, and backed her request for funds, then debts would come due left and right, other ships to *Finity*, *Finity* to other ships and to Pell—and Mallory. Favor-points in a merchanter crew meant owing someone a drink, a duty-shift. On this scale, one favor nudged another until it shook the recently settled universe all over again.

"I don't truly ask your business or your destination at the moment," she said. "I don't ask why you've drawn what you have from the bank. That's Mallory's business or it isn't and I won't put you in the position of lying to me. But I'll tell you what's no news to you, and something *we* have to deal with. We both know that Union is getting past the Treaty. What may be news is that there are fourteen more ships pending construction. Union is building ships to put us out of business, and it's doing it while we bicker." Having mapped out her arguments for her ship in advance, oh, for sleepless nights and seven years, she tapped a finger on the table surface to make her points and ignored all logic of why a Quen ship should be first.

"I can name you the ships," she said. "I can tell you which shipyards." She'd almost lay odds that *Finity* could name them, too. But James Robert gave her not an iota of help or encouragement, the old fox. "One. The Treaty says Union won't build merchant ships and Alliance won't build warships. Two: Union is hauling cargo on military craft they're suddenly building with damned large holds. I'm sure it's no news. Three: We're throwing our budget into armaments for our merchant ships and we haven't built a single ship to counter the real danger. Don't hand me the official denial: I wrote it. Four: We have a pie of a given size, but we can have a larger one." *Damn* him, did he never react? She'd faced him in negotiation before, and remembered only now how hard it was. "*Five*, cold facts and you know them: *We'll have no damned pie at all if we let Union build military merchanters and build nothing but guns, ourselves.* The plain fact is, we're in a new war, a war for trade, and guns won't win it. We need new *ships* licensed. And we can grit our teeth, take the pain in the budget, adjust our trade routes and *do* that—or we can bicker on till we're *all* Union ships and we have no choice."

Captain James Robert Neihart—who decades ago had refused Union and the Earth Company officials alike the right to enter and inspect his ship. Captain James Robert, who'd started the merchanters' strike that had made any merchant ship a sovereign government, James Robert, who'd unified the merchanters finally against Union and started the Company Wars . . . didn't so much as blink.

Neither did she, who'd settled on Pell, not Earth, for the new Merchanters' Alliance headquarters, an independent Pell Station, as *she'd* demanded exist. Together they'd dealt with double-dealing Earth and powerful Cyteen to keep their independence, and they'd stood, James Robert and Elene Quen, as opposite pillars holding the whole structure of the Alliance in balance: ship rights and station rights, defined and agreed to, with a damn-you-all alike to Union's claims to have won the War—and Earth's claims not to have lost it.

With the remnant of the Fleet preying on shipping, with civilization on the brink of ruin, it had simply been more expedient for Union to agree to a neutral Pell and a free Merchanters' Alliance. Now it was becoming less so. Now that the pirate threat was less, Union was pushing the Treaty with the Alliance to exercise every loophole for all it was worth and the merchanter captains of the Alliance Council still temporized with the fraying of the treaty, aware something should be done to prevent Union running over them, but never quite willing to say this was the year to do it.

"You know what Union's going to say," James Robert said. "To get them to accept Alliance merchanters in *their* space, we have to stop the smuggling."

Back to the old argument from Unionside. She *wasn't* prepared to hear it from James Robert.

"Can't be done," she said. In spite of herself she'd rocked back at the very thought, and became conscious of her body language, braced at arm's length from the table. At the same moment James Robert had leaned forward, taking up the space she'd ceded, pressing the argument.

"Has to be done," James Robert said.

"On Union's say-so? Union's cheating every chance it gets."

"Union has a point. Mallory agrees. The black market is supplying Mazian."

Merchanters *were*, almost by definition, smugglers. Everyone ran their small side business of trade that didn't go through station tariffs. It was a piddling amount compared to what flowed through stations. It always had been. It was a merchanter *right* to trade off-station and duck the taxes that were supposed to be paid on two ships trading goods.

But she hadn't intended to talk about smuggling. She was thrown off her balance, off *her* point of negotiation, and found herself still wondering why James Robert, historic father of merchanter rights, had taken Union's side. "We can't talk trade," she said, circling doggedly to the flank, "if we're facing a fleet of non-Alliance merchant ships. Smuggling be damned. We'll be working from Union's rule book and *only* Union's rules if we sit idle and let them build ships to out-compete the free merchanters. I want my ship, *Finity*. That's the issue, here. I'm calling in debts. All I've got." If change was coming, if a whole new phase of human life really was dawning, one *without* the Fleet, one in which even James Robert Neihart would argue to curtail merchanter rights because they couldn't otherwise get their share of Union's wealth and Earth's resources, then maybe in the long run the pessimists were right. Maybe they'd end up, all of them, with half of what they'd bargained for, and an age of less, not more, prosperity, with fewer starstations, fewer centers of population, smaller markets.

But, if for a brief while more, it might still matter to someone that Elene Quen was a hero of the Alliance; she'd trade on that or anything else she owned to get her Name back in space and get her descendants' share of the markets that remained. "I want my ship. *Yes*, I want this to be the first ship of other ships we build. Yes, I want us, the Alliance, and Pell *and Earth* to challenge Union on what they're doing. I want us to go head to head with them and not let Union pick our pockets for another twenty years. Maybe we'll be short of funds for a while. But we'll survive as independents if we have ships. That's my proposal."

"I'll give you mine," James Robert said. "The smuggling has to be cut off. If the Fleet's getting supply from *us*, we've become our own worst enemy. And to enable that . . . the Merchanter's Alliance will ask all Alliance signatories for lower tariffs."

There was the stinger. Less tax. At a time when the stations needed funds for modernization and competed to get the merchanters to stay longer, spend their funds at this starstation rather than another. "How much lower?"

"Starting at ten percent, and pegged to the *increase* in trade coming through the stations when we're *not* trading off the record."

"That's difficult."

"So is persuading our brother merchanters. But if stations don't lower port charges, and if we don't put moral force behind getting *our* people out of the smuggling trade, we're going to see the Fleet has become *us*, that's the danger. I can name you six, seven ships that are operating in that trade—hard evidence. We want the tether reeled in. We want arrests threatened, ports sealed, where documentation exists. And *that* will take a united Council of Captains, and it will take a solid agreement from all the stations."

She envisioned the fuss that would raise, the Merchanter's Alliance trying to keep all its own ships from doing what ships had always done, on the grounds some few would supply Mazian. *Some* had always supplied Mazian.

But she could also envision a scenario in which, if the Treaty started deteriorating, more would do it. If Mazian swore undying repentance for raiding merchanter shipping, and if Union pushed merchanters too hard with its notion of hauling cargo with state crews, in its own far routes, yes, she could envision all of civilization blowing up. The War all over again. Once James Robert aimed her eyes down that track it wasn't hard at all to envision it. If Union or Pell or the merchant trade pushed too hard at each other and relations blew up, Mazian didn't have to attack. He'd come in to the rescue, reputation refurbished. A hero of Earth and Pell again—nightmarish thought.

There was a prolonged silence, in which Elene felt a chill in the constantly cycling air, the slow dance of stars about the room.

"If we should back this ship of yours," James Robert said, "—let's have a clear understanding . . . you're not talking about going back to space yourself. We couldn't show that much favoritism. This *is* an act of principle you're proposing. Do I understand that?"

They were far too old in this to be fools. There'd been a time when she'd planned to stand fast on the name of her ship, on another *Estelle*.

"Let the Council name the ship. There are competent, reliable crew *begging* for a berth. But my *daughter* will go to space."

"We could back that," James Robert said; and granted in that simple willingness to talk that they were suddenly beyond initial negotiations. "We *need* you where you are."

"My daughter will contribute her station-share," she opened the next round, half-sure now of Neihart's support, because beyond that one point granted, all else was inevitable, the whole cascade of debate among spacers—and the agreement won the necessary outcome, in Union's backing off the building of merchant ships. All, that was, if they could get Alliance united and *agreed*, God help them, on a single program. Her daughter's station-share, millions, when no other stranded spacer could come up with thousands, would make her owner-operator. Not pilot, but policy-maker. "Can I count on you in Council?"

"I'll hear more about it."

James Robert was a trader first and foremost. And talk ran on to agreement and dwindled to inconsequentials clear to the bottom of the second bottle.

James Robert, champion of merchanters against station governments, would use his bully pulpit with other merchanters. She would use hers with Pell Station. The immoveable negatives miraculously stood a chance of moving. An end to the smuggling and black market that, dire thought, might be supplying Mazian?

It was possible that that flow of goods added up, somehow, to enough leakage of goods through the system to be significant. They'd operated on the theory it was Sol doing it; or that there were secret bases, supply dumps they had yet to find.

But if there was a supply flow that they could cut off— then, then Mazian would start suffering.

If they could *have* supply or non-supply to Mazian as a club to wield, *keep* Union worried about a Mazianni resurgence if they threatened to collapse Alliance trade, and if somehow by hook or by crook James Robert could get the fractious merchanter captains in line one more time . . . it was a house of cards, precariously balanced, but if they could do all that, they could argue with Union to back off their construction of their own merchant fleet.

And that would create safe routes for new, tariff-paying merchanters, while employing the shipyards of Pell, which would be the key argument to move the industrial interests of Pell to agree to lower the tariffs and dock charges that would increase merchanter profit and sweeten the deal . . .

It all fell miraculously in line, and her skin felt the fever-chill of almost miracles. She'd invited James Robert and his fellow captains here to talk urgently about the future. They'd come here equally eager to talk and to deal, at this hinge-point of change in the universe.

And because she was here to put forward her requirements, she had everything. Everything, because it *was* sane and it was right to build more ships, and it *was* in everyone's best interests.

Even Earth's, in the long run, because it was good for the peace. They could have their prosperity—if James Robert was right. They could gain everything.

Then James Robert said:

"There's one sticking-point. The *old* problem. The lawsuit."

She hadn't utterly forgotten. She'd even been prepared to have it float to the surface early in the dinner—but not now, not on the edge of agreement. It was Damon's department, Legal Affairs. And her stomach was moderately in a knot. "Francesca's case."

"Third time," James Robert said moderately, "third time we've tried to settle the matter with Pell. We sue, you counter-sue. Your bursar, I'm sure some clerk in your office, just sent us a bill for a station-share."

"You're joking," Elene said.

"As we sent you one. I'm sure it will eventually cross your desk."

It hadn't yet. She was completely appalled. Her fingers, locked on Damon's, clenched, begging silence. She was sure Damon was disturbed at the impropriety.

But James Robert was far too canny a man directly to suggest a linkage.

"A very basic question of merchanter sovereignty," James Robert said. "I'm sure our own Legal Affairs office made the point to yours some seven years ago that we are prepared to go to court, —which with other matters at hand, is a very untimely flare-up of an issue that should have been settled. We do not owe Pell Station any station-share. We will not pay living expenses. We will pay Francesca's medical bills. That is my statement." A wave of James Robert's hand, a dismissal. "Just so you know there's no ill will."

A ship-share of *Finity's End* was an immense amount of money—and so was a station-share on Pell. Francesca Neihart had run up medical bills, living expenses. So had her son.

"The boy is a year from his majority," Damon said.

"And seven years older than the last time we sued. We're in the middle of cargo purchase. But here we are, with what seven years ago was a simple wash: your debt for our debt. Now we're dealing with real money, fourteen point five million credits of real money, which you will *not* see, I assure you in a very friendly way, and which your courts will *not* attach, *or* freeze, because we will sue the bloody clothes off you—so to speak."

James Robert did not bluff.

"The boy," Damon said, "is a ward of Pell courts."

Madison cleared his throat, in what became a very long silence. The Konstantins were also known for stubbornness.

"He is *our* citizen," James Robert said. "And we no longer operate in harm's way. I believe that was the exact objection of the court in prior years. We cannot afford to debate this particular issue, Konstantin. Not at this particular moment. Yet on principle, we will sue."

Damon, who'd never contradict his wife in the midst of negotiations—Damon viewed the concept of law in lieu of God; and Damon was going to hit the overhead when they got home tonight. Elene could feel it in the rock-hard tension of his hand, his sharp, almost painful squeeze on her fingers. No children in a war zone, the Children's Court had held, in spite of the fact that there were children on every family merchanter ship out in space. The Children's Court had its hands on *one* of those children and in a paralysis of anguish over the War one judge and her own husband's office wouldn't let that child go. But in those critical words, *no longer operate in harm's way*, the advocacy system, the judiciary, which couldn't resolve its technical issues over Francesca Neihart's son because the court-appointed social workers and psychiatrists wouldn't agree, had just had its point answered.

Fletcher Robert Neihart had always been caught in the gears. It wasn't the boy's fault that elements in Pell's administration resented being a trailing appendage to the Merchanter Alliance, and some noisy few fools even thought that Pell should assess merchant ships to see whether they were fit for children. It was a ridiculous position, one that would have collapsed the whole merchanter trade network and collapsed civilization with it—but they were issue-oriented thinkers.

To complicate matters, years ago some clever child advocate in the legal office had thought it a fine argument to claim a station-share and sue *Finity* during wartime on the boy's behalf. In further bureaucratic idiocy, filing said claim with the court thereafter had made no difference after that that 14.5 million credits was a figure that never had existed, either in cash or in any official assessment of actual debt. Once that sum had gotten onto the documents, politicians and bursars alike were afraid to take the responsibility of forgiving a fourteen-million-credit debt. So it was in the court records, and it would persist until someone somewhere signed papers in settlement.

Now, to cap a macabre comedy teetering on the verge of tragedy, it sounded as if the Pell Bursar's office, unstoppable as stellar gravity, had just billed *Finity* for the amount outstanding on Pell's books and thereby annoyed the seniormost and most essential captain in the Merchanters' Alliance, a man to whom Pell and the whole Alliance owed its independence. And done so at the very moment the peace and the whole human future most needed a quiet, well-oiled, dammit, even slightly illegal personal agreement to fly through the approval process before Pell's enemies knew what was going on.

Her long-suffering husband knew where she stood. Her children—both near grown—they knew. Her son said she cared only for her daughter; her daughter said bitterly that her own birth was nothing but a means to an end.

Far too simple a box, to contain all the battles of a lifetime. Pell Station knew what it wanted when it persistently elected a spacer and a zealot to the office she held . . . that in her soul there were places of utter, star-shot black.

Means-to-an-end certainly covered part of her motives, yes.

Chapter
— III —

The next day—the next *days*—were glorious.

"This you female," Melody said, in their third meeting on the riverbank, and peered into Bianca's faceplate in very close inspection, perhaps deciding Bianca, this third day, was more than a chance meeting. "She young, good, strong come back see you." Melody patted Bianca's leg. "You walk?"

This spring was what Melody meant: mating, the Long Walk. And Bianca didn't understand. Bianca murmured something about coming from the Base, but Fletcher blushed behind his mask and said, "Not yet, not yet for us."

Then Bianca was embarrassed. And indignant. "*What* did you tell her, Fletcher?"

"That I sort of like you," Fletcher said, looking at his feet. And Melody and Patch flung leaves at them and shrieked in downer laughter.

He *did* sort of like her. At least he liked what he saw. What he'd imagined he'd seen in Bianca's willingness to come back here twice. And on that grounds he was suddenly out of his depth and knew it. He saw v-dramas and vid, and imagined what it would be like to have a girl who liked you and who'd maybe—maybe be part of the dream he'd dreamed, of living down here.

He hadn't gotten a lot of biochem done the last two nights.

This wasn't someday. This wasn't just dreaming. When he'd been a juvvie and thought almost everything was impossible he'd had fantasies of coming down to the world—he'd stow away on a shuttle. He'd pirate supplies and make an outlaw dome, and get all the downers on his side.

Then the downers would join them and humans at the Base

would never again *see* a downer unless he said so. And the stationmasters would have to say, All right, we'll deal. And he'd
be king of Downbelow and Melody and Patch and he together
would run the world.

God, he'd been such a stupid juvvie brat in his daydreams,
and now, realtime, just having embarrassed himself, he had to
admit he'd caught another case of the daydreams almost as
fantastical. She was embarrassed; he was. And if you shone
light on some daydreams they evaporated.

No Family girl was going to keep on hanging around him.
She was probably just trying to make Marshall Willett leave
her alone. It had been two days of happiness interspersed with
anxiety and a biochem test he might have blown. That was a
pretty good run, as his runs went.

He'd sounded like a fool. Reality was the best medicine for
a case of daydreams, and he went off in his acute embarrassment to go over to the water and squat down and poke at
stones at the river-edge, real stones, real world, important
things like that.

His real life wasn't like the vids, and daydreams didn't
come true for somebody who wasn't anybody, somebody who
for most of his life couldn't guarantee where he'd be. It was
mortally embarrassing to have to go back to your instructors
at school and have to say, with other kids listening, that, no,
the reason you didn't know about the test was your mail wasn't
getting to you and, no, you weren't still living at 28608 Green,
you'd moved, and you were back at the shelter again, or you
were out and living with the Chavezes this week.

Then about the time the stupid teacher got the records
straightened out you still weren't getting your e-mail because
you "just hadn't worked out" with the Chavezes. It was pretty
devastating stuff when you were eight.

It was doubly devastating if you'd just had a counselor so stupid
he didn't even shut his office door when he was talking about you
to your foster parents—who didn't want you anymore because
they were pregnant and thought you'd interfere with the baby.

It hadn't been fun. The administration eventually changed
his psychiatrist to somebody who still asked stupid questions

and put him through the same getting-to-know-you routine
that by then had just about stopped hurting. It had bored him,
by then, because he'd been switched so often, to so many
people with court-ordered forms to fill out, you got a sample
of the routines and you knew by then it was just business, their
caring. They were paid to care, by the hour.

The station paid foster-families.

They paid downers, but not in money, and not to take care of
stray station kids: Melody and Patch had cared for him for free.

A hand slipped over his shoulder. He thought it was
Melody, and felt comforted.

But it wasn't Melody. It was Bianca who knelt down by
him and touched her head to his so the faceplates bumped
edges, and he was just scared numb.

"What's the matter?" she asked. "What did I do?"

God, the world was inside out. What did *she* do? She was
kidding. She had to be. But Bianca hugged her arm around him
and he hugged her, and if it wouldn't have risked their lives he'd
have taken the mask off and kissed her.

"Oh," Melody said, from somewhere near. "Look, look,
they make love."

"Dammit!" he said, breaking the first ten rules of residency
on Downbelow, and never would willingly curse Melody. He
broke his hold on Bianca to rip up a stick and fling, and double
handfuls of flowers. "Wicked!" he cried, thinking fast, and
turning his reaction into a joke.

Melody squatted down, out of range of flower-missiles,
and turned solemn, watching with wide downer eyes. "Fetcher
no more sad," Melody said. "Good, good you no more sad."

What did you say? What *could* you say, in front of the girl you
hoped to impress, and who knew what an ass you'd just been with
downers you were here to protect from human intrusions?

"I love you," he said to Melody, and fractured the rest of the
rulebook."You my mama, Melody. Patch, you my papa. Love you."

"Baby grow up," Melody said. "Go walkabout soon, make
me *new* baby."

God, what did it say about him, that he was so suddenly, so
irrationally hurt?

He shifted about on one knee to see what Bianca thought, but you could hardly see a human face through the mask.

As she couldn't see his. "Melody used to take care of me," he said to explain things. The truth, but not all of it. To his teachers and the admin people and his psychs and everybody, he was just trouble. *They* had families and Bianca had Family, and he was always just *that boy from the courts.*

"Where was this?" Bianca asked, not unreasonably confused.

"A long time back on the station. I got lost, and they sort of— found me. And got me home." He'd no desire to go into the sordid details. But he couldn't get a reaction out of her masked face to tell him where he stood in her opinion. He committed himself, totally desperate, a little trusting of the only girl he'd ever really gone around with. "I used to sneak into the tunnels, to be with them. And first thing I wanted when I got down here was to find Melody and Patch."

"You're kidding," she said.

He shook his head. "Absolute truth."

"Is he making fun?" she asked Melody, breaking the first rule: never question another human's character.

"He very small, very sad," Melody said. "Long time he sad. You happy he."

Sometimes you didn't know what downers meant when they put words together. He guessed, with Melody, and thought that Melody approved of Bianca.

"Make he walk lot far," Patch chimed in helpfully.

"This is way too far," she said, teen slang . . . which you weren't supposed to use, either. He guessed Bianca was overwhelmed with it all, and maybe adding it up that she was with a kid who wasn't quite regulation. Or respectable. Or following the rules. She sat there looking stunned, as far as a body could who was wearing a mask, and he took a wild chance and put an arm around her.

She pushed him back, sort of, and he let go, fast, deciding he'd entirely misread her.

But she patted his arm, then, the way they learned to, when they wanted someone's serious attention.

"I believe you," she said, and slipped her hand down and

held his fingers, making them tingle, just touching her bare skin.

And by sunset walking home, not so long after, she held his hand again.

"I went through the program over in Blue," Bianca said, apropos of nothing previous as they walked along the river-edge. "Did you ever go to the games?"

"Sometimes."

They had the big ball games on Wednesday nights. And the academy in rich Blue Sector played schools like his, over in industrial, insystemer-dock White, where he'd lived with the Wilsons. Sometimes the games ended with extracurricular riot.

"Isn't it funny, we probably met," Bianca said.

"I guess we could have."

She couldn't imagine, he thought. From moment to moment he was sure she'd turn on him when she got safely back to the domes and tell everything she'd heard. But her fingers squeezed his, bringing him out of his fantasies of dismissal and disgrace. She talked about ball games and school.

He wanted to talk to her about his feelings. At one wild moment he'd like to ask her if she was as uncertain as he was about the line they'd crossed, holding hands, walking holding tight to each other.

But what did he say? He felt as if his nerves and his veins were carrying a load they couldn't survive.

Maybe normal people felt that way. Maybe they didn't. He wasn't ever sure. If Melody didn't know and peer wisdom didn't say, he didn't know who he could ask.

Damn sure not the psychs.

Two legal papers waited Elene Quen's signature. *In the matter pending before the Court of Pell* . . . lay atop: *In final settlement of the aforesaid claim against the merchant ship* Finity's End, *James Robert Neihart, senior captain,* Finity's End, *her crew and company tender 150,000 credits to be held in escrow against all charges whatsoever and of whatever origin, public or private, as of this date pending, said amount*

*to be placed in the Bank of Pell to clear all debts of Fletcher
Robert Neihart, a national of* Finity's End.

The last descriptive represented a controversy settled at a
fraction of the claim's 14.5 million value. The 150,000 represented a reasonable valuation of Francesca's intended stay on
Pell, one year, plus her medical bills for a normal birth,
excluding interest.

Debt paid. *Finity's End* simply sent the agreed amount to
the Bank of Pell, and the legal dispute that had troubled all
Finity's wartime dockings, was done with. Further claims and
debts of any sort would be judged against that 150,000 fund.
It focused the political infighters and their lawyers on a single,
achievable prize, not a kid and his surrounding issues.

She signed the papers, stood up, and gave them to *Finity's*
legal representative, a young man they called, simply, Blue.

"It's done," she said. And had qualms about the one
remaining step in Fletcher's case. She'd never agreed to a
spacer going downworld in the first place; it had just stopped
being easy to prevent him. With some degree of guilt she
remembered how she'd not objected strenuously when, four
years ago, she'd become aware Fletcher's juvenile fascination
with downers now aimed at planetary science. The study program had kept the boy off the police reports and given her
four years without a crisis with Fletcher. And now things
came due.

Finity's backing in the Council of Captains would build a
merchanter ship for the first time since the Treaty of Pell.

Union wouldn't have its way. That was the down-the-line
outcome. Union thought the Council of Captains couldn't
reach a disinterested decision, or a unified action, or get any
two merchant ships to agree.

If Mallory of *Norway* was right and the black market was
in fact Mazian's pipeline to supply and funds, the notion that
ships were slipping over into Mazian's camp was very disturbing and very plausible. The War had been between the
Earth Company and Union in its earliest days—and the
Alliance hadn't yet existed. Merchanters had declared
neutrality in what had been then a small-scale dispute.

Merchanters had served both sides, excepting those merchanters actively enlisted as gunships.

Meanwhile Earth had built the Fleet to enforce Earth's hold
on the colonies and to break Union's bid for independence;
Earth had typically failed to realize what it took to sustain a
war on that scale, hadn't supplied the Fleet it had launched,
declaring that to be the colonies' job; the Fleet had taken to
relying on merchant shipping—buying off the black market
during the War and engaging in occasional outright piracy
even *before* the Battle of Pell. The Fleet had alienated the merchanters and it was the merchanters who had risen up against
them to drive them out—out far into the dark, when their bid
to take Earth itself had met Mallory and Union's and merchanter opposition. The Fleet, having lost all its allies, had had
to retreat into deep space . . . to obtain supply by means that,
indeed, no one had quite proved.

Most merchant ships had dealt with Mazian before the
Battle of Pell; and once James Robert raised the specter of continued merchant supply far more widespread than anyone had
added up, yes, it was chillingly reasonable that some merchanters, to whom personal independence was a centuries-old
ethic, might still be willing to cut other merchanters' throats by
continuing that trade on a large and knowing scale. That trade,
not conducted on station books, had historically been hard to
track—hard to develop statistics on what no station could
observe. And what James Robert suggested was that Mazian
had found large-scale ways to tap into the whole shadow trade,
the meetings of ships at isolated jump-points, where manifests
and cargomasters' stamps miraculously changed, and goods
mutated or vanished on their way to the next port, altering the
very records on which the statistics and the tariffs were based.

It was also a network that extended routes beyond what any
station tracked as regularly existing—no station could maintain records that covered every ship contact, and every ship
movement, when only station calls registered in the ships'
logs. The shadow market was a network where, theoretically,
you could buy anything that moved by ship. Union, obsessed
with order, had never liked it. Union didn't want Alliance mer-

chanters serving its far, colonial ports—internal security, Union insisted. Others said it was because Union didn't want Pell and Earth to know how rapidly and how far it was expanding. At the same time Union was aggressively building ships, Union had selected Alliance merchanters it *would* allow to reach Cyteen, and favored them with deals designed to pro-voke divisive jealousy among merchanters. That increased demands on Pell to lower dock charges to match the favorable rates Union offered. But now James Robert came saying that Union should gain its point, and that merchanters should restrict *themselves*, and that all stations should lower tariffs in exchange for a merchanter pledge to conduct all trade inside the tariffs.

That, James Robert implied, or watch the whole Alliance slide blindly into Mazian's grasp—as *she* was worried about it sliding into Union hands.

But both of them had to admit that hard times would make some merchanters desperate enough to trade with the devil—or to call him back as a hero, a savior from grasping station politicians.

Conrad Mazian, hero. Themselves all as outlaws and trai-tors. The War renewed. It wasn't a new thought. Just the resur-gence of an old, old worry.

All stakes became far, far higher, in that thought. Union didn't want that scenario for a future, either.

Finity going back to trade because the War was over? No. She'd lay odds that there'd been no far-off victory. She'd also lay odds Mallory *had* sent *Finity* back to merchant trade—for one urgent reason, to do exactly what James Robert had done with her: cut deals only James Robert could cut. He'd evi-dently come to her first, to get Pell lined up behind him, counting on her ability to deliver Pell's vote.

After that, he was going to seek general merchanter approval—and where better to do it but along the string of stars that were the stations *almost* Union and *almost* Alliance, and doing a delicate ballet of relationship with both.

Mariner. Voyager. Esperance.

Then the merchanters themselves. No station, no govern-ment, no military organization could sway several hundred highly independent merchanter captains from a trade they thought was their God-given right to conduct, as no one could get the same merchanter captains to agree to set up other merchanter captains in business to compete with them.

But this man might.

In the vids that came from Old Earth there were blue sky days. There never were on Downbelow. The clouds had endless patterns, sometimes smooth, sometimes with bubbled bottoms, sometimes with layers and sheets that traveled at different speeds in the fierce winds aloft. Great Sun usually appeared through thick veils—so that if the sun ever did show an edge of fire the downers took it for an event of great importance.

But while downers revered Great Sun, and wanted to stand in polite respect and wait for Great Sun's rare appearances, the time between those appearances was just too long to endure.

So they made the Watchers, great-eyed and reverent statues that sat gazing at the sky in lieu of living downers.

There were several such statues on a forested hill near the Base, only knee-high, so you'd trip over them if you didn't know they were there. Two looked up. One looked a little downward from the hill, and if you looked where it was looking, you could see the Base itself through the trees.

Fletcher already knew where the site was, so he knew where Melody and Patch were going when they climbed that hill. He followed, and Bianca trekked after him.

"Where are they going?" Bianca panted. And then stopped cold as she saw the images mostly hidden in the weeds. "Oh, —my."

She was impressed. Fletcher felt a warmth go through him.

"Bring watch sky," Patch said, with a wave of his arm all about. "Good see sky!"

Great view, was what Patch meant, and today it was on the downers' agenda to look at the sky, for some reason—or maybe to show Bianca this special place, as they'd shown it to him early last fall.

"It's wonderful," Bianca said. "Do they know at the Base, I mean, do they know this place is here?"

"I don't know," Fletcher said. "It's none of the researchers' business, is it, if the hisa don't tell."

He had that attitude about it. He didn't know whether if he looked it up on the computers back at the Base he'd find it was known to the researchers, and off-limits especially to juniors in the program; but juniors in the program didn't have personal hisa guides to bring them here, either.

It was a mark of how much Melody and Patch had accepted Bianca, he thought, that all of a sudden this morning they'd snagged him away from brush-cutting and wanted him to get Bianca.

"Banky," they'd called her when she came, addressing her directly. "Walk, walk, walk."

That meant a fair hike. Three walks.

So Bianca had slipped out of her work this morning, too. It was easy. The job got done sometime today. On the station they'd have had inquiries out after two teens under supervision who took a morning break.

Here, they found a secret place and watched the clouds scud overhead.

"The clouds are really moving," Bianca said, pointing aloft as they sprawled flat on their backs beside Melody and Patch. "There must really be a wind up there."

"Rains come," Melody said, and reached out her hand and held Fletcher's tightly in her calloused fingers.

Rains. The monsoon.

The weather reports at the Base had been saying there was a low in the gulf, up from the southern continent. But those were advisements relayed from the station; the station watching from space was never that good about figuring out the weather—ultimately, yes, the conditions were changing, but they were never right. There were so many variables that drove the weather, and real ground-level data came only from four places in the world, from the farms to the south, the port, from a research station on the gulf shore, and from the Base, from a primitive-looking little box full of instruments. The staff was in the habit of joking that if you wanted to know the weather, the downers always knew and the atmospherics people used dice.

But the clouds were darkening with a suddenness that raised the fine hair on his arms. The monsoon was coming: born in space as he'd been, even he could feel disturbance in the sudden change in the sky and in the air. *That* was why they'd brought him and Bianca here. Melody and Patch pointed at the sky and talked about the wind blowing the clouds. Maybe, he thought with a sinking heart, they were feeling whatever drove downers to go on their wanderings. They would go into danger in their preoccupation.

Maybe this was the last day he would ever see them. Ever.

"River he go in sky," Patch said with an expansive wave of a furry arm. "Walk with Great Sun. Down, down, down he fall, bring up flower, lot flower."

Melody inhaled deeply. "Rain smell."

What might rain smell like? He wondered, among other things he wondered, but he didn't dare risk it even for a second. The clouds were uncommonly gray today, and if he'd had to guess the hour in the last fifteen minutes he'd think it more and more like twilight, even though he knew it was noon. In one part of his mind he was scared and disturbed. In another—he was suddenly fighting off a feeling it was near dark. An urge to yawn.

A danger sign, if your cylinder was giving out. But he thought it was the light. Light dimming did that to you, whether it was the mainday-alterday change on station or whether it was the rotation of the planet away from the sun.

"Feels like night," Bianca said without his saying anything.

"Yeah," he said.

"Rain," Melody said, and in a moment more a fat drop hit Fletcher on the hand.

More hit the weeds with a force that made the leaves move.

"We'd better get back," Fletcher said. He was growing scared of a danger of a more physical sort, lightning and flood. He'd seen occasional rain, but they'd all been warned about the monsoon storms, about the suddenness with which floods could cut them off from the paths they knew—dangers station-born people didn't know about. From a sameness of weather, highs and lows, days and nights, they were all of a sudden faced with what informational lectures told him was not going to be the full-blown monsoon, not all in one afternoon.

Light flashed. Lightning, he thought. He'd rarely seen it except from the safety of the domes.

Then came a loud boom that sounded right at hand, not distantly as he'd heard it before. They'd both jumped. And Melody and Patch thought it was funny.

"Thunder," he insisted shakily. He was sure it was. Shuttles broke the sound barrier, but only remotely from here. "I think we'd better think about moving."

"We take you safe," Melody said, and ran and patted the statues, talked a sudden spate of hisa language to the statues, and left a single flower with them.

Then they scampered back, grabbed them by a hand apiece, and hurried them back toward the Base as droplets pelted down, let them go then on their own and just scampered ahead of them. A strong wind swept through the trees, making a rushing sound he thought at first was water rushing.

A faint siren sound wailed through the woods, then, over the pelting rain: that was the weather-warning, late.

The Base itself hadn't seen it coming. Not in time. Someone was scrambling for the alarm switch. Someone was red-faced.

And they were a long way from shelter.

Chapter
—IV—

The adventurer teetered on the edge of a blue-edged pit.

Fell in. Slid, with heart-stopping swiftness, whipped a scary spiral through stars, and shot out onto an unforgiving desert.

A dinosaur pack was on the horizon. Coming this way.

JR looked around for advantage, kicked the rocks around him.

A purple glow came from under the sand.

That was either another Hell level or a way out. He saw a big rock not so far away, and moved it with improbable strength. Actinic light flooded up at him through the sand, and he eased his feet into it. Slid in and down as the dino pack roared up over his head and lumbering bodies shook the ground. Teeth snapped and hot breath gusted after him.

Snaky purple ropes sprouted tendrils around him as he shot through the shapeless black, retarding his fall.

He shot through their grasp and with a sudden drop his tailbone hit a soft surface. Lights dimmed. And brightened. Three times.

Game done.

He took off the helmet, raked a hand through his sweaty hair, and sat there on the floor below the exit chute, breathing hard for a moment. Shaking. Telling himself he was safe. Games were good. Games honed the reflexes. And no one's life depended on him.

The adjacent chute spat out a cousin, Bucklin. And a second one, Lyra.

Equally exhausted, equally shaky. It was a rush, one that didn't mean life and death, but combat-weary nerves didn't entirely believe it.

"Pretty good, for purple lights," Lyra said, out of breath.
"Yeah."

They hadn't done a vid ride since they were kids—vid rides had existed at Earth's Sol Station, but there'd been, thanks to that station's morality ordinances, only kid themes or mocked-up combat, and they'd seen mostly youngsters doing the one and wouldn't let their potential pilots do the other. This ride mandated at least five feet in height, and adult spacers were doing it, so they'd delved up the chits from their pockets and given it a try, as they said, to test it out and see whether they'd clear the establishment for the three youngest cousins.

JR got to rubbery legs. You had to *work* up there in the sim. Stupid as it all was, it was, as Lyra had said, pretty good for purple lights and dinosaurs. He was sweating and breathing hard. And had a few bruises from knocking into real, though padded, walls.

This place advertised 47 rides, software-dependent. Some were hand-to-hand combat. Some were relaxing. Some were workouts. This one, rated chase-and-dodge, proved that true. They were still sweating when they went out to a noisy little soft-bar—no alcohol in this establishment, which had strict rules about doing the ride straight. There was a place down in White Sector that didn't check sobriety, and that had a lot wilder adult content than the Old Man would like to know about, JR strongly suspected.

But *Finity* had been gone from Pell too long, out where they'd been had been real ordnance, real guns, and it wasn't sex he was principally worried about as an influence on their youngest crew, although that was a concern with juniors mentally old enough but physically not. What the Old Man restricted most for the juniors on moral grounds were the space combat themes and, in the realm of reality, contact with the rougher element of some docksides. JR, in direct charge of the juniors, didn't want to let the junior-juniors unsupervised into any establishment without knowing what the place was like—or (figuring that even very young *Finity* personnel had reflexes other people might lack) whether there were liabilities to other users.

It was fantastical enough, JR judged. The juniors wouldn't confuse it with reality. It wouldn't give them nightmares—or encourage aggressive behavior.

It didn't mean he and the senior-juniors weren't going to slip down to Red or White Sector when the junior-juniors were safely in their rooms and see what the adult fare was like on the seamier side of Pell docks. The senior-juniors, his own lot, had crossed that line to anything-goes maturity in the seven years since they'd last made this port. They'd been out where combat was real, and they'd walked real corridors where surprises weren't computer-spawned. They came back to their port of registry after seven station-measured years of hard living and real threats in deep space, and sat and sipped pink fruit drinks in a soft-bar with painted dinosaurs and garish dragons on the walls as the rest of their little band found their way out to the bar area and found their table.

Chad, Toby, Wayne, and Sue showed up, sweaty and flushed and admitting it actually had been a little wilder than they expected.

"Won't hurt the juniors," was JR's pronouncement, between sips of his fruit juice. Sweet stuff. Almost sickeningly sweet. It brought back kid-days with a bitter edge of memory.

The whole trip brought back memories, a nightmare that wouldn't quite come right, because the dead wouldn't come back and enjoy the things they'd known and shared the last time they'd been at Pell. A lot of the crew was having trouble with that, ghosts, almost, the eye tricked, in a familiar venue, into believing one face was like another face.

Or remembering that you'd been at a theater, and finding your group several short of a momentary expectation, a memory, a remembrance of things past.

Ghosts, far more vivid than any computer sim . . . poignant and provoking dreams. But you had to let them go. At his young age, he knew that. He'd just expected a bit more . . .

Dignity.

Pell had been a grim, joyless place during the war, so the seniors said; he'd seen it make its docks a rowdy, neon-lit carnival in the years since. Now . . . now the place had dinosaurs, as if the place had finally, utterly, slipped its moorings to reality.

So the Old Man said they were going back to trading, making an honest living, the Old Man said, now that Mazian's pirates had gone in retreat and seemed apt to nurse their wounds for some little time. At least for now, the shooting war was over.

So where did that leave them, a combat-trained crew, brightest and best and fiercest youth of the Alliance?

Testing out the facilities—desperate hard duty it was—that they were going to let the junior-juniors into. Babysitting.

Well, that was the reversion the Old Man had talked about in his general speech to the crew. They could have a *real* liberty this time, the Old Man had said, and the Old Rules were in effect again, rules that had never been in effect in JR's entire life, and he was the seniormost junior, in charge of the younger juniors. The dino adventure was now the level of the judgment calls he made, a little chance to play, act like fools . . . or whatever the easy, soft station-bred population called it, when grown men sweated and outran imaginary dragons, while paying money for the privilege.

This was station life, not much different than, say, Sol, or Russell's, or any other starstation built on the same pattern, the same design, down to the color-codes of its docks, an international language of design and function. Pell was richer, wilder, fatter and lazier. Pell partied on with post-War abandon and tried to forget its past, the memorial plaques here and there standing like the proverbial skeletons at the feast. *On this site the station wall was breached . . .*

This was Q sector . . .

People walked by the plaques, acting silly, wearing outlandish clothes, garish colors. People spent an amazing amount of money and effort on fashions that to his eye just looked odd. Station-born kids prowled the docks looking for trouble they sometimes found. Police were in evidence, doing nothing to restrain the spacers, who brought in money; a lot to restrain station juveniles, who JR understood were a major problem on Pell, so that they'd had to caution their own junior-

juniors to carry ship's ID at all times and guard it from pick-pockets.

There was so much change in Pell. He couldn't imagine the young fashioneers gave a damn for anything but their own bodies. His own generation was the borderline generation, the one that had seen the War to end all wars . . . and even at seventeen, eighteen ship-years, now, still a mere twenty-six as stations counted time, he saw the quickly grown station-brats taking so damn much for granted, despising money, but measuring everything by it.

Hell, not only the station-brats were affected. Their own youngest were quirky, strange-minded, too fascinated by violence . . . even shorter of decent upbringing than his own neglected peers, —and that was going some.

Dean and Ashley showed up. Nike and Connor came next. The waiter, forewarned, was fast with the drinks, while they talked about the strangling plants effect and the swamp and the engineering.

"Effex Bag," Bucklin said. "Same one, I'll bet you." It was a full-body pocket you dealt with. The things fought back as hard as you could provoke them to fight, but a feed-back bag was self-limiting and you learned a fair lesson in morality, in JR's estimation: at least it taught a good lesson about action and reaction, and the effects here were more sophisticated than the primitive jobs they'd met in their repair standdown at Bryant's, a notable long time ashore. The quasi-dangers in any Effex Bag were all your own making. Hit it, and it hit back. Struggle and it gave it back to you. Go passive and you got a tame, boring ride.

"Pretty good jolt at the end," Dean said. "They drop you real-space."

"Yeah," Nike said. "About a meter. Soft."

"Junior-juniors'll like this one," JR said, deciding he couldn't take more of the pink juice. He listened to his team wondering about trying the Haunted Castle for another five credits.

Vid games and sims. Earth's cultural tourism run amok. You could experience a rock riot. Swing an axe in a Viking

raid, never mind that they equipped the opposing Englishmen
with Renaissance armor.

The reapplication of the pre-War Old Rules on *Finity's End*
had let them out without restrictions for the first time in three
decades, after the rest of the universe had been war-free for
close to twenty years, and this senior-junior, listening to his
small command discuss castles and dinosaurs, had increasing
misgivings about their sudden drop into civilian life. The fact
was, *he* hadn't had an unbridled fancy in his life and didn't
know what to permit and what to forbid, but after an education, both tape-fed, and with real books, that had taught him
and his generation the difference between a dinosaur, a Viking
and Henry Tudor, he felt a little embarrassed at his assignment. Foolish folly had become his job, his duty, his mandate
from the Old Man. And here they were, about to loose *Finity's*
war-trained youngest on the establishment.

Under New Rules or Old Rules, however, they *didn't*
wear *Finity* insignia when they went to kid amusements or
when they went bar-crawling, or doing anything else that
involved play. It was a Rule that stood. Break it at your peril.
Finity insignia, in a universe of slackening standards, sloppy
procedures, almost-good instead of excellent, still stood
for something. *Finity* personnel wouldn't be seen falling on
their ass in a carnival, not in uniform. But there *was* one in
his sight at the moment, a junior cousin violating the no-
uniforms rule. He indicated the cousin with a nod, and
Bucklin looked.

"That's in uniform," Bucklin declared in surprise.

That was Jeremy, their absolute youngest: Jeremy, who
eeled his small body among the tables of sugar-high youth,
wearing his silver uniform and *with* the black patch on his
sleeve.

He went for their table like a heat-seeking missile.

Business. JR revised his opinion and didn't even begin a
reprimand. Jeremy's look was serious.

"They got Fletcher," was Jeremy's first breath as Jeremy
ducked down next to them. "We *got* him. They signed a
paper."

"Cleared the case?" JR was, in the first breath, entirely astonished. And in the next, disturbed.

"Well, damn," Bucklin said.

It was more than Bucklin should have said to a junior-junior. But Jeremy's young face showed no more cheerful opinion.

"What terms?" JR asked. "Is there any word how? Or why? Did he apply to us?" The Fletcher Neihart case had gone on most of his life. They'd never worked it out. Now with so many things changing, the Rules upending, the universe settling to a peace that eroded all sensible behavior, *this* changed.

"I don't know what they agreed," Jeremy said. "I just heard they signed the papers and he's on the planet or something, but they're going to get him up here and we're taking him."

How in hell? was the question that blanked other thinking.

They, the junior crew, were not only turned loose among dinosaurs—all of a sudden they had a station-born stranger on their hands.

"That all you know?" JR said.

"Yes, sir, that's all. I just came from the sleepover. Sorry about the patch. I'm getting out of here."

"This place is on the list," JR said, meaning it was all right for junior-juniors, and Jeremy's eyes flashed with delight that didn't reckon higher problems.

"Yessir," Jeremy said. "Decadent!"

"Vanish," JR suggested. And should have added, Walk! but it was too late: Jeremy was gone at a higher speed than made an inconspicuous exit. Even the over-sugared teens in this place stared, knowing who they were, and seeing that in this lax new world, *Finity* crew played like fools and sat and drank with the rest of the human race.

Observers who had jobs besides games might have noticed, too, and know that *Finity*'s seniormost juniors had just gotten a piece of not-too-good news on some matter. That could start rumors on the stock exchange. If it ricocheted to the Old Man, the junior crew captain would hear about it.

The junior crew, meanwhile, didn't break out in complaints, just looked somberly at him—waiting for the word, the

junior-official position from him, on a situation that had just
suddenly cast a far more uncertain light not only on their liberty in this port, but on their whole way of working with one
another.

"Well," JR said to his crew, moderately and reasonably, he
thought, and trying to put a cheerful face on the circumstances, "—this should be interesting."

"He's a stationer," was the first thing out of Lyra's mouth.

"He may be," JR said, "but you heard the word. If it's true,
we've got him." He tossed a money card at Bucklin and got up.
"Handle the tab. I've got to talk to the Old Man."

Rain blasted down. The clean-suits were plastered to their
bodies as they hurried down a scarcely existent path, and
Fletcher's breath came short. The light-headedness he suffered
said he was needing to change a cylinder, but he didn't want
to stop for that, with the lightning ripping through the clouds
and the rain making everything slippery. They were already
going to be late getting back, and he knew their truancy was
beyond hiding.

He had to get Bianca back safely. He had to think of what
to say, what to do to protect himself *and* her reputation; all the
while his breaths gave him less and less oxygen even to know
where he was putting his feet.

His head was pounding. He slipped. Caught himself
against a low limb and tried to slow his breathing so he could
get *something* through the cylinders.

"What's the matter?" Bianca wanted to know. "Are you
out?"

"Yeah." He managed breath enough to answer, but his head
was still swimming. He had to change out. The rules said—
they were posted everywhere—advise your partner if you felt
yourself get light-headed: if you were alone, shoot off the
locator beeper you weren't supposed to use in anything but life
and death emergency. But they weren't to that point. If he
hadn't been a total fool. A hand against his thigh-pocket
advised him he was all right, he'd replaced the last one—
when? Just yesterday?

"Need one?" Bianca's voice was anxious.

"Got my spares. Let's just get there. Don't want to be logged any later than we are." He kept moving to push a little more out of the cylinders he was using: you could do that if you got your breathing down.

"They're gone!" Bianca said, then, looking around, and for a second his muddled brain didn't know what she was talking about. "I didn't see them leave."

He hadn't seen Melody and Patch go, either. Desertion wasn't like them. But downer brains grew distracted with the spring. Did, even on the station . . . and was this it? he asked himself. Was it the time they *would* go, and had they left him? Maybe for good? Or were they just scared of the storm?

The lightning flickered hazard above their heads . . . *danger, danger, danger,* a strobe light would say on station. It said the same here, to his jangled nerves. He walked, light-headed and telling himself he could make it further without stopping for a change—at least get them past the place where the trail looped near the river: *that* was what scared him, the chance of being stranded or having to wade. The tapes they'd had to watch on what the monsoon rains did when they fell chased images through his head, of washouts, trees toppling, the land whited out in rain.

Melody and Patch, he said to himself, must have sought shelter. There were always old burrows on the hillsides, and hisa grew afraid when the light faded. When Great Sun waned, there was no place for His children but inside, safe and warm and dry.

Good advice for humans, too, but they daren't bed down anywhere but at the Base. He heard his heart beating a cadence in his ears as, through the last edge of the woods and the gray haze of rain, he saw the fields and the frames.

"We'll make it," he gasped.

"But we're late," Bianca moaned. "Oh, *God,* we're late!"

They were fools. And Bianca was right, they were going to catch it, catch it, catch it.

They reached where he'd been working—close to there, at any rate. He'd left a power saw up on the ridge, and if he didn't have it when he checked in, he'd catch hell for that, too.

"Keep going!" he said to her. "I'll catch up!" And when she started to protest he shouted at her: "I left my *saw* up there. I'll catch up!"

She believed him, but she was arguing about the failing cylinder he'd complained of, about how he was already short, and he couldn't run. "Change cylinders!" she said, and held onto him until he agreed and got his single spare out of his pocket.

Rain was pouring down on them and you weren't ever supposed to get the cylinders wet, even if they had a protective shell. You got them out of the paper they were in and all you had to do was shove them in, but you had to keep your head and eject one and replace one, and then go for the other one. You weren't supposed to run out of both cylinders at the same time, but he realized he'd been close to it, and light-headed, as witness, he thought, the quality of his decisions of the last few minutes.

Bianca tried to help his fumbling fingers, and opened the packet on one cylinder of little beads. She was stripping it fast to hand it to him and he ejected one of his.

Her tug on the packet spun the cylinder out of her wet hands and she cried out in dismay. It landed in water, with its end open. Ruined. In the mask, it would have survived a dunking. Not outside it.

And he was on one depleted cylinder, with his head spinning.

"All right, all right," he tried to tell her.

"I've got mine," she said, and got out one of her spares, and opened it while he sucked in hard and held his breaths quiet, waiting for her to get it right, this time, and give him air enough to breathe.

She got it unwrapped and to his hand this time. Shielding the end from the rain, he shoved it in, then drew fast, quick breaths to get the chemistry started.

Then the slow seep of rational thought into his brain told him first that it was working, and second, that they'd had a close call.

He let her give him the second cylinder, then: they still had one in reserve, hers. You could lend a cylinder back and forth if bad came to worse, but you *never* let both go out together.

He was all right and he'd cut it damned close.

"Fletcher?" Bianca said. "I'm going with you. We're down to three. Don't argue with me!"

"It's all right, it's all right." He pocketed the wrappers: you had to turn them in to get new ones, or you filled out forms forever and they charged you with trashing. Same with the ruined cylinder. He was going to hear about it. It was going on his record.

"Just leave the saw," she pleaded with him. "Say we were scared of the lightning."

It was half a bright idea.

"We were late because of the cylinders," he said, with a better one, "and we can still pick up the saw. Come on."

She picked up on the idea, willingly. She went with him down the side of one huge frame to where he'd been cutting brush. They couldn't get wetter. The lightning hadn't gotten worse.

It was maybe ten minutes along the curve of a hill to where he'd left the saw in the fork of a tree. Safe. Waterproof.

But it wasn't there.

For a moment, he doubted it was the right tree. He stood a moment in confusion, concluding that someone had gotten it, that it might have been—God help him—a curious downer— a thought that scared him. But it most likely was Sandy Galbraith, who'd been working not in sight of him, but at least knowing where he was.

If it was Sandy checking on him and if she'd found the saw but not him, she'd have been in a bad position of having to turn him in or having to explain why she had his equipment.

If she'd been half smart and not a damn prig, she'd have left the saw where it was and pretended she didn't see anything unless she needed to remember.

Damn.

"Sandy probably got it," he said, and that meant they were later and he had to come up with a story for the missing saw, too.

He'd gone to look for Bianca because of the rain coming, that was it.

"Look," he said, as lightning whitened the brush, and they started slogging back the ten minute walk they'd come out of the way already. "I'm going to catch hell if somebody turned it in. What happened was, I knew you were by the river, and I was worried about the rain, and I ran down there to warn you, and that was why I left the saw."

She was keeping up with him, walking hard, and didn't answer. Maybe she didn't like lying to the authorities. Maybe she was mad at him. She had a right to be.

"I know, I know," he said. "I don't want to lie, either, but I didn't plan on the rainstorm, all right?" That she didn't leap at the chance to defend him made him—not mad. Upset—because of the cascade of stupid things that had gone wrong.

Maybe he'd spent too much time with psychs in his life, but he could say 'displacement' with the best psych that was out there: he and the psychs had talked a lot about his 'displacement.' And he was having a lot of displacement right now, to the extent that if he really, really had the chance to pound hell out of somebody, he would. He was upset, short of breath, and as they slogged through the mud washing from the sides of the frame, and on to the road, which was a boggy mess, he didn't know whether Bianca was mad at him or not. They didn't have any breath left to talk. They just walked, until they were on the approach to the domes.

"Remember what you've got to say," he said on great, ragged breaths. "If we've got the same story they'll have to believe us. I left the saw to go after you and I was running low on the cylinders and we were taking it slow coming back so we'd save the cylinders so as not to run without a spare apiece." They didn't let them have any more than a spare set, but they were supposed to come back to the Base immediately if they were out without a spare. You were supposed to stick with your buddy so you could share a set if you had to. And not run. That part was important. That was the core of the excuse. "Got it?"

"Yes," she said, out of breath.

The domes were close now, veiled in rain as the doors of the admin dome opened and a figure came out toward them.

Deep trouble, he thought. Administration knew. It was his fault.

JR stepped off the slow-moving ped-cab in front of number 5 Blue Dock, where a gantry with skeins of lines and a lighted ship-status sign was the only evidence of *Finity*'s presence the other side of the station wall. Customs was on duty, a single bored agent at a lonely kiosk who looked up as he came through the gate. Customs manned such a kiosk in front of limp rope lines at every ship at dock—and, at Pell, ignored most everything on a crew activity level.

The flash of a passport at the stand, a quick match of fingerprints on a plate, and he made his way up the ramp, past the stationside airlock and into the yellow ribbed gullet of the short access tube. The airlock inside took a fast assessment of the pressure gradient between ship and station and, as it cycled, flashed numbers and the current sparse gossip at him . . . *I'm moving to the DarkStar—Cynthia D.* Someone had met up with someone interesting, gone off and advised the duty staff of the fact she wasn't where she'd first checked in.

Finity personnel didn't do much of that.

Hadn't done much of it. Correction.

It was in a lingering sense of uncertainty that he walked out of the airlock and into the lower corridor of his ship at dock. The Ops office door was open, casting light onto the tiles outside, a handful of seniors maintaining the systems that stayed live during dock, and whatever was under test at the moment. JR put his head in, asked the Old Man's whereabouts.

The senior captain *was* aboard, was in his office, was at work, would see him.

He went ahead, down the short corridor past Cargo and by the lift into Administrative. Senior captains' territory. Offices, and the four captains' residences in B deck, directly above, all arranged to be useable during dock, when the passenger ring was locked down.

It was a moment for serious second thoughts, even with

honest administrative business on his mind. Business he'd gotten by scuttlebutt, not official channels.

He was damned mad. He realized that about the time he reached the point of no retreat. He was just damned mad. He knew James Robert Sr. would have policy as well as personal reasons for what he'd done. He even knew in large part what the policy decisions were.

But the result had landed on *his* section.

He signaled his presence, walked in at the invitation to do so, stood at easy attention until the Old Man switched off a bank of displays in the dimly lit office and acknowledged him by powering his chair to face him.

"Sir," JR said. "I've just heard that Fletcher's coming in. Is that official?"

The light came from the side of the Old Man's face, from displays still lit. The expression time had set on that countenance gave nothing away. The Old Man's eyes were the reliable giveaway, dark, and alive, and going through at least several thoughts before the sere, thin lips expressed any single opinion.

"Is it on the station news," James Robert asked, "or how did we reach this conclusion?"

"Sir, it came on two feet and I came over here stat."

"Sit down."

JR settled gingerly into a vacant console chair.

The silence continued a moment.

"So," James Robert said, "I gather this provokes concern. Or what *is* your concern about it?"

"He's in my command." He picked every word carefully. "I think I should be concerned."

"In what way?"

"That we may have difficulty assigning him."

"Is *that* your concern?"

"The integrity of my command is a concern. So I came here to find out the particulars of the situation before I get questions."

Again the long silence, in which he had time to measure his concerns against James Robert's concerns, and James Robert's demands against him and a very small rank of juniors.

James Robert's grand-nephew, Fletcher was. So was he.

James Robert's unfinished business, Fletcher was. James Robert said there were new rules, the new Old Manual they'd been handed, and about which the junior crew was already putting heads together and wondering.

"The particulars are," James Robert said, "that a member of this crew will join us at board call. He'll have the same duties as any new junior, insofar as you can find him suitable training. And yes, you *are* responsible for him. On this voyage, with the press of other duties, I have no time to be a shepherd *or* a counselor to anyone. In a certain measure, I shouldn't be. He's not more special than the rest of you. And you're in charge."

"Yes, sir." Same duties as a new junior. A stationer *had* no skills. His crew, already unsettled by a change in the Rules, was now to be unsettled by the news. "I'll do what I can, sir."

"He's *not* a stationer," James Robert said directly and with, JR was sure, full knowledge what the complaints would be. "This ship has lost a generation, Jamie. We have nothing from those years. We've lost too many. I considered whether we dared leave him—and no, I will *not* leave one of our own to another round with a stationer judicial system. We had the chance, perhaps one chance, a favor owed. I collected. We are *also* out from under the 14.5 million credit claim for a Pell station-share."

"Yes, sir." Clearly things had gone on beyond his comprehension. He didn't know what kind of an agreement might have hammered his cousin loose from Pell's courts. He understood that, along with all other Rules, the situation with Pell might have changed.

"So how far has the rumor spread?" James Robert asked him.

On Jeremy's two feet? Counting the conspicuous dress? "I think the rumor is traveling, sir, at least among the crew. It came to me and I came here. Others might know by now. I'd be surprised if they didn't."

"Jeremy."

"Yes, sir."

"Let a crew liberty without a five-hour check-in and they think the universe has changed. Drunken on the docks, I take it, when this news met you."

"No, sir. Fruit juice in a vid parlor."

The Old Man could laugh. It started as a disturbance in the lines near his eyes and traveled slowly to the edges of the mouth. Just the edges. And faded again.

"Life and death, junior captain. Ultimately all decisions are life and death. It's on your watch. Do you have any objections? Say them now."

"Yes, sir," he said somberly. "I understand that it's on my watch."

"The generations were broken," James Robert said. "From my generation to yours there was birth and death. There was a continuity—and it's broken. *I want that restored*, Jamie."

"Yes, sir," he said.

"You still haven't a chart, have you?"

"Sir?"

"You're in deep space without a chart. We didn't entirely get you home."

He understood that the Old Man was speaking figuratively, this business about charts, about deep space, expressions which might have been current in the Old Man's youth, a century and more ago.

"Too much war," James Robert said. The man who, himself, had begun the War, talked about charts and coming home. About charts for a new situation, JR guessed. But home? Where was that, except the ship?

The Old Man got up and he got up. Then the Old Man, still taller than most of them, set his hand on his shoulder, a touch he hadn't felt since he was, what?

Ten. The day his mother had died—along with half of *Finity*'s crew.

"Too many dead," the Old Man said. "You'll *not* crew this ship with hire-ons when you command her. You'll run short-handed, you'll marry spacers in, but you'll never let hire-ons sit station on this ship, hear me, Jamie?"

The Old Man's grip was still hard. There was still fire in

him. He still could send that fire into what he touched. It trembled through his nerves. "Yes, sir," he said faintly, intimately, as the Old Man dealt with him.

"I've given you one of your cousins back. I've agreed to Quen's damned ship-building. It was *time* to agree. It's time to do different things. Time for you, too. You're young yet. You— and this lost cousin of ours—will see things and make choices far beyond my century and a half."

"Yes, sir." He didn't know what the Old Man was aiming at with this talk of crewing the ship, and building ships for Quen of Pell. But not understanding James Robert was nothing new. Even Madison failed to know what was on the Old Man's mind, sometimes, and damned sure their enemies had misjudged what James Robert would do next, or what his resources were.

"Making peace," the Old Man said, "isn't signing treaties. It's getting on with life. It's making things *work*, and not finding excuses for living in the past. Time to get on with life, Jamie."

The Old Man asked, and the crew performed. It wasn't love. It was Family. And Family forever included that gaping, aching blank where a generation had failed to be born and half of them who were born had died. It was the Old Man reaching out across those years of conflict and training for conflict— and saying to their generation, Make peace.

Make peace.

God, with what? With a station obsessed with games and dinosaurs? With Union more unpredictable as an ally than it had been as an enemy?

That prospect seemed suddenly terrifying in its unknowns, more so than the War that had grown familiar as an old suit of clothes. The universe, like his whole generation, was in fragments and ruin.

And the Old Man said, without saying a word, *Do this new thing, Jamie. Go into this peace and do something different than you've ever imagined in the day you command.*

He was back on that cliff again. Jump off, was James Robert's clear advice. Try something different than he'd ever known.

And to start the process, of all chancy gifts, the Old Man gave him the new Old Rules and a rescued cousin who wasn't any damn *use* to the ship except the bare fact that getting Fletcher back closed books, saved the Name, prevented another disaster in Pell courts.

And maybe redeemed a promise, a loose end the Old Man had left hanging. Francesca herself had shattered, lost herself in a fantasy of drugs. But she'd kept her kid alive and under her guardianship, always believing, by that one act, that they'd come back.

Now they had. Maybe that was what the Old Man was saying, his message to Pell, to everyone around them.

They'd come back. They'd kept the ship alive. They'd survived the War. And no one had ever believed they'd do that much.

Chapter

V

There was no chance to slip into the domes unnoticed. Administration had come looking for the two of them, an irritated Administration in the form of one of the seniors, who stood suited up and rain-drenched, waiting as they came breathlessly up the path.

"Ran out of cylinder," Fletcher began his story before Bianca had to say a thing. "It was my fault. I left my saw." They weren't supposed to leave power tools where hisa could get them in their hands. Responsible behavior was at issue. "We went back after it and ran low on time. Somebody must have taken it on in. Sorry."

The rain made a deafening lot of noise. The mask hid all expression. The man from Staff Admin waved a hand toward the women's dorm. "Get in out of the rain," he told Bianca. Then: "Neihart, you come with me."

It clearly wasn't the casual dismissal of the case he'd hoped for. It didn't sound even like the forms and reports to fill out that led to a minor reprimand. The staffer led him toward the Administration dome.

So they nabbed him as responsible and sent the Family girl off without a reprimand. He was both glad they had put the responsibility on him—he'd talked Bianca into going out there—and resentful of a system settling down on him with familiar force. He figured he was on his own now, in more serious trouble than he'd bargained for, and as he walked he calmly settled his story straight in his head, the sequence, the way it had to work to make everything logical. He'd done no harm. He could maintain that for a fact. He had hope of calming things down if he just kept his head.

They walked in through the doors, out of the rain. And the senior staffer—the name was Richards, but he didn't remember the rest—waved him through to the interview room, where you could deal with Admin without going through decon, if you didn't have long business there. It was a room where you could go in and talk to someone through a clean-screen, or apply for a new breather-cylinder, or fill out paperwork.

Left alone there, he sat on one of the two hard plastic chairs, rather than appear to pace or fret: he was onto psychs with pinhole cameras. He knew the tricks. He sat calmly and wove himself a vivid, convincing memory of seeing a team member by the river when the rain started, a stand of trees that was real close to the water, where somebody could get cut off by rising water.

Yes, he'd been stupid in leaving the saw: if you were dealing with administrators, you always had to admit to some little point where you'd been stupid and you could promise you'd never do that again, so they'd be happy and authoritative. They could say he'd learned a lesson—he had—and he'd be off the hook. He'd learned a long time ago how to make people in charge of him go off with a warm glow, having Saved him yet again and having Made Progress with their problem child. He had the mental script all made out by the time the director walked in from the other side of the transparent divider and sat down, sour-faced, on the other side of the desk.

His bad luck it was Nunn; he had rather it had been the alterday director, Goldman, who had a little more sense of humor.

Nunn had brought a paper with him. Nunn passed it through the little slot in the divided desk.

"Mail, Mr. Neihart."

Mail? Complete change of vectors.

Different problem. *Stupid* change of direction. What was this, anyway?

Station trouble? If it was mail for him it was either his last set of foster parents upset about something or it was lawyers. And a first glance at the address at the top of the folded fax sheet said *Delacorte & McIntire*.

Lawyers.

His sixth set of lawyers. Four had resigned his case. Two had retired, grown old in his ongoing legal problems. He went through lawyers almost faster than he'd gone through foster-families.

Nunn was clearly waiting for him to read it in front of him and wanted some kind of reaction. Admin had to know every time you sneezed down here and every time you had a cross word with anybody. The rules that protected the downers didn't let anybody go around them who had any personal or job problems, and if the letter was anything the director considered bad news, he'd be yanked off duty till he'd been a session with the psych staff.

Which with his other problems wasn't good. So he prepared himself to be very calm, no matter what, and to convince the man there wasn't a thing in relation to any human being or situation on Pell Station that could possibly upset him.

Except—the one thing that reliably *could* upset him.

Finity was in port. Here they went again. Seven years since the last lawsuit from *that* quarter.

None of them, he told himself, had ever meant a thing.

The lawyers' letter said, after that opening tidbit: *This is to apprise you . . .* ran down to: *refiling of the petition to the Superior Court of Pell;* and, like a high-speed impact: *The official reopening of your case . . .*

He read it to the end. McIntire wanted him to be aware, that was all: the legal wars were starting again. They'd want depositions. Maybe another psych exam. Dammit, he was one year short of past all this: one year short of his majority, and they could mandate another psych exam, see whether his best interests were being served . . . that was the way they always put it. His best interests.

Only this time—this time he wasn't exactly within walking distance of his lawyer's office.

"They want you to take the next shuttle up," Nunn said. "Tomorrow."

He folded it again as it had been and gave it back to the director in the pretense that the director hadn't read it first.

And he tried to assume a nonchalance he didn't feel, while his heart raced and his mind scattered. "That's ridiculous. Respectfully, sir. That's ridiculous. How much money are they going to spend on this?"

"They want you to take the flight."

"For a week on station? Two, at max? This is *stupid*. They do it whenever they're in port. Don't they know that? This isn't any walk down to the court."

"Do you resent it? Do you think it's unfair?"

Oh, *that* was a psych question. Nunn wasn't real clever at it.

"I'm not real happy," he said calmly. "They don't say a thing about how long I'm going to stay up there."

"Well, their idea, of course, is that you'll board their ship, isn't it?"

A cold day in hell was what he thought. Nunn's calm voice made his skin crawl. "They sue every time they're in port. They always lose. It's just a waste of time and money. They're worried because the station wants them to buy me a station-share. They don't want to spend fourteen million. So everybody sues. That's what this is about."

There was a little silence, then, a troublesome silence. He hadn't a notion why, just—Nunn looked at him, and for some reason he thought Nunn knew something Nunn wasn't telling him.

The man wanted him on that shuttle, and they wanted to get him out of here, that was the first consideration. And if Bianca's family on the station had heard about him and knew his history—God knew what strings *they* could pull. The trouble he'd thought he was in for being late back from the field was nothing against this trouble. And he didn't dare let Nunn see how upset he was. If you were emotionally upset they sent you away from the downers. Fast.

A seventeen-year-old with no credentials in the program and a continuing prospect of emotional upset? They'd send him Upabove with no return ticket. And lawyers couldn't help him. Not even the court could overrule the scientists in charge of downer welfare.

"I'd better go pack." His voice almost wobbled. He turned

a breath into a theatric sigh and cast Nunn the kind of exasperated, weary look he'd learned to give police, lawyers, judges, authority in general. He didn't break into a sweat and he didn't blow up. "So where's the shuttle schedule?" He feared one was onworld. It was midweek. One should be. "What time does the shuttle go?"

"Tomorrow morning. You'd better pack all your stuff, all the same. Oh-seven hundred, weather permitting, the car will pick you up at the dorm."

"Yes, sir," he said. He wasn't going to have days to get ready, then. And, pack all your stuff. Nunn thought he'd be staying Upabove, then.

He'd think of something. He'd surprise them.

He'd make them fly him back.

Make them. He hadn't had a great deal of luck *making* anybody do anything. He'd gotten in here only because he'd been a straight, clean student since he'd reformed, and because he'd half-killed himself scoring high on the exams, but that was getting *into* the program. Now, in a lawsuit, they weren't going to look at his future. They were going to look at his past, which was nothing but trouble. All his records were going to end up in court, public. They were going to ask how somebody with a juvenile record had gotten into the program in the first place. Everything he'd lived down was going to reappear. All his records. A drug-dosing mother. All his sessions with station cops. His psychs had vouched him clear of that; if only he could show a clean record in his work down here he might have a chance.

Instead he'd lost equipment and been late. He'd picked one hell of a time to slight the rules down here . . . with the lawsuit coming up again, and himself going under the psychological microscope again to try to prove, no, he couldn't go to space, he wasn't fit to go to space. He was too fragile to be deported.

How could he simultaneously prove he was rehabbed enough to be down here and not fit to go with his relatives and get shot at along with his mother's ship?

And what did he say when they asked him what he'd been up to reporting late? I lost my head? I was infatuated with a girl? And drag Bianca's name into it, and let *her* Family in on it?

He hated his relatives with a fury beyond reason. He hated all humanity at the moment.

He went out the doors, one after another, realizing, in a colder panic since the test that brought him here, that they— the *they* in station administration who lifelong had ordered him around—could now get him up to the station for their own convenience in their lawsuit, but *they* might not get around to bringing him back all that quickly, even if all things were equal and he *hadn't* just gotten Bianca Velasquez into trouble—a shuttle ticket up, they'd pay for. Down, he couldn't afford. That meant even if things went absolutely flawlessly, his lawyers were going to have to sue to make them send him back, which would take time, a lot of time.

They could ruin his life while they messed around and made up their minds. They *were* ruining his life, just filling out their damned forms and sending him up to the station again because the *law* said he had to be in court to say so.

Seven hundred hours. That was when the shuttle broke dock, flew, did whatever it did. He heard the shuttles go over in the early mornings when the staff was having breakfast. They'd roar overhead and people would stop talking for a few beats and then they'd go on with their conversations.

Where's Fletch? they'd say tomorrow morning.

Bianca would miss him for a couple of weeks. Maybe longer.

But what good would it do?

He'd never see Melody and Patch again, and they *damned* sure wouldn't understand where he'd gone. The monsoon was coming. They could *die* in their long walk and he wouldn't be here, he wouldn't know.

Rain washed over him and lightning whitened the door of the men's dorm as he opened it and shoved his way through into the entry. In a shattered blur of white he saw the usual pile of clean-suits for the cleaning crew to take, all the masks hanging, clustered on their pegs. His mask should join them. He should unsuit, go in, pack, as he was told.

But he didn't want to unsuit. Not yet. Not yet for going inside and facing the questions he'd get from supervisors and the others in the program when he started packing up. Emotions would answer. And that was no good, not for him, not for his future. He wanted an hour, one hour, to walk in the rain—just to get himself together, not to have a fight with Marshall Willett on his record.

And he'd reported to the Base. He'd checked in with Admin. He wasn't on anyone's list as missing any longer. You could be outside. There wasn't a curfew on. If he wanted to get wet, it was his choice, wasn't it?

His mask was on one cylinder.

Hell, he thought, and opened another mask, one on the pegs, and borrowed one, in the thought he'd annoy someone, but nothing against the necessity of getting himself a chance to cool down before he had to deal with anybody.

Then, to be safe, he borrowed one from another mask—it would risk whoever it was to take both, in case they were stupid enough to ignore how light the mask was and go out thinking they were set . . .

But then he wasn't as trapped. And in a fit of anger he raided a third and a fourth mask. A fifth and a sixth. He wouldn't *be* trapped. He was going to *miss* that shuttle. Maybe his lawyers could fight it through the court: they'd take his side, and it was time for them to earn their station-given stipend. Get himself up there in reach and some court order could get him set aboard his relatives' ship, and then no court order could get him off. That was one thought. The other was that right now he wanted not to have to see Marshall's smug face and that most of all he wanted not to have to tell Bianca that he was sorry, he wasn't like other people, lawyers owned him and they could deport him if the courts didn't rule he was mentally unstable.

In which case they'd throw him out of the program anyway, and the station would give him some makework job because his mental state made him unemployable at anything else he was qualified to do.

He resettled his mask. He'd stuffed his pockets with cylinders until they wouldn't hold any more. He walked out the door into the rain and the lightning of a world that, until a quarter hour ago, had been happy and promising him everything he could ever want.

He walked down the puddled gravel path toward the river, and no one stopped him.

If they caught him he could still lie and say he'd left the saw and only then remembered it and didn't want to leave the Base with a black mark on his record. He still had an escape. He always left himself one way to maneuver.

But he was scared this time, more than all the other times he'd been snatched up by the system. He'd usually had enough of whatever home they'd put him into, and it was certain by the time he'd heard it taken apart and analyzed and argued pro and con in court, that he was ready to be put elsewhere. You couldn't maintain an illusion that you were normal when your foster-family got up in front of a judge and answered questions about their private lives and your private life, and lied right in front of you to make them sound better and you sound worse.

And you'd say, in a high childish voice, That's a lie! And sometimes the court believed you, but by then you knew it wasn't better, and wouldn't ever be better, and things that hadn't been broken before the lawyers got into it would be broken by the time they got through hashing it up in public. Or if there was anything left of ties to that family he'd break it up in his own stupid actions—he'd go immediately and get in trouble of some kind, just to hit back, maybe, because it hurt. He could see that from where he was now, and after Melody had told him that truth about himself. He'd always come out of the hearings worse than he went in, usually with a family in ruins—and this time—

This time it wasn't anything so ephemeral as one more human family that he'd lose. This time it was everything he'd ever worked for. It was Melody and Patch themselves.

Just Melody, just Patch. Just a couple of downers. Quasi-humans. Just the only living beings that had ever really loved him. And Bianca, who made him stupid and excited and set him tripping over his own tongue and still for some reason liked him. Bianca was the first ever of anybody who fit that category of 'people' the psychs were so set on him making relationships with, but when he thought about it, it wasn't a seamless relationship, even so. Nothing was seamless when the courts made you hold a microscope to it and asked you if it was valid.

Bianca was what he'd say to the psychs when they got around to arguing about his motives for making trouble. He'd say, *I've been working on developing relationships.* That was one of their own phrases. They'd like that. You couldn't use words like *transference* and *displacement,* because they knew you were psyching them when you did that, but *relationships* was a word that you could use. He'd say he was just working things out about relationships—

The dicing-up had in that sense already begun—as if he knew the track things had to take now and couldn't help himself. He couldn't bear for the court psychs to get their hands on him, so he ripped himself up and handed them the pieces in the order *he* controlled. But, hell, it still meant that nothing stayed whole. If they found out about Melody and Patch they'd dice *that* up, too, until, like his foster-families, there wasn't any clean feeling left.

And he'd told Bianca. *She* knew. She'd talk. People always did, when the psychs wanted to know. They betrayed you to help you.

"You!" someone shouted, thin and far away. It was a male voice, and angry. Somebody *had* seen him. And he ran. He knew that he'd made a choice the moment he'd started running, and it felt like freedom, and he didn't stop.

"Come back here!" the staffer shouted. Desperate.

So was he. He ran for the path by the river, where the trees and the rocks hid him and he kept running and running, while the breathing mask failed to keep up with the need for oxygen and started feeding him CO_2.

Red and gray warred in his vision. He slowed only because he had to. He walked, blind and gasping, because he knew someone was behind him who might not run as fast, but who'd be there, nonetheless.

The river roared beside him, swollen with the falling rain. When the man chasing him got the notion he couldn't find him in the thicket and went back to report that there was a fool out running in the woods, they'd send out more people with more cylinders to look for him in a systematic way.

Old River's rising might cut them off, cover his tracks, keep him safe.

Old River he strong, Melody would say, Old River he drink all, all down he catch.

Old River was both friend and enemy, god and devil to the hisa, stronger than human courts or decrees or all the forces the Base could bring to bear. It might kill him, but he didn't care. He knew he was stupid for running, and right now, he didn't care. Back there at the Base, in the next few minutes, the word would get around. Where's Fletch? Where's Fletch, the buzz would start. And then they'd all start saying it.

And he didn't want to be there to hear it. Yes, they'd have the people out searching. But slower than they'd be out searching, under other circumstances. *Their* masks were missing cylinders. They'd have to fill out all that paperwork, do all those reports. It gave him a strange, light-headed satisfaction. Die? They wouldn't. Be inconvenienced? A lot. He felt a light-headedness not from shortness of air, but from a single moment of victory he knew he'd pay for.

He'd worked all his life to get here, and in the end, it wasn't lawyers that took him away, it was himself, because he'd blown it—and chosen to blow it—at least he'd chosen it. Stealing those cylinders and running, that wasn't going to be a minor rules infraction. But it was a *choice,* damn them all. It was *his* choice. When things fell apart, he at least had that to say.

Lightning flashed and thunder cracked right above his head, above the tops of the trees. His heart jumped and his knees wobbled with the adrenaline rush it gave him. A planet's surface where electricity flew around like a loose power line, that was a dangerous thing: water coursed beside the path, not tame Old River any longer, but a rough-surfaced flood, Old River in one of his killing moods.

Old River he mad, the downers would say.

Old River he catch you foot, drag you down. Melody had warned him of the treachery of soft banks among the very first things she'd ever warned him when he came to the planet. Old River was the devil who always lurked to take the unwary, and Great Sun was the god—if downers had a religion. Which human experts argued about in stupid technicalities.

You couldn't ask the downers that. They said if you asked you'd give them ideas and it might pervert the whole course of downer development, turning it toward something human.

So what were the domes, fools? Puffer-balls? Nature falling from the sky? They didn't know about Old River. They recorded downer beliefs about Old River, they knew the words, but Old River wouldn't cover for them, wouldn't protect them, wouldn't take care of them, father and devil both.

He'd told Bianca—he'd told Bianca—his thoughts were tumbling wild as the water near his foot—to say that they were late because he'd gone back to see about the saw. Wasn't that what they'd agreed to say? That was what she'd have said, if they went to her. As they would. He'd thought through so many variations on the lie he'd confused himself.

But that was it, wasn't it? She was supposed to say that, if they questioned her about being late. So he *couldn't* use the saw excuse.

He could say, well, he wasn't sure where he'd put the saw, and he remembered later putting it somewhere else and he wanted to find it—

The hell, after that interview with Nunn? after being told to pack up?

He could still make a case for himself, he could say he'd just been that shaken and wanted to keep his record clear in case he and Bianca had just missed finding it out here, but, damn, nobody was going to believe that, and he was never going to get reassigned down to the Base, never again. He'd blown all the trust, all the credit he had for common sense . . .

His foot went in. Cold water pressed the one-way fabric to his leg, and, sweat-osmosed, a trickle got through and into his boot before, one hand holding a branch, the other braced against the moss, he hauled himself out and up to squat on the bank.

Close. Soberingly close. Adrenaline had spiked. It fell,

now, leaving tremors, leaving a side aching and lungs burning with effort.

He knew he'd be smarter to go back on his own, and say— just say he was spooked, and he'd been a fool, but he'd come back on his own, hadn't he?

If he was Marshall Willett, he'd get a second chance, no problem. Mama and papa would buy it for him, pull strings, use up favor-points, and Marshall would get one more chance.

But he was Fletcher Neihart, a spacer-brat, son of no one, and he'd used up all his second chances just surviving his mother's inheritance.

Disaster. The kid had run. Spooked. Elene Quen had the report on her desk, a personal fax from Nunn, down at the Base, and she sat staring at it, reading it for any wisdom she could get from it.

Damon had been upset with what she'd done in getting the court order.

Not as upset as she'd expected about the fact of her trading her influence on Pell for *Finity*'s support: that was a merchanter way of doing business and it regarded merchanter relations. It was diplomacy, in which diplomats used every card they had to use and did it in secrecy.

But about *what* she'd traded, about interference with the Children's Court, he'd been unexpectedly upset—a distress about the boy's case which she hadn't predicted, and still, after all these years on station, didn't understand. Damon was a lawyer, before anything, and believed in processes of law as important for their own sake, a viewpoint she flatly didn't share in her heart of hearts—only took his advice, generally, when she crossed from port law, which she did understand, into station law, which she detested on principle. Perhaps that was the heart and soul of what was at issue.

The fact that *Finity* had a right to the boy? In Damon's eyes, that might be disputable. In her eyes, that was absolute. That the station court had repeatedly held against that right? In her mind, that was an outrage. Not her outrage, because it wasn't her ship—*she ain't my ship, she ain't my fight* was the rule on dockside—but now a deal had set her firmly on *Finity*'s side in the matter.

Process for its own sake? Importance of the process? The law might be Damon's life. But it was an ornament, a baroquerie of station life. In space it just might kill you.

Maybe, now, by the facts in this report, she'd just lost a kid, following the station's damned *processes.* A letter from the boy's independent lawyers, acting *in his interest,* had gotten to Nunn *before* her letter; and dammit, Nunn had handed that letter to the kid and then let that kid walk out the door, *trusting* he was dealing with a stationer mentality who'd tamely, because it was the orderly thing to do, walk over and pack his belongings and surrender to the law.

Hell if. Fletcher Neihart might have lived on a station, but he hadn't been brought up by Nunn's rules or Damon's law, not for the first five years of his life. Not so long as Francesca Neihart had had her kid in hand. He might have been born on a station, stuck on a station, educated on a station, but one stationer family after the other had come back to the Children's Court saying *they* couldn't handle him.

Now, enterprising lad, he'd stolen a bunch of cylinders, each one about eight hours of oxygen—if you didn't push it. Three, or less, if you pushed it hard. And a scared, mad kid didn't know moderation. The cylinders weren't fresh ones, either. They added up the total use-hours from work records on the people he'd stolen them from and came up with three days *if* he was pushing it.

The kid was trying to wait till *Finity* had left port, was what he was doing: he was *doing* things that weren't totally bright on an adult level but that made perfect sense to a kid. She'd brought up two of her own, she knew station-born sixteen- and seventeen-year-olds from personal and recent experience, and right now the desire to shake the runaway till his teeth rattled mingled with the fear that spacer directness and stationer legality together might have pushed Francesca's kid into deeper danger than his limited experience could comprehend.

The fact was, Fletcher Neihart was trying to stand off the whole Alliance court system *and* her authority simultaneously, and he was doing a pretty good job of it—because a starship couldn't sit at dock extra days. *Finity* couldn't wait. It had schedules, obligations, operations, God *knew*, critical operations, with desperate issues at stake. Fletcher *was* a Neihart. And he was holding off the lot of them. Like mother, like son, and like the legendary man whose name he carried.

And if Nunn had lost that kid, if thanks to people she'd put in charge of critical operations, station management didn't deliver a live body to *Finity* before undock, she would be in a hell of a mess. The agreement she and James Robert had made for good and solid reasons of policy might stand, but the decades-long friendship she had with the politically essential Neiharts might not survive the event.

Hell of a thing for the kid—who right now was wandering a Downbelow woods on three days worth of cylinders, in a state of mind she could more accurately imagine than any court could. She knew what it was to be ripped loose from everything and set adrift in a world that was never going to make gut-level sense.

But she hadn't done wrong in signing the order or anything else she'd arranged with the Neiharts of *Finity's End*. *She* was right—ethically, morally, historically right. Leave things to Damon's precious law, and the whole human race could go down the chute. They'd come near enough in the last phase of the War: nobody had thrown a planet-buster, but they'd lost a station. They'd nearly lost two. They could lose a planet the next time the human race went to war. In order to prevent that happening, she had no illusions. Her enemies claimed she wanted to destroy Union. That was so. But practically she knew she couldn't do that. In plain diplomatic reality, the Merchanters' Alliance had to keep the tight balance of power between themselves and Union, and they had to keep it balanced no matter how frightening and uncomfortable the attempts of Mazian to destabilize the Alliance and rebuild his power base, no matter the near-time choices in terms of her political future, even of her own determination to save the Quen name—let alone one kid's personal wishes about his domicile.

Fight the microbattles, the ones on paper, on conference tables, sometimes in public posturings—so they never, ever had to fight another hot war or—the alternative—lose what was human by acquiescing to Union's high-speed expansionism.

Instant populations. Cultures planned and programmed by ReseuneLabs on Cyteen. Ariane Emory. *That* was what she was fighting, with no knowledge even of their enemy's internal workings, not at the level they needed in order to make negotiation work. Emory was a name she knew very well, but the tight control Union had maintained over ships near Cyteen had limited what she knew. She planned in the absence of good intelligence information.

Time was what they had to gain. They'd faced, in Azov, in Emory, a faceless enemy. An alienated humanity Earth had alienated over centuries. An alienated humanity that didn't operate by the same rules. The very history and *process* Damon venerated didn't work out there in the Beyond.

The Fletcher Neiharts of the universe, along with her long-time problem child, were precious, every one of them. Her throwaway problem couldn't live under Pell's law . . . and now that she devoted half an hour's sustained consideration to the boy as he'd grown to be, she knew why he'd been inconvenient all his life—that he couldn't thrive in a sealed bubble of a never-changing, zero-growth world where every decision was for the status quo. He couldn't live in it unless and until the system crushed him—and she had never let it do that. The mentalities to respond to the problems Cyteen posed the rest of humanity couldn't come out of Pell. Neither, for what she could see, could that response come out of Earth, whose distance- and culture-blinded dealings had driven Cyteen to become the alien culture it was in the first place.

She had such a narrow, narrow window in which to give a civilization-saving shove at the clockwork of the system—in things gone catastrophically wrong between Earth and its colonies in the earliest days of Earth's expansion outward. The timeliness that had brought her *Finity's End* in its mission to reconcile merchanters and Union was the same timeliness that demanded the Alliance finally wake up to the economic challenge Union posed. It was the pendulum-swing of the Company Wars: they'd settled the last War, they'd banded together and shoved hard at the system to get it to react in one way; now the reactionary swing was coming back at them, the people with the simplistic solutions, and they had to stand fast and keep the pendulum from swinging into aggressive extremism on one hand and self-blinded isolationism on the other.

She hadn't forever to hold power on Pell: a new election could depose her inside a month. People too young to have fought the War were rabble-rousing, stirring forces to oppose her tenure, special interests, all boiling to the top.

And they might topple her from the slightly irregular power she held if she'd just killed a kid. James Robert Neihart hadn't forever to live in command of *Finity's End*. He was pushing a century and a half, time-dilated and on rejuv. Mallory's very existence was at risk every time she stalked the enemy, and she never ceased.

At least one set of hands on the helm of state were bound to change in twenty years. That was a given, and God help their successors. Madison, James Robert's successor, was a capable man. He just wasn't James Robert, and his word didn't carry the Old Man's cachet with other merchanters.

The whole delicate structure tottered. Time slowed. *Finity's End* would have to wait on a teenaged boy to come to his senses . . . or lose him, to its public embarrassment, and her damnation, as things were running now.

And damn him, *damn* the kid.

They lost him, the word floated through the meetings of *Finity* personnel on dockside, and there were quiet meetings in cafes, in bars, in the places seniors met and the junior-seniors could go, circumspectly. JR heard it from Bucklin in one of those edge-of-reputable places you couldn't go with the juniormost juniors. The honest truth, because he *couldn't* sort out how he felt about them losing Fletcher, was that he was glad it was only Bucklin with him.

All the Old Man's hopes, he thought. To start this voyage by finally losing Fletcher . . .

What you want to happen, the saying went . . . What you want to happen is your responsibility, too. He'd heard that dictum at notable points in his life, and he wasn't sure how he felt right now.

Guilty, as if he'd gotten a reprieve, maybe. As if the entire next generation of Neiharts had escaped dealing with a problem it could ill afford.

I will not lie. I will not cheat. I will not steal. I will never dishonor my Name or my ship . . .

That pretty well covered anything a junior could get into. And as almost *not* a junior, and in charge of the rest of the younger crew, he was responsible, ultimately responsible for the others, not only for their physical safety, but for their mental focus. If there was a moral failure in his command, it was *his* moral failure. If there was something the ship had failed to do, that attached to the ship's honor, the dishonor belonged to all of them, but in a major way, to him personally.

The ship as a whole had all along failed Fletcher. His mother individually and categorically had failed him.

And what was the woman's sin? A body that had happened to carry another Neihart life, at a time when the ship hadn't any choice but put her ashore, because to fail the call *Finity's End* had at the time hadn't been morally possible. *Finity's End* had always been the ship to lead, the ship that *would* lead when others didn't know how or where to lead; and she'd had both the firepower and the engines to secure merchanter rights on the day that firepower became important, when *some* ship had had to follow *Norway* to Earth.

It was impossible to reconstruct the immediacy of the decisions that had gotten Francesca Neihart into her dilemma. It was certain that they'd had to go to *Norway*'s aid, and as he'd heard the story, they'd vowed to Francesca, leaving her on Pell, that they'd be back in a year.

But it had been more than that single year, it had been five; and in that extended wait, Francesca had failed, or whatever was happening to her had conspired against her sanity. He didn't himself understand whether it was the dubious pregnancy or the overdoses of jump drugs she'd taken while she was ashore, or whether by then Francesca had just consciously chosen to kill herself.

And worse, she'd done it with a kid involved, a *Finity* kid, that the station wouldn't, in repeated tries and reasoned appeals and lawsuits, give back to them.

In the sense that he was related to that kid and in the sense that he'd talked himself into accepting responsibility for that kid, he felt a little personal tug at his heart for Fletcher Neihart, his might-have-been youngest cousin who was lost down there. The three hundred six lives that *Finity* had lost in the War—three hundred seven if you counted Francesca, and he thought now they should—were hard to bear, but they were a grief the whole ship shared. The most had died in the big blow when the ship's passenger ring had taken a direct hit. Ninety-eight dead right there. Forty-nine when they'd pulled an evasion at Thule. Sixteen last year. Since they'd left Francesca, half the senior crew was dead, Parton was stone blind, and forty-six more had some part of them patched, replaced or otherwise done without. Juniors had died, not immune to physics and enemy action. His mother, his grandmother, three aunts, four uncles and six close cousins had died.

So on one level, maybe those of them who'd been under fire for seventeen years were a little short on sympathy for Francesca, who'd suicided after five years ashore. But in figuring the hell the ship had lived through, maybe no one had factored in what Pell had been during those years. Maybe, JR said to himself, she'd died a slower death, a kind of decompression in a station growing more and more foreign and frivolous.

And with a son growing up part of the moral slide she'd seen around her?

Was *that* the space she'd been lost in, when she started taking larger and larger doses of the jump drug and getting the drug from God knew where or how, on dockside?

Out there where the drug had sent her, damn sure, she hadn't *had* a kid. Or cared she had.

That was what he and Bucklin said to each other when they met in the sleepover bar, in the protective noise of loud music and cousins around them.

"The kid's in serious trouble. Down there is no place to wander off alone," Bucklin said, "what I hear. There's rain going on. One rescuer nearly drowned. I don't think they'll ever find him."

"Board call tomorrow," he said over the not-bad beer. "They're finishing loading now. Cans are hooked up."

"They're holding the shuttle on-world," Bucklin said. "It's supposed to have lifted this morning. Can you believe it? So much fuss for one of us?"

The stations didn't grieve over dead spacers. Didn't treat them badly, just didn't routinely budge much to accommodate spacer rights, the way station law didn't extend onto a merchanter's deck. Foreign territory. *Finity's End* had won that very point decades ago, with Pell *and* with Union.

But right now, the whisper also was, among the crew—they'd found it out in this port—Union might make another try at shutting merchanters out. Union had launched another of the warrior-merchanters they were building, warships fitted to carry cargo. The whisper, from the captains' contact with Quen and Konstantin, was that there were many more such ships scheduled to be built.

Meanwhile Earth was building ships again, too, for scientific purposes, they said, for exploration—as they revitalized the Sol shipyards that had built the Fleet that had started the War. The whole damned universe was unravelling at the seams, the agreements they'd patched up to end the War looked now only like a patch just long enough for the combatants to renew their resources and for Union to try to drive merchanters out of business. The rumor on Pell was that of shipbuilding, too, ships to counter Union and maybe Earth.

And now cousin Fletcher had taken out running, the final,

chaotic movement in a bizarre maneuver, while the finest fighting ship the Alliance had was loaded with whiskey, coffee, and chocolate she hadn't sold at Pell, and now with downer wine.

"Luck to the kid," JR said, on a personal whim, and lifted his mug. Bucklin did so, too, and took a solemn drink.

That was the way they treated the news when they heard it was all off, they'd not get their missing cousin.

But by board call as *Finity* crew who'd checked out of sleepovers and reported to the ship's ramp with baggage ready to put aboard, they met an advisement from the office that boarding and departure would be delayed.

"How long?" JR asked their own security at the customs line, giving his heavy duffle a hitch on his shoulder. "Book in for another day, or what?"

"Make it two," the word was from the cousin on security. "Fletcher's coming."

"They found him?" JR asked, and:

"He's coming up," the senior cousin said. "They got him just before he ran out of breathing cylinders. I don't know any more than that."

There were raised stationer eyebrows at the service desk of the sleepover when all the *Finity* personnel who'd just checked out came trooping back in with bag and baggage. The Starduster was a class-A sleepover, not a pick-your-tag robotic service. "Mechanical?" the stationer attendant asked.

"Unspecified," JR said, foremost of the juniors he'd shepherded back from the dockside. The rule was, never talk about ship's business. That reticence wasn't mandated clearly in the Old Rules, but it was his habit from the New Rules, and he'd given his small command strict orders in the theory that silence was easier to repair than was too much talk.

"What *is* this?" Jeremy asked, meeting him in the hallway of the sleepover as he came upstairs. The junior-juniors were on a later call, B group. "We've got a hold, sir?"

There was no one in the corridor but *Finity* personnel. "We've got an extra cousin," JR said. "They found Fletcher."

"They're going to hold the ship for him?"

They'd always told the juniors they wouldn't. Ever. Not even if you were in sight of the ramp when the scheduled departure came.

"She's held," JR said, and for discipline's sake, added: "It's unusual circumstances. Don't ever count on it, younger cousin."

There was a frown of perplexity on the junior's face. Justice wasn't done. A Rule by which *Finity* personnel had actually died had cracked. There were Rules of physics and there were *Finity*'s Rules, and they were the same. Or no one had ever, in his lifetime, had to make that distinction before. Until now, they'd been equally unbendable. Like the Old Man.

"How long?" Jeremy asked.

"Planets rotate. Shuttles lift when they most economically can."

"How long's that?"

"Go calc it for Downbelow's rotation and diameter. Look up the latitude. Keep yourself out of trouble. I *will* ask you that answer, junior-junior, when we get aboard. And stay available!" There were going to be a lot of questions to which there was no answer, and Jeremy, to Jeremy's misfortune, had pursued him when he was harried and out of sorts. The junior-juniors were going to have to stay on call. They all were going to have to stay ready to move, if they were on a hold. That meant no going to theaters or anywhere without a pocket-com on someone in the group. That meant no long-range plans, no drinking, even with meals, unless they went on total standdown.

Francesca's almost-lamented son had just defied the authorities and the planet.

Beaten the odds, apparently.

As far as the cylinders held out.

Just to the point the cylinders had run out, by what he'd heard. By all calculations, Fletcher should have died by now.

He didn't know Fletcher. No one did. But that said something about what they were getting—what *he* was getting, under his command.

Pell and the new Old Rules had felt chancy to him all

along. He'd felt relief to be boarding, with the Fletcher matter lastingly settled; guilty as he'd felt about that, there had been a certain relief in finality.

Now it wasn't happening.

And nothing was final or settled.

Customs wasn't waiting at the bottom of the ramp. Police were. Fletcher knew the difference. He shifted an anxious grip on the duffle he'd been sure he was going to have to fight authority for—again—and knew the game had just shifted rules—again.

He walked ahead nonetheless, from the yellow connecting tube of the shuttle and down onto the station dock, into the custody of station police.

He didn't know this batch of police. Many, he did know, and no few knew him by name, but he was glad he didn't have to make small talk. He handed over his papers, a simple slip from Nunn and his shuttle authorization, and halfway expected them to put a bracelet on him, the sort that would drop an adult offender to his knees if he sprinted down the dock, but they didn't.

"Stationmaster wants to see you," one informed him. "Your ship's waited five days."

Maybe one or the other piece of information was supposed to impress him. But he'd met Stationmaster Quen far too many times at too early an age, and he didn't give an effective damn what kind of dock charges *Finity's End* was running up waiting for him. So his interfering relatives had held a starship for him. They could sit in hell for what he cared.

"Yes, sir," he said in the flat tone he'd learned was neutral enough, and he went with them, wobbling a little. After the close, medicine-tainted air in the domes and the too-warm sterile air of the shuttle, the station air he'd thought of as neutral all his life was icy cold and sharp with metal scents he'd never smelled before. Water made a puddle near the shuttle gantry, not uncommon on the docks. The high areas of the dockside had their own weather and tended to condense water into ice, which melted when lights went on in an area and heated up the pipes.

Splat. A fat cold drop landed in front of him as he walked. It turned the metal deck plates a shinier black was all. On Pell Station it had rained, too, clean and bright gray just a few hours ago. It had been raining nonstop when he'd left, when he crossed from the van into the shuttle passenger lounge. He'd been able to see out the windows, the way he'd had his first view of Downbelow from those doublethick windows, half a year ago.

He'd rather think of that now, and not see where he was. He had no curiosity about the docks, no expectations, nothing but the necessity of walking, a little weak-kneed, with the feeling of ears stuffed with cotton. They'd stopped up in the airlock and the right one hadn't popped yet, petty nuisance. Down at the shuttle landing, they'd given him a tranquilizer with the breakfast he hadn't eaten. He'd had no choice about the pill. Not much resistance, either. Things mattered less than they had, these last few days.

He went with the cops to the lift that would take them out of White Sector, where the insystem traffic docked—the shuttles among them. He'd gone out the selfsame dock when he'd made the only other trip of his life, down to Pell's World. He came back to the station that way. If nothing intervened to prevent his being transferred, he'd never use White again. He'd be down in Green, or Blue, where holier-than-anybody *Finity* docked, too good for Orange or Red. Fancy places. Money. A lot of money. Money that bought anything.

Anyone.

They took the lift. The lift car was on rails and sometimes it went sideways and sometimes up and down or wherever it had to take you. This time the car went through the core, around the funny little turn it did there and out another spoke of the station wheel.

Hold on, the cops told him at one point, and he dutifully tightened his grip, not arguing anything, not speaking, not looking at them.

During recent days, flat on his back in infirmary, while they dripped fluids into him and scanned his lungs for damage he half wished he'd done, he'd had ample time to realize the fix had been in before he ever ran, and to realize that his lawyers weren't going to intercede this time. He'd sat by the window on the way up, unable to see much but the white of Downbelow's clouds, until they put the window-shields up and stopped him seeing anything of the world. Necessary precaution against the chance tiny rock as they cleared Pell's atmosphere. But he'd looked as long as he could.

Now, with cold and unfeeling fingers, he clung to the rail of the car while the car finished its gyrations through the station core and shot down a good several levels.

It jolted and clanked to a stop and let them out on more dockside, the cops talking to someone on their audio. They brought him out onto the metal decking, with the dark wall of dockside on one side, with its blinding spotlights and ready boards blazoning the names and registries of ships. A group of people were standing by a huge structural wall, ahead of him. One, the centermost, was the Stationmaster.

Dark blue suit, aides with the usual electronics discreetly tucked in pockets; security, with probably a fancy device or two—you couldn't always tell about the eye-contact screens, or what the men were really looking at, but they weren't station police, that was sure. He'd never met Elene Quen in her official capacity. He guessed this was it.

"Fletcher," Quen said in a moderate, pleasant tone, and offered her hand, which he took, not wanting to, but he'd learned, having been trained by lawyers. When you were in something up to the hilt, you played along, you smiled so long as the authorities were smiling. Sometimes it got you more when you'd been reasonable: when you did pitch a fit on some minor point, you startled hell out of them, and consequently got heard if you didn't also scare them.

But that wasn't his motive right now. Right now all he wanted was not to lose his dignity. And they could take his dignity from him at any time.

"Do you have your visa?" she asked.

He had. He'd expected to use it for customs. He fished it out of his coat pocket and she held out her hand for it.

She didn't look at it. She slipped it into her suit pocket and handed him back a different one.

He guessed its nature before he looked at the slim card in his fingers. It hadn't Pell's pattern of stars for an emblem. It was the space-black of *Finity's End*, a flat black disc for an emblem, no color, no heraldry, not even the name. The first of modern merchanters was too holy and too old to use any contrived emblem, just the black of space itself.

It was a fact in his hand. A done deal. *This* was his new passport.

"You all right?" Quen asked him.

"Sure. No problems."

"Fletcher, . . ." Quen wasn't slow. She caught the sarcasm. She started to say something and then shut it down, nodding instead toward the dockside. "They're boarding."

"Sure."

"You went where you weren't supposed to go," Quen said, as if anything he'd done or could do had changed their intentions.

"I was invited to go." He ought to say *ma'am* and didn't. "I was coming back on my own when they found me."

"You risked lives of your fellow staff members."

"It was their choice to go out there. No one died."

That produced a long silence in which he thought that maybe, just maybe, he could still throw his case back to the psychs.

"I tried to kill myself," he said, "all right?" He knew a station, even with its capacity to absorb damage, didn't want a suicide case walking around loose. A ship going into deep space couldn't be happy at all with the idea. And for a moment he thought she really might send him off to the psychs and have a meeting with the ship. If he just got beyond this current try then he'd be at least eighteen by the time *Finity* cycled back again, eighteen years old and not a minor any longer.

"Fletcher," Quen said, "you're good. I'll give you that. But you don't score."

She knew his game. Dead on. And he was too tired, too rattled, and too sedated to come up with another, more skillful card.

"Yeah," he said. "Well, I tried."

"Fletcher, I've tried to help you, I've set you up with people where I used up favors to get you set. And you'd screw it up. Reliably, you'd screw it up."

"Yeah, well, *they'd* screw it up. How about that?"

"It's a possibility they did. But you never gave anyone a chance."

"The hell!" he said. Temper got past the tranquilizer, and he shut it down. She wasn't going to needle him into reaction, or salve her conscience, either. "The Neiharts aren't going to be happy with me. You know that."

"It's not a place to screw up, Fletcher. There's no place to go. —You look at me! Don't drop your eyes. You look straight at me and you hear this. You give it a good chance. You give it a good *honest* try and come back with no complaints from them and after a year, in the year it's going to take them to get back here, you can walk into my office as a grown man and say you want to be transferred back. *And I'll intercede for you.* Then. Not now."

His heart beat faster and faster. He didn't say anything for the moment. She waited. He threw out the next challenge: "I screwed up down there. Can you fix *that?*"

"I can fix it up here enough to give you a post in the tunnels. You'd work with downers. You'd stand a chance of working your way back to Downbelow."

It was too good. It was everything handed back to him. On a platter. Everything but the downers that mattered. Years. Human years. A long time for them. Maybe too long for Melody and Patch.

"But," Quen said, as firmly, "if you come back with anything on your record, I'll give *Finity* the chance to decide whether they want you, and if they don't, we'll see about an in-depth psych exam to see what you *do* need to straighten you out. Do you copy, Mr. Neihart? Is that plain enough?"

"Yes, ma'am." All cards were bet. *Straighten you out.* That meant psych *adjustment*, not just psych tests. It wasn't supposedly a big deal. Just an instilled fear of sabotage was what they gave you, just a real horror of messing up the station. But they'd find out, too, what he thought of the human species. And they'd straighten *that* kink out of him. They'd rip the heart out of him. Make him normal, so he could never, ever want to go back to Downbelow.

"It's serious business, Mr. Neihart. It's very serious, life-and-death business. *Are* you unstable? Did you try to kill yourself?"

"No, ma'am. Not really."

"Logical decision, was it, to run off into the outback?"

"No. But I'd duck the ship. Miss the undock. Get sent to the psychs."

"It'd lose you your license, all the same."

"Yes, ma'am, but you were taking it away anyway. At least I wouldn't go on the ship."

She thought about that a moment. She thought about *him*, and held his life and sanity in the balance. The noise and clang and clank of the dockside machinery went on around them, inexorable clank of a loader at work.

"That bad, is it, what we're doing to you?"

"I don't *want* them. I never wanted them. Hell if they want me."

"Wanting had nothing to do with it, Fletcher. By putting your mother off the ship, they gave you and your mother a chance to live."

"Well, she died and none of them did damn well by me!"

"They were kind of busy saving this station. Earth. Humanity. In which, if I do say so, they saved *you*. *And* saving the downers, if that scores with you. If the Alliance had gone under, Mazian's Fleet would have had Downbelow for a source of supply. They'd have employed very different management methods with the downers. Or did they cover that in your history courses?"

They had. And he was glad Mazian wasn't at Downbelow, and that someone had kept the Fleet far away. But the fact that the Neiharts were heroes in that fight didn't mean anything on a personal level. It didn't bring his mother back. She'd never been crazy enough the courts didn't dump her kid back with her. And she'd never been sane enough to sign the papers that would give him up for adoption—and for Pell citizenship. He didn't forgive her for that.

"Look at me," Quen said. He did, reluctantly, knowing that this was the other woman largely responsible for his life— every screwed-up placement, every good, every bad: Quen had personally intervened to *keep* him from the trouble he'd gotten into any number of times. The fairy godmother. The magic rescue for him, that had enabled him not to compete with the likes of Marshall Willett but to stay out of complete disaster.

And the primary reason, maybe, his mother *hadn't* gotten psyched-over before she killed herself. He didn't know what he felt about Quen. He never had understood.

"I'll tell you something," Quen said. "You've got the best chance of your life in front of you. But it's not going to be easy. You've walked off from every family you've been put with. Aboard ship, you can't walk off; and no matter what you think, you can't stop being related to these people. These are the *real thing*, Fletcher. They're every fault you see in the mirror and every good point you own. Give them a fair chance."

"Screw them!"

"Fletcher, get it through your head, *I envy you.* You've *got* a family. And they want you. Don't be an ass about it, and let's get over there."

Her ship was destroyed in the War. With everybody on it. And he thought about taking a cheap shot on that score, the way she'd come back at him, but she'd held out hope to him, damn her, and she was the only hope. She gathered up her aides and her security and the cops and they all walked over to the area of the dock where the board showed, in lights, *Finity's End.* There was customs; she walked him past. It was that fast. The gate was in front of him, and he looked back, looked all around at Pell docks.

Looked back, in that vast scale, even imagining the Wilsons might show up. That was his last foster-family, the one he was still legally resident with. The one he even liked.

But the dockside was vacant of anybody but dockers and, he supposed, *Finity* crew. Even his lawyers and his psychs were no-shows. Just Quen. Just the cops. All the little figures, dwarfed by the giant scale of the docks, were strangers.

When he gave it a second thought he guessed he was hurt—hurt quite a bit, in fact, but the lack of well-wishers and good-byes didn't entirely surprise him. Maybe Quen hadn't told the Wilsons where he was. Or maybe the Wilsons had heard about him running away on Downbelow, and just decided he was too crazy, too lost, too damned-to-hell screwed up.

He didn't know what he'd say to them if they did show up, anyway. *Thanks?* Thanks for trying? In the slight giddiness of vast scale and the fading tranquilizer, he hated his lawyers, hated his families. Every one of them. Even the last.

"Good-bye," Quen told him. "Good luck. See you." She didn't offer her hand. Didn't give him a chance to refuse it. "You go on up, give your passport to the duty officer. Follow instructions. You're out of our territory from the time you cross that line. —Matter of fact, this is the ship that won that particular point of law as a part of the constitution. That was what the whole War meant. Welcome to the future."

Screw you and your War, was what he thought as hydraulics wheezed and gasped around the gate, and the huge gantry moved above him, like some threatening dragon making little of anything on human scale. He had nothing to back up any reply to Quen. He owned no dignity but silence and to do what she'd said, go ahead and go aboard. So he left her standing and, passport in hand, took that long, spooky walk, up that ramp and into a cold, lung-hurting tunnel far thinner than the station walls.

He was aware there was black space and hard vacuum out there, beyond that yellow ribbing. Walking down the tunnel looked like being swallowed by something, eaten up alive. And it was. The cops would still be waiting at the bottom of the ramp to be sure he went all the way down this gullet; but when he reached the lock and confronted a control panel, he wasn't even sure what to do with the buttons. They said he was spacer-born. And this damned thing had not even the courtesy of labeling on the buttons.

Hell if he was going to walk back down and ask the Stationmaster which one to push. Damn ships didn't ever label anything. The *station* hadn't labeled anything until the last few years they finally put the address signs up, because they'd been invaded once and didn't want to give the enemy any help.

He hated the War, and here he was, sucked into a place like a step backward into a hostile time, right back into the gray, grim poverty of the War years. He resented it on *that* score, too.

And since nobody did him the courtesy of advising *Finity* he was here, he could stand here freezing in the bitter cold, or he could punch a button and hope the top one was it and not the disconnect that would unseal the yellow walkway from the airlock.

The airlock opened *without* his touching it.

So someone *had* told them he was here.

But no one was in the airlock to meet him.

He'd never seen a starship's airlock up close, except in the vids, and it was unexpectedly large, a barren chamber with lockers and readouts he didn't understand. He walked in and the door hissed shut. Heavily. He was *in* a spaceship. Swallowed alive.

Not a citizen of Pell. He never had been. They'd never let him have more than resident status and a travel visa. He knew all the ins and outs of that legality. Entitled to be educated but not to vote. Entitled to be drafted but not to hold a command. Entitled to be employed but not tenured.

Now after all his struggle to avoid it, he'd achieved a citizenship. He became aware he had a citizen's passport in the hand that held the duffle strings, and this was where he was born to be.

But Quen hinted that, too, could change.

Lie. They all lied.

The inner door opened, and he walked out of bright light into a dimmer tiled corridor. No one was there. The corridor went back, not far, before four lighted corridors intersected it, and then it quit. A ship's ring was locked stable while they were at dock, and the four side corridors all curved *up*. The *up* would be *down* when the ship broke dock and the ring started to rotate, but until it did, this seemed all there was, a utilitarian hallway, showing mostly metal, insulated floor, the kind of insulated plating you used if you thought a decompression could happen.

A door to the right was open. He walked that far, his boots making a lot of metal racket, but a woman came out and met him. So did another woman, and a man.

"Fletcher, is it?" the woman said, and put out a hand.

So, hell, what did he do? He purposely misunderstood and handed her the passport.

"Welcome aboard," she said without a flicker, and pocketed it without looking at it. "Not much time. I'm Frieda N. This is Mary B. And Wes. There's only one. There's no other Fletcher, either. You're just Fletcher."

He'd never been anything else. Frieda N. held out her hand a second time, and he took it, finding himself lost in the information flow, wondering if she was related, how she was related and how any of these people were related to his mother. *His* mother had talked about *her* mother. He had a grandmother. He didn't know whether she was still alive or not, but spacers lived long lives, and stationers aged faster. He supposed she might be here.

For the first time it came to him . . . there was something personal about these people who assumed they owned him. These people who'd owned his mother. And left her.

Others came into the hall. "This is your cousin June, Com 3. And Jake. Jake's chief bioneer, lower deck Ops."

June was an older woman, with a dry, firm handshake, and communications didn't seem to add up to anybody he needed to deal with. Jake had a thin face, a sober face, and looked like a cop he knew: not unnecessarily an unpleasant man, but somebody who didn't have much sense of humor.

Then another man came in, in the kind of waistlength, ribbed-cuff jacket spacers wore over their coveralls where they were working near the cold side of the docks. Silver-haired. A lot of stripes on the sleeve.

"Fletcher," Jake said, "this is Madison, second captain."

He'd already spotted authority, and took the hand when it

was offered him, feeling overwhelmed, wobbly in the knees, wobbly in his mental state, knowing he was going to want to settle how to deal with these people, but all his scenarios of defiance had evaporated, in Quen's little advisement, her outright *bribe* for good behavior.

Not smart at least to screw things up from the start. Start friendly, start sane, *try*, one more stupid time, to make the good impression with one more damned family—his own family.

"Welcome aboard."

"Yes, sir," he said, and *Finity*'s second captain held onto his hand, a cold-chilled, dry clasp. He felt trapped for good and certain. I don't know you people, he wanted to shout. I don't give a damn. And here he was doing the safe, the sensible thing, as somebody else arrived to take his hand. It was a cousin named Pete, a cargo officer, nobody, in his book. It was one more introduction, and he wanted just to escape to somewhere private and shut the door.

"Welcome in, Fletcher." Pete was a dark-haired man with a trace of gray in a beard unusual on dockside—you only saw them on spacers; and it was worth a stare; he was aware he was staring, losing his focus, while strangers' hands patted his shoulders, welcomed him in a chaos of names and emotions.

"Pete," Jake said, "you want to show Fletcher to the safe room?"

"Yeah, sure," Pete said, and indicated the duffle. "That's all the baggage you brought? I'll stow it for you."

"Nossir," he said, and held onto it. Desperately. "No."

Pete relented. Jake said, "Get Warren to make him up a patch set soon as we leave dock. —What's your height, son? Height and weight, Pell Standard. Six feet?"

"About. Eighty-five kilos."

"Baggage weight?"

He knew what he'd come downworld with. What they let you bring. "Twenty-two."

"Got it." And with no more fuss and no more word about the duffle Pete took him out to the corridor and to another room at the next cross-corridor, no simple room, but a vast curved

chamber, a VR theater, he thought, with railings where everybody stood. Old people, younger ones. A theater full of relatives,
hundreds of them, all staring in sudden quiet in their conversations. "This is Fletcher," Pete called out, and someone cheered.
"He's late, but he's here!" Pete said. Others called out hellos and
welcome aboard, and, grotesquely enough, applauded.

"Ten minutes," Jake called out, and Pete showed him to a
place to stand in the third row, where people leaned and reached
out hands to shake, or patted his back or his shoulders, throwing
names at him. At distances out of reach, they all talked about
him: there couldn't be another topic in the room. Of the ones in
earshot, who called out names to him or introduced each other,
there was a Tom R., a Tom T., a Margaret, a Willy and a Will,
there was Roger Y., Roger B., and a single Ned; there was a
Niles senior, a man with silver at the temples, and Jake's brother
was Louis down in cargo, *not* to cross him with Lou on the
bridge, who was Scan 2, third shift.

Bridge ranks. Post designations. Old people. Senior crew,
with hairline wrinkles that spoke of rejuv.

Then a handful of crew trooped in with their quilted
jackets literally frosted with cold, ice cracking as they moved.
There was a Wendy who looked barely in her twenties, and a
William and a Charles who wasn't Charlie because Charlie
was his uncle, chief medtech, who was at his station, and his
mother was Angie. There were half a dozen Roberts, Rob,
Bob, Bobby, and Robbie and a kid they just called JR, not to
cross him with his uncle *Captain* James Robert, senior captain, who besides being famous all over the Alliance always
went by both names.

Pretentious ass, Fletcher said to himself.

Jim, James and Jamie were all techs of various kinds, old
enough to have a touch of gray; and there was McKenzie,
Mac, Madden, and Madison that he'd already met.

He got the picture, if not most of the names. You carried
Names, and there wasn't much creativity about it inside a line
of relations: the ones that carried the same Names tended to be
close cousins, the way they were introduced.

Close cousins as opposed to remote cousins, which *everybody* was to each other.

Hi, he said uneasily to each out of reach introduction, saved by distance from shaking hands, resenting the welcome, resenting *them* with all the integrity he could muster. He'd had about half a mother, that was the way he thought about it: he'd had about half her attention half the time, but that was all the real relative he ever acknowledged. And here were a ship full of people all claiming he was tied to them in some miraculous way that didn't mean a damn to him.

Friendly, he supposed so. People had been friendly before, in schools where it was *welcome in* until they got to know him up close and discovered he wasn't up to their standards in some way or another. Not part of the right clubs. Not part of the right experiences. The right family. The right mother. The right attitude.

He'd fought his sullen tendencies for years just to get into the program, no reform, no real change in him, just in his objectives. *God*, he'd been friendly. He'd watched how the accepted ones did it and he'd learned the lessons and copied—*forged*—good behavior. And here he was doing it all over again, new start, one damned more time, one damned more try. Stunned, shocked, still marginally battling the tranquilizer they'd given him, he did it by now on autopilot, acting the shy, reserved, *pleasant* fool with every one of them while his brain, behind a chemical shield the shuttle authorities had given him, was passing from numbed shock to outright anger.

Hate you, he kept thinking while he smiled and shook hands. But that wouldn't get him home again. Wouldn't ever get him to Downbelow.

The monsoons were starting. The shuttle had almost delayed launch because of the weather and teased him with a last, aching hope that it couldn't get off the ground and he'd miss his ship even yet.

Hadn't worked, had it?

The monsoons were starting and Melody and Patch were off, by now. He'd not seen them again.

He ran out of hands to shake, and people close enough to shout introductions at him. "One minute," someone said, and he knew then that this was it: it was countdown. Pete showed him a toe-hold, a long slot in the carpet, and encouraged him to settle his toes there. He did, and gripped the safety rail, watching the tendons on his own hands stand out as white as the knuckles.

Then someone started singing, for God's sake, one of those rowdy old spacer songs, and the whole company started in, more men than women, deep voices. Cousin, uncle, whatever-he-was Pete elbowed him in the ribs and grinned at him, wanting him to pick up on the words and join in. It was a spooky sound: he'd never heard singers who weren't hyped with sound systems, but this went through the air and off the walls, and it was a lot of men's voices, singing about space, singing about going there—when he didn't in the least want to.

That segued to another song that rocked and rollicked, that caught up his basic fear of space and began with its music and moving beat to break into parts of his soul he didn't want broken into right now, painful parts, aching with loss at a parting he didn't want.

Came a powerful thump and clank, and a light started flashing in the overhead. But that singing drowned other sounds as they started to move, and bodies swayed. For a moment there wasn't any up or down, and he grabbed the rail hard. Pete, next to him, grabbed him and held on, a human reassurance—nobody even missing a beat except to laugh, and he had his toe hooked in the slot, but he wasn't sure it was enough.

Terror whited out all other thoughts, then, terror that things were moving so fast, that it was all real, and all his objections were spent to no avail. They'd just broken their connection to Pell. They were backing away.

The floor began just slightly to be the floor again, but he was afraid to let go, not clearly reasoning what had just happened, because Pete didn't let go of his arm and something more might be coming. People were laughing, and the song was rowdy and wild, while something in his heart went numb and the outer body was shaking. He was afraid Pete knew how scared he was, and that they'd all make some joke of it. But down, down, down his body settled, force pressing his feet to the floor, while a terrified fraction of his mind told him the passenger ring was rotating now, and the ship was still drifting back from the station dock, inertial.

Came a stress then that made him lose his sense of up and down. Bodies, tightly packed all around, swayed at the rails. People cheered, excited, glad to be going.

The singing had stopped, with that. He kept a white-knuckled grip on the rail, not knowing how long it would go on. Then it did stop, and there was thundering quiet, as if he'd gone deaf.

"Good lad," Pete said. "We're away. Duty stations. Stay by the door and somebody'll post you somewhere. Mind, if there's a take-hold, hang on to the rails."

He unbelted amid snicks and snaps from all over the hall. He got shakily to his feet as Pete hurried off, as people began moving for the door, everyone exiting into the corridor with a buzz of talk and a feeling that everybody except him knew where they were going and had to be there. Urgently.

He was scared of what they called take-holds, motion alarms. He'd seen enough disasters in vids to make him nervous. He lost Pete in the rush and set himself beside the door where Pete had told him to be, standing with his duffle beside him as people moved hurriedly by him. He could see up the curved floor that was walkable now and lighted in either direction, curves sharper than the vast curves of Pell Station. If the scale was shorter, their rotation rate had to be higher, and he felt sick at his stomach.

Cold. Chilled through. Everything was browned metal. Noisy. All around him, hurrying bodies, sharp shouts of orders or information he didn't begin to grasp.

"Fletcher!"

He jerked about at the sharp address. The kid named JR came up to him. The captain's nephew. Fa-mi-ly. Highest of the high on this ship.

"Stow that fast," JR said pointing at the baggage. "For future information, you're not to carry baggage aboard. You turn it in at the cargo port. You get around to your quarters first thing, get your stuff put away, don't leave any latches open—"

"I'm not stupid," he said.

"I didn't ask if you were stupid. I said latch the lockers tight."

"Look here . . ."

"I'm an officer," JR said. "Junior captain. You're excused for not knowing that. Clean slate, fast orientation, pay attention. This is A deck. Up above is B. Stay off B deck. Everything you want's on A until you've got orders to be on B. Your quarters number is A26. You copy?"

"Yes."

"That's yes, sir, Fletcher, if you'll kindly remember."

"Yessir," he muttered, too tired to fight. This JR didn't look a day older than he was. But he was the captain's nephew. He got the picture.

"Get your stuff tucked in, get down to A14—that's the laundry, same corridor, down ten doors—and get some work clothes before we hit the safety perim and do another burn. You've got time. That's about an hour. You draw three sets of coveralls, underwear, what you need; and when we're underway that's where you'll report for duty. A14."

"Laundry?"

"Laundry and commissary. You start out there, work your way up to galley. We'll see later what you do know."

"Biochem. Life sciences." He didn't want a job. But he had most of his degree. He'd worked for it. And he didn't do *laundry*.

"You'll get a chance at whatever you're qualified to do," JR said, tight-lipped and tight-assed, about his size, maybe ten kilos less. And self-important as hell. "While I'm at it, let me explain something to you as politely as I can. This whole ship delayed five days for you. It never will again. If you're on a liberty and you don't answer board call, you're on your own. We won't buy you back twice. You know what two hundred twenty-four hours at dock *costs* this ship?"

"Damn you all, you can leave me at *this* station and I'll be happy. Give me a suit. I'll take my chances station'll rake me in. That's the only favor you could do me!"

JR gave him a look as if maybe he hadn't quite understood that part of the equation. "Then you're out of luck," JR said then. "If it were up to me, you'd *be* on the dockside. But you're here. You're in *my* crew, and what I ask of you is simple: show up on time, do your job, wait your turn and ask if you don't understand something. This ship's on a schedule, it moves, and physics doesn't care what your excuse is. If you hear a siren, you see these handholds?" JR gripped a handle inset in the wall. "You grab one and hang on. That'd be an emergency. It happens. If you don't hold on, you could die. Fourteen did, last year. End warning. Go pick up your clothes at the laundry window. That's A14, down to your right."

He picked up the duffle and started off.

"Yessir," he muttered, "yessir. Yessir." And walked off.

He had something material to lose if he got on the wrong side of this officer who looked his age and acted as if he owned the ship. He learned fast. He took the cues. He knew now the guy was a tight-assed jerk. He knew sooner or later they'd come to discuss it again.

He went where he was told, feeling sick at his stomach and telling himself Quen was probably conning him and had no intention of putting him back on station. He wasn't *important* enough to matter to people on her level. He never had been.

The Neiharts were far more important to Quen, collectively. For their sake, that jumped-up jerk nephew of the captain would be. And if by then they had an active grudge, JR would use every influence to see him set down. He knew that equation, in his heart of hearts.

Lies. Lies that moved him here, moved him there. When the world stopped shifting on him for an hour, he'd think, and when he learned the new rules well enough to know how to maneuver in this new family, he'd do something. Not yet. Not now.

Not soon enough to prevent being shipped out of the solar system. He had no hope now except to live that year,

and get back, and see if the court or Quen had another round
to play.

That wasn't, JR said to himself, watching the retreating
view, the most auspicious beginning of a situation he'd ever set
up . . . and truth was, he *hadn't* handled it as well as he could.

That was a seventeen-year-old, not someone in his mid-
twenties. You forgot that when you looked at him. It was too
easy to react as if he were far older.

The Old Man had told him, when they knew the shuttle
was on its way, "He's all yours." And then added: "All these
years. All these years, Jamie. The only one of all the lost kids
we'll ever get back."

Five days. Five *days* they'd held in port, with cargo in their
hold, the heated cans drawing power, the systems up, because
until the third day, they hadn't gotten a medical go-ahead on
Fletcher's shuttle ride up, and they hadn't been sure they could
get a shuttle flight out through worsening atmospheric conditions. *Then* it had been more expensive to bring systems down
again and go back on station power than it was to stay on their
own pre-launch ready systems. That meant that crew had had to
board to run those systems, cycling in and out of a departure-
ready ship to the annoyance of customs and the aggravation of
crew stuck with the jobs and having to suit and clamber about
in the holds.

Fletcher was welcome aboard and politely, even warmly,
welcomed aboard, but it was with a certain edge of irritation
with their fast-footed cousin, from all of them who'd been put
on that unprecedented hold.

Fletcher had also broken ten thousand regulations down on
the planet and fled into the outback of Downbelow, just in case
holding up a starship wasn't enough.

He'd been picked up at death's door and lodged in a
Downbelow infirmary while the planetary types and batteries
of scientists tried to figure out what he'd done, what he'd
screwed with, what he'd screwed up and what damage he
might have done to the only alien intelligence in human reach.

A *Finity* crew member had done that. That was how the outside would remember it, and Fletcher, an honorable name, would be notorious in rumor forever if he had in fact lastingly harmed anything on the planet.

Quen had shoved Fletcher toward the ship at high speed, keeping him out of station custody by taking him directly across the docks, not ever bringing him into administrative levels and procedures where Pell administration could get their experts near him for another round of questioning. Fast work from a canny administrator.

And, thank God, *Finity* had been able to make departure on the schedule they'd finally been able to set, while all Pell Station had to be buzzing with speculation regarding the delay that kept *Finity* in port—speculation that was no longer speculation as the news filtered through the station legal department and the rumor mill that *Finity* was recovering a long-lost crew member. Then the story had been all over station news.

Notorious in *Finity*'s affairs from the day he was born, an embarrassment and a tragedy on *Finity*'s record from the hour his mother had begun her downward drug-induced slide— Fletcher was all theirs now. Captain James Robert set great store by recovering him, and he was somehow supposed to make something of him.

Meanwhile the report up from the medics on the planet said Fletcher's lungs were clear.

So his guess was right and despite the speculation to the contrary, Fletcher hadn't half tried to kill himself rather than be taken to the ship. Fletcher could have walked out of the domes with *no* cylinders if he'd wanted to do that, as best he understood the conditions down there.

No. It had been no suicide attempt, regardless of the speculation in the station news. Fletcher simply had tried to lie low until schedule forced them to abandon him again, and hell if the Old Man was likely to give him up on that basis. It had come down to a test of patience, an incident now with an unwanted publicity that could harm Quen at the very least.

He found it significant that the Old Man hadn't even asked

to see the nephew on whom they'd spent such effort. It was a fair guess it was because the Old Man's temper was still not back from hyperbolic orbit.

That meant, in the Old Man's official silence toward young Fletcher, the whole business of settling Fletcher in was definitively *his* problem.

His problem, his unit, his command, and his job to fix.

"So what do you think?" Bucklin stopped beside him to ask as he stood thinking on the Fletcher problem.

Bucklin had a temper where it came to junior misbehaviors; and he already knew Bucklin was annoyed. But Bucklin was also the one who'd stand by him, next-in-command, as Madison had stood by the Old Man in the last century of time, come hell or high water. They were right hand and left, both in the captain's track, both destined for backup to Alan and Francie when they succeeded Madison and the Old Man. They'd always been a set—and became closer still over years that had seen their mothers lost, when half the juniors alive had died in the blow-out, when they'd *had* no juniors born for all of Fletcher's seventeen years.

The last kid. The very last until one of the women got *Finity* another youngest, and until stationside encounters began to fill the long-darkened kids' loft: that also was part of the change in the Rules. Real liberties. Unguarded encounters. *Finity's* women were going off precautions, and some talked excitedly, even teary-eyed, about babies—the scariest and most irrevocable change in the Rules, the one that, at moments, argued that the Rules change was permanent.

But the need for children born was also absolute. The ship had to, at whatever risk, repopulate itself.

What do you think? Bucklin asked. What he thought was tangled with yesterday and bitter losses.

"Just figuring," JR said. "Ignore the face. The guy's seventeen. Just keep telling yourself those are station-years. The Old Man said it. Out of all those years, he's all the replacement we've got. So here we are."

Chapter
—VII—

Number A26. At least they believed in posting numbers *inside* the ship. Fletcher found the door of his quarters and elbowed the latch. It wasn't locked. And it slid open on a closet of a room with two bunks, barely enough room between them for a person to stand up. A couple of lockers at the end. God, it was a *closet.* And two bunks? He had to share this hole? With one of *them*?

He wasn't happy. But it was a place, and until now he'd had none. He walked in and the door shut the moment he cleared it. He stood there, appalled and this time, yes, he tested it out, *angry.* He wanted to throw things. But there wasn't a single item available except the duffle he'd brought, no character to the place, just—nothing. Cream and green walls, lockers that filled every wall-space above the mattresses and bed frames. Cream-colored blankets secured with safety belts. *That* promised security, didn't it?

A check of the lighted panel at the end of the room, which looked to fold back, showed a toilet and a shower compartment, a mirror, a sink, a small cabinet. The place was depressingly claustrophobic. He checked the lockers out, found the first right-hand one full of somebody's stuff—bad news, that was—and slammed it shut, tried the left-hand side and found it empty, presumably for the clothes he'd brought.

There was more storage under the bunk, latched drawers that pulled out. He unpacked his duffle and stowed his dockside clothes, his underwear, his personal stuff, where he figured he had license to put them.

Most carefully, he unwrapped what he really wanted to put

away safely, the most precious thing—the hisa stick he'd wrapped in layers of his clothes.

The stick that customs hadn't found. That the authorities on Downbelow hadn't confiscated. That everything so far had conspired to let him keep. It was hisa work. It was a hisa gift.

It was illegal to touch, let alone to have and to take off-planet. But hisa bestowed them on special occasions—deaths, births, arrivals. And partings.

He smoothed the cords that tied the dangling feathers. The wood—real wood—was valuable in itself. But far more so was the carving, the cord bindings, the native feathers—only a very, very few such items ever left Downbelow, and the government watched over those with jealous protection from exploitation of the species, their skills, their beliefs.

But this particular one was his. He'd told his rescuers how he'd gotten it, and where he'd gotten it, and wouldn't turn it loose. The planetary studies researchers had grilled him for hours on it, and he'd thought *they* might try to take it—but they'd only asked to photograph it, and put it through decon, and gave it back after that, and let him take it with him. He'd expected customs would confiscate it and maybe arrest him for trying to smuggle it out, a hope he actually entertained, thinking that maybe a snafu like that would get him snagged in the gears of justice again and maybe keep him off the ship—but Quen's intervention had meant he hadn't even had to deal with customs.

So one obstacle after another had fallen down, maybe Quen's doing all along, and by now he supposed it really was his. And it was all he'd managed to take away that meant anything to him.

It meant all the hard things. It meant lessons Melody had tried to teach him—and failed.

It meant parting from where he'd been. It meant a journey. It meant eyes watching the clouded heavens. It meant faith, and faithfulness.

Maybe a human who was born to space couldn't *have* the faith hisa had in Great Sun. Maybe he couldn't believe that Great Sun was anything but what they said in his education, a nuclear furnace. Maybe Great Sun wasn't a god, maybe there was no god, or whatever hisa thought or expected when they looked to the sky. But Melody was so sure that Great Sun would take care of his children, that Great Sun would always come back, that the dark never lasted . . .

The dark never lasted.

For him it would. Forces he couldn't control had shoved him out where the dark went on forever, where even Melody's Great Sun couldn't walk far enough or shine brightly enough. That was where he was now.

But this stick he touched had lived, once. These feathers had flown in the fierce winds, once. Old River had smoothed these stones. All these things, Great Sun had made. And they were real in his hand, and he could remember, when he felt them, what the cloud-wrapped world felt like. They were his parting-gift.

Hisa put such sticks on the graves of the dead, human and hisa. They put them near the Watcher-statues. And when the researchers asked, bluntly, why, the hisa didn't have the words to say.

But he knew. He knew. It was when you went away. It reminded you. It was a memory. It was the River and Great Sun, it was weather and wind. It was all those things that he'd almost touched, that the clean-suit only let him imagine touching without a barrier. It was waking up to a sunrise, and watching the world wake up. It was sleeping in the dark with no electric lights and waiting for Great Sun to find his child again—*knowing* that Great Sun would come for him the way Melody had come in the darkest hour of his childhood, when he was hiding from all the crazed authorities.

That was the faith the hisa had. That was what he took away with him.

Bianca had sworn she'd wait for him. But he knew. People didn't keep such promises. Ever. And hisa couldn't. Their lives were too short, too precious for waiting. It was why they made the Watchers.

And now Quen had tried to psych him with this last-minute offer of hers . . . just a psych-out. A ploy to get Fletcher to behave, one more time.

He wound the dangling cords about the stick and put it away in the back of the underbunk drawer, behind his spare station clothes, so no prying roommate would find it.

He quietly closed the drawer, telling himself he was stupid even to think of falling for Quen's line. He knew the drill. He could almost manage a cynical amusement past the usual little lump in his throat that conjured all the other bad times of his life. Have a fruit ice, kid. Have another. You'll like it here. Look, we've got you a teddy bear.

Ten weeks later the new family'd be back to the psychs saying he was incorrigible.

This one was already a disaster.

Work in the laundry, for God's sake. He'd pulled himself from police-record *nothing* into a degree program in Planetary Studies, and his shiny new family had him doing laundry and matching socks. *That* was damn near funny, too, so funny it made the lump in his throat hurt like hell.

He latched the drawer. The locker didn't have a lock. The bath didn't have a lock. When he looked at the door to the outside, it didn't have a lock. There wasn't anywhere that was his.

All right, he said to himself for the tenth time in five minutes, all right, calm down. A year. A year and he'd be back to Pell and he'd survive it and if Quen reneged, he'd go to court. Do what they said, keep them happy until, back at Pell after that year, he ran for it and held Quen to her word.

Meanwhile the captain's nephew had said go back down to the laundry and check out some clothes. He could do that, while his heart hammered from anger and his ears picked up a maddening hum somewhere just below his hearing and he wasn't sure of the floor. He told himself he was going to walk around, telling himself he wasn't going to be sick at his stomach, he wasn't even going to think about the fact that the ship was moving. He walked out to the hall and down to A14, to the laundry.

He wasn't the only one looking for clean clothes. He stood in a line of six, all of whom introduced themselves with too damn much cheerfulness, a Margot with a -t, a Ray, a Nick, a

Pauline, a Johnny T., and a John Madison who, he declared, wasn't related to the captain. Directly.

He didn't intend to remember them. He wasn't remotely interested. He was polite, just polite. He smiled, he shook hands. Their chatter informed him you could pick up more than laundry at the half-door counter. You could buy personal items on your account, if you *had* an account, which as far as he knew he didn't. As he approached the counter he could see, beyond the kid handing out the clothes, a lot of shelves with folded clothing sorted somehow. He saw mesh sacks of laundry left off and folded stacks of clean clothes picked up, and this supposedly was going to be his post. Big excitement.

"Fletcher," he told the kid at the desk.

"Wayne," the kid said. He looked no more than sixteen. "Glad you made it. So you take over here after next burn."

"Seems as if." He mustered no false cheerfulness. The other kid on duty, Chad, went and got the size he requested. "*Finity* patch is on," Chad said of the ship's blues he got. "Personal name patch, Sam'll get to it as he can. He makes 'em. He'll get it done for you before we go up."

Up meant leave normal space. He knew that. He knew it was regularly about five days a ship took between leaving dock and exiting the system. "Yeah," he said. "Thanks."

A small plastic bag landed on top of the stack of folded blues, toiletries, and such. "There you go."

"Thanks," he said again, and carried his stack of slippery-bagged new clothes back the way he'd come, along a corridor that curved very visibly up.

That was it. He was assigned, checked in, uniformed, and set.

His gut was in a knot. He wanted to hit the first thing he came to. Nothing made sense. His stomach was sending him queasy signals that up and down were out of kilter, the horizon curves were steeper than he'd ever dealt with, and he was going to be a little crazy before he got off this ship, crazy enough he'd have memorized JR, James Robert, John, Johnny, Jake, Jim, and Jimmy, Jamie and all his damn relatives.

He opened the door to his room. This time there was a kid on the other bunk. A kid maybe twelve, dark-haired, dark-eyed, eyeing him with equal suspicion.

"Hi," the kid said after a beat. "I'm Jeremy."

"Yeah?" Defensively surly tone.

Defensively surly back. "I got lucky. We're bunkmates."

He must have frozen stock still a heartbeat. His heart speeded up. The rest of the room phased out.

"No, we're not," he said, and threw his new issue down on the other bunk.

"I live here," was the indignant protest, in a pre-adolescent voice. "First."

"No way in hell. This does it! This is the limit!"

"Well, I don't want you here either!" the kid yelled back.

"Good," he said. His voice inevitably went shaky if he didn't let his temper blow and the struggle between trying to be fair with a hapless twelve-year-old and his desire to punch something had his upset gut in an uproar. It was the whole business, it was every lousy, *stinking* decision authorities had made about him all his life, and here it was, summed up, topped off and proposing he was rooming with a damned *kid*.

He dumped his new clothes on the bed. The door had closed. He went back and hit the door switch.

"They're about to sound take-hold," the kid's voice pursued him as he left. "You can't find anybody! You'll break your neck!"

He didn't damn care. He started down the hall, and heard someone shout at him and then footsteps coming.

"Don't be stupid!" Jeremy said, and caught his sleeve. "They're going to blow the warning. You haven't got time to get anywhere else! Get back in quarters!"

The kid was in earnest. He had no doubt of that. He didn't want to give up or give in, but the kid was worried, and maybe in danger, trying to stop him. He yielded to the tug on his arm and went back toward the room, wondering if he was being conned, or whether the kid knew what he was talking about. It was convincing enough.

And they no sooner were back in the room with the door shut than a warning sounded and Jeremy dived for his bunk.

"Belt in," Jeremy said, and he followed Jeremy's example, unclipped the safety belts and lay down, with the siren screaming warning at them all the while.

"Got time, there's time," Jeremy said, horizontal and fastening his belt. "*God*, you don't ever do that!"

He ignored the kid's concerns and got the belt snugged down, telling himself if this turned out to be minor he was going to be madder than he was.

Then force started to build, not downward, but sideways, and the mattresses tilted sideways, so that he had a changing view of the inside bottom of the bunk beside him. His arms weighed three times normal, his whole body flattened and he could only see the bottom of Jeremy's bunk, both rotated on the same axis, both swung perpendicular to the acceleration that just kept increasing.

He couldn't fight it. He found himself shaking and was glad Jeremy couldn't see it. He was scared. He could admit it now. He was up against something he couldn't fight, caught up in a force that could break him if he ran out there in the hall and pitted himself against it. It went on, and on.

And on.

And on.

There wasn't that much racket. Or vibration. Or anything. He shivered from fear and ran out of energy to shiver. He couldn't see Jeremy. He didn't know what Jeremy was doing. And finally he had to ask. "How long do we do this?"

"Three hours forty-six minutes."

Shivering be damned. "You're kidding!"

"That's three hours fifteen to go," Jeremy's high voice said. "We like to clear Pell pretty quick. Lot of traffic. Aren't you glad you didn't go in the corridor?"

He couldn't take being squashed in his bunk for three hours with nothing to do, nothing to view, nothing to think about but leaving Pell. Or the ship hitting something and everybody dying. "So what do you *do* when you're stuck like this?"

"You can do tape. Or read. Or music. Want some music?"

"Yeah."

Jeremy cut some on, from what source he wasn't sure. It was loud, it was raucous, it was tolerable. At least he could sink his mind into it and lose himself in the driving rhythm. Inexorable. Like the ship. Like the whole situation.

It occurred to him finally to wonder where they were going. He'd never asked, and neither Quen nor his lawyers had told him. Just—from Quen—the news he'd be gone a year.

He asked when the music ran out. And the answer came from the unseen kid effectively double-bunked above his head:

"Tripoint to Mariner to Mariner-Voyager, Voyager, Voyager-Esperance, Esperance, and back again the way we came. There's supposed to be real good stuff on Mariner. Fancier than Pell."

Partly he felt sick at his stomach with the long, long recital of destinations. And he supposed he had to be glad their route was inside civilized space and not off to Earth or somewhere entirely off the map.

But he felt his heart race, and had to ask himself why he'd felt this little . . . lift of spirits when the kid said Mariner— which *was* supposed to be a sight to see. As if he was *glad* to be going to places he'd only heard about and had absolutely no interest in seeing.

But they were places Pell depended on. It wasn't the Great Black Nothing anymore. He knew what places were out there. And Mariner was civilized.

"How you doing?" Jeremy asked in his prolonged silence.

"Fine." The compulsory answer. The polite answer. But he got a feeling Jeremy at least considered him part of his legitimate business. And for a scruffy, skinny twelve-year-old, Jeremy was level-headed and sensible. There were probably worse people to get stuck with.

For a twelve-year-old. The obvious suddenly dawned on him. He knew that spacers didn't age as fast as stationers. Sometimes they'd be ten, fifteen years off from what you thought—little that the difference from stationers' ages had ever mattered to him, and little he'd dealt with spacers except his mother. But—on a kid—even a fraction of ten or fifteen years—was a major matter.

He was moderately, grudgingly curious. "Mind me asking? —How old are you?"

"Seventeen," was Jeremy's answer.

Good God, was his thought. Then he thought maybe the kid knew *he* was seventeen and was ragging him.

"Same age as you," Jeremy's voice said from the bunk above his head. "We'd have been agemates. Except your mama left."

"You're kidding. Right?"

"Matter of fact, no. I'm actually couple of months older than you. I was already born when your mama left to have *you* on Pell, and there was question about leaving me, but they didn't. So you're kind of like my brother. —We'd have *been* close together, anyway."

He didn't know what he felt, except upset. He'd been through the *this is your brother* routine four times with foster-families. He'd tried to pound one kid through the floor. But this was not only an honest-to-God relative, this was the kid he really would have grown up with, and been with, and done kid things with, if his mother hadn't timed out on him and left him in one hell of a mess.

This was the path he really, truly hadn't taken.

"I wish you'd been born aboard," Jeremy said. "There weren't any kids after us two, I guess you know. They couldn't have 'em during the War. They will, now. But our years were already pretty thin. And then we lost a lot of people."

Fletcher found a queasiness in his stomach that was partly anger, partly—he didn't know. He could see what he might have grown into by now, a scrawny twelve-year-old body that was so strange he couldn't *imagine* what Jeremy's mind was like, seventeen and stuck at physical twelve.

It wasn't natural.

It wasn't natural, either, their being separated. He didn't know. He didn't know, from where he was lying, what kind of a life he'd missed. He only knew the life he was leaving, with all it did mean.

Besides, all the sibs people had tried to present him had ended up hating him, the way he hated them . . . except only Tony Wilson, who was in his thirties and his last foster sib. Tony'd been distant. Pleasant. The Wilsons had recognized he was a semi-adult, and just signed his paperwork, had him home from school dorms for special holidays, provided a legal fiction of a family for him to fill in school blanks with. Tony hadn't ever remotely thought he was a rival. He supposed he'd liked Tony best of all the brothers he had, just for leaving him the hell alone most of the time and being pleasant on holidays.

Their not showing up when he was shipped out . . . that hurt. That fairly well hurt.

So who the hell was Jeremy Neihart and why should he care one more time?

"So," Jeremy said in another long silence, "did you *like* it on the station?"

The question went right to the sore spot. "Yeah," he said. "Yeah, it was fine."

"You have a lot of friends there?"

"Sure," he said. Everything was pleasant. Everything was fine. Never answer How are you? with anything but, and you never got further questions.

"So—what'd you do for entertainment?"

There hadn't been any entertainment, hadn't been any let-up. Just study. Just—all that, to get where he'd been, where they ripped him out of all he'd accomplished.

There wasn't an, *Oh, fine* . . . for that one.

"I've got a lot of tapes," Jeremy said when he didn't answer. "We kind of trade 'em around. I got some from Sol. We can pick up some more at Mariner, trade off the skuz ones. I spent most of my money on tapes."

"I don't have any," he answered sullenly. Which wasn't the truth, but as far as what a twelve-year-old would appreciate, it was the truth.

"You can borrow mine," Jeremy said.

"Thanks," he said. He was too rattled and battered about any longer to provoke a deliberate fight with the kid. The *kid*.

His might-have-been brother. Cousin. Whatever they might have been to each other if not for the War and his addict mother.

On a practical level, Jeremy's offer of tapes was something he knew he'd be glad of before they got to Mariner. He needed something to occupy his mind if they had to lay about for hours like this, or he'd be stark, staring crazy before they cleared the solar system. Tapes to listen to also meant he didn't have to listen to Jeremy, or talk about might-have-beens, or deal with any of them. Plug in, tune out. He didn't care what Jeremy's taste in music turned out to be, it had to be better than dealing with where he was.

He was going to see the universe. Flat on his back and feeling increasingly scared, increasingly sick at his stomach.

He did know some things about ships. You couldn't breathe the air on Pell Station without taking in something about ships and routes and cargo. Besides knowing vaguely how they'd travel out about five days and jump and travel and jump, he knew they'd load and unload cargo and the captains would play the market while the crew drank and screwed their way around the docks. Just one long party, which was why he had absolutely no idea who his father was. His mother had just screwed around on dockside because, sure, no spacer gave a damn who his father was. Mama was everything.

As he guessed Jeremy had a mother aboard, but he didn't know why Jeremy wasn't living with her, or for that matter, what he was supposed to be to his roommate's mother. Everybody aboard was related. It was all the J's. Jeremy, James, Jamie and Johnny, Jane, Janette, Judy, Jill and Janice. Who the hell cared?

What was it like for a mother to have a seventeen-year-old kid Jeremy's size?

What was it to have your mind growing older and your body staying younger than it was?

Or *was* Jeremy more than twelve mentally? The voice didn't sound like it. Jeremy wouldn't have lived those seventeen years, he guessed, but he'd have watched seventeen

years of events flow past him, in the news and on the ship.
He'd—

Force just—quit. The bunks swung, and he grabbed the
edges of the mattress with the feeling he was falling.

"Takehold has ended," came from the speakers. *"Posted
crew, second shift, you lucky people. All systems optimal."*

Jeremy was unbelting and sitting up. He figured he dared.
His head was still feeling adrift in space.

"You play cards?" Jeremy asked.

"I can." He didn't want to. But he didn't want to do anything else, either. "Can we go in the halls?"

"Corridors. Stations have halls. We have corridors. Just so
you know. Vince'll snigger, else. And we're off-shift right now.
Best stay in quarters if you don't want to work. You wander
around, some senior'll put you to work. Poker?"

"How long do we have to stay lying around like this?"

"Oh," Jeremy said, "about another couple of hours. Till we
clear the active lanes."

"I thought that was what we were doing."

"Just gathering *V.* We'll run awhile at this *V.* Then step up
again. Four or five times before we get up to speed. We could
do it all at once. But that's real uncomfortable."

"Deal," he said glumly, and Jeremy bounced up, got into
his bunk storage and rummaged out a plastic real deck.

Twelve-year-old body, he thought, watching the uncon-
scious energy with which Jeremy moved. There were advantages to being twelve that even at seventeen you'd lost.

"Favor points or money?" Jeremy asked.

He knew about favor points. If you lost you ended up doing
somebody's work for him. He had no money. He didn't know
where he'd get any. He'd rather play for no points at all,
because Jeremy handled those cards with dexterity a dockside
dealer could envy.

"Points," he said.

"You haven't got an assignment yet."

"Yes, I do. Laundry."

"Oh, we all do that." The cards cascaded between Jeremy's

hands. Fletcher bet he could do it under accel, too. "Future points. How's that?"

"Fine," he said.

He lost an hour to Jeremy. And was trying to win it back when a buzzer went off and scared him.

"Dinner," Jeremy said, scrambling to his feet to get the door.

Somebody, another kid, whose name Fletcher didn't bother to listen to, had a sack, and out of that sack the junior handed them two box suppers, little reusable kits containing— Fletcher's hopes crashed as he looked—cold synth cheese sandwiches.

"Is this all we get?" Fletcher asked.

"Galley's shut down," Jeremy said. "It'll be up next watch."

"How's the food then?"

"Real good," Jeremy said. "We got *real good* cooks. Or we space 'em."

Tired joke, but reassuring. Fletcher ate his synth cheese sandwich and drank the half-thawed fruit juice, trying to calm down. Very basic things had started mattering to him. He'd just about lost his composure, finding out food this evening was a sandwich. Shaky adjustment. Real shaky.

And here he was again. Been here before. Everything was new. Everything was the same as it had ever been. Worse than it had ever been. Spent half his seventeen years climbing out of the mess mama had left him in and here he was, back at the starting point.

The real one this time.

The lump in his throat went away. Sugar and protein helped. He figured he'd get good at poker on this cruise, if nothing else. Jeremy *wasn't* so bad, for mental twelve—or a little more than that. Probably others weren't.

When they ripped you out of one home and put you some-place else you tried never again to think of where you'd been, or miss anything about it. You just built as solid a wall as you could. So there was just a wall. Just a blank behind him. At least until the pain stopped.

• • •

Two hours into maindark and the Old Man finally asked. "How's Fletcher?"

And JR, on the when-you're-free summons to the Old Man's topside office, gave the answer he'd predetermined to give: "Autopilot. He's functioning. He's not happy with this."

"One wouldn't think so," James Robert said. James Robert wasn't at his desk, but in the soft chair from which he did a great deal of his business. Cargo listings on the wall display screens had given way to system status reports and navigational data. "Has Jeremy complained?"

Jeremy had a beeper. With instructions to use it. "No, sir. He hasn't." Jeremy had seemed the best choice, over the junior-juniors there were. Vince was a heller from the cradle, always had been, and Linda, female and thirteenish, wasn't an option.

A lot of empty cabins. There'd easily been a place to put Fletcher alone, as Jeremy had been alone, as Vince and Linda were alone. But he didn't rate it safe for an uninformed, inexperienced passenger. Jeremy would warn him. Jeremy would take care of him.

"You had an encounter with him," the Old Man said.

Not surprising that that news had made it topside. "I'm zeroing it out. Waiting to see. Can't blame the guy for being on edge."

The Old Man just nodded, whether approving his attitude, or whether sunk in some other thought. The Old Man brought up other business, then, the general schedule, the maintenance windows, the expectations of other crew chiefs when the junior command would have to supply hands and bodies. The jump would come on main shift. Sometimes it did, sometimes it came during alterday. He'd expected alterday this time, but no, apparently not.

There wasn't a mention of Fletcher's life-and-death problems in facing jump for the first time, no special caution to be sure Fletcher got through it sane and in one piece. JR accepted it, then, as all on his watch, literally, as all things were that the sitting captains didn't specifically cover in other assignments. The juniors were all mainday schedule. There weren't enough of them for two commands, and they'd be working right up to the pre-jump. JR wondered whether that schedule were just possibly tailored around the new cousin.

And some things, like non-spacers, weren't within his experience or his observation.

"On the Fletcher question," JR said, in the Old Man's silence, "does he get tape, or not, during jump? Should *I* take him into my quarters and see him through it?"

All of them had experienced hyperspace in the womb. Experienced it until their lives were strung out in it.

Fletcher was definitely a question mark.

"Leave tape study off," the Old Man said. "I'd say, not this trip, for him or for Jeremy. I'd say—you stay off tape, too. I want you able to respond."

"Yessir," he said.

"Where he rides it out," the Old Man said, "is your discretion. You're closer to the situation than I am. Tell him—"

Rare that the Old Man failed to have exactly what he wanted to say, exactly as he wanted it.

But the last few days of "Fletcher's lost" and "Fletcher's found" and "Fletcher will be another day late" had worn on everyone, and based on past events, he began to suspect the Old Man knew the uneasy feeling in the junior crew, and saw deeper into his personal misgivings than he liked.

The Old Man's chain of consequences, on the other hand, went right back into the decision to join *Norway* and leave Francesca.

The hero, the old warrior, said they had a peace to fight now, and they'd taken on non-military cargo as well as an outsider, both for the first time in nearly two decades.

But Mallory's War wasn't over. Mallory and the Old Man had had words of some kind when last they'd met, out in the remote fringes of Earth's space. And whatever they'd said, it was solemn and sobering in its effect on the Old Man, who'd come back solemn and sad, and not one word had filtered down to his level.

Tell him—the Old Man had begun, and found no words for what to tell Francesca's heir, either.

So there was no information for him, just an urging to make the situation work . . . somehow . . . within the junior crew, where the Old Man didn't, on long-standing principle, interfere. It was the future relationships of the members of that crew to each other that they were hammering out in their conduct of a set of duties and responsibilities all their own, the way *Finity* crew had done for more than a century. In a certain measure the Old Man *couldn't* reach into that arrangement to settle and protect one special case without skewing every relationship, every reliance, every concept of personal honor and chain of command the junior crew maintained.

Fletcher had to make a Fletcher-shaped place in the crew. There couldn't be less. Or more. And it wasn't the Old Man's job to do it. He got that from the silence, when he knew that the Old Man had thought a very great deal about Fletcher *before* he came aboard.

"I'll take care of him," JR said, and received back only a sidelong look from the Old Man. When JR looked back in leaving, the Old Man was busy at his work again, clearly with no intention of asking or saying further in the matter.

Morning mess hall was another collection of cousins, mostly seniors. Fifty people ate at a set time, on schedule—be hungry or skip it entirely, unless you had an excuse or a favor-point with the cook, so Jeremy said.

Fletcher ate at the same table with Jeremy and two other only moderately pubescent juniors, Vincent and Linda, both doubtless older in station years than they seemed, but mentally like the age they looked, they mostly jabbered about games or what they'd done on Pell docks, their speech larded with *wild*, *decadent*, and *fancy*, juvvie-buzz that seemed current among their small set. Mostly they ignored him, beyond the first exchange of names, turned shoulders to him without seeming to notice it in the heat of their conversational passion, and Jeremy's eyes lit with the game-jabber, too.

Being ignored didn't matter to Fletcher. He'd lain awake and tossed and turned in his bunk. Jeremy had lent him music tapes and those had gotten him through the dark hours.

But today he had to work with these kids who admittedly knew everything he didn't; and he went with them when they'd had their breakfast—a decent breakfast, if he'd had the appetite, which he didn't.

They all went, still jabbering about dinosaurs and hell levels, down to A14, and in the next few hours he learned all about laundry, how to sort, fold, stack, and keep a cheerful face right along with the two other juniors in the mess pool with him and Jeremy.

They'd drawn Laundry as their work for this five-day stint . . . but not *every* day. You didn't get stuck on one kind of job as a junior. That was a relief to learn.

The junior-juniors, the ship's youngest, the seventeen- and eighteen-year-olds among whom he was unwillingly rated, drew such jobs relatively often. But so did the mid-level techs, from time to time. Juniors, so Jeremy said, rotated through Laundry to Minor Maintenance, to Scrub, to Galley, but there were jobs all over the ship that were rotating jobs, or part-time jobs, or jobs people did only on call.

Junior-juniors inevitably got the worst assignments, Fletcher keenly suspected. Laundry was *everybody's* laundry; laundry for several hundred people who'd been out on liberty for two weeks was a *lot* of laundry, sonic and chemical cleaning for some tissue-fabrics, water-cleaning for the rough stuff, dry, fold, sort, and stack by rank.

It filled the time that otherwise would have required too much thinking, and it was a job where you did meet just about everybody, as people came to the counter for pickup of what they'd sent in at undock and to pick up small store items like soap refills for their showers, and sewing kits, and other odd notions.

Fletcher didn't remember all the names by half—except Parton, who was blind, and who had one mechanical eye for ordinary things, Jeremy said, and the other one was a computer screen for cargo data or anything else Parton elected to receive. He didn't think he'd forget Parton, who asked him to stand still a moment until his mechanical vision had registered a template of his face. He'd never met a blind person. But Jeremy said Parton's left eye was sharp all the way into situations where the rest of them couldn't see, and Parton didn't always know whether there was light or not. His mechanical eye could spot you just the same.

Laundry pickup was a place to hear gossip—all the gossip in the ship, he supposed, if you kept your ears open. He picked up a certain amount of information on certain individuals even with no idea who he was hearing about, and he heard how various establishments on Pell didn't meet the approval of the senior captain.

Vincent and Linda talked about various places you'd go *in civvies*, and restaurants you'd *wear a patch to*, meaning the ship's patch, he guessed. Someone dropped by the counter and gave him his own, ten black circular ship's patches, and small patches that said *Finity's End* and *Fletcher Neihart*. It was, he supposed, *belonging*. He wasn't sure how he felt about them.

Jeremy handed him a sewing kit from off the shelf of supplies. "You stitch 'em on," Jeremy said. "The shiny-thread ones are for dress outfits, the plain-thread are for work gear. If they start looking tatty you get new ones or the watch officer has a fit. I'll show you how, next watch."

Labels got your laundry back to you, that was one use of them he saw. You also had a serial number. He was F48, right next to his name. He saw that in a roll of tags that was also in the packet the man had given him. Those were just for the laundry. It was a lot of sewing on tags.

Even in the underwear and the socks.

Labeled. Everything. Head to toe.

He didn't say anything. He didn't like it. On Base he'd had to do his own laundry. Everybody did. You got your clothes back because you sensibly never dumped them in bins with everybody else's. He'd never learned to sew anything in his life, but he figured he'd learn if he wanted his socks and underwear back.

Labeling right down to his socks as *Finity* crew, though, he'd have skipped that if he could. But counting they'd lose your underwear if you didn't, it seemed a futile point on which to carry on a campaign of independence, or make what was a tolerable situation today harder than it was. Nobody had done anything unpleasant—or been too intrusively glad to see him. Vincent tried to engage him about where he'd been, holding up the ship and making them late on their schedule, but Jeremy told Vince to stop and let him alone and Vince, who came only up to mid-chest on him, took stock of him in a long look and shut up about it.

Jeremy wanted to talk about Downbelow when they got back to quarters after mess, and that was harder. They sat there stitching his labels into his socks, and Jeremy wanted to know what Downbelow looked like.

"Real pretty," he said.

"There's trees on Pell," Jeremy said.

"Yeah. The garden. The ones on Downbelow are prettier." He jabbed his finger with the needle, painfully so. Sucked on it. He and Jeremy sat on their respective bunks, with a stack of his entire new wardrobe and all the clothes he'd brought with him plus a pile of the clothes he'd gotten dirty so far, and he wasn't sorry to have the help doing it.

He daydreamed for an instant about puffer-ball gold and pollen skeining down Old River, beneath branches heavy with spring leaves. Rain on the water.

Jeremy chattered about what he'd seen in Pell's garden. And segued nonstop to what he wanted to do after they got the patches stitched on. Jeremy wanted him to go to rec with him tonight: there was a rec hall, with games and a canteen, Jeremy said.

"I don't want to."

"Oh, come on. What are you going to do, else?"

It was a point. He'd be alone in this closet of a room. He was tired, but he'd get to thinking about things he didn't want to think about.

He went. It was the same huge compartment they'd all been in during undock, only now there were no railings. There were game machines. A vid area. Tables and chairs, senior as well as junior crew playing cards, playing games, watching vids. He suffered a moment of dislocation, and almost balked at the transformation alone.

But the entertainments offered were very much like at the Base. Familiar situation. You mixed with senior staff and techs and all. They just generally didn't talk with junior staff.

"What do you play?" Jeremy asked him.

Dangerous question. He'd already lost ten hours to Jeremy at cards; but when he glumly decided on vids, and looked through the available cards in the bin to the side of the machines, he found an Attack game he hadn't seen since he was a small kid. The card itself when he pulled it out was old, showing a lot of use; but he remembered that game with real pleasure, and recalled he'd been pretty good at it—for a seven-year-old. He might have a chance at this one.

He appropriated a machine. Meanwhile Vince and Linda had shown up, and thought they'd join him and Jeremy.

He wasn't delighted, but he kept the expression off his face; he linked up with the three of them, a little suspecting ambush. He *didn't* play vids, not for the last four years, being short of opportunity and short of time, and he dropped into the semi-world of state-of-the-art interactives with a little caution.

Blown. Blown in two seconds. He made four tries, but he couldn't come *out* of the drop into the game fast enough with these kids to avoid getting blasted.

"This is enough," he said. But Jeremy jollied him out of quitting, said they'd play partners, and after that he lived for maybe the equivalent of a station hall block before he blew up.

He just wasn't very good at it. Or the point was, they were *very, very* good and their reflexes were astonishingly fast. When he exited the game and took the visor off he was a little disoriented from the intensity of the play they'd forced him to. *They* were different when they took theirs off, hyped, nervous, so much so that when they went for soft drinks at the bar he didn't know the Jeremy he was dealing with. Jeremy's fingers twitched, his small body was like a wound spring, and he sat and sipped a soft drink with Vince, who was a little saner, while Jeremy and Linda went back into the game and had it out. A long game. You could elect to watch the game on the screen where they were sitting; and Vince, who said he was tired, did . . . while Jeremy and Linda were nearby, two people just sitting at a table opposite each other, twitching occasionally, fingers moving on the pads. But on the screen two fighters were stalking each other.

"They're good," he said to Vince, aware first of a twelve-, thirteen-year-old boy's face, and second that Vince was, chronologically speaking, a year older than he was.

And third that Vince was himself too hyped for rational conversation, arms and shoulders twitching to the moves on the screen, jabbering strategy at Linda, who was, he'd found out, Vince's fairly close cousin and year-mate.

He didn't react the way these twelve- and thirteen-year-olds did—but he'd never seen any kid react the way these kids did, not the most dedicated gameheads who'd haunted the vid parlors on Pell. Something in him said *dangerous*, and something said *alien*. Something in his gut said he was going to be out-matched at anything but cards with these kids, and that there was something direly skewed about these seventeen- and eighteen-year-old twelve-year-olds.

Baby faces. Tiny bodies. High, pre-change voices. He could pick any of the three of these kids up in one hand; but their reactions in games were tigerish. He'd heard the word, and knew the association. *Tigerish*. Predatory, low brain function, and fast.

Vince and he watched and drank soft drinks and ate chips as Jeremy and Linda kept it up for another hour and a half before watch-end mandated their return to quarters—a return which, like a lot of other odd things, said to him that these weren't ordinary twelve-year-olds, who voluntarily delayed a game to sew patches on clothes, who made their beds without a wrinkle, who didn't duck out on rules—and kept a single Attack game going an hour and a half because nobody could score.

He walked the steeply curving ring beside Jeremy, who still couldn't walk like a normal human being, who was still electric and jumping with an energy he hadn't discharged. And when they got into quarters Jeremy wasn't relaxed until he'd spent a long time in the shower.

"You all right?" he asked Jeremy when the kid came out, stark naked, to dress for bed.

"Yeah." Jeremy gave a little laugh and pulled on a tee and briefs to sleep in. But there was something still a little breath-less, a little strange about him.

Fletcher took his own shower and scrubbed as if he could scrub out the sight he'd just seen, and asking himself how he felt about room-sharing with a hype-head. *That* was what it reminded him of. He *had* seen people react that way. On drugs.

He didn't remember his mother playing kid games with him. He remembered his mother drugged out, but languid, most of the time. Remembered her more than once sitting at the table in the apartment and staring into space *she* didn't need a visor to see. But her arms would be hard like that, as if she were waiting for something, and her face would be—

He couldn't remember her face anymore. Not clearly. He came closest he'd come in years to remembering it with the women, senior crew, who came and went around him today. They looked *like* her. All the people on this ship looked *like* her in some subtle way, until those recent faces washed over what his mother had looked like to him.

And he remembered the times, the scariest times, when she'd been as scarily hyped as Jeremy had been in the game. How, at the last, she'd prowl the apartment and bump into walls that weren't there for her. She'd held him in her arms, the only times he could remember her holding him, and she'd say she saw the stars, she saw all the colors of space, and she'd ask him if he could see them, too.

He couldn't. Aged five, he'd thought there was something wrong with him, and that he was stupid, because he hadn't been able to see the stars the way she could. Thank God she hadn't given him any of what she was taking. She'd never gone that far down.

He let the shower fans dry his skin and his hair. He came out of the bath, abandoning the Base-induced modesty that had had him, on prior days, dressing in the cramped bath space. Jeremy didn't give him more than a glance, so he guessed it was nothing new in the intimacy of a crowded ship. Jeremy sat on his bunk letting the cards cascade between his hands, cards flying between his fingers and piling up again, sheer nervous energy.

Jeremy had already proved he was good at cards.

He lost three more hours. He won one back. And when he did win, Jeremy didn't sulk about it like some twelve-year-olds he'd known, just said, well, he was improving, and dealt another hand.

He was still sure he could swat Jeremy and his cousins aside in a straight-on fight. But he wasn't sure, now, that he could exit without damage. He hadn't factored in the possibility that his roommate was outright crazy. He hadn't figured that others might be, that it might go with the territory, just being out here, dealing with space. He'd known no spacers intimately but his mother and Quen. All his life, he'd heard people say spacers were *different* or *strange*, usually meaning it came in the blood and it accounted for his misbehaviors or his quirks.

Maybe there was something to it. He no longer denied there could be reasons besides upbringing that made spacers rowdy and made station police nervous when spacers intruded into residential areas. They bullied people. They went in groups and were loud and disorderly. They got drunk and knifed each other in bars and the police just contacted ships responsible, never arrested anybody unless they had the ship's officers present . . . because there'd been riots when a station attempted to intervene in spacer troubles, and what a riot was like when you got one, two thousand, ten thousand Jeremys all hyped *and* mad, he didn't ever want to see.

The final tally of favor-points was thirteen hours. He lost the last time and went to bed, with the prospect of another tomorrow exactly like this one.

He had no idea where the ship was by now. There were sounds he couldn't identify, occasionally hydraulics, but they were flying along at what Jeremy and his physics course called inertial. He lay in his bunk thinking about that until he made himself queasy with the thought of running into something; and reminded himself they weren't going through the ecliptic like insystemers, but nadir of the system, clear of the planets and stations, clear of the star, out there where *only* starships went.

On the next day he found his appetite for breakfast had increased. His stomach had gradually settled to the feeling the ship gave him. His sinuses had quit protesting the change in air pressure. At work, the frantic pace in the laundry detail that had kept them moving during the first days had abated, and that meant time on their hands. They talked. He didn't. They all folded sheets and stacked them up and they talked about the vid game last night, which at least was common ground,

but he wasn't inspired to add any observations, past their rapid
chatter.

They talked on and he handed out shower soap to a cousin
named Susan, who came to the counter. She wanted to talk and
make acquaintances: she was pretty, dark-eyed, looked twenty
and was just curious, he thought, and then reminded himself
this wasn't a pretty girl, it was a cousin, and you couldn't have
thoughts like that aboard, even if he was having them, and was
far more interested in her than in the game-chatter behind him.
She said she worked in cargo. He said he was in planetary
studies.

She said she didn't know what there was to study about a
planet. She wasn't joking, he decided. His ardor cooled
instantly, the conversation died a rapid, distracted death as the
game-chatter actually became more interesting than talking to
her, and maybe he managed to offend her. He was depressed
after she'd left.

Truly depressed. The new had worn off. The body and
brain had stopped having to move fast. Realization was settling in. He was among total strangers.

"What's the matter?" Jeremy asked him after a while.

"Tired," he said. And Vince took that as a cue to try to bait
him:

"A little work get to you?"

He didn't answer. "Let him alone," Jeremy said, and then
Jeremy engaged Vince and Linda in a game of cards in the
other room—which was one of the thousand little things that
hinted to him that Jeremy might be wiser than twelve—or at
least more mature than Vince was. They played cards. He did
small squares on the handheld that he'd brought among his
personal gear, a cheap, field-battered handheld that held a
couple of games, all his personal notes from classes and sessions in the field. He didn't want to access those. He couldn't
face the memories. He just built squares on the sketchpad,
trying to forget cousins.

JR came by and stopped at the counter, the first time he'd
seen JR since boarding. "So how are you feeling?" JR asked.

JR, who looked to be *his* age, and he was sure now both was and wasn't.

"Fine." He shut the handheld down and pocketed it, as inconspiciously as he could, fearful they might object either to his using it or having an unauthorized computer. Some places were touchy about it.

JR ignored it and took something from his breast pocket. He laid three little sealed plastic packets on the counter. "Jump drugs. It's regulation you have them on you at all times. You didn't report to infirmary when you boarded."

They were inevitability, staring him in the face. The event he most dreaded. "Nobody told me."

"Fine. I'm telling you now, for all future time. Scared to give yourself a shot?"

"No." He'd never done it. But he'd watched it.

"You just put it against your wrist and push the button. Kicks. If you have one malfunction . . . they don't, but if it should happen, you're supposed to have a second. Whenever you use one, you've got to drop by medical, that's A10. Day before jump, there'll always be a box sitting out for you to take what you need. One packet on your person at all times when the ship is out of dock, an extra when you're going for jump."

"There's three."

"This time, yes. Tripoint's supposedly safe as a dockside stroll these days, but nobody on this ship would bet his sanity on it. A jump-point's a lot of dark where you can still meet somebody you don't want to meet, and if we do, if we *should*, you'd hear the siren blowing when you come out of jump, and you'd have just enough time to hit yourself with that second shot. You've got to keep clear-headed and do that or you're in serious trouble. Not to scare you, but this ship has enemies. And people have gone into hyperspace without trank, but most don't come down the way they went in."

He'd been scared of a lot of things in the last number of days. Being shot at by pirates hadn't been on the immediate list. Coming awake in hyperspace hadn't been. Now it was.

"When you board, for the record, next thing after you turn

in your baggage at the dock, the packets are on the counter, pick 'em up."

"Yeah, well, I had cops attached."

"No excuses next time. As you board, you take your duffle to the counter, pick up the drugs, sign the list."

"You're going to let me off this ship?"

"Only seniors stay aboard. No deck space during dock. Unless you're sick. You don't plan to be sick. And just once, and just for the record, never take this stuff except when you're told to by an officer. That box sits on the counter on the honor system. Take only what you're supposed to."

He'd been getting along well enough until cousin JR said that.

"My mother was an addict," he said. "That what you mean?"

"Never take it except when told by an officer. Standard instruction. That's the rule. Nothing personal."

"Like hell."

There was the laundry counter between them. It was probably a good thing. The card game was going on in the next room. There was nothing else to separate them.

The silence between them went on a moment. JR's jaw muscles stood out in shadow. But JR didn't inform him it was Like hell, *sir*.

"Obey the regulations," JR said. "Go back to work."

JR walked off.

He didn't know who was in the right about that encounter. He stood there with a pocketful of what had killed his mother. The ship was going into jump with him aboard, and if he didn't take the drug he'd meet whatever it was in hyperspace that drove people crazy. The drugs were ordinary, they were what you had to take to get through the experience, and his mother had died only because she overdosed and depressed her nervous system. He knew all that.

And he knew that the clock was running down close to that event and that through an oversight he'd almost not had the drugs he was supposed to have. That was a fact, too, and if somebody hadn't checked and there'd been some kind of emergency he knew he could have been in bad trouble. JR had come by to make sure he had the drug and knew what to do, so he couldn't fault that as hostile behavior. It was just the little extra remark that just hadn't been necessary.

He was scared. Scared of the event, terrified of the drug—he'd been tested for it: the court had wanted to know if his mother had given it to him, to a five-year-old. But her suicide had been solo. Probably not intended to happen while he was home. She'd loved him. She kept getting him back from the social system no matter how many times she gave him up. Wasn't that love?

"So what'd JR want?"

The card game was over. Jeremy was back at his elbow. Assigned to be there: he suddenly drew that conclusion. Jeremy was always looking out for him not because Jeremy gave a damn but because Jeremy had orders.

He opened the counter and left, walking fast, nowhere, and then toward his quarters, which he realized was no refuge from Jeremy. He was cornered, and stopped, in mid-corridor.

"You can't just walk off-duty," Jeremy said. "What *happened*?"

"Nothing happened," he said, and drew a couple of calmer breaths. He didn't want to explain it. He didn't want to deal with it. And he didn't want to have to hold together incipient panic with a twelve-year-old hanging on his arm. "When are we going into jump?"

"About four hours."

"Today?"

"Is there a problem?"

Is there a problem? He wanted to laugh. Or cry. "No," he said. And turned back toward the laundry. "Just keep Vince off me. I'm not in a good mood."

"Sure," Jeremy said, and walked with him.

He couldn't walk in with no commotion. Vince had to say something.

"Well, is cousin Fletcher going to take a walk?"

He grabbed a fistful of Vince's jumpsuit.

"Fletcher, stop!" Jeremy said, and tried to push him and

Vince apart, no luck where it came to budging his arm. "No fighting. Vince, cut it, don't hassle him! Hear me?"

"Vince," Linda said, in what sounded like real fear, and pushed at Vince as if Vince had a choice about it. She acted as if she might have prevented Vince swinging at him. At least she gave Vince an excuse to take his thirteen-year-old self in retreat about five paces and toward the next section of the laundry.

Jeremy and Linda did the age-old part of friends, calming Vince down as if he'd been fierce and unrestrainable, just on the verge of swinging on somebody two heads taller.

Vince had been flat pissing scared. Fletcher realized that, now, as he realized the kid had gotten him angry enough to do damage, which wasn't called for. They *were* kids, and it wasn't their fault the captain or whoever had put him down with them. He wished on the one hand he'd gone ahead and hit Vince and improved his attitude. But he told himself that a warning had settled it. He went back to folding sheets, telling himself that whatever a batch of snot-nosed kids took in stride, he could, and his mother's case wasn't his case, and he wasn't going to panic or let the kids see how scared he was.

That was the trouble. He was scared. Scared of the drug as much as the jump, and telling himself, rationally, there wasn't anything to be scared of. Sad about, upset about, yes, but not scared.

Not in front of Jeremy.

"So how's he doing?" Bucklin asked before jump, and JR didn't find a ready reply.

"Calm," JR said, "mostly." They were both on last moment patrol of the corridors. The ship was about to do another burn, this one of short duration, getting up to V enough to preserve vector and assure they didn't make a momentary anomaly in the local sun. The warning had sounded, an order for all but jump crew to go to their cabins and stay there. The endless, upward-curving corridor was deserted, the doors all shut. They'd just passed the room Fletcher shared with Jeremy, on their way to their own quarters, senior and second-senior, the last two moving about down on A corridor, while upstairs, in

B, much the same process would be going on. They'd collected their e-rations, they had their trank, and they were about to head for Tripoint, a set of three large mass-points that would anchor their jump toward Mariner.

Relatively busy as jump-points went. You followed the same procedures as at a star, but the triple mass made precise navigation tricky there. You could find out where you were after you'd arrived, but your precise arrival was just a little hard to coordinate. You got the latest navigational charts just before the ship left, charts shot to you in the final informational packet. *Finity* hadn't been through Tripoint recently, but some ships at dock had, and the information they had on Tripoint's precise numbers had gone to Pell Central along with the stock market data and civil records from Viking and Mariner and everywhere else in the network.

Tripoint had its hazards, and a ship arriving there even these days was careful who they met and who might be lurking. Since the War, this ship was always careful, and went in with someone ready at the guns.

But he didn't think that was information their new cousin needed to know on his first jump.

Feet appeared on the horizon. Two pair. Legs followed. Chad and Lyra were walking the opposite direction in the ring, and they were meeting up. Circuit complete.

"No ball of flame in A28?" Lyra asked.

"Nothing exciting," Bucklin reported. "We don't have to sit on him."

"Damn," Lyra said. "There goes my chance."

Joke. There wasn't any bunking about on board, New Rules, or Old. But cousin Fletcher's felicitous sorting of the family genes—and his status as a stranger—had drawn remarks among the femme-cousins.

Fletcher might be just seventeen, but he was a well put together and mature seventeen, which, given he was *new*, was triggering interest spacers didn't ordinarily feel toward a shipmate. He knew he probably ought to talk to Fletcher about that. It wasn't something he could easily tell Jeremy to explain, Jeremy, whose body didn't yet inform him what it would abundantly explain in the next few years.

But given how Fletcher had exploded, given the level of tension Fletcher was already carrying, it didn't seem quite the moment.

When their brand-new and fine-looking cousin *did* mix with spacers on a foreign dockside in about ten days, subjective time, Fletcher would get offers . . . offers that would presume experience to match the face and body. It was going to be interesting.

They parted company, to separate quarters, the privilege of all the senior-juniors in a ship with too many vacant cabins. They hauled cargo in some of their unused space, right along with the huge shipping cannisters in the hold and the rim. It was Earth goods and downer wine they carried inside, high-priced cargo that needed not only gravity such as they could provide in the outer rim but specific temperatures, for its safety.

They were moving slowly, this trip, laden with, besides their luxury goods, plain staples: flour. They were vulnerable economically, vulnerable in terms of self-defense . . . not as heavy mass as they'd ever hauled, but heavy enough a feel to the ship to let them know they had cargo.

The last reports into Pell, from a ship inbound eight hours ago, said Tripoint was safe, free from lurkers. But that could change with any heartbeat. A starship could arrive at Tripoint from various places, one of them a deep route, the sort only non-cargo ships used, reachable by a ship that had a very high engine/mass ratio. That deep route intersecting with a busy commercial route was what made it so valuable in the War, and valuable after to the black market, and to those just keeping an eye out—for various causes.

He was anxious about that place, on edge about this jump more than any except the one into their turnaround point, at Esperance. The bridge could ill afford distractions, like a medical from A deck.

Chad and Lyra went on to their separate quarters. His and Bucklin's were side by side, A20 and 21. They'd roomed together since they were knee-high to Jeremy. They had separate quarters now, using the spare space as office, each of them, but they stayed together. They walked in that direction.

"Well," Bucklin said, "here we are, on our way to respectable trade."

"Here's to it," JR said, and opened his own door, went in, sat down on a bunk he hadn't visited in . . . how many hours?

There'd been staff meetings. Reviews about their handling qualities: the Old Man wanted that hammered home to everybody who was used to *Finity* moving with a lot more response than she'd have under these circumstances. Different set of rules, both navigational and defensive. In an emergency, since the captain had officially ordered him on standby and not on tape, he would be on-shift backup to Madison, leaving Alan and Francie to enjoy a little deeper sleep and the chance to do tape.

As short-handed as *Finity* had run, it could come on any given jump, any one of the captains failing to make it—and the Old Man was pushing it with every jump, stretched thin, year upon year upon year. Madison wasn't that far behind, himself, and a rough exit and Alan and Francie doing tape at the time, could put him *in* the Old Man's chair, giving orders to Helm simply because there wasn't another alternative.

So he had the numbers to memorize, the instructions and locations in navigation as well as the figures on their laded mass and moment in exit, and by the very nature of his assignment memorizing them the old-fashioned way, the way they'd done before the Old Man had given in and admitted that tape-study wasn't going to turn the crew and particularly the juniors into Unionized automatons.

God, they'd even gotten hypermath through Vince's head since that blessed change in the Rules.

And they couldn't short Jeremy his education the entire pass around their course, not even a significant number of jumps. Jeremy was going to go on study again in a couple of jumps or spend some of his rec evenings later this year locked in a room with Fletcher and *both* of them doing deep-study.

He hadn't broken that small piece of news to the boys yet.
Jeremy was still delighted with his new roommate, with an
almost-brother who was large, inept with the routines, and
mentally—

—different. Say that much for dealing with a stationer.

Much as he didn't like it.

He stowed the boots in his locker and tugged on the light-soled
jumpboots that would protect his feet if he had to move and still
wouldn't cramp up during a quasi-sleep that, in his body's time,
would amount to about two weeks.

You didn't want tight clothing during that time, because
your body wouldn't do much of anything while the drug
stayed in your body—you wouldn't move, but you were just
marginally aware. Your mind could process things, like
dream-state, and you could learn things of a factual sort, and
if you were vastly disturbed, at the edge of the state, as you
were coming out, sometimes you could get up off your bunk
and do things marginally under the control of your conscious
mind.

That was the spooky part—and never having known anyone
who'd not been through the experience of a hyperspace jump
from way before birth, when pregnant women had to get off
mild thymedine and onto hyprazine, a drug which *would*
intentionally get to the fetal bloodstream, he had extreme last-
minute regrets about leaving Fletcher to Jeremy. Jeremy had a
generally calming effect on Fletcher—unless Fletcher hyped
instead of tranked down, and thought he'd met the devil in
hyperspace.

Maybe he *should* pull Fletcher into his quarters. The rest of
the crew wouldn't take it as exalting Fletcher, but Jeremy
would take it as a slap in the face.

Jeremy had a beeper; Jeremy was unfazed by jump and had
been known to be up on his feet *during* the dump-downs,
which the young smart-ass still illicitly did, he was all but certain. Nobody among the juniors, including himself or Bucklin,
would be faster to have their wits about them if Fletcher did
spook; he was sure of that. Jeremy also had two extra doses of

trank and knew what to do with them, right through the plastic envelope on any available surface of his roommate if he had to.

You didn't track a kid toward Helm if he didn't have the killer reflexes. And Jeremy had them, better than anybody in years.

It remained to prove what they'd make out of Fletcher.

Chapter
— IX —

Fletcher sat on his bunk putting on the lighter boots and the light sweater Jeremy advised, a lot calmer than he thought he'd possibly be now that the event was on him. Jeremy's juvenile cheerfulness was reassuring. "It gets kind of cold," Jeremy said matter-of-factly. "And you can't get up to get anything. You might want to, but you'd lose your balance, even if you can think that far. They really advise against it."

He'd thought people slept through it, numb to anything that happened to them. But his mother had been aware enough, walking around. She'd talked to *him* when she was on it. He didn't know how high a dose she'd been taking.

Too much, the last time . . . *that* was for damned certain. But it wasn't poison. It was just a drug. A drug that thousands of people took regularly with no ill effects.

The takehold sounded. He scrambled to get belted in, to get a pillow under his head. *And* to get the book set up, which Jeremy had lent him. It fed out into a game visor, for when he wanted it. It was an adventure story, something called *War of the Worlds*. He wouldn't spend the hours with nothing to do but think about his situation.

"Usually we take tape," Jeremy said, "usually it's math—or biology." A wrinkle of Jeremy's nose. "But they want to kind of, you know, make sure you're all right with this before they let you take tape during it. So I'm staying off tape for the meanwhile, so I can help you if you, you know, need something."

"What's dangerous about it?" Stupid question. He knew the answers there were.

"Just, you know, if you didn't get set right and needed something."

"I thought you couldn't move."

"You *shouldn't* move. I mean, you can scratch your nose or something. You try not to think about it, but your nose always itches. If you can find it and not hit yourself in the eye. Best is just to relax. Watch the pretty lights. There's usually lights."

"Usually?"

"If you're not doing tape. Or you think about stuff. Think about happy stuff. Think about the happiest stuff you can think of. That's the best."

He damn sure didn't want nightmares. A solid month of nightmares. He didn't want to think about it. "How many of these have you been through?"

"Oh, I don't know. Maybe . . . maybe fifty, sixty. And Tripoint. Tripoint's a cinch now. You come out with shooting going on, alarms going off—that's where you just lie there wondering . . . "

"Where's that?"

"Oh, Tripoint once. At Earth."

Somehow, on this ship, he didn't think the kid was lying. "*On* it?"

"Not *on* it. They were shooting, you could see it on the scopes. They were shooting, just all hell going on." Jeremy was winding tighter, the way he'd been with the vid games, muscles tight, hands balled into fists, beating a short, small rhythm as if there were music Jeremy could hear. "Like, if you get hulled, —we did, once—there's this *sound*—there's this sound goes through everything. You don't hear it. And the lights going off. Everything's red when you wake up, those emergency lights—"

"That happened?" He didn't think that was a lie, either. He'd hit a nerve of some kind, touched off something, and the kid was scared—of what, he didn't know—staring at sights he didn't see.

"Yeah, it happened." Breath came through Jeremy's teeth and he seemed clenched tight, every muscle. "But we got 'em back. We got 'em back at Bryant's." The beat of hands continued, a drumbeat against his drawn-up legs, rapid, tight movements. And the engines cut in. "We're going. We're going. Here we go."

The kid was spooked. *He'd* expected *he'd* be crawling the walls in panic, but Jeremy was wired, wound, caught up in memory Jeremy had just advised him not to access: *think of happy things.* Jeremy wasn't thinking of happy memories.

"We don't take the drug now?" he asked Jeremy, any question, to gain some doorway into Jeremy's private terror. The bunks were tilting, making their whole cabin one double-deck bunk the way they did when the ship was accelerating. He couldn't think of anything else to say but to question what he was trying, in his own fear, to remember to do. "We wait for the announcement. Right?"

"Yeah," Jeremy's voice came to him. "Yeah, wait. Just wait. They'll say when."

He imagined Jeremy up above him, still spooked, still wound tight as a spring. He didn't know whether Jeremy was always like this on jumps, or whether his own fears were rational, or whether that last memory still haunted the kid. The ship getting hulled . . .

That wasn't something ships survived. But *Finity* was a big ship; among the biggest. And it had been, for years, fighting the Fleet, hunting the hunters that preyed on shipping, firing and being fired on . . .

"Are we looking for any trouble?" he called up to Jeremy, trying without seeing him, to test whether the kid was all right. "Are we really going to Mariner? Is that where we're really going?"

"Yeah," Jeremy said back. "On this vector? Yeah. Mariner via Tripoint. We're hauling cargo. This time it's real cargo. For us, not for Mallory. Tons of Scotch whiskey and coffee and chocolate. We used to haul missiles and hard-rations."

Mallory. Mallory of *Norway.* The rebel captain who'd defended Pell. Cargo for Mallory, whose ship had docked only rarely at Pell in his lifetime.

Supplying Mallory with necessities? Making cargo runs to the warships out in space?

That was for history books. The War was something you heard about in documentaries and vid games.

But Jeremy, at twelve, had been out on the fringes for seventeen years. This ship had gotten hit during the War. Or after. During the pirate hunts, which had danced in and out of the news all his life, just part of the background of his life.

But it was real, out there.

Correction. Out *here*. On this ship he was on. It was very real to Jeremy. It had never been *un*real to Jeremy.

He wasn't hearing anything out of the kid. He wanted a voice. Wanted truth. Wanted an estimation of what to expect out here. "You see any pirates?"

"What do you mean?" Jeremy asked.

"I mean, you ever come close to any? Recently?"

The force was slamming them into the mattresses. It wasn't easy to move, but Jeremy had rolled over and looked over the edge of his bunk.

"Where do you think we've been for seventeen years? They *teach* you anything on that station?"

He'd been a fool. "I guess not enough."

"Half this ship died," Jeremy said fiercely, hair hanging, face reddening. "My mama and half of everybody aboard, some of them juniors who never knew what hit 'em. We got a decompression in half the ring and we had damn-all getting back to a port where we could get us put back together. I wish we was still hunting them and not going on this stupid trade run, massed up so we can't handle worth a damn at an insystem wallow. Captain-sir wants us back to trading, and Captain Mallory says the War's over, but they're still out there, there's pirates still out there we haven't got, and Mallory's still hunting 'em. When I make senior, *damn-all*, and if we haven't gotten after those bastards again, I'm going to jump ship and join Mallory's crew."

"You think they could try to raid us on this run?"

"I don't know." Jeremy's face had gone an alarming color from the strain of hanging over the edge. "They say it's quiet right now and the stations don't want to give us any more money to keep us out hunting. Madison says they haven't got hit, is what. They've been safe for seventeen years and they don't want to pay, and we're the *reason* they haven't been hit for seventeen years. Year we were born and we left Pell, the station was a wreck."

The first years on Pell had been lean, that was sure. His childhood memories were scarce food and a lot of construction.

"Let a ship get hit," Jeremy said out of the air above him, finally back all the way in his bunk, "and you bet the merchanters are going to be yelling. Where's *Finity*? They'll say. Why isn't *Finity* on the job? And maybe they'll pay the dock charges for us, or all the ships will go on strike so the stations have to *let* us dock and fuel on station-charge. That's what the Old Man did before. He shut down all merchant traffic and nobody hauled. He did it when Union wanted to Unionize us and he did it when the Earth Company wanted us not to trade Union-side, and he did it to cut the Fleet off so the Fleet couldn't get supply. We could do it again."

The merchanter strikes were famous. It was something he knew from school. "So why don't you?"

"I don't know," Jeremy said, and then said, in a lower voice: "I think the captain's getting old."

Captain James Robert Neihart. *The* Captain. The one who'd hauled him aboard and wrecked his life. It seemed to him that the captain had power enough to get his way. And that Quen did.

Jeremy didn't say any more. The acceleration kept up, and kept up. Fletcher put the visor on and turned the book on, and moved only his thumb to change pages.

He was still scared. Maybe more so, but less so of the jump itself. The pirates sounded more active than the station news had had the story. He hadn't meant to tread on Jeremy's sensitivities. Jeremy had lost a mother, too, in the War, or what passed for the peace, and they had that in common, as well as their birth.

He didn't know enough about history. He'd gotten through his courses without having to know that much. He was good on the governments of Earth, far off things that were more exotic than evocative of real pain. The construction had been an inconvenience of his childhood, places you couldn't go, because there was always construction in the way, but he'd actively avoided knowing about the War, or his mother's reason for being where she'd died. He'd understood that Q section had been pretty bad, and some of the people that had been in Q section were still visiting the psychs. Some had even asked for a minor wipe, to purge that time from their memories. Which said it had been pretty bad, because the psychs had granted a wipe to some, and they hadn't even considered it for his mother. Even if she later killed herself.

"This is James Robert. Jump in five minutes. First warning. Trank down. Fletcher, welcome aboard, and have a sound sleep."

Me? he asked himself. The high and mighty senior and universally-famous captain talked to him, in front of the whole damn crew?

"Trank down," Jeremy said from above him. "Now. You all right?"

"Yeah. Yes." He'd mapped out every move he needed to make. His hands were shaking as he pulled the visor off and stowed it the way he'd been warned to stow everything loose, shoved it in the tight elastic pocket at the edge of the bunk. "Where's best to give it?" JR had said shoot it in the wrist, but Jeremy knew easy ways for everything.

"Anywhere below the neck. Arm's fine. Push up your sleeve and just hit it."

He pulled out the packet with nightmares of dropping it, fought with the tear strip, got his sleeve up and froze . . . just froze, hand shaking so he almost did drop it.

"You give it yet?" Jeremy called down to him.

He pushed the packet hard against his bare forearm. The spring kicked. He didn't feel it as sharply as he thought he should. It didn't sting. He held up the clear packet to his eye. The plastic was flat against the backing, fluid depleted. It had gone in. It looked as if it had. Maybe he should take the other one. In case. Maybe it had ejected on the bedclothes instead of in his arm. . . .

"Fletcher? Did you do it? Are you all right?"

"Yes!" He was shivering. But things were growing distant. He felt the drug insinuating itself through his veins. It *had* gone in, he'd just been so scared he hadn't felt the sting. He was getting slower . . .

Slower and lighter at the same time. Maybe the ship had cut the engines. It felt that way . . .

"Fletcher . . ." he heard someone say. . . .

They were looking for him. . . .

Rain swept the trees in sheets, and battered the mask, making the seal against his face slippery and uncertain as he traded cylinders—the first trade-out he'd had to make, and sooner than he'd expected. That early depletion of a life-and-death resource scared him; rather than squander another, he replaced just one, just the one with the end gone dark red, all the way expired.

His hands were trembling as he shoved the replacement in, and he couldn't get the rain-wet facial seal to take and reseal the way it ought. So he pressed it hard against his face as he walked, mad, now, mad at all the world above and half the world of Downbelow and knowing he had to focus down and get his wits about him before he had an accident Downbelow just wouldn't forgive.

It was getting dark, now: simple fact in the domes, or on the station, where twilight happened as a technological choice and a human hand could revise it.

Not out here. A dozen times he'd tell himself he had to just turn around, go back, follow River home. But he'd long passed any hope of using any excuse he could think of but one: he was lost.

And that was the truth. He'd gotten himself in such a mess now he didn't know how to get out.

Couldn't blame anyone—not for the *lost* part. That was stupid. And if he died of it, he couldn't pass the blame for that. He had a locator. And he walked without losing it, because dammit, he wasn't giving up. Not yet. Not until he was a lot closer to being out of cylinders than he was.

And maybe—maybe—it was a tiny idea, a forlorn and hopeless hope—maybe somebody would find him, and maybe he *would* hold out until the ship undocked, or until—remotest of all hopes—until they were so glad he was alive they'd understand how hard they'd pushed him, and maybe he could engineer something if he just got a chance to talk to the psychs.

He'd hated them lifelong. But right now he saw them as a chance: he was *good* at talking to them. He'd say he'd spooked because of being followed and that at first he'd really meant to get the saw before it went on his record. And then he could break down and say it wasn't the idea, and he'd lied, and it was just immaturity. He had *just* turned seventeen. You got some license to be immature, didn't you? They gave plenty to Marshall Willett. Or Jim Frantelli. Jim had a book full of reprimands on stupid things, and he didn't have *any*. Not one. Wouldn't that count for something? Somewhere?

Or if they got onto him and said he couldn't come back to the program he could talk to the downers. He'd tell Melody and Patch if he wasn't there after they came back from the walk, they should sit down and strike. They'd get all the downers behind him and they'd say no downer would work if they didn't have Fletch—

He was kidding himself. It wasn't going to happen. Melody and Patch couldn't organize something like that even if he could make them understand. They'd try to help him, but they weren't the kind of downer that ran things. He didn't even know if he'd find them out here, or if the rains had started the spring and they'd have gone off somewhere he didn't know, all unknowing that their Fetcher was in trouble.

He'd just needed—just needed to have some breathing room. A day or two before people started invoking courts and lawyers and sending him through it all again. . . .

He'd worked hard. He'd be happy to work hard all his life, and earn the station-share the ship was suing the station about and never spend a credit except on food. He'd be good down here.

It just wasn't damn all fair, and he hated their damn ship and he hated the family that had left his mother on the station.

Intellectually he knew they'd had no choice, sick as she was; but there was a childish part of him that was mad about that; and a much more rational part that hated them for their damned *persistence*, coming back again and again with their lawsuits, and the station for its stupid automated accounting systems that kept kicking the bill out again—when all they wanted was not to be billed for fourteen and a half million c and all the station wanted was a quittance so they could either put him on the books or get him *off* the books. It was two authorities playing games with each other, all technicalities, for a stupid ship that refused to pay his mother's bills and a station that refused to admit he was born to a station-share and kept billing *Finity* for his existence here.

Stupid games. All these years that he'd been trying to get on the level and have a life of his own, for God's sake, what did they want of him, except to go one more round of lawsuits and make points on each other. He hated—

Mud sent him skidding, down, down, down in the twilight, and River was below. He grabbed at things in fright, and got his hand on a branch, and held, having torn muscles and scared himself. He hung there and slowly began to get his feet under him, and crawled up the slope on his hands and knees, asking himself why it mattered, and wouldn't it have been better after all if he'd just gone in and saved everybody the bother.

It took him a long time to get his feet under him. When he walked again it was with a knot of pain in his throat and a knot of fear around his heart, with no notion where he was going.

To see as much of the world as he could see, he decided, before he pushed the come-get-me button on the locator and admitted the dream was over. There wasn't much point in wandering in the dark and using up cylinders. So he'd just sit down and stay warm and not lose his head.

He was shivering when he did find a place to sit. The suit had a flash lining, and you could pull a patch off and it would heat up. It would only do it once, and then that suit was done and a discard, but he was going to be at the halfway point of cylinders by tomorrow and he'd have to go back or he wouldn't come back.

You wouldn't die of Downbelow's air right away. If you breathed it you got medical problems.

Maybe if he just lied and told them he had breathed the air they'd keep him on the station. They'd put him in the hospital, and they'd find out he hadn't, and he'd be in a lot of trouble, but he wouldn't be on the ship.

Or maybe he'd just really do it, just take the mask off and come back really sick and not have to think about the ship. He'd be a medical case, then, maybe for the rest of his life, just like his mother.

But he'd seen that. He didn't want it.

He'd think about solutions tomorrow, he decided. He'd think when he had to think. He pulled the patch to heat the suit, and felt the warmth spread in the folds, first, then, gradually to the rest of his body.

Then there was nothing to do but sit there, while the rain roared in the trees and River roared in his banks nearby.

Nunn would have gotten in a lot of trouble, Fletcher imagined, for thinking he was going to walk tamely back to the dorm-dome. He was sort of sorry about that. Nunn never had done anything to him.

It was damned hard not to think what a mess he'd gotten himself in. He wished he had the strength to keep walking so he didn't have to listen to his own mind work, and to his own common sense say how badly he'd screwed up.

If you had a cylinder go out while you were sleeping you just got slower and slower and maybe didn't wake up. He should have checked out how far gone the cylinders were before it got dark. He wasn't *used* to places that became dark with no light switch to flip. It *was* dark, now, and he couldn't check them. That was what they said. If you get lost, don't go to sleep. He could go by feel and change out to ones he knew were new; but if he ran around with a bunch of unwrapped cylinders in his pockets he could ruin a few, or he could get them wet in the rain and the damp.

Hell with it, he thought. He *thought* he had enough time left on the ones that were in.

The scare when he'd nearly fallen in Old River a while ago

had begun, however, to drive something of his self-preservation out of him. It had been a sharp, keen danger, not the sickly kind of terror he hated so much worse—sitting in a lawyer's office and listening to people disposing of his life. He'd nearly fallen in the river and he began slowly to realize now he wasn't scared. Just toss the dice, and maybe he'd decide to come back and maybe he wouldn't.

If he passed the safe limits of choice, then maybe he'd make it, and maybe he wouldn't. In either case, he had more control over his life than the people who ran things would ever give him.

He was screwing them up good, was what he was doing. They'd be upset, and he wasn't damned sorry.

Probably Bianca would be upset, too, but then, Bianca didn't know his record. When people found that out they quit caring, and most of them got away from him so fast their tracks smoked.

Melody and Patch would be upset. Melody most of all. But Melody hoped for a new baby. Hoped he'd grown up and found a girl of his own kind only so she could have a baby and quit taking care of a messed-up human kid.

When he thought about that, he hurt inside. Aged seventeen, safe and secret in the dark, he hurt, for all the things that had ever gone wrong . . . .

They were calling him again . . .

Wouldn't let him be alone, and it was all he wanted . . .

. . . "Fletcher . . ."

"Fletcher," someone said from outside, and he blinked, shaky, sick. Someone—his eyes were blurred—lifted his head up after several tries and succeeded after he began to coop-erate with the effort to lift him. Someone put something to his lips and said, "Drink," so he closed his lips on the straw and drank. It was what his body needed, a taste told him that.

The somebody was a younger cousin. Jeremy. The place was the ship.

The arm he was holding himself up with began to shake. The place smelled like sweat and old clothes. "Something wrong with the ship?" He found the strength to panic, and tried to sit up.

"No," Jeremy said, and slipped his arm free and let him struggle with the belts that were holding him. "Keep drinking the juice. I'm senior by a month. I get the shower first."

"Well, did something happen?" he called after Jeremy, thinking because it had been so short a time, they must have aborted the run. . . .

But things had changed. He felt his face—the little trace of beard, dead skin that rolled off under his fingers. His clothes were disgusting. Like month-old laundry. The smell was *him*.

"We're at Tripoint," Jeremy called back from inside the shower. "Drink the juice! You'll be sorry if you don't! We're going to be blowing *V* in a bit. Don't panic if the ship sort of goes away. It just does that. It's kind of wild. About two, three times."

He had three packets of the stuff. He drained the first. There was a terrible moment of giddiness, where the deck seemed to dissolve under him and the walls went nowhere. He was utterly disoriented, and slumped down on the bed until the feeling went away.

"That was the first," Jeremy called out. "Damn, that was hard!"

"First what?" He felt sick at his stomach.

"*V*-dump," Jeremy yelled back. There was the sound of the shower. "Braking, hyperspace style. We don't go up all the way, we just kind of brush it. Slows us down."

He knew something about hyperspace. He'd never imagined feeling it. They'd just touched the hyperspace interface. He felt shaky and ripped open another juice, so thirsty his mouth felt dusty.

Things tasted too sweet, and too sour. The green walls had a flavor. The smell had a color, and not a pretty one.

Most of all, the dreadful thing had happened, he was no longer at Pell, he was out of reach of home, and the only thing he could think of was a desperate need for liquid and what taste told him was in that liquid. He ripped open another drink packet. He sat there sipping mineral-reinforced juice until Jeremy came out to look for a change of clothes.

The intercom came on. What sounded like a mechanical voice called their names, and Vince's and Linda's, and said, *"Galley duty."*

"Shower's yours," Jeremy said. "We've got galley this round. All those pots and pans. Lucky us. But it's not bad. Rise and shine."

He felt like hell. And they were going to be working. The rebel part of him said ignore it, lie here, make them come get him. But it was better than lying in a bunk thinking. He stripped off and went to the shower, and was in the middle of a steamy, lung-hydrating deluge when the siren sounded.

"Takehold!" Jeremy screamed from outside. "Stay put! Damn, what's he *doing* up there?"

He didn't know what to do or which wall to brace himself against. The world dissolved and reformed. The water hit him, boiling hot. Or the world had come back. He leaned against the shower wall hoping to drown and not to be blown to atoms. Shaking head to foot.

"You all right?" Jeremy yelled.

"The emergency has ended," a calm voice said on the intercom. *"The ship is stable. That was a second precautionary reposition on receipt of an unidentified, now ID'ed as Union military* Amity. *All clear. Request roll call and safety check."*

"Well, damn all, what are *they* doing here?" Jeremy said from outside the door. "Bridge wants us to call in. You all right, Fletcher?"

"Fine," he said. He stood there while the fans dried him off and he shook and shivered in the warm air. He managed to ask, meekly, "Is something wrong?"

"Must be all right," Jeremy said through the door. "Helm must've not liked the look of things. But we got our all clear. We can move about."

Move about? He was in the God-help-him *shower.* "Do we do that a lot?"

"Pretty rare we see anybody," Jeremy said. "It's empty out here. We didn't nearly hit her, understand. We just, if we see anybody, we change *V.* In case they, you know, aren't up to any good. In case they fired. That is a Union carrier out there."

"So?"

"So this is sort of *Alliance* territory. They can come here, just kind of nosing around, but that's one big ship out there. Usually they'd send just a cruiser to look around. That's a whole damn command center."

"Friendly?"

"Yeah. Sort of. It's pretty wild. Helm must've forgot we were hauling."

He opened the shower door and felt the chill outside. He dressed in clean coveralls, trying to conceal the shakes he was suffering. He'd dropped weight, he'd noticed that when he'd been in the shower. He felt hollow inside, and wanted another fruit juice, but they were out.

"So are we still likely for a takehold?" he asked Jeremy. "Can we go down to the galley, or are we stuck here?"

"We're supposed to be on the new Old Rules," Jeremy said, "whatever *that* means. That everything's supposed to be looser and if we get a takehold it's not a takehold like they're going to be shooting. Not unless they say 'red.' Then it's serious and we're back on the old New Rules. But I guess the old New Rules still apply on the bridge all the time. Damn, that was a stop! I bet they rearranged the galley good and proper. Cook's going to be cussing the air blue."

They were crazy. The whole ship and its company was crazy, and he was still shaking.

"But I guess it's all right to go," Jeremy said. "You ready? Guess they're not going to shoot."

Chapter

— X —

Pure nerves, JR discovered when he reported in on the bridge. Nobody blamed Helm. Their pilot had made a precautionary move when he picked up a carrier's large presence in the local buoy information, maintaining V.

Then a fast drop to non-combatant stance, all before the rest of them knew anything was going on and before the carrier's advanced, fire-linked systems could read and confirm their ID off stored files. The deep spacetime punch and quick relocation of their larger than average mass could, unhappily, have given them a warlike, carrierlike, appearance—a paradoxical faster-than-light presence that would propagate through the spacetime sheet in the same way a pin-drop could make itself heard in a still room.

But they weren't, in that instant, helpless and spotted in the fire-path of the carrier's hair-triggered defense systems. For one thing, in the hand of cards that Old Man Inertia dealt, an entering ship always had the ace if they had a pilot who knew how to use it. The entering ship could fire downslope if they chose; reposition if they chose. If they hadn't been willing to meet the carrier, they'd have gone silent and unlocatable somewhere along a track dictated only by physics and the local mass—a track that carrier could calculate, but not soon enough or precisely enough, on a ship that still carried enough V to jump out again on the Viking heading. And fire as they did so.

That rapid stutter of presence they'd made, however, was delay enough to let their systems determine that the presence in the jump-point was Union, not Mazianni, and their subsequent stop let the carrier find out the same about them, since they'd been lawfully using their ID when they came in.

It was still a jittery feeling, a once-enemy dreadnought in possession of the Tripoint system and themselves in its crosshairs. By what JR detected on the displays, the carrier didn't look at all to be in transit of the jump-point. It was low-energy on a vector that said it had come from Viking, but it wasn't proceeding. It was just sitting. Looking around. Logging traffic.

Prowling the edges of Alliance territory it wasn't supposed to visit . . . except on specific invitation of Pell, which he didn't think it had.

Mallory's invitation, however, in the deep uncertainties of this post-War period, might be the answer. The carrier was possibly—possibly—moving out of its territory in order to back up Mallory in Earth space after *they'd* left Mallory unattended. That would imply *Finity*'s decision had been made many months earlier than he thought it had—but it wouldn't be the first time he'd been caught ignorant of *Finity*'s high-level operations.

Junior officers were expected to guess, and to hone their strategic skills against real situations, trying to outfigure senior officers. But it didn't help junior officer nerves. He'd taken himself up to B deck at breakneck speed, unshaven, still in flight-slippers, and checked in on the bridge. So had Madison, who was supposed to be the next shift, and who obviated all necessity for him to stay here—but stay he did.

In the duty of second-guessing command without disturbing operations, JR went up to Scan 5's post and simply observed for a moment, in order not to disturb the critical, multilevel operations of that post.

"Rider status," he asked Scan 5 after a moment of stable display.

"Uncertain," Five reported without turning in his chair. "Carrier ID confirmed as *Amity*. Output normal, range 5 minutes."

The carrier, five minutes away as light traveled, had resumed ID output, a measure of confidence as it looked them over. Scan and passive-recept alone, however, couldn't entirely confirm what *Amity* was doing, whether it was sitting there with its several rider-ships still attached and therefore harmless, or whether it had already deployed them as heavy-fire platforms, lying transmission-silent and ready at various points about the area. *Finity's* optics were surely in play, along with other methods of search.

The carrier hadn't obliged their optics by turning a profile that would make its status clear, either. He saw the fuzzy image and the enhancement and didn't take that situation for a chance arrangement in their relative positions. Five minutes was close, as ships reckoned entry positions. It was not close in targeting.

They had had an uneasy working arrangement with Union military that had held for nearly two decades. They'd even worked, though not lately, with this particular carrier. Both Alliance and Union protected their secrets, and Union was still very wary, particularly of Mallory's intentions, even after two decades.

Bucklin and Lyra showed up to take their stations: apprentice-posts, unassigned chairs, like his, that left them able to observe, not necessarily to work at this critical juncture. He made a quiet approach to his own regular post, near the Old Man and Madison, noting that by now in ordinary procedure their bridge shift should have changed. Madison's team was held, not yet called to duty, and that changeover might be delayed indefinitely.

Then the Old Man engaged Com. Voice meant that senior officials had now made station on the carrier, if they hadn't been there at the moment of their entry. JR sat beside Bucklin and Lyra and put in his earpiece to catch the drift of that message, relieved to hear the Old Man's voice addressing the Union captain in a casualness that didn't betoken hostility.

Reassuring. There was code passing, now, he'd bet, words that didn't quite fit the conversation, and there was at the same time he noted a relaxation of the Old Man's features, a little hint of humor.

Madison spared JR a direct glance, a nod, a handsign that meant, ordinarily, Ours, but meant, here, JR believed, Friendly approach.

A time-lagged response from *Amity* came then, that said:

"Greetings from the admiral and his respects for your efforts at Wyatt's, Captain Neihart. You may pass that along to your colleague on Norway. *I must say your appearance is a surprise. I trust it forecasts success and not bad news at Earth. Where are you bound?"*

"Esperance. We've resigned from the chase, sir. We've gone simply to routine cargo-carrying on this run, and we'll be back in the trade from now on if things go as we plan. The pirate hunt is growing thin, success in that regard. Now we have to teach these young people of ours the merchant trade, give them a new view of the universe. Greetings to the admiral and our hopes for future cooperation. We'll be quick to respond if we do spot trouble—sorry about that reposition— but we're hauling cargo now and we'll even be taking mail from time to time. Earth's as stable as I've seen it and we hope to have eliminated some of the flow of goods we were concerned about. Salutations from our colleague and expectations of good news from your arena."

Time-lagged conversations tended to run simultaneously and to change topics multiple times in the same paragraph, following the informational wavefront that had just come to the speaker.

"I wish I'd had the wherewithal to load full at Sol," the Old Man said. *"A load of whiskey, chocolate and wood on our last run, however. I'll send you over a bottle of Mallory's favorite Scotch. Her compliments. And mine."*

Audacious. And from Mallory? A Union carrier might not want to swallow a pill *Finity* dispensed, fearing bombs or biologics. But it was a handsome gift at the prices that prevailed past Pell.

A startling implication of connections and conduits of information. The *hell*, then, they hadn't known *some* Union contact might be here. Yet it had startled Helm, appearing as it did? Revise all estimates: they'd expected a smaller ship, but *some* ship.

The junior officer, kept in the dark and fed whatever data he could find by feel, could at least surmise the fact that they'd expected someone, and spooked for fear of the size of what they'd found. Helm might not have picked it up from buoy input. Helm *might* have read the interface itself, and been just that fast reacting to the unexpected.

"Delighted to receive fire," one of the most powerful warships in space answered that offer. *"Good voyage to you,* Finity."

A Union carrier was going to search empty space for a beeper-can and a bottle of Scotch whiskey?

Orders were passing. The ops crew down on A deck was finding a cannister, basically a smuggler's rig, certainly not something you could buy at a station outfitters—and an item which they did chance to have, by some cosmic and unsuspected luck.

As he listened, Lyra, as the available junior-most crew, found herself dispatched on an unusual mission to the captain's private bar.

"Is Scotch all of it?" he asked Madison as the attenuated conversation wound down to sign-offs.

"Smart lad," Madison said, and nothing more.

So there was something from Mallory that didn't involve Scotch, something that they'd been carrying in event of some such meeting somewhere along their course, and that a Union carrier was now going to pick up.

Curious dealings they had. No, they wouldn't poison-pill a Union carrier. Not on their fragile lives. There was something going on in this voyage that he'd lay odds wasn't in the line of trade: Mallory's business, almost certainly so, and Mallory was always a wild card in the affairs of Pell Station, apt to take any side that served her purpose. She was a former merchanter, former Fleet officer and bitterly opposed to Union. And had worked with Union against the Fleet. There was no side she hadn't been on, at one time or another, including Earth's.

If Mallory was out there keeping an eye on something, even *expecting* this carrier, or *a* carrier to be operating on this border, then there was something afoot. He *thought* Mallory was back near Sol.

But there were some things for which the senior captains

gave no answers because there was no need-to-know, and because crew on liberties were vulnerable and sometimes too damned talkative. Even Family crew.

The more people involved, the more chance of accidents. Clearly if Madison wanted to tell him what was in that packet besides a bottle of extravagantly expensive Scotch, Madison would have said, directly. And it was still the junior's job to figure things out.

Foolish question he'd asked Madison. Pursuing confirmations, he checked his output from Nav, and then got up to walk past Nav's more junior stations and confirm their exact arrival point at the dark mass. He should have asked . . .

"How'd the kid make it through?" Helm 1 asked, Hans Andrew, blindsiding him on the other matter of his reasonable concern as he passed the helmsman's chair. Fletcher. If there'd been a problem in that department, it had been a junior problem, and no one in senior crew had had time to ask him—until now. Odd and eclectic, the concerns that sometimes came out of Helm, who more than anyone on the ship was focused on the shadow of that carrier and on space at large.

"Fine. Jeremy reported in, they're fine." Jeremy had called him as his direct report-to station while Fletcher was in the shower, and reported himself and Fletcher as in good order. In the crisis, JR hadn't yet checked on the specific details. Fletcher was alive, God hope he was sane.

Things were still questionable on the bridge.

"Sorry to do that to him," Helm muttered: Hans Andrew, peppershot gray and eyes that, focused on his console, still frantically darted to small side motions with the marginal come-down off a pilot's hype. JR suspected that Hans was still tracking little if any of the intership communications—nor cared. When a pilot decided to move his ship in reaction to a developing situation, he did so on the situation, not on plan, not on policy, and sometimes not on the captain's orders: had to, at the speeds Hans' mind dealt with. The active pilot was in one sense the most *aware* individual on the ship; the gunner and Scan chief were right behind, with guns autoed live the nanosecond *Finity* dropped into system.

Meanwhile Helm would ask about the new kid on A deck, but not about the carrier, and Helm's eyes—one of them with a VR contact—would dart and track minutiae of the ship's exterior environment on his instruments, alive to that with a focus that concentratedly ignored any micro-dealings of ops. Unless you were the captain, you didn't talk to Helm unless addressed by Helm. You didn't bother him when he was hyped.

And he didn't answer Helm's comment except to dismiss a concern Helm had evidently carried into hyperspace with him, a stray thought from a month ago. It cleared an item from Helm's agenda. At the speed Helm's mind thought, mere human transactions, the negotiations of captains and admirals, must take an eternity.

He walked on to the empty chairs at Nav. Bucklin joined him after about ten minutes in which not much happened but routine and chatter back and forth with the carrier regarding a month-ago solar flare off EpEri, Viking's sun. "We've just dropped the beeper-can," Bucklin said in a low tone as he sat down in the vacant chair beside him. "What do you make of this crazy goings-on?"

"An interesting voyage," JR said.

"I thought we'd retired."

"The Old Man's *full* of surprises."

"You think Mallory's out there at the moment?"

He thought about it, all the deep dark fringes of the sprawling mass-point where whole Fleets could hide, a hundred ships a mere pinprick on the skin of the universe. Lose something out here? Easy as not knowing what tiny arc to sweep with your scan, in a universe noisy with stars and blinded by local mass.

But he shook his head.

"No. Personally, I don't. I think she's somewhere at the other end of Earth's space. While we lump along like an ore-hauler, on the merchant routes. *That* ship won't use them." Meaning the carrier, meaning the commercial short hops. There were further routes, that ships like that one, with its powerful engines, could use. And he envied that Union ship its capacities, its hair-trigger systems, with all his War-taught soul. State of the art, start to finish. Beautiful. A life remote from a future of slogging about trading stops and loading cargo.

"There is the deep route out of here," he said to Bucklin. "The other thing that carrier has, besides riders, is an admiral. They might be working *with* Mallory."

"She's telling that carrier where to look for trouble. That's what I'm thinking. I think we're a go-between. I don't think Union wants their ships near her any oftener than they can avoid it."

It was likely true, in principle. There were a lot of bitter grudges between Union and Alliance, even between specific Union and Alliance ships—resentments from the War years. Mallory very possibly stood off at one end of Alliance space, telling Union where a Fleet operation might pop out of hyperspace in their side, doing nothing that would bring her under Union guns . . . in these years when the pirate operations were dying down and when, consequently, Union might perceive their need for Mallory as less—as less, that was, if they were fools.

JR drew a long breath in speculation, thinking of the Hinder Stars, where their patrols failed to keep universal security. That strand of stars, the same set of stars that had enabled the first starships to reach out from Earth to Pell, was a bridge that no firepower man had yet invented could blow out of existence. Stellar mass was damn stubborn in being where it was at any given moment.

If you moved like a carrier, on huge engines, and took those long-jump routes only a light-laden ship could take, you could, however, bypass that bridge entirely, take the direct route out of Tripoint to Earth—or out of it. Something big could be coming.

A major battle, maybe.

And, God, *God!* for *Finity* to be read *out* of those universe-defining decisions? Leave the big choices to the big carriers, and devil take the merchanters, after all the dead they'd consigned to scattered suns?

A knot gathered in his throat as he saw nothing *Finity*

could do right now in what was important in the universe, not if Mazianni carriers arrived this second full in their sights.

Finity couldn't maneuver. A closed-hold hauler couldn't dump cargo on a minute's notice, the way a can-hauler could release the clamps and spill everything it had into the shipping lanes.

And if they *could* dump cargo, they couldn't afford to: the Old Man had seen to that first when he'd withdrawn their repair reserve at Sol for this cargo and all those bottles of Scotch whiskey and crates of coffee and other highly expensive items they'd taken on—and then lawfully declared at Pell, a little honesty at which he'd winced when he learned it. No other merchanters willingly paid all that tax, they *always* hedged the question on cargo-in-transit and just didn't declare it.

What was in the Old Man's mind? he'd asked himself then. Playing by outmoded rules? Acting on honor, as if that could carry them in a post-War universe that was every ship for itself? He ached to see the Old Man, who said they had to trade to survive, play by rules the universe didn't regard as important any longer, and said to himself they were going to find themselves out-competed, if that was the case.

He'd entertained hope it was only a short-term run, to sell off the luxury goods for moderate profit at Pell.

But at Pell, they'd withdrawn their other major reserve and bought high-mass staples as well as Pell luxuries, to carry on to Mariner, with the stated objective of Esperance, the back door to Cyteen itself. He'd have hoped they *were* a courier—except that some of *Finity*'s women had believed the senior captain and gone off their birth control. *That* was a scary decision. He couldn't imagine the mindset it took to vote with one's own body to risk Francesca's fate.

Their run to Mariner and beyond felt, in consequence, unhappily real. They'd left Pell as mercantile and committed as the captain had indicated, and he'd never *felt* so helpless, sitting fat and impotent in front of a potential enemy. As a future commanding officer of a significant Alliance merchant-warrior, he'd never in a million years contemplated he'd see his ship absolutely helpless to maneuver.

Finity signed off its transmission, signaling the carrier that it was about to make its routine course change for Mariner. If there was an objection to that procedure they were about to learn it. They'd fired a ridiculous missile. Now they had to walk past the predator and see if it jumped.

The takehold sounded. Crew that happened to be standing found places to belt in. He and Bucklin found theirs side by side, on the jump seats beside Helm.

In five minutes more they did a realspace burn that took them out of relational synch and bow-on orientation to the carrier, and started the process of finding inertial match relative to their next target.

Unlike Pell, Mariner had a different traveling vector than Tripoint. Their climb out would be a burn, then a little space of heavy but automated computer work, another few takeholds possible, and then a steep climb back to jump, shorter than the struggle with a fair-sized star that they routinely had at Pell. Tripoint mass was complex and tricky, and could give your sensors fits if you didn't zero it all the way out as you set yourself up as sharing a packet of spacetime with contrarily moving Mariner. That was Nav's job.

Madison switched their console output over to the Old Man's screens and put both him and Bucklin on watch, while Madison and the Old Man engaged in urgent discussion. The captain's data feed was a constantly switching priority of input, from whatever his number two thought significant, and whatever a crew chief in a crisis bulleted through on a direct hail.

Things stayed quiet. The screens switched in regular rotation, then one rapid flurry as nav data started to come in.

He didn't sit the chair often, even figuratively, as when the captains passed him the command screens. Now the third and fourth captains, Alan and Francie, had come to the bridge, moving between takeholds. He saw their presence in the numbers that showed on the Active list whenever a posted officer or tech arrived on duty. All four captains were now in conference on the encounter, and he, with Bucklin, sat keeping an eye on the whole situation with the real possibility of them, momentarily more current than the captains, actually ordering Helm to move.

Definitely a planned encounter, he concluded. Perhaps Mallory was positioning *Finity* via Mariner clear to Esperance, their turn-around point, and calling *Amity* to hold that intersection, hoping to trap something in the middle or drive quarry to an ambush. There was hope yet that *Finity* was engaged in trade purely as cover, and they *wouldn't* sit helpless in that encounter.

The steady tick of information past him tracked the beeper-can on a lazy course that would ultimately intersect the carrier. The same screen said the carrier had launched something considerably larger, at slow speed, probably a repair skimmer, a far cry from any rider-ship, in pursuit of the Scotch.

Nothing threatened them. There were no other arrivals. It might be days, even a week or two, before another ship came through Tripoint. The system buoy didn't, a matter agreed on by treaty, inform them of the number of ships that were recent, although ships left traces in the gas and dust of the point that their instruments could assess for strength and time of passage. It was a security matter, out here in the dangerous dark. All merchanters that came and went had just as soon do so without overmuch advertisement to other merchanters—and didn't want the buoy politicized—or information given to the military, especially considering the Alliance military included potentially rival merchanters. It was the age of distrust. And it was the age of self-interest succeeding the age of self-sacrifice, as ships and stations alike fought for survival in a changed economy.

Aside from the worry about pirate lurkers, and raids, smuggling went on hand over fist in such isolation, goods exchanged in direct trade, without station duty, illicit or restricted items, pharmaceuticals from Cyteen, rare woods from Earth's forests. Nothing that ships that habitually paused and lurked here were doing would bear close examination by station authorities.

That carrier out there was, in its way, another authority that would frown on such free enterprise: ships that arrived here under that grim witness would be intimidated, and wouldn't make the shadow-market exchanges common in such meetings.

But stop the furtive trade? It would move to some other point until the carrier was gone. And the carrier *would* go.

That carrier, rather than tracking what merchanters did, was going to be moving somewhere the light of suns didn't reach. And *Finity's End* continued on, slogging her way to jump.

A month and four days had passed. It was on the galley clock.

Seeing the date on that clock was when the fact came home to Fletcher that this wasn't Pell, and Fletcher stood and stared a moment, knowing that the thin stubble he'd shaved off his face in the shower wasn't a month's worth . . . but half that, as much as a spacer aged.

Both were facts he'd known intellectually before he reported for work. But that that disparate aging was happening to him as it had happened to Jeremy and all the rest—it took that innocuous wall clock to bring the shock home to him. Spacers weren't just *them*, any longer. It was *himself* who'd dropped out of the universe for a month, and wasn't a month older.

But Pell was. And Bianca was. They'd never make up that time difference.

The rains were mostly done, now. The floods would be subsiding.

The grain would have started to grow. Melody and Patch would have made their mating walk, made love, begun a new life if they were lucky.

But he wouldn't be there when they came back. *If* they came back. If Melody ever had her longed-for baby. He wouldn't know.

"Yeah," Vince said, juvenile nastiness, "it's a clock. Seen one before?"

"Shut up," he said.

It was crazy that this could happen. They'd changed *him*. He wasn't Fletcher Neihart, seamlessly fitted into Pell's time

schedules, any longer. He was Fletcher Neihart who'd begun
to age in time to Jeremy's odd, time-stretched life.

It was a queasy, helpless feeling as he went to work at the
cook-staff's orders, and he kept a silence for a while, a silence
the seniors present didn't challenge.

They weren't bad people, the cook-staff: Jeff and Jim T.
and Faye, all of whom had been solicitous of him when he first
came aboard. They'd worried about his preferences, been
careful to see he got enough to eat—a concern so basic and at
once so dear to Jeff's pride in his craft that he couldn't take
offense.

Now he was their scrub-help, along with Vince and Linda
and Jeremy, and he took heavy pans of frozen food from the
lockers, slid cold trays into flash ovens, opened cabinets of
tableware trays and food trays and handed them up to Linda,
who handed them to Vince and Vince to Jeremy.

At least in all the hurry and hustle he didn't have to think.
They had nearly two hundred meals to deliver to B deck mess, as
many to set up here, on A, in the mess hall adjacent to the galley.
There were, besides all that, carts of hot sandwiches to take up to
B, for crew on duty in various places including the bridge.

He didn't do that job. They didn't let him up into operations areas—they didn't say so, but Vince ran them down to
the lift and took them up. And there were special, individual
meals to serve as people came trailing in from cargo and
maintenance, wanting food on whatever schedule their own
work allowed. It was a busy place, always the chance of
someone coming in. It was hard work. But hungry people
were happy people once they had their hands full of food, at
least compared to the duty down in laundry.

Fletcher snatched a meal for himself, and the others did the
same, then had to interrupt their break to get more trays out,
because all of technical engineering had unloaded at once
from a meeting, and there were hungry people flooding in.

That group came in talking about a ship they'd met. A
Union ship.

Aren't we in Alliance territory? he wondered. Then he felt
queasy, remembering in the process that if he did have a view

of the space outside the ship, it wouldn't be anything like the Pell solar system schematic he'd learned in school. No planets. No sun. Great Sun was far behind him.

They were at what they called a dark mass, a near-star and a couple of massive objects that still wouldn't go to fusion if you lumped them all together.

The nature of the Tripoint mass was a fact to memorize, in school, a trade route on which Pell depended. Fact, too, that Tripoint had been a territory they'd fought over in the War. He'd grown up with the memorial plaques. *On this site . . .*

But here he was in the middle of it, and so was a Union ship, and the kid across from him, his not-kid roommate with the twelve-year-old body, and Vince and flat-chested Linda the same, they all chattered with awed speculations about what a Union carrier was doing, or why, as the rumor was, the captain had talked with it and fired a capsule at it.

"We might see action yet," Jeremy said happily. Fletcher didn't take it for cheering news. But, the techs said, nothing had developed. The Union ship had stayed put.

Another takehold warning came through. *Finity* had moved once, and then again, and now it fired the engines again. They spent an hour in the safety-nook of the galley playing vid games while the engineering people went to their quarters, off-shift and resting. There was no hint of trouble.

Then there was cooking to do for future meals, mixing and pouring into pans and layering of pasta and sauce while the end-shift meal cooked.

Pans from storage, thawed and heated, produced fruit pastry for dessert, with spice Fletcher had never tasted before. Jeff the cook said it came from Earth, and that gave him momentary pause. He was being corrupted, he thought. Fed luxuries. He thought how he couldn't get that flavor on Pell, or couldn't afford it; and he asked himself if he ever wanted to get to like it.

But he ate the dessert and a second helping, and told himself he might as well enjoy it in the meanwhile and be moral and righteous and resentful later. Shipboard had its advantages, and it was a moral decision to enjoy them while they were cheap and easy: the spice, the tastes, the novelty of things. He was mad, yes, he was resentful, and he was caught up in affairs he'd never wanted, but he didn't, he told himself, need to make any moral points, just legal ones, and only when he got back to Pell. Anything he chose to enjoy for the time being—the fruit dessert, the absolutely best shower he'd ever had access to, a better mattress than he'd ever slept on, all of that—he could equally well choose to forego when the time came, nothing of his pride or his integrity surrendered.

And the taste, meanwhile, was wonderful.

Galley duty, he decided, beat laundry all hollow. Laundry was work. On this detail there was food. As much as you wanted. It was, besides, a duty with the freedom of Downbelow about it—a work-on-your-own situation, with amicable people to deal with as supervisors. He especially liked Jeff, the chief mainday cook, a big gray-haired man who'd evidently enjoyed a lot of his own desserts, and who bulked large in the little galley, but who moved with such precision in the cramped space you were safer with him than with any three juniors. Jeff liked you if you liked his food, that seemed the simple rule; and Jeff didn't ask anything complicated of him—like assumptions of kinship.

Cleanup after the cooking wasn't an entirely fun job, but it wasn't bad, either. Word came to Jeff by intercom that the carrier had held its position and they were going to do a run up to V in an hour, so the galley had to be cleaned up, locked up, battened down, every door latched. Then, Jeff said, they could go to quarters early, at maindark, that hour when the lights dimmed to signify a twilight for mainday and dawn for alterday crew. Before, they'd have had two hours for rec and rest, but tonight the captains had declared no rec time. It was early to bed, stuck in their bunks while the ship did whatever it did to get where they were going.

He was moderately uneasy when the engines fired. He and Jeremy lay in their bunks while the next, relatively short burn happened, a long, pressured wait. After that, during what was announced as a fifty-minute inertial glide, Jeremy played vid games, lying in his bunk, so hyped on his fantasy war it was hard to ignore him, in his twitches and his nervous limb-moving and occasional sound effects.

Jeremy might act as if he were on drugs, but Fletcher knew as a practical fact of living with the boy that that wasn't the case. At times he was convinced that Jeremy sank into his games because he was *scared* of what the ship was doing, and he tried not to dwell on that thought. If Jeremy was scared, then he had no choice but assume a kid used to this knew what to be scared of. But at other times, as now, he wondered if that line blurred for Jeremy, as to what were games and what weren't.

Join Mallory's crew when he grew up, Jeremy had said. Trade wasn't for Jeremy. No such tame business. Jeremy wanted to fight Mazian's raiders.

History and life had shot along very fast in the seventeen station-side years Jeremy had been alive—and for all the twelve violent and brutal years Jeremy had actually been waking, Fletcher surmised, Jeremy had been right in the thick of it, in that situation the court on Pell had refused to let him enter.

Jeremy had a dead mother, too. This ship had death in abundance to drive Jeremy; as he guessed Vince and Linda were also driven—all of them stranger than kids of twelve and thirteen ever ought to be.

And not even a precocious twelve *or* a fecklessly ignorant seventeen. Jeremy, Vince, Linda all had the factual knowledge of those years. Jeremy indicated that, unlike the present situation, they usually had tape during the couple of weeks they did live during jump—briefing tapes making them aware of ship's business, educational tapes teaching them body-skills and facts, informational tapes informing them of history going on at various ports, all those very vivid things that tape was, and all the vivid teaching that tape could evidently do even more efficiently on the jump drugs than it did on the other brands of trank that went with tape-study stationside. Tape could *feel* like reality, and if he added up the tape Jeremy must have had in all those months tranked-out lying in his bunk, he figured he could tack on a virtual college education and a couple or three waking years of life on Jeremy's bodily twelve.

But while it was knowledge and technical understanding Jeremy had gained during those lost, lifeless weeks, life lived at the time-stretched rate of two weeks to every month of elapsed universal time while a ship was in jump, it still wasn't real-life experience. It wasn't any kind of emotional maturity, or physical development. They were mentally strange kids, all of the under-seventeens, sometimes striding over factual adult business so adeptly he could completely forget how big a gap his own natural growth set between them and him—and sometimes, again, as now, they acted just the age their bodies were. Humor consisted of elbow-knocking and practical jokes. Sex was to snigger at. War and death were vid games, even in kids who'd seen their own mothers and sibs die—that was the awful part. Jeremy had seen terrible, bloody things—and went right back to his games, obsessed with bloody images and grinning as he shot up imaginary enemies. Or real ones. Think what you're doing, he wanted to yell at Jeremy, but by what little he'd been able to understand, Jeremy's whole life was no *different* than those bloody games and Jeremy was fitting himself to survive. That was the most unnerving aspect of the in-bunk vid wars. *Linda* wanted to be an armscomper and target the ship's big guns. About Vince, he had no idea.

Himself, during the ship's maneuvering and slamming about, he shut his eyes and listened to the music Jeremy lent him. He asked himself did he want to risk his tape machine and *his* study tapes by using them during such goings-on, when if they came unsecured they could suffer damage.

But without his tapes, even without them, if he ignored Jeremy's occasional sound effects, he could see Old River behind his eyelids, and didn't need the artificial memory to overlay his own vision.

A month gone by already. He was two weeks older and remembered nothing of it; the planet was a month along, and after a few down, glum days, Bianca would have put him and his problems away and gotten on with her life. The everlasting clouds would have brightened to white. Melody and Patch would come back to the Base.

They'd know now beyond a doubt that he'd gone. He thought

about that while the ship, having finished its short bursts and jolts, announced another long burn of two hours duration.

He drew a deep breath as the buildup of pressure started, and let the music carry him. It was like being swept up by Old River, carried along in flood.

Jeremy fought remembered battles and longed for revenge. He rode a tide of music and memory, telling himself it *was* Old River, and Old River might have his treacheries, but he had his benefits, too.

Life. And springtime.

Puffer-balls and games on the hillside, and skeins of pollen on the flood, pollen grains or skeins of stars. They weren't going for jump yet. They were just going to run clear of the mass-point. He was learning, from Jeremy, how the ship moved.

It was safer to think of home . . . of quitting time in the fields, and the soft gray silk of clouds fading and fading, until that moment white domes all but glowed with strangeness and the night-lights around the Base walks, coming on with dusk, were very small and weak guides against the coming dark.

Back to the galley *before* maindawn: the ship had built up a high velocity toward Mariner, and now they were scheduled for two days of quiet, uninterrupted transit before their jump toward that port.

The cooks, so they declared, never slept late, and neither did the juniors helping out in the galley. They made a break-fast for themselves of synth eggs and fruit after they'd delivered breakfast in huge trays to the service counters on A and B deck. The work had a feeling of routine by now, a comfort-able sense of having done things before that, once he was moving and doing, also gave him an awareness of what the ship was doing, rushing toward their point of departure with a speed they'd gained during last watch.

A smooth, ordinary process, except that jolt when they'd come into Tripoint. And he tried to be calm about the coming jump. How could he be anxious for their physical safety, Fletcher asked himself, when a ship that had survived the War with people shooting at them, did something it and every other merchanter ship did almost every two months of every year?

He decided he could relax a little. The gossip among the cook-staff still said the Union carrier that had startled them on entry was watching their backs like a station cop on dockside, and it still didn't seem to be bad news: there was no move to hinder them, and if there'd been any Mazianni about, they'd have been scared off by the Union presence, so they could dismiss that fear, too.

He was, he realized, already falling into a sense of expectations, after all expectations in his life had been ripped away from him. Vince and Linda were, hour by hour, tolerable nuisances. Jeremy was his reliable guide and general cue on the things he had to learn, besides being a cheerful, decent sort of kid when he wasn't blowing up imaginary pirates. Jeff the cook didn't care if he nabbed an extra roll, or, for that matter, if anybody did. It was like deciding to enjoy the fruit desserts. Life in general, he decided, was just fairly well tolerable if he flung himself into his work and didn't think too hard or long about where he was.

He even found himself caring about this job, enough to anticipate what Jeff wanted and to try to win Jeff's good humor. No matter how he'd previously, back at Pell, resolved to stay sullen and just to go through the motions in his duties for his newest family, he found there was no sense sabotaging an effort that fed them fruit and spice desserts. Jeff Neihart appreciated with a pleasant grin the fact that he stacked things straight and double-checked the latches the same as people who were born here. It was worth a little effort he hadn't planned to give, and he ended up doing things the careful way he could do something when he cared.

Disorientation still struck occasionally, but those occasions were diminishing. Yes, he was in space, which he'd dreaded, but he wasn't *in* space: it was just a comfortable, spice-smelling kitchen full of busy people.

When, late in the shift, he took a break, he sat down to a cup of real coffee at a mess hall table. He understood it was *real* coffee, for the first time in his life, and he drank it, rolling the taste around on his tongue and telling himself . . . well . . . it was richer than synth coffee. Different. Another thing he daren't get too used to.

A ship, he was discovering, skimmed some real fancy items for its own use, and didn't count the cost quite the way station shops would. On this ship, while they had it, Jeff said, they had it and they should enjoy it.

There were points to this ship business that, really, truly, weren't half bad. A year was a long time to leave home but not an insurmountable time. There were worse things to have happened. A year to catch his balance, pass his eighteenth year, gain his majority . . .

Jeremy came up and leaned on the table. "Madelaine wants you."

"Who's that?" he asked across the coffee cup.

"Legal."

His stomach dropped, no matter that there wasn't anything Legal Affairs could possibly do to him now. He swallowed a hot mouthful of coffee and burned his throat so he winced.

"Why?"

"I don't know. Probably papers to clear up. She's up on B deck. Want me to walk you there?"

He didn't. It was adult crew and he didn't want any witnesses to his troubles, particularly among the juniors. Particularly his roommate. All the old alarms were going off in his gut. "What's the number up there?"

"I think it's B8. Should be. If it isn't, it's not further than B10."

"I can find it," he said. He drank the rest of the coffee, but with a burned mouth it didn't taste as good, and the pain of his throat lingered almost to the point of tears, spoiling what had been a good experience. He got up and went down the corridor to the lift he knew went to B deck.

It was a fast lift. Just straight up, no sideways about it, and up to a level where the Rules said he shouldn't be except as ordered. It was a carpeted blue corridor: downstairs was tiled. It was ivory and blue and mauve wall panels.

Really the executive level, he said to himself. This part of the ship looked as rich as *Finity* was. So *this* was what you lived like when you got to be senior executive crew . . . and lawyers were certainly part of the essentials. *Finity* didn't even need to hire theirs. It was one more damn cousin, and since lawyers had been part and parcel of his life up till now, he figured it was time to get to know this one.

This one—who'd stalked him for seventeen years and who he suddenly figured was to blame, seeing how long spacers lived, for every misery in his life.

Madelaine? Such an innocent name. Now he knew who he hated.

It was B9. He found *Legal Affairs* on a plaque outside, and walked into an office occupied by a young man in casuals one might see in a station office, not the workaday jump suit they wore down where the less profitable work of the ship got done.

"You're not Madelaine," he observed sourly.

"Fletcher." The young man stood up, offered a hand, and he took it. "Glad to meet you. I'm Blue. That's Henry B. But Blue serves, don't ask why. Madelaine's expecting you."

"Thanks," he said, and the young man named Blue showed him into the executive office, facing a desk the like of which he'd never seen. Solid wood. Fancy electronics. A gray dragon of a woman with short-cropped hair and ice-blue eyes.

"Hello," she said, and stood up, came around the desk, and offered a cool, limp hand, a kind of grip he detested.

She looked maybe sixty, old enough that he knew beyond a doubt she was one of the lawyers behind his problems and that apparent sixty probably represented a hundred. She was cheerful. He wasn't.

"So what's this about?" he asked. "Somebody forget to sign something?" He feigned delight. "You've changed your minds and you're sending me home?"

Unflapped, she picked up a blue passport from off her desk and handed it to him. "This is yours. Keep it and don't mislay it. I can reissue but I get surly about it."

"Thanks." He tucked it in his pocket and was ready to leave.

"Sit down. —So how *are* you getting along?"

She knew he wasn't happy here and didn't give a damn.

Good, he thought, and sat. That judgment helped pull his temper back to level and gave him command of his nerves. It was another lawyer. The long-term enemy, the enemy he'd never met, but always knew directed his life. She was cool as ice.

He could be uncommunicative, too. His lawyers had taught him: don't fidget, look at the judge, don't get angry. And he wasn't. Not by half. "Am I having a good time?" he countered her as she sat down and faced him across her desk, her computer full of business that had to be more important to her than his welfare. "No. Will I have a good time? No. I'm not happy about this and I never will be. But here we are until we're back again."

"I know it's a hard adjustment."

"And you *had* to interfere in my life." He hadn't found anybody aboard he could specifically blame. He'd have expected something official from the senior captain, at least a face-to-face meeting, and hadn't gotten it—as if they'd snatched him up, and now that they'd demonstrated they could, they had no further interest in him. He resented that on some lower level of his mind. He wouldn't have unloaded the baggage in her office, he hadn't intended to, but, damn it, she asked. She wanted him to sit down and unburden his soul to her, in lieu of the real authority on this ship—when she was the person, the one person directly responsible for ten and more years of lawsuits and grief in his life, not to mention present circumstances. He drew a deep breath and fired all he had. "My mother was a no-good drughead who ducked out on me, *you* wouldn't leave me in peace, and here I am, just happy as you can imagine about it."

"Your mother had no choice in being where she was. She did have a choice in refusing to give up your *Finity* citizenship."

"She died! And excuse me, but what in *hell* did you think you were doing, ripping up every situation I ever worked out for myself?"

There was a fairly long silence. The face that stared at him was less friendly than the hisa watchers and just as still.

"I'm sorry you wanted the station, but you weren't born to the station, Fletcher, and that's a fact that neither of us controlled. This universe doesn't let you just float free, you know. There's a question of citizenship, your birthright to be in a particular place, and birth doesn't make you a Pell citizen. You were always ours, financially, legally, nationally. Francesca wouldn't let you be theirs. She wanted you here. They just wouldn't let you leave."

"The damn courts, you mean." In the low opinion he held of Pell courts they could possibly find one small point of agreement. And she hadn't flared back at him, had, lawyeresque, held her equilibrium. He even began to think she might not be so bad, the way nobody on the whole ship had really turned out to be an enemy. In giving him Jeremy, they'd left him nothing to fight. Nothing to object to. In sending him here, to this woman, they gave him, again, nobody he could fight with the anger he had built up. It was robbery, of a kind he only now identified, that he really didn't want to hurt this woman.

"The damned courts," she said quietly, "yes, exactly so."

"Did you pay fourteen million?"

"You heard about that."

"Damn—excuse me—right I heard."

"They sued us to buy you a station-share and kept the case in limbo; meanwhile, their own Children's Court wouldn't release you to us so long as the War continued, or so long as we were working with *Norway*. And we don't give up our own, young sir. Learn that first off. For good or for ill, this ship's deck is sovereign territory and we don't give up our own and pay a fourteen million credit charge on top of the outrage. If you want to know who put obstacles in your path, yes, the Pell courts, who saw no reason to credit this ship for the very fact there *is* a Pell judiciary and not an outpost of Union justice in its place. Your mother fought tooth and nail to maintain custody of you. We would have taken you at any pass through this system. Pell courts thought otherwise, but they gave you no rights within Pell's law."

It had been a good day going, before Madelaine the lawyer
called him in to tell him what great favors they'd done him.
Nothing to fight? She'd given him something. Fourteen million credits and his *life* at issue. Civilization was cancelled for
the day. And he turned honest. "I don't want to be here.
Doesn't that count? "

"But the fact is, you had no right to be at Pell, either."

"I had every right!"

"Not the important right. Not the legal right. And they
wouldn't give it to you unless we paid for it because your
rights lie on this ship where, from your mother, you have citizenship and financial rights."

"Well, that's not my fault. I don't owe this ship. And I
damned sure don't owe my mother. She never did anything but
mess up my life."

"She had little enough of her own. Your mother was my
daughter's child. Your grandmother died at Olympus.
Unfortunately for both of us, it seems, I'm your great-
grandmother. Your closest living relative."

He'd fired off his mouth without knowing what he was
firing at. He'd insulted his mother as he was in the habit of
doing with strangers rather than having others do the sneering
and the blaming and him do the defending. Lifelong habit, and
he'd just done it to the wrong person. He'd wondered what it
would be like to have a grandmother, or a godmother, back
when he was reading nursery rhymes. Stationers had them. If
he had one he wouldn't ever be in foster homes. Would he?

His godmother, however, wasn't a soft, plump woman with
a wand and a pumpkinful of mice. It was a spacefaring lawyer
with eyes that bored right through you. And not his *god*-
mother, either. Not even his grandmother. His grandmother's
mother, two generations back.

"Francesca died when you were five," Madelaine said.
"That's too young really to have known her. Or to have formed
a good judgment."

He was prepared to back up a couple of squares and admit
he'd been too quick. But her judgment of him drew a shake of
his head. He couldn't help it. "No. I was there. *I remember*."

He remembered police, and his mother lying on the bed, not moving. He remembered realizing something was wrong with her. Her hand had been cold, terribly cold when he'd touched it. He'd known that wasn't right. And he'd called the emegency squad. He remembered textures. Sensations. Everything, every tiniest detail, was branded in his consciousness.

"She was a good woman," Madelaine said. "Good at what she did. She'd taken jump drugs all her life with no trouble. The simple fact was, she was pregnant, too late to abort, too early to deliver except to a birthlab, which she chose not to do; we knew what we were facing—it's declassified now, so we can talk about it. But it wasn't then, and going to a birthlab at her stage of pregnancy—we didn't have the time for her to do that and recover. We just couldn't wait for her, if she did it without us she'd still be stranded ashore, and she was in a hell of a mess. There was nothing for anyone but bad choices. We said we'd be back in a year. That didn't happen. We missed our appointment with her, and she crashed. Just crashed, physiologically, psychologically. Depression sometimes follows a birth. She started self-medicating. The hyprazine, particularly the hyprazine, if you've taken it in jump, it gives you an illusion of *being* in space, and that's what you take when you're pregnant. That illusion was what she was after, Fletcher. Just so you know."

"You and JR have been talking. Right?"

Madelaine shook her head. "No. We haven't. What about?"

"The truth—" He could hardly breathe. He kept his voice calm. "She kept sending me to welfare—and getting me back—until she finally went out on a trip and never came down. And left *me* tangled in the damn court system. Then *they* couldn't put me anywhere permanent and let anybody get attached to me because *you* kept suing the station. Let me tell you. I made it through six foster-families, five of them before I was fifteen. I made it through school. I made it through the honors program and into graduate. I licensed to work on Downbelow in Planetary Science, which is what I want to do, and where you called me from, and where I left everything I care about. And you come along and jerk me up and out of that to do your damn laundry and scrub mess hall tables, because you could *do* that and I'm your property! Well, screw all of you! I'm trying to keep my head straight because I *know* we can't turn this ship around, I haven't got money to buy passage on any other ship, and I have to live out this year, but that's *all*! That's *all*. Because when we get back to Pell I'm going to sue you to get off this ship."

"It still won't give you Pell citizenship."

It failed to knock the wind out of him, as she clearly expected. He didn't want to tell her about Quen's promise to him. She'd be the lawyer fighting him. He'd already been stupid and said too much. His lawyers would certainly have told him so.

"I had a girl back there," he said.

"Oh, is *that* it?"

"No! That's *not* it. It's not all it is." Naturally they wanted to wrap all his problems up in that. But what he felt wouldn't be understandable to people who didn't know what there was on a planet. He'd had a grandmother. She'd died. A lot of people on this ship had died . . . along with Jeremy's close relatives. And Madelaine—his grandmother . . . his *great*-grandmother—just stared at him, maybe amused, maybe hurt by the truth he'd told, maybe not giving a damn for anything but the ship's fourteen million. Since his mother died he'd never had to deal with anybody who owned the same set of emotional entanglements to him that his mother had had, and then he'd been five. Slowly the emotional shock of meeting this woman reached through to him, the feeling of an emotional pain somewhere he wasn't sure of, bone-deep and about to become acute, and tangled somewhere in his mother's death.

"I was in Planetary Studies," he said. "That doesn't mean anything here. But it mattered to me. It mattered everything to me."

"The stationmaster told us what you'd done. Both your extraordinary work to get into the program, and the ruinous thing you did at the end." Madelaine's face was sober. Her hands were steepled loosely before her, a tangle of fingers, an attitude that somehow echoed a habit of someone else—his mother—he wasn't sure. "Fact is, in your tender love of the planet, you broke laws, you fractured rules designed to protect it and the downers from the well-meaning *and* the callous users. I'm interested in why you'd do such a thing."

The lawyer. Wanting to know about laws. And asking into what wasn't her business, except that the question also involved his attitude toward rules-following, his behavior in a ship full of critical procedures. He was tempted to lie, to make things far worse than they were.

But he didn't want to find himself restricted from the freedom he did have, either.

"Did you *have* a reason for running off from the Base?" she pursued, and he tried to organize his thoughts to give her the answer she'd both believe and take for reassurance.

"Being pushed further than you can push me now," he said. "Further than anyone can ever push me again. That's all. You can only lose so much."

"Were you thinking of suicide?"

"Maybe. Maybe not."

"Did you care about the downers? The stationmaster said you'd been consorting rather closely with two of them."

Bianca talked. The information hit him like a hammer blow.

And then, on a next and shaky breath, *Of course Bianca talked. I was gone. She had a right to talk.* It was nothing but expected—only the ruin of something else important. Another support of his life kicked out from under him.

She was scared. She was involved and I involved her. A Family girl with a Family on her back. Sure, she had to get straight with them. I had to be the one at fault. I was gone, she had to be practical about it.

He'd hoped for a little more fortitude from her. Just a little heroism. But she'd saved her own hide. Everyone did, when the chips came down.

"Despite your heritage, —you trained to work with the downers," Madelaine asked sharply. "Why?"

"Because—" He almost said, Because I *love* them, but he

wasn't going to let *that* information loose. Because I never thought you'd get me away from Pell. Never give a psych or a lawyer a handle to hold to. Not a real one. "Because they're different. *Because I don't like human beings much.* How's that?"

"Sad if true."

"Downers don't *kidnap* people."

"And, as I know from brief experience, they don't understand human relationships. It's very much the contrary of what you're supposed to be doing with them. But you were intent on your own reasons."

"Reasons that they invited me to be with them. For years. I *know* the downers. I know the two I dealt with."

"You know them better than the scientists and the researchers. You know them well enough to defy the rules and endanger a half a hundred rescuers."

"It was their choice to be out there chasing me."

"Was it?" A shake of the lawyer's head. "Fletcher, I think you're better than that. Difficult. So was my granddaughter. It's why you were born. She was in love, in a year when any child was a hostage to fate. She knew that. She ran a risk."

In *love.*

It's why you were born.

He had a merchanter for a mother and that meant he *had* no father. It was one of the facts of his life: he *had* no father. How *dare* she throw that out for bait? His mother *knew* who the father was and it wasn't some chance encounter in a sleepover?

He wouldn't take that bait. Not if his life depended on it.

He stood up. "I've got work to do."

Madelaine looked at him as if he were something on her agenda. No longer cool, no longer remote. "God, you're like Francesca."

That, too, was a gut blow. He didn't know how hard until he'd walked out, through the office, past the cousin named Blue, and out into the fancy carpeted corridor.

Like Francesca. She looked at him with age-crinkled eyes and dismissed his best shot with *God, you're like Francesca. . . .*

He wasn't like his mother. He wasn't anybody's copy. His mother hadn't been like him.

She was in love. . . .

He'd not known his mother when she was seventeen. She might have sat in that same chair. She might have used this same lift. Walked these same corridors . . .

Been in love . . .

He had a father somewhere. His great-grandmother *knew* who it was. She had all the names, and held them as bait to draw him out, to get pieces of him in her reach, more deft than any psych.

He was used to the station as his mother's venue. *That* was where she'd lived, and *Finity's End* was where she'd come *from.*

But this corridor, these places, all this was a place she'd walked in, too, like some hidden room of her life where she'd been as young as *he* was now and where people remembered *her* in the same awkward, mistake-making years he was trying his best to grow out of.

It shook him.

It totally revised his concept of where he was and what he'd come from and who that seventeen-year-old twelve-year-old he roomed with really might have been to him. Here he was wandering around blind, in *her* young years, meeting people who'd wanted him because they'd lost *her* and to whom the whole reality of the station was a locked room *they* couldn't get into, either. And Jeremy was the bridge. Jeremy was the might-have-been, the one he'd always have been with. His mother would be dead, maybe, with Jeremy's mother, with half the people on the ship . . . and things would be a lot the same, but different, vastly different, too.

He rode the lift back to A deck and walked back where he'd come from. His nerves weren't up to a challenge of things-as-they-were or a confrontation with Madelaine Neihart. He just wanted to go back to the mess hall and to Jeremy, that was all; even to go back to Vince and Linda. He couldn't feel the ship moving, but they were shooting unthinkably fast toward the nadir of the Tripoint mass-point, where another event he didn't understand would happen and they'd more than accelerate: they'd plunge a second time out of the known universe into a state his mother had chosen to live in, that she'd ultimately chosen to die in.

He'd failed that unit in his physics class—how the universe didn't like the state they'd be in, and spat them out reliably somewhere else. He agreed with the universe: he didn't like the state they'd be in and he didn't want to imagine it. He didn't know whether he *could* understand it, but when he'd had to study it, he'd pleaded with his physics instructor he didn't want to take that tape again, please God, he didn't want to . . . and the psychs had gotten into it. Finally the school had exempted him and let him study it and just barely pass it realtime, with pencil and paper, because the psychs said there were special psychological reasons that the instructor and the school weren't equipped to deal with. They'd offered to *help* him deal with it. And he'd said no. And somehow it hadn't come up again.

No more exemption, now. No more psychs to step in and say let Fletcher alone: he can't deal with it. The court had forgotten all about that fear when it gave him up and stripped him of his Pell ID. His bitter guess was that it had stopped mattering to most people the second somebody mentioned fourteen million credits. Quen had reached out and tapped some judge on the shoulder and said, Let them have him this time.

And ironically, completely unexpectedly, the only person in the whole affair who cared—personally, cared, as it turned out—might have been the lawyer, Madelaine. The crew at large, meanwhile, didn't know what he'd grown into, but thought the courts were holding from them some poor stupid kid it was their *right* to have, a kid whose spacer heritage would leap to the fore and instantly make him love them.

The ship unfortunately didn't turn around to undo its mistakes. It only went forward and it didn't stop for anything, that was what that long-ago physics tape had told him . . . the universe abhorred their situation half in hyperspace and half here and spat their bubble along the interface until a mass-point snatched them into its gravity and jerked their bubble remorselessly flat. When he thought about it, walking a cor-

ridor on a ship courting that event, the space that connected
him to Pell felt stretched thinner and thinner, as if his whole
universe could just tear and vanish.

His mother had died like that, hadn't she? Her mind had
just—stretched thin until one day there wasn't enough left to
get her home again.

Madelaine had all the wit he hoped his mother had had,
needle-sharp and quick as he imagined now his mother might
have been if she hadn't been out on drugs and if he hadn't been
a feckless five-year-old. He couldn't ever know her, clear-
eyed—couldn't ever sit in a room with her as he'd just sat with
Madelaine, to have clear memories, or to sort out her pluses
and minuses. He had memories of his mother being happy, and
smiling, but he'd told himself in the maturer, more brutal judgment of his teenage years that those had all been days when
she'd been high as the drugs could make her and still function—when the body was on Pell Station, but *she* wasn't.

Love? She'd exuded just enough to rip the guts out of a kid.
She loved somebody whose name Madelaine dangled before
him? Had his kid?

Then why in hell had she lost herself in drug-hazed space?
Post-birth depression? He wished it were that simple.

He went back to the mess hall and, finding there was
nothing doing at the moment, had a soft drink. They were free.
It was one benefit of a situation that felt, again, like the trap it
was.

"So what'd Legal want?" Jeremy wanted to know.

"Just passport stuff," he said. He didn't talk about it. He
didn't want Jeremy for a confidant on this point. He didn't at
all want Vince and Linda, who were lurking for gossip. If
Vince had opened his mouth right then, he'd have hit him.

He fought for calm. He tried to settle down and just go
numb about the situation, telling himself that a year, like all
other periods of time, would pass. He'd learned to wait in doc-
tors' offices, in psychiatrists' offices, in court. "Don't fidget,"
the adult of the month would say, and he'd stay still. When he
stayed still nobody noticed him. A year was long, but his fight
to get to Downbelow had been longer. He did know how to

win by waiting. Don't feel anything. Don't say much. Don't engage anybody the way he'd engaged the lawyer. He'd made the one mistake up in Madelaine's office . . . made the kind of mistake that gave manipulative people and lawyers levers to use.

No. She'd already known him, before he ever walked in that door. He was her *great-grandson,* and she'd lost her daughter and her granddaughter and now she wanted a try at him, seeing his mother in him. That was something he'd never faced. She was his honest-to-God real great-grandmother, and his mother had *lived* on this ship.

She'd just *died* on Pell.

The shift went to bed, an exhausted mainnight in which visions of rain-veiled river danced in Fletcher's eyes; and playing cards cascaded like raindrops, inextricably woven images, in which somehow he owed days, not hours, and in which he chased Jeremy through tunnels first of earth and then of garishly lit steel and pipe, the latter of which looked miraculously like the tunnels on Pell.

Next morning it was back to the galley before maindawn, help Jeff set out the breakfast trays and get the carts up to B deck, but they were still cooking huge casseroles for next jump . . . things that could warm up in a hurry, a lot of red pepper involved. Taste was pretty dim after jump, so Jeff said, and by Fletcher's estimation it was true; spicy things perked up the appetite. While they were doing that, they'd had no further alarms, no changes in velocity. Jeff said the ship's long, even run under inertia would give them the chance to get some baking done. Cakes in the oven during a high-V run were doomed, so Jeff said.

So whenever they hit an onboard stretch where they could spread out and cook, they cooked for all they were worth: fancy pastries, casseroles, pies, trays of pasta and individual packets for those hours people came in scattered. There were onions and fish from Pell, there was keis and synth ham, there was cabbage and couscous and what they called animal protein, which was a kitchen secret nobody should have to look at before it cooked. It came in pieces and mostly the cook-staff ground it. There was rice from Earth and yellow grain from Pell; there were sauces, there were gravies, there were fruit jellies that came from Downbelow and wine solids and spices and yeasts that came from Earth. There were keis sandwiches, fish sandwiches, and pro-paste sandwiches which Fletcher swore he'd never eat again in his life; there were pickles and syrups and stuffed pasta, string pasta, puff breads and flat-breads and meal and pro-paste pepper rolls with hot sauce, and there were sausage rollups, which were their lunch, and keis and ham rollups which were supper. The galley had rung with the battering of pans and trays, swum in pots of sauce that went steaming into forms of given sizes and had to be trundled on carts into the galley lift, where in coats you put the stuff in deep-freeze on the very outer level of the rim in what they called the skin. Out there among the structural elements of the passenger ring, cold was the natural, cheap environment, requiring only a rack for storage, no mechanism but a light; and you felt that cold burning right through your boot-soles when you walked the grids. Fletcher made one trip down with Jeff just to see what it was like, his closest approach to the uncompromising night outside the hull; he was glad to get back up into warmth and light of the ring.

All this day they worked on sandwiches, and of course, tastes of the current batch. Nobody on regular cook-staff ever seemed to eat a meal: they sampled; and the last job they put together, just before supper, was a giant pyramid of tasty little sandwiches and another of sweets. Which to Fletcher's disap-pointment didn't turn up on *their* menu. It went to B deck.

"We'll get some," Jeremy said as he watched the cart go. "Topside in the senior mess. There's a get-together coming. Everybody's there."

"So?" he said. He wasn't at all enthusiastic about meetings. He remembered board-call, and everybody together for that. It had been particularly uncomfortable. And he'd worked hard today. He thought he had a right to those desserts. "I'd rather read or something. Thanks."

"You're really supposed to go. It's all of second and third shift, and a lot of first will come. That's why they've been handing us fast food today. Eat light."

"Is it a meeting, or what is it?"

"Not a *meeting*," Jeremy said as if he were a little slow. "Food. The fancy food. It's a *party*. You know. People. Music. Party."

"Why?"

"'Cause that Union bunch is just sitting back there not bothering us, 'cause we're in a big boring jump-point and we don't have anything much to do. Why *not*? When you're downtimed and there's no pirates going to bother you, you throw a party. Come on, Fletcher, you'll enjoy it. Be loose. Jump before maindawn, but tonight we shake things up, man. Be loose, be happy, it's got to be somebody's birthday! That's what we say, it's somebody's birthday somewhere! Celebrate for George."

"Who's George?" There was such a thing as ship-speak: the in-jokes sometimes flew past him.

"King George V."

He'd thought, with his fascination with old Earth history, there was no way a twelve-year-old from *Finity* was going to know King George of England. Or England, for that matter, in spite of Jeremy's tape study. He was amazed. And enticed. "Why George?"

"Well, because he's old and he's dead, and nobody throws him parties anymore, so we do on *Finity*. When it's nobody else's birthday, it's for old King George!"

He'd walked into that one. "Why not?" he said. "Seems logical."

He still didn't entirely want to go, but he considered the food they'd been working on all day; and he knew himself, that once he was committed to being alone, knowing full well there was a party going on elsewhere, he'd feel lonelier. *I'd rather stay in my room and hate all of you* might be the real answer, but it wasn't, in Jeremy's clear opinion, going to be the accepted answer.

Besides, Jeremy had, against all odds, made it sound like fun.

So they showered and put on clean, unfloured, unpeppered clothes without grease spots, and went up to B deck. Fletcher's most dire apprehension in the affair was that he might have to suffer through some formal introduction of himself, standing up in front of people he didn't want to be polite to. "They're not going to introduce me again, are they?" he'd asked Jeremy. "I don't want to be introduced."

"They won't if you don't like," Jeremy said. "I'll tell them and they won't."

He still, riding up the lift to B deck, feared he couldn't escape another round of j-names: *John, James, Jerry and Jim.* He was resigned to that idea, if not the idea of another introduction, or any sentimental *This is Francesca's baby* on anybody's part. As long as it stays George's party, he'd told Jeremy, when he'd agreed. No surprises.

And when they walked up around the ring to the senior mess, he could see the food laid out, he could see tables spread with linen; and he could see people, the Family, all walking around or talking at random: no special recognition looked to be in the offing, no ceremony, no conspicuous embarrassment and no formality, either. The B deck rec hall turned out to be connected to the B deck mess hall, a wall-to-wall segment of the whole ring, carpeted, the area that was rec furnished with vid-game sets, not in use at the moment; a bar, which was in use; and maybe fifty tables with linen tablecloths like some high-class restaurant. The whole arrangement filled two segments of B deck's ring, with only a little half-bulkhead and a drawn-back section door to separate rec from the mess. There were maybe a hundred, two hundred people—all, God save him, relatives—milling around in casual familiarity, with more arrivals coming in from either end of the area.

There was a pool table, a game going there, in the rec section. That had drawn a row of kibitzers. A couple of women played quiet, not-bad guitar in the background, up at the end of the mess hall, and the sweets and snacks from the mess hall were going fast. The bar opened up, and various mixed drinks and wine glasses ready to be picked up were going off the counter as fast as the kids serving could set them out, fifty, a hundred of them.

Held off on cheese sandwiches all day. Fletcher raided the

dessert stack instead and filled his mouth with sweet cream pastry.

"Fletcher."

He knew that voice. He turned and frowned at Madelaine. She had a glass of wine in hand and was clearly not official at the moment.

"Glad you came, Fletcher," Madelaine said.

"Thanks," he said, and knuckled a suspected smear of cream off his lip. He wouldn't have come at all if he'd known he'd run into her first off.

"Enjoy things," she said. And to his relief and gratitude, she didn't engage him in intrusive, personal conversation, just smiled and walked past him, wine glass in hand, leaving him free to wander around with Jeremy.

Jeremy, who was bent on telling him who was who.

"No good with the names," he said after six or seven. "There's too many J's in the lot. I'm not going to remember. Unless you can point out King George. Who *is* a G, isn't he?"

Jeremy thought that was funny. "Everybody *is* J's," he said, as if he'd never added it up for himself. "Most, anyway. 'Cept you're Fletcher. Probably the first Fletcher in fifty years."

"Why? Why's Fletcher the exception?"

"He was shot dead, a long time ago," Jeremy said. "He was the one getting the hatch shut when the Company men were trying to board, and he did it and died on the deck inside. Or there wouldn't *be* any of us. No Alliance. No Union."

He knew about the incident. He'd learned it in school, but he didn't know it was a Fletcher Neihart who'd been the one to get the door shut when they tried to trap *Finity* and arrest Captain James Robert. He knew about *Finity's End* saying the Earth Company authorities weren't going to board, and the captain and crew had sealed the ship and left the station *and* the authorities behind them, refusing them authority over the ship and refusing station law on a merchanter's deck. It was where the first merchanter's strike had started, when merchanters from one end of space to the other had made it clear that trade goods didn't and wouldn't move without merchant ships.

In a long chain of events, it was the incident that had started the whole Company War.

History. Near-modern history, which he detested. He'd passed the obligatory quiz on the details to get into the program. The Company War. Treaty of Pell, 2353, and that had left civilization where it was when he'd been born, with Union on one side and Alliance on the other and Earth not real happy with either of them. And him stranded and his mother dead. That kind of history.

So, Jeremy said, somebody he was named after had gotten a critical hatch shut in the original fracas between Company ships and Family ships, without which either the ship wouldn't have gotten away or the cops who shot this long-dead Fletcher would have died in the decompression that would have resulted if he hadn't shut that hatch.

Pell knew about that kind of event. And he'd known about the start of the Company War.

So the guy's name had been Fletcher. He didn't know why he should be proud of some spacer who was a hundred years dead—but, well, dammit, he'd lived all his seventeen years around the snobbery of the Velasquezes and the Willetts, the Dees and the Konstantins, who'd been important because of *their* names, and important mostly because of what dead people in *their* families had done, while he'd never before had a sense of connection to anything but an addict mother and a lawsuit.

Somebody died closing an airlock and did it with pieces of him shot away, knowing otherwise there'd be vacuum killing more than the people shooting at him—that was a level-headed brave guy, in his way of thinking. While the Willetts—they'd donated a warehouse full of stuff to the war effort. Big deal. No one had been shooting at them.

And Fletcher Neihart *meant* that man, on this ship. Fletcher wasn't just a name. It was a revision of who he was—for a moment.

He never had meant much. And that, he'd told himself when he'd been at a low point of his teenaged years, scared spitless of the program placement tests, that *never meant much* was the source of his strength: not giving much of a damn. Like a gyro—kick it off balance a second and it swung right back. That realization had kept him sane. Kept him aware of his own value, which was only to himself.

Maybe that was why Madelaine's being here had upset him—why *Madelaine* had upset him and why even yet he was feeling shaky. He'd instinctively seen a danger when Madelaine had dangled the lure of his mother's motives and his father's name in front of him yesterday.

He'd been in danger a second ago when he'd thought about famous relatives.

He was in danger when he began to slip toward thinking . . . being Fletcher Neihart wasn't that bad a thing.

Yes, and Jeremy wasn't a bad kid, and they could get along, and maybe Jeremy could make this year of enforced servitude not so bad. But he'd thought he could rely on Bianca, too, and yesterday in the same conversation in which he'd learned he had a great-grandmother and the lawyers he hated really loved him, in the very same conversation Madelaine had proved Bianca had talked to authorities and betrayed everything he'd shared with her about Melody and Patch.

It was nothing to get that angry about. Bianca had behaved about average, for people he'd dealt with. Better than some. She hadn't talked *until* she'd been cornered and until he'd already been caught and shipped off the planet.

So forget falling into the soft traps of potential relatives. Figure that Jeremy would keep some secrets and advise him out of trouble, but he shouldn't get soppy over it or mistake it for anything special. Jeremy had his orders, and those orders came from authority just like Madelaine, if it wasn't Madelaine herself. She wanted him to ask who his father was. He didn't damn well care. Whoever it was hadn't come to Pell. Hadn't cared for him. Hadn't cared for his mother.

Spacer mindset.

Safer just to disconnect from all of them, Jeremy too. He could be pleasant, but he didn't have to commit and he didn't have to trust any of them. And that meant he didn't have to get mad, consequently, when they proved no better and no worse than anyone else. He'd learned that wisdom in his half a dozen family arrangements, half a dozen tries at being given the nicely prepared room, the nicely prepared brother, the family who thought they'd save him from his heritage and a mother who hadn't been much.

In that awareness he walked in complete safety through the buzz of talk and the occasional hand snagging him to introduce him to this or that cousin . . . screw it, he thought: he wasn't possibly going to remember anything beyond this evening. The names would sink in only over time and with the need to deal with one and another of them. If he really, truly needed to know Jack from Jamie B., he'd ask for an alphabetical list. In the meantime, everyone wore name tags.

He'd had a hard day, however, and what he did want to quiet his nerves and dim the day's troubles wasn't on the dessert tray. He strolled over to the bar, lifted a glass of wine, turned his shoulder before he had to deal with the bartenders and walked off with it, sipping a treat he hadn't had at the Base but that he had had regularly in the latest family. The Wilsons had collected their subsidy from the station for taking care of him, he hadn't caused them trouble (he'd been a model student who ate his meals out), he'd done his own laundry . . . fact had been, he'd *boarded* at the Wilsons', and they were pleasant, decent folk who'd had him to formal dinners on holidays at home or in nice restaurants, and who hadn't cared if he hit their liquor now and again as long as he cleaned up the bar and washed the glasses.

The wine tasted good. His nerves promised to unwind. He told himself to relax, smile, have a good time, get to know as many of the glut of relatives as seemed pleasant. Like Jeff. Jeff was all right. Even great-grandmother Madelaine was on an agenda of her own, nothing really to do with him as himself, except as the daughter-legacy Madelaine hoped he'd turn into. He would disappoint her, he was sure.

But if she refrained from exercising authority over him and just took him as he was, as she'd done when she'd failed to make a fuss over him here, he could refrain from resisting her. He could be pleasant. He'd been *pleasant* to a lot of people once he knew it was in his interest, as it seemed generally to be in his interest on this ship.

He'd like to find a few cousins who were somewhat above twelve years of age. He'd like to have someone to talk occasionally to whose passion wasn't vid-games.

"God, you're not supposed to have that," Jeremy said, catching up to him.

"Had it on station."

Jeremy was troubled by it. He saw that. But he had it now, and he wasn't going to turn it in. He drank it in slow sips. He had no intention of gulping multiple glasses and making an ass of himself.

"What's this?" He knew that young, high, penetrating voice, too. Vince had showed up, with Linda. Inevitably with Linda. "You can't drink that."

Vince and his holier-than-thou, wiser-than-everyone attitudes for what Vince wouldn't dare do when he was taller and older. He gestured with the three-quarters full glass. "Have drunk it. When you grow up, you can give it a try. Meanwhile, relax."

"You'll get on report," Vince said. "I'll bet you get on report."

"Fine. Let them ship me back. I'll cry tears."

"I wish they would," Vince said, one of his moments of sincerity, and about that time a larger presence came up on him. JR.

"He's drinking," Vince said as if JR had no eyes. Fletcher looked straight at JR.

"Somebody give you that?" JR asked in front of Jeremy *and* Vince *and* Linda. He'd had enough family togetherness for the day. He drank three-quarters of a well-hoarded glass down in three swallows.

"Here," he said, and handed the empty glass to JR. JR almost let it fall. And caught it on the fly, not without spilling a couple of last drops to the expensive carpet.

Fletcher walked off. He'd had enough party and celebration, and beyond that, he wasn't in a frame of mind to stay around to be discussed or reprimanded in front of his room-mate, a twelve-year-old jerk, or a couple of hundred of his worst enemies. It was easy to leave in the open-ended mess hall section. He just kept walking to the lift, out where the light was dimmer and the noise was a lot less.

JR held a glass he didn't want to be holding. He handed it to Vince, restraining himself from immediate comment. He didn't know what exchange had preceded Vince's complaint to him. Clearly cousin Fletcher had just overloaded on some-thing, be it wine or family.

He refused to get into he-saids with immediately involved junior-juniors and walked to the bar to learn the plain facts. "Nate. Did you give Fletcher wine?"

Nate was one of the senior crew, now, lately of the junior crew, and Nate looked distressed. "No. He just took it. I didn't know what to do. Has he got leave?"

"Not officially, no. You did right. You didn't make an inci-dent. Vince and the junior-juniors called him on it, though, and he flared and left."

"The guy wasn't real straightforward about asking for per-missions, what it seems to me. I think he knew it was off limits."

"Yeah. You and I both noticed. If he does it again just let him. I'll talk to Legal and we'll find out whether there were agreements with him before he boarded, or what."

"Trouble?" Bucklin turned up by him at the bar. Bucklin couldn't have missed Fletcher's leaving.

"Vince sounded off about the drink. Fletcher's pissed."

"Cousin Fletcher came aboard pissed. Counting he was hauled here by the cops *and* the stationmaster, I'm not per-sonally surprised he and young Vince should go critical."

"It's on our watch," JR sighed. "We got him, he's ours."

"Maybe we could have airlock drill." Bucklin's tone was wistful, the suggestion outrageous.

"I'm afraid that won't solve it." He couldn't quite joke

about it, tempest in an infinitesimal teacup though it might be.
"Captain-sir wants him. Madelaine wants him. I'm afraid we
ultimately have to work him in."

"Between you and me only, this has a bad feeling." This
time Bucklin wasn't making a joke at all. "This guy doesn't
want to be here. I mean, it's hard enough to work him in if we
wanted him. We're busy. We've got nothing but unskilled labor
in him. We had a fine thing going before we got lucky in the
court, and I appreciate we had a legal problem, but—where
are we going to fit him in?"

Bucklin left his complaint hanging after that, and after a
moment, in his silence on the issue, Bucklin walked away.
Bucklin wasn't of a rank to say what was floating in the air
unsaid. *We* don't want him didn't half sum up the feeling
among the senior-juniors. They had had an integrated team
that was turning their last-born batch of juniors, ending with
Jeremy, into a tight-knit unit that would put the senior-juniors
in crew posts in another couple of years, with Jeremy and
Vince and Linda their best backup for what was going to be,
with adequate luck, a sudden crop of babies forthcoming
from this run. The senior-juniors were a team tested literally
under fire. However thin they were in numbers, he saw the
makings of a damned *fine* command in what his seniors had
left him and what he'd spent the last seven years putting
together. Supposing now that women did become pregnant,
and that the nursery did acquire a new batch of kids, he and
Bucklin and Lyra had plans to set Jeremy and Vince and
Linda in charge of the ones who'd come out of the nursery as
junior-juniors at just about the time that trio hit physical
maturity. It had all been going to work out neatly, and *then*
they got cousin Fletcher, of a physical size to fit with senior-
juniors, basic knowledge far beneath that of junior-juniors,
and a surly attitude to boot. Add to that a late-to-board-call
stunt unprecedented in the history of the ship, for which
Fletcher had proved nothing but self-righteous and angry.

It was wrong, the whole blown-out-of-proportion incident
just now with the wine glass was just damned *wrong*, both

what Fletcher had done walking out and what Vince had done lighting into him and what Jeremy had done standing confusedly in the middle. It wasn't the drink. It was Fletcher's attitude that made no way for anybody to back down; and as the saying went, it had happened on his watch.

On one level the Old Man didn't want to know the details, the excuses, or the extenuating circumstances of the junior captain's failures; on another level, the Old Man would rapidly know every detail that *he* knew the minute he walked in here and wanted to know where Fletcher was, and there was nothing worse in God's wide universe than an interview with Captain James Robert Neihart, Sr. when your tally of mistakes went catastrophic—as it had just done in that little damn-you-all gesture of Fletcher's.

He, supposed to handle things, had thought that in putting Fletcher with the junior-juniors he had arranged Fletcher a berth that wouldn't expose his ignorance, put demands on his behavior, or burden his own essential and often working team with constantly babysitting Fletcher.

Yes, the senior crew including the Old Man had a load of personal guilt over cousin Francesca, over the fact they *hadn't* made it back in time to prevent what they were relatively sure had been a suicide.

Yes, Francesca had named her kid one of the signal names in *Finity*'s history, one of the names which, like *James Robert*, you didn't just bestow on your kid without asking and without the bloodline to permit it.

Yes, Francesca had named him that name before she'd known she'd be left—she had done it, he guessed, not out of bitterness, or to imply a guilt they all felt, but to declare to a station who otherwise despised spacers that this was no common kid.

Unfortunately that name had stayed on after her suicide to confound *Finity* command, attached to a kid in the original Fletcher's line, a kid caught in the wheels of jurisdiction and power games, a kid who *by* that name and *Finity*'s reputation necessarily attracted attention in spacer circles.

And *yes*, James Robert had wanted to get a kid named

Fletcher, his grand-nephew, out of the gears and out of station view. There'd be no shameful appendix to the life of the first Fletcher, to append his name to a kid hellbent——JR had seen the police reports——on conspicuous and public disaster, right down to his dive for the outback.

Yes, Francesca's situation had been a tragedy. But a lot of people on *Finity* had had a lot harder situation than Francesca's, in his estimation.

His mother was one, dead in the decompression. And Jeremy's. And Vince's half-brother. Or ask Bucklin, who'd lost every close relative in his whole line except Madison, and Madison, who'd lost everyone but Bucklin.

Damn right they were close, the ones left of the old juniors' group, the ones like himself and Bucklin, who'd huddled together in nursery while the ship underwent stresses that killed the weak. They'd seen kids grow weaker and weaker until eventually they just didn't come out of trank at a given jump.

Damned right they'd earned the pride they had and damned right they didn't like all they'd won handed to a stranger on a platter, particularly when the stranger bitterly, insultingly rebuffed what welcome he was given.

He had a situation building, a resentment in his command. And it was his job to find a way to deal Fletcher in.

"So how is he?" Madison asked, second captain, and JR felt heat rise to his face, wondering what answer he possibly could find.

"He's not happy." To his left a guitar hit a quiet passage, strings ringing with a poignantly soft tune he'd heard since he was small; "Rise and Go." Parting of lovers. Partings of every kind. It was cliché. It never failed to send the chills down his arms and the moisture to his eyes. It disturbed logic. Prompted frankness. "Neither are we with him, sir, plainly speaking, sir."

"We had to take him," Madison said. "This was our chance. We couldn't leave him."

"I'm aware of our obligation, sir. And mine. I'm not begging off from the problem, only advising senior command that I've not made significant headway with him."

"Not only *our* obligation," Madison said. *"Elene Quen* had a part in this."

That small, added information, so directly and purposefully delivered, struck him off balance. And at that moment Madelaine wandered over with a drink in hand.

"Jake's called ops downside," Madelaine said, "just to be sure, you know, that Fletcher made his quarters without incident."

"I think he did," JR said. The kid was angry. Not stupid. And if Madison's information bore out into something besides Family determination to recover one of their own, there might be justification for that anger. Quen. Politics. Deals.

"He swiped a drink," Madelaine said to Madison. "Pell Station let him, I'd be willing to bet. Station rules. He didn't know he needed a go-ahead."

Madison frowned. "The body's old as JR, here. It's the mind that's under-aged. Your call, junior captain. What *will* you do with him?"

"My call," JR said. "But this is a new one. Where do you rate him, sir? Junior-junior, or not? He's Jeremy's age and far less experienced."

"And physically the same as your age. Look up the statutory years." Madison spotted someone coming in by the up-ring entry, and drifted off with that quandary posed, information half-delivered.

JR gazed after him in frustration. *He* drank, judiciously and seldom, and *he* had twenty-six years for mental ballast. He also had the responsibility for issuing such privileges to juniors under him. Was Madison saying give Fletcher senior-junior privileges right off? He didn't think so.

And this hint of deals with Quen, that might have complicated the situation with understandings and arrangements . . . no one had told him.

"What's this," he asked Madelaine, "that the name of *Quen* came up just now? I know why we took him, on principle. He's *Fletcher*. But what are we *doing* taking him in on this run, not asking for him after he's local eighteen and the court's off his case? Is there something essential that I'm not hearing, here?"

"Oh, there's a fair amount you missed that night at dinner."

"With Quen? What did I miss?"

"The fact Quen very ably moved the courts to give us Fletcher when she wanted to, after telling us for twelve years that she couldn't budge them. Now, that may be an unfair suspicion. Possibly her position has changed: possibly she has more power now; perhaps she simply called in a tall stack of favors." Madelaine stopped—he knew that silence of hers: she was suddenly wondering how much to tell the junior captain on a particular point, and a blurted question from him right now would make her sure he wasn't qualified to know. So he stood quietly while Madelaine took a sip of wine and thought about her next piece of information.

"Quen wants a ship. She wants a *Quen* ship. And she wants James"—Madelaine was one of a handful who called the senior captain *James* and not *James Robert*—"to stand with her and get it approved."

"That, I already know."

"But it's more than that. Like Mallory, Quen is worried about Union's next moves. Thinks the next war is going to be a trade war. Union's building ships it proposes to put into trade and saying they don't violate the Treaty. We of course say differently. Fletcher's an issue on his own and always has been, but he's become an issue of trust between us and Quen. Quen proves to us she's got power on Pell by delivering Fletcher to us, maneuvering past Pell's red tape—and we'll stand by her in the Council of Captains and use our considerable stack of favor-points with other ships to swing votes on the issue she wants—if she backs us. We want tariffs lowered. An *unrelated* understanding, mark that."

He did. There was no linkage between the two events because both parties agreed there wasn't a linkage. Yes, *Finity* could fail to carry out their part of the deal, take Quen's gift of Fletcher *and* go on to oppose Quen in Council, because there wasn't a linkage. But if *Finity* betrayed her, Quen wouldn't be their ally on something else they wanted *her* vote on.

And what was there to deal for? Quen wanted a Quen ship: understandable. What was there that *Finity* would be wanting from Quen? Lower tariffs didn't sound at all related to the battle they'd been fighting against Mazian. It affected merchanter profits and the price of goods. That was all that he saw.

Tariffs affected trade; trade affected international affairs. Did the question have any relation to that Union ship out there, the most notable anomaly in this voyage besides their own declaration they were going back to merchanting? Quen detested Union, so he'd heard. And Quen had traded them the kid they'd held hostage for seventeen years because *now* Quen wanted to build ships.

Build ships to keep Union from building ships to operate essentially on trade routes within Union. That was a delicate and sticky point: pre-War and post-War, all commercial trade routes in existence had been independent merchanter freighter routes—all, that was, except the two routes between Cyteen and its outermost starstations. On those two routes Union had always used its own military transport, in supply of, the merchanters were given to understand, fairly spartan stations, probably populated by Union's tailor-made humanity, for what he knew. No merchanter in those days had been interested in going there. That mistake had given Union a foothold in merchanter operations.

"So . . ." he asked Madelaine, "what *is* going on? How did Fletcher get into it, besides as a bargaining chit? And why are we making deals with Quen? Or is that what we're *really* doing on this voyage? Who are we fighting? Mazian? Or Union?"

"This is topside information," Madelaine said, meaning what she told the junior first captain didn't go to the junior-juniors or even to Bucklin. "We were always anxious to get Fletcher out. We didn't expect to get Fletcher this round. We took him because we *could* take him. Quen happens to hold a general view of the situation with Union *we* want her to act on, but we don't tell her that. We have to let her persuade *us* at great effort, or she'll start arranging other deals with other

parties because she'll believe we folded too easy and we're up
to something. So Fletcher wasn't at issue . . . we snatched him
up because we could; we just didn't plan on him becoming a
high-profile problem on this voyage."

Aside from the damage done his tight-knit command, he
didn't like the ethical shading of the transaction he was
hearing about, for Madelaine's own great-grandson. They
were merchanters, and they bought and sold, but people
shouldn't fit into a category of goods. In that regard he felt
sorry for anyone caught in the turbulence around their dealings, Mallory's and Quen's. And if Fletcher detected the nature
of the dealings, it could certainly explain Fletcher's state of
mind.

"You're not to tell that," Madelaine said, extraneous to any
prior understandings she'd elicited of him. Madelaine was
drinking wine and maybe just a little bit more open than she'd
have wanted to be. "Especially to Fletcher."

"You don't like Quen," JR observed. It seemed to him that
Quen was an unanswered question, and what her dealings had
been were never clear.

"I don't," Madelaine said. "Not personally. I admire her. I
don't like her. She got personally involved with a stationer,
kited off from *Estelle* because she was head over heels in love
with a bright young station lawyer and nobody could prevent
Elene doing any damn thing. It's uncharitable to say it, but
that's the case. Elene was on station when her ship died
because Elene was having her way in one of her romantical
fancies. My Francesca was on station because she had no
damn choice, medically speaking, and we had to transfer her
off and go in fifteen minutes." Another sip of wine. "Now
Elene's a hero of the Alliance and my granddaughter's dead of
an overdose. Quen didn't do one thing to make her life easier
while she was alive and alone there. Not one."

He was shocked, and tried to hide it. Madelaine had never
unburdened that opinion to him. But he hadn't been in the line
of command the last time they'd visited Pell and Madelaine's
temper hadn't been ruffled by a sordid trade to get her great-
grandson back, either.

"I blame Elene," Madelaine said. "I blame Elene that she left her own ship. I blame Elene that she didn't take Francesca in tow and provide a little personal friendship. Granted Elene was busy and Elene was pregnant, too, but if she ever extended a hand of friendship to my granddaughter before she hit the bottom I have yet to hear it. If my Elizabeth had lived to get back to Pell, she'd have had words for Quen. I reserve what I say. I'm only the girl's grandmother."

Francesca's mother, Elizabeth. Dead at Olympus. There were so many.

Madelaine nudged JR's arm with her wine glass. "Take a little extra care of my great-grandson. Don't waste him in the junior-juniors. I know he's an ass, but he's got possibilities. Personal favor."

JR drew in a slow, deep breath. He'd gotten snagged, broadsided, and boarded. Aunt Madelaine *was* the ship's chief lawyer.

"I'll try," he said.

"All you can do," Madelaine agreed.

"Any special advice?" he asked Madelaine.

"For dealing with him? Grow all-over fur. The boy's had no *human* ties. Damned Pell courts." Sip of wine. The bottom of the glass, a little straw-colored liquid remaining. "Get me another wine, there's a love. James has come. I won't tell him what Fletcher did. None of us will. It just isn't important."

James Robert had come in, perhaps thinking he'd find a grateful, happy new member in the Family. Madelaine went in that direction, damage control, protection of her great-grandson, leaving him to get a refill at the bar, and one for himself while he was at it.

James Robert and Madelaine were in heavy discussion when he brought the wine. He put the glass in Madelaine's outheld hand, offered his other on the moment to the Old Man, who hadn't gotten across the room before Madelaine's interception, and the Old Man murmured an abstracted thanks and took it.

Talk among the seniors: a Union ship just sitting out there, having run recovery on a bottle of Scotch. Quen and some high-powered agreement in their own vital interest. Madelaine said it was tariffs, which pointed to a political agreement inside the Alliance. The secrecy smelled to high heaven of some kind of operation of Mallory's, while, third question, they were very publicly taking up trade again, in a move that had to be gossiped wherever merchanters docked . . . and the Fletcher incident had to dominate the gossip on Pell and everywhere else.

He had surmised their return to trade might be intended as a demonstration of Alliance power, a demonstration of the safety they hoped they'd created in the shipping lanes . . . at a critical moment when support of the starstation councils for the continued pirate hunt was wavering.

And at a time when Union was handing out special privileges to merchanters who wanted to sign on to wealthy Union instead of the economically struggling Alliance. He didn't want to focus his career on fighting Union activity: he'd trained all his life to fight Mazianni, and that was where his interest was, but he could see that Union's actions, actions which Quen would find of interest, constituted a smart move. Getting enough merchanters voluntarily signed into Union would win for Union without a shot what the War hadn't gained for them by all the ordnance expended. If merchanters started drifting over the Line and signing with Union in any significant numbers the universe could see humanity polarized again into two major camps. Then, depend on it, merchanters would see themselves first regulated to the hilt, then entirely replaced by Union's own ships: a merchanter desperate enough to clutch at Union financial support wasn't analyzing his future further than the next set of bills.

It was the very situation that had started the War, the move to take over the merchanters this time coming not from Earth's side, but from Union's side of the border. One would think Union might have learned from Earth's experience with the merchanters. Not so. The merchanters had formed their own state, at Pell, and with a handful of stations balancing commitment between the Merchanter Alliance and Union, and now Union started pushing to get the merchanters. The starstations' independence would go next, and then they'd reach for Earth.

If Mazian didn't step in.

Or if Mallory and Quen and the Old Man of *Finity's End* didn't draw a line and say: no further.

And was *that* the message that went with the bottle in a black, starry sea? A warning—from Mallory *and* from *Finity,* Stay our allies? Don't provoke us with your recruitments and your ship-building? Yours is the glass house?

It was certain in their own minds that Mazian had a secret base, somewhere within 20 lights of Pell, and that was an immense volume of space to search for someone determined not to be found. The rest of human habitation was concentrated in a comparatively small sphere at the center, where Mazian could strike without warning—and escape to that remote base.

It required a network of informants to establish any kind of security. Union didn't have that network. Mallory did. Mallory—who was once *of* the Fleet. And they were such a network, they, the merchanters . . . who wouldn't talk to Union or Alliance stationside officials with anything like the freedom with which they talked to each other.

From Mazian's view, however, finding the heart of human civilization wasn't a question of searching a 40-light sphere. It was a concentrated area Mazian could easily strike, without warning and with a choice of targets that could send chills down any civilized backbone. If a junior could venture a guess of his own, it was worse than that: Mazian's aim might be to establish multiple bases, scattered points from which to threaten the center—and Mazian's overriding strategy might not be a crushing military strike but rather evading Mallory, waiting for Union to get overconfident, and then maneuvering the Alliance or Earth into so deep a diplomatic crisis with Union that the Alliance had no hope *except* to forgive Mazian and recall him to take over the government. Then Mazian could use those bases to hit Union. But merchanters would bleed in the process.

Against that backdrop, the captains of *Finity's End* had held their meeting with Quen and gotten some agreement out of her that they had wanted. Meanwhile they were going back to trading, Union was still refusing to let Alliance merchanters into its internal routes without them signing up as Union-based, and the Old Man had *wanted* Quen to bribe him into supporting her in some scheme of her devising.

What in *hell* game were they playing?

He went back to the bar, picked up a glass of wine for himself. Bucklin and Chad intercepted him on their own inquiry, having been out of the loop.

"So was that all about Fletcher?" Bucklin asked.

"Some of it. Madelaine being his grandmother." Great-grandmother, but in a Family's tangled exogamous web of greats, second and third cousins and nieces and nephews on lives extended by time dilation and rejuv, you compressed generations unless you were seriously trying to track what you were to each other. "She's taking a personal interest. She wants this kid in very badly."

Silence greeted that revelation.

"About the drink," JR said. "Let it slide. He didn't know the rules. I'll think about where he fits. He's *not* Jeremy's size. The body's as mature as we are. The education's just way behind."

"Yeah, well." Bucklin sighed, and they took their drinks and walked over to the rest of the junior-seniors, who'd staked out a table for eight. They pulled more chairs over, until it was a dense, tight group, Lyra, Toby, Ashley, Sue and Connor, Nike, Wayne, and Chad: as many different looks as they had star-scattered fathers. Lyra, a year younger than Bucklin and third in command, was the family's sole almost redhead, sporting an array of earrings and bracelets she couldn't wear in ops. Lyra, and beside her, Toby, whose brown complexion and shoulder-trailing kinky locks made that pair of cousins about as far apart as the Family genes stretched.

Lyra and Toby had brought a dedicated bottle of wine from the bar. Bucklin and he also had wine. The rest had soft drinks and fruit juice, and that was the line Fletcher had crossed without permission: Fletcher had assumed, maybe because he'd done it on station, that he had a right.

"Fletcher," JR said by way of explanation, "had a run-in

with Vince, you'll have noticed. He opted for his quarters. Presumably he got there. Jake checked."

"So did you explain the rules?" Connor asked over his own soft drink. By custom, they didn't follow formal courtesies in rec hall or in mess. Complaints were allowed; and he could have figured it would be Connor and Sue that spoke up for the rule book.

"Fletcher's got a possible Extenuating." He saw frowns settle not only on those two faces but all around. "He's a junior-junior, but Madison said it. The body physiologically isn't."

"Body's not mind," Nike said, and swept an indignant hand from Wayne and Connor on her right to Chad, Sue, and Ashley on her left. "When do *we* get wide-open liberty on the docks? When do *we* sleepover where we like? Or take a wine off the bar in front of the seniors and everybody?"

"You know when." He didn't want this debate over the issue, and their challenge to him *was* the answer. No, maturity wasn't identical from ship to station on the biological or the mental level, and there wasn't a neat equivalency. The off-again on-again hormonal flux of time-dilated pubescent bodies that was the number one reason they didn't get bar privileges was precisely the hormonally driven emotional flux that set their nerves in an uproar when they were crossed. His physical-sixteens and -fifteens were a pain in the ass; he was just emerging from that psychological cocktail himself, and while at physical and mental seventeen-to-eighteen and chronological and educational twenty-six he was just getting his own nerves to a calm, sensible state. Yes, he still flared off, a besetting sin of his. But the infinite wisdom of the Way Things Worked on a short-handed ship had made him senior-most junior, responsible for all the junior crew that was still in that stage.

Keep them busy picking nits, his predecessor in the role had warned him; never let them take on the real rules. Give them nits to worry at and they'll obey the big ones. Then Paul had added, smugly: *You* did.

Nits, hell. His predecessor had commanded the juniors

through the dustup at Bryant's, when so many had died—
among the juniors as well. That had been no waltz.

They gave *him* Fletcher on a damn milk run. It seemed, on
the surface, a tame, and minor, duty, one that shouldn't set *his*
lately pubescent hormones skewing wildly through the whole
gamut of adrenaline charge. He'd had his last personal snit, oh,
exquisitely dissected and laid out for him by Paul, right down
to temper as his personal failing.

Not this time.

"Give him some leeway," he said to the others. "Just give
him some leeway. He's not the same as having grown up here.
He's not the same as anyone we've ever personally known."

"I hear he gave *you* trouble," Ashley said.

"Not lately."

"Not in fifteen minutes," Sue said. "He shoved that glass
on you in front of everybody."

"Fine. I gave it to Vince. Who set up the situation, if we
have to talk about fault." His temper *was* getting on edge. Sue
had a knack for stirring it up. He hauled it back and put on the
brakes. "I saw the drink and I was dealing with it. I didn't need
a snot-nosed junior-junior to tell me that was a wineglass.
Vince interfered. It blew. That's the end of it. We've got
Fletcher, he's physiological seventeen, he probably drank on
station, and somewhere, somehow in the plain fact he doesn't
know a damn thing useful, we've got to fit him in at the
bottom of the senior-juniors—"

"No!" from Nike.

"—or see him someday in charge of the junior-juniors.
Vince is chronologically a year older than he is; but Fletcher's
seventeen years weren't time-dilated. So do you want *my*
orders, or are there other suggestions?"

"He's the baby," Connor said. "I think we ought to do a
Welcome-in."

Loft-to-crew-quarters transition. Scare the new junior. It
wasn't the idea he had in mind, though it was arguably a
fair proposition: Fletcher wanted crew privileges and he
hadn't been through the process and the understandings

and the acceptance of authority that all the rest of them had.

"He's a little old for that," JR said.

"We did a Welcome-in for Jeremy," Sue said. "Jeremy was the last. Jeremy took it. So how's this guy holier than any of us?"

"He's upset, that's one difference. He wasn't born here. He's not one of us . . ."

"That's what a Welcome-in's *for*, isn't it?" Chad asked, with devastating reason.

But a bad idea. "Not yet. This isn't somebody straight down from the kids' loft. This isn't a green kid."

"Plenty green to me," Chad said.

"He can't *do* anything," Lyra said. "He's not trained to do anything. He's a stationer. He's a stationer with stationer attitudes. And he's got to appreciate what he's joining."

JR cast a look aside, where the captains and Madelaine talked with Com 1 of first shift. And back again, to frowning faces. A kid coming up out of the nursery, yes, always got a Welcome-in when he or she officially hit the junior ranks. It was high jinks and it was a test. It was, among other things, a chance for senior-juniors to get their licks in and, outright, bring the new junior into line. But it also put the new junior in the center of a protective group, one that would see him safely through the hazards of dockside and take care of him in an emergency.

"So when do we do a Welcome-in?" Chad asked, and he knew right then by Chad's tone it was an issue the way Fletcher's encounter with him over the wine glass was going to be an issue with Chad.

"Not yet," JR said. "Ultimately we have to bring him in. But push him and he'll blow, and *that's* no good."

"Everybody blows," Connor said.

"Everybody is straight from nursery and not this guy's size," Bucklin muttered, finally, a dose of common sense. "Somebody could get hurt. Fletcher. Or you."

There were sulks. They hadn't done a Welcome-in on anybody since Jeremy, three shipboard years ago, a wild interlude in the middle of dangerous goings-on. They hadn't known whether *Finity* would survive her next run, and they'd Welcomed-in Jeremy the brat a half-year early, because it hadn't seemed fair for any kid to die alone in the nursery, the ship's last kid, in years when they hadn't produced any *other* kids.

Jeremy and Fletcher. The same crop, the same year. One theirs, one lost to station-time.

And very, very different.

"I say we go easy with him," JR said in the breath of reason Bucklin's clear statement of the facts had gained, "and we give him a little chance to figure us out. Then we'll talk."

There was slumping, there was clear unhappiness with that ruling.

"Square up," JR said. "Don't sulk like a flock of juvvies. This is a *senior* venue."

Heads came up, backs straightened marginally.

"I say with JR," said Lyra, who was usually a fount of better judgment, "we give him a little time. If he comes around, fine. If he doesn't, we talk again at Mariner."

"Just don't take him on," JR said. "If you've got a problem with him, refer it to me."

He thought maybe he should go down to Fletcher's quarters this evening and try to talk it out with him. But he didn't trust that three-quarters of a wine glass in three gulps had improved Fletcher's logic. Or his temper. There were constructive talks, and there were things bound to go to hell on a greased slide.

He supposed he'd tried to fix things too fast. And putting him with Jeremy maybe hadn't been the ideal pair-up.

But putting him with him or Bucklin would inspire jealousy. Put him with Chad? There were two tempers in a paper sack. Connor, the same. Ashley or Toby would go silent and there'd be offense there. He couldn't think of anybody better than Jeremy, who could outright disarm the devil.

The Old Man and Paul both had warned him there weren't fast fixes for personal messes once they went wrong. You didn't just go running down to a case like Fletcher and tell him how to fix his life and expect cooperation, especially after a public scene such as they'd just had. Fletcher had to figure a certain amount out for himself, and meanwhile he and his crew had to figure out what a mind was like who'd been more than content to sink into a gravity well and never see the stars again.

Stranger than the downers, in his own opinion. Downers at least had been born to endless cloud and murk.

Wood, a slim wand of it brought into space where wood was a rarity, feathers, where birds never flew . . . and spirals and dots and bands carved by hisa fingers—fingers no longer content to carve wood with stones, the scientist reminded them. Hisa of these times were quite glad to have sharp metal blades. Hisa accepted them in trade and called metal cold-cold. That had become the hisa word for it.

No matter how hard you tried to keep the Upabove out of Downbelow, humans didn't give up their ties to the technology they depended on and hisa learned to depend on it, too. But humans found it difficult to go down to a world again.

Fletcher lay on his bunk, his head a little light from the wine. His fingers drew peace from the touch of the feathers, damaged by a Downbelow rain. The touch of wood evoked memories far happier than where he was.

He didn't give up his resentments. He didn't give up his dreams, either. And maybe the experts *weren't* right that he'd done actual harm by going where he'd gone. Expert opinion had backed another theory, once, right up to the time before he was born. Then the idea had been to get the hisa into space, teach them technology, give them the benefits of the steel and plastics world above their clouded world. Hisa had been very clever with machines, quick to learn small jobs like checking valves, changing filters, reading dials.

Pell Station, short of personnel in its earliest days, and overwhelmed by events cascading about it, had *begun* with hisa at the heart of the operation, and they'd built the station around the presumption there'd always be hisa on Pell.

But human greed had tried to push things too fast on

Downbelow. People had multiplied too fast. Had brought demands on the hisa for more, more, more of their grain, for organized work, for controlling Old River's floods and doing things on schedule.

Hisa hadn't taken to schedules and human demands. A hisa named Satin had led a hisa uprising—well, as uprisen as patient hisa ever got—back during the War.

Then a new set of experts had moved in, declared humans had done everything wrong and shut down a lot of operations the Base had used to have, restricted more severely the rotation of hisa up to the station, and dashed all expectations of hisa and humans working together.

Was it wrong that Melody and Patch had rescued a human child?

Was it wrong he'd grown up and found them again?

Was it wrong he'd dreamed of working with them—maybe a little closer than he should have gotten?

(But he *knew* them, and they knew him, his gut protested. He hadn't hurt them. He'd never hurt them.)

His fingers traced designs no human understood. He knew what scientists surmised the designs were: day-night in the pattern of black dots, Great Sun in the circles, Old River in the long curves and branches.

But maybe the curling patterns meant vines and seeds. Maybe it was fields and maybe it was hisa paths the lines meant. You could see anything you believed in, in hisa carving, that was the thing. And if he ever could ask Melody and Patch to read the stick for him, as sure as he knew their minds, he'd bet they'd read him something completely different every time he asked.

So who was smarter? Hisa, with their patterns that could mean anything the day felt like meaning? Or humans who, in their writing and their image-making, pinned a moment down with precision, like a specimen on a board?

Was one better, or smarter, and ought hisa *not* to work on the station as much as some of them, individuals with preferences like every human, wanted to work?

He didn't think natural was better. He didn't think hisa

should die young from infections, or lose their babies in floods or to fevers, or die of broken legs. But the authorities ruled there were hisa you could contact, but hisa who didn't work at the Base were completely off limits. And they went on dying of things station medicine could cure.

Experts said—better a few die like that than have another contact the way it had been when the Fleet military had invaded Downbelow. Humans never should have landed on Downbelow at all, was what one side said. Everything humans had ever done was harmful and wrong. They'd already robbed an intelligent species of their unique future and further contact could only do worse.

But wasn't a human-hisa future unique in the patterns of a wide universe, too? Wasn't it a surer chance for the hisa to survive, when worlds with life were so few? And wasn't it as important in the vast cosmos that two species had gotten together and worked together?

Seemed sensible to him that he'd done no harm.

They'd given him a gift that meant—surely—they weren't harmed.

But when he remembered that he was lying on a bunk in a ship speeding toward nowhere, and *away* from every meaning the stick had to anyone, a lump came up in his throat and his eyes stung.

Rotten stupid was what it was.

More experts. Quen, this time. Nunn.

Friends, he and Bianca. Running around together. Thinking of things together. For maybe fifteen whole, oblivious days, with disaster written all around them.

It shouldn't surprise him when it all fell apart. Things always did. He wrapped the feathered cords around the stick and put it away in the back of the drawer.

Then he fell back on his bunk and stared at the ceiling, chasing away the ache in his chest with the remembrance of sunglare through green leaves. Jeremy came in from the party, late, and he pretended to be asleep as Jeremy clattered about and took a late shower.

When Jeremy had dimmed the lights and gone to bed, he got up and stripped his clothes off to go to sleep.

"There's a lot of the guys mad at you," Jeremy said out of the dark.

"Doesn't matter to me," he said.

"You shouldn't have taken the drink," Jeremy said.

"I don't want to hear about it," he said coldly. "They set 'em out, yeah, I'll drink one. Nobody had a sign up. Nobody told me stop."

"Vince was an ass," Jeremy said finally.

"Yeah," he agreed, feeling better by that small vindication. "Generally. So how was it?"

"Oh, it was fine." Jeremy settled, a stirring of sheet and a sighing of the mattress. A silence then, in the dark. "JR said everybody should lay off you and be polite."

"That so." He didn't believe it. But he couldn't see Jeremy's face to test the truth of it.

They were going to jump at maindawn. He was worried about sleeping through it. Forgetting the drug. Going crazy.

They were going to Mariner from here. They'd actually be at another star.

"Are they going to warn us tomorrow morning?" he asked Jeremy.

"About the jump? Yeah, sure, I'll guarantee you can't sleep through it. They'll be on the intercom. Fifteen minutes before. You got your drugs?"

"Yeah." When he was out of his clothes, he had the drugs in the elastic side pocket, on the bed, the way Jeremy had advised him. Always with him. "They're right here." He was still wobbly about the experience. Going into it out of the dark, he supposed one shift or the other had to have it in the middle of their night, but it was a scary proposition.

"Anybody from the party have a hangover," he said. "That'd be bad."

"The Old Man wouldn't show 'em any mercy," Jeremy said. "How are you, drinking that wine? You won't have a headache, will you?"

"Not usually." Stupid, he said to himself. He'd forgotten about the jump when he drank it all. He hoped he wouldn't.

He figured if he did he wouldn't, as Jeremy said, get any pity for it.

He shut his eyes. He didn't sleep, for a long, long time.

When the warning came it was loud, and scared him awake.

"Fifteen minutes," it said. *"Rise and shine. We're on our way. Pull your pre-jump checks, latch down, tuck down, belt in, all you late party-goers. No sympathy from fourth shift . . . you get the next jump and we get the rec hall . . . move, move, move . . ."*

Chapter
—XII—

The light came back. Melody would say Great Sun came walking back above the clouds. As soon as Fletcher could see trunks of trees in the dawn he took up walking, just following River; and River led him, oh, far, far up through the woods. Rain drizzled down, but still not a downer appeared. Downers on such a day would stay to their burrows, having more sense than to get wet and cold.

Or they'd gone wandering for love, walking as far as a female could, and farther than some of the males, those less able, those less strong. That was the test.

That was what he was looking for, he began to think. That was the test he'd set himself, the challenge, to overtake what he loved, lusted after, longed for with a remote and bewildered ache. He was a young male. He'd been confused. But now, beyond any psych's pat answers, he had a clear idea what he hoped to find in this tangled woods, with its huge trees and its banks of puffer-globes glistening with the mist. Like the downers who walked until a last suitor followed, he was looking for someone who cared. Simple quest. Someone who cared.

He wasn't going to find that someone, of course. And ultimately, being only human, he'd have to push that rescue button and let the ones who didn't give a damn chase him down and bring him back, because the station paid them to do that. His thinking was muddled and he knew it was, but it was comfort to think the ache was common to all the world.

The sun grew brighter. The rain grew less.

He heard strange whistling calls, such as came constantly in the deep bush. No one was sure what made some of those sounds. Sometimes he'd heard downers imitate them.

There were clicks, and rising booms, and whistles.

A creature stared at him from the hillside. He'd heard of such big, gray diggers, but they came nowhere near the Base, being shyer than the downers and given to be harmless to humans if unmolested. It was a marvelous sight. It moved on all fours, unlike downers, and chewed a frond of herbage, staring at him with a blandly curious expression. It wasn't afraid of him. He wasn't quite afraid of it, but the advice from lectures was not to go close or get in their way, and he walked off the path and across to another clear spot to avoid it.

A shower of fronds came down on him, startling him and making him look up. A downer was in the tree near him.

And his heart soared.

"Hello," he called it, hoping it might be a friend. He didn't think he knew this downer, but he called out to it. "Good morning. Want Melody and Patch! Name Fetcher." He ventured their hisa names, that he'd never used to another hisa. "Tara-wai-sa and Lanu-nan-o my friends I want find."

"You come!" the downer said, decisively.

So it did understand, and that meant it was one who'd worked with humans and one that might help him. Maybe the downers had heard a human was missing; but he'd given a request, and rarely would a downer refuse. This one scrambled down the fat, white-and-brown tree trunk and skipped ahead of him through the fronds that laced over the trail.

So after all his fear he was rescued. Downers knew where he was. His imaginings, his wild constructions of hope, the constructions of fantasy and rescue he'd built in the dark to keep him going—his daydreams so seldom came true, and he'd begun to believe this one would come to the worst, the most calamitous end of all.

But now, instead, the last, the wildest and most fanciful hope, was taking shape around him: *yes*, Melody and Patch knew he was lost. They'd whistled it through the trees, or simply sent younger, quicker downers running to look for him. They hadn't forgotten him. They still cared.

On and on the downer led him, until he was panting, short on oxygen and staggering as he went.

The way it led him wasn't back the way he'd come. Or perhaps he'd gotten oriented wrong with River: he'd been following the water, and perhaps in the winding paths he could find on the high forested hills, away from observing the direction of River's flow, he'd just turned around and started walking back again. He'd be disappointed if that proved so, if suddenly between the trees he found himself back at the Base, among the human-tended fields, nothing gained.

But the walking went on and on for hours, beyond anything he thought he could do. He changed out mask cylinders. By then he had no idea where he was. But the downer never quite lost him. He'd think he was hopelessly behind, and then the whistling would guide him, past the thumping of his own pulse in his ear. He'd fall, tripped in the awkward vision of the mask, and a shower of leaves would fall around him, like a benediction, a gentle urging to get up again.

I'm using up the cylinders, he wanted to say to the downer, who never came close enough long enough. He began to fear he was in danger after all, and that with the best will in the world the downer would kill him, only from the walking.

A long, long walk (another cylinder-change along, it was) he saw the giant trees of the forest began to grow fewer. Am I back after all? he asked himself. Was I that far lost? And am I only back at the Base?

He was exhausted and in pain, and struggling to breathe, trying not to give up a cylinder sooner than he'd wrung the last use out of it. He was ready, now, to be back in safety.

But a bright gold of treeless land showed between the trees.

It *wasn't* the cleared hillsides around the Base. There was no white of domes or dark green of trees, and Old River was far from him. It might be the further fields, where humans grew grain in vast tracts, at Beta Site, near the shuttle landing.

But those wouldn't be gold yet, just brown, turned earth.

It was the forest edge, for sure. And when he'd followed his guide to the last fringe of forest giants he saw below him a hill sweeping on for a great distance, down to a plain of last year's golden grass. In the heart of a pollen-hazed distance, something like a set of figures stood, thick and strange, and impossible to be alive.

Scale played tricks with his eyes. Tiny figures moved among the greater ones, hisa, dwarfed by skyward-looking images.

He knew, then, what he saw—what he'd heard reported, at least, and seen only in photographs.

It was the Spirit-place, the great holy place. The stone figures that watched the sky, the great Watchers, of which their little ones on the hill were the merest hint.

Humans didn't come here.

"Come-come," the downer said, beckoning as humans beckoned. "Come-come, you come, Melody child."

He walked a golden hill, that tore beneath his feet. He was losing the vision. There was a feeling of falling . . .

. . . down and down.

Of arrival. He knew it now. The dream escaped his mind. Breaths came faster. There was no cylinder restraining his air. There was no clean-suit. There was no world . . .

He'd been in the best moment of his life. And wasn't there. Would never be. Tears leaked between Fletcher's shut lids, and he drew tainted breath, and knew why his mother had kept the dream, bought it on dockside. Knew why his mother had loved it more than she'd loved him.

There'd been no future in the dream. He'd not known it could turn darker.

That moment, that very moment he'd want to hold, that was the one the arrival ripped away from him, after all the pain.

There was just Jeremy scrabbling in his drawer, after clothes, there was just Jeremy saying, "Drink the stuff. You've got to have it."

He'd have ignored Jeremy. But he couldn't ignore his stomach. It wanted; and he reached numbly after the drink packets, the synth that pulled electrolytes back into balance after hyperspace had done its worst to a human body.

After the dream was done.

"You shower first or me?" Jeremy asked him.

"You." He didn't want to move. It wasn't a favor Jeremy

offered him. He wanted to keep his eyes shut and try to recover that sight, that moment, when he'd met all his hopes.

He could have them back. Could have had them forever. If something hadn't pulled the ship in.

It was another month. What had pulled them in, if they weren't doomed to die in empty space, had to be the star they'd been looking for.

They were at Mariner.

He gulped down his remaining drink packets, drowsed while Jeremy showered and his own stomach settled. They made two more touches at the interface that almost made him sick, and then he slept again. He came to with the intercom talking to them.

"*Jeremy, Vincent, Linda, Fletcher.*" It was the synthesized voice he'd heard last time. Jeremy had told him there was a set-up in the computer where a random-sort program juggled the electronic dice and put the scut-crews on whatever assignment their luck assigned them. It activated the intercom to call your team's cabins and even left mail in your mailbox.

"*Laundry detail,*" it said.

"Damn!" Jeremy cried from inside the bath, and came out still damp and stark naked. "No fair!"

At least, Fletcher thought, he knew how to do that job.

"Stupid machine!" Jeremy shouted at the ceiling and kept swearing.

Fletcher rolled out of bed, his clothes at that particular stage of sticking to his body and dragging across dead skin that made him sure he didn't want to linger in them. The effects of a month-long near dormancy weren't pretty on the human body inside or out, he'd discovered. This time his gut wanted to protest, and he made the bathroom in some haste.

Officers' meetings. Numbers that pertained to ship-sightings, stock reports, futures and commodities . . . the same kind of information they'd tracked for military purposes for nearly two decades, and from before JR had sat on staff; but the information was never sifted down to military intelligence: the availability of supply and the activity and origin of suspect ships—questions which JR's brain kept following off-track of what his seniors were discussing.

Seniors reminisced instead about old port-calls, pre-War, early War. They talked about the early days of Mariner Station, when everything had been bare metal, and the details swirled around in a junior mind not quite sure whether this was needful information or just the pleasurable talk of old crew, recalling hard times which juniors nowadays didn't remember.

When they'd put into Mariner before, in his recollection, they hadn't traded. The Old Man had had meetings with Mariner authorities and military authorities, they'd had meetings with other captains and senior crew off other ships and taken in the kind of information ships wouldn't ordinarily trade with each other, information on the market more freely shared than made sense . . . if they were rivals. They'd been no one's rivals, then.

Now they were going in to compete and consequently they wanted prices for what they carried as high as possible.

Now secrecy mattered not because they didn't want Mazian and the Fleet to know what they hauled and where they hauled it, but because they wanted to keep the price of goods, apparently scarce, as high as they could manage until they sold what they were carrying. Let somebody speculate that their load was *all* downer wine (it wasn't) and the price of wine would plummet, taking their profit. Let them speculate that they carried Earth chocolate and coffee (they did) and the price of those goods would drop in three seconds on the electronic boards.

They were legally restrained from entering their goods on the market until they'd reached a certain distance from Mariner, and Helm had run them as close to that mark as they could at near-light before he'd dumped them down to the sedate crawl at which they approached Mariner Station.

At 0837h/m local their goods had gone up for sale on the Mariner Exchange, and they had a vast amount of printout from Mariner, which was just old enough (two hours light-speed) to make buys hazardous. The new guessing game was not what *Finity* carried but what *Finity* wanted or needed. The price of goods would react. Any ship dropping into Mariner system was going to affect prices when they began to make their buys and as traders reassessed goods 'in the system' and their effect on each other. And there was a ship, *Boreale*, already approaching dock.

Boreale was from Cyteen. That was interesting in the engineering and the political sense: it was one of those new Cyteen quasi-merchanters with a military, not a Family crew, coming from a port which specialized in biostuffs (rejuv, plant and animal products, pharmaceuticals) as well as advanced tech. Also a factor to consider on the question of that ship's cargo and the futures market: farther ports deep in Union territory did produce metals and other items that could drive down the prices of goods inbound from say, Viking, heavily a manufacturing system.

It was, in short, a guessing game in which Mariner futures and commodities traders could suffer agonies of financial doubt, a game on which *Finity*'s profit margin ticked up or down by little increments every time someone made a buy or sell decision and changed the amount of goods available.

The market also reacted in a major way to every ship docking, because the black box that every ship carried shot news and technical statistics to the station systems, news derived from all starstations in the reporting system. The black boxes wove the web that held civilization together. A single ship's black box reported every piece of data from the last station that ship had docked at, and thus every piece of data previously brought to that last station from other ships of origins all over space. The information constituted pieces of a hologram reflecting the same picture at different moments in time, and the station's computers somehow assembled it all: births and deaths, elections, civil records, deeds, titles, rumors, popular songs, books in data-form for reproduction by local packagers, mail, production statistics, news, sports, weather where applicable, star behaviors, navigational data, in-space incidents, the total picture of everything going on anywhere humans existed so far as that particular ship had been in contact with it. A last-minute load went into a ship when it undocked and went out of a ship when it docked elsewhere, weighted by the computers as most accurate where the ship had just been and least accurate or least timely regarding starstations farthest from its last dock. The station computers heard it all, digested it all, overlaid one ship's black-box report over another and came up with a universe-view that included the prices of goods at the farthest ports of the human universe . . . one that faded in detail considerably regarding information from Cyteen or its tributaries—or from inside Earth—but it was good enough to bet on, and pieces let a canny trader make canny wagers.

The black box system also continually affected the local station-use commodities market, as a shortage of, say, grain product on Fargone affected the price of grain product everywhere in known space. A tank blew out at Viking and a major Viking tank farm shut down a quarter of its production: the price of fish product, that bane of a small-budget spacer's existence, actually ticked up ^{19}/100ths of a credit everywhere in the universe, in spite of the fact that every station produced it and there was no food staple cheaper than that: somebody might actually have to freight fish product to Viking.

JR told himself this truly was a thrilling piece of news and that he should be pleased and proud that *Finity* was at last occupied with details like that rather than figuring how they could best spend the support credits they had to supply ships like *Norway* with staples and metal, out in the deep, secret dark of jump-points a ship laden the way they were loaded now couldn't reach. They still would haul for Mallory—one run scheduled out when they were done with this loop, as he understood—but there were other ships appointed to do that, a few, at least, who regularly plied the supply dumps that Mallory used.

What was different from the last near-twenty years was that their schedule to meet Mallory at a rendezvous yet to be arranged *didn't* call on them for their firepower.

And at Pell, they'd officially given up the military subsidy that fueled and maintained them without their trading. That was the big change, the one that shoved them away from the public support conduit and onto the stock exchange and the futures boards not with an informational interest in the content of the boards—but with a commercial one.

Safer, Madelaine had argued, to haul contract. That meant hauling goods for someone else who'd flat-fee them for haulage and collect all the profit, with a bonus if their careful handling and canny timing, or blind luck ran the profit above a pre-agreed amount, and liability up to their ears if something happened to the cargo. It was steady, it was relatively safe, it guaranteed they got paid as long as the goods got to port intact.

But it didn't pay on as large a scale as a clever trader could make both hauling *and* trading their own goods. They had the safer option; but *Finity* had never done contract haulage as a primary job, and maybe it was just the Old Man's pride that he disdained it now. James Robert and Madison had been doing trading in ship-owned goods for a lot of years before the War, they'd watched the market survive the War and blossom into something both vital and different, and by what JR saw now, they just couldn't resist it.

The Old Man and Madison were, in fact, as happy as two kids with a dock pass, going over market reports. JR felt his brain numbed and his war-honed instincts sinking toward rust. All he'd learned in his life was at least remotely useful in what the two senior captains were doing, but not with the same application. He wasn't even engaged in strategy thinking, like whether the ship near them might be reporting to Union command. They knew that *Boreale* would do exactly that—report to Union command—so there wasn't even any doubt of it to entertain him.

Trade. Real trade. He still entertained the unvoiced notion that they were engaged in information-gathering and intrigue about which neither the Old Man nor Madison had told him. He went over the political and shipping news with a trained eye and gathered tidbits of speculation that—were no longer useful in the military sense, since they'd be outmoded by the time they got near someone who reported to Mallory.

That ship they'd met at Tripoint continued to haunt him, and after the staff meeting—knowing he'd lose points in the strange non-game they played, but not as many as if he asked on a current situation—he snagged Madison to ask with no hints about it whether that encounter had been scheduled.

"No," was Madison's answer. "They're watching, is all."

"Watching us."

"Watching for anything the Alliance is doing. Seeing what our next step is. Being sure—odd as it might sound—that *we* aren't negotiating with the Fleet for a cease-fire and a deal with Mazian independent of them. Earth's made some provocative moves."

Mark that for a blind spot he should ponder at leisure. It wasn't enough to know the honest truth about one's own intentions toward the enemy: an ally still had to plan its security in secret and without entirely trusting anyone. One's allies could take a small piece of information, foresee double-crosses and act, ruinously, if not reassured.

And, true, Earth was building more ships, launching new explorations in directions opposite to the Alliance base at Pell.

That *Earth* might someday make peace with the Fleet and amnesty them into its service again . . . that was, in his book, a very sensible fear for Union or Pell to have; but that *they themselves*, *Finity*, and *Norway*, would someday make peace with the Fleet? Not likely. Not with Edger in the ascendant among Mazian's advisors. Damn sure Mallory wouldn't. Union didn't remotely know Mallory *or* Edger if they ever thought that.

But then . . . Union hadn't had experienced military leaders when the War started. They'd learned tactics and strategy from the study tapes on which Union's education so heavily relied. But most of all they'd learned it from the Fleet they were fighting, as the whole human race hammered out the tactics and strategy of war at more than lightspeeds and with relativistic effects and no realtime communications at all. *He'd* learned Fleet tactics by apprenticeship to the Old Man and strategy from Mallory. The Fleet had developed uncanny skills and still did things Union pilots couldn't match. Union, on the other hand, sometimes did things that surprised you simply because it wasn't what one ought to do . . . if one had read the ancient *Art of War*, or if one had understood the Fleet.

Union was always hard to predict. Sometimes its actions were just, by traditional approaches, wrong. Union was now their ally.

"Where do you suspect Mazian is right now?" he asked Madison. The estimation could change by the hour. Like the market, only with more devastating local consequences.

"I have absolutely no idea," Madison said. "The way I don't know where Mallory is, either."

On the fine scale of the universe, that was not an unusual situation. "Do you think *she* knows where Mazian is?"

There was a longer silence than he'd expected, Madison thinking that one over, or thinking over whether it was needful baseline information, or a truth a senior-junior ought to figure out for himself. "I think Mallory knows contingency plans she'll never divulge. I think she knows a hell of a lot she'll never divulge. I think they're her safety, even from us. Loose talk could reach Union. I don't think their amnesty is worth a damn in her case."

"You think they'd go after her?"

"They'd be fools *right now* if they did. And I don't think they're fools. I think they'd like to know a lot more about her operations than they know. I think they lose a lot of sleep wondering whether someday we'll turn tables, make an understanding with Earth, and go after them. Earth trying to get a foothold back in space, establishing new starstations . . . in other directions . . . they view that with great suspicion."

"Do you think Earth might become a problem?"

"We don't think so currently. But after the War, when we couldn't get a peace to stick . . . you aren't old enough to remember. But we space farers had been homogenous so long we flatly had forgotten how to deal with divergent views, contrary interests, traders that we are. One thing old Earth is good at: diplomacy."

"Good at it!" He couldn't restrain himself. "Their diplomacy started the War!"

"Not on *their* territory," Madison said with a nasty smile. "The War never got to them, did it? When we and Union chased Mazian's tail back to Sol space and we lost him, it looked as if we were going to square off with the Union carrier . . . Earth mediated that little matter. We frankly didn't know what hit us. First thing we knew, we agreed, the Union commander agreed, each of us separately with Earth; then we had to agree with each other or Earth would have flung us at each other and watched the show from a distance. Learn from that. It's all those governments, all those cultures on one world. They're canny about settling differences. And we'd forgotten the knack. Four, five thousand years of planetary squabbles have to teach you something useful, I suppose." Madison folded up his input board and tucked the handheld into his operations jacket, preparing to leave. "I don't know if we could have made peace without Earth."

"Would we have made *war* without them, sir? In your opinion."

"Far less likely, too. We'd have been an adjunct of what's now at Union. But James Robert would have spit in their eye, still, when they tried to nationalize the merchanters. We'd have fought them. We'd have had every merchanter in space on our side. As we did. And we'd still have gained sovereignty on our own decks. As we did. Think about it. It's all we merchanters ever really gained from all the fighting we ever did. I just don't think we'd have blown Mariner doing it."

A Union spy had sabotaged a station—this station. Mariner. Pell had lost a dock during the War. Mariner had depressurized all around the ring, and tens of thousands of people who hadn't made it to sealed shelter had died. It was the worst human disaster that had happened outside of Earth. Ever.

And, *we merchanters*. It was the first time he'd ever heard anyone on *Finity* use that particular *we*. Or talk about a balance sheet, a profit-and-loss in the War. It was a sobering notion, that the War wasn't just the War, immutable, always there. There'd been a before. Was it possible there *would* be an after—and that they wouldn't have gained a damned thing by all they'd done, all the blood they'd shed?

Was it true, that even if you shoved at history and fought and struggled with its course, the universe still did what it was going to do anyway?

Hell if.

He couldn't accept that.

Madison went on his way to the bridge, needed there, and he went his.

He hadn't found his way past Madison's reticence to ask what no one had yet told him . . . the reason they'd split from Mallory, which he began to think held all the other answers. No better informed than before he'd snagged the second captain, JR picked up his own handheld and clipped it to a belt that did little else but hold it—a great deal like the pistol he'd once worn, back in the bad old days when fifteen-year-olds had gone armed everywhere on the ship.

They'd stopped doing that when they'd gotten through the business with Earth and when it was sure they'd moved Mazian's raiders out of the shipping lanes. What the likes of *Africa* and *Europe* had done when they boarded a merchanter didn't bear telling their younger crew, but he'd grown up with a pistol on his hip and instructions how to use it in corridors where you had to worry about a pressure blowout.

At fifteen he'd been instructed to blow out the corridor where he was *himself* if his only other prospect had been capture by the Fleet.

Helluva way to grow up, he supposed. It was the only life he'd known. And when they'd gotten past the worst of the mop-up, and when they could go through a jump-point without being on high alert—then the Old Man had called the guns in, and arranged that they'd be in lockers here and there about the ship, with no latch on the cabinets (nothing on *Finity* was locked), but not to be carried again. He'd felt scared when they'd taken the guns away. It had taken him this long to get over being scared.

And they hadn't ever had to use them. Their in-ship stand-down from arms had lasted and the Old Man had been right.

Maybe this stand-down from arms would last, too, and

maybe he needed to bear down harder on the study of Viking fish farms.

Laundry wasn't anybody's favorite assignment. After-jump meant a load of sweaty clothes. But it was better, Jeremy had said, than drawing the duty after liberty, because there was no limit to how many outfits somebody could get dirty on a two-week liberty, and there was a limit to how many clothes anybody totally tranked out could get dirty during jump. So they had the light end of things, and consequently they'd washed everything they had in the bins inside four hours. The better and worse of such assignments was a detail of spacer life Fletcher had never quite, somehow, imagined as potentially an item of curiosity and least of all his problem.

But he'd learned how to manage his personal property, on this particular detail. He'd learned, for instance, that by rules and regulations you left your last work clothes for cleaning in the laundry on your way out to liberty, like at Pell, and who-ever got next laundry duty (it *couldn't* be them, because the computer *never* doubled you on the same assignment) did all of it as they'd done, on the run out from dock.

So there were rhythms to the jobs they did. The laundry didn't always operate at the mad pace it had the last time. It was a burst of activity in this particular period, and then last-minute special cleaning for officers' uniforms.

He learned, for instance, that a crew member on *Finity* had an issue of clothing of which at least one dress and one work outfit stayed in the locker ready for board-call and undock schedules or a senior officer talked seriously to you about your wardrobe. A regular crew member took only flash stuff and civvies ashore on a liberty, and wasn't *allowed* to wear work stuff on dock unless he was working, which junior-juniors didn't have to do.

"So what if you wear work clothes?" he asked Jeremy as Jeremy worked beside him, having given him this piece of information. "Another talk with an officer?"

"Why don't you try it?" Vince asked from behind his back.

That was at least the third snide and uninvited remark. Vince was still on him about the drink from the bar last main-dark, from what he could figure; somehow that really bothered Vince.

"After all," Vince said, "you don't have to follow the rules. Not you."

"Cut it out," Jeremy said.

"Vince," Linda said.

"Well, he didn't, did he?"

"Vince," Jeremy said.

"I want to talk to you," Vince said to Jeremy, and those two went out in the corridor and stayed gone awhile.

"Is Jeremy all right?" Fletcher asked Linda, and Linda didn't look at him, quite. "Yeah. Fine," Linda said.

He was worried. Vince and Linda both were a little senior to Jeremy and he had the idea they were both leaning on the kid. His agemate. Him.

He'd personally had enough of Vince's notion of subtlety. Adrenaline was up, vibrating through him so he'd like to put Vince through the nearest wall if Vince crossed him one more time about the drink issue. But Vince was too small. At best he'd have to settle for bouncing Vince off the wall, which wasn't satisfying at all, or holding him a few inches off the deck, which had possibilities. But either would likely get him confined to the ship for a long, boring couple of weeks and he found he was looking forward to liberty. He really was. He figured he'd write home. He'd promised Bianca he'd write. Yes, she'd caved in, she'd saved her neck, her career. He couldn't blame her, now that he'd had time to think about it. He had a lot to tell her.

He'd write his foster-family, too. The Wilsons. Tell them he was all right. He owed them that. He'd heard that junior crew had an allowance and he'd asked Jeremy how much a letter cost: the answer was simply that letters didn't mass at all, in a ship's black box, and if you didn't want physical copy to go, it was ten c per link for handling.

That was a little more than he'd hoped, but a lot less than he'd feared, and Mariner was a single-hop from Pell as you

counted postage: jump-points, Jeremy said, didn't count, only
station hookups did; and for that ten c, they let you have a fair
amount of storage per letter.

He'd see Mariner and he'd write Bianca about it like a
diary. He was a little doubtful about the Wilsons, even shy
about writing to them, in the thought maybe they didn't want
a letter from him after the trouble he'd caused at the end, but
he'd eaten enough of their holiday dinners: he could afford the
cash at least to tell them he was all right, even if none of them
had come to see him off—for one thing because he didn't
depend on Quen to have even told them. She'd have known
they were a legal convenience—she'd set it up. But she probably didn't know, because he'd not mentioned it even to the
psychs, that they were the one batch he'd really liked, and
really called some kind of home.

He could write to Quen. One of those picture messages, the
really neon, garish ones, the sort spacers bought, if he were
going to send one to Quen. If it wouldn't cut seriously into his
spending money he'd be downright tempted just for the hell of
it. But something nice and sentimental for the two really he was
going to send, maybe the picture sort that you could print out in
holo. He didn't know whether Bianca or the Wilsons had ever
gotten a message from outside Pell, and he figured they'd keep
it and maybe like a picture they could repro and look at.

Jeremy and Vince came back. He looked at Jeremy for
bruises or signs of ruffling, but Jeremy didn't look to have
been disturbed, just a little hot around the edges and not
looking at anybody.

He couldn't ask Jeremy then and there what Vince had
wanted, or whether Vince had given him a hard time. Things
seemed peaceful. Vince and Jeremy settled to playing cards.
Business was so slow there wasn't an alterday crew into the
laundry once they closed up shop for the shift: their instructions
were to leave the laundry door open and the light on, however,
and put a check-sheet and a pen in the holder for people that
took soap and other things, so they could keep the reorder
records straight and know who'd picked up their clothes.

Doesn't anybody ever steal? he wondered, and then he

asked himself, Steal shower soap? And decided it was silly. It was free. Their own job as guardians of the laundry was largely superfluous once the washing and folding was all done: they had to clean up, latch down, be sure cabinet doors were shut tight and otherwise safed. Mostly they played cards. He figured at a certain point it was just a place for them to be, out of the way and bothering no one essential to the ship. Or maybe, at this stage of things, heading in, maybe everyone aboard was taking a breather. Traffic in the corridor was the lowest and slowest it had been.

As it happened, they didn't go straight to the mess hall this end of shift. Jeremy and he were supposed to check in with medical . . . again. It was a few minutes standing in line, but the staff didn't do anything but prick your finger, weigh you, and ask you a few questions, like: How are you sleeping? How are you feeling? With him it was, Glad to see you, Fletcher. Had any problems? How are the lungs?

In case he'd inhaled something on Downbelow. But he could say, for the second time, he hadn't. They stuck his finger, looked at his lungs, listened to him breathe . . .

"All fourteen million credits are safe," he said to the Family medics, and the medic looked at him as if it was a bad joke. Probably it was pretty low and surly humor.

"Do I get a liberty?" he asked.

"See no reason not," the medic in charge said.

"Thanks." He'd no desire to offend the medics, or get on somebody's report to JR. Clean record was his ambition right now, just get through it. Stay out of run-ins with JR, who alone of the officers seemed to be in charge of his existence. Get back to Pell. He had to produce a calm pulse for the medics and he'd done that, forgetful of Vince: he thought of green leaves and sun through the clouds, and when they dismissed him, he supposed they called him healthy.

Jeremy didn't get his lungs looked at. Jeremy just watched, cheerful again.

"So what was that with Vince?" He sprang the question on Jeremy as they walked toward the mess hall. And Jeremy's good mood evaporated.

"Oh, Vince is Vince," Jeremy said.

"If he gives you a hard time about me, you know, —let me know."

Jeremy looked at him, a dark eye under a shelf of hair that was usually shading his eyes. "Yeah," Jeremy said as if he hadn't quite expected that. "Yeah, thanks."

He'd felt obliged to offer. He guessed Jeremy hadn't expected much out of him and he knew Jeremy hadn't been completely happy to give up his (he now knew) single room to be the only junior-junior with a roommate. But Jeremy had been cheerful all the same, and stood up for him and tried to make the best of it, and that was fairly unusual in the string of people he'd lived with. In this kid, in this twelve-year-old body and combat-nerves mind, he had something ironically like the guys he'd used to hang out with when he was a little younger than Jeremy, guys well aside from what the sober adults in his life had wanted him to associate with. He'd been into a major bit of mischief until he'd wised up and gotten out of it.

But, along with the mischief he hadn't gotten into any longer, had gone the fellowship he hadn't had in the competitive Honors program. He'd invested in no friendly companionship since he'd gotten involved so deeply in his goals, except, well, Bianca, which had started out with a rush of something electric. But no guys, no one to play a round of cards with or hang about rec with. He'd evaded females in the crew. He'd let himself fall back into an earlier time when girls were something the guys all viewed from a distance, when guys were mostly occupied with looking good, not yet obsessed with hoping their inadequacies didn't show . . . he'd been through all of it, and he could look back with, oh, two whole years' perspective on the really paranoid stage of his life.

And maybe—he decided—maybe dealing with small-sized Jeremy in that sense felt like a drop back into innocence and omnipotence.

Like revisiting his own brat-kid phase, when vid-games and running the tunnels had been his total obsession. Getting away with it. Telling your friends how wonderful you were. Yes, he grew tired of hearing blow-by-blow accounts of maze-monsters and flying devils while Jeremy was beating him at cards, and the words *wild* and *dead-on* and *decadent* were beginning to make his nerves twitch; but there was something genuine and real in Jeremy that made him put up with the rough edges and almost regret that he'd lose Jeremy when his year of slavery was up. A few years ago, bitter and sullen with changes in his living arrangements, he'd have declined to give a damn—or to invest in a quasi-brother he'd lose. But he'd grown up past that; he'd had his experience with the Wilsons, and finally the Program; and somewhere in the mix he'd learned there was something you gained from the people that chance and the courts flung you up against, never a big gain, but something.

So, for all those tentative reasons, walking back to mess, he decided he *liked* his designated almost-brother, this round, among all the foster-brothers they'd tried to foist off on him. And if Vince leaned on Jeremy again tomorrow, he'd rattle Vince's teeth with no real effort and damn the consequences.

They played cards in the rec hall after supper this first evening in Mariner system, and he won his time back from Jeremy plus six hours. Jeremy blew a hand. That was something. Or he was getting suddenly, measurably better.

"Want to play a round?" It was one of the senior-juniors coming up behind his shoulder as he collected the cards. He'd forgotten the name, but the convenient patch on the jumpsuit said, *Chad.*

Jeremy scrambled up from the chair when Chad asked, dead-serious and looking worried. The room was mixed company, seniors out of engineering watching a vid, a couple of other card games, the senior-juniors over in the corner shooting vid-games, and this guy, one of their group, wanted to play.

It wasn't right. Jeremy's behavior said it wasn't right.

"Maybe you'd better play Jeremy," Fletcher said. "He's better."

Chad settled into the chair anyway, determined to have his

way. Chad looked maybe a little younger than JR, not much, big, for the body-age. Chad picked up the cards and dealt them. The stakes were already laid: get up and walk off from this guy, or pick up the cards. Jeremy's distress advised him this was somebody to worry about. He picked up the cards, hoping he could score that way.

Chad won the hand, a lapse of his concentration, his own fault. The guy didn't talk, didn't ask anything, just played a hand and won it. They'd bet an hour.

"My hour," Chad said. "You clean my room tomorrow, junior-junior."

"I guess I do," he said. He'd lost, fair and square. He didn't like it, but he'd played the game. He'd satisfied Chad's little power-play, didn't want another hand, in any foolish notion he could win it back against a good, a very good card player. He got up and left, and Jeremy caught him up in the corridor, not saying anything.

He felt he'd been played for the fool, though he was grateful for Jeremy's cues, and didn't want to talk about the bloody details of the encounter. More than embarrassed, he was angry. Chad was one of JR's hangers-on, crew, cronies, whatever that assortment amounted to, and JR hadn't been there; but at the distance of the corridor, he saw the game beneath the game, and he knew winning against Chad wouldn't have been a sign of peace.

"Did he cheat?" he asked Jeremy. He didn't think so, but he wasn't sure he'd have caught it, and he wanted to know that, bottom-level.

"No," Jeremy said, "but he's pretty good."

It was better than his suspicion, but it didn't much improve his mood. "Why don't you go on back?" he said. "There's no point. I'm going to bed."

"Me, too," Jeremy said, for whatever reason, maybe that things weren't entirely comfortable for a roommate of his in the rec hall right now. There'd been a pissing-match going on. My skull's thicker than yours head-butting. And why Chad had chosen to come over to their table and pick on him was a question, but it wasn't a pleasant question.

They got to the cabin, undressed.

"When we get to Mariner, you know," Jeremy said, awkwardly enthusiastic, "there's supposed to be this sort of aquarium place. It's wild. Really worth seeing, what I hear."

"Yeah."

"Well, we could kind of go, you know."

He let his surly mood spill over on Jeremy and Jeremy was trying to make the best of it. Least of anybody on the ship was Jeremy responsible for Chad's unprovoked attack on him.

He sat down on the bed; he thought about aquariums and Old River and how the fish had used to come up in the shallows, odd flat creatures with long noses. Melody had told him the name, but like no few hisa words, it was hisses and spits. They had an aquarium on Pell, too.

But it was an offer. It was something to do. Mostly he wanted to send his letters home. He didn't want Chad or anybody else setting him up for something. And the coming liberty was a time when they might be out from under officers' observation.

"I'm sorry," he said. "I'm kind of in a mood."

"Yeah," Jeremy said.

"You know I didn't want to be here. It's not my fault."

"Yeah," Jeremy said. "But you're all right, you know. I wish you'd been here all along."

He didn't. Especially tonight. But he couldn't say it to Jeremy's earnest, offering face. There was the kid, the twelve-year-old man, the—whatever Jeremy was—who wanted to go with Mallory and fight against the Fleet, the kid who got so hyped on vid-games he shook and jerked with nerves, and who wanted to tour an aquarium on Mariner—probably, Fletcher thought, a whole lot more exotic to Jeremy than it was to him. Jeremy shared what *he* wanted to do. Shared a bit of himself.

Wished he'd had his company. That was saying something.

And because the moment was heavy and fraught with might-have-been's, he ducked Jeremy's earnest look and bent down instead and pulled open his under-bunk storage.

Where more than next morning's socks resided. Where what was important to him resided.

In that moment of emotional confidences he took the chance, dug into the back of it and took out what Jeremy probably had never seen, something hands had made that weren't human hands.

"What's that?" Jeremy asked in astonishment, as he sat up and brought out the spirit stick. The cords unwound, feathers settling softly in the air, and the unfurling cords revealing the carvings in wood.

"Something someone gave me," he said. He was defensive of it, and all it was to him. He thought to this moment he was a fool for unveiling it. But Jeremy's reaction was more than he expected. It wasn't puzzlement. It was awe, amazement, everything he looked for in someone who'd know what he was looking at and appreciate what he treasured.

"It's hisa work," Jeremy said. "Where'd you get it?"

"It was a gift to me. That's where I lived. That's what I did. That's what I worked all my life to get into." He handed it across the narrow gap and Jeremy took it carefully in his hands, stick, cords, feathers, and all.

Jeremy handled it ever so carefully, looked at the carvings, at the cords, fingered the wood, and then looked closely at a feather, stroking it with his fingers. "I figure about the cords, maybe, but how'd they make *this*?"

He didn't know what Jeremy was talking about for a moment, and then by Jeremy's fingers on the center spine and the edges of the feather he realized. "It's a *feather*," he said, hiding amusement, and Jeremy instantly made his hands gentler on the object.

"You mean like it came off a bird?"

"Not quite like the birds on Earth. They don't fly much. They kind of glide. Some stay mostly on the ground. Downbelow birds."

"I never saw a feather close up," Jeremy said. "It's soft."

"Feathers from two kinds of birds. The wood comes from a little bush that grows on the riverbank. Cords are out of grasses. You soak it and put a stick in it and twist real hard while it's wet and it makes cord. There's a trick to sticking the next piece in just as you're running out of the last one, so they make a kind of overlay in the twist. I've watched them do it. They don't braid, that's not something they invented. But they do this twist technique. If you do a lot of them, you've got rope."

"Wild," Jeremy said, and fingered the cord and, irresistibly, the feathers. "That's really wild. I've seen vids of birds. I never saw a feather, like, by itself. Just from a distance."

"They fall off all the time. You're not supposed to collect them. Hisa do. But humans can't collect them."

"A bird with its feathers falling off." Jeremy thought that was funny.

So did he. "Not all at the same time. Like your hair falls out in the shower. A piece gets tired and falls out and a new one grows. It's kind of related to hair. Biologically speaking."

"That's really strange," Jeremy said. "Do you have a lot of this stuff?"

He shook his head. "I'm not supposed to have this one, but it was a gift and the authorities didn't argue with me. The cops somehow got me past customs."

"What's this stuff mean? It's not writing."

"They don't write. But they make symbols. I'm not sure in my own head what the difference is, but the experts say it isn't writing."

"This is so strange," Jeremy said. "What's it mean?"

"Day and night. Rain and sun. Grain growing." He became aware that rain and sun, day and night, were words like the feather, alien to Jeremy, with all they meant. Spacers didn't say morning and evening. It was first shift, second shift. They didn't say day and night. It was mainday, maindark, alterday, alterdark. And twilight was a time the lights dimmed and brightened again, mainday's twilight, alterday's dawn. Stationers were like that, too. But on Downbelow you rediscovered the lost words, the words humans had used to have, words that clicked into a spot in your soul and took rapid, satisfying hold.

Maybe that was why they had to bar humans from Downbelow, and let down only a privileged, special few who could agree not to pick up feathers or stones.

"The little stones," he remembered to say, "water smoothed

them. They tumble over one another in the bottom of Old River as the water flows, just rubbing against each other." He took account of Jeremy's literal interpretation of molting feathers, and remembered a question he'd asked of a senior staffer. "You don't ever see them move. But when Old River floods, it tumbles them."

Jeremy looked at him as if to see if that was a joke of any kind, and felt the smoothness of the stones. "I was going to ask how," Jeremy said. "That's so, so wild. I'm used to old rocks . . . but these must have been tumbling around a long time."

"Rocks in space are older," he said. "Water's just pretty powerful. It carves out cliffs, changes course, floods fields. Gravity makes it fall from high places to low places and whatever's in the way, it flows around it or over it."

"How's it get high in the first place?"

"Rain. Springs." More miracle words to Jeremy. He didn't think Jeremy knew what a spring was.

But Jeremy wanted to know things. That was what engaged him. Jeremy wanted to know. He could liken some things to what Jeremy did know: condensation on high dockside conduits. The big drops that hit you on the head when you were near the gantries.

"It's just past monsoon, now," he said, dazed to admit the unfelt time-flow that *Jeremy* took for granted. "Hisa females will be pregnant, grain will be sprouting in the fields and in the frames. There's a kind that only grows with its roots in mud. There's a kind that only grows on dry land, in the open fields. We interfered to improve the yield, but the thinking now is that we shouldn't have, that it'd be a lot better if we'd left the hisa alone and not had them working on the station or anything."

Jeremy handed the stick back carefully. "Do you think so?" Maybe Jeremy heard the disbelief in his voice. Do you think so? Jeremy asked straight into his privately-held, his cherished heresy. None of the staffers had ever seen it. But Jeremy did. And deserved an answer he'd never give, in hearing of Pell authorities, who could bar him from the planet as dangerous.

"I think maybe they'd gain something from developing at their own pace." The cautious apology to official policy. But he plunged ahead. "Or maybe they'd gain things from us we never thought of. Or they might die out without us. You know there aren't that many sites in the world where there *are* hisa. World population's given to be, oh, maybe twenty million."

"That's a lot."

"Not for a planet. Not at all for a planet."

Jeremy was quiet for a moment. "Dead-on that Earth's got a lot." Jeremy had been there, Jeremy had said so. The fabled and unreliable motherworld. Wellspring of everything they knew about planets. All the preconceptions, all the right and wrong perceptions.

"Yeah," he said. "That's our model. That's what we know in the universe. That's *all* else we know and it's a pretty small sample. Twenty million hisa on Downbelow. A lot fewer platytheres on Cyteen."

"They're not intelligent."

"They don't seem to be." What he knew said that Cyteen's platytheres had gotten too successful for their own environment, deforested vast tracts that then became prey to weather patterns. And human beings on Cyteen had determined the planet was more useful and more viable if they killed them all. Environmental scientists on Pell were aghast.

But nature sometimes killed itself. Not all life succeeded. Could life intervene to save life, when the end result would be extinction, or did nature know best?

He wasn't sure. It was *all* human judgment. The hisa had watched the sky for as long as hisa remembered, from before humans left Earth. Waiting for something to happen from their clouded, starless sky. Was it a cultural dead end they'd reached?

"You know a lot of stuff," Jeremy said.

"I'm two years short of a degree in Planetary Science. You know? It's my *life*. It's what's important to me. And somebody aboard asked me why study planets."

"Because you want to know!" Jeremy said, which did a lot to patch that young woman's careless dismissal. "Because you want to know stuff. I do, anyway."

"I don't think what I know is real useful here."

"You know science, don't you?"

"A lot of life science."

"Well, tell JR. I'll bet he'd be interested. Life science is what keeps us breathing, case of what's important, here. You probably ought to talk to Jake. He's the bioneer."

"Probably I should," he said, "talk to Parton, that is." Dealing with JR, he preferred to keep to a minimum. "Maybe I *could* do something besides laundry."

"Oh, everybody does laundry sooner or later," Jeremy said. "Just the chief engineer sends all the junior engineers to do it, right along with maintenance, and the chief doesn't unless he loses a bet. But you 'prentice to Jake, is what you do. Me, I'm off studies for the last couple of jumps because I'm watching you so you don't turn green and die. Usually I'm on study tape. That's where Vince goes after shift. That's where Linda goes. You just do sims until there's a rush on, and then they call you in, like me, I do beginner pilot sims and scan sims, because if I don't make the cut when I'm big enough, you know, for the real test stuff, there's got to be something for me to do. God, I *really* don't want to do scan. I really hate it." Jeremy was slapping his fist against his leg, that nervousness he got from vid-games; now Fletcher knew where it came from. "But even if I make Helm, I'll have to sit Scan in a crisis. Same as Linda. She likes it, though. She thinks it's great."

"What's Vince?" He had to know. The set wasn't complete.

"Vince, he's Legal. That's what he wants to do, can you believe it? That and archive and files and library. It's about the same. Records."

Vince at a desk, doing painstaking work. A lawyer. A librarian. Their hothead wanted to keep books? The mind didn't easily form that image. Plead in court? The judge would throw *Vince* in jail.

"I think you ought to talk to Jake, though," Jeremy said.

"I'm sure they've got my records." They don't care, was in his mind. But also there was the glimmer of a use for himself. Not the use he wanted, but it was using something he knew and having contact with the systems on a ship that did technically interest him. A foam-steel planet, in those respects, recycling its atmosphere and doing so in systems he wanted to see.

"You want *me* to talk to Jake?" Jeremy asked.

"I'll talk to him, sooner or later." He tucked the stick back into the drawer, and shut it. "Right now I guess it's enough I don't turn green and die."

"Medical said let you go through maybe four, five jumps before you do anything like tape. The captains used to not let any of us do it. Used to make us learn with books. But the information just comes too fast, that's what Paul said. Helm said if pilots could do tape-sims to keep their skills up then the rest of us weren't going to go azi-fied on a calculus tape. I'm glad. Dead-on I'd *be* an azi if I had to learn calculus out of a book. You'd just see the blank behind the eyes . . . " Jeremy gave his rendition of an automaton. "Did you learn from books on Pell?"

"Tape, mostly. Lots of tape. Same thing. They've come round to thinking it's all right. I brought some with me, —All right, I lied. I've got tapes. Some of the environmental stuff. My biochem." Just the pretty ones, those first of all. The ones with pictures of home. His home. He didn't think he could take them right now. It still hurt too much. "You can try one if you want." Turning Jeremy into somebody he could really *talk* to about Downbelow was a bonus he hadn't expected when he'd packed the tapes. But that seemed possible, and his spirits were higher than they had been since he'd boarded.

"Yeah," Jeremy said. "Sure! Wild! Can I borrow one tonight?"

He opened the drawer, took out his tape case, took out a pretty one.

And hesitated. "It could be scary for you. I don't know. It's a planet. You feel the weather. Thunder and all. It's a pretty good effect."

"Oh, hell," Jeremy said. "Can't be that bad." Jeremy took the tape and opened the wall panel at the side of his bunk, looking for pills.

"Take a quarter-dose, no more. This is stationer tape. *Planetary* tape. Lightning and reverse-curve horizons. If you climb the walls tonight it won't be my fault."

Jeremy grinned at him and shook out a pill. He split it. Offered the other half to him.

He opted for the biochem tape for his own reader. It wasn't jump they faced, just a night's sleep, and a night of no dreams but the ones the tape provided—a Downbelow tour for Jeremy and a night of life process chemistry for him.

He didn't care that he was into Chad for a room cleaning. He settled down with the headset and the tape going and with the drug that flattened out your objections to information coursing through his bloodstream.

It was the first time he'd taken tape aboard. It was the first time he'd trusted the people he was with enough to take that drug that made you so helpless, so compliant, so ready to believe what you were told. You didn't learn around strangers. You didn't, in his own experience, do it anywhere but locked in your own private room, safe from outside suggestion, but he felt safe to try, finally, in Jeremy's presence.

It meant a good night's sleep, a night in which he was back in things he knew and terms he understood. You forgot little details if you didn't use what you learned; tape could sharpen up what was getting hazy in your mind, and if he talked to Jake in engineering as Jeremy suggested, about getting into something that offered a little more headwork, he wanted to be sharp enough to impress Jake and not sound a fool if Jake asked him questions. This time through the old familiar tape he set his subconscious to wonder about things that a closed system like a ship's lifesupport might find problematic, and he wondered what tapes the ship's technical library might have that would let him brush up on specifics of the systems. The ship *had* a library. They might let him have tapes to study. If they trusted *him*, which had become an unexpected hurdle.

Talk to JR? Not damned likely.

Chapter XIII

"There's a problem," Bucklin put it, warning JR what was coming, and after that there was a junior staff meeting, a quiet and serial staff meeting, pursued down corridors, anywhere JR could find them. JR found Vince and Linda, among the first, in A deck main corridor, and made them late reporting to breakfast.

"What's this with a Welcome-in?" he asked. "I said, did I not, let him alone?"

There were frowns. There were no effective answers.

He found Connor topside, B deck, and said, "It's off. No hazing. My orders."

He found Sue and Nike in A deck lifesupport, and asked, "Whose damn idea was it in the first place?"

He didn't get a satisfactory answer. What he got was, "He's a problem. He's a problem in everything, isn't he?"

He found Chad, and said, "If he cleans your room, Chad, he just cleans it. You keep your hands off him or you and I are going to go a round."

Chad wasn't happy.

He went the whole route. Lyra and Wayne, Toby, and Ashley, all glum faces and unhappy attitudes.

And after he thought that he'd made the issue crystal clear, at mid-second shift he had a delegation approach him in the sim room, next to the bullet-car that reeked of the cold of the after holds. He was going in, not out, but he was still mentally hyped for the pilot-sims his career-track mandated—sims that *didn't* have anything to do with Pell's vid-game amusements. It was high-voltage activity that maintained his ability to track on high-V emergencies, just as Helm had had to do when it met the Union carrier, and his state of mind at the moment was not optimal for intricate interpersonal politics. Bucklin had to know that.

It was Wayne and Connor, Toby, Chad and Ashley who pulled the ambush, and they'd done it in the cramped privacy of the core-access airlock, a small sealed room with a pressure door between it and the main A-deck corridor. It was only them, they could talk without senior crew in the middle of it, and *Bucklin*, damn him, had unexpectedly chosen to become their spokesman. JR found himself ready to blow, given just a little encouragement.

"The question is," Bucklin said as JR stood with his hand on the call-button that would give him the sim-car and take him away from their bedeviling. "The question is, this is what we've always done. Omitting it says something."

He dropped his hand from the button. Clearly he wasn't going to solve this in two seconds. Clearly, like dealing with Union carriers, sometimes the situation tested not one's speed in handling a matter, but one's self-control.

"Always isn't this time," he said to the group. "The guy is *not* one of us, he *didn't* grow up in our traditions, he *doesn't* know what we're up to, and we don't communicate all that well with that stationer-trained brain of his."

"It seems to me," said Ashley, "that those are *exactly* the reasons for having a Welcome-in."

"No," he said, and drew a calm breath. "The answer is *no*. It's an order."

"We did it for Jeremy," Wayne pointed out. Wayne, next to Bucklin and Lyra, was their levelest head. "It was important then. It made lot of difference."

"And I'm telling you we can't do it for Fletcher. For one thing, the Old Man would have the proverbial cat. For another, he's a *stationer*."

"That's the problem, isn't it, up and down the list?" Chad said. "He's a stationer. He doesn't give a damn about this ship. He walks up, does as he pleases in front of everybody at the bar and thumbs his nose at you, and all of us—and nobody ever called him on it."

"I called him on it. Immediately."

"Yes, and he walked off. He roughs up Vince, he doesn't stay for gatherings . . . say hello to him and you get stared at."

"Did you hear the word *order,* Chad? I *order* you to let this drop."

"Yessir, we hear, but—"

"We don't think a Welcome-in is as important as it used to be," Toby said, all earnestness, "or what? Is this part of the Old Rules? I thought it *was* the Old Rules. I thought that was what we were always hanging on to. I thought it was important to do the traditions. We're going to have babies on this ship. Are we not going to welcome *them* in when they come up, or what?"

"I'm saying—" He faced a handful of juniors who'd survived all the War could throw at them. Who'd kept the traditions intact. Who hadn't given up the principles, the history, the *honor* of the ship. And who could tell them that the practices of a Welcome-in, centuries old, were stupid, silly, ridiculous?

The junior captain, the officer in charge of the juniors, wasn't even supposed to be involved in this, and *traditionally* speaking, hadn't been and hadn't sought it. He'd gotten involved at all, point of fact, because he'd given an order first not to do it in this case, and then to wait, and now they'd come back to him to argue for now rather than later, because his order was in their way. It was crew business and not *his* business, by centuries-old habit. There was a tradition in jeopardy here just in their having to confront him.

And more serious to the welfare of the ship, their unity, their way of defining who was who, their way of including someone new in the traditions—all that was threatened. His position, like Bucklin's, was defined by the lofty track toward the captaincy, but theirs was a network of relations with each other that would define all of their lifetime of working together. And he was looking down on it all from officer-height and saying, It's not that important—at a time when the crew as a whole was facing the greatest and most profound change in its mission since it had become, de facto, Mallory's backup.

They were feeling robbed. Robbed of their war, their victory, their outcome. He understood that. None of them liked what they saw as being sent away from a conflict that had cost them heavily. And he saw, staring into that lineup of faces, and taking in the fact that they were all male, that there was also the men-women issue. Lyra and Linda, female, made a small but separate society: their children, when they chose to get them, from whomever they chose to get them, were the hope of the ship, the hope, the future of *Finity's End*. Young men, and it was specifically the young men of the crew who'd come to him . . . they were the tradition-keepers, the teachers: men had their importance to a merchanter Family not in getting children, but in *being* Family, in bringing up their sisters' and their cousins' children. They were the guardians of tradition; and they were, potentially, men on a ship with a damaged tradition, a shattered ship's company, too *damn* many dead *Finity* brothers with too little memory on the part of the outside as to who'd died and what heroic sacrifices they'd made away from the witness of stationers and worlds. There were all too many small, funny, or touching stories that had died with this uncle or that cousin, stories of the ship's finest hours that never would find their way into *Finity's* archive, or into the next generation.

The men of *Finity's End* alone knew *what* they were. The ship hadn't been able to leave Fletcher to the ordinary existence of a stationer, but they hadn't brought him in, either. Only the men could do that.

They were right. And after giving a halfway yes, he'd delayed too long. He'd weakened. He'd already gotten himself on the gravity slope by agreeing it had to be done.

"I'm still saying *wait*," he said, trying to recover what authority his wavering had undermined. Unpleasant lesson and one he was determined to remember. "I'm saying—just— whenever you do it, go easy. He's *not* a kid *or* a senior. He's had all those several years of waking transactions Jeremy hasn't had, and for all I can figure, his mind did something during those years besides learn algebra, all right? He's not a ship kid. Give him some credit for the age he looks—the way I did, dammit, over the damn drink. I think he's due that."

"He looks like you and me," Bucklin was quick to remind him. "When he hits Mariner dockside, nobody but us is going to know how old he is. And we're responsible for him."

"I say he's gained a little more maturity than Jeremy. You're right he's got a body that mixes with adults, not kids. A body that's mostly done with its growing. He's Jeremy with a body at its fastest and his nerves a lot more under control. It's got to make a difference. He's been dealing with adults as an adult on station. Jeremy hasn't."

"You're not supposed to know about what goes on," Chad said, "officially speaking. You don't know about it."

"I'm saying use your common sense!"

"That's fine," Wayne said, "and we agree, sir, but you still don't know about it. You're not supposed to have been this far involved with it. Let us. That's what this is about. He's not *one* of us yet. He doesn't know us. We don't know him."

"Yeah," he said reluctantly, "I still don't know about it."

They left. He stood there, wired for the sim, literally. And telling himself he shouldn't interfere.

Then that the potential for someone getting hurt was high. And that they'd probably do it sometime during evening rec. An ambush in one's quarters was the usual. A gang showed up, hauled you off to a storage area and ran you through the same silliness everybody endured once, during which you agreed who was senior and who wasn't.

If he interfered and the crew found out he had, he could create a major problem, in their sense of betrayal.

But a *Finity* youngster knew exactly what was happening to him. He knew he wasn't being killed. He knew it was a joke.

He put in a call to legal, to Madelaine's office. "Call Fletcher up there," he said to Blue, who took the call. "I want to talk to him. I don't want the whole ship to know."

"Problem?" Blue asked.

"Not yet," he said.

The laundry was still quiet, so quiet it was down to cards, Jeremy teaching him the trick shuffle and Fletcher about to concede that small fingers had their advantage. Linda was watching—"Never got it myself," Linda said—when Vince drifted in, and one of the seniors came with him.

"Thought you were going to clean my cabin," Chad said.

"Yeah, well," Fletcher said, and decided he wasn't going to learn the shuffle in another round and he might as well do what he'd gotten himself into. He got up, gave Jeremy his cards back and Chad gave him the cabin number, A39, a fair distance around the rim.

"You do a good job," Chad admonished him.

"Yeah," he said, and left, telling himself he wasn't playing cards with Chad again until there was revenge involved. He stopped by his own cabin and picked up cleaning cloths, in the case Chad's place wasn't supplied, and told himself Chad had probably trashed the place just to make his life difficult.

A39. He opened the unlatched door. Stared in shock at Chad, among a gathering of cousins packed into the room. "Sorry," he said, thinking at first blink he might have interrupted some private gathering.

"No, come on in," one said. He didn't recall the name. The family resemblance was close and common among all of them. He thought, well, maybe they were being friendly, walked the rest of the way in, had just the least second's inkling of something wrong in their expectant expressions, and was standing there with the cleaning supplies in his hands when the cousin at the end of the bed bounced up between him and the door and pushed the shut button. The door closed. Still, joke, he thought.

The lights went out.

He ducked. He'd been in ambushes before. He knew one when it came down around him, and he dropped the cleaning packets and tried to get at the door button by blind accuracy in the dark. They were just as canny, and grabbed him as he was trying to reach it, piled on him, shouting at the others that they had him as they carried him painfully down to the floor between the end of the bunk and the wall.

He got an arm free. He hit somebody. They pinned him down and then came a loud ripping sound like cloth torn. They tried to hold his head as somebody tried to tape his face and got his hair. He bucked as they continued sitting on him, he tried to get knees or a foot into action, scored once someone else sat on his legs, but they still managed to get tape wrapped around his face.

"Watch his nose, watch his nose," somebody said, "don't cut his air off."

It was a stupid kid game and he was It. He'd been It before, and he didn't want any part of it or them. He kept fighting, but it was a cramped space and somebody was winding cord around his feet, struggle as he would.

At the same time they pasted tape across his eyes and one cheek, hard, got it across his mouth in spite of his spitting and cursing. He was running out of wind and there were enough of them finally to twist his arms together and get cord around his hands, and sloppily around his body. He couldn't get enough air past the tape and a nose gone stuffy from being hit, and meanwhile they picked him up like a half-limp package and slung him onto the bed. He hit his head on somebody's leg and stars shot through his vision.

"Fights damn good," somebody said, and there was a lot of panting and spitting and sniffing, while the cousin he'd collided with swore and while he tried to find a target to kick with both feet. "Hey, enough of that!"

They flung bedclothes around him, wrapped him, as he guessed, in blankets, and then hauled him up and over somebody's shoulder, for another toss—he had no idea. Being head down with someone's shoulder in his gut made it hard to breathe. Blood rushing to his head made his nose stuff up worse. He tried to kick, tried to advise the damn fools holding him he was having trouble breathing, but they carried him— out the door, because there was nowhere in the room to go with him. Out the door, down the corridor with him blind-folded to the light and choking and struggling all the way.

"Stay still," somebody said, slapping him on the back, and they went onto a different-sounding floor, like metal. Sounds reached him then of elevator doors closing, then of a lift working, as the floor dropped.

He kicked wildly, tried to score in the cramped space, running out of air as they reached the bottom. They carried him out of the lift into the ice-cold he'd felt only in the freezer, and he heard the ring of their steps on metal grid as they walked.

It was the freezer, it *was* the damn galley freezer they'd brought him to. He began to think he'd pass out, maybe die in their stupidity. Or of purpose. He didn't know now. He might never know. He'd be dead and they'd catch hell.

The guy carrying him dumped him down and let his feet hit the floor. The pressure in his head shifted as they pushed him back against cold pipe, and somebody tore the tape off his mouth.

He sucked in a fast deep gasp of ice-cold air and found something like pipe and steps against his back, metal so cold it burned the bare skin of his hands. He was still blind, he was still tied hand and foot, his head was still pounding and his brain was hazed from want of oxygen.

Something touched his face, burning hot or burning cold, he couldn't tell.

Then they left him. He thought they did.

"Hey!" he yelled, and tried to hold himself up, unbalanced as he was, lost his balance and fell—into someone's arms. They shoved him and he fell toward somebody else, and around, and around. He knew the game. At any moment somebody *wouldn't* catch him and he'd hit the metal floor, but he couldn't save himself, couldn't do a damned thing unless he could get his balance.

They laughed. There were at least ten, twelve of them. High voices, girls, among the others.

One caught him, held him upright. He hung there shivering and heard the quiet shuffling of steps, the panting breaths around him.

"We have here Fletcher," that one said. "Who am I, Fletcher? Do you know?"

"Chad." He knew the voice. He'd never in his life forget it.

"You're right." Chad tossed him off balance. Another caught him.

"Do you know me?" another voice asked.

"Go to hell," he said. He'd like to bring a knee up. With his feet tied, he couldn't. They spun him around and tossed him from one to the next, until they stopped and somebody sawed free the cords holding his feet.

He kicked. And missed, being blind.

"Temper, temper," the voice said.

"Find us, Fletcher," a female voice called to him, echoing in distance and metal dark. "Find us and name us and you're free."

"He doesn't know our names." Male voice, on his left. Footsteps echoing on metal grid.

"Fletcher." A voice he did know. Vince.

"Damn you, brat." It was still another direction. He was blind. He had no concept what the place was shaped like, whether he could blunder off an edge, down steps . . .

"Fletcher." Another voice. Older.

"Fletcher!" Jeremy. "Fletcher, come to *me*!"

Jeremy was in on it. He stopped turning, stopped playing their game at all, no matter how they called.

"Fletcher, come here, come this way."

"Fletcher!"

"I said go to hell!" he yelled.

An icy bath of liquid hit him, full in the chest. He jerked, and convulsed, and spat, and fell, hard, helplessly, on the grating.

"Dammit!" a male voice yelled. "Sue!"

He heard movement around him. He was drenched, in bitter, burning cold. He couldn't get his legs to bear under him, he began to shiver so, muscles knotting so it drove his knees together and his elbows against their ordinary flex. He'd hurt his arm on the grating. It burned with a different fire.

"Who am I?" a female voice said. "Try again."

He couldn't talk coherently. He was shivering so violently he couldn't get his jaws to work.

"Hey, guys," somebody said in a warning tone. Someone was close to him. He tried to defend himself with a kick, but that one touched his face, got the edge of the tape on his cheek, and then pulled away the tape across his eyes, ripping brows and strands of hair along with it.

He was lying soaked, still with his hands tied, in the dark, and their faces were lit with a lantern on the echoing metal grid, so they assumed a horror-show aspect, gathered all around him against tall cannisters and girders and machinery. It wasn't the freezer. It was somewhere else. Chad was there. He knew that broad face. Vince and Linda were there. *Jeremy* was there, not saying a thing.

He just stared at Jeremy. Even when they introduced themselves, one by one, and said he had to learn the names to get loose, he just stared at Jeremy.

"My name's Jeremy," Jeremy said when it was his turn to talk, "and I was the last they did this to. It's a Welcome-in, Fletcher, you got to go along with it, you got to say what they say and learn the stuff and then you're one of us, that's all, for good and ever. Welcome in."

He didn't know whether he ever wanted to talk to Jeremy again. What Jeremy said he didn't doubt in the least: it was some form of Get the New Guy and he was supposed to bend to the group and kiss ass until they'd gotten their bluff in.

But it wasn't just roughhousing. They'd put bruises on him and half-frozen him, soaking him with water, they'd dumped him on the burning cold deck, and he didn't give a damn what else they were doing, or threatened to do, he wasn't playing their silly games to get In with them, not if he froze to death.

He started memorizing names and faces, all right. They wanted him to, and he would, to remember where he owed what and for how long. He knew Chad, who'd started this and set him up, and he learned Wayne who was the second voice, who'd shoved him, and Connor, and a thin-faced girl named Lyra. Ashley was another thin one, the quietest voice, Sue was a broad-faced girl with a cleft in her chin, and that voice and her name had accompanied the water; Wayne had protested it. *There* were two different scores. They sat there in the dark, lit up like a horror show and going on with their stupid game, while he shivered and his hair stopped dripping, probably frozen. They told him how he was welcome to the ship, and how it was a great ship, and how he was lucky to be a Neihart and how he'd put up a good fight.

Fine, he thought. They hadn't seen *fight* yet.

He didn't talk, not even when Jeremy tried to get him to say it was all right.

At least he was getting numb, and the fingers had stopped hurting.

Wayne got up and so did Ashley; the two of them took hold of him, pulling him to his feet. "We'd better get him warm," Wayne said.

"He never said the names," Sue protested.

"He's freezing his ass off!" Wayne said. "Get the knife, get the damn cords off."

The lift thumped into operation. It was coming down. Connor was saying it wasn't good enough. He was trying just to stand, telling himself if they'd just listen to Wayne he might get out of this.

"Ease off," someone said. "Someone's coming."

Rescue? He asked himself. An officer?

His knees were shaking so they almost tore the ligaments. He staggered off to the side, and hit a pole and leaned on it, that being all he could do to stand up.

"What in hell are you doing?" Male. Young as the rest. He was losing his ability to stay on his feet. He wanted to fall down, and all that saved him was the fact his chilled knees wouldn't unlock. "God, he's *frozen*! He's all over ice. Get him topside, into the warm!"

"We can't take him topside!" Connor said. "Clean him up, first, get him some clothes or there'll be hell."

There was argument about it. He stopped following it. The consensus was take him to the cargo office where they could bring down heat; but he couldn't walk on his own—they dragged him across to the wall, and opened a door, and flung a light on that blinded him after the scant light of the lantern. Wayne had him stand with his forehead against the wall, his eyes sheltered from the punishing light, and cut the cords on his upper body, and his hands—that was all right. Then somebody yanked his coveralls off his shoulders. They cracked with ice. Warmer cloth landed on his back, somebody's coat tucked around him, a coat warm from someone's wearing it.

They fussed about getting heat started, and a fan began blowing warm air in. They stripped the coveralls the rest of the way off and wrapped coats around him, made him sit in an ice-cold chair, at which he protested, and they contributed another coat. He was starting to shiver so his teeth rattled.

"He could lose his ears," somebody said, the new one, the junior officer; after that there was a lot of protest back and forth around him, about who'd thrown the water and how he'd fallen and cut his arm and whether his fingers and ears were all right. Chad maintained that they were and they hadn't had time to freeze, but Lyra, more to the point, held her warm hands close to his head and tried to warm them up, and it hurt.

Then Jeremy showed up, out of breath, with dry clothes and a blanket.

"I got them from the room," Jeremy said, his kid's voice shaking whether from the running or from fright. "I got the heavy ones."

He took the clothes. He levered himself out of the chair and a tumble of coats in his soaked and mostly frozen under-wear, no longer giving a damn about females present. He dressed, beginning as he struggled with the clothes to feel pain in his hands again, and in the joints he'd sprained simply in shivering. The cord had left marks on his skin. His elbow was cut from his fall. The tape had ripped his face and left it sore. His hair trailed around his face, dripping again, after being stiff with ice.

"Are you all right?" Jeremy wanted to know. "Fletcher, God, —are you all right? It was a joke. That's all, it was sup-posed to be a joke."

Jeremy was upset. Jeremy *was* sorry. Jeremy alone of all of them had meant it for a joke. Stupid kid.

Wayne had seen things going to hell and used his head. The young officer had found out and come after them. The rest—

They were somewhere in the depths of the passenger ring rim. It was uncompromisingly dark and cold outside the little office. It was hard to think of braving that dark and going out there again to get to the lift they'd come down in; but he wanted to get out of here in one piece and back to A deck, if they'd just let him, if they weren't going to try to cover up what they'd done or try to threaten him to silence.

He took an uncertain step toward the door. Two. He could have gone hypothermic if they'd left him much longer, and he'd given them all a show, because he'd really been scared. He was still scared, because he didn't know what they'd do, and because if he didn't get himself away from them, maybe they didn't know yet, either.

"Fletcher," the newcomer said. Bucklin. That was the name. JR's shadow. Bucklin had caught his arm. "This went too far. Way too far."

"Damn right it did." He managed that much coherently, and shook off the hand, wanting the door.

"Just a minute," Bucklin said.

Just a minute was too long, way too long to spend with them. But when Bucklin made him look back, he saw the one he wanted, zeroed in on Chad right behind Bucklin's shoulder, and hit Chad square in the jaw. Chad teetered over a chair, fell back into the office wall and knocked another conference chair over.

Fletcher touched the door control with a throbbing knuckle, only wanting out of this place and away from their welcomes and their double-crossing.

"Chad!" Lyra yelled out, and he spun around as Chad barreled past Bucklin and startled cousins tried to stop him. He used the chance the grappling cousins gave him and punched Chad in the face.

Cousins grabbed him, too, and held on.

"Easy, easy, easy." The one holding his right arm was Bucklin.

"I'll kill him," he said, and Chad charged back at him, dragging cousins with him. He got hold of Chad's collar and the collar ripped; Chad hit him in the gut and he kept going, lit into Chad with a left and a head-shot right, out of breath, crazed, until two cousins had his arms in separate locks and Chad tried to use that to advantage. Fletcher kicked out, caught Lyra by accident as she was trying to back Chad up.

"Easy!" Bucklin said into his ear, dragging back at him. He

was sorry to have hit Lyra, who'd warned him in the counter-attack. Chad never had laid a good hit on him, but Chad's face was bloody. And Jeremy was in the way now.

"Easy," Jeremy said. "Fletcher, Fletcher, —easy. It's all right. We're getting out of here, all right? We're getting out of here . . . we'll go home."

"Name's Bucklin," Bucklin said, and put pressure on the arm. "Lieutenant over the juniors. This is officially over. It got way out of hand. Way beyond what anybody intended. I'm going to let you go, now, Fletcher. I want you to stand still a minute. I want you to hear apologies, and I want everybody involved in this to stand and deliver loud and clear. Do you hear me, Fletcher?" There was a pat on his shoulder, and he was trembling, partly with the strain on an arm he didn't want broken and partly from unresolved nerves. "They'll apologize. No more fighting. Have I got that, Fletcher?"

"I don't want *anything* from them," he said, out of breath. Bucklin's hold on his arm let up anyway. "Let him go," Bucklin said, and had to repeat it: "Let him go," until the other guy—it was Wayne—let go from his side.

"Apologies," Lyra said before he could bolt. She was limping. "Major sorry, here, Fletcher. Bucklin's right. Way too much."

It was hard to walk out on a girl he'd kicked in a fight by accident. He stood still, burning mad. Linda apologized, a sheepish mumble. Sue did. "I threw the water," Sue said. "Bad judgment."

Damn premeditated, he thought, regarding Sue. Liquid water? Out there in that cold? She'd brought it down here, with clear intent to use it.

The rest of them, the guys, he wasn't even interested in hearing. He opened the door and walked off, blind in the dark except for the dim glow of the lift call button that guided him across the gratings. He hit ice. His foot skidded, costing his knee on the recovery.

"Fletcher!" Jeremy called after him, but he kept walking. Jeremy came clattering over the grids, overtook him and tried to hold his hand from the call button. He had such an adrenaline load on he hardly felt it, and could have brushed Jeremy off, oh, three or four meters into the dark without half trying.

"I'm sorry," Jeremy said. "Fletcher, we're *all* sorry."

"That's fine," he said, and the lift door opened. He saw the choices, RIM, A, and B. He took A, and rode it up alone to an astonishingly normal corridor, where nothing had happened and two seniors walking by didn't notice anything unusual about him.

He went to his cabin, took off the clothes he'd just put on, and showered until he'd both warmed up and cooled off.

When he came out of the shower, still with the trap replaying itself in shadows in recent memory, he found Jeremy had come home, and was sitting on his bed shuffling cards.

He gave Jeremy the cold eye and picked up his clothes and started dressing.

"I'm sorry as hell," Jeremy said. Expressions like that jarred, from a twelve-year-old's mouth. But Jeremy *was* twelve. He hadn't bucked his cousins to warn him, but what could he expect of a twelve-year-old?

Still, he let the silence continue, if only to learn what would fall out of it.

"They always do it," Jeremy said plaintively. "To welcome you in."

"Is *that* what it is?" He fastened his coveralls and sat down to pull on his boots. The adrenaline still hadn't run out. He could put his fist through something, but Jeremy was the only target he had.

"They shouldn't have thrown the water," Jeremy said. "That was pretty stupid."

"The whole thing was pretty stupid," he said, with a bitter taste in his mouth. "I know the game. You could have said something to warn me. You know that? You could have said something."

"You aren't supposed to know," was Jeremy's lame excuse.

"So everything's fine now. You just beat hell out of me, damn near suffocate me with the tape, cut my arm so I bleed all over a pair of coveralls, play a hell of a nasty joke and finish it up by throwing ice water on me, and now I'm your long-lost cousin and glad to be one of the guys, is that the way it works? You're not damn smart, you know that? Even for twelve, you're just not damn smart."

"You didn't need to hit Chad like that," Jeremy said.

"What do you expect? What in *hell* did you expect, if you jump on a guy?"

"I'm *sorry*, Fletcher. You were supposed to say our names and we'd welcome you in and nobody was supposed to get hurt at all. Not you, not anybody. It's just what they always do when you come in."

"Well, it didn't work, did it?"

"No. I guess not."

He was mad. He was damned mad, and sore, and his hands were bruised and he still wanted to kill Chad, who'd set him up with his room-cleaning and the card game.

Probably Jeremy had been in on it for days. Probably if there was somebody to be mad at it *ought* by rights to be Jeremy. But Jeremy wasn't principally responsible and Jeremy had been scared spitless and upset at the turn things had taken. So had Wayne.

Of all of them he didn't choose to hate, Jeremy and Bucklin were on his list; Bucklin who'd broken it up, Wayne, who'd used his common sense, and Lyra, whom he'd kicked hard, not meaning to, and who'd taken it in stride and not held it against him. Lyra, maybe.

Sue with her water-bucket was right on his list with Chad.

He drew a calmer breath. And a second one.

Jeremy sat there, dejected, in a long, long silence.

"Got a bandage?" he asked Jeremy, his first excuse to break the silence. "I ripped my arm."

"Yeah," Jeremy said, and scrambled up and got him a plastic skin-patch. Jeremy put it on for him. "There."

"Got my knuckle, too." He had. He didn't know whether he'd caught it falling or cut it on Chad. "Chad better keep out of my way," he said. "At least for right now. It's a long voyage. But right now I'm pissed. I'm real pissed."

"I think you broke Chad's tooth."

"He had it coming."

"If the captain finds out there was fighting, we're all going to be in his office."

"It's not my problem." He stared Jeremy straight in the eye. "And if he asks me I'll say be damned to the whole ship."

"Don't say that."

"Why shouldn't I say it? You ambushed *me*. I don't recall it was the other way around."

"I mean don't say that about the ship."

"The hell with the ship!"

"No," Jeremy said with a shake of his head. "No! You never say that about a ship. You never say that, Fletcher! We're your Family. You're *in*, now. Maybe it was screwed up, but it counted, and you're *in*, you're part of us."

"Do I get a *vote* about it?"

"Come on, Fletcher. Nobody meant anything bad. Nobody ever meant anything bad. You were supposed to say the names and learn what they tell you—"

"No."

"Well, you were supposed to."

"That wasn't what they were after, Jeremy. Wise up. They wanted me to kiss ass. That it was Chad and not me that got a broken tooth, no, Chad didn't plan on that, did he? But that's what he got."

"Nobody meant you should get hurt."

"Oh, let's add things up, here. Vince wouldn't shed any tears. Chad wouldn't. Sue—"

"Oh, Sue's an ass. Vince is an ass. They know they're asses. They're trying to grow out of it."

From the twelve-year-old mouth. He had to stare.

"I'm an ass, too," Jeremy said. "I try not to be."

"Then I forgive *you*," he said. "Bucklin and Wayne tried to use common sense and Lyra warned me about Chad. But the others can go to hell."

"Ashley's all right."

"I'll take your word on Ashley." He'd hit a moment of magnanimous charity and extended it likewise to the girls, excepting Sue. "Linda's not bad."

Jeremy shook his head. "Don't trust Linda. Especially not if you're on the outs with Vince."

Jeremy was serious. And with spacers, it was probably true, there were connections and he could get himself knifed. He'd heard stories off Pell dockside. Read accounts in the news and congratulated himself he wasn't part of it.

Now he was.

"A happy, loving family," he said, and felt the wobbles come back to his legs. There were more than fears. There was betrayal. The captain wanted him aboard because he didn't want to pay fourteen million. He understood that. Madelaine wanted him because of her dead daughter. He understood that, too. But the two of them with their reasons had rammed him down everyone else's unwilling throats, and he'd tried to make himself useful and get along where they put him and, *sure*, they were going to welcome him in. The hell.

"I think you should talk to Bucklin," Jeremy said, "and get stuff straightened out. JR didn't want them to do this. Everybody else thought it was, you know, like maybe it would solve things."

"Solve things."

"Like, you'd fit in."

"You think that'd do it, do you?"

Jeremy was out of his depth with that. And so was he. If JR had tried to stop it, it was because JR knew it was going to go the way it did and that certain ones were laying for him, not like Jeremy, a little naïve, but seriously, to get their bluff in and make it stick. Those were the terms on which he'd have fitted in. He'd been hazed before. You got a little of it in school. You got a little of it in any new situation. But held upside-down and threatened with hypothermia? He'd punched Chad with no thought whether he'd kill him. And Chad had come after him the same way.

"Maybe I'm a little old for fitting in," he said to Jeremy, with a bitterness that welled up black and real. "Maybe there isn't any fix for it. I don't belong here."

"There could be a fix."

"There *isn't*. Get that through your head. This is real. It isn't a game. I'm not playing games. Next batch of cousins lay a hand on me is going to be damn sorry. You can pass that word along. But I think they know that."

"You can't go fighting on board," Jeremy said.

"It's not *my* choice."

"Well, nobody's going to fight you."

"Fine. Go on to work. Get. Go."

Jeremy lingered.

"I'm not damn pleased, Jeremy! Get your ass to work! I'll be there when I want to be there!"

Jeremy ducked out, fast. He'd upset the kid. Scared him, maybe—maybe upset his sense of justice.

He figured he should go face down the job, the cousins, the situation, rather than have it fester any longer. He reported to the laundry not too long after Jeremy, met Vince and Linda and didn't say a word about the last hour and all they'd been involved in together. Instead he went cheerfully about folding laundry and let them sweat about what he thought or what he'd do, Vince and Linda and Jeremy alike. He figured plenty of talking had gone on in the few minutes after Jeremy arrived and before he did, and that plenty of talking was going on elsewhere. He looked to get called by Legal or the captain at any moment, maybe with the whole junior crew, maybe solo.

What they'd done, hurt. It hurt for reasons that had nothing to do with the cut arm, the split knuckle and the cord-marks and the one blow Chad had gotten in on him. It hurt in a way he wouldn't have expected, because he truly *didn't* give an effective damn about his welcome or non-welcome on the ship. He didn't know why he should be upset as profoundly as he was.

Or maybe it was just the injustice of it. Maybe it was having them take everything, for one reason and then once he got here and tried to make the best of it, to gang up and try to take his self-respect.

Because that was what they'd wanted to break. His dignity. His self-control. All those things he'd put up between him and a random universe. They'd struck consciously and deliberately at what kept him whole. And he couldn't tolerate that. They'd asked him to give up the last defenses he had, and turn himself over, and play their game, and he wouldn't do that, or give up his pride, not for anybody's asking.

Chapter
——XIV——

If the junior captain, on A deck, wasn't supposed to know about a Welcome-in, the senior captains, on B deck, damn certain weren't supposed to know about such an event; or to have to question the junior captain's common sense or ability to command unless or until he gave them reason to think the junior command had made a mistake.

In a few years, JR was well aware, the ship's entire existence might ride on the wisdom of his decisions. Right now he found the entire crew's welfare still did, the welfare not alone of one Fletcher Neihart, or even of the junior crew in isolation from the rest, or of Chad, who was getting a broken tooth repaired in sickbay.

There *was* no isolation of juniors from seniors once things had gone wrong, and they had gone very seriously wrong.

"They jumped the gun and I didn't find out," Bucklin said, outside sickbay, when JR had answered the call, "until somebody cued me the laundry was empty. That was when I called you. And I had two places to look before I found where in the rim they were. Chad didn't want the tooth fixed. Oh, no. *Chad* didn't want a report filed with you, but I didn't give him that grace."

He heard out the whole story, the bucket of water, Sue's notion of getting a fast agreement out of an argumentative customer she'd been scared was too strong and too tall to handle: *Sue* had feared someone was going to get seriously hurt in a melee, and she'd taken action to assure Fletcher folded.

Not a bad idea, if it had worked.

His call to Legal Affairs had gotten a call out for Fletcher, but Fletcher hadn't answered the call they sent. His hoped-for clandestine talk with Fletcher hadn't happened. Chad and the crew hadn't waited. Fletcher had been dragged down to the rim directly after Chad and the crew had approached him for a go-ahead, with the result they now had; and Fletcher's failing to respond to a call . . . that had assured that Madelaine was aware something odd was going on. It was a short jump from Madelaine's office to the Old Man's.

"I want Fletcher here."

"Fletcher seems undamaged," Bucklin said, but added, hastily, "but he'll be here."

JR walked into sickbay and stood, quietly, while senior cousin Mary B. finished the dental work. Chad rolled a disconsolate eye in the direction of judge and jury.

"There," Mary said, giving Chad a mirror. "Two stitches and a bond on the tooth. *Don't* eat hard candy today."

"Is he in pain?" JR asked Mary.

"He's numb," Mary said. "Hit a wall, so I hear."

"The wall hit back," JR said. "Would you call Charlie down?" Charlie was the medic of the watch, when he wasn't on com. "I'd like him and the wall both looked at."

Mary gave him an arch look and went to do that before she tidied up her equipment.

"You owe Mary some scrub time," he said as Chad climbed out of the chair. "About ten hours of scrub time, including her quarters, I'd say."

"Yes, sir." Chad's mouth was numb. Chad met his eyes without flinching, credit him that, JR thought. He just stood there a second, and Chad just stood.

"So?" JR said. "You jumped the gun on Bucklin, you got a little too enthusiastic in your goings-on, and Sue resourcefully chucked a bucket of water on Fletcher. Where did it go wrong?"

"I set him up," was what he guessed Chad said, past the deadening of the lip. "He didn't go along with it. He told us go to hell. Then Bucklin got him loose, and he took exception to me."

"Fletcher did."

"Yes, sir."

"So, was there a particular reason for him to take exception beyond that you set him up? Just the color of your eyes? The idea of the moment?"

"I don't know, sir, but I apologize, sir."

"Did you apologize to him?"

"He walked out, sir."

"Do the words fucked-up clearly apply here?"

"Yes, sir. Fairly fucked-up."

"Thank you." He caught Mary's nod. She'd snagged Charlie and the medic was coming down to give Chad the once-over.

Cousin Fletcher was not a slight young man. Neither was Chad, both of them towering over him by half a head. There was the potential for cracked ribs, cracked teeth, or slightly more subtle damage, like the level of trust available within the crew.

"You go sit over there." A nod toward the medic's station, the sliding doors of which stood open, tables that were surgery when they had to be. "When Fletcher gets in here, I want no repetition of the problem, do we have it clear, Mr. Neihart?"

"Yes, sir, we do." It was a pathetic mumble. The stitches, two neat electronic clips, were going to smart when the painkiller wore off.

Bucklin showed up. With Fletcher. An undamaged Fletcher, to look at him. A brittle and angry Fletcher, ready to damn all of them to hell.

Jeremy trailed after, and hung about in the doorway.

"You," JR said, "out of here."

Jeremy vanished.

"You"—to Fletcher—"I want to talk to. Relax."

"Is this about the fight?"

Fletcher *would* manage to come at things head-on and with guns live. Not his best feature. "If you've got any arena for improvement, Fletcher, it's your slight tendency to meet people with a challenge, just one of those small problems I'm sure you can improve. At this particular moment I'm sure there's some reason for what I see here, which I'd rather not officially notice. How *are* you getting along, in general?"

"Fine."

"Jeremy's all right with you?"

"Fine. Just fine."

"No problems with Jeremy?"

"No."

"That's good. How about the rest of the crew?"

And that got a direct look of Fletcher's dark, same-genetics eyes.

"You know what happened."

"Chad's report." He nodded to the end of the room, where Chad sat on the end of a surgery table.

"I'm in here for a medical. Is that an excuse, or what? Or do I get another round with him?"

"I want a medical report. And some common sense. *Listen* to me, Fletcher." The tone had Fletcher's attention to himself for about two heartbeats. "We have a tradition on this ship, welcome-in the new guy. *As you know*—" Another gathering of Fletcher's temper and Fletcher got past it. "Usually it's straight out of the nursery, transition into the crew. Jeremy was the last. Kidnap the kid, play a few pranks, a little ceremony, that's about the size of it. Two damn fools your size going at each other weren't in the plan." He couldn't tell Fletcher's state of mind at the moment. Fletcher's face was absolutely rigid. "It's a test—a test of your sense of humor among other things."

"I got a taste of your jokes."

"I understand so. There were some pretty light-weight kids involved in what went way out of parameters. You and Chad are a fair match. You kept it to that. I respect that. They *know* they took it too far. I frankly tried to dissuade them from the idea, but they wanted to welcome you in, in the serious sense. That's the tradition."

"Welcome, is it?"

"It's what they meant. Know us. Fall into the order of things. Find a place. *With* the crew. In the crew."

"It's a stupid tradition."

"It may be, but I'm asking you to take it the way it *should* have gone. No grudges. They've done what they insisted on doing. It's over. You're in."

"I don't *want* to be in."

"That's another problem, but they've no right now to treat you as an outsider. You understand that? There is a difference. And *they* made that difference, so *they* have to accept you in with whatever privilege I grant."

"Damn if I care. Sir."

"Calm down, I say. You've got a right to be mad, but if you exercise it you'll do yourself damage."

"More than they'd like to do? I don't think so. Welcome in, hell! I'm not welcome here! That's real clear!"

"It was a bad start. Best I could do. I wasn't going to leave you alone for your first jump; and me taking you in—that would put you in with the senior-juniors where you *don't* fit. That was my thinking. Jeremy's a good kid. He reacts fast. He'd keep you out of trouble. *Do you want to be moved?*"

"Jeremy's fine." Fletcher seemed calmer, and stayed fixed on him without evidence of skittering off into temper. "No problems with him."

"You're sure. Even after what happened."

"He's a kid."

"He is a kid. On the other hand . . . you're not. And you are. Coming off a station where you don't cope with ship-time . . . you don't fit the ship's profile, that's what we say. You're not in our profile. It's hard to figure where to put you."

"That's too bad."

Fletcher had a way of trying to get under his skin. Or he outright didn't understand. And Charlie had shown up. Charlie—whose job was spacer bodies in all their diverse problems.

"Fletcher, I want you, first of all, to get checked out. Go right over there and sit down. Chad's been in getting his mouth fixed. No lasting damage. —Then, Charlie, if you'd check out Chad. We're looking for dents."

It meant both Fletcher and Chad sitting on two adjacent

tables in the surgery, a traffic management pricklier than two rimrunners at a jump-point, and the same possibilities of shots fired. "I'm not going to ask for any handshaking," JR said, while Chad sat still and Fletcher stripped to the waist and got up on the other table, jaw set.

"Hurt?" Charlie had provoked a wince, pressing on ribs, then bent an arm, bringing a deeply gashed and bandaged forearm to view. "Lovely. So what did we have here?"

"We had a small discussion," JR answered for both participants. "Charlie, we have here one stationer, aged seventeen, one spacer, Chad, aged twenty. How old are we?"

"Which one?" Charlie asked, having a close look meanwhile into Fletcher's right eye, preoccupied with inventory. "Our spacer is, what, a little short of seventeen?"

"Sixteen," Chad muttered, "sir."

"So how old are we?" JR asked. "For our stationer's benefit, —how old are we?"

Charlie backed off from the inspection of the other eye and gave Fletcher a slow scrutiny, the same, then, to Chad. "The stationer is a mature seventeen, probably having most of his height, not his ideal adult weight by about fifteen kilos. The spacer is a mature and very tall sixteen-year-old physique, grew, what was it? An inch since Bryant's?"

"Yessir," Chad said.

"And putting on a couple of kilos off Jeff's fancy desserts," Charlie said. Chad blushed. He *was* putting it on around the middle. "But the stationer," Charlie said, "our stationer lad is a different maturity, been through puberty, long bones are stopping growth, secondary sexual traits normal at my last examination . . ." Fletcher's mouth was a thin line, he was staring at the edge of the table, possibly with a flush on Fletcher's face, but Charlie didn't proceed to the comparative clinical details. "Emotionally, however," Charlie said, "the equation is more different between them now than it will ever be in later life. Fletcher, at seventeen, has lived every day of his seventeen years. He's not grown up having the purge of emotional stress Chad's undergone every month or so in hyperspace: his experience hasn't been subject to that deboot.

It's all been continuous, interrupted only by ordinary nightly dreamstate and whatever psych counseling he's had." Fletcher shot Charlie a hard, burning look, which Charlie didn't look to see. "Our spacer, now, has seen twenty years of history; he was born during the War; he's seen combat for all his years. Our stationer's seen three less years and his station's been at peace, whatever internal events it's suffered. Our spacer's nineteenth and twentieth years were spent in a sixteen-year-old body in the last stages of puberty, and he's not expected to finish that process until he's at least twenty-one or twenty-two depending on our travel schedule; he won't be posted to adult crew until he's at least twenty-six or twenty-seven and won't enter apprenticeship until he gets at least another physical year's growth. Meanwhile our stationer's already past the growth spurt, the rapid changes in jaw, hair, primary and secondary sexual development. Body and hormones reach truce. He's pretty well started on his adult life, as stationers tend to be at his age. —On the other hand, when Chad reaches his ship-time twenties, advantage pitches in the other direction. Our spacer won't suffer the stress disease a stationer has: he *has* that monthly emotional purge, granted he's not one of the rare poor sods that comes out of jump depressed, and our Chad is not depressed. He'll be sixty station-years before he needs to think about rejuv, and look forty, with the historical experience of sixty, when our stationer who stayed on station-time for his first seventeen years is just a little sooner on rejuv. If he doesn't want to ache in the mornings." Charlie patted Fletcher's bare shoulder. "You survived. Congratulations. But let's put a better bandage on the elbow."

"It's fine."

"Shut up, Fletcher," JR said. "Just sit still."

Fletcher sat, and gazed fixedly at the wall, endured the neoplasm Charlie shot on for a patch, and the bandaging.

"You can shower with that."

"Thanks."

"Go and thrive. You're released. Done. Unless JR wants you."

Fletcher slid down from the table and began to pull his

clothing to rights, determinedly not looking at any of them, as
Charlie moved on to Chad and the mouth.

It *was* hard to judge Fletcher's limits and capabilities. Add
everything Charlie had said, plus bone-ignorant of safety procedures and any useful trade.

Try again, JR thought. "Difficult call, Fletcher. Difficult to
judge where you are."

"Where I don't want to be, is the plain fact."

"You were right at the start of everything, were you?" He'd
known intellectually that Fletcher was called up out of a study
program. How adult it was, how much career it might be, was
all guesswork to him. "Now a career restart."

"I'm not interested in a restart," Fletcher said.

And, frankly, Fletcher was late to be starting anything. At
any given jump, the senior captain or third Helm or Scan or
Com 1 might not wake up, and the senior-juniors would be
moving up, into real posts. It could make bad, bad blood on
that point if he couldn't finesse what Fletcher was, or might
be. But he'd made his initial determination, a junior personnel
decision, and it was his decision.

"Behind my unit and ahead of Chad's," he said, "there's no
personnel from those years. No one survived. *That's* the problem.
There's no one to assign you with, you're too far behind my set,
and you and Chad, who'd be somebody to put you with, have just
pounded hell out of each other. That makes things somewhat
hard for me trying to put you somewhere constructive."

"How about back on Pell?" Fletcher asked, in hard, insub-
ordinate challenge.

"Not my option. Not yours. I said you were *in*. I've got the
job of finding you a spot. You want some senior privileges—"
It was the damned drink incident at the bar that had touched
off the mess, that and his failure to lay the law down absolutely
on one side or the other. He was aware Chad was listening, and
Chad would report exactly what the disposition was. So would
he, faster than that. A memo would hit the individual mail-
boxes within the hour. And this time he didn't count on their
lifelong connections to straighten out the details: he knew

where he'd assumed it would happen with Fletcher. It hadn't worked itself out; and decision, any decision, was better than no decision. "I'm creating a class of one. Solo. You want your unique privileges, you've got bar rights at family gatherings, but I'm insisting you stay in the approved junior-juniors' sleepovers and not overnight elsewhere during liberty. More than that—I'm giving you a duty. *You* take care of Jeremy, Vince, and Linda. It takes them off my hands and gives me and my team a break from junior-juniors."

Fletcher gave him a straight-on look, as if trying to decide where the stinger was.

"I don't know the regulations."

"They do. Jeremy won't con you. Vince will almost assuredly try." He made a shift of his eyes to Chad, who was getting off the table. And back to Fletcher. "You don't have to make apologies to each other. A love fest isn't required. I do expect civil behavior. And a concentrated effort to settle your differences."

Fletcher absorbed that observation in long silence. He looked across the gap at Chad, on whom Charlie had interrupted his examination.

"Chad," JR said, and Chad got down, jump suit bunched around his waist.

"Yessir."

"Chad, this is your cousin Fletcher."

"Yessir." It was a mumble, still. Chad drew a deep breath and offered his hand.

Fletcher took it, not smiling.

"Pretty good punch," Chad said magnanimously.

Fletcher didn't say a thing. Just recovered his hand.

"Go on," JR said, and Fletcher left.

"Damn station prig," Chad said when he'd gone. "But he sure learnt to fight somewhere."

"Evidently he did," JR said dryly, and Chad got back on the table and endured being poked and prodded.

"Ow," Chad said.

It wasn't a perfect solution, but it tied things down. Charlie had put a finger on one significant matter. Tempers on what had been a burning issue almost always settled a little after jump: hyperspace straightened out perspectives, lowered emotional charges, made things seem trivial against the wider universe—acted, in most instances, like a mood elevator. Some quarrels just dissipated, grown too tenuous to maintain, and others fizzled after a few half-hearted spats the other side of where they'd been.

Unfortunately they weren't approaching a jump where things would cool down. They were on the inbound leg of the Mariner run, coming *into* port, where he had to turn junior-junior crew loose on a dockside that had notoriously little sense of humor with rule-breakers—a dockside made doubly hazardous because it was a border zone between Alliance and Union and a minefield of political sensitivities and touchy cops.

Finity on a trade run as an ordinary merchanter was going to be damned conspicuous. He'd caught discussion among the senior crew, how various eyes were going to be watching her and her crew for signs that she wasn't really engaged in commerce, signs, he could fill in for himself, such as the absence of underage crew on the docks, when all other ships let their youngsters go to the game parlors and the approved kid haunts.

They had to let the junior-juniors go out there. They had to look normal. And he had to get them back again, in one piece.

Put Fletcher *in charge* of the juniors who'd more or less been in charge of *him*? It might straighten out the accidental kink that had developed in the order of things. He'd have Fletcher report to him once daily about the state of the juniors, *he'd* threaten Jeremy's life if they gave Fletcher a hard time, and he'd have a daily phone call from Fletcher coincidentally confirming Fletcher's own well-being and whereabouts, and necessitating the learning of rules and regulations—which would have galled Fletcher's independent soul if he'd asked Fletcher to report on himself, or to read the rule book and learn it.

It was as good as he could manage. Better than he'd hoped.

He went to B deck and filed a report with the Old Man's office, not a flattering one to himself. "I've put Fletcher in charge of the juniors," he began it. And explained there'd been an incident. He'd hoped not to face the Old Man directly, but unfortunately the robot wasn't taking calls.

Vince and Linda gave Fletcher a speculating look when he came back to the laundry. Jeremy stood and stared, his face grave and worried.

There wasn't enough work to keep them busy. There was nothing but cards. Fletcher made a pass about the area looking for work to do, anything to keep him from answering junior questions. But in his concentrated silence even Vince didn't blurt questions or smart-ass observations, maybe having learned he could get hurt.

"Not enough work to justify four of us," Fletcher announced. "*You* handle what comes in. I'm going to the room."

"You better not," Jeremy said in a hushed voice. "You'll catch hell."

"It's my room," he said. "I'll go to it."

But the intercom speaker on the wall came on with: *"Fletcher."*

Jeremy dived for it. "He's here," Jeremy volunteered, as if that was the source of all help.

"Fletcher R., report to the senior captain's office."

"Shit," he said, and Jeremy instantly blocked the reply mike with his hand.

"He's coming," Jeremy said then. "He'll be right there."

"Going to catch hell," Vince muttered.

Fletcher thought of going to his room anyway, and letting the captain come to him. But, he told himself, this was the person he wanted to see, the person who should have seen *him* when he boarded and who never yet had bothered. This was the Goda'mighty important James Robert who'd built the Alliance and fought off the pirate Fleet, who finally found time for him, and who might be annoyed to the point of making his life hell and fighting him on his hopes of leaving this ship if he didn't report in.

"So where do I find him?" he asked Jeremy.

Vince, Linda *and* Jeremy answered, as if they were telling him the way to God.

"B7. There's these offices. All the captains. His is there, too."

Right near Legal. He knew his way. He walked out of the laundry station and down to the lift, rode it to B deck, trying not to let his temper get out of control, telling himself this *was* the man who could wreck him without trying.

Or finally understand the simple fact that he didn't want to be here, and maybe . . . maybe just let him go.

The kids' description matched reality, an office setup a lot like Legal, a front office where several senior crew worked at desks, all staff, offices to the side.

And JR.

"You set this up," he said to JR, and was ready to turn and walk out.

"I don't make the captain's appointments," JR said. "Report the situation? I was obliged to."

"Thank *you*," Fletcher said. So he wasn't to meet with the captain alone. He had JR for a witness, to confuse anything he wanted to say. It wasn't going to be an interview. It would be a reading of the rules.

He was here. He held onto his temper with both hands as JR opened the door and let him in.

The Old Man everybody referred to wasn't that old to look at him, that was the first impression he had as the Old Man looked up at him. He was prepared to deal with some dodderer, but the eyes that met him were dark and quick in a papery-skinned and lean face. The hand that reached out as the Old Man rose was young in shape, but the skin had that parchment quality he'd seen on the very long-rejuved. It felt like old fabric, smooth like that; and he realized he hadn't consciously decided to take the Old Man's hand. He just had, suddenly so wrapped in that question that he hadn't consciously noted whether JR had stayed or what the office was like, until the Old Man settled back behind his desk and left him standing in front of it. JR *had* stayed, and stood behind him, slightly to the side.

It wasn't a big office. There was a thing he recognized as a sailing ship's wheel on the wall between two cases of old and expensive books. There was a side table, and a chart on the wall above it, a map of stations and points that had lines on it in greater number than he'd ever seen.

Mostly there was the Old Man, who settled back in his chair and looked at him, just quietly observed him for a moment, not tempting him to blurt out anything in the way of charges or excuses prematurely.

Like a judge. Like a judge who'd been on the bench a long, long time.

"Fletcher," James Robert said, in a low, quiet voice, and made him wonder what the Old Man saw when he looked at him, whether he saw his mother, or was about to say so. "A new world, isn't it?"

He wasn't prepared for philosophy. Could have expected it, but it wasn't the angle his brain was set to handle. He stood there, thoughts gone blank, and the Old Man went on.

"We're glad to have you aboard. You've had a chance to see the ship. What do you think?"

What did he think? What did he *think*?

He drew in a breath, time enough for caution to reassert itself, and for a beleaguered brain to tell him not to go too far. And to stop at one statement.

"I think I don't belong here, sir."

"In what respect?" Quietly. Seriously.

List the reasons? God. "In respect of the fact I prepared myself to work on a planet. In respect of the fact I'm totally useless to you. In respect of the fact I'm no good anywhere except what I trained all my life to do."

"*What* did you train to do?"

"To work with the downers, sir." The man knew. And was trying to draw him out. While he had JR at his shoulder for an inhibition. "It's what I want to do."

"What's the nature of that work?"

He wasn't prepared to give a detailed catalog of his jobs, either. "Agriculture. Archaeological research. Native studies. Planetary dynamics."

"All those things."

"I hadn't specialized yet."

"What *would* you have chosen?"

"Native Studies."

"Why that?"

"Because I want to understand the downers."

"Why would you want that?"

"Because I want to help them."

"How would you do that?"

Question begat question, backing him slowly toward a corner of the subject with truth in it, a truth he didn't want to tell.

"By being a fair administrator."

"Oh, an administrator. A fair one. Just what they need."

The tone had been so quiet the barb was in before he felt it.

"Yes, sir, it beats a bad one. And they've had *that*, too."

"I'm very aware. So you were going into Native Studies. Getting a jump on the administrator part, it seems. You'd formed acquaintances among the downers."

Bianca. It was the same thing Madelaine had hit him with. But now it had lost its shock value.

"Yes, sir. I did. I knew them before I went down. And there's nothing in the rules that covered that."

"I take it you checked."

"They're friends of mine! There's nothing I did that would harm them."

"Including going into the outback. Including endangering others. Including meeting with downer authorities."

He'd told that to the investigators. He remembered lying in the bed, and them recording everything he said. He'd had to explain the stick. That he hadn't stolen it. So it *hadn't* been all Bianca.

"Why," the captain asked him, "would you break the regulations?"

"Because you pushed me."

"We weren't there. I don't think so. You made a decision. You went where you were forbidden to go, you stole lifesupport cylinders—"

"One from each. If anybody got out there compromised it was their own stupidity. You can feel it in the masks. They'd be too light."

Was that a slight smile on the captain's face? He didn't take it for one. And JR was hearing entirely too much.

"You also," the captain said, "went out there to outwait us. Endangering your downers, about whom you care so much."

"Outwait you, yes. But not to endanger the downers."

"How do you know that?"

"Because it wouldn't."

"You were sure of that."

"I know them. I was looking for the two I knew."

There was a long silence then. James Robert leaned forward, elbows on the desk, fingers steepled in front of his lips. "Then," James Robert said, "you thought it wouldn't hurt them. You took conscious thought."

"Yes, sir. If I'd thought I'd do them any damage I'd have turned around and given up. Right then."

"Are you sure you didn't?"

"I am absolutely sure I didn't." He was scared, however, that the captain knew more than he was saying . . . about what he'd boarded with. He waited to be accused.

"You invaded a downer shrine, on your own decision."

"It's not a shrine." Had he *said* that part of it? God! He didn't know now what he *had* said to the investigators, or how much more they'd inferred. "It's a ritual site. There's a difference."

"That's what they say."

"Yes, sir." They knew what he'd brought aboard. They were going to take it away from him.

"And why did you go there?"

"A downer led me."

"Your friends did."

"No. A different one."

"And you still say you didn't do damage."

"I know I didn't. They accepted me there. They *brought* me there." There was more that he hadn't said, but he wasn't willing now for the Old Man to direct the conversation where he wanted it, chasing him into every corner of what he knew. "I talked to *Satin*."

"So have I," James Robert said.

For a moment he didn't believe it. And then did. This was James Robert who'd *been* on Pell when the foremost of downers had been on the station.

"I've *met* Satin," James Robert said. "An extraordinary creature. She went all the way to Mariner, and came back talking about war."

He was impressed. In spite of everything.

"Do you know," James Robert said, "they had no word for war until we told them?"

"She wasn't on *this* ship."

"On another merchanter ship. On a far more ordinary voyage. But even so she found the outside too threatening. She said the heavens were too troubled for hisa. She came back to her world, by what I understand, to sit by the Watchers and add her strength to the Watchers' strength. To dream the future."

A chill went over his arms. "What do *you* know about it?"

"I met her. I talked with her."

He was vastly more impressed with this man than he'd planned to be. He'd tried to act righteous and the man turned out to know things that made him look like the rules-infracting fool he knew in his heart he'd been. A fool that deserved booting from the program—as they'd done with him, so thoroughly that Quen couldn't even use reinstatement as a bribe.

Quen knew. Quen had told James Robert. And James Robert hadn't met with him until now, when he'd have thought the captain who sued for his return would have been at the head of the list.

"What I know," the captain said, "is the old ones sit by the

Watchers and believe for the people. They *expect* things from
the sky. Hell, *we* showed up. Something else might happen.
There even might be peace. If you want my opinion, that's
what she's looking for. That's why she went back."

"They say don't attribute anything to them. That we can't
know what they're looking for."

"Bullshit. I know what she's looking for. All of us who
dealt with her know what she's looking for. You don't look so
blind, either."

His heart was beating very fast.

"And what's that?" he challenged the captain. "What do
you know that they don't?"

"The meaning of not-war. We taught her the word for war.
They didn't have it. But they don't have a word for peace
either. And *that's* what she waits to see. She's got to be really
old by now, in downer terms."

Silver. Like an image. The captain made Satin so real in his
mind it hurt.

"Yes," he said. "She is."

"You know *what* this ship is, Fletcher, besides a recurring
inconvenience in your life?"

"No." The captain preempted what he'd have said. Diverted
talk to the ship. Which he didn't want.

"This ship," the captain said, "*your* ship, Fletcher, the way it
was your mother's, is the oldest merchanter still working. It's
the one that broke open the rebellion against the Earth
Company. It had been started before, but we made it inevitable.
Your predecessor helped make it happen."

"I know that." He didn't want a history lesson. He knew
about this ship, God, he *knew* about this ship. He'd learned
about his almost-immediate ancestor. This ship was armed, it
went God knew where, it was a warship in disguise, and it was
probably lying (he began to fear so, counting that carrier that
had spooked the ship back at the last jump) when it claimed it
was going back to merchant trade.

"This is the ship," the captain continued in dogged

patience, "that secured the right that no matter what law a station is under, a merchanter's deck is sovereign territory. Without that, merchanters would have been sucked right into the War, or coopted by Union."

"I know that part, too."

"This is the ship that led the merchanter strikes, the first to resist Earth's imposition of visas."

"At Olympus."

"Thule. Learn your Hinder Stars. There are those of us who remember, Fletcher. And you have to. People who meet one of our crew expect you to remember, so be correct on that point."

"I wasn't born then. You may have been, but I wasn't."

"I know other things, in your world. This ship, Fletcher, *is* what Satin hopes for."

"No. Satin doesn't. Satin doesn't *care* what humans do."

"Yes, she does."

"It's a cheap try. The downers have no connection to us. They don't know why we do what we do and we shouldn't confuse them."

"Did Satin tell you that?"

A shot straight to the gut.

"What did she say?" the captain asked. "Did she tell you that their culture is equivalent to but aside from protohuman development and that she's a mirror of ourselves?"

"No."

"I don't think it's her job, either. No more than it's your job to run her planet for her."

"I never said it was."

"You have to take that line if you want to be an administrator. You have to work with the committee, play with the team, and leave the downers alone. If the committee had found out what you were doing they'd have had you on a platter, and by now they probably *do* know and they've got three study groups and a government grant to try to find out what happened. You were doomed. They'd have had you out of that job in a year."

"It wouldn't have gone the way it did."

"Yes, it would. Because you questioned the most basic facts in the official rulebook . . . that Satin's people have to be left alone and her people can't learn anything they don't think of for themselves. Those are the rules, Fletcher. Defy them at your own risk."

"I never risked *them*." It was the one thing he could say, the one thing he was, in heart and head, sure of, that Nunn never would believe.

"I know that. *I* know that. And Satin won't talk to the researchers. Not to the researchers. Not to the administrators. Do you think she's stupid? She has nothing to say to them."

"What do *you* know? You talked to her once."

"Like you. You talked to her once."

"I've studied them all my life. I do know something about them."

"Something the researchers don't know?"

It sounded ludicrous. He was no one. He knew nothing.

"You love them?" the captain asked. That word. That word he didn't use.

"Love isn't on the approved list. Ask the professors."

"I'll give you another radical word. *Peace*, Fletcher. It's what Satin's looking for. She doesn't know the name of it, but she went back to the Watchers to wait for it. That's why she's there. That's why she folded downer culture in on itself and gave not a damn thing to the researchers and the administrators and all the rest of the official establishment. It was her dearest wish to go to space. But *we* weren't ready for her."

"Satin went back to her planet rather than put up with the way we do business!" Fletcher said. "Wars and shooting people on the docks didn't impress her. And she didn't like the merchant trade. Downers *give* things, they don't sell them."

"When you met her, what did she tell you?"

His voice froze up on him. Chills ran down his arms. *Go*, she'd said. For a moment he could hear that soft, strange voice. *Go walk with Great Sun.*

"We talked about the Sun. About downers I knew. That was all."

"Peace, Fletcher. That's the word she wants. She knows the word, but we haven't yet shown her what it means. She knows that the bad humans have to leave downers alone. But that's not peace. We haven't been able to show it to her. We showed her war. But we never have found her peace. And that's what we're looking for, right now. On this ship. On this voyage."

"Fancy words."

"Peace is a lot more than just being left alone."

"You couldn't give it to her down there," the Old Man said. "You're a child of the War. So is JR." His eyes shifted beyond Fletcher's shoulder, to a presence he keenly felt, and wished JR had heard nothing of this. "Neither of you have any peace to give her. And where *will* you get it, Fletcher? Your birthright is *this ship*. This ship, that's trying to make peace work real-time, in a universe where everybody is still maneuvering for advantage mostly because, like you, like Jeremy and his generation, even like Quen at Pell, you're all too young to know any better. You're as lost as Satin. You don't know what peace looks like, either."

"What do you know about me *or* her? What the *hell* do you know?"

"The hour of your birth and the prejudice of several judges. The fear *and* the anger that sent you running out where you knew you could die . . . we never wanted you to be that afraid, Fletcher, or that angry."

"You don't want me! You wanted your fourteen million! And I was *happy* until you screwed up my life! Besides, I wasn't trying to kill myself."

"But if you hadn't run out there, Satin would have come to the end of her life without talking to Fletcher Neihart."

"What does that have to do with it?"

"Nothing, if you don't do anything. A great deal if you commit yourself to find out what peace is, if you *learn* it, if you find it and take it to your generation. Satin's still looking at the heavens, isn't she? Still waiting to see the shape of it, the color of it, to see what it can do for her people, Fletcher. Right now only a few of us remember what peace looked like, tasted like, *felt* like."

He caught a breath. A second one. He'd never been up against anybody who talked like James Robert. Everything you said came back at you through a different lens.

James Robert did remember before the War. Nobody he knew of did.

"Work for this ship," he said in James Robert's long silence. "Is that what you mean? Do the laundry, wash the pans . . ."

"All that we do," James Robert said, "keeps this ship running. I take a turn at the galley now and again. I consider it a great pleasure."

"Yes, sir." He knew he'd just sounded like a prig.

"What good were you at laundry anyway? You think the first strike happened at Olympus."

"Thule, sir."

"Good. Details matter. If it wasn't Thule everything would have been changed. The borders, the ones in charge, the future of the universe would have been changed, Fletcher. Details are important. I wonder you missed that, if you're a scientist."

"Biochemist."

"Biochem? Biochem isn't related to the universe?"

"It is, sir. Thule."

"Precisely. I detest a man that won't know anything he doesn't imminently have to. Just plod through the facts as you *think* you know them. 'Approximate is good enough' makes lousy science. Lousy navigation. And keeps people following bad politicians. Are you a rules-follower, Fletcher?"

The Old Man was joking with him. He took a chance, wanting to be right, aware JR was measuring him and fearing the Old Man could demolish him. "I think you have my record, sir."

A small laugh. A straight look. "A very mixed record."

"I'm for rules, sir, till I understand them."

"I knew your predecessor," the Old Man said. "There's a similarity. A decided similarity."

He hoped that was a compliment.

"So JR tells me he's assigned you to keep young Jeremy in line."

"Jeremy's been keeping *me* in line, mostly."

A ghost of a smile. And sober attention again. "Biochem, eh?"

He saw the invitation. He didn't know whether he wanted it. James Robert had a knack for getting through defenses, with the kind of persuasion he wanted to think about a long time, because he'd gotten his attention, and told him the truth in a handful of words, the way Melody had, once: *you sad.*

James Robert told him plainly what he'd always seen about the program: that if you didn't believe what they said, follow their rules, you were out. And he'd hedged it all the way, being new, following his dream, living his imaginings . . . not looking at . . .

Not looking at what James Robert told him, that the Base *wanted* someone like Nunn, someone who'd follow rules, not push them—because what ran the human establishment on Downbelow wasn't on Downbelow. It was on Pell.

"You get a few ports further," the Old Man said. "We'll talk again. You have a good time in this one, that's my recommendation."

The Old Man hadn't ever mentioned the fight. The hazing. Any of it. Or changed JR's assignment of him.

"Yes, sir," he said. "I'll try to. Thank you."

The Old Man nodded. JR opened the door, let him out.

And came outside with him.

"Fletcher," JR said.

He turned a scowling look on JR, daring him to comment on personal matters.

"I didn't set you up to fail," JR said. "Any help you want, I *will* give you."

"Thank you," he said. He couldn't beg JR to forget what

he'd heard. He had to leave it on JR's discretion, whatever it
might be, without trusting it in the least. He left, back to the
laundry, thinking . . . they'd talked about *peace*, and he'd
believed everything the Old Man said while he was saying it.
It gave him the willies even yet, when he considered that this
ship hadn't been trading for a living for seventeen years.

The Old Man said they were looking for peace, and that
none of them knew what it looked like.

He thought of Jeremy, talking of going to Mallory, carrying
on the fight. Of Jeremy, shivering in the bunk approaching jump,
because the kid was *scared.*

The youngest of them had seen the least of what the Old
Man said they were looking for. They called it *peace*, when the
Treaty of Pell had stopped Union from going after the former
Earth Company stations, when the stations agreed to host the
Merchanters' Alliance and Earth disavowed the Fleet . . . but
the Fleet hadn't surrendered. And there wasn't any peace.

And the oldest downer had gone back to her world to watch
the heavens and believe for her people.

Believing that there was something more, though she'd seen
what war looked like. Believing there'd be something else—
when for thousands upon thousands of years the Watcher-
statues had watched the heavens, waiting . . .

For what? Visitors?

What peace? he should have asked the Old Man when he
had the chance. *What does this ship have to do with it, when
all it's done is fight? What are we doing, when you say we're
looking for peace? None of the juniors know what it is, for
very damn sure.*

When did I say yes? When did I even start listening?

Anger tried to find another foothold. Resentment for being
conned.

But this was a ship that *had* meant important things in the
recent past.

What if? he began to ask himself. He, who'd met Satin, and
looked into her eyes.

"Got chewed out, hey?" Vince asked when he got back to the laundry, and he just smiled.

"No," he said in perfect good humor. "I just got put in charge of you three."

Vince's mouth stayed open. And shut.

"You're kidding," Linda said.

"No," he said. Jeremy grinned from ear to ear.

Chapter
—XV—

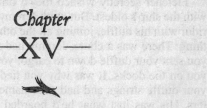

Liberty was coming. The mood all over the ship was excitement, anticipation. The junior-juniors' attention for anything
was scattered: liberty and stationside and games were coming
after days of duty and sticking by their posts.

It was, Fletcher thought as the ship prepared for docking,
air to breathe—wider spaces, not corridors, not the unsettling
pervasive thrum that he'd grown used to and that he now knew
was the ring in its constant motion. Where they'd exit in less
than an hour wasn't going to be Pell, but it was a place that
would look like Pell, feel like Pell, *be* like Pell. He could do
things ordinary people did on stations, walk curves less steep
than *Finity*'s deck—go to a shop, look at tapes. Maybe buy
one. He was due a little money, a little cash, they'd said, for
incidentals. If he skipped a meal or two, he could buy a tape.

A third of personnel, including the bridge, and older crew,
whose personal quarters were in areas that would be downside
during dock, could simply sit in quarters during docking and
undock, if they chose to do that. For the seniormost crew not
so blessed by the position of their cabins during ring lockdown, there was the small theater topside, where a pleated
floor (Jeremy had explained this wonder of engineering), solid
seating and safety belts were available. The whole theater
became stairsteps.

But for the able-bodied, they packed them into rec like sar-
dines, and they rode it through with takeholds and railings,
just the way they'd done in undock. The junior-juniors disdained the theater. Jeremy said docking was more fun than
undock.

Fletcher secretly wished they'd offered him a theater seat with the ship's oldest. But, with Jeremy, he went down the corridor with his duffle, joining all the other crew doing the same thing. There was a chute, Jeremy had forewarned him, where you sent your duffle down to cargo; your baggage would meet you on the docks. It was why you tied silly personal items to your duffle strings and had your name stencilled in large letters. His was just what he'd boarded with, plain, distinctive only in that it wasn't worn and stencilled. He'd put a ship's tag on it, Jeremy's recommendation. He'd tied a bright civvy sock to the tag strings, the only thing he owned amenable to serving as ID. He'd not brought anything in his baggage but clothes and toiletries. And watching the way the duffles went down the chute he was glad he'd packed nothing else.

"They're not damn careful," he said.

"Warned you," Jeremy said brightly. "They're more careful coming back. That's the good thing. They know the incomings got fragiles."

The rec hall was transformed again. Machines and tables were out. The safety railings were back. He and Jeremy stood, indistinguishable from the mob of other silver-suited Finity crew, Linda and Vince each with senior crew protectively spaced between them as Finity glided toward dock and occasional decel forces shoved gently at the ship.

"Decoupling," the intercom said. "Condition yellow take hold."

That meant real caution. Next thing to Belt-in-if-you-can. Don't let go to scratch your nose.

Gravity ebbed. Fletcher's stomach went queasy. Don't let me be sick. Don't let me be sick. It's nerves. It's just nerves. Nothing out of the ordinary's going on.

"Condition red take hold."

"Hold on tight," Jeremy said.

Big jolt. Not too bad, he thought.

Then a giant's hand grabbed them and suddenly slung everyone in the room hard against the rails with a crash and a bang that echoed through the frame.

No one came loose. No one screamed. Fletcher thought his

sore fingers had dented the safety rail and his neck felt whiplash.

"That was the grapple," Jeremy said cheerfully, on the general exhalation and mild expletives in the room, and added, "We're carrying a *lot* of mass."

"I could live without that." Fletcher congratulated himself he hadn't screamed. His stomach was the other side of the wall. Jeremy had let go the rail to stretch his back. "We didn't hear an all clear."

"We will," Jeremy said in cocky self-assurance, and in the very next instant the intercom came on to give it:

"The ship is stable. We are in lock. Mainday three to stations."

Jeremy constantly scanted the rules. Fletcher had begun to notice that small defiance of physics and warnings. Jeremy was confidently just ahead of everything; he'd taught *him* some of his unsafe habits, which he knew, now that he'd actually seen the written regulations for himself. And one part of Fletcher's soul said the hell with it, the kid knew, while another part said that since he *was* nominally in charge he ought to call the kid on it . . .

In a system the kid knew from before his birth.

He had his instructions from JR, all the same. Yesterday at shift-end a brand new bound print of ship's rules had arrived in his quarters, a gift which Fletcher acknowledged to himself he'd have chucked in the nearest waste chute a day ago in disdain of the whole concept. Instead, knowing he had Jeremy to oversee, he'd fast-studied it and memorized the short list in the front; he had it in his duffle, and meant business. He'd advised the junior-juniors so: *he'd* take no shots from the Old Man due to their putting anything over on him.

"Section chiefs report forward for passport procedures."

"There you go," Jeremy said.

Jeremy not only hadn't resented his appointment over him, the kid had actually seemed to take pride in it—as well as in the fact he'd gotten that rise in rank directly after the rough Welcome-in, when he'd, as Jeremy so delicately put it, knocked the fool out of Chad.

"Meet you out there," Jeremy said as he extricated himself

from the row of cousins. He felt a pat on his back, a pat from other, older crew as he passed them to get to the door . . . they *knew* he'd gotten an assignment, and they encouraged him. *Him*, the outsider.

He made the door in a flutter-stomached disorganization, telling himself, without feeling of his pocket, that, yes, he had his passport, and Jeremy's and Vince's and Linda's, for which he was responsible.

He joined the other section chiefs, far senior, over sections far more important to the ship. It was simply his job to get the junior-juniors through customs and to get them back through customs on the way out. To save long lines when there was no particular customs slow-down, section chiefs handled passports, ID'ed their people for customs in a mass, and passed them through; but junior-juniors, being minors, didn't handle their own passports at any time. He had to. In the sleepover, being minors, they didn't sign their own bills.

He had to sign for them. He had to authorize expenses for the junior-juniors, and he was to dole out credit in a reasonable way for pocket change, but meal and authorized purchase bills went to his room. He'd thought it was a watch-the-kids kind of baby-sitting JR had handed him. It had turned out to have monetary and legal responsibilities attached. A lot of money. Several thousand c worth, that he was supposed to dispense and account for.

There'd been a visicard hand-clipped to the front of the manual, a quick and easy condensation of the rules, specific advisements for this port, even a good fast study for the arcane procedures of getting into a sleepover—one of those dens of iniquity stationers viewed as exotic and dangerous and about which teenaged stationers entertained prurient curiosity. *He* was going to such a place with a parcel of apparent twelve-year-olds forbidden to drink or to consort with strangers. He took the card out of his breast pocket, thumbed the display on and double-checked it while the line advanced another set of five, right down to his group.

Phone the ship with your sleepover address code and enter it into your pocket com first thing after registering and

*reaching your room. Do not carry cash chits above 20 c at any
time. Memorize the date and hour of board-call and report no
later than one hour before departure. If you overnight in
another sleepover, phone the ship. If injured or ill, phone the
ship. If arrested, phone the ship. Note: White dock is off-limits
to all deep-space personnel by local statute. Junior personnel
are limited to Blue and Green by order of the senior captain.
The senior staff reminds the crew that this is a tight port with
strict zoning. In past years, we have had military privilege.
That is not in force now. Be mindful of local regulations. Have
a pleasant stay.*

Sleepover rules and do's and don'ts were in the next screen.
Third screen provided a crewman other specific procedures in
case of disaster, how to avoid getting left here by his ship.

His ship. God. *His ship.* His independence was gone. He'd
begun to rely on *his ship.* He looked no different than the rest
of them. His uniform made no distinction of rank: he wore
silver coveralls, with the black patch that had no ship-name
beneath it. They were instructed, all of them, the manual said,
to write simply *spacer* if asked for rank on any blank the station handed them, as even the captains did, despite stations
wanting to know more than that about the internal business of
merchanters, and wanting, historically, to regulate them. Some
ships complied. But *spacer* and *Neihart* was enough for the
universe to know.

Arrogant. Stationers called *Finity* that.

At least, for his peace of mind, *Finity* personnel had
booked a block of rooms close together in the same sleepover.
JR had told him personally no drinking on station, and with
the kids in tow and with Vince to keep an eye on, it seemed a
good idea. JR *hadn't* told him don't go sleep with any chance
stranger who walked up on him . . . but he had very soberly
figured it out for himself that that practice of free sex which so
scandalized station-dwellers was not a good idea for him, not
in a situation the rules of which he was desperately studying,
and not with three kids he was responsible for getting back in
one piece, and not with strangers whose motives he could
guess far less than he could guess those of his shipmates.

The airlock cycled them through, letting them out into the cold yellow passage to the station airlock, and through to the elevated ramp.

All the docks spread out in front of him from that vantage, the neon lights of unfamiliar shops and establishments displaying an unfamiliar sign-age above the heads of his fellow *Finity* spacers as they walked, down, down, down to the cordoned area with the small customs kiosk.

He'd seen this procedure all his life . . . looking up, from the other end of the proposition, standing, say, by one of the big structural pillars, watching the arrival of a ship. This time he was one of the distant visitors, the customers, the marks to some, the fearsome strangers to others.

The scene inside the airlock wouldn't be mysterious to him, now. Ever. He knew the routines, he knew the names of the people around him—and this station didn't know his name or have him in its records. No one on this station knew who he was except as *Finity* crew, no one would answer familiar phone numbers. His station looked exactly the same—but at home there was a neon Kittridge's Bar sign opposite Berth Blue 6. Here it was the sign for Mariner Bank.

The shift and counter-shift of perspectives as his feet touched the dock itself had him halfway numb. But he resolved not to gawk at the signs, not even to think about them, for the sake of the butterflies holding riot in his stomach. He waited his turn and reported his own small team through customs and registry as *Finity* juveniles on liberty, four, counting himself.

Hands only moderately trembling—he'd feared worse—he slipped the passports through the scanner, a modest number compared to what section chiefs in Engineering had to present. Jake from Bio had a stack of passports, as a customs officer read off *James Thomas Neihart, James Robert Hampton-Neihart, Jamie Marie Neihart, Jamie Lynn Neihart,* and proceeded to *June* and *Juliana* in a patient, mind-numbed drone. His agent handed him slips with each passport, slips that said—he looked when he had walked clear of the line, still within *Finity*'s customs barriers—*The importation or export*

*of radioactive materials, biostuffs and biostuff derivatives
including genetic mimes is strictly controlled.*

He'd been among the last crew chiefs. JR came behind him
and, as he supposed, took the senior-juniors' passports through
the kiosk; by the time the airlock spilled out JR's bunch, his
own three crew members were already lugging their duffles
down the ramp. The press of Engineering midlevel crew had
largely cleared out; there was still a crowd at the crew baggage
chute.

Bucklin walked past him, paused and slipped two messages into his hand. Fletcher looked at them, mildly surprised,
thinking one at least, maybe both, were from JR. But one had
Finity's black disc for a source, that was all. He read the first
slip as Bucklin walked away.

From the senior captain. *Jr. Crew Chief Fletcher R.
Neihart,* it said. *The senior officers extend good wishes and
willing assistance in the assumption of your new duties.
Should you have any need of assistance do not hesitate to call
senior staff. —James Robert Neihart.*

He read it twice, first assuming it was routine, and then
suspecting it might not be and looking for meanings between
the lines. *It's your call,* was what he saw on that second
reading. *Call too early and you're incompetent; call too late
and you're in my office.*

Maybe he was too anxious. Maybe it *was* just a routine
letter and a computer had done it, the same way a computer
called their names for duty assignments.

The other message was a sealed letter. He pulled the edges
open. A credit slip was inside.

Two credit slips. A pair of 40 c slips made out to him.
Wrapped in a note. *No young person should go on first liberty
without something in his pocket. Don't spend it unless you find
something totally foolish. This is personal money. Allow me to act
like a grandmother for the first time in years. —Love. Madelaine.*

He didn't want charity. He didn't want Madelaine's money,
personal or otherwise, even if 80 c had to be a trifle to her personal wealth.

Grandmother.

And *Love? Love, Madelaine?* Her daughter was dead. Her *granddaughter* was dead. *Allow me to act like a grand-mother . . .*

A lot of death. How did he say No thank you?

How did he avoid getting in her debt? How dared she say, *I love you,* his great-grandmother, who didn't know damn-all about him.

And who knew more than anybody else aboard.

He pocketed the money with the messages, told himself forget it, enjoy it, spend it, it wasn't an irrevocable choice and money didn't buy him, as he was sure Madelaine didn't think it did— Say anything else about her, the woman wasn't that shallow and it was just a gesture.

"Fletcher!" he heard, Jeremy's voice, and in a moment more Vince and Linda rallied round. "We got to get our bags!" Jeremy said.

They walked over where baggage was coming out the conveyor beside cargo's main ramp. The cargo hands, family, were tossing duffles to cousins who were there to claim them, and Jeremy snagged all four in short order, for them to take up.

"Where do we go?" Linda wanted to know. "Where, where, where have they got us? What's the number?"

"We're all at the Pioneer," Fletcher said. "It's number 28 Blue, that way down the dock." He pointed, in the smug surety of location that came with knowing they were docked at berth number 6 and the numbers matched.

"They got a game parlor at number 20," Vince said, already pushing. "It's on the specs. I read it. There's this high-gee sim ride. It's just eight numbers down. We can go there on our own. . . ."

"The aquarium," Jeremy reminded him.

"Who wants stupid fish?" Linda asked. "I don't want to look at something I've got to eat!"

"Shut up! I do!"

"Game parlor this evening," Fletcher said. "First thing after breakfast, the Mariner Aquarium, all three of you, like it or not. Vids in the afternoon, and the sim ride, if I'm in a good mood."

"You're not supposed to go *with* us," Vince said. "Go off to a bar or something. You can get drinks. We won't say a word. Wayne did."

"Find JR and complain," Fletcher said. He heard no takers as he shepherded his flock past the customs kiosk, a wave-through, as most big-ship arrivals were.

JR was even in the vicinity, with Bucklin and Chad and Lyra, as they cleared customs, and he didn't notice Vincent or Linda lodging any protest.

You know stations, JR had said in his brief attached note, explaining the general details of his duties and telling him the name and address of the sleepover they'd be staying in. It gave him something to be, and do, and a schedule, otherwise he foresaw he was going to have a lot of time on his hands.

He'd also been sure at very first thought that he didn't want to consider ducking out or appealing to authorities or doing anything that would get him left on Mariner entangled in *its* legal systems. That was when he'd known he'd settled some other situation in his mind as a worse choice than being on *Finity*, and that a grimly rules-conscious station one jump from where he wanted to be was *not* his choice.

So, amused, yes, he'd do JR's baby-sitting for him, grudgingly grateful that he was shepherding Jeremy and not the other way around. And JR's statement *you know stations* went further than JR might expect. He knew Pell Station docks upside and down. He knew a hundred ways for juveniles to get into trouble even Jeremy probably hadn't even thought of, like how to get into service passages and into theaters you weren't supposed to get to, how to bilk a change machine and how to get tapes past the checkout machines without paying. He hadn't been a spacer kid occasionally filching candy and soft drinks he wasn't supposed to have, oh, no. He'd been on a first name basis with the police, in his worst brat-days; and when JR had said, *Watch Jeremy*, his imagination had instantly and nervously extended much further than JR might have expected, and to a level of responsibility JR might not have entirely conceived. Jeremy's liberty wasn't going to be nearly that exciting, because he wasn't going to let his charges do any of those things. They gave him responsibility? *He* was going to come back to the ship in an aura of confidence and competence that would settle all question about whether Fletcher Neihart could be taken for a fool by three spacer kids. The converse was not to be contemplated.

Confined to *Blue and Green*? That eliminated a whole array of things to get into. It was the high-rent area, the main banks, the big dockside stores, government offices, trade offices, restaurants and elite sleepovers.

It was where stationers who did venture into the docks did their venturing. It also was where the well-placed juvvie predators looked for high-credit targets, if this long-out-of-trade ship's crew was in any wise naïve on that score. *Finity* juniors as well as the high officers had their pre-arranged sleepover accommodations in *Blue*, where, no, they wouldn't get robbed in a high-priced sleepover, but short-changed, bill padded? They might as well have had signs on their heads saying, Rich Spacers, Cash Here. It was a tossup in his estimation whether *Finity*'s reputation would scare off more of the rough kind of trouble than it attracted of the soft-fingered kind.

The junior-juniors weren't going to handle their own money, not even the 20 c cash chits: he'd dole it out at need, and he was very confident the local finger artists couldn't score on him. He almost hoped they did try, on certain others of the crew, notably Chad and Sue; he was confident at least the con artists would flock. Pick-pockets. Short-changers, even at the legitimate credit exchangers. Credit clerks would deal straight for stationers they knew were going to be there tomorrow, and who'd surely be back to complain if they got the wrong change. Spacers in civvies they might be just a little inclined to deal straight with . . . in case they were stationers after all. Spacers in dock flash and wearing their patches were a clear target for the exchange clerks; and God help spacers at any counter who might be just a little drunk, and whose board calls were imminent. Crooks of all sorts knew just as well as station administration did which ships were imminently outbound. When a ship was scheduled outbound, the predators clustered to work last moment mayhem.

He checked in at the desk, in this posh spacer accommodation that didn't at all look like the den of iniquity stationer youngsters dreamed of. Blue and dusky purple, soft colors, neon in evidence but subdued. There was a sailing ship motif and an antique satellite sculpture levved above a bronze ship on a bronze sea, the Pioneer's logo, which was also on the counter. A sign said, *We will gladly sell you logo items at cost at the desk.*

"Can we go to the vid-games before supper?" Jeremy asked.

"Maybe." He distributed keys. They had, for the duration, private rooms, an unexpected bonus.

He also had a pocket-com. So did the juniors. There were three stories in this hostel, all within what a station called level 9. The junior-juniors and he all had third floor rooms, and this time they had locks.

He shepherded the noisy threesome upstairs via the lift, sent them to the rooms, with their keys, to unpack and settle in and knock at his door when they were done.

It was the fanciest place he'd ever visited. He opened the door on his own quarters, and if the ship was crowded, the sleepover was a palace, a huge living space, a bedroom separate from that, a desk, vid built-ins, a bath a man could drown in.

He knew that Mariner was new since the War, but this was beyond his dreams. Two weeks in this place. Endless vid-games, trips to see the sights.

He suffered a moment of panic, thinking about the money Madelaine had given him, and everything really necessary already being paid for—

And then thinking about the ship, and home, and the hard, cold chairs in the police station, and the tight, small apartment his mother had died in, in tangled sheets, down the short hall from a scummy little kitchen where they'd had breakfast the last morning and where he'd been looking for sandwiches . . . but she hadn't made any . . .

He sat down on the arm of an overstuffed chair and looked around him in a kind of stunned paralysis, his duffle with the sock for an ID dumped on immaculate, expensive carpet at his feet. *This* kind of luxury was what she'd been used to.

He saw the barracks beds of the men's dorm, down at the Base. He heard the wind outside, saw the trees swaying and sighing in the storm the night before he'd left . . .

Came a different thunder. The kids knocked at the door, all three wanting to go play games.

"God bless," Jeremy said, casting his own look around.

"Are they all like this?" he asked. "Are your rooms this big? This fancy?"

"About half this," Jeremy said. "Kind of spooky, i'n't it? Like you really want to belt in at night."

He had to be amused. "Stations don't brake."

"Yeah, stupid," Linda said. "If this place ever braked there'd be stuff everywhere."

"Pell did, once," Jeremy said. "So did this place. It totally wrecked."

"In the War," Fletcher said. "They didn't brake. They went unstable. There's a difference."

"Shut up, shut up," Linda said, and shoved Jeremy with both hands. "Don't get technical. He'll be like JR, and we'll have to look it up!"

He was moved to amusement. And a sense that, yes, he could be the villain and log them all with assignments.

But he wouldn't have liked it when he'd been anticipating a holiday, and if he hadn't forgiven Chad for the hazing, he didn't count it against Jeremy, who'd have to be included in any time-log he might be moved to make against Vince and Linda.

"So what do you want to do?" he asked the expectant three-some, and got back the expected list: Vids. Games. Shopping. And from Jeremy, over Linda's protests, the aquarium.

He laid down the schedule for the next three days, pending change from on high, and distress turned to overexcitement. "Settle down," he had to say, to save the furniture.

The Pioneer was a comfortable lodgings—good restaurant, good bar—game parlor to keep the junior-juniors occupied at all hours, which was no longer JR's concern.

Well . . . not officially his concern.

He was mirroring Francie this stop. That meant that whatever Francie did—*Captain* Frances Atchison Neihart—he did, mirrored the duties, the set-ups, everything. He didn't bother Francie with asking how he'd performed. He just ran ops on his handheld just as if it were real, and, by sometime trips out to the ship, checked the outcome against Francie's real decisions. Every piece of information regarding crew affairs that Francie got, he got. Every page that called Francie away from a quiet lunch, he also got. Every meeting with traders that Francie set up, he set up in shadow, with calls that went no further than his personal scheduler; without ever calling ship's-com on the unsecured public system or betraying *Finity*'s dealings to outsiders who might have a commercial interest in them, he continually checked his own performance against a posted captain's.

It was occasionally humbling. The fact that he'd been in a noisy bar and hadn't felt the pocket-com summon Francie to an alterday decision on a buy/no-buy that would have cost the ship 50,000 if he'd been in charge . . . that was embarrassing.

Occasionally it was satisfying: he'd been able to flash Francie real data on a suddenly incoming ship out of Viking that had a bearing on commodities prices. That had made 24,000 c.

And it was just as often baffling. He'd never done real trade. Madison and Hayes, their commodities specialist, had schooled him for years on the actual market theoreticals he'd not paid adequate attention to, in his concentration on the intelligence of ship movements they also provided. But the market now became important. He usually didn't lose money in his tracking of his picked and imaginary trades, but he wasn't in Hayes' class, and didn't have Madison's grasp of economics. Madison *enjoyed* it. The Old Man enjoyed it. He tried to persuade himself he'd learn to.

Anything you were motivated to buy came from somebody equally convinced it was time to sell. That was one mock-expensive thing he'd learned at Sol. And a good thing his buys were all theoretical.

But trade was not the only activity senior crew was conducting. He first began to suspect something else was going on, by reason of the unprecedented set of messages _Francie_ was getting from the Old Man. Meeting at 0400h/m; meeting at 0800. Meeting not with cargo officers, but with various captains of various other ships, at the same time Madison and Alan were holding similar meetings. The Old Man had been socializing with the stationmaster, very much as the Old Man had done at Pell . . . but more surprisingly so. The Old Man had a historical relationship with Elene Quen. It would have been remarkable if they hadn't met.

It was understandable, he supposed, that the Old Man wanted to meet with Mariner's authorities, considering that _Finity_ was a new and major trader in this system.

But there was anomaly in the messages that flew back and forth, notes which didn't to his mind reflect interest in trading statistics. There was nothing, for instance, that they traded in common with several of those appointments; there was a requirement of extreme security; and there were requests for background checks on every ship on the contact list, checks that had to be run very discreetly, via an immense download of Mariner Station confidential records—which were open to both Alliance and Union military, by treaty, but they were not part of the ordinary course of trade.

All these meetings, a high-security kind of goings-on. Whatever the captains were saying to other captains didn't bear discussion in the Pioneer's conference rooms.

He could miss items when it came to trading. He _didn't_ fail to notice a care for security far greater than he'd have judged necessary. A ship traded what it traded. She _didn't_ need to consult the captains of other ships in such tight security. She didn't need to consult the stationmasters of Mariner in private meetings that lasted for ten hours, in shifts.

She didn't need to have an emergency message couriered by a spacer from a shiny alleged Union merchanter that happened to be in port—the quasi-merchanter _Boreale,_ which if it hauled cargo only did so as a sideline. It was a Union cargo-carrier, it wasn't Family, and it set the hairs on JR's neck up to find himself facing a very nice-looking, very orderly young man who just happened to drop by a hand-written and sealed message at *Finity*'s berth.

Union military. He'd bet his next liberty on it. The physical perfection he'd seen in aggregations of Union personnel made his skin crawl. But the young man smiled in a friendly way and volunteered the information that they'd just come in from Cyteen.

"I'm pleased to meet you," the young man said, shaking his hand with an enthusiasm that cast in doubt his suspicions the man was azi. "You have my admiration."

"Thank you," was all he knew how to say, on behalf of *Finity* crew, and stumbled his way into small talk with a sometime enemy, sometime ally who wasn't privileged to set foot aboard. He was sure the courier was at least gene-altered, in the way that Cyteen was known to meddle with human heredity, and he was equally sure that the politeness and polish before him was tape-instructed and bent on getting information out of any chance remark he might make.

They stood behind the customs line, short of *Finity*'s entry port, where he'd come to prevent a Union spacer from visiting *Finity*'s airlock, and talked for as long as five minutes about Mariner's attractions and about the chances for peace.

He couldn't even remember what he'd said, except that it involved the fact that Mariner hit your account with charges for things Cyteen stations provided free. On one level it was a commercial for their trading with Union—a ridiculous notion, considering who they were. On the other, considering they were discussing details about Cyteen's inmost station, about which Cyteen maintained strict security, he supposed the man had been outrageously talkative, even forthcoming. Had the man in fact known what *Finity* was? Could their absence in remote Sol space have taken them that far out of public consciousness.

No. It was not possible. People did know. And it had been decidedly odd, that meeting. Like a sensor-pass over them, wanting information on a more intimate level.

When he conveyed the envelope to the ops office inside the ship and the inner seal proved to be a private message to the Old

Man—he was on the one hand not surprised by the address to the captain in the light of all the other hush-hush going on; and on the other, he became certain that the whiskey bottle was only the opening salvo in the business.

"Sir," he said, proffering that inner message across the desk, in the Old Man's downside office, next door to ops. "From *Boreale.*"

"Thank you," the Old Man said, receiving the envelope, and proceeded to open it with not a word more. The message caused the mild lifting of brows and a slightly amused look.

The junior captain was not informed regarding what. "That's all," the Old Man said, and JR felt no small touch of irritation on his way to the door.

He walked out with the dead certainty that he'd not passed the test. He'd gotten far enough to know something was going on: his mirroring of Francie's duty time told him the details of everything and the central facts of nothing, and he was starting to feel like a fool. If he, inside *Finity,* couldn't penetrate the secrecy, he supposed the security was working; but he had the feeling that the Old Man had expected some challenge from him.

It was trade they were engaged in. It involved meetings with Quen, meetings with Mariner authorities, meetings with other merchant captains, to none of which he was admitted, and the Old Man, sure sign of something serious going on, had never briefed him.

Definitely it was a test. He'd grown up under the Old Man's tutelage, closely so since he'd come under the Old Man's guardianship. In a certain measure he was the accessible, onboard offspring no male spacer ever had—and which the Old Man had taken no opportunities to have elsewhere. While the Old Man had a habit of letting him *find out things*, figuring that an officer who couldn't wasn't good enough . . . he'd often reciprocated, letting the Old Man guess whether and when he'd gotten enough information into his hands. And he wondered by now which foot the Old Man thought he was on, whether he was being outstandingly clever, or outstandingly obtuse.

Meetings. All sorts of meetings. And a whiskey bottle from Mallory.

What they were doing came from Mallory, was agreed upon with Mallory . . . and ran a course from Earth to Pell to a Union carrier there was no human way to have set up a meeting with—unless it had been far in advance, at least a year in advance.

Nothing he could recall had set it up, except that a year ago a courier run had gone out from Mallory to Pell.

If something had gone farther than Pell it wouldn't necessarily have gone through Quen. It could have gone through a merchant captain and through Viking or Mariner to reach Cyteen, to bring that ship out to wait for them. . . .

Had Fletcher's delay in boarding at Pell meant a *Union carrier* was sitting idle for five days?

Remarkable thought. It might account for Helm's nervousness when they'd gone in.

A bottle of whiskey from Mallory and then all these meetings at a port which accepted a handful of carefully watched, carefully regulated Union ships.

But if one counted the shadow trade—

If one counted the shadow trade, and a hell of a lot of the shadow trade went on along their course, Mariner had a *lot* of shady contact. The next station over, Voyager, was a sieve, by reputation: it couldn't communicate with anything but Mariner, it was a marginal station desperately clinging to existence, between Mariner and Esperance. The stations of the Hinder Stars, the stepping-stones which Earth had used in the pioneering days of starflight to get easy ship-runs for the old sublighters, had seen a rebirth after the War, and then, hardly a decade later, a rapid decline as a new route opened up to Earth trade, a route possible for big-engined military ships and also for the big merchant haulers, which were consequently out-competing the smaller ones and close to driving the little marginal merchanters out of business and out of their livelihood.

There was a lot of discontent among merchanters who'd suffered during the War, who'd remained loyal, who now saw their interests and their very existence threatened by big ships taking the best cargo farther, and by Union hauling cargo on military ships. They'd won the War only to see the post-War economy eat them alive.

And the Old Man was dealing with one of those cargo-hauling Union warships, and talking to merchanter captains *and* station authorities?

What concerned *Finity*? The Mazianni concerned them. That and their recent spate of armed engagements, not with Mazian's Fleet, but with Mazian's supply network. He knew *that*, as the condition which had applied during *Finity*'s most recent operations.

They'd crippled a little merchanter named *Flare*, not too seriously. Left her for Mallory . . . just before they'd made their break with pirate-hunting and come to Sol and then to Pell. *Flare* was, yes, a merchanter like other merchanters, and like no few merchanters, dealing with the shadow market. But *Flare* had been operating in that market in no casual, opportunistic way: she'd been running cargo out beyond Sol System, a maneuver that, just in terms of its technical difficulty and danger, lifted the hair on a starpilot's neck: jumping out short-powered, deliberately letting Sol haul them back. It gave them a starship's almost inconceivable speed at a short range ordinarily possible only for slow-haulers, freighters that took years reaching a destination. But it was a maneuver which, if miscalculated, or if aborted in an equipment malfunction, could land them in the Sun; and what they were doing had to be worth that terrible risk.

Flare had six different identities that they'd tracked at Sol One alone. You didn't physically *see* a ship when it docked behind a station wall, and Mars Station was another security sieve, a system rife with corruption that went all the way up into administration and all the way back into the building of the station.

He stopped in the hallway, saying to himself that, yes, Mazian was indeed getting supply from such ships as *Flare*, well known fact of their recent lives; and, second thought, it was after that interception that the Old Man had gone to such uncommon lengths to put *Finity* into a strict compliance with the station tariff laws which every merchanter operating outright ignored, cheated on, or simply, brazenly defied—using the very principle of merchanter sovereignty which *Finity's End* had won all those years ago.

That a ship couldn't be entered or searched without permission of the ship's owners put a ship's manifest on the honor system. A ship could be denied docking, yes, and there'd been standoffs: stations insisted on customs search or no fueling; but a ship then told the customs agents which areas it would get to search, and in tacit arrangements that accompanied such searches, their own cabins full of whiskey, as crew area, could have gone completely undetected.

Third fact. Their luxury goods weren't getting offloaded even this far along their course, and they were still paying those transit taxes, confessing to their load and paying. They'd laded their hold with staples, sold off a little whiskey and coffee at Pell and kept most of it. Added Pell wines and foodstuffs, which were high-temperature goods and which had to take the place of whiskey in those cabins.

And they weren't offloading all those goods at Mariner, either. The plan was, he believed now, to carry them on to Esperance, where there was, as there was at Mariner, a pipeline to Union.

But hell if they had to go that far to sell whiskey at a profit.

Pell, Mariner, Voyager, Esperance. They were the border stations, the thin economic line that sustained the Alliance. Add Earth, and the stations involved were an economic bubble with a thin skin and two economic powers, Earth and Pell, producing goods that kept the Alliance going. Mariner was the one of the several stations that was prospering. Yes, those stations all had to stay viable for the health of the Alliance, and yet . . .

Union wouldn't break the War open again to grab them: the collapse of a market for Union's artificially inflated population and industry was too much risk. Union always trembled on the edge of too much growth too soon and expanded its own populations with azi destined to be workers and ultimately consumers of its production; but populations ready-made and hungry for Union luxuries and the all-important Union pharmaceuticals were too great a lure. Union had ended the War with a virtual lock on all the border stations. Now Union kept a mostly disinterested eye to the border stations' slow drift into the Alliance system, because Union didn't want to lose markets. Union was interested in Viking; *interested* in the border stations, which had gone onto the Alliance reporting system with scarcely a quibble. *Nobody*, not even Union, profited if the marginal stations collapsed, and the vigorous support of Alliance merchanters also moved Union goods into markets Union otherwise couldn't reach.

The Old Man was talking to Union this trip. And they'd left an important military action to go off and enter the realm of trade. Madelaine, the night of the party, had talked about tariffs, just before she went off the topic of deals and railed on Quen.

He must have looked an idiot to Jake, who passed him in the corridor. He was still standing, adding things up the slow way.

But he stood there a moment longer reviewing his facts, and then turned around and signaled a request for entry to the Old Man's office.

The light gave permission. He walked in and saw James Robert look at him with a little surprise, and a microscopic amount of anticipation.

"Trade talks with Union," he said to the Old Man. "About the shadow market. Maybe the status of the border stations. Am I a fool?"

The Old Man grinned.

"Now what ever would make you think that?"

"Esperance and Voyager are leakier than Mars, in black market terms, and if we really wanted profit, we'd round-trip to Earth for another load of Scotch whiskey."

"Is that all?"

"So it's not money, and we've suddenly become immaculate about the tariff regulations. I know we have principles, sir, but it seems we're making a point, and we're agreeing to Quen's shipbuilding and paying her station tariffs by the book."

There was a moment of stony silence. "We don't of course have a linkage."

"No, sir, of course we don't. We got Fletcher for the ship. We got Quen to agree to something else and we're talking to Union couriers. I'd say we advised Union as early as last year we were shifting operations, and we promised them that Quen can pull Esperance and Voyager into agreement on whatever-it-is without her really raising a sweat, unless Union makes those two stations some backdoor offer to become solely Union ports. And Union won't do *that* because they're a military bridge to Earth and it would as good as declare war. Mariner, though, could play both ends against the middle. Except if the merchanters themselves threaten boycott. That would make Mariner fall in line."

A twitch tugged the edge of the Old Man's mouth. "Mariner isn't going to fight us. But Mariner *will* play both sides. Security-wise, you just don't tell Mariner anything except what you expect it to do. Its police are hair-triggered bullies, on dockside. But its politicians have no nerves for anything that could lead to another crisis or a renewal of Union claims on the station. The populace of Mariner is invested in rebuilding, trade, profit. They're squealing in anguish over the thought of lowered tariffs, but they're interested in the proposition of merchanters doing all their trading on dockside."

"All their trading."

"If the stations lower tariffs the key merchanters will agree to pay the tax on goods-in-transit and agree that goods will move on station docks. *Only* on station docks. That lets us trace Mazian's supply routes far more accurately. It stops goods floating around out there at jump-points where they become Mazian's supply. And it stops Union from building merchant ships . . . that's the quid pro quo we get from Union: we hold up to them the prospect of stopping Mazian and stabilizing trade, which they desperately want."

He let go a breath. Stopping the smuggling . . . a way of life among merchanters since the first merchanter picked up a little private stock to trade at his destination . . . revised all the rules of what had grown into a massive system of non-compliance.

"Are the captains going with it, sir?"

"Some. With some—they're agreeing because I say try it. That's why the first one to propose the change had to be this ship. We're the oldest, we're the richest, and that's why *we* had to be the ones to go back to trade, put our profits at risk, lead the merchanters, pay the tariffs, and call in debts from Quen. The shipbuilding she wants to launch is an easy project compared to bringing every independent merchanter in space into compliance. But her deal does make a necessary point with Union— we build the merchant ships and they don't. Building that ship of hers actually becomes a bonus with the merchanters, a proof we're asserting merchanter rights against Union, not just giving up rights as one more sacrifice to beat Mazian. The black market is going to go out of fashion, and merchanters are going to police it. Not stations, and not Union warships. Esperance and Voyager are, you're right, weak points that have to get something out of this, and the promise of their clientele paying tariffs on all the wealth passing through there on its way to Cyteen is going to revise their universe."

"I'm amazed," was all he found to say.

"Mazian, of course, isn't going to like it. Neither are the merchanters that are trading with him. As some are. We know certain names. We just haven't had a way to charge them with misbehaviors. Consequently we are a target, Jamie. I've wondered how much you could guess and when you'd penetrate the security screen. Pardon me for using you as a security gauge, but if you've figured it, I can assure myself that others with inside knowledge, on the opposing side, can figure it out, too. So I place myself on notice that we have to assume from now on that they do know, and that we need to be on our guard. We're about to threaten the living of the most unprincipled bastards among our fellow merchanters. Not to mention the suppliers on station."

"Sabotage?"

"Sabotage. Direct attack. Between you, me, and the senior crew, Jamie-lad, I'm hoping we get through this with no one trying it. But if you hear anything, however minor, report it. I don't want one of you held hostage, I don't want a poison pill, I don't want a Mazianni carrier turning up in our path between here and Esperance. The danger will go off us once we've gotten our agreement. But if they can prevent us securing an agreement in the first place, by taking this ship out, or by taking *me* out, they'd go that far, damn sure they would."

"I've put Fletcher out there on the docks with three kids."

"Oh, he's been watched. He's being watched." The Old Man gave a quiet chuckle. "He's got those kids walking in step and saying yes, sir in unison."

It was literally true. He'd been watching Fletcher, too, on the quiet.

"But we've got *Champlain* under watch, too," the Old Man said. "*Champlain's* listed for Voyager. They're due to go out ahead of us, six days from now."

JR was aware of that schedule, too. *Champlain* and *China Clipper* both were suspect ships on their general list of watch-its. A suspect ship running ahead of them on their route was worrisome.

"Once they've cleared the system," the Old Man said, "you'll see our departure time change for a six-hour notice. *Boreale* can out-muscle them on the jump, and *Boreale* is offering to run guard for us. I think we can rely on them. Let somebody else worry for a change. We'll carry mail for Voyager and Esperance. We can clear the security requirements for the postal contract and I'll guarantee *Champlain* can't."

Mail was zero-mass cargo. It made them run light. The Union ship *Boreale,* perhaps in the message he'd just hand-delivered to the Old Man, was going to chase *Champlain* into the jump-point and assure that they got through safely.

How the times had changed!

"Yes, sir," he said. "Glad to know that."

So he took his leave and the Old Man returned to his cor-respondence with *Boreale.*

So they were pulling out early, to inconvenience those making plans. It had the flavor of the old days, the gut-tightening apprehension of coming out of jump expecting trouble. And it was chancier, in some ways. With Mallory you always knew where you stood. The other side shot at you. You shot at them. That was simple.

Here, part of the merchanters who should be working on their side was working for the Mazianni and at the same time, representatives of their former enemy Union might be working for Mallory.

He supposed he'd better talk to the juniors about security. The juniors, especially the junior-juniors with Fletcher, were, on one level, sacrosanct: any dock crawler that messed with a ship's junior crew was asking for cracked skulls, no recourse to station police, just hand-to-hand mayhem, in the oldest law there was among merchanters. Even station cops ignored the enforcement of simple justice.

But he didn't want to deliver the Old Man any surprises. And Fletcher was worth a special thought. Attaching Jeremy to him with an invisible chain seemed to him the brightest thing he'd done at this port.

340   C. J. CHERRYH

The lift was without him, the lock upward bound, and he
turned for the stairs. . . .

"Educated," a raspy voice said behind and he caught himself
with his hand on the rail.

It was Vance, with a foolish smile.

". . . What's the problem?"

"Not a thing." Wayne said cheerfully, and brushed off the
importunate contacts with a wave of his arm.

He was just well on . . .

Chapter

—XVI—

Games, vids, more games, restaurants with a perpetual sugar
high. It was everything a kid could dream of . . . and that was
when Fletcher began to know he was, at stationbred seventeen,
growing old. The body couldn't take the sugar hits. The ears
grew tired of the racketing games. The stomach grew tired of
being pitched upside down after full meals. So did Vince's,
and the ship's sometime lawyer lost his three frosty shakes in
a game parlor restroom, and didn't want to contemplate anything lime-colored afterward, but Vince was back on the rides
faster than Fletcher would have bet.

It meant, when he took them back to the sleepover nightly,
that they were down to the frazzled ends, exhausted and laying
extravagant plans for return visits.

Linda had bought a tape on exotic fish.

And he'd gotten them back alive, through a very good meal
at the restaurant, past the sleepover's jammed vid parlor. He
loaded them into the lift.

"Hello," someone female said, and he fell into a double
ambush of very good-looking women he'd never met, who had
absolutely no hesitation about a hands-on introduction.

"On duty," he said. He'd learned to say that. Jeremy and the
juniors were laughing and hooting from the open elevator, and
he ricocheted into a third ambush, this one male, in the same
ship's green, who brushed a hand past his arm a hair's-breadth
from offense and grinned at him.

"What's your room number?"

"I'm on duty," he said, and got past, not without touches on
his person, not without blushing bright red. He felt it.

The lift left without him, the kids upward bound, and he dived for the stairs.

"Fletcher!" a *Finity* voice called out, and he caught himself with his hand on the bannister.

It was Wayne, with a grin on his face.

"What's the trouble?"

"Not a thing," Wayne said cheerfully, and brushed off the importunate incomers with a wave of his arm.

"The kids just went up."

"They'll survive," Wayne said. "Join us in the bar."

"I'm not supposed to."

"JR's with us." Wayne clapped him on the shoulder. "Come on in."

He'd not had a better offer—on first thought.

On second, he was exceedingly wary it was a set-up.

Except that Wayne had been one of the solid, the reliable ones. He decided to go to the door of the bar and have a look and risk the joke, if there was one.

It was as advertised, the senior-juniors with a table staked out and a festive occasion underway. Wayne set a hand on his back and steered him toward the group. JR beckoned him closer.

He took it for an order, set his face and walked up to the table . . . where Lyra cleared back, Bucklin pulled up a chair, and JR signaled service. Chad was there, Nike, Wayne, Sue, Connor, Toby, Ashley . . . the whole batch of them.

"Our novice here just shed three offers," Wayne announced. "They're in tight orbit about this lad."

"Not surprised," Lyra said. "I would, if he weren't off-limits."

"You would, if *you* weren't off-limits," Connor gibed. "Come on, be honest."

He wasn't sure whether that was a joke at his expense or not, but the waiter showed up and asked him what he was drinking. He took a chance and ordered wine.

Talk went on around him, letting him fall out of the spotlight. He was content with that. They talked about the sights on the station. They talked about the progress of the loading, they talked about the rowdy arrival—it was a freighter named *Belize,* a small but reputable ship, no threat to anyone—and he had his glass of wine, which tasted good and hit a stomach long unaccustomed to it. Chad ordered another beer. There were second orders all around.

"I'd better get up to the kids," he said, and got up and started to move off.

"Good job," JR said soberly. "Fletcher. Good job. If you want to stay another round, stay."

"Thanks," he said, feeling a little desperate, a little trapped. More than a little buzzed by the wine. "But I'd better get up there."

"Fletcher," Lyra said. "Welcome in."

Maybe it was a test. Maybe he'd passed. He didn't know. He offered money for his share of the tab, but JR waved if off and said it was on them.

"Yessir," he said. "Thank you." He escaped, then, not feeling in control of the encounter, not feeling sure of himself in his graceless duck out of the gathering and out of the bar.

But they'd invited him. His nerves were still buzzing with that and the alcohol, and if spacers from *Belize* tried to snag him he drifted through them in a haze, unnoticing. He rode the lift up to the level of his room, got out in a corridor peaceful and deserted except for a slightly worse for wear spacer from *Belize,* and entered his palace of a room, where he had every comfort he could ask for.

He'd written to Bianca. *Things aren't so bad as I'd thought...*

This evening he undressed, showered, and flung himself down in a huge bed that, as Jeremy had said, you almost wanted safety belts for ... and thought about Downbelow, not from pain this time, but from the comfort of a luxury he'd not imagined. Memories of Downbelow came to him now at odd moments as those of a distant place—so beautiful; but the hardship of life down there was considerable, and he remembered that, too—only to blink and find himself surrounded by the sybaritic luxury of an accommodation he'd never in the world thought he could afford. He had so many sights swimming in his head it was like the glass-walled water, the huge fish patrolling a man-made ocean. His worlds seemed like that, insulated from each other.

His hurts tonight were all in that other world. He'd felt *good* tonight. He'd been anxious the entire while, not quite believing it was innocent until he was out of that bar without a trick played on him, but his cousins had made the move to include him, and he discovered—

He discovered he was glad of it.

He shut his eyes, ordered the lights out . . .

A knock came at the door. A flash at the entry-requested light.

Cursing, he got up, grabbed a towel as the nearest clothing-substitute, and went to see who it was before he opened the door.

Jeremy.

"What's the trouble?" he asked, and didn't bother to turn the lights on, standing there with a bathtowel wrapped around him and every indication of somebody trying to sleep.

"Vince and Linda went downstairs. I told them not to. But you weren't here. And they said they were going down to check . . ."

"I'm going to kill Vince," he said. "I may do it before breakfast." The lovely buzz from the wine was going away. Fast. He leaned against the doorframe, seeing duty clear. "Tell you what. You go downstairs, you tell them we just got a lot of strangers off another ship, some of them are drunk, and if they don't get their precious butts back up here before I get dressed and get down there, they're going to be sorry."

"I'm gone," Jeremy said, and hurried.

He dressed. There was no appearance at the door. He went downstairs, into the confusion of more *Belize* crew of both genders in the lobby, wanting the lift, noisy, straight in from celebrating their arrival in port—and their collection of spacers of different ships, not *Belize* and not *Finity*. He escaped a drunken invitation and escaped into the game parlor where Belizers were the sole crew in evidence—except the juniors, in an open-ended vid-game booth in which Jeremy, not faultless, was an earnest spectator.

Then Jeremy spotted him, and with a frantic glance tugged at Linda to get her attention to approaching danger. Vince, his head in the sim-lock, was oblivious until he walked up and tapped Vince on the shoulder.

Vince nearly lost an ear getting his head out of the port.

"You're not supposed to be down here without me."

"So you're here."

"I'm also sleepy, approaching a lousy mood, and the crowd in here's changed," Fletcher said.

"You don't have to be in charge of us," Vince said. "You're younger than I am!"

"So act your age. Upstairs."

"Chad never chased after us."

"Fine. I'll call Chad out of the bar."

"No," Linda said. "We're going."

"Thought so," he said. "Up and out of here." He'd been a Vince type, once upon a half a dozen years ago. And it amazed him how being on the in-charge side of bad behavior gave him no sympathy. "Come on. I'm not kidding."

"We weren't doing a damn thing!" Vince said.

"Come on." He patted Vince on the rump. "Still got your card wallet?"

Vince felt of the pocket. Fast. Frightened.

"Your good luck you do," he said, and gave it back to Vince.

"Yeah," Jeremy said mercilessly. And: "That's wild. How'd you do that?"

"I'm not about to show you." He put a hand on Jeremy's back and on Vince's and propelled them and Linda through the jam of adult, drunken Belizers at the door. "Up the stairs," he said to them, figuring the lifts were likely to be full of foolishness, and unidentified spacers. He thought of resorting to JR, then decided it was better to get the juniors into their rooms. He escorted them up three flights, unmolested, onto their floor, just as a flock of spacers arrived in the lift and came out onto the floor, with baggage, checking in, he supposed, but the situation was clearly different than what seemed ordinary.

"In the rooms and stay there," he said, with an anxious eye to the situation down the hall, where somebody was fighting with a room key. "Is it always like this?" he had to ask the juniors.

"No," Jeremy said.

It was supposed to be a tight-rules station. He knew Pell would have had the cops circulating by now. "Keep the doors locked," he said, saw all three juniors behind locked doors, and went back down the stairs.

A *Finity* senior in uniform met him, coming up: the tag said *James Arnold*.

"We've got kind of a rowdy lot up there," he said to his senior cousin.

"Noticed that," Arnold said. "Where are *you* going?"

"JR," he decided, his original intention, and he sped on down the stairs to the lobby, eeled past a couple more of the rowdy crew, and started through the lobby with the intention of going to the bar.

JR, however, was at the front desk talking urgently to the manager.

He waited there, not sure whether he'd acted the fool, until JR turned away from the conversation, the gist of which seemed to be the *Belize* crew.

"We've got them on our floor," he said to JR without preface. "James Arnold just went up there."

"Good," JR said. "Were they all *Belize*?"

"Some. Not all."

"It's all right. Management screwed up, but we've checked some personnel out to other sleepovers and they just put ten Belizers up where we'd agreed they wouldn't be. They're a little ship, an honest ship, that's the record we have. Just louder than hell. Just keep your doors locked. It's not theft you have to worry about."

He didn't understand for about two beats. Then did. And blushed.

"Seriously," JR said, and bumped his upper arm. "Go in uniform tomorrow. Juniors, too. That'll cool them down. Their senior officers know now there are *Finity* juniors on the third floor. Keep an eye on who comes in, what patch they're wearing. We've got lookouts on *China Clipper*, *Champlain*, *Filaree*, and *Far Reach*, for various reasons. If you see those patches, I want to know it on the pocket-com."

"What about the ones that aren't wearing patches?"

"We can't tell. That's the problem. But it's what we've got. Keep the junior-juniors glued to you. The ships I named are a serious problem in this port. Most are fine. But some crews aren't."

JR went off to talk to senior crew. He went back upstairs, not sure what to make of that last statement, thinking, with station-bred nerves, about piracy, and telling himself it might be just intership rivalry, maybe somebody *Finity* had a grudge with, and it wasn't anything to have drawn him in a panic run down-stairs, but JR hadn't said he was a fool. He picked up more propositions on his way through the crowd near the bar. A woman on the stairs invited him to her room for a drink—"Hey, you," was how it started, to his blurred perception, and ended with, "prettiest eyes in a hundred lights about. I've got a bottle in my kit."

"No," he said. "Sorry, on duty. Can't." He said it automat-ically, and then it occurred to him how very much the woman looked like Bianca.

He was suddenly homesick as well as rattled. He gained his floor, where Arnold, in *Finity* silver, was conspicuously on watch. He felt strangely safer by that presence, and his mind skittered off again to a pretty face and an invitation he'd just escaped just downstairs.

Gorgeous. Not drunk. And part of a problem that his ship's officers had sallied up here to head off. A problem that had chased the small-statured juniors to their rooms.

Interested in *him*, he thought dazedly as he put his keycard in the door slot. Interested not because he was from *Finity* and *Finity* was rich. He was in civvies. He could have been anybody. She was interested in *him*. That absolutely beautiful woman had wanted him.

His door opened. He made it in. Undamaged. Alone. Safe with the snick of that lock, and telling himself there had to be something critically wrong with his masculinity that he hadn't said the hell with the three brats and gone off with the most glamorous—hell, the *only* invitation of his life, including Bianca.

Intelligence, something said. Even while the invitation stayed a warm and arousing thought. He'd made it through a spacer riot, well . . . at least a moment of excitement that had gotten the officers' attention. His encounter on the stairs was probably a wonderful young woman. He might even meet her in the morning . . . but no, he had specific orders to the contrary. And what she wanted was too far for a stationer lad on his first voyage and she was . . .

What was she, really, looking maybe late twenties? Thirty? Forty?

He felt a little dazed. Not just about her. He'd caught invitations from *all* over. He, Fletcher Neihart, who'd only in the last year gotten a real date. He didn't know why the woman had looked at him, except *here* he didn't have a rep as a trouble-maker working against him.

Maybe he had *shiny-new* written all over him. Maybe—

Maybe what that woman had seen was a man, not a boy. Maybe that was who he *could* be.

He phoned the kids to be absolutely sure they were in their rooms and assured them there was a *Finity* senior on watch. He had another shower after all that running up and down stairs, and flung himself down in bed, in soft pillows, with his hands under his head.

The ceiling shifted colors subtly, one of the room's amenities—something just . . . just to be pretty. Something you had to pay for. And spacers lived like this. Rich ones did . . . unlike anything he'd ever experienced.

But that was a bauble. The warmth in the bar tonight, the acceptance with JR's crowd, that they hadn't been obliged to offer him—the pretty young women trying to attract his attention, that was the amazing thing in his days here. And tonight, the knowledge, dizzying as it was, that when things went chancy he wasn't alone, he wasn't counted a fool, and he had a shipful of people to turn up as welcome as Arnold and JR had done, to fend off trouble and know solidly what to do.

It was damned seductive, so seductive it put a lump in his throat despite the thin sounds of revelry that punctured the recent peace.

Did he still miss Downbelow? He conjured Old River in his mind, saw Patch laughing at him from the high bank, and yet . . .

Yet he couldn't hear the sound, not Patch's voice, not Melody's. He could only see the sunlight and the drifting pollen skeins. He couldn't remember the sounds.

And Melody and Patch by now believed he'd gone . . . Bianca had gone on with her studies, passed biochem, he did hope. What could she possibly know about where he was?

He'd written to the Wilsons. *I'm fine. I've done a lot of laundry. Now they've put me in charge of the kids. Who are older than I am. You'll find that funny. But my station years count, and they're far smaller than I am. I'm back doing vidgames and losing . . . I know you'll be amused . . .*

To Bianca he'd begun to write *I love you . . .* and he'd stopped, in the sudden knowledge that what they'd begun had never had time to grow to that word. He'd agonized over it. He'd not even been able to claim a heartfelt *I miss you . . .* because he'd gotten so far away and so removed from anything she'd understand that he didn't think about her except when he thought about Downbelow.

He'd written . . . instead . . . *I think about you. I wish you could see this place. It seems so close to Pell, now. Before, it seemed so far . . .*

He'd written . . . in a crisis of honesty . . . *I've kind of bounced around, people here, people there. I've never dealt with anybody I didn't choose. . . .*

If he added to that tonight, he'd write . . . *I don't think any group of people since I was a kid ever looked me up and invited me in . . . but they did that, tonight. It felt . . .*

But he wouldn't write that to Bianca, no admission she wasn't the one and only of his life . . . you weren't supposed to tell a girl that. No admission he'd had a dozen offers tonight. No admission he'd felt excited . . .

No admission he'd been scared as hell walking up to that group in the bar, and sure they were going to pull one on him, but he'd gone anyway, because he wanted . . . *wanted* what they held out to him. He wanted inclusion. A circle closing around him. He'd never felt complete in all his life.

He disliked Chad and Sue and Connor with less energy than he'd felt before he'd spent a few days ashore. Now they were familiar faces in a sea of strangers. He'd ended up talking to the lot of them, who'd made nothing of any grudge he had. He'd just been *in,* and the double-cross and the pain and the bruises and everything else had added up simply to being asked to that table to break one of JR's rules and to be regarded as one of them, not one of the kids.

That event was unexpectedly important to him, so important it buzzed him more than the wine, more than the woman trying to make connection with him, more than anything that had happened.

It's a setup, he kept saying to himself. He'd believed things before. He'd even believed one of his foster-brothers making up to him, best friends, until it turned out to be a setup, and a fight he'd won.

And lost. Along with childish trust.

He was dangerously close to believing, tonight, not the way he'd believed in Melody and Patch, nothing so dramatic . . . just a call to a table where he'd not been remarkable, just one of the set. He was theirs, because they had to find something to do with him. Making his life hell had been an option to them, but not the one they'd taken.

It was better than his relations with people at the Base, when he added it up. He'd come in there determined to succeed and George Willett, who'd planned to do just the minimum, had instantly hated him, so naturally the rest had to. He'd come aboard *Finity* mad and surly, and JR, give him credit, had been more level-headed than he had been, more generous than he had been . . .

He didn't exactly call truce or accept his situation on *Finity.* But for the first sickening moment . . . he wasn't sure if he knew how to get home again. The first actual *place* he'd visited, and he felt . . . separated . . . from all he had known, and *connected* to the likes of JR and Jeremy and a grandmother who gave him a handful of change on a first liberty.

He didn't know what was the matter with him, or why a handful of change and a drink in a bar could suddenly be important to him . . . more important than two downers he'd come to love. It was as if he had Downbelow in one hand and *Finity* in the other and was weighing them, trying to figure out which weighed the heaviest when he couldn't look at them or feel them at the same time.

It was as if the sounds had come rushing back to him and he could see Melody saying, in her strange, lilting voice, You go walk, Fetcher?

You grow up, Fetcher?

Find a human answer, . . . Fletcher?

Maybe he had to take the walk. Maybe the answer was out there.

Or maybe it was in that unprecedented *come and join us* he'd, for the first time in a decade, gotten from other human beings.

• • •

"If Pell reaches agreement," the Mariner stationmaster said, and James Robert declared, "Then bet on it. It's surer than the market."

Senior captains of a significant number of ships in port had happened to have business on Mariner's fifth level Blue at the same time, and found their way to a meeting unhampered this time by *Champlain*'s attempts to get into the circuit of information. *Champlain* was outbound this morning, and good riddance, JR thought, if *Champlain* weren't headed to *their* next port.

But in the kind of dispensation *Finity* had long been able to win on credentials the Old Man swore they'd resigned, the Union merchanter *Boreale* changed its routing and prepared an early departure.

In the same direction.

"If the tariff lowers *and* the dock charges lower," the senior captain of *Belize* said, "we'd sign."

Talk of tariffs and taxes, two subjects JR had never found particularly engaging until he saw the looks on the faces around him, senior captains of ships larger than *Belize* looking as if they'd swallowed something sour.

Belize, a small, old ship, incapable of doing much but Mariner to Pell, Pell to Viking and back again, saw its economics affected if the agreement of Mariner and Pell pulled Viking into line with that agreement. Viking's charges, JR was learning, were a matter of complaint among Alliance merchanters—while Union willingly paid the higher fees, for reasons Alliance merchanters saw as simply a pressure against them, encouraging the stations to excess.

A junior supplying water and running courier, as he'd been asked to do, he and Bucklin, could learn a great deal of tensions he'd known existed, but which he'd never mapped—the narrow gap between a station's charges for supplying a port and a ship's costs of operation, a slim gap in which profit existed for the smaller carriers.

But there were the windfall items: the few ships that had the power to make the runs to Earth, in particular, had enormous opportunity . . . and to his stunned surprise, the Old Man put that extreme profit up for trade as well.

A cartel, skimming off that profit, would assure the survival of the marginal ships, the old, the outmoded. An entire *system* of trade, giving critical breaks to the smaller ships.

"It won't work," Bucklin had said in the rest break after they'd first heard it. "We'll take less for our goods?"

"If the little ships fail," he'd said to Bucklin, the argument he'd heard from the Old Man, himself, "Union's going to move in."

Bucklin thought about that in long silence.

When that argument was advanced to them, the other captains had much the same reaction—and came to much the same conclusion.

Then it seemed the major obstacle would be Union.

But, JR reasoned for himself, and saw it borne out in arguments he was hearing, Union, growing among stars they had only vague reports of, responded to the pirate threat with a fear out of all proportion to the size of the Mazianni Fleet.

Probably it had to do with the fact that Union had been consistently outpiloted, outgunned, and outflanked.

Possibly it even had to do with fear of a third human establishment in space, an admittedly unhappy situation they'd all talked about aboard, but only in the small hours of the watches and not in public. Union set great importance on *planning* the human future, and a third human power arising from a base somewhere outside their knowledge might not be a comfortable thought for them.

"What we have," the Old Man said now in his argument to the gathering of captains and Mariner Station administration, "is a shadow route and a shadow trade that's running clear from Earth, dealing in exotics like whiskey, woods, that sort of thing, biologicals funneled on the short routes out of Sol . . . one ship we did catch, *Flare*, a Sol-based merchanter doing short-haul trade—not necessarily *with* Mazian, but *for* Mazian."

"Mazian's getting the profit, you mean." That was Walt Frazier of *Lily Maid*, a small hauler, an old acquaintance of Madison's and the Old Man, by what JR guessed.

"There's a well-developed shadow trade at Earth," the Old Man said. "As you may know. Mars is a rich market. Luxury goods get off Earth, they go toward Mars. A certain amount doesn't get there . . . written up as breakage during lift, just plain left off the manifests. And the mini-network leaks a certain amount via short-haul suppliers right on the docks of Sol One . . . but there's a fairly brazen trade—or there's *been* a fairly brazen trade—siphoning off goods to ships the like of *Flare* and several others we've been watching. They've been short-hopping their illicits out just to the edge of the system where others are picking it up and trading it on. We think certain interests in the Earth Company are supporting Mazian by running cargo for him, and that there's a link between thefts and smuggling in Sol One district—not war matériel: luxury goods. Paintings. Foodstuffs. It's high money. Money *does* buy Mazian what he wants."

Among the captains, among four, there were a few exchanged glances and slow nods, sharp interest from the others.

"And *Flare* is no longer operating," *Joshua* asked.

"Not *Flare*, but a ship named *Jubal* is. Was when we left Sol. Operating under Mallory's close curiosity. We want to know where the goods are coming from, but we also have an interest in tracing the route through the black market, and figuring how it translates into supplies. We find it ironical that the primary market for illicit luxuries is Cyteen. And the second-largest is Pell. Every credit spent in the black market has a good chance of coming back as ammunition and supply for the Fleet. It's picked up, run through the Hinder Stars, comes into this reach not necessarily at Mariner: more likely at Voyager, where security is less exacting, and then it travels on to Esperance, where it connects to Cyteen. But those are the heavy items. Big-time smuggling. In the same way, and adding up, money out of

the whole shadow market is drifting into Mazian's hands
through the *honest* merchanters. People just like you and me.
It's a situation that can collapse stations. Collapse our markets.
And have Mazian and Union going at it hammer and tongs
again across Alliance routes. *All* of us will be fighting, if that
happens, either that, or we'll be hauling for Union trying to beat
Mazian, and hoping to hell we don't get hit by raiders the first
voyage and the second and the third . . . That's the situation we
came from, and if we don't get fairness out of the stations
regarding our needs, and if we don't get compliance out of our
own brothers and sisters of the merchant Alliance to stop the
trade that's feeding Mazian, we'll see the bad days back again
and *hell* staring us in the face. You remember the feeling. You've
been out in the dark, at some jump-point with a hostile on the
scan and with no support in ten lightyears. *Don't leave Mallory*
in that condition. We're decent people. Let's stick to principles,
here. Let's realize how much the shadow-market does amount
to, and who's profiting."

God, the Old Man could rivet the rest of them. And he
could use words like *principles*, because he had them and
acted by them. Nobody moved. JR thought, This is how it was
all those years ago. This is how he got them to unite in the
action that started the War.

"So what percentage are we talking about?" *Lily Maid*
asked, to the point.

The Mariner stationmaster thought he was going to answer.
The Old Man said:

"Pell's talking ten."

There was a slow intake of breath.

"No higher," *Lily Maid* said, and *Genevieve* agreed.

"Are we talking about ten across the board?" the stationmaster wanted to know. "The luxury goods—"

"The point is," the Old Man said, "voluntary compliance.
We *voluntarily* confess the true manifest. If we install incen-
tives to hedge the truth, if we need a rulebook to tell what's right
and wrong, there won't be universal compliance. Flat ten."

There were long sighs, frowns, shiftings of position, literal and maybe figurative. A junior witness to a major turn in human history didn't dare take so much as a deep breath.

"It's a talking point," the stationmaster said. "If Pell agrees on a universal ten. If the black market stops. If *Union* agrees on the same percentage."

"We believe we can negotiate that point. They don't want a resurgence of raids. And they're worried about *what's* getting onto the market. The luxury trade is sending *biologicals* right back down the pipeline, right to Earth. Surprisingly, Cyteen shares one thing with us: the belief that the motherworld, as our genetic wellspring, *should be sacrosanct.* In that regard, and in what it takes to cut Mazian off cold, we will have their cooperation. The fact that they may harbor notions of cutting harder deals after we eliminate Mazian as a threat means that we have *two* jobs to do, one of which is to strengthen, not weaken, our weakest and slowest ships. This proposal of ours answers both needs."

They were listening. JR stood unmoving during discussion. He saw, from his vantage, Bucklin, who stood guard outside the meeting room, talking with Thomas B., who'd arrived with some news. Thomas B. left.

Then he saw Bucklin signal him, a fast set of hand-signals that said, in the way of spacers who sometimes worked in difficult environments, Talk, Urgent, Official.

He made his way around the edge of the room, and outside.

"Champlainers were in the Pioneer last watch," Bucklin said. "And *Champlain's* on the boards for depart in two hours. Alan just found it out."

"God." Their security was breached and the perpetrators were headed out toward a dark point of their next route. *Armed and hostile* perpetrators. "Where were they?"

"Came in with *Belize*. Spent the night and left this morning. *Belize's* captain doesn't know. They didn't have access to the ID we got from customs."

"Damn." They'd used their military credentials to get official records on the *Champlain* and *China Clipper* crews. *Belize* couldn't do that. And even knowing hadn't enabled them to spot everybody that came and went, any more than they could go about warning other ships about ships that hadn't committed any actual crime. "Just last watch, you're sure."

"Best I know, yes. Alan's handling it. And they're outbound; they went up on the boards in the last thirty minutes. Apparently it was two of the Champlainers, sleeping over with one *Belize* crew, on her invitation."

"Some party." He cast a look back through the glass where the meeting was still going on, still at a delicate point. It wasn't a time to disturb the Old Man and Madison. It wasn't a time to confront the *Belize* senior captain, who'd helped support their proposals, among others. "I suppose it's too much to ask that the Belizer remembers exactly what he told them, or what they discussed."

"She. And no, by what seems, she *thinks* there were two and she *thinks* they never left the room."

Belize was a lively ship, say that for them.

"Can't interrupt right now," he said, "but five'll get you ten we get an early board call. We might overjump that tub if we got moving. Let them stare down *our* guns." He had his back to the windows to preclude lip-reading and didn't want to create more distraction than his extended receipt of some message from Bucklin might have done already. "I'd better get back in there," he said. "Nothing we can do from here. Where's Tom gone?"

"Just passing the word about. Alan's orders."

"We'll go on boarding call. Just watch."

He went back into the meeting, took up a quiet, confident stance a little nearer the door.

Belize had had a particularly hard run from Tripoint, and a mechanical that had risked their lives getting in. To the *Belize* family's delight, they'd sold their cargo right off the dock, the problem had turned out to be a relatively inexpensive module, and he had every sympathy for the Belizers' desire to celebrate, in a sleepover far fancier than they ordinarily afforded. They'd lodged their juniors at the more junior-friendly Newton, and hadn't remotely expected youngsters in a fancy lodging like the Pioneer. That was easily sorted out, and they weren't bad people. The adult and randy Belizers, however, had proceeded to drink the bar dry, and gone down the row, looking for assignations the hour they'd docked—some of *Finity*'s own had cheerfully taken them up on the offer. They'd been quieter neighbors since the first night, goodnaturedly gullible as they were, and now, damn! one of them had taken up with a ship their own captain had put the *avoid* sign on.

Meanwhile the *Belize* senior captain had had a very cordial session with the Old Man of *Finity's End*, and word was that bottles from *Finity*'s cargo, duly tariffed and taxed, were making their way to various ships. If spies were taking notes of the number of captains who got together in a shifting combination of venues, they must have a full-time occupation; what worried him, and what he was sure would worry the Old Man, was the likelihood that *Belize*'s internal security was as lax as its concept of restricted residency.

If the *Belize* captain had talked too much to his own crew, some of their business could have gotten into that sleepover room last night and right into the ears of curious Champlainers.

Who now were outbound.

It had to be a successful stay on dockside, Fletcher said to himself: Jeremy had a stomachache and all of them had run out of money. Here they were, standing in line for customs three days earlier than their scheduled board call, a moving line. Customs was just waving them through.

Their loading must have gone faster than estimated. And Fletcher was relatively proud of himself. He'd had the pocketcom switch in the right position; he'd gotten the call, figured out the complexities of the pocket-com to be able to key in an acknowledgement that they were coming, and gotten the juniors to the dock with no more delay than a modest and reasonable request from Jeremy to make a last-minute dive into a shop near the Pioneer to get a music tape he'd been eyeing. And some candy.

So Jeremy wasn't so sick as to forswear future sweets.

And instead of the slow-moving clearance of passports in their exit, they advanced through customs at a walk, flashed the passport through the reader on the counter, only observed by a single customs agent, tossed their duffles uninspected onto the moving cargo belt for loading, and walked up the ramp to the access tube, where for brief periods the airlock stood open at both ends to let groups of them walk through.

"They *are* in a hurry," Linda said when she saw that.

"New Old Rules," Vince said. "Maybe they're going to do that after this. No more lines."

"We've got a security alert," a senior cousin behind them said, breath frosting in the chill of the yellow, ribbed access.

"About what?" Jeremy asked.

"Just a ship we don't like. But we're not going out alone." The cousin ruffled Jeremy's hair and Jeremy did the time immemorial wince and flinch. "No need to worry."

"So who are they?" Fletcher asked, not sure what *security alert* entailed, whether it was a trade rivalry or a question of guns and something far more serious.

"What we've got," the cousin behind that cousin said—one was Linny and the other was Charlie T.—"what we've got is a rimrunner for the other side. But we've *also* got an escort. Union ship *Boreale* is going to go our route with us."

A *Union* ship?

"Do we trust them?" Fletcher asked.

"Sometimes," Charlie T. said. And about that time the airlock opened up and started letting them through, a fast bunch-up and a press to get on through and out of the bitter cold. They went through in a puff of fog that condensed around them. They'd put down a metal grid for traction as they entered the corridor, and it was frosted and puddled from previous entries.

Mini-weather, Fletcher thought, his head spinning with the possibilities of Union escorts, an emergency boarding. But the cousins around him remained cheerful, talking most about Mariner restaurants and what they'd found in the way of bargains in the shops. A cousin had a truly outlandish shirt on under the silvers. And it was a strong contrast to his last boarding in that he knew exactly where he was going, he knew they'd been posted to galley for their undock duty—laundry would have been entirely unfair to draw this soon—and he was actually looking toward *his* cabin, *his* bunk, *his* mattress and the comforts of his own belongings after the haste and nonstop party of dockside, which he'd thought would be hard to leave, when he'd gone out. He'd bought some books he was anxious to read, he'd bought games that promised hours of unraveling, and even a block of modeling medium—a long time since he'd had the chance to do any model-making; he'd used to be good at it.

He took the sharp turn into the undock-fitted rec hall, herded his three charges in to the rows of rails and standing cousins, but he had second thoughts about Jeremy.

"Are you all right?" he asked, delaying at the start of the row and holding up traffic. "You want to talk to Charlie, maybe get something for your stomach? Maybe go to the sit-down takehold?"

"No," Jeremy said, and flashed a valiant grin. "I'm fine."

"If he gets sick everybody'll kill him," Linda said helpfully as Jeremy went on into the row.

"Just if you don't feel right, tell me."

"No, I'm fine," Jeremy said, and they all packed themselves into the eighth row among an arriving stream of cousins.

Everybody had called to confirm they were on their way, customs was expediting, and the ship was go when ready, that was the buzz floating in the assembly. It was the kind of thing *Finity* had used to do, or so the talk around him indicated; and

at the rate the prelaunch area was filling up they were going to
be clearing dock . . . the estimate was . . . maybe in twenty
minutes.

Boreale, their Union escort, was on the same shortened
schedule.

"What did this ship do?" Fletcher asked of Charles T.
"Why are we suspicious?"

"It left dock early. Going our way."

"Is it going to shoot at us, or what?"

"It could have that intention," Charles T. said. "That's why
Boreale is going with us."

"What they think," said another cousin, turning around
from the row in front, "is that *Champlain*—that's the ship in
question—is going to report somewhere ahead of us. It's an
outside possibility it might want to take us on. But not two of
us. *Boreale*'s a merchanter only in its spare time, and it'd *like*
that ship to make a move. If we can build a case that ship's
Mazianni, there are alternatives we can take at Voyager."

"They've had a watch on our hull the whole time we're
here," a third cousin said. "So we're clean."

Watching for what? Fletcher wondered uneasily, but his
mind leapt to uneasy conclusions.

"Don't suppose they've watched *theirs*?" Charles T. said
with a wicked grin.

"Tempting," Parton said.

The juniors were all ears. Even Jeremy.

Another flood of cousins poured in. *"Ten minutes,"* the
intercom said in the same moment. *"We've got a potential
bandit, gentle cousins, but our intrepid allies out of Union
space are going to pace us in fond hopes of getting the goods
on the rascals. We'll make specific safety announcements
before jump, but we're clearing dock in plenty of time for*
Champlain *to figure the odds, which we think will discourage
a wise captain from lingering to meet us in the jump-point. We
will be doing an unusual system entry just in case our pirat-
ical friends have strewn our path with any hindrances, and we*

*will post the technicals on the maneuver for those of you who
have a curiosity about the matter. Welcome aboard, welcome
aboard, welcome aboard. We hope your hangovers are less
than you deserve. Fare well to Belize and Mariner, and fond
hopes for Esperance. Voyager will be a working port, we regret
to say, with restricted liberty and fast passage.*"

There were groans.

"We're going to *work*?" Vince cried indignantly.

"Sounds like an interesting stop," a cousin said. "Are we
hauling this trip, or how much *did* we load?"

Time spun down. A last few cousins ran in, JR and Bucklin
among them. Chad, Connor and Sue followed, and then the rest
of the juniors . . . probably on duty, Fletcher said to himself.
The icy mess in the corridor was a likely junior job, of the sort
that wouldn't wait for undock, during which icemelt could run
and metal grids could slide.

Odd thought . . . how much he'd gotten to figure out
without half thinking about it. *His* ship. *His* junior-juniors. *His*
roommate. He'd been out on liberty, he'd come back in charge
of three kids who'd come around somehow to admitting that
seventeen waking years beat twelve and thirteen in a lot of
respects: he'd been in *his* element, and the one he was coming
back to wasn't foreign, either, now.

He knew these people. He knew the sounds he'd heard before,
and wished there were a way to ask, when the undocking started,
exactly what sound was what. He'd stood and watched ships
undock, from outside, and the lights would be flashing and the
hatches would seal, and the access tube would retract. Then the
lines would uncouple, the gantry arm would pull back.

Then the grapples. That was the loud one. The jolt.
Somebody started a loud and rowdy song, that subbed in the
word *Belize*, and he found himself with a grin on his face as
Finity's End came free and powered back from dock.

One song topped another one, and they ran out of the
rowdy ones and into the sentimental, good-bye to the port,
good-bye to lost loves . . .

He had an urge to chime in, but he was too conscious of the juniors beside him and he couldn't sing worth a damn. He could listen. He could feel a little shiver of gooseflesh on his arms, a little shortness of breath when the song wound on to foreign ports and lost friends.

They knew. He wasn't different. He knew he was slipping under a spell, and that Downbelow was getting farther and farther away. He'd heard about meetings, in the chaff of conversation before undock. He'd heard about the captains getting together and talking about peace.

And now *Union* was escorting an Alliance ship?

He'd thought he understood the universe, or all of it he needed to know. And things weren't what he thought.

"Clear to move," the intercom said. *"Twenty minutes to get your baggage and ten to take hold, cousins. Move, move, move."*

The front row filed out to the corridor and the next row was hot on their heels, everybody moving with dispatch when it was their turn.

Cargo spat out baggage at high speed and fair efficiency. He'd bought a silly cartoon trinket to hang from the tag, a distinction easier to spot, he'd learned, than the stenciled name; and Jeremy had urged him to buy it. Other people had colored cords, plastic planets, tassels . . . Jeremy's was a metal enameled tag that said Mars, and a cartoon character of no higher taste than his. Jeremy's duffle was already in the stack, but his wasn't.

Jeremy carted his off. Fletcher saw his own come down the chute and grabbed it, double-checking the tag to be sure.

"Fletcher," JR said, turning up beside him, and instinct had him braced for unpleasantness as he straightened and looked JR in the eyes.

"Good job," JR said. "I can't say all of it, even yet, but we've had a situation working at this port . . . same that put that ship out ahead of us, and it wasn't a place to let our junior-juniors in on the matter, or to let them wander the dockside on their own. Toby and Wayne kind of kept an eye in your direction, you may have observed at first, but you didn't *need* help, so they just pretty well left things to you and after that we got swept into running security for the captains' business and *didn't* check back, in the absence of distress signals. But we didn't feel we had to. So we do appreciate it, and I'm speaking for all of us."

He wasn't used to well-dones. He didn't have a repertoire of suitable polite remarks. His face went hot and he hoped it didn't show.

"Thanks," he said. If he was one of the Willetts or the Velasquezes he'd have learned how to shed compliments like water. But he wasn't. And stood there holding a duffle with a plastic, large-eyed cartoon wolf for an identifying tag. The one JR had against his leg sported a classy Sol One enamelled tag, which *he'd* undoubtedly bought above Earth itself.

"We got out all right," JR said, "and regarding what the captain was talking about to you before we made dock . . . and the *reason* we're running with an escort right now . . . I'm warning you in advance we're not going to get much of a liberty at Voyager. We can't guarantee their cargo handling and we're going to have to search every can. This is not going to be a fun operation. But we have to do it. We have to look as if we trust Voyager without actually *trusting* Voyager. Again, that's for you to know. The junior-juniors aren't to know the details."

"And I *am*?" He couldn't help it. He didn't see himself in the line of confidences.

JR looked him straight in the face. "You need to know. *You're* watching the potential hostages. And you need to know."

"You don't know *me*. Where do you think I'm so damn trustworthy?"

JR outright grinned. "Because you'd warn me like that."

He'd never been outflanked like that. He shut his mouth. Had to be amused.

"Takehold in ten minutes," the intercom advised them, and JR picked up his baggage.

"Got to walk my quarter," JR said. And set off. "Don't forget your drug pickup!" JR called back.

He would have forgotten. Remembered it by tomorrow, but he would have forgotten. Fletcher took his duffle, slung it over his shoulder and walked in JR's direction far enough to reach the medical station and the drug packets set out in bundles.

Take 6, the direction said, a note taped to the side of the bin on the counter, and the bin was three-quarters empty. He came up as JR was initialing the list as having picked up his. JR took his six, and Fletcher signed in after and filled his side pocket with the requisite small packets, asking himself, as his source of information walked away, what circumstance could demand *six* doses.

Precaution on the precaution, he said to himself, and, drugs safely in pocket, and feeling proof against the unknown hazards of yet another voyage, he toted his duffle back the other direction, past the laundry and past a sign that instructed crew not to leave laundry bundles if the chute was full.

Piled up on the floor inside, he well guessed, glad it wasn't his job this turn. Galley was a far better duty.

He walked on to A26, to his cabin, anticipating familiar surroundings—and almost reached to his pocket for a key as he reached the door, after a week in the Pioneer. He reached instead to open the door.

Beds were stripped, sheets strewn underfoot. Drawers and lockers were open, clothes thrown about. Jeremy, inside with his arms full of rumpled clothes, stared at him with outright fear.

"What in hell is this?" he asked.

"I'm picking it up," Jeremy said.

"I know you're picking it up. Who did it? Is this some damn *joke*?"

"It's your first liberty."

"And they do *this*?"

"I'm picking it up!"

"The hell!" His mind flashed to the bar, to Chad sitting there with all the others. Butter wouldn't melt in their mouths. He stood there in the middle of the wreckage of a cabin they'd left in good order, feeling a sickly familiarity in the scenario. No bloody *wonder* they'd been smiling at him.

He saw articles of underwear strewn clear to the bathroom, his study tapes and what had been clean, folded clothes lying on a bare mattress. The drawer where he kept his valuables was partially open, the tapes were out—the drawer showed empty to the bottom, the drawer where he'd had Satin's stick; and he bumped Jeremy aside, dropping to his knees to feel to the back of the storage.

Nothing. He got up and looked around him, rescued his tapes and the rumpled clothes to the drawer and lifted the mattress, flinging it back against the lockers to look under it.

"I'll check the shower," Jeremy said, and went and looked and came back with more of his clothes.

No stick.

"Shit!" Fletcher said through his teeth. He looked in lockers, he swept up clothes, he rummaged Jeremy's drawers.

Nothing. He slammed his hand against the wall, hit the mattress in a fit of temper and slammed a locker so hard the door banged back and forth. A plastic cup fell out and he caught it and slammed it into the wall. It narrowly missed Jeremy, who stood, white-faced, wedged into a corner.

Fletcher stood there panting, out of things to throw, out of coherent thought until Jeremy scuttled out of his corner and grabbed up clothes.

He grabbed the clothes from Jeremy, grabbed Jeremy one-handed and held him against the wall. "Who did this?"

"I don't know!" Jeremy said. "I don't know, they do this sometimes, they did it to me. First time you go on liberty—"

"Fletcher and Jeremy," the intercom said. *"Report status."*

"We hit the wall," Jeremy reminded him breathlessly. "They want to know if we're all right. Next cabin reported a noise."

"You talk to them." He wasn't in a mood to communicate.

He let Jeremy go and Jeremy ran and, fast talking, assured whoever it was they were all right, everything was fine.

It took some argument. *"One minute to take hold,"* another voice on the intercom said then. *"Find your places."*

Jeremy started grabbing up stuff.

"Just let it go!" Fletcher said.

"We have to get the hard stuff!" Jeremy cried, and grabbed up the cup he'd thrown, the toiletry kit, the kind of things that would fly about in a disaster. Fletcher snatched them from him, shoved them into the nearest locker and slammed the door.

Then he flung himself down on the sheetless bed and grabbed the belts. Jeremy did the same on his side of the room.

The intercom started the countdown. He lay there staring at the ceiling, telling himself calm down, but he wasn't interested in listening.

They'd gotten him, all right. Good and proper. They'd probably been sniggering after he left the bar.

Maybe not. Maybe *Chad* had. Chad and Connor and Sue, he'd damn well bet. They'd cleared the cabins and the *senior*-juniors were still running around the ship, well able to get into any cabin they liked, with no locks on any door.

"I'm real sorry!" Jeremy said as the burn started.

He didn't answer. The bunks swiveled so that he was looking at the bottomside of Jeremy's, and so that he had a good view of the empty drawers and the underside of the bunk carriage, and Satin's stick wasn't there, either. He even undid the safety belts and stuck his head over one side of the bunk and the other, trying to see the underside. He held on until acceleration sent the blood to his head and, no, it wasn't stuck to the bottom of the bunk carriage, wasn't stuck to the head of the bunk—wasn't stuck to the foot, which cost him a struggle to search. He lay back, panting, and then snapped at Jeremy:

"Look down to your right, see whether it's down in the framework."

A moment. "It's not there. Fletcher, I'm sorry . . ."

He didn't answer. He didn't feel like talking. Jeremy tried
to engage him about it, and when he didn't answer that, tried
to talk about Mariner, but he wasn't interested in that, either.

"I'm kind of sick," Jeremy said, last ploy.

"That's too bad," he said. "Next time don't stuff yourself."

There was quiet from the upper bunk, then.

Chad. Or Vince. And he'd lean the odds to it being Chad.

He replayed everything JR had said, every expression,
every nuance of body language, and about JR he wasn't sure.
He didn't think so. He didn't read JR as somebody who'd
enjoy that kind of game, standing and talking to him about
how well he'd done, and all the while knowing what he was
walking into.

He didn't *think* JR would do it, but he wanted to talk to JR
face to face when he told him. He wanted to see the reactions,
read the eyes, and see if he could spot a liar: he hadn't been
damn good at it so far in his life.

It hurt. Bottom line, it hurt, and until he talked to the
senior-junior in charge, he didn't know where he stood or what
the game was.

Chapter
—XVII—

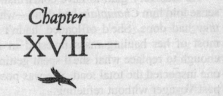

Boreale was also out of dock, likewise running light, about
fifteen minutes behind them. That made for, in JR's estimation, a far better feeling than it would have been if they'd had
to chase *Champlain* into jump alone.

It also made their situation better, courtesy of the station
administration, for *Finity* to have had access to *Champlain*'s
entry data, data on that ship's behavior and handling charac-
teristics gathered before they'd known they were under close
observation. They had that information to weigh against its
exit behavior and its acceleration away from Mariner, when
Champlain knew they were carefully observed.

That let them and *Boreale* both form at least some good
guesses both about *Champlain*'s capabilities and the content of its holds. And at his jump seat post on the bridge, JR
ran his own calculations on that past-behavior record,
keeping their realtime position and *Boreal*'s as a display on
the corner of the screen, and calling on a large library of
such records.

Finity's End, in its military capacity, stored hundreds of
such profiles of other ships of shady character, files that
ordinary traders couldn't access and which (he knew the Old
Man's sense of honor) they would never use in competing
against other ships in trade. The data included observations
of acceleration, estimates of engine output, maneuvering
capacity, loading and trade information not alone from
Mariner, but black-boxed information that came in from
every port in the shared system—and they had that on
Champlain.

He was very glad to have confirmation of what common sense told him *Champlain* had done—which was exactly what *they* had done. She'd offloaded, hadn't taken in much, had most of her hauling mass invested in fuel: she'd taken on enough to replace what she'd spent getting to Mariner, but no one inspected the total load. She was possibly even able to go past Voyager without refueling.

Finity had to fuel at Voyager. If they delayed to offload cargo and take on more fuel, they'd lose their tag on *Champlain* even if *Champlain* did put into that port. But *Finity*'s unladed mass relative to their over-sized engines meant they'd still handle like an empty can compared to *Champlain*, unless *Champlain*'s hold structure camouflaged more engine strength than the estimate persistently turning up in the figures he was running.

Boreale was likewise high in engine capacity, and she was also far more maneuverable than *Champlain*, if the figures they had on their ally of convenience were right. They'd been hearing about these new Union warrior-merchanters. Now they had their chance to observe one in action, and *Boreale* couldn't help but be aware of their interest and who they reported to. . . .

The com light blinked on his screen. Somebody wanted him. He reached idly and thumbed a go-ahead for his earpiece.

Fletcher. A restrainedly upset Fletcher, who wanted to talk.

"I'm on duty," he said to Fletcher. "I'm on the bridge."

"That's all right," Fletcher said. "I'll wait as long as I have to."

The quiet anger in the tone, considering Fletcher's nature, said to him that it might be a good idea to see about it now.

"I'll come down," he told Fletcher. "Where are you?"

"My quarters."

"I'll be there in a moment." He signaled *temporarily off duty,* and stored and disconnected on his way out of the seat.

Fletcher sat on the bed, in the center of the debris. And waited.

Jeremy had left to report to Jeff, in the galley, for both of them.

Fletcher sat, imagining the time it took to leave the bridge, walk to the lift and take it down to A deck . . .

To walk the corridor.

He waited. And waited, telling himself sometimes the lift took a moment. People might stop JR on the way . . .

The light by the door flashed, signaling presence outside.

Fletcher got up quietly and opened the door.

JR's face said volumes, in the fast, startled pass of the eyes about the room, the evident dismay.

JR hadn't expected what he saw. And on that sole evidence Fletcher held on to his temper, controlling the anger that had him wound tight.

"Jeremy went on to duty," he said to JR in exaggerated, careful calm. "This is what we came back to."

"This . . ." JR said, and seemed to lose the word.

"This is a joke, right?"

"Not a funny one. Clearly."

He hadn't been able to predict what he himself would do. Or say. Or want. He was angry. He wasn't, he decided now, angry at JR. And that was not at all what he'd have predicted.

"I'd discouraged this," JR said. "It's supposed to be a joke, yes. Your first liberty. But it shouldn't have happened. Was anything damaged?"

"Something was stolen."

JR had been looking at the damage. His eyes tracked instantly back again, clearly not comfortable with that charged word. He'd deny it, Fletcher thought. He'd quibble. Protect his own. Of course.

"*What* was?" JR asked.

He measured with his hands. "A hisa artifact. A spirit stick. Wood. Carved, tied up with cords and feathers."

"I've seen them. In museums. They're sacred objects."

"I had title to it."

"I take your word on it. You had it in your cabin. Where?"

"In the drawer." He indicated the drawer in question with a backward kick of his foot. "At the back of the drawer. Under clothes. I've been over every inch of the room. Including under the bunk frames as they'd tilt underway. It's not here. I don't give a damn about them tearing up the room. I don't like it, but that's not the issue. The stick is. The stick is *mine*, it was a gift, and it's not something you play games with."

"I'm well aware." JR looked around him and frowned, thinking, Fletcher surmised, where it might be, or very well knowing the chief suspects on his own list.

"I don't even know it's on this ship," Fletcher said. "I don't know why they thought it was funny to take it. I don't even want to imagine. I *can* point out that the market value is considerable, for someone who might be interested in that sort of thing. And that we've been in port."

He'd hit home with that one. JR frowned darker still.

"No one on this ship would do *that*," JR said.

"You tell me what they would and won't do. Let me tell you. Somebody sitting at your table, in the bar the other evening, looked me straight in the eye knowing damned well what he'd done. Or *she'd* done. They kept a real straight face about it. Probably they had a good laugh later. I'm serving notice. I can't work with people like that. I want *off* this ship. I gave you my best shot and my honest effort. And this is what I get back from my *cousins*. Thanks. If you want to do me a personal favor, sell me *back* to Pell and let me get back to my life. If you want to do me a bigger favor, get me passage back from Voyager. But don't ask me to turn a hand to help anybody on this ship. I want my own cabin, the same as everyone else. I don't want to be with Jeremy. I don't want to be with anybody. I want my privacy, I want my stuff left alone, I don't want any more of your jokes, and I don't want any more crap about belonging here. I *don't*. I think that point's been made."

JR didn't come back with an argument. JR just stood there a moment as if he didn't know what to say. Then:

"Have you discussed this with Jeremy?"

"*No*, I haven't discussed it with Jeremy. I have nothing against Jeremy. I just want the lot of you off my back!"

"I can understand your feelings. If you want separate quarters, I can understand that, too. But Jeremy's going to be affected. He's taken to you in a very strong way. I'd ask you give that fact whatever thought you think you ought to give. I'll talk to the captains; I'll explain as much as I can find out. I'll find the stick, among other things. And if you want someone to clean this mess up, I'll assign crew to do that. If you'd rather I not, . . ."

"No." Short and sharp. "I've had quite enough people into my stuff. Thanks." He was mad as hell, charged with the urge to bash someone across the room, but he couldn't fault JR on any point of the encounter. And he didn't hate Jeremy, who'd left with no notion of his walking out. "I'll think about the room change. But not about quitting. It's not going to work. You've screwed up where I was. I don't ask you to fix it. You can't. But you can put me back at Pell."

"There's no way to get you passage back right now. It wouldn't be safe. You *have* to make the circuit with us."

He wasn't surprised. He gave a disgusted wave of his hand and turned to look at the wall, a better view than JR's possibilities.

"I'm not exaggerating," JR said. "We have enemies. One of them is out in front of this ship likely armed with missiles."

"Fine. They're your problem."

"Fletcher."

Now came the lecture. He didn't look around.

"Give me the chance," JR said, "to try to patch this up. Someone was a fool."

"Sorry doesn't patch it." He did turn, and stared JR in the face. "You know how it reads to me? That my having a thing like that on this ship was a big joke to somebody on this ship. That the hisa are. That everything the hisa hold sacred and serious is. So you go fight your war and make your big money and all those things that matter to you and leave me to mine!

You know that hisa don't steal things? That they have a hard time with lying? That war doesn't make sense to them? And that they know the difference between a joke and persecution? I'm sure they'd bore you to hell."

"Possibly you're justified," JR said. "Possibly not. I have to hear the other side of this. Which I can't do until I find out what happened. Let me be honest, at least, with our situation—which is that we've got a hostile ship running ahead of us, and there may be duty calls that I have to answer with no time for other concerns. On time I do have control of, I'm going to find the stick, I'm going to get answers on why this happened, and I'm going to get your answers. I put those answers on a priority just *behind* that ship out there, which is going to be with us at least all the way to Voyager. I *don't* consider the hisa a joke and I don't consider anything that's happened a joke. This ship can't afford bad judgment. You've just presented me something I don't like to think exists in people I've known all my life, and quite honestly I'm upset as hell about it. That's all I can say to you. I *will* follow up on it."

"Yessir," he found himself saying, not even thinking about it, as JR turned to leave. And then thinking . . . so far as he had clear thoughts . . . that JR was being completely fair in the matter, contrary to expectations, that he had just said things that attacked JR's personal integrity, and that he had the split second till JR closed the door to say something to acknowledge that from his side.

But with a flash on that meeting in the bar, he didn't *trust* JR, in the same way he didn't trust anyone on the ship.

And the second after that door had closed . . . he knew that that wasn't an accurate judgment even of his own feelings, let alone of the situation, and that he should have said something. It was increasingly too late. The thought of opening that door and chasing JR down in the corridors with other crew to witness didn't appeal to him.

Not until he'd have to go a quarter of the way around the ship to do it; and by then it was hard to imagine catching

JR, or being able to retrieve the moment and the chance he'd had.

It didn't matter. If JR hated his guts and supported his move to get off the ship, it was all he wanted. Make a single post-pubescent *friend* on this ship, and he'd have complicated his life beyond any ability to cut ties and escape. That was the mathematics he'd learned in court decisions and lawyers' offices, time after time after godforsaken time.

There was a sour taste in his mouth. He saw that meeting in the bar as a moment when things had *almost* worked and he'd *almost* found a place for himself he'd have never remotely have imagined he'd want . . . as much as he'd come to want it.

He couldn't go home. But he couldn't exist here, where clearly someone, and probably more than one of the juniors, had not only expressed their opinion of him, but had done it in spite of JR's opposition—not damaging *him*, because the petty spite in this family no more got to him than all the other collapsed arrangements had done. The illusions he'd had shattered were all short-term, a minimum amount invested—so he only felt a fool.

What that act had shattered in JR was another question. He saw that now, and wished he'd said something. But he hadn't done the deed. He hadn't chosen it. He couldn't fix it. His being here had drawn something from JR's crew that maybe nothing else would have ever caused.

Now it had surfaced. It was JR's job to deal with it as best he could. And he'd let the door shut on a relationship it would only hurt JR now to pursue. If he chased after it—he saw the damage he could do in the crew. He was outside the circle. Again.

He began to clean up the room, replacing things in drawers and lockers, Jeremy's as well as his own. And he saw that JR was right. Jeremy was in a hell of a situation. Jeremy had latched on to him in lieu of Vince and Linda, with whom Jeremy had avowed nothing in common but age; and now when he left, Jeremy would have to patch that relationship up as a bad second choice.

Worse still, Jeremy had set some significance on his being the absent age-mate, Jeremy's lifelong what-if, after Jeremy had, like him, like so many of this crew, lost mother, father, cousins . . . all of the relationships a kid should have.

The last thing the kid needed was a public slap in the face like his moving out of the cabin they shared, in advance of the time he made a general farewell to the ship.

Jeremy was the keenest regret he had. In attaching to him, the kid had done what he himself had done early in his life. The kid had just invested too much in another human being. And human beings had flaws, and didn't keep their promises, and all too often they ducked out and went off about their own business, for very personal reasons, disregarding what it did to somebody else.

That was what it was to grow up. He'd always suspected that was the universal truth. Now, being the adult, he did it to somebody else for reasons *he* couldn't do anything about. And maybe understood a bit more about his mother, who'd done the chief and foremost of all duck-outs.

He went to the galley when he'd finished the clean-up.

"Did you find it?" was Jeremy's very first question, and there was real pain in Jeremy's eyes.

"No," he said. "JR's looking for it."

"We didn't do it," Linda said, from a little farther away.

Vince came up beside her.

"We'd have *done* it," Vince said, "but we wouldn't have *stolen* anything."

He'd never have thought he'd have seen honesty shining out of Vince. But he thought he did see it, in the kids whose time-stretched lives made them play like twelve-year-olds and look around at you in the next instant with eyes a decade older.

"I believe you," he found himself saying, and thought then he'd completely surprised Vince.

But he saw those three faces looking to him—not *at* him, but *to* him—in a way he'd never planned to have happen to him or them. And he didn't know what to do about it.

• • •

Bucklin was the first resort. Wayne was the second. Lyra the third. If one of those three would lie to him, JR thought, there was no hope of truth, and Bucklin said, first off:

"I can't imagine it."

Wayne simply shook his head and said, "Damn." And then: "What in hell was he doing with a hisa artifact? Aren't those things illegal?"

Lyra, when he found her in the corridor at B deck scrub, had the stinger. "Is it remotely possible Fletcher faked it?"

He supposed he hadn't a devious enough mind even to have thought of that possibility.

Or something in Fletcher's behavior had kept him from thinking so. He entertained the idea, turned it one way and another and looked at it from the underside. But he *didn't* believe it.

He tracked down the junior-juniors, who were *with* Fletcher, working in the mess hall. "I want to talk to them," he said to Fletcher, and took Jeremy to a far enough remove the waiting junior-juniors couldn't see expressions, let alone overhear.

"What happened?" he asked Jeremy.

"We got back and it was just messed," Jeremy said.

He was tempted to ask Jeremy who he thought had done it. But a second thought informed him that the last thing he wanted to do was start an interactive witch hunt. "Any observations?" he asked.

"No, sir," Jeremy said.

"How's Fletcher behaving?"

"He's being real nice," Jeremy said, and looked vastly upset. "You think maybe we should call back to Mariner, maybe, if somebody sold it?"

He had to weigh making that call, to inform Mariner police. He didn't say so. He didn't want to log it as a theft on station: it would taint *Finity*'s name, no matter what spin he put on it: possession of a forbidden artifact, theft aboard the ship. It was excruciatingly embarrassing, at a time when

Finity's good name had just secured agreements from other captains and from the station that were critical to peace, and at a time when—he was constantly conscious of it—the captains had life and death business under their hands.

At any given instant, the siren might sound and they might be in a scramble to stations regarding some maneuver by the ship in front of them.

Meanwhile all their just-completed agreements hung on *Finity*'s unsullied reputation for fair, rigorously honest dealing. Taint *Finity*'s good name with a sordid incident aboard and captains and station management back at Mariner had to ask themselves whether *Finity* was as reliable and selfless in her dealings as legend said of the ship. *Finity* had been meticulously honest. Other captains and the various stations had contributed to the military fund that kept *Finity* and *Norway* going without limit, repaired their damage, fueled them, armed them, trusted them—and he had to call station police and say there'd been a theft on a ship no one else could get aboard?

Silence about the matter was dishonest toward Fletcher. But telling the truth could damage the ship *and* the Alliance. There was no clean answer. And the matter was on his hands. He had to take the responsibility for it, not pass it upstairs to the senior captains; and that meant he had to answer to Fletcher for his silence, in his absolute conviction that, whatever else, if it had ever existed, it was aboard, because no member of this crew would have sold it ashore.

One last question, one out of Lyra's question: "What did this artifact look like?"

"About this long." Jeremy measured with his hands, as Fletcher had, exactly as Fletcher had. "Brown and white feathers, sort of greenish twisted cords . . . it's carved all over."

"You did see it?"

"He let me hold it. He let me touch it. They're *real feathers*."

"I'm sure they are." Until Jeremy's description he had no evidence but Fletcher's word that such a stick actually existed, and he set markers in his mind, what was proved, what was assumed, and who had said it. The stick now went down as a fact, not just a report. "Did he say where he got it?"

"A hisa gave it to him. He said the cops got him through customs. He says the carvings mean something."

So much for Wayne's question whether it was legal. Fletcher claimed to have met Satin, who had authority; Fletcher had come off-world and through customs. Fletcher was entitled to have it, if Jeremy was right. He didn't know what the black market was in such items, but it had to be toward fifty thousand credits.

And in any sane consideration, what did somebody in the Family want with fifty thousand credits, when *Finity* paid for everything that wasn't pocket money on a liberty, and where, if someone truly wanted something expensive, the Family might vote it? There was nothing to buy with fifty thousand credits. There'd been no requests for funds made and denied to anyone. There was just no motive regarding money.

Fifty thousand might get Fletcher a passage back to Pell. *That* unworthy thought had flitted through his mind.

But Fletcher hadn't missed board-call, hadn't skipped down the row of berths to seek passage on some other ship bound back to Pell, and most significantly, Fletcher hadn't even minutely derelicted his assigned duty to the juniors, and he knew far more minute to minute where Fletcher had been during the liberty than he could answer for anybody else in his command, including Bucklin.

And the juniors, as for their whereabouts, had been with Fletcher, the most conscientious, the most rigorous supervision the junior-juniors had ever had in their rambunctious lives.

He couldn't say that about the senior-juniors, who'd been scattered all over the docks, running back to the ship on errands for senior command, a whole string of errands which had put them aboard in a ship mostly vacated, a ship in which, if you were aboard and past security, there was no watch on the corridors, beyond the constant presence in ops and the captains intermittently in their offices.

That *senior* crew would do something so stupid was just beyond belief. It was most assuredly his own junior crew that had done it—and it added up to an act not for money but aimed at Fletcher.

He sent Jeremy back and had Jeremy send Linda to him.

"Do you know anything about this?" he asked Linda, and Linda shook her head and returned her usually glum expression.

"No, sir. I don't. They shouldn't have done it, is what."

"What, they?"

"The they that did it. Whoever did it."

"No, they shouldn't. Go back and send Vince."

She went. Vince had stood at the threshold of the mess hall, looking this direction, and when Linda went back, he started forward, walking more slowly than the others, looking downcast.

"I didn't do it," Vince said before he even asked the question.

"You didn't do it."

"No, sir."

"Look at me."

Vince looked him in the eyes, but not without flinching.

"So what do you know that I ought to know?" he asked Vince.

"Nothing. I didn't do it."

"The pixies got in and did it, did they?"

"I don't know who did it," Vince said hotly. "I don't do everything that goes wrong aboard this ship, all right?"

"Sir," he reminded the kid.

"Sir," Vince muttered. "I didn't do it, *sir.*"

"I didn't think it was likely," he said, and Vince gave him a peculiarly troubled look.

In the same moment he saw Fletcher coming toward them. Fletcher came up and set a hand on Vince's back.

"He'd have told me," Fletcher said. "Sir."

He shut up, prevented by the very object of his charity. He saw a cohesive unit in front of him. Linda had followed Fletcher halfway back and stood watching. Jeremy had come up even with her, both watching as Fletcher violated protocols to come to Vince's defense. It was Vince on whom suspicion generally settled—in most anything to do with junior-juniors.

Which wasn't just. And Fletcher had just made that point.

"I take your assessment," he said to Fletcher. And to Vince: "Thank you, junior."

"Yes, sir," Vince said; and JR left, with a glance at Fletcher, who met his eyes without a qualm, in complete, unassailable command of their fractious junior-juniors—the tag-end, the motherless, grown-too-soon survivors of the last liberties *Finity* had enjoyed before these last two ports.

He didn't know what exactly had happened in the last couple of weeks on Mariner, or what spell Fletcher had cast over the unruly juniormost, but he knew loyalty when he saw it. Fletcher said he was leaving. If he did leave—he'd do lifelong damage to those kids in the same measure he'd done good.

It was hard to conceive of the mental vacuum it would take even for a junior-junior to have done the deed. For one of his crew to lay hands on something that unique, that clearly, personally valuable—he almost thought it of Sue . . . and even Sue's spur-of-the-moment notions fell short of the mark. Whoever had taken it had known, even if it were perfectly safe, even if it was meant as a joke, he had to assume some crueler intent far more like the charges Fletcher had leveled. Whoever had done it, above the age of children, had to know the minute they saw a wooden object that it was valuable, in fact irreplaceable, and that meddling with it went beyond any head-butting welcome-in rituals.

Start through his own circle in the same way, in a hierarchy of suspects? Vince had known, automatically, that he was the chief suspect, even when *he* knew that Vince hadn't had an access that made it likely. Vince just assumed because everyone else assumed. And in a society composed only of family, —he felt damned sorry about the spot he'd just put Vince in, letting him sweat until the last.

Granted Vince had helped build that unfortunate position for himself over the years. Sue and Connor had built theirs in exactly the same way; but damned if, having done an injustice to Vince, he now wanted to charge in and put them publicly and automatically at the head of his list of suspects.

He asked himself what he did want to do as he walked the corridor back to the lift, and that list was unhappily short of resources.

The circuit took him past the laundry, which was in full operation, Connor receiving bundles at the half-door that was the counter, a half-dozen cousins in line to toss their laundry in.

"Get those six customers," he said to Connor, at the counter, and waved the line on to do their business and clear out. "Then put the chute sign out and fold up."

"What's this?" Chad asked, as he and Sue turned up from inside.

Chad. Connor, Sue, the whole threesome.

"Shut down for a quarter hour," he said. "Meeting in rec."

"What about?" Sue asked.

"No questions. Just show up." He went down to the nearest com-panel and used his collective code to page all the senior-juniors at once, immediate meeting, shut down and show.

Then he went to rec himself. Toby and Nike had been breaking down the boarding config in rec and restoring the area's open space. They had rails in hand, and the inflexible rule was that those long rails and the stanchions went into storage one by one and immediately as they were dismounted, being the kind of objects that, end-on, could deliver small-point impact with a high-mass punch.

"Got your page," Nike said. "What's up?"

"Wait for all of us. Stow that rail and wait."

"Trouble?" Toby asked, with what seemed genuine lack of information.

And, dammit, he was having to ask himself bitter questions and read nuances of expression, forming conclusions of guilt or innocence on people he'd have to rely on for his life. He'd known Nike when she was Berenice in the cradle. He'd known Toby when he was scared of the dark in his new solo cabin, alone for the first time in his life.

Bucklin arrived with Wayne. Chad and Connor and Sue came in. Dean, Lyra, and Ashley came in, and there they were, every member of the crew under thirty and over shipboard seventeen.

All that survived, except for four junior-juniors, the ship's whole future.

"Something happened among us," he said, standing, arms tucked, and made himself watch the faces. "Somebody seems to have played a joke on Fletcher, and he's not real upset about the stuff in the lockers or the bedsheets, but he wasn't prepared for it. If he'd been expecting something like that he might have gotten back to his quarters posthaste. He didn't. As a consequence, he and Jeremy spent a couple of very bad hours under heavy accel with loose objects all around them while we have a hostile ship in front of us and a Union stranger running on our tail."

Very serious faces. Fully cognizant of the danger. Fully cognizant of the fact they had trouble among themselves in ways no one had reckoned.

"Nobody got hurt," he said. "It was their good luck we didn't have an emergency. But there's more to it than that. A keepsake disappeared, something personal that can't be replaced. That's why Fletcher's upset. Now I've talked to the junior-juniors. And I'm going to suggest that if possibly—possibly—this was just extremely bad judgment, and somehow the object got misplaced—even damaged—it would be a good idea if it turned up in my quarters. Or Fletcher's. I'm going to hope on my faith in this crew that this event will happen within the hour. I'm going to give this crew half an hour off-duty and I'm going to go back to the bridge in the hope that this will in fact happen and we can find a way to patch what's happened. I'm not going to answer any questions. If one of you knows what I'm talking about and can solve the problem expeditiously I would be personally grateful. If one of you wants to talk about it, you can page me. If anyone has anything to add to the account, I'll listen right now."

There was absolute quiet. Bucklin and Lyra and Wayne looked at him. Sue looked to Connor, and Chad looked at her, and for a moment he thought someone was going to say something.

But heads shook in denial, Chad's, Sue's, and the ones who had looked to that silent exchange looked back at him.

No answers. There was still hope, however, of a miraculous appearance.

"That's all, then," he said, and left and went to the lift, rode it up to A deck in a mood that drew glances from senior crew he passed on his way to the bridge.

"How's it going?" he asked when he took his seat at the console. Trent, next over, said, "No change."

He wished he could say that about the junior crew.

No missing artifact turned up in his cabin. JR went down to A deck, to his own quarters, hoping and fearing . . . and fears scored. Hope got nothing. The missing item wasn't on his bed, not on the sink.

He began to get angry, and to ask himself who in his command would be afraid to come to him. *Scared* had to describe the perpetrator by now.

Except if someone from outside the ship *had* gotten past all their security . . . and in that case why target Fletcher's room? The lifts all required a key when the ring was locked down, a key that had to be gotten from the duty officer, so the bridge couldn't be reached. The operations center would be a target, but that had been manned around the clock, and nothing else was missing in the whole ship.

He began to entertain again the notion that Fletcher might be a very good actor, even that his exemplary behavior during the liberty was a set-up. There was no one in the crew he wanted to suspect. That did leave Fletcher, maneuvering everything, first to show the item to Jeremy and then to arrange to have it missing and himself the wronged party.

Why? was the next question. Some notion of giving the ship hell?

Some ploy to get himself shipped back to Pell with apologies? It was the first thing Fletcher had asked for.

Some bogused-up stick out of materials Fletcher could have gotten onplanet very easily, carvings Fletcher could have done, the whole thing his ticket to Pell if he could con a gullible junior-junior into serving as witness and setting the whole crew at odds with each other.

He sat alone in A deck rec and enjoyed a cup of coffee that didn't entail going down to the mess hall where Fletcher was working, because the thoughts that were beginning to replay in his brain kept pointing to Fletcher as the origin of the problem.

His pocket-com had, however, messages. A lot of messages. From Toby: *I didn't hear anything about it. It seems to me the junior-juniors might be playing a prank, and it got out of hand.*

From Ashley: *I didn't hear anything. I assure you I would tell you if I had.*

Nike came quietly up to him, and settled into the seat opposite his at the table.

"I don't know who particularly had it in for Fletcher, but if you could kind of tell us what's missing maybe we could look for it, in case, you know, somebody's kind of scared to come forward?"

"In the whole ship? We're not talking about something the size of a shipping cannister."

"So what is it?" Nike said. "If it was in Fletcher's cabin it was smaller than a shipping can. But how big could it be? Like a piece of jewelry?"

"Bigger." He was down to games with people who'd be his life and death reliance when they replaced senior crew. "Tomorrow," he said, hoping that the long hours of mainnight would weigh on someone's conscience. "Tomorrow I might be more specific."

Nike was the sort who'd badger after an answer. But she didn't. She got up quietly and left. He saw her at the edge of the area talking to Bucklin, and saw Bucklin shake his head.

Bucklin came to him after that, sat down in the seat Nike had vacated and leaned crossed arms on the table.

"This," Bucklin said, "is poisonous. Jamie, let me tell them at least what we're trying to find."

"I'm not *sure* what we're trying to find. I'm not sure I trust Fletcher."

"You think he's putting one over on us? Why?"

"To get back to Pell! I don't know."

"Possible," Bucklin said. "But it's also possible Vince—or Linda—"

"*Or* Sue. Or Connor, or Chad. Maybe we should just post armed guard. You and I stand in the corridor and shoot the first one that stirs toward another cabin."

Bucklin's shoulders slumped. "I'd rather think it was Fletcher."

"So would I. That's why I distrust my own wishes. Either he's the best liar in lightyears about or he's suffered an extreme injustice, and I don't know which. I don't know whether he's laughing at us or whether someone in this crew has completely lost his senses."

"I think we ought to pull a search."

"For an object you could fit in a duffle and over an entire ship that's been opened up to crew at dock."

"If someone hid it during dock you can eliminate half the ring."

"But not the entire damn hold."

"Possible. But you'd have to suit to go in the hold. In the ring skin you don't have to. If Fletcher hid it, it'd be in places Fletcher knows, right near the galley. If somebody else did it, that still means they'd play hob getting to half the ring during dock, and they'd probably not want to stay long or climb high to do it. I say we search the parts of the ring skin that are convenient during dock, and search in the storage lockers and the office near the galley stores first of all. That's where Fletcher was hazed. That could be the place somebody might put it."

It made sense. "But we've got *Champlain* out there."

"I'd say if we're going to find that thing we look *now*, while we're still in Mariner space. If we wait till the deep dark, damn sure it's going to be more dangerous to go larking about in the ring. But if we don't do something to find it, we've got to live with that, too. —And maybe—maybe somehow it'll materialize so we *can* find it. It's a lot easier for it to turn up out there, you know, just kind of—by happenstance."

"What's the matter with walking in and laying it on my bunk?"

"Your bunk is in your cabin, and your door is visible up and down the corridor where we have cameras."

"What do they think? I'd say go in and do it anonymously and then sit on the bridge and use the cameras?"

"I think everybody thinks this is a real serious issue that reflects pretty badly on whoever did it, and maybe right now somebody is real scared that he's completely lost your trust. I think whoever did it had rather die than have it known."

He looked up at Bucklin. "You don't know who that someone is, do you?"

Bucklin's face registered—something. "Listen to us," Bucklin said. "*Listen* to us talking to each other."

"Hell," JR said. Bucklin was his right arm, his friend, his closer-than-brother. And he'd just asked if Bucklin was hiding something from him.

"We've got to do something," Bucklin said. "Yeah, we've got serious trouble out in front of us. But we've got guns for that, and we've got a warship riding beside us, protecting us. We've got defenses against the outside. This is right at our heart."

"Go search where you think we ought to search." He'd told Bucklin what the object was. It was time to relinquish that card regarding the rest of the crew. "Send the crew by twos to do it."

"Including Fletcher?"

He drew a slow breath. "Everybody. Pair Jeremy with Linda for that duty. *I'll* go with Fletcher, if nothing turns up right off."

"Do the seniors know what's going on?"

"I don't think so. Alan does. I told him. But this is a nasty, distracting business. Bridge crew doesn't need to know, if we can clean it up. Let's just keep this quiet. We're locked down during alterday. There's *just* this next watch to look."

"When did you hear that?"

"That's the word that just came. We're going to do a hard burn during mainnight, third watch. Straight into jump." A thought occurred to him. "If it *was* in the ring skin and somebody didn't secure it before we spun up, hell, no telling where it could get to."

"Damn. That is a thought. Not to mention where it could get to during the burn. If somebody did hide it for a joke, and it slid under something, or into something, they might not be *able* to find it."

"Wood and feathers. Low mass. God knows where it could get to." It was frustrating, not even to know whether Fletcher could have chucked it down the waste disposal. *Surely* nobody on *Finity* had grown up without knowing about the hisa. *Surely* nobody on *Finity* could go into a cabin on a prank and taken something made of wood and real feathers, in ignorance the thing was valuable. *Surely* no one would destroy a thing like that. Take somebody's entire stock of underwear and dispose of them in some unusual place, yes, in a minute. But not real wood. Everybody aboard had *seen* wood, —hadn't they? Nobody was stupid enough to mistake its value. Nobody aboard disrespected the hisa, the only other intelligent life they'd found in the universe. That was just unthinkable, that someone in the Family would have that attitude.

Bucklin nodded and got up. "I'll get started on it."

Word came to the galley: they were going *up* before maindawn. Jeremy fairly bounced with the news, and shoved a set of pans into the cupboard and latched it tight, nerves, Fletcher thought, feeling his own nerves jangled, but no part of Jeremy's fierce anticipation.

"What's going on?" he asked Jeff the cook—unwilling, at least uneasy, in appearing to be more ignorant than the juniors he'd had put in his charge.

"That ship," Jeff said. "I imagine."

Fletcher didn't know what to imagine, and found himself peevish and short-fused. Stations behaved themselves and stayed on schedule, and so did station-dwellers. He habitually felt a tightness in the gut when even ordinary, minor things swerved slightly off from an anticipated schedule, perhaps the fact that so many truly sinister events in his life had begun that way. He was leaving Mariner, going even farther from Pell. He had an enemy who wanted to spite him, he'd tried to duck out of association with the family, and the *juniors* had conspired to hold on to him.

He didn't say a word to Jeff. He just quietly left the galley and took a walk, as circular a proposition as on a station, a long stroll past the machine shop, the air quality station, lifesupport, all the gut and operations areas of the ship, where things were quieter and the feeling of urgency settled. Read-outs were on the corridor walls here. The noise of the machine shop working made him wonder what in all reason someone could be doing on the edge of destruction. It made him wonder so much he put his head in to look. And it was Tom T. using a drill press on a small metal plate.

"So what's that?" he asked.

"Shower door latch."

"Oh," he said. It looked like one when he recalled their door. It was the socket of the door. He was almost moved to ask why Tom would be fixing a shower door if they were all going to be blown to hell and gone. But he just stood and watched. He'd never been in a machine shop. There was a certain comfort in knowing someone's leaky shower was going to get replaced.

"Did you make that?"

Tom pushed up his safety goggles and wiped his nose. Tom had gray hair, large, strong-veined, competent hands. "We make about everything. Hell to get parts for old items, and most of this ship is old."

"I guess it is." A ship that traveled from port to port wasn't going to find brands the same, that was certain. "Interesting place."

"Ever done shop work?"

"No, sir."

Tom grinned. "You want to take a turn at it sometime, you come on in. The youngers of this generation are all hellbent on pushing buttons for a living."

"I might." He figured he'd better get back to the galley before Jeff was hellbent on finding out where he'd gone or what he was up to. "I'll give it a try. I'd better get back."

"Any time," Tom said. "Extra hands are always welcome."

He'd wanted to ask—Have you heard about us going to do a burn tonight? but he didn't end up asking. People just did their jobs. Jeremy was wired. Linda and Vince were jumpy. Tom fixed a shower door and Jeff was making lasagna.

He supposed it made a brittle kind of sense to do that. He, the stationer, he decided to take the long way back to the galley, and to go all the way around the ring.

Cabins, mostly, in the next two sections. After that, doors with numbers, and designations like Fire System and two more just with yellow caution tags and Key Only. And more cabins, everything looking so much like everything else he began to be uneasy.

But after that he saw the medical station, and the main downside corridor, and he felt reassured. He knew where he was now, beyond a doubt, and he walked on toward the familiar venue of the laundry. It was a farther walk than he'd thought, and he was moving briskly, thinking he really should have gone back the way he'd come.

Running steps came from behind him, all out running. "Fletcher!"

Jeremy's voice. Jeff must have gotten worried and sent Jeremy the whole walk around, after him.

He stopped, as Jeremy came panting up from off the curvature. "Where are you going?" Jeremy gasped.

"In a circle," he said.

"Damn," Jeremy said. "You could've said."

"Sorry," he said, and clapped Jeremy on the shoulder as they walked, together, on what was now the shortest way to reach the galley.

"You mad, or something?"

"No," he said, but ahead of them, the crew manning the laundry had come out to stare at who had been running and making a commotion.

Chad. Connor. And Sue.

"What in hell's going on?" Connor said. "You running races out here?"

"We're doing what we damn well please," Fletcher said, feeling the anger rise up in him, telling himself get a grip on it.

"Hey," Chad said as he passed, "we're looking for that stick thing."

He whirled around and hit Chad, hard, and didn't find two words in a string to describe what he thought about Chad, the missing stick, and Chad's sympathy all in one breath; Chad slammed into the wall and came back off it aimed at him, and he drove his fist into Chad's rock-hard gut.

He heard people yelling, he felt people grabbing his shirt, pulling at his arms, and meanwhile he and Chad went at it, hitting the walls, staggering back and forth when Chad got a punch through and he shot one back with no science to it, just flat-out bent on hammering Chad into the deck.

"Hey, hey, *hey*!" someone shouted close to his ear, and he paid no attention. It was every damned sniping attack he'd ever suffered, and he hit and took hits until he began to red-out and run out of wind, and to lean into the blows as the opposition was leaning into him. Another flurry and they were both out of breath. He took a clumsy roundhouse at Chad and glanced off, and Chad took one at him and he took one at Chad. People were all around them, and when Chad swung at him and halfway connected, somebody got Chad and another got him and pulled them apart.

"I didn't steal your damn stick!" Chad yelled at him, spitting blood.

"I said shut up!" JR yelled. It occurred to Fletcher that JR had been yelling at him, and JR had hold of him; Bucklin had Chad.

"He started it!" Sue said.

"I'm not damn well interested! Fletcher, straighten the hell up!"

Fletcher wiped his mouth and stretched an arm to recover his shirt onto his shoulder. The hand came away bloody. His right eye was hazed and he couldn't tell whether it was sweat or blood running into it. Chad was bloody. There were spatters on the walls.

"Fletcher!" Jeremy said. "Fletcher, don't fight anymore."

"All I said was . . ." Chad began.

"Shut *up!*" JR said, and jerked Fletcher back out of reach. "Madelaine wants to see you."

"I'm not interested."

"You get the hell up there before *she* comes down here. Now!"

"I'll clean up, first."

"Just go on topside. Right now."

"Yessir," he said, because he still believed JR, out of a handful of people he would listen to, and because he hadn't any other clear direction while the universe was still far and hazed. He blotted at the eye with the back of his hand, sniffed what tasted like blood down his throat, and shot a burning look at Chad before he walked on toward the lift.

Light, quick steps ran behind him, and he spun around.

"Jeremy," JR said in a forbidding tone, and Fletcher looked at Jeremy through his anger as if he saw an utter stranger—a scared and junior one, one he had no motive to harm, but not one he wanted to touch him at the moment.

Not when he was like this and wanting nothing more than to finish what he'd started.

But the fire was out of the encounter at the moment, and

the lift car came to the button and he got in and rode it up to B deck. A startled senior stared at him as he wiped his nose to keep the blood off the carpet and walked into Legal.

Blue, at the desk inside, gave him a startled look, too.

"You want a tissue?" Blue asked pragmatically, and offered one.

"Thanks," he said, and as pragmatically took it and blotted his nose before he went into Madelaine's office.

Madelaine just stared at him. Shocked.

He stared back, still mad, but not mad enough to drip on his grandmother's carpet. He fell into a chair and made careful use of the tissue.

"Have another," Madelaine said, offering one. "JR?"

"Chad." His nose bubbled. "We were discussing my missing property."

"The spirit stick. I heard about it. I'm very sorry."

"Not your fault."

"I was dismayed. It's not like this crew."

"I'm not a good influence." He had to blot again. But the flow was less. "I made my try at joining in. It's no good. I don't belong here."

"We don't know the whole story."

He didn't fly off. He took a careful, deep breath. "I do."

"What happened, then?"

"What, specifically, happened? Chad's pissed that I exist."

"Did he say that?" Madelaine asked.

"I don't think he's real damn happy at the moment!" He laughed, a bitter, painful laughter. "It's the same damn thing. You think all everybody on this ship is glad I'm here? Not half. Not half. I told JR I want to go back to Pell."

"But?"

"I didn't say but."

"I heard but. You told JR you wanted to go back to Pell, but . . ."

He let go a soft, bubbling breath. And blotted a flow down his upper lip. And shook his head, because he thought about

Jeremy and his throat acquired an unexpected and painful knot.

The silence went on a moment.

"A but, nonetheless," Madelaine said. "There are people on this ship disposed to love you, Fletcher."

"Yeah, sure." She was trying to corner him with the love nonsense. He'd heard it before.

"Is that so common?"

"Not so damn common," he said harshly. "I've heard it. *This is your new brother, Fletcher. You'll be great friends. This is your room, Fletcher, we fixed it just for you. We're sorry, Fletcher, but this just isn't working out . . .*"

He ran out of breath. And composure. And found it again, not quite looking at Madelaine.

"Great intentions. But I'm getting to be a real connoisseur of families. I've had a lot of them."

"We still haven't gotten to the but. —You wanted to go back to Pell, but—"

"I've forgotten."

"Do you want to go back to Pell?"

He didn't find a ready answer. "I don't know what I want. At this point, I don't know."

"All right," she said, and got up. He took it for a dismissal, and he rose.

Madelaine came and put her hand on his arm; and then put her arms around him, and gave him a gentle hug. And sighed and bit her lip when she stood back and looked at him.

"Tell Charlie put a stitch in that or I'll be down there."

"It doesn't matter."

"Listen to your grandmother. James Robert wanted to talk with you about the stick . . . I said let things ride a little, let the juniors try to work it out. We have concerns outside our hull right now, and the captains *can't* divert themselves to settle a quarrel. Operations crew can't. So they leave it to us. And you to me, as the person responsible. Promise me. Peace and quiet. We'll work it out."

"I'll try," he said.

"Fletcher. We're going up, third watch. Don't *take* anger into jump. Let it go, this side. Let go of it."

Spooky advisement. He didn't take it as a platitude.

"All right," he said. And took his leave, and went out and down the lift again, headed for sickbay, where he wasn't surprised to find JR, and Chad.

"Wait your turn," Charlie said.

"Yessir," he said, and set his jaw and gave Chad only an intermittent angry glance.

It wasn't patched. Charlie did take the stitch, and it hurt. Charlie said he had to cauterize the bloody nose because it was dangerous to take that condition into jump, and that was even less pleasant. JR simply stood by, watching matters, and when Charlie was done, relieved him to go off-duty and to his quarters the way he'd sent Chad.

"And stay there," JR said shortly. "I don't care who's to blame, both of you stay in quarters until after jump. That ship in front of us is going up, this ship is engaged, and we can't afford distractions. I don't think Chad did it. Do you hear me?"

By then the bruises were starting to hurt, and he didn't argue the question. Charlie had shot him full of painkiller, and it had made the walls remote and hazy. He was having trouble enough tracking what JR was saying, and had no emotional reaction to it. He didn't even hate Chad anymore. He just thought, with what remained to him of self-preservation, that he was going to have trouble getting through jump, the way he was.

Fact was, when he got down off the table, he missed the door, and JR grabbed him and walked him to his quarters, opened the door, and got him to his bunk.

"Sleep it off," JR said. "We'll talk about it the other side."

Jeremy came in. Fletcher didn't know how long he'd been there, but he pretended he was still sleeping. He heard Jeremy stirring about, and then Jeremy shook his shoulder gently.

"I brought your supper."

"Don't want it."

"Dessert. You better eat. You'll be sick coming out of jump if you don't eat, Fletcher. I'll bring you something else. I'll bring you anything you want. . . ."

That was Jeremy, three new programs offered before he'd disposed of the first one. Dessert . . . a heavy hit of carbohydrate . . . was somehow appealing, even if his mouth tasted like antiseptic.

He struggled up to a sitting position. His eye, the one with the stitch in the eyebrow, was swollen shut. His ribs felt massively abused. Jeremy set a tray in his lap, and the offering was a synth cheese sandwich.

Considering the condition of his mouth, the detested synth cheese wasn't a bad choice. He ate the sandwich. He ate the fruit tart dessert while Jeremy jabbered on about the ship they were chasing having started a run, and how *Finity*'s engines were more powerful than any little pirate spotter's and how Jeremy thought they didn't need the Union warship that was running beside them. If *Champlain* tried a duck and strike maneuver, they'd scatter *Champlain* over the jump-point.

He wasn't so sure. And his head was spinning. The sugar tasted good. The rest was just palatable. He supposed that he should be terrified of the possibility of the ship going into combat, but maybe it was the perspective of just having been there himself, on a smaller scale: he didn't care. Jeremy took the tray and he lay down again and drifted out.

At some time the lights had dimmed. He slitted his eyes open on Jeremy moving about the room, trying not to make a racket, checking locker latches. He couldn't keep awake. Whatever Charlie had shot into him just wasn't going away, and he thought about Chad and Connor and Sue, and the scene at the laundry pickup. "We ever get our laundry turned in?" he asked, thinking that Chad was going to have to do it, whatever he liked or didn't like, the work of the ship had to go on. And Jeremy answered:

"Yeah, I took it down."

He drifted again. And waked with the intercom blaring warning.

"... ten minutes, cousins. Wake up. Wake up. Wake up. Get those packets organized. Our spook friend went jump an hour ago and we're going early. Wake up and acknowledge, on your feet and get belted in. This is going to be a hard dump on the other side. You juniors belt in good and solid. Helm One says easy done but the captain says we'll flatten pans in the galley. If you have any chancy latches, tape 'em shut."

"Hot damn," Jeremy said. "We're on 'em."

"On what?" Fletcher asked thickly. And then he remembered Champlain, JR's talk about missiles, and the chance there might be shooting. Then the fear that hadn't been acute at his last waking seemed much more immediate. He tried to sit up, looking for the packets, with the cabin swinging round on him. He was aware of Jeremy doing the call-in, reporting to the computer they were accounted for.

Jeremy came back to him and had the packets, and some tape. "Going to fix these so they don't slide out of reach," Jeremy said, and taped them to the edge of the cot, except one, which Jeremy stripped of its protective coating. "You want to take it yourself, or do you want me to shoot it?"

"A little early."

"It'll be all right. You take it. I got to see you do before I tuck in."

"Yeah," he said. Admittedly he was muzzy-headed. "Charlie gave me a hell of a dose."

"One of those time-release things," Jeremy said as Fletcher put the packet against his arm and let it kick. He didn't even feel the sting, he was that numb.

"Double-dosed," he said. "Is that all right?"

"Charlie knows," Jeremy said, and found the ends of the safety belt for him as he lay back. Fletcher snapped the ends, tucked a pillow under his head, asking himself if he was going to wake up again, or if anything went wrong, whether he'd ever know anything again. Did you have to wake up to die? Or if you died in your sleep, did you ever know it had happened?

He couldn't do anything about it. He'd taken the shot. And Jeremy still sat there. Watching him.

Just watching, for what seemed a long, long time.

What are you looking at? Fletcher asked, but he couldn't muster the coordination to talk, feeling the uncertainty of one more drug insinuating itself through his bloodstream. Jeremy set a hand on his shoulder, patted it but he couldn't feel it. He was that numb.

"Five minutes. Five minutes, cousins. Whatever you're doing, get it set up, we're about to make a run up."

"I don't want you to leave," Jeremy said distressedly. "I don't want you ever to leave, Fletcher. I don't *want* you to go back to Pell. Vince and Linda don't want you to go."

He was emotionally disarmed, tranked, dosed, numb as hell and spiraling down into a deep, deep maze of dark and shadows. He heard the distress in Jeremy's voice, felt it in the pressure, no keener sensation, of Jeremy's fingers squeezing his shoulder.

"Most of all *I* don't want you to go," Jeremy said. "Ever. You're like I finally had a brother. And I don't want you to go away, you hear me, Fletcher?"

He did hear. He was disturbed at Jeremy's distress. And he began to be scared for Jeremy sitting there arguing with him long past what was safe.

"Get to bed," he managed to mumble. After that the pressure of Jeremy's hand went away, and he drifted, aware of Jeremy getting into his bunk.

Aware of the last intercom warning . . .

Gravity increased. The earth was soft and the sky was heavy with clouds . . .

"I don't want you and Chad to fight," a young voice said, and called him back to the ship, to the close restraint of the belts, the pressure hammering him into his bunk.

"I'd really miss you," someone said. "I would."

A long, long time his back pressed against the ground, and he watched the monsoon clouds scud across, layers and layers of cloud.

Then he walked, on an endless wooded slope . . . in an equally endless fight for air . . .

Going for jump, he heard someone say . . .

The Watcher-statues towered above the plain, large-eyed hisa images like those little statues on the hill. But these were far larger, tricking the eye, changing the scale of the world as Fletcher walked down toward them. Living hisa moved among them, very small against the work that, when humans had seen it, revised all their opinions about the hisa's lack of what humans called civilization.

He knew that part. Only a very few artifacts ever left Downbelow. Everybody was curious about the hisa, and if nothing prevented the plunder of hisa art, so he understood, hisa artifacts would be stripped off the world and the culture would collapse either for want of critical objects of reverence (or . . . whatever hisa did with such things); or it would collapse because of the influx of culturally disruptive trade goods and environmentally disruptive human presence.

Researchers didn't ordinarily get to go out to the images. Only a handful had come here to photograph, and to deal with hisa.

And now, culmination of his dreams, he was here, approaching the most important site humans knew of on Downbelow. His youthful guide brought him closer and closer. He walked at the speed the scant air he drew through the mask would let him move, with the notion that before he got to those statues surely some authority, hisa or human, would stop him. It was too reckless, too wondrous a thing for a nobody like him to get to see this place close up.

And yet no one did stop him. As he walked down the long

hillside, he saw strange streaks in the grass all around the cluster of dark stone images, and wondered what those patterns were until he noticed that his guide's track was exactly such a line, and so were his steps, when he cast a mask-hampered look back. They were tracks of visitors, coming and going from every direction.

Hisa sat or walked among these images, some alone, some in groups, and they had made the tracks across the land, most from the woods just as he did, but some from the river, or the hills or the broad plain beyond. The rain that sifted down weighed down the grasses, but nothing obliterated the traces.

Tracks nearer the images converged into a vast circle of trampled grass all about the images and in among them, where many hisa feet must have flattened last year's growth, wearing some patches nearest the base down to bare dark earth. It struck him that from up above, this whole plain bore a resemblance to a vast, childishly drawn sun: the circle of stone images, the tracks like rays going out. But hisa didn't always see the sense of human drawings, so he wasn't sure whether they saw that resemblance or that significance. They venerated Great Sun, who only one day in thirty appeared as a silver brilliance through Downbelow's veil of clouds, and that veneration was why they made their pilgrimages to the Upabove: to look on the sun's unguarded face.

As these Watchers were set here to stare patiently at the sky, in order to venerate the sun on the rare occasions the edge of the sun should appear: that was the best theory scientists had of what these statues meant.

There were fifteen such Watchers in this largest site, huge ones. There'd been three very much smaller ones on the hill to which Melody and Patch had led him and Bianca. And what did that mean, the relative size of them, or the number?

He found himself walking faster and faster, slipping a little on the grass, because his guide went faster on the downhill; and he was panting, testing the mask's limits, by the time he came down among the images.

He stared up at the nearest one. Up. There was no other impulse possible. For the first time in his life a hisa face towered above his, but not regarding him, regarding only the heavens above. He felt the hair rise on the back of his neck.

And when he looked around his guide was gone.

"Wait!" he called out, disturbing the peace. But his hisa guide might have been one of ten, of twenty hisa of like stature. Three in his vicinity wore cords and bits of shell very like his guide's ornament. Wide hisa eyes stared at him, of the few hisa who remained standing and of the most who sat each or in clusters at the front of a statue.

"Melody?" he called out. "Patch?" But there was such a stillness around about the place that his calling only provoked stares.

What was he supposed to do? His guide had failed to tell him.

Where did he go? Push the button and call the Base for help?

He wasn't ready to do that. He wasn't ready to give up the idea that Melody and Patch would come here at least for him to bid them good-bye; more than that, getting past the administrative tangle he knew he'd added to his troubles—his mind shied away from fantasies of hisa intervention, last-moment, miraculous help. It didn't seem wrong, at least, to explore the place while he waited. Hisa weren't ever much on boundaries, and, after the novelty of his shouting had died away, hisa were wandering about among the images at apparent random, seeming untroubled by his presence.

So he walked about unhindered and unadmonished, looking up at the statues, one after the other, seeing minute differences in them the nature of which he didn't know. Looking up turned his face to the misting rain, and spotted his mask with more water than the water-shedding surface could easily dispose of, water that dotted the gray sky with translucent shining worlds, that was what he daydreamed them to be: this was the center of the hisa universe, and he stood in that very center, by their leave.

He spread wide his arms and turned, making the statues move, and the clouds spin, so that the very universe spun as it should, and he was at the heart of the world. He did it until he was dizzy, and then realized hisa were staring at him, remarking this strange behavior.

He was embarrassed then and, being dizzy, found a statue at the knees of which no one sat; he sat down like the others, exhausted, and realized he was beyond light-headed. A breathing cylinder wanted changing. But not urgently so. He set his hands on his knees and sat cross-legged, back straight. He was shivering, and had a hollow in the middle of him where food and filtered water would be very welcome. Excitement alone had carried him this far. Now the body was getting tired and wobbly.

He breathed in and out in measured breaths until he at least silenced the throbbing in his head and the ache in his chest. Still, still, still, he said to himself, pushing down his demand on the cylinders until he could judge their condition.

He'd been cold and hungry many a time in his foolish childhood. He remembered hiding from maintenance workers, back in his tunnel ventures. He'd gone without water. Kid that he had been, he'd gotten on to how to manage the cylinders with a finesse the workers didn't use, and pretended ignorance through the instruction sessions when he'd come down to the world. He'd known oh, so much more. He'd read the manuals understanding exactly what the technical information meant, as he'd wager the novices didn't.

He leaned his head back against the stone, face to the sky. And drew a slow breath.

In time he knew in fact he had to change one cylinder out, and did. He slept a while, secure in two good cylinders.

Once, in an interlude between fits of rain, a hisa came over to him and said, "You human hello," and he said hello back.

"You sit Mana-tari-so."

"I don't understand," he said.

"Mana-tari-so," the hisa said, and pointed up, to the statue.

It wasn't a word he'd learned, of the few hisa words he did know.

"He name," the hisa said.

"He name Mana-tari-so?" The statues, then, had names, like people, or stood for people. He rested against the knees of Mana-tari-so.

"Do you know Tara-wai-sa and Lanu-nan-o?" He didn't pronounce Melody's and Patch's names well. But he thought someone should know them.

"Here, there," the hisa said, and patted the statue. "Old, old, he." And wandered off in the way of a hisa who'd said what he'd wished to say.

He knew something, he suspected, just in those few words, that the scientists would want very much to know, but he could only ponder the meaning of it. Old? Going back how far? And did it stand for a specific maker? And if that was the case, how did a hisa merit the making of such a huge image, with only stone tools? It was not the effort of one hisa. It couldn't be, to shape it and move it and make it stand here.

He sat there cold and hungry and thirsty while the gray clouds went grayer with storm. He sat there while lightning played overhead and thunder cracked. His suit had passed its one flash heat, and had nothing more to give him except to retain some of his body heat. But Mana-tari-so sheltered him from the wind, and ran with water. . . .

The earth shook. Heaved. . . .

Became the ship . . . and a giant fist slamming at him.

He lay there, half-smothered by his own increasing weight, thinking . . . with startled awareness where he was . . . We're going to die. We're out of jump. We're going to die here . . .

Second slam.

"Fletcher!" he heard from Jeremy. "You all right, Fletcher?"

"Yeah," he said, as his stomach threatened to heave. "Yeah."

A third drop. A wild, nerve-jolting screech from Jeremy.

The damned kid took it like a vid ride. Enjoyed it. Fletcher caught a gulp of air.

Told himself he couldn't take the shame of being sick. There was a way to take it the way Jeremy did. He tried to find it. Tried to hold onto it.

"Stay belted! Stay belted!" the intercom said. *"We're in, we're solid, but stay belted. You juniors, this is serious."*

The hell, Fletcher thought. The hell.

"I don't think we'll use the shower yet," Jeremy said. "Drink all those packets! Fast!"

The backup shift on this jump was second to first, Madison to James Robert, Helm 2 to Helm 1. Both shifts were on the bridge.

But JR, riding it out below, fretted and occupied his time shaving, flat in his bunk, and taking a risk on a lightning-fast wash before he dressed. The Clear-to-move was uncommonly late in coming, but the audio off the bridge was reaching him while he lay there, and the captain's station echoed to a monitor setup he had on his handheld, a test of fine vision, but what he heard, fretting below, was a quarry fleeing the point, trying to elude their fast drop toward the dark mass of the failed star that was the point.

They'd gone low, toward the mass, because a bat out of hell was going to come in after them and above them, and *Champlain* must guess it.

He wanted to be on the bridge, but there wasn't a useful thing he could do but watch, and he was watching here, as Bucklin would be watching, as Lyra would be watching, and all the rest of them who had handhelds in regular issue. They were held in silence, not disrupting the essential com flow, not even so far as chatter between stations.

He waited. Waited, with an eye on the clock.

Saw, utterly silent, the appearance of another dot on the system scheme, and the fan of probability in its initial plot, rapidly revising.

"There she rides!" Com was unwontedly exuberant. *"Announcing the arrival of Union ship* Boreale *right over us and bound after* Champlain *for halt and question.* Champlain *is at a one-hour lag now, and projected as one and a half hours and proceeding. We do not believe that* Champlain *has made a second V-dump."*

He wouldn't slow down to exchange pleasantries, JR said to himself, if he were in the position of *Champlain's* captain, with an Alliance merchant-warrior and a Union warrior-merchant on his tail.

What the Old Man and *Boreale* could do to a suspected pirate spotter inside Mariner space was one thing. Outside that jurisdiction there was no law, and *Champlain* knew it was no accident they'd gone out on the same vector and tagged close behind her.

He had a bet on with himself, that almost all *Champlain's* mass was fuel and that *Champlain* was going far across the local gravity well and away from them, before she dumped *V* and redirected for Voyager. They were doing a light skip in and out, light-laden themselves, in the notion of jumping first, transcending light while *Champlain* was still a moving dent in space-time, and possibly beating *Champlain* to Voyager. There was additional irony involved: that both they and *Boreale* could do it, and that neither they nor *Boreale* wanted to show to each other how handily they could do it in case their respective nations one day ended up in conflict. And that they didn't entirely trust one another. There was just the remotest chance it might be politically useful to one party or another inside Union for one of the two principle ships defending the Alliance to disappear mysteriously and just not make port.

Dangerous ally they'd taken. The Old Man had chosen that

danger instead of the sure knowledge *Champlain* was no friend, and possibly did so precisely to demonstrate trust.

More compelling persuasion in the affairs of nations, JR thought now, the cessation of smuggling the Old Man proposed, the acceptance of Union negotiating demands: to have Alliance suddenly accept Union proposals threw such a new wrinkle into Union/Alliance affairs that *Boreale* wouldn't dare turn on them without reporting that fact to Union headquarters. Unlike that carrier they'd passed (and he was sure it was no coincidence: the two ships were almost certainly working together), *Boreale* wasn't a zonal command center, and couldn't act without authority.

But even the carrier *Amity*, back at Tripoint, couldn't set Union policy. A Union commander in deep space had to act with some autonomy, but conversely the restrictions policy laid on that autonomy were explicit. The Old Man had turned all Union certainties into uncertainty by complying with what Union had asked of them, and therefore it was likely the ship operating with them on this run was going to protect them until it could get word there and back again from Cyteen.

He'd grown up in the tangled shadows of the Old Man's maneuvers, military and diplomatic, and he'd learned the principles of Union behavior: Uncertainty paralyzes: self-interest motivates. That, and: No local commander innovates policy.

Mallory innovated with a vengeance. It had made her highly unpopular with every nation, and annoyed the Alliance whose self-interest dictated they take the help of the only carrier and the only Fleet captain they or Earth could get. But even Pell didn't entirely trust Mallory.

Let it be a lesson, the Old Man had used to say when he was a junior Jeremy's age. Unpredictability has its virtues. But it has its negotiating drawbacks.

Union's strategy hadn't always worked. Mallory's did more often than not. Mazian had been betrayed by his own masters: and Mallory had said in his hearing, Never serve Earth's interests and succeed at anything. Nothing touched off Earth's thousand-odd factions like the suspicion that some one faction's policy might really succeed.

Pell was a Quen monarchy primarily because Pell had Earthlike tendencies, with one important difference. They chose an outsider to govern their outsider affairs because they couldn't agree on one of their factional leaders holding power. Mariner was, again, a monarchy masquerading as a democracy: since the War, the same administrator had held power and set up an increasingly entrenched group, the only ones who knew how to govern. Voyager, tottering on the edge of ruin all during the War and fearing that peace might kill it . . . Voyager remained an enigma. While Esperance, a consortium of interests, as best he'd been able to figure its internal workings, clung to the Alliance only so long as it successfully played Alliance against Union.

What they carried, something the Old Man had to hope the Mariner stationmaster had not let leak in any detail to *Boreale*, was a firm proposal to shore up Voyager's economy.

Voyager's survival was not in Union's short-term interest. If Voyager went bankrupt, Esperance would have no choice but to swing into Cyteen's political and economic Union a situation which the consortium on Esperance itself surely couldn't want to happen, though individual members of that consortium might have other notions. In helping them carry out their mission, however, *Boreale* not only abetted the effort to close the black market, which was in Union's interest, but aided Voyager's economy, which wasn't altogether in Union's economic interest but was in interest of the peace, which was in Union's long-term interest.

Higher policy. *Boreale*'s captain, even if he knew both halves of the equation, was going to be damned by his high command if he failed to render aid to *Finity* if the question went one way and damned if he did render it, if the question went the other, but as Union generally operated, that captain's career salvation was going to be the simple fact *Boreale* had acted to uphold current policy.

So *Boreale* wouldn't blow them to hell out here away from witnesses, and would concentrate instead on its proper target, a merchanter on the wrong side of Union policy and Alliance law.

The Old Man bet their lives on it, but it was a good bet and a better bet than being out here alone in the case that *Champlain* might have dumped down hard and *Finity* would have exited jump into a barrage of fire. Might have won, all the same, but this way there wasn't a shot fired. The Old Man's bet was won.

"Crew has one hour," the intercom said. *"One hour to prepare for run up to jump. We are not spending time here. Cargo is stable. Ship is stable. Rise and shine, cousins, and get yourselves set. Our colleague is now in front of us and we're on the track. Note: the captain regrets there will be no bar open at Mariner-Voyager Point."*

"What are we doing?" The junior apprentice appointee in charge of Jeremy and company was no better informed than he'd ever been. He was reassured by the levity on the Intercom, but the situation was far from clear.

"We're chasing that ship," Jeremy said happily. "Burn their ass, we will, if they lag back."

"We're going to shoot?"

"Probably," Jeremy said. "Sure as sure that we're not running from it. Got to move quick. You want me to get the sandwiches and you take the shower?"

"Yeah," he said. An hour, the announcement had said. An hour before they either shot at somebody or went right back up again, still wobbly from the last jump. Taking a shower under the circumstances was on one hand the stupidest thing he could imagine, and on the other, he couldn't imagine anything more attractive than getting out of the sweaty clothes he'd worn for a month unless it was the news they weren't going to jump or shoot after all, and that didn't look forthcoming.

He stripped and stuffed the old clothes into the laundry bag, hit the shower and set the dial for five minutes.

The bruises were faded green. The stitched eyebrow felt healed and no longer swollen. The cut lip felt normal.

He remembered how he'd acquired them, remembered he wanted to beat hell out of Chad Neihart, but the heat of anger was as dim as weeks could make it . . . dim as a weeks-neglected chemistry of anger could make it. He knew biology, and was halfway glad to have the intervening cool-off, the diminished hormonal surges, but he felt robbed by that elapsed time, too, robbed of something basically and primally human, as effectively as he'd already been robbed of his sole tie to home and the first girl he'd almost loved. Feelings went cold as yesterday's breakfast. Human concerns diminished until he could contemplate going into a fight as a technical problem, remote from A deck.

They probably wouldn't find the stick. The pranksters had probably gotten scared, probably chucked it down a waste chute rather than get caught with it.

When he thought that, he could halfway resurrect the anger he'd felt a month ago. Fight Chad Neihart again? It was inevitable that he would.

Trust him again? He didn't think so.

Love the girl he'd thought he loved? He wasn't sure what he'd felt and what he did feel.

But he recalled something as recent as slipping into jump, Jeremy's *I'd miss you* still echoed in his thinking. Jeremy would in fact miss him, as he'd miss Jeremy, and as strange, he thought he'd miss Madelaine, who'd fought to get him aboard, and who'd given him a tissue for a bloody nose.

He missed Downbelow.

But he'd miss people on *Finity*, too.

He'd never felt that, going away from the station to Downbelow.

He scrubbed hard, peeling away dead skin and scab and leaving new skin beneath. He raced the shower dial, which would finish with a warm all-over wash-off. His stomach remained queasy, not alone from the jump, but from the divergence between mind and body, that just didn't muster the intensity of feeling he'd had before. As if the water sluiced away passions and left conclusions intact but without support. People on this ship wanted him. Others didn't. How much of their feelings had jump leached out of them . . . and what would a second jump leave? A placid acceptance of the theft?

Hell, no. He wouldn't let it. There'd be a reckoning. There'd be justice.

But did it take runaway hormones to make anger viable? Was it cowardice to let it fall, or to find it was falling what did a sane human do, who'd gone off where humans were never designed to go?

The water cycle hit from all sides, stung his skin in a short burst. Blinded him.

He loved Melody and Patch, but that passion was fading, too, no more immune to the onslaught of jump-space than his anger was. Spacers' loves flared in sleepovers and died between jumps and became someone else in the next port, nothing eternal but the brother- and sisterhood on the ships. Family wasn't meeting someone and marrying; it was your relations, your shipmates, the attachments close as Jeremy. I'd miss you . . . and that would resurrect itself.

Bianca was further and further behind. He was what, now? six weeks ahead of her and three months further on?

Melody's pregnancy would be showing now, if she and Patch had succeeded. Her new baby would be a visible fact. She'd spend her time in a burrow. She'd have gone away from him of her own volition, grown absorbed in her future, not his past. His love for them didn't diminish—their beginnings with him were almost as old as his sense of self—but they were his foundation, not his present reality.

He came out into the cold air, found Jeremy had gotten back from what must have been a sprint to the mess hall, with synth cheese sandwiches and cold drinks in plastic containers. Jeremy finished his in a gulp, started stripping and went to the shower, stuffing his laundry in the bag. "I'll take it to the laundry chute," Jeremy said from the shower, before it cut on.

Fletcher dressed and tucked up on his bunk with the sandwich and fruit juice, feeling not too bad and finding it hard to track on where they were in what could be the edge of a firefight. Ordinary things went on, the ordinary pleasures of clean clothes, a cold, sweet drink. Went on right down to the moment it might all be over. And he'd fallen into the understanding of it.

He'd finished his sandwich when Jeremy came out and dressed.

"How are you feeling?" Jeremy asked.

"Mostly healed up," he said.

Jeremy wasn't surprised. "You got that *Introspect* tape? You think you could lend it?"

He'd bought it at Mariner. He'd played it several times. And Jeremy liked it.

"Yeah," he said, and asked himself if he wanted to set up a tape himself.

But visions of Downbelow still danced in memory, a day unlike no other day he could ever imagine. Maybe he could recover that dream.

"Hello, cousins," came from the intercom, a different voice. *"Here we are, second shift taking over, a rousing applause for first shift which dropped us neatly where we hoped to be and all the way down to synch with our port. Thanks to the galley for a heroic effort, and all those sandwiches. We're on to Voyager, where, alas, we're going to have to be on long hours. But the galley promises us herculean efforts during our Voyager run-in. We are able to reveal to you now, seriously, cousins, that we were engaged in negotiations with both Pell and Mariner, and with numerous captains of the Alliance, who concurred in a plan that now has Union working with us. This ship has become valuable to the peace, cousins, in a way that command will explain in more detail*

past Voyager, but Captain James Robert has a word for you in
advance of our departure. Stand by."

"Wild," Jeremy said quietly. "He only does that when we're
going in to fight."

"This is James Robert," the next voice said, and a chill
went over Fletcher's skin. *"As Com says, more later, but this*
we do know. We're couriering in a message Voyager will very
much wish to hear. We're assuring its continued existence in
the trading network, one additionally assuring that Mazian
will lose the heart of the supply network that's kept him going.
There's been a black-market pipeline funneling Earth goods to
Cyteen and war matériels to Mazian, and that's about to stop.
I'll fill you all in at Voyager, but console yourselves for a very
hard stay at Voyager that we're about to deal Mazian a blow
heavier than any he's had in years. Peace, cousins. Tell your-
selves that when you're on three hours of sleep and your backs
hurt, and you're tired of watching console lights that don't
change. Voyager liberty is cancelled. We may manage a few
hours, but we're going to work like dockhands at this next
port. As an additional piece of news, our running partner
Boreale is in hot pursuit of Champlain, and if Champlain
doesn't have the extra fuel we think she has, and does pull in
at Voyager, we can deal with that, too."

"We ought to hit them," Jeremy said in a tone of disap-
pointment. "Why's *Boreale* get all the fun?"

"It's not fun, Jeremy!" Nerves made him speak out, and he
gained a shocked look in return. "It's not fun," he reiterated.
"Listen to the captain who's done more of hitting them than
anybody."

"Maybe he's getting old."

"Maybe he always knew what he's been fighting for! And
maybe you're too young to know."

"I'm not too young!"

"I'm too young! Pell's been at peace, but the idea of no
enemy anywhere? I've never known that. But I lived with creatures who never fight each other, who don't steal from one

another, and people on this ship do! I've at least seen peace, and you haven't!"

Jeremy looked at him, just stared, as if he'd become as alien as the downers.

"Maybe we can't be like that," Fletcher said, sorry if he'd hurt Jeremy's feelings, and sorry to be at odds with him. "But we can be happy living a lot closer *to* that, where people don't get killed for no good reason, and where you're not taking what we could spend on building places for forests and blowing it all up."

Jeremy didn't look happy. Or informed.

"Take hold," the intercom said. *"Belt in, cousins. We're about to move."*

"Somebody's got to get Mazian," Jeremy said. "Downers couldn't get him."

"Did you hear the captain? We *are* getting him. We're getting him worse than if we blew up a carrier. Downers didn't get him. But they watch the sky and wait."

The count started. Then the pressure started and the bunks swung.

"I still wish we got that ship!" Jeremy shouted.

"I'm going to be happy if we get there in one piece!" Fletcher yelled back. "It's no game, Jeremy. Get your head informed! You never saw what the captain's looking for, you've never been there. But you've seen that tape I've got. They didn't take that. You want to borrow it again? I can get it up to you!"

"No!" Jeremy shouted back. "I got a study tape to do."

"Scare you?" he challenged the kid. "Doesn't scare me."

"You scared of *Champlain*? I'm not!"

"Scared of a thunderstorm? I've walked in one!"

"Seen a solar flare? That's scary! I've seen Viking spit!"

He grinned, in this war of top-you. "I've seen the Old Man in his office!"

"That's scary," Jeremy said, and he could hear the grin in Jeremy's voice. They played the game in increasing silliness until they'd reached bilious vats of synth cheese, and the pressure made talk difficult. They were moving. Faster and faster.

"My sides hurt," Jeremy said, and they were quiet for a while.

Then Jeremy said, "I don't know what it'd be like, to just have liberties all the time."

"Is that what you think we do, on station? We work jobs!"

"No, I mean, if we just went around to stations having liberties and trading and going to dessert bars and seeing girls and that."

"And *that*. What's *that*?"

"*You* know."

He knew. Another grin. "Kid, your body's going to catch up to your ambitions someday and the universe will make sense to you."

"It makes perfect sense now!"

"Out there without a chart, junior-junior. Someday you'll know."

"You sleep with any of those Belizers?"

"If I had I wouldn't tell you!"

"I bet you didn't."

"You'd be right. I'm particular."

"You ever?"

"Maybe."

"What was it like?"

"Like you've read in those books you're not supposed to be looking at in that Mariner shop!"

"No fair. I was looking at the next row!"

"I'll bet you were." His ribs were getting tired from talking, but it whiled away the time, and fought the discomfort as *Finity* climbed toward jump. Finally voices gave out, and Jeremy resorted to his music tape.

He lay and stared at the underside of the bunk, then shut his eyes, asking himself how he'd worked his way into this, and suddenly thinking no one at home would even understand the exchange with Jeremy. That was, he supposed, when you knew you'd become different, when you started sharing jokes with *Finity*'s youngest . . . and knowing nobody back home would understand.

It was . . . when you settled in to a run like this, knowing you could make a fireball in the night, five or so lightyears from making a glimmer in anyone's telescopes, and do it with a philosophical turn that said, well, it was more likely you'd get to Voyager instead.

And, it was a place he'd never remotely imagined going. It was mysterious and dark and primitive, by all he knew. It was a doomed and damned kind of place.

He'd say that to his stationer cronies of his junior-junior years and they'd say, Wild, and talk about going. But when they got to his age, they'd begin to talk about savings and getting more apartment space and whether to work extra hours for the bigger space or take the free time and live in a closet.

On *Finity* you got damn-all choice what you'd work, what you'd wear, and you didn't retire. He did live in a closet, and shared it, to boot. They were out here with someone who was trying to kill them. For real.

God.

What made him settle in and say they'd probably make it?

What made him say to himself he didn't need the stick to read Satin's message, and that they might in fact be what Satin was waiting for? He was in the heavens Satin looked to for her answers.

"Approaching jump," the intercom said. *"Trank down, and pleasant dreams, cousins."*

"You awake?" he asked Jeremy. He hadn't heard a sound out of the top bunk for the last hour.

"Yeah," Jeremy said. "I got it. How are you?"

"Fine," he said, and pulled the trank packet from where Jeremy had taped it a month ago.

Stuck it to his arm and felt the kick, not even having worried about it.

"Pleasant dreams," he said.

"You too," Jeremy called down.

"We are in count, plus five minutes," Com said. *"Boreale has gone for jump and we believe* Champlain *has gone out of the continuum ahead of us. We have had no indications of hostile action. Stand by for post-jump crew assignments. We will transit Voyager space in ordinary rotation, third shift to the bridge, fourth to follow. Operations in all non-essential stations are suspended for the duration. Galley service will go on, that's Wayne, Toby B., and Ashley. Laundry, scrub, filter change all will be suspended. Translate that, get your rest, cousins. You're going to need it when we dock. That's four minutes, twenty-nine seconds . . ."*

Fletcher drew a deep breath, listening to the periodic reading of the count.

"I bet we could have gotten *Champlain*," Jeremy said at the one-minute mark.

"Maybe we could," Fletcher retorted, feeling the creak in ribs long protesting the acceleration. "But Mazian's going to be madder if we cut off his supply."

"You really think we can do that?"

"You got to study something besides vid-games, kid! You can't make bread without flour, and you can't get flour if the merchanters don't move. And flour's far scarcer than iron for missile parts in this universe!"

"That's thirty seconds. Twenty-nine . . ."

He tilted his head back against the strain. The engines cut out for that moment of inertial drift that generally preceded a jump.

"Sweet dreams," he yelled at *Finity's* warlike youngest. "Think about it! Grain and flour, Jeremy! What the downers grow, what they lend us the land to grow! Bread's a necessity for us, far more than ice and iron!"

The ship spread out to infinity and lifted . . .

That was the way it felt . . .

He sat there all through the dark, aware of hisa around him, in the night. There was no shelter but the images. There was no talk. Hisa waited, sitting much as he sat, in the intermittent rain.

Is this a place where old hisa come to die? he began to wonder.

Did the young hisa mistake what I was looking for? Do hisa just wait here, and starve, and die?

He grew more and more uneasy. His legs kept going to sleep. He'd been told that lightning tended to hit the highest thing around, and he sat at the base of an image that was one of fifteen highest points in the immediate area, exactly what the Base seniors had said was not wise in a rainstorm.

Were all of them waiting for lightning to kill someone? Was *that* the kind of game this was? Divine favor? Judgment from the clouds?

The rain came down in torrents for a while, then slacked off, as if nature had grown weary of its rage.

After a long, long while he could see the shadows of the tall Watchers by some source of light other than the lightnings.

He'd seen the sun go down. He'd been in the thick of the woods. He'd never in his life really seen the sun rise from an unobstructed horizon, not as it did now, just a gradual, soft light that at first he could scarcely detect. He could never point to a moment and say that this was dawn. Light just became, and grew, and defined the world around him.

He shifted sides: the leg nearest the ground had chilled to the point of pain, and he could protect one side at a time. He changed out a cylinder, carefully pocketing the spent wrapper.

He slept, then, perhaps simply from weakness. He truly slept, and waked in an unaccustomed warmth. He opened his eyes and realized Great Sun was brighter than he was accustomed to be, comforting the land.

He sat, absorbing the warmth, leaning on the knees of the statue, on Mana-tari-so. He said to himself then that he should just wait, and never push the button that would call for help at all. It wasn't a scary place. He was with the hisa, and whatever this place was: it waited, it watched. It was all expectation, and in a light-headed way, at this moment, so was he.

But a hisa took his arm, and wanted him to rise and walk, where, he had no idea. A hisa never meant harm, at least. They were utterly without violence. And he went, curious, wobbling on his feet from hunger and light-headedness and cramped legs.

The hisa brought him to the base of the largest Watcher, and a little gray-furred hisa, older than any hisa he'd ever seen.

"You walk in forest," the old hisa said—female, he thought. And he sank down to his knees on the mat of golden grass, before this old, old creature. "You name Fetcher."

"Yes." Something held him from blurting out a request for Melody and Patch. He'd been before judges—and this was one, something told him so, with a sense of hushed reverence that distant thunder could not disturb.

"Satin, I."

Satin! A shiver went down his spine. Satin, the downer who'd led in the War. *Satin*, who'd been to space and come down again.

A very thin, elderly hand reached out to him, brushed dust from the mask faceplate, then touched his bare, muddy fingers.

"You boy come watch Great Sun."

"Yes."

"What he tell you?"

"I don't know." Was he supposed to know something? Was he supposed to be wiser? There was a time downers had made him better than he was. There was a time downers had given him far better sense than he had. But what should he know now? He didn't think there'd be an easy answer for the ship above their heads and for the rules he'd broken.

"Not you place," Satin said, and lifted her chin, looked up then at the heavens with eyes tireless as the Watchers themselves. "*There* you place, Fetcher."

"I'm Melody's," he said, fearful of disrespecting this most important of hisa; but Satin was wrong. He *didn't* belong up there. That was all the trouble. "I belong to Patch and Melody. I don't want to go back up there. Ever."

A chill went down his back as those eyes sought his, with the mask between them. "You walk with Great Sun. I walk with Sun my time, bad time, lot shoot, lot die."

The War. *War* wasn't a word they were ever supposed to use with hisa.

"I know," he said.

"You walk with Sun," she said, and from the grass beside her took up a spirit stick, a carved stick as long as a human's forearm, a carved stick done up with woven strands and feathers and stones. He'd seen them on gravesites, at boundaries, at important places hisa meant to mark. "Take," she said, and offered it to him.

Humans weren't supposed to touch such things. But she offered it, and he took it carefully in one hand. He saw intricate carvings, and the wear of age and the discoloration at one end that said it might have been set in dark earth once.

"You take," she said.

He didn't know what to say. He couldn't own such a thing. Or maybe—maybe it was a grave marker. They were, sometimes. Maybe it was his dying she meant.

"Why?" he asked. "Do what with it?"

"Go you place. You sleep with Mana-tari-no, make he no rest. You dream Upabove. All you dream belong Upabove. You go there."

He didn't know what to say, or to do. He didn't *want* this answer.

"I want to see Melody and Patch," he said as clearly as he could, as forcefully as he dared object.

"Not you dream," Satin said.

"I *didn't* dream. I didn't have a dream!" It was what hisa came here to do, that was what the researchers said. They dreamed and the wise old ones interpreted those dreams. They believed the old ones dreamed the world into reality. They were primitive beings.

He looked into those old, wise eyes and saw—pity?

He grew angry. Or wanted to. But Melody had told him the truth all those years ago. He wasn't angry. He was sad.

"You find dream up *there*." Satin gestured toward the sky. "Go walk you springtime. Melody and Patch go walk. Time you go, Melody child."

It hurt. It hurt a great deal. But he knew the truth when, after a period of self-delusion, he got the straight word from somebody who could see it.

Go away. Go back. You're hurting Melody.

It *was* true. He'd invited himself into Melody's life and never left. And downers didn't live as long as humans. It was a big piece of Melody's life he'd taken with his need, his problem.

Downer females didn't get pregnant until their last infant grew up.

Did Melody think that he was hers? In her heart of hearts, was that the reason, that she *wanted* to be rid of him and couldn't—and couldn't *have* her baby until he was out of her life?

He offered the stick back, with all it meant, every tie, every connection to the hisa. He did it in hurt, and in what his pride insisted was anger and what Melody had always insisted wasn't.

But Satin refused the stick. "You take," she said. "Belong you."

He couldn't speak for a moment. He didn't know the exact moment in their talking together when the realization had happened, just that at a moment amid the pain he felt assured that he'd been—not cast out: the gift of the stick proved that. But *sent* out by them. Graduated. Dismissed, with his own business unfinished; his messages unspoken; his plans shifted to a totally different course.

And by what he knew now, he had to go.

It was a good thing he wore a mask. The bottom seal was getting slick. And there was a painful lump in his throat.

"Tell Melody and Patch I love them," he said finally. "I hope they're all right this spring."

"Spring for them," Satin said, saying it as plainly to his ears as any human could: it was too much for a hisa to bring up a human. Spring came. It carried hope for Melody. And a hisa wise in the ways of the Upabove explained what Melody and Patch were too kind, too gentle to say: Melody should forget her human child, quit her lifetime of waiting for him and get on with the years she had, she and Patch. *Spring for them.*

"I understand," he said, and got up, weary and weak as he'd grown. He made the proper little bow hisa made to those they owed respect, and held the stick close as he walked away.

He sighted toward the dark line of the woods, a long, long climb of the hill, on mist-slicked grass. He was well clear of the trampled circle when he reached into an inner, safe pocket, and found the locator device, and contrived, tucking the precious stick under his arm, to push the complex button.

He could do two things, then. He could throw it away and let it simply advise rescuers where he'd been.

Or he could start walking home, toward his assigned fate, wondering if he'd already stayed too late, and whether the cylinders would last.

"Fletcher? Fletcher, wake up!"

"You're scaring me, Fletcher! Don't play games . . ."

He blinked, angry at life, at peace with dying. He couldn't remember why, until a junior-junior started shaking him.

"You were *out*," Jeremy said. "God, Fletcher!"

"I'm fine," he said harshly, annoyed at being shaken, and then realized Jeremy had already showered and changed.

He'd been on Downbelow.

He'd been lost, dismissed. Sent away.

"We're *here*! —Are you all right?"

"Yeah," he said. "Yeah, I'm fine."

He'd had Satin's gift in hand. Her gift, her commission.

But he'd lost it, had it stolen, whatever mattered at this point.

Go away. You too old, Fetcher. Time you go.

Had she known? Was there any way her images had whispered the future to her?

She hadn't said . . . go Upabove, to the station. She'd said . . . go walk with Great Sun. Go to *space*. And giving him her token, she sent him away from Melody and Patch, and into her sky.

To be robbed, by a crew supposed to be the best of the merchanters. By his relatives.

His lip wasn't cut anymore. He'd almost forgotten Chad, *and* the theft, until he searched with his tongue for that physical tag of his last waking moment, and met smoothness and no pain.

"Fletcher?"

"I'm fine," he said harshly, the universal answer. He moved. He sat up. He felt—he'd gone back there. He'd been there. He hadn't wanted to leave.

And when he came upright and tried to sit on the edge of his bunk, his stomach tried to turn itself inside out.

Jeremy opened a drink packet, fast, made him drink it. The taste told him he needed it. Jeremy pressed the second on him. He almost threw up, drew great breaths of unhindered air.

"You had me scared."

"I was walking home," he said. "But I wake up *here*, and I didn't remember the fight, I *forgot, dammit*!" He sat on the edge of his bunk in a frantic search inside after pieces, trying desperately to find the anger, not at his fate, not at Quen, or at the ship, but specifically with Chad . . . and it wouldn't come back. It wouldn't turn on.

You not angry . . . Melody had said, remembered in his dream, and turned his feelings inside out. But this time he wasn't sad, either—he was *scared*. Twice robbed. Ten-odd lightyears had come between him, Chad, and the fight, and Mariner, and all of it. It was two months ago . . . and the brain had cooled off and the anger had gotten away despite his concentrated effort to remember it, and left only panic in its place.

He'd failed a trust Satin had given him. He'd lost the stick. He didn't know where to find Satin's gift. Didn't know where to find a piece of himself that had just . . . slipped away in his sleep, leaving his intellect aware but his body uninformed. Even his pain at losing Melody and Patch was getting dimmer, as if it had been long ago, done, beyond recall—as it truly was.

He flung himself to his feet, stripped as if he could strip away the dreams. He went to the shower and scrubbed away at the stink of loss and fear. He slammed the shower door open and came out into the cold clear air determined to resurrect his sanity and his sense of place in the universe, on this ship, whatever the rules had become.

And to fight. To *fight*, if he had to.

He dressed. He contemplated doing his duty. He went through the motions of anger, as if that could breathe life into it; but his brain kept saying it was past, left behind, and his fear said if he didn't care, nobody cared. Intellect alone tried to urge the body into rage, but all it achieved was disorientation.

He wanted—he didn't know what, any longer.

"Have we got a duty?" he asked Jeremy. They hadn't waked before without one. He didn't know what the routine was, aside from that.

"We're supposed to stay in our bunks."

"Hell." The one time he *wanted* work to do. There was nothing. He was in a void, boundless on all sides. He sat down on his bunk and raked hands through his wet hair.

Satin. The stick he'd carried through hell and gone . . .

His brain began to look for bits of interrupted reality. Finally found the key one.

Voyager. "Where's the ship we were following? Where's *Champlain*?"

"I don't know," Jeremy said in a hushed voice. "Nobody's said yet. Fletcher, you're being weird on me. You're scaring me."

"I want the stick back. I don't care what kind of a joke it is, it's over. I want it back. You think you can communicate that out and around the ship?"

"JR's been looking for it. Everybody's been looking. I don't think they're through—"

"Then where is it?" He scared Jeremy with his violence. He'd found the anger, and let it loose, but it didn't have a direction anymore, and it left him shaken. "I don't know whether *JR* might know all along where it is. And say I should just have a sense of humor about it. But I don't. And for all I know the whole damn ship thinks it's funny as hell."

"No," Jeremy said faintly. "Fletcher, —we'll find it. We'll look. They haven't got us on any duty. We'll look until we find it."

"Yeah. Why don't we ask *Chad* along?"

"We'll find it."

"I think we'd have hell and away better shot at finding it if JR put out the word it had better be found."

Jeremy didn't say anything.

And he was being a fool, Fletcher thought. The vividness of the Watcher dream was fading. The feeling of loss ebbed down.

But the feeling of being robbed—not only of Satin's gift, but of his own feelings about it—lingered, eating away at his peace. He'd come out of sleep in a panic that wasn't logical, that was a weakness he'd gotten past. He'd changed residences before and thrown away *everything* when he got to the new one . . . photographs, keepsakes, last-minute, conscience-salving gifts. All right into the disposal, no looking back, no regrets. And yet—

Not this time.

Maybe it was the spite in this loss.

Maybe it was the innocence and the stern expectation in the giver . . .

Maybe it was his failure, utterly, to unravel what he'd been given, or why he'd been given it, or even whose it was.

Downers put them on graves. Put them at places of parting. Gave them to those who were leaving, and the ones who carried them from a parting or a death would leave them in odd places—plant them by the riverside, so the scientists said, in utter disregard that Old River would sweep them away next season . . . plant them in a graveyard . . . plant them on a hilltop where no other such symbols were in sight and for no apparent distinction of place outside the downer's own whim.

And sometimes such sticks seemed to come back again. Sometimes a downer took one from a gravesite and bestowed it on another hisa and sometimes they returned to the one that had given the gift. One researcher had asked why, and the downer in question had just said, "He go out, he come back," and that was all science had ever learned.

He go out. He come back.

To a graveyard, with more strings and feathers added. Researchers took account of such things, in meticulous studies that noted whether the sticks were set in the earth straight, or slanted, or if the feathers were tied above or below certain marks . . .

All that would mean things in the minds of the researchers, perhaps. He didn't trust anything they surmised—he, as someone who'd been *given* one—someone who'd carried one as a hisa had to carry such a gift. He'd had no place to store it, no place to carry it . . .

And had the researchers with their air-conditioned domes and their cabinets and their classifying systems never thought what it was to carry one, with no pockets, ridiculous thought? When you had one in your trust, you just carried it, was all, and it was with you, and at some point in the next day or so after, he supposed downers felt a need to complete the job of carrying it, taking it to a grave, or to Old River, or to stand on some hilltop, nearest the sky, just to get on with their lives, get a meal, take a drink, do something practical.

He never got to find a place to let it go, that was the thing.

Satin gave it to him, laid the burden of it on him, saying . . .
go to space, Fletcher.

He'd brought it here and in that sense he'd carry it forever
if he couldn't find it. He'd carry the burden of it all his life, if
the people he'd been sent to, his own people, made a joke of
it—if the ones who should accept him thought so little of him
and all he'd grown up to value.

He raked the hair back, head in his hands, had, he thought
to himself, a clearer understanding of Satin's gesture and of
his banishment than any behaviorist ever could give him.

Take this memory and go, Fetcher.

Be done with old things. Be practical. Feed yourself. Sleep.
Let Melody go.

But that wasn't all of it, even yet. It was *Satin's* gift. It came
from the one hisa who'd gone to space, and back again. It
wasn't just from *any* hisa. It was from the authority all hisa
knew and all humans recognized. It was Satin's gift and Base
administration hadn't dared say otherwise.

Then some stinking lowlife stole it, because an unwanted
cousin came in as an inconvenience, one who had had some
other life than the ship.

He didn't think now that JR would have done it or countenanced it, but protect the party responsible and try to patch it
all up? That was JR's job, to keep the bad things quiet and
keep the crew working. He figured the Old Man might not
even have heard yet—if it was up to JR to report.

But no—he recalled now, piecing the details of pre-jump
together: *Madelaine* knew. And if Madelaine knew, he'd bet
the Old Man did know.

He didn't think that the senior captain would approve such
goings-on. In that light, it was well possible that JR had had to
explain the situation.

A weight came on the bunk edge beside him. Jeremy. With
an earnest, troubled look, itself an unspoken plea. He'd been
seeing Downbelow, in his mind.

"The hell of it all is," he said to Jeremy, "the stick was like a trust. You know what I mean? And if I get it back, I don't know what I'd do with it . . . something Satin would want; but I don't know. —But it's for me to choose when and where to do that. Somebody else doing it . . . just tucking it away somewhere . . . "He was talking to a twelve-year-old, who, even with his irreverence, believed in things dim-witted twelve-year-olds believed, in magic, and a responsive universe, things somebody older could still in his heart believe, but never dare say aloud. "You know what that means? That *they* carry that stick. And that *they've* taken on responsibility for something they probably wouldn't choose to carry, but I'll tell you something about that stick. It won't turn them loose. That thing's an obligation, that's what it is. And this ship won't ever be quit of it if it doesn't give it back to me." He saw Jeremy's face perfectly serious, absolutely believing. "And—no," he said to Jeremy, "I'm *not* going to look for it. It's going to come back to me or this ship will change and change into what somebody aboard wants it to be. I'm not going to play games with Chad about it. He'd better hope he finds it and gets it to me before the captain steps in to settle it, and I kind of think that's the instruction the captain's given JR. You understand me? If the ship doesn't find it—it's going to be the *ship's* burden, and the ship's responsibility, and as long as I live I won't trust Chad Neihart. Maybe no one else will, either."

"What if it's not his fault?" Distress rang in Jeremy's voice. "What if he, like, meant to give it back and something went wrong?"

"I said it. It's something you carry until you can lay it down. Downer superstition, maybe. But it's true. I can tell you, either I'm going to forgive Chad and his hangers-on, or I'm not. And I'm going to trust this ship or I'm not. That's the kind of choice it is. You can pass that word where you think it needs to be passed. Things people do don't altogether and forever get patched up, Jeremy, just because they're sorry later. If Chad destroyed it . . . that says something it'll take years for me to forget."

There was a long and brittle silence.

"He's not a bad guy," Jeremy said faintly.

"Can I trust him after this?" he asked. Yes, Jeremy believed in miracles, and balances. And maybe it was callous to trade on it, but, dammit, he believed such things himself, and maybe belief could motivate one other human being in the crew. "Can I ever trust him? That's the question, isn't it?"

Jeremy didn't have an answer for him, even with a long, long wait. Just: "I'll put the word around. This *shouldn't* have happened. It shouldn't, Fletcher. We're not like that."

"I want to think so," Fletcher said. It was, at least in that ideal world of these few moments' duration, the truth. Then, because the ensuing silence grew uncomfortable: "Are they going to open rec, do you think, or not?"

"I think we're supposed to sit in quarters. At least until they give us a clear. I'll lend you my tapes."

Fletcher got up and walked the six steps the cabin allowed before he fetched up in front of the mirrored sink alcove. He saw Jeremy standing, too, watching him with a distressed look on his face.

"Cards," he said to Jeremy, foreseeing otherwise Jeremy worrying at the matter and himself pacing twelve steps up and back, up and back, for a long, long number of hours. It was a situation Jeremy knew how to endure, this being pent in quarters. He imagined the rule in force at other chancy moments, on *Finity*'s exits into lonely star systems, and the too-wise twelve-year-old with nothing and no one to confide in.

Don't leave. He remembered Jeremy pleading with him, in a way that, maybe hearing it when he was tranked, the way it did with tape-drugs, had settled into his consciousness with peculiar force. He'd had borrowed brothers all his life. He'd never had a foster brother as desperate, as lonely as Jeremy. There'd never been a rivalry between them. Now—he began to see Jeremy adopting *his* trick of leaving the coveralls collar undone, his trick of how he did a hitch in the belt—

Even the cuff turn-up. The obsession, when they'd been on

liberty, with finding a sweater, a *brown* sweater, like his. God, it was laughable.

And enough to grab his heart, when he looked at the kid's face, the eyes that searched his for every hint of advice, and, having just evoked it and brought it into the open, how did he ignore it?

He didn't know how he felt now. Trapped, yes.

And at the same time gifted with something he'd never had, and now couldn't walk away from . . . no more than Melody had walked away from a lost boy that day on Pell docks.

Chapter
—XX—

Voyager lay ahead, a spark against a starry dark, swinging in orbit about a stony almost-planet itself orbiting a smallish star.

No *Boreale*. No *Champlain* when *Finity* had broken out of hyperspace here. Just the ion traces of ships that had come in . . .

And gone. Both. *Champlain* in the lead, one guessed, and *Boreale* in pursuit. A nominally Alliance ship fleeing; and a Union ship, which without their permission couldn't hunt in this space, in hot pursuit.

The feeling on *Finity*'s bridge was one of frustration. It was second watch in charge of the jump out of Mariner-Voyager Point. That was Madison's crew, with Francie's watch coming on—third watch; and for a buffer, and to handle emergencies, and the senior-juniors, who'd fought the ravages of a double-jump and hauled their depleted bodies out of bunks faster than no few of the seniors could . . . anticipating the remote possibility of battle stations, and moving to be there in case one of the seniors *couldn't* make it to station.

JR held the lead of that set.

But nothing. Just nothing. They turned out to be alone in the jump range, and that was, for the ship, good news. JR told himself so—even if Madison hovered after turnover with a general glum look, and even if Helm 2 had stayed around to be a problem to Helm 3.

Battle nerves, with no battle, no answer, even, for simple human curiosity—and the suspicion that a Union ship had just slipped their witness in Alliance space with full opportunity to carry out an attack on what was, nominally, still an Alliance ship.

That was JR's suspicion, at least. And at a time when they were trying their damnedest to persuade Alliance merchanters to surrender to the Alliance station-based government at Pell some of the rights *Finity's End* had once been pivotal in winning.

Ignore the fact our Union ally just took out after an Alliance ship . . . and did it one jump short of Esperance, the hardest sell they'd face? No matter that that Alliance ship might be guilty of aiding the enemy, the enemy that had not that long ago been their own Fleet; and no matter that some Alliance merchanters were caught on the wrong side of the line. The Alliance found it hard to forgive Union, who'd roughly handled some merchanters during the War and whose territorial lines were now trying to choke some merchanters out of business.

Alliance was very ambivalent about rimrunners, ships skirting the edges of the modern international alignments; and about dealings with Union; and while they wanted Mazian kept at bay, it was not a universal sentiment that the Alliance could exist without the bugbear of Mazian out in the dark—because that fear kept Union behaving itself.

A Union ship taking on a merchanter would harden Alliance merchanter attitudes at the same time it might incline Esperance Station attitudes *toward* an agreement with Union. Get-tough policies regarding merchanter compliance weren't going to win points with the small merchanters who were one economic catastrophe away from having to run cargo they wouldn't ordinarily choose to be running. JR didn't know what the Old Man thought of the situation. He *hoped* that the ion signature they picked up was of a passage, not a battle shaping up to happen in the witness of Esperance and anyone docked there.

He'd bet first that the Old Man, who was not on the bridge this jump, was well aware, and second, that the Old Man was not amused at *Boreale*'s giving chase past Voyager without consultation. Likely he was already considering how he was going to counter the negatives if the situation blew up.

They had, JR concluded, a potential problem. They'd given *Boreale* what *Boreale* couldn't otherwise have gotten: a straight short-cut through Alliance space to warn the Union's own presence at Esperance—reputedly there was a major one at all times—that there was something in the offing. And that could be bad news—or good.

There was no possibility that the carrier they'd met at Tripoint had sent *Boreale*: arrival times at Mariner didn't make it possible, but he was curious enough to sit down and call up Mariner data to confirm that *Boreale* had, indeed, been in port for a week before they'd gotten in. No. Even granted ships could over-jump one another in hyperspace, that theory didn't fit the timeline.

Boreale had come in from Cyteen vector and it had no possibility of having been sent by *Amity*. So its being there was honest.

Boreale's guarding them in the understanding that they were trying to get merchanters into compliance with the customs regulations, that was honest, too.

So it was perfectly reasonable, aside from chasing *Champlain*, that they would want to get on through to Esperance where, unlike at Voyager, they had a straight shot to carry a message to Cyteen and could equally well contact other ships whose black boxes had been in very latest communication with Cyteen, to check out what was going on elsewhere. In *Boreale*'s situation, they'd have done exactly the same.

The Old Man had played it safe, and here they were. *They* had to go in at Voyager, refuel, do their business of meetings with station administration, and go through the routine motions of trade. They wouldn't slight Voyager by bypassing it.

The good break was that, in the slight imprecision of ship

arrivals in a gravity well, Helm had used the belling effect of
a ship still at the interface to skip a moderately loaded and
very powerful ship well out even from the center of system
mass, which wasn't the center of the star . . . and the direction
of that skewing was toward the position Voyager station happened to be at this time of its year. It was a beautiful job both
from Nav and from Helm, a piece of skill that had, all at the
same time, simplified their dive toward the station, let them
speed faster longer than they'd dare at larger stations, and
given them a chance of making up time in what had become a
race with *Boreale* toward Esperance.

Ahead was the least modern station still functioning this
side of Union, a small station, with part of its ring under construction before the War, a construction, their files said, which
was now abandoned.

Pell, Mariner, Earth . . . Cyteen, as well, had strung multiple
establishments through the ecliptic of their stars. But impover-
ished Voyager was just Voyager, in orbit about a tiny planet near
a debris ring unpleasantly perturbed by a smallish gas giant.
Voyager had built a watchful defense not originally against
piracy but against high-velocity visitors. But its capabilities
had found dual use during the War—use which had kept it alive
and kept it a port of call for whatever side could hold it.

And that had been Mazian, for most of the War years.

Prior to the War, in the days of shorter-hopping ships,
Voyager had been a bridge toward the hope of more exotic
mining at Esperance, but in post-War years, mining had turned
out less lucrative for Esperance than the lure of trade with
Cyteen. *Mariner* also wanted the promise of traffic between
Pell and Cyteen, if the peace held. Now, poised between
Mariner and Esperance, Voyager was the unfortunate waystop
between two stars only fragilely interested in trading with each
other.

There was a time crunch on. They had a very little time at
this star to turn that situation around.

The Old Man arrived on the bridge. Madison and Alan

alike stood up. JR did, and all the other juniors on the bridge, in respect of the senior captain, who waved them to be seated.

Madison delivered the first report, of which JR caught the salient details. Alan delivered the second one. Frances had shown up in James Robert's wake, to hear the general reports, and JR listened on the edges, aware of Bucklin having moved up near him.

"Well," the Old Man said with a wry expression that framed official reaction, "we have a need to get through this port and get our job done. We *are* going to get turned around and get out of here in record time. All senior crew to round the clock hull watch, all able-bodied to transfer of cargo, senior staff to what I hope will be short meetings. I don't anticipate station will object to our proposals at all, but the local merchant trade is likely to. And I'd rather have had *Boreale* here with us. But we don't have that. What does the schematic show us? Who's in port?"

"That's three interstellars, sir," Alan said, "end report."

That was incredibly thin traffic.

"We mustered better than that at our last conference with Mallory," the Old Man said with a shake of his head. "Jamie. Who are they? Mariner origin or Esperance?"

"*Velaria* left Mariner for Voyager a week ago, sir, *Constance* and *Lucky Lindy* were before that. Nothing but ourselves, *Boreale*, and *Champlain* the last five days. No ships from Esperance in port."

"Counting that a week's rated a long stay here, it's a reasonable expectation, three ships. Voyager's apt to berth about five ships on any given twenty-four hours, rarely ten. We're the fourth. *Boreale* and *Champlain* would have made it almost to traffic congestion, for this port."

"Yes, sir," JR said. He'd been ready. It was a struggle, on a two-jump, to have mental recall on everything you'd been supposed to track. It was a job skill. A vital one, and he hadn't failed it.

"Four empty cans," the Old Man said, "food grade and

clean, ride in the hold. The job will be to test and transfer whatever we pick up on the local market to assure ourselves a clean cargo, one can to the other. Senior crew will not have forgotten this drill, our compliments to the junior crew, who will carry out a great deal of the transfer. We will secure lodgings for all crew near the ship, and crew will not separate from assigned groups, no matter what the excuse. We will make an additional issue of clothing, purchased at the station. We will forego ship's rules on patches and tags. Wes, you'll treat the details in a general announcement. The station could use the trade, and we won't have access to the laundry. Junior-juniors will stay particularly close, within safe perimeters, and *only* senior staff will deal with food procurement, clothing issue, all other activities where something from the outside comes aboard this ship, including personal baggage, which will be extremely limited. Security Red applies. Cargo will, however, be inert."

It was the old New Rules. Nothing came aboard without being scanned through, logged, accounted for, and the crew member in question absolutely able to vouch for its integrity. Security Red usually applied when they were hauling touchy cargo . . . explosives, not uncommonly in the past. This time it wasn't the cargo's volatility that prompted the precautions against sabotage. It was Voyager's.

The Old Man walked about then, taking a short tour past the number one stations, the general boards, spoke a word with the Armscomper, who'd only begun to shut down the hot switches, and with Tech 1, who'd handled the tracking on the emissions signatures.

Habitually the Old Man also said a word to the observing staff, as they called it: the senior-juniors, and JR waited, standing.

"I had a memo from Legal before jump," the Old Man said in a lowered voice. "I'd like to see you in my office. Now."

"Yes, sir." It was not a topic he wanted to deal with on the bridge. It wasn't a topic he wanted to deal with. And had to.

The Old Man left the bridge. JR looked at Bucklin, who cast him a look of sympathy, and went to report a situation he'd hoped, pre-jump, to have solved.

"The situation on A deck," the Old Man said with no preamble, as JR stood in front of that desk in the Old Man's office, the one with the bookcases, the mementoes of old, wooden ships. Past the Old Man's iron control, JR had no difficulty detecting distress: personal, distracting distress, which the senior captain could well do without when he faced life and death decisions, peace and war decisions.

"Not the captain's immediate concern, sir. I hope to have a solution."

"We've never had to use the word 'theft.' "

"I'm well aware, sir. I don't know what to say. I don't have an answer." At that moment a message began on the intercom, a general advisement to the ship that *Boreale* and *Champlain* had slipped through Voyager system and that they were proceeding to dock and refuel.

"Security Red will apply here," the intercom said, Alan's voice, *"and we will be shifting cargo. The fact that* Boreale *has gone on in close pursuit of* Champlain *remains a matter of concern, but it is not, at the moment, our concern . . ."*

James Robert's finger came down on the console button and the announcement fell silent in the small office.

"I think we know those details."

"Yessir," JR said.

"A spirit stick as I understand it?"

"Yes, sir."

"Smuggled aboard."

"Technically, yes, sir." It wasn't the illegality of it that he felt at question, but the very question how anything of that unusual a nature had gotten past his observation. "Legally in his possession."

Sometimes in the tests the Old Man set him he had to risk being wrong. "Sir, I haven't considered what the case is.

Evidence points to someone taking it, I've requested its return, and no one's come forward."

"And there's been a fight."

"Yes, sir. There was a fight." Sometimes, too, the challenge was to hang on to a problem and keep it off B deck. And conversely to know when to send it upstairs. "I'd like to continue to handle this one, sir, on my own resources."

There was a long, a very long silence. If there was a space under the carpet he'd have considered it. As it was he had to stand there, the subject of the senior captain's very critical scrutiny at a time when a very tired, very worn-looking senior captain took spare moments out of his personal rest time, not his duty schedule.

"I take it the investigation is not at a standstill."

"No, sir. Ship movement took precedence, but this can't end with an acceptance of this situation. That won't solve it."

The captain nodded slowly, in concurrence with that assessment, JR thought.

They risked losing Fletcher. That was one thing. They risked setting a precedent, a mode of dealing with each other that might destroy them.

"Ship's honor," JR said faintly, in the Old Man's continued silence. "I know, sir."

"Ship's honor," the Old Man said. "It's the means by which we dare ask those other ships, Jamie, to put aside self-interest. In the last analysis, it's the highest card we have. Think about it. Do we wish to give that up?"

"No, sir." It was hard to make a sound at all. Hard to breathe, until the Old Man dismissed him to the relative safety of the corridor.

Five minutes later he gave Bucklin and Lyra orders.

In fifteen minutes, every unassigned junior including Fletcher was on intercom-delivered notice that the Old Man had inquired about the object; and juniors were spreading out through the ship this time on independent, not team, search.

Give the culprit the opportunity to find the object, in whatever way he or she wished. It wouldn't end it, but it would enable him to put the focus on the interpersonal problem and discover what they were actually dealing with: a theft, or the ruse, or the destruction of something irreplaceable.

Fletcher, however, was with the junior-juniors, all three, when he came on them going through A deck's vacant cabins a search that, in the example he saw, had boxes of whiskey moved, storages opened, bunks swung to look underneath, all with amazing dispatch.

"Fletcher," JR said, and drew Fletcher outside the door to 40A. "The Old Man expresses extreme concern. It's not a property issue. I don't consider it one. He doesn't. If you want to file a complaint with him, that door will be open. I'm asking you, personally, give me time to unravel this."

Fletcher had been moving boxes. His breaths came deep. "I didn't intend to get involved," Fletcher said, and gave a move of the eyes toward the flurry of activity inside. "They wanted to."

If it had been any other circumstance, he would have been dismayed at the thought of the inexpert junior-juniors disarranging cargo. Thumps continuing to come from inside the disused cabin. "I'm impressed with their enthusiasm," he said.

And in the uneasy silence that followed between them: "Fletcher, we're approaching a very dangerous dock. I hope we can resolve things prior to docking. If not, I'm asking you, as I'll ask Chad, to refrain from confrontations. Very serious negotiations are riding on it. Alliance-Union negotiations. They could be adversely affected if two of our crew engage on dockside." There was a moment more of silence, and diminishing hope of Fletcher's understanding. "I'm asking your cooperation for a handful of days. We're going to be working hard, tempers are going to be short. You're assigned to watch the junior-juniors, the same as before, but I can take you off that if you feel you'd be better separated from other personnel. You and the junior-juniors can sit in a sleepover together and watch vids, if that's your choice, and you won't have to work."

Fletcher stood their considering what he said. He increasingly expected Fletcher to choose to stay to the sleepover, the safest choice, and the one, in the absence of Fletcher's desire to cooperate, he still might order.

But Fletcher let go the frown, and glanced instead toward the doorway, where the junior-juniors were conducting their search. Then he looked back.

"Even if provoked," Fletcher said. "As long as we're in dock. You've got my promise."

"I'm glad to take your word," he said, and left the junior-juniors to their activity. He hunted down Chad with the same proposition, and that quest required a trip out into the rim, where in coats and gloves and with flashlights, Chad had paired up with Wayne. Another glow, from around the girder-laced curve, showed where Nike and Lyra were operating, in cold deep enough to get through boots.

"I don't know why he picked me," Chad said. "That's twice he's come at me like I was the only one."

"I don't know why," he said. "I can't defend it. I only know how important it is we keep the peace. On both sides of this."

"I don't even know what the damn stick looks like," Chad said. "It's hard to search for something when you only have a description of it. And that's all I have."

Chad wanted to convince him he was innocent. He wished he believed it himself. And yet he couldn't dismiss the possibility it was the case.

"It's all I have, too," he said to Chad.

"I think he did it," Chad said, breath frosting in the light, "and he's just putting us to running rings. I think it's going to turn up somewhere and he'll be the only one not surprised."

"If that's the case," he said. "If it's not the case, the real way this is going to get solved is when we sit down together and look at each other without suspecting the worst. Him. You. Wayne. Me. All of us."

"Chad's taking the brunt of this," Wayne said. "And I don't think he's to blame."

"He doesn't want to be here, anyway," Chad said.

"And I just talked to the Old Man, and asked for more time. Give me some help, Chad."

"Yessir. I won't fight."

He had a confidence in Chad he couldn't have in Fletcher, who hadn't been a presence all his life. Chad might be on the wrong side of something, but he wouldn't go against the answer he'd just given.

"Not even if he jumps you, Chad. If he does I'll settle it. I know it's hard what I'm asking, but you're both of you strong hands we need, and I'd rather not have you sitting it out in quarters."

"I got my tooth chipped the first time station-boy threw a punch out of nowhere!"

"Chad."

"Yessir," Chad said.

"And don't call him that. No words, Chad, same as no fighting."

"Yessir," Chad said the second time.

"I take your word on it," he said, wishing it weren't Chad's word that was utterly at issue.

And that Chad wasn't the only potential explosive in their midst. There was Connor. There was Sue. There was Nike.

Vince seemed to have fallen in on the side of the offended, not the offenders. Vince was, at least, off his mind.

No sign of the stick, not the first twenty-four hours, not the second, and the junior-juniors, early and enthusiastic in their burst of energy, grew frustrated and short-fused.

"We're not going to find it," Linda said.

"Probably," Fletcher said, "we have less chance than the ones in the outer ring."

"We can go out there," Jeremy declared.

"No, we can't. I'm not being responsible for you clambering around in the dark. Senior-juniors are searching that."

Jeremy's shoulders slumped. The junior-juniors were tired to the point of exhaustion. They all had blisters.

And senior crew had found out, unofficially. A number had volunteered extra hours, and hiding places they'd known when they'd been young and foolish.

Some of those searches surprised the junior-juniors, that anyone but them did know those nooks and crannies.

Jake came, having gotten the general description, and said there'd been no stones in the recycling traps, which indicated it hadn't gone into biomass, unless somebody had thought of that and removed the stones before chucking it into a disposal chute.

That was a logical place to search, one Fletcher hadn't thought how to handle in terms of the chemistry; and Jake, the bioneer, had disposed of the question by something so basic his school-fed theory hadn't even considered it.

Notes from all four of the captains turned up one by one in his personal pager, saying, essentially, that the captains were aware, and that official issues aside, if he wanted to discuss the matter, they stood ready to listen.

Fletcher didn't know how to answer, so he delayed answering. The first impulse had been to say, Get me off this ship; and the second one had been a hesitancy to say what might not, even yet, answer where he wanted to go, or what he wanted to do.

He hadn't expected the flurry of senior help in the search.

He hadn't expected the junior-juniors, patching blisters, to keep looking.

He hadn't expected the senior-juniors to show up in the mess hall, half-frozen from the ring skin, looking for hot coffee and looking exhausted as his own small crew. That included Chad, who avoided looking at him, who pointedly looked the other way when he stared.

It's destroyed, he said to himself, and Chad's scared to say so. It's destroyed or it's lost and Chad can't find it.

But none of the senior-juniors talked much, least of all to him, and not that much to each other. There was no rec, meals were catch-as-catch-can, and no one associated together.

This is wrong, Fletcher said to himself, sitting in the A deck mess hall with a coffee cup cooling between this own hands. Jeremy had gotten himself a cup of coffee, and then Vince and Linda had, not their habit. Caffeine wouldn't, Fletcher thought, improve Jeremy's already hair-trigger nerves. He wasn't sure any of the junior-juniors were used to it. But he drank it; and they drank it, a warm-up from the chill of places they'd searched.

Jeremy had fallen asleep yesterday night with the suddenness of a light going off. He'd lain awake with the increasingly heavy responsibility of the ship's search lying on his pillow, and he thought, today, *This is wrong,* with the notion that if he stood up, said, Forget it, it's lost, it may never turn up . . . he might free everyone, and relieve everyone's nerves, and just let it pass.

He got up, finally, with the notion of doing exactly that, and immediately the junior-juniors wanted to jump up and follow.

"No," he said. "An hour alone. All right? And don't do anything stupid."

"Yessir," Jeremy said.

He went over to that other table, where Chad and Wayne and Connor were sitting. "Where's JR?" he asked in a carefully neutral tone. "Do you have any notion?"

"Bridge," Wayne said, "last I heard. What's the problem?"

He couldn't go to the bridge. No one could go there without an authorization.

"Thanks," he said, frustrated in his resolution.

"What do you want?" Wayne asked, and he looked at Wayne, and the two he had most problem with, and took resolution in both hands.

"To stop this. Just give it up."

"Why?" Wayne asked.

"Because it's getting nowhere! Somebody lost it. I accept that. Just everybody quit looking. It may turn up ten years from now. It may never turn up. That's the way it is."

"I'll relay that to JR," Wayne said carefully. Neither Chad nor Connor said anything. Chad did look at him, an angry look, a wary one. Connor didn't do that much.

He went back to the juniors and sat down.

"We can't give it up," Jeremy said.

"Even if we stop looking," Linda said, "we can't give it up."

It was, he thought, the truth, however Linda meant it. He had the captains' messages stacked up and waiting, that he hadn't heard from Madelaine meant only that Madelaine was either under orders or trying to restrain herself, and in all the things that had happened aboard the ship, he could only fault a bad situation and a natural resentment.

It was natural that the senior-juniors wished he'd never come aboard; and maybe it was natural Jeremy and Madelaine and maybe the Old Man wanted him never to leave. He'd become the center of a situation he'd never wanted, and everything had gotten out of hand to the point it had damaged the ship.

Even if we stop looking we can't give it up. . . .

He knew now what a delicate, interconnected structure he'd arrived in, and how it had tried to fit him in, and how he'd damaged it without understanding it . . . irrevocably so, perhaps. Stopping the search wouldn't cure it.

Getting rid of him might relieve the pain, his and theirs, but it wouldn't cure it. There wasn't even an organized evening mess in which he could snag JR into private converse.

In another hour the intercom announced the docking schedule, and particulars of assignments, and they were in their quarters packing duffles reversed in the usual proportion of flash and work clothes: this time it was one dress outfit and the rest work blues.

"*This is James Robert Senior,*" the intercom said unexpectedly. *"We have completed cargo purchase and fueling arrangements prior to dock. Senior officers will be engaged in negotiations vital to the peace of the Alliance. We have been alert for any merchanter inbound from Esperance in the notion that such a ship might have information on the two ships who jumped close to us. Keep your eyes occasionally toward the station schedules and be aware that if such a ship should come from Esperance vector, the situation might change rapidly and dangerously. Be aware that this station has numerous black marketeers doing business on the docks and that they may feel we threaten their interests. Be alert. Do not violate the schedule and do not leave the accommodations except to come straight to the ship for work. The sleepover is the finest we were able to obtain, and it has some recreational facilities, but we do not believe there will be extensive time aside from sleep and meals. We will not stow any can we have not verified.*

"You are all by now aware that there has been an incident aboard unprecedented in this ship's history. I call on all involved to set aside the matter for the duration of our stay, in the interests of all aboard, and I continue to express confidence that the parties involved will find it in their capacity to resolve the issue in a manner considerate of the ship's best interests and traditions of honor.

"Enjoy your stay."

He had continued to fold clothing, Jeremy to tuck in small items like his tape player.

Neither of them said anything. He wished now he'd never reported the theft or made an issue. He said to himself he wanted it forgotten, beyond their next jump, that, in the way of mystical things, he'd gained all he could from his loss and stood to lose all he had, if he insisted on finding it.

The intercom droned on with assignments and shifts. The junior-juniors and Chad were at opposite ends of a twenty-four-hour clock. They went down to the assembly area and took their places, Vince and Linda attaching themselves from somewhere farther back in the large, rail-divided rec hall; and Madelaine and others noted their passage through the mob of cousins, giving them small pats on the shoulder, as others did with him.

Fletcher ducked his head and studied the rail in front of him, not wanting to communicate. The junior-juniors stood fast about him through the procedures, like some fiercely protective bodyguard, until it was time for the section chiefs to go out and down to take care of customs.

It was, Fletcher discovered, *not* Pell, *not* Mariner. It looked more barren than Pell's White Dock at the dead hours of alterday, as seedy as any between-shop alley in White. And it had a look of danger, the way White Dock had been dangerous, the domain of insystemers and cheap hustlers and those who wanted to sink in among them for safety.

Customs was a wave-through. For everyone.

Baggage pickup was fast. Everyone had packed as lightly as possible and bags came down the exit chute from cargo as if the handlers had slung them on six at a time.

"The bag-end of stations for sure," he said to the junior-juniors when they set out for their sleepover, a short march across the docks to a frontage of gray-painted metal.

Definitely not Mariner. The promised Safe Harbor Inn was squeezed in between a bar's neon light and a tattoo parlor.

Fifteen minutes later, with scant formality, they had their keys and found themselves sandwiched into what they'd called a suite on the second level—with a note from JR on his pager that occupants on the same floor were known smugglers and that senior staff would walk the whole junior-junior contingent to their duty shift *every* shift.

Their so-called luxury suite was one room, two beds, and a couch.

"God," Vince cried. "This is brutal. We're *stuck* in here?"

"We've got a vid," Jeremy said in desperate cheerfulness, and turned it on. The program selection was dismal and, at one channel, Fletcher made a fast move to stand in front of the screen.

Then he thought . . . what the hell. They were spacer juniors. They'd tossed Linda in with him and Jeremy and Vince, and he figured it was because she was safer with them than elsewhere, tagging around after some preoccupied senior crewwoman and trying to catch up with her age-mates for duty.

"The hell with it all," he said, and gave up on censorship with the vid. Then turned it off. "Yes, we're stuck. I brought my tapes. Vince and Jeremy, the bed on the left, Linda, the right, I get the couch cushions and probably I've got the better bargain. We'll splurge on supper, go to duty. It's three days max."

"Walking us to duty like babies," Linda sighed, and collapsed on the end of the bed, her feet on her duffle. "Skuz."

It was, Fletcher thought, the other side of the spacing life. It wasn't all palaces. His mother had known places like Mariner. But this was *like* post-War Pell, this was like the apartment he'd shared with his mother, right down to the plumbing that rattled. It wasn't a place he wanted to remember, in its details, the cheap scenic paneling. The place had had a plastic tri-d painting, pink flowers, right over the couch that was a makedown bed.

And he'd gotten those couch cushions for his bed, on the floor. Odd thing to be nostalgic about. But that was how little space they'd had. He'd had to walk on the cushions to get past the arm of the couch, his mother had fitted him in that tightly against the wall. His nest, she said. And then when welfare complained, she'd gotten a bed for him, but he'd preferred the cushions, his homey and comfortable spot. So after all that fuss they kept the cot behind the couch and never set it up.

They ate supper, he and the juniors, they walked the only circuit they had, in the lobby, they played a handful of game offerings in the game parlor. At 1200 hours a part of *Finity* crew formed in the lobby and walked, in a group, to the dock, and to the cargo lock.

The instructions arrived, written, for each section head. He read them three times, because it made no particular sense to be emptying one container into the other. He went to the head of Technical over at the entry, a little sheepish.

"Are we emptying one can into another or is it something I'm missing in the instructions?"

"Vacuuming it from one to the other. That's why we took on only food grade and powders." Grace, Chief of Cargo Tech, the coat patch informed him. "Easier to clean the vacuum with powders." He must have looked as bewildered as he felt, because Linda, who'd tagged him over to ask, nudged his arm.

"They can kind of put a foreign mass in stuff, even powder like flour, and they sort of make it assemble by remote, or sometimes it's on a timer. It's real nasty. But it's got to have this little starter unit."

"It blows up," Grace said. "That's why we're analyzing the content on every can and sifting through everything. Security Red. There's those with reason to wish we'd fail to reach our next port."

"Because of the negotiations," he said.

"Because of that, and because some just had rather on general principles that we didn't exist."

All the junior-juniors had gathered around. People wanted to blow up ships with kids on them. That was why the court had kept him off *Finity*. Maybe the court had saved his life. They talked about so many dead, the mothers of these three kids among them, dying in a decompression.

He didn't ask. He lined the fractious juniors up to go in and get the coats they were supposed to have. The cans were sitting outside on the dock, huge containers, the size of small rooms. The message to the section heads said something like fifteen hundred of those cans.

And they were going to transfer cargo from one to the next so they could be sure of the contents?

He'd never been inside a ship's hold. He'd only seen pictures. He went up the cargo personnel ramp, was glad to snatch a coat from the lockers beside the access and to see the juniors wrapped up, too, on the edge of a dark place with spot-lights illuminating machinery, rows and rows of racks.

"Back there's hard vacuum," Jeremy said, pointing at another airlock with Danger written large in black and yellow. Machinery clanked and clashed as a can came in, swung along by a huge cradle. No place for kids, his head told him, but these three knew better than he did.

"You got to keep to the catwalks," Vince yelled over the racket, breath frosting against the glare and the dark. Vince slapped a thin rail. "Here's safe! Nothing'll hit you in the head! Lean over the edge, wham! loader'll take your head off!"

"Thanks for the warning," he said under his breath, and said to himself of all shipboard jobs he never wanted, cargo was way ahead of laundry or galley scrub. His feet were growing numb just from standing on the metal. Contact with the rail leached warmth from his gloved hands. The proximity of a metal girder was palpable cold on the right side of his face. "Colder than hell's hinges."

"You got a button in your pocket lining," Jeremy said, and he put his hand in and felt it. Heated coat. He found it a good thing.

They were mop-up, was what the duty sheet said. Every can had to be washed down and free of dust, as it paused before its trip into the hold. Cans that had been set down, behind the concealment of the hatch, had to be opened, the contents sampled, shifted to another can, and that can, its numbers re-recorded on the new manifest, then had to be picked up by the giant machinery, and shunted to *their* station while Parton and his aides were running the chemistry to prove it was two tons of dry yeast and nothing else.

The newly filled cans acquired dust in the process. Dust was the enemy of the machinery and it became a personal enemy. They took turns holding a flashlight to expose streaks on the surface, on which ice would form from condensation even yet, although the cold was drying the raw new air they'd pumped into the forward staging area. Ice slicked the cat-walks, a rime hazardous as well as nuisanceful. Limbs grew wobbly with the cold, hands grew clumsy.

Fletcher called for relief and took the junior-juniors into the rest station to warm up with hot chocolate and sweet rolls and sandwiches, before it was back onto the line again.

"Wish we had that bubbly tub from Mariner," Jeremy said, cold-stung and red-nosed over the rim of his cup. "I'd sure use it tonight."

"I wisht we had the desserts from Mariner," Vince said.

"You and your desserts," Linda said. "We'll have to roll you aboard like one of the cans."

"Not a chance," Vince said. "I'm working it all off. A working man needs a lot of calories."

"Man," Linda gibed. "Oh, listen to us now."

"Well, I *do*," Vince said.

Fletcher inhaled the steam off the hot chocolate and con-templated another trip out into the cold. He looked at the clock. They'd been on duty two hours.

They had four more to go.

The gathering in the Voyager Blue Section conference room was far smaller than at Mariner, hardbitten captains, two women, one man, who wanted to know why they'd been called, and what they had to do with *Finity's End*.

"Got no guns, no cash, nothing but the necessaries," the man in the trio said.

Carson was the name. *Hannibal* was the ship-name, a little freighter not on the Pell list of ordinary callers, but on Mariner's regulars: JR had memorized the list, had seen the -s- and ques-tion mark beside both *Hannibal* and Frye's *Jacobite*, the one that was sharing the sleepover with them. That -s- meant *suspect*. *Jacobite* did just a little too well, in their guesswork, to account for runs only between Mariner and Voyager and maybe Esperance at need, but Esperance was pushing it for a really marginal craft, no strain at all for *Finity's End*.

There was reason the small ships took to trading in the shadows, bypassing dock charges, maximizing profits.

"We hope," the Old Man began his assault, "that we have a good deal in the offing. We've got a problem, and we've got a solution, and let me explain the making-money part of it before I get to the cost. It's not going to be clear profit, but it's going to be a guarantee Voyager stays in business; it's going to mandate your ships keep their routes, as the ones that have kept Voyager solvent thus far. There's also going to be a repair fund, meaning credit available for the short-haulers. Mariner's backing it. So's Pell. Voyager stationmaster will speak for himself. We have a list of twenty-five small haulers that stay within this reach. Those ships will see protection."

"The cost."

"You serve this reach and you make a profit doing it. You keep the trade only on the docks and you pay the tariff."

"We pay the tariff," *Hannibal* said.

"On all trades," the Old Man said, and there was a little silence. The captains liked the one part of it. Salvation for the small operator, vulnerable to downtime charges and repair charges, was inextricably linked to cession of ship's rights. Anathema.

"Who's going to say our competition pays the same?" That from *Jamaica*, captain Wells, whose eyes darted quickly from one side to the other in arguments. "Who's inspecting? *Finity*, arguing to let station inspectors on our decks?"

Difficult point, JR thought. Difficult answer, but the Old Man didn't pull the punches.

"They'll pay," the Old Man said, "because there'll be a watch on the jump points."

"No," *Hannibal* said.

"You're supplying Mazian," the Old Man said, more blunt and more weary than he'd been at Mariner, and the captain of *Hannibal* sat back as JR registered a moment of alarm. "Not necessarily by intent," the Old Man said in the next second. "But that's where the black market's going, and that's why there's going to be a watch at those jump points. The money that's not going to the stations will have to get to the stations. And this is where the profit will be for *you*."

Totally different style with these hardbitten captains than the Old Man had used at Mariner. JR took mental notes.

"We have an agreement in principle by Voyager, and the stationmaster will be here within the hour to swear to it: there will be provision for ships that register Voyager as their home port. Uniform dock charges, to pump money into Voyager and do needed repair. More freight coming in, going out, more loads, more profitable goods . . ."

"Too good to be true," *Jacobite* said. "What if we sign and we comply and here comes a big fancy ship, say, *Finity*'s size . . ."

"*You* get preference on cargo. You're registered here. *You* load first."

"Voyager's going to *agree* to that?" Clear disbelief.

"Voyager *has* agreed to that."

"Way too good to be true," *Jamaica* said. "Say I got a vane dusted to hell and gone, and I'm going to borrow money, get it fixed and the Alliance is going to come across with the money."

"In effect, yes."

"I'm already in hock to the bank."

"The idea is to preserve the ships that preserve this station. The Alliance is not going to let a ship go, not yours, not any ship registered here. Fair charges, fair taxes, stations build up and modernize and so do the ships that serve them. You may have seen a Union ship go through here in the last few days. That did happen. The Union border is getting soft. Union trade will come through, possibly back through the Hinder Stars again."

There was alarm. The smaller ships couldn't make a jump like that. Then *Jamaica* said:

"They open and they shut and they open. I don't ever bet on the Hinder Stars. Waste of money."

"It's getting to be a good bet, at least for the Earth trade.

Chocolate. Tea. Coffee. Exotics of all sorts. Cyteen's two accesses to trade are Mariner and Esperance. Voyager is right in the middle. If Esperance opened up a second access to the Hinder Stars and on to Earth, Voyager could be in a position to funnel goods along the corridor to Mariner, in a damned lucrative trade competing with Pell's Earth route. If you survive the transition. That's the plan. Shut down the black market, cut Mazian out of deals and the local merchanters in."

There was consideration. There were thinking frowns, and a general pouring of real coffee, which *Finity* had provided for the meeting. JR moved to assist, and Bucklin set down a second pot to follow the first.

They were working as hard to sell three scruffy short-haulers on the plan as they'd worked to sell far larger ships on the concept.

But these ships were the black marketeers, the shadow traders. This *was* Mazian's pipeline, among the others, and these captains were beginning to listen, and to run sums in their heads in the very shrewd way they'd dealt heretofore to keep their small ships going.

They wouldn't say, aloud, we'll try to do both, comply and maintain ties with Mazian. JR had the feeling that was exactly the thought in their heads.

But half compliance was better than no compliance, and half might become whole, if the system began to work.

He went outside to bring in another platter of doughnuts. *Hannibal*'s capacity for doughnuts was considerable, and *Jacobite*'s captain, in the habit of common spacers at buffet tables, had pocketed two.

"Loading's going smoothly," Bucklin found time to say. "We've moved ahead of schedule on that. But fueling's going to take the time. The pump's not that fast."

"Figured," JR said, and had. The high-speed pumps at Pell and Mariner were post-war. Practically nothing on Voyager was, except the missile defenses.

To a place like this, ships, if they would forego the shadow

trade and pay standardized dock charges, offered more than a
shot in the arm. Ships to follow them brought a transfusion of
lifeblood to Voyager, which until now had seen ships just as
soon trade in the dark of the jump-points as stay in its dingy
sleepovers and spend money in its overpriced amusements. In
the War, the honest trade had gotten thinner still, as Union had
taken exception to merchanters supplying the Fleet and tried
to cut off Voyager, as a pipeline to Mazian's Fleet.

It had been one hell of a position for station and merchanters to be in, and one which Alliance merchanters
resolved never to get into again. Abandon Voyager? Let
Esperance slide into Cyteen's control?

No. Starting from a blithe ignorance at Pell, JR had
acquired a keen understanding of the reasons why small, mori-
bund Voyager was a key piece in keeping Esperance in the
Alliance, and keeping trade going between Mariner and
Esperance inside Alliance space.

He knew now that Quen's deal about the ship she wanted
to build would put her in complete agreement with the position other Alliance captains had to take: new merchant ships
were useless if all trade ebbed toward Cyteen; and shoring up
Voyager would protect Pell's territory more effectively than
the launch of another Fleet.

That was why they'd agreed with her. The danger to the
merchant trade now was in fact less the Fleet than a resur-
gence of Union shipbuilding with the clear aim of driving
merchanters out of business.

So Voyager fish farms and an infusion of money to refurbish
the Voyager docks were part and parcel of the new strategy.
Voyager could become a market, a waystation: a station, given
the wide gulf between itself and the Hinder Stars, that might
revive the Hinder Stars for a third try at life, if they could establish a handful of ships capable of making that very long transit.

If the Hinder Stars could awake for a third incarnation free
of pirate activity, there was a future for the smaller merchanters after all.

Get Voyager functioning, the Fleet cut off, Union agreeing not to compete with Alliance merchanters and get Union financial interests on the side of that merchanter traffic, and they had the disarmament verification problem solved. Alliance merchanters threaded through Union space, every pair of merchanter eyes and every contact with a Union station (to some minds in Union) as good as a Fleet spy recording their sensitive soft spots. But odd to say, they felt a lot the same about Union ships carrying cargo into Mariner and Viking. There were Unionside merchanters, honest merchanter Families whose routes had just happened to lie all inside Union territory, and who now got more favorable docking charges and privileges and state cargoes now that those ships had come out and joined the Alliance.

To his personal knowledge none of those Families had succumbed to Union influence and none would knowingly take aboard a Union operative. But love happened, and you could never be sure there wasn't some stationer spouse of some fourteenth-in-line scan tech on a ship berthed next to you whose loyalties were suspect and who might be gathering data hand over fist.

That was the bright new age they'd entered.

He saw the years in which he might hold command on the bridge as a strange new age, a time of balances and forces held in check.

With less and less place for the skills of the War. The Old Man, who remembered the long-ago peace, had shown him at least the map of that future territory—and it was like nothing either of them had ever seen.

Bed, the couch cushions arranged on the floor as a bunk, or the bare carpet, if they'd had nothing else—a chance to lie horizontal came more welcome than any time in Fletcher's life. The junior-juniors, past the giggle-stage and into complaints, mixed-gender accommodations and all, went down and fell mostly silent.

It was the second night, the second hard day, doing the same thing, over and over, until Fletcher saw can-surface and felt the protest in his feet even when he shut his eyes. The Vince-Jeremy argument about cold feet gave way to quiet from that quarter, darkness, and an exhaustion deeper than Fletcher had ever felt in his life.

Drunken spacers couldn't rouse any resentment, careening against the door, or whatever they'd done outside. Fletcher just shut his eyes.

Hadn't had supper. They'd had too many rest-area sandwiches and too much hot chocolate in the cargo hold office, and still burned off more energy than they'd taken in.

They'd showered once they got back to the Safe Harbor, was all, for the warmth, if nothing else, and Fletcher hoped the next shift got an immense amount done that they wouldn't have to do.

He shut his eyes . . . plunged into black . . .

. . . wakened to dimmest light and twelve-year-old voices telling each other not to wake Fletcher.

In the next second he saw a flash of light on the wall, moving shadows against it, and heard the door shut. He rolled over, saw nothing but black, got up, and banged his shin on a table.

"System. Light!" he ordered the robot, and, seeing the beds vacant, and hearing nothing from the bathroom: "Jeremy? Dammit!"

He flung on clothes, not bothering with the thermal shirt, just the work blues and the boots, and headed for the lift. Which didn't come.

He took the bare metal stairs and arrived down in the lobby. Third shift was coming in, a scatter of juniors.

Chad and Connor.

"Fletcher!" Connor said.

He ignored the hail and went into the dining room, hoping for junior-juniors in the press of spacers in the breakfast line.

"Fletcher." Connor. And Chad.

"I don't see the kids," he said.

"What'd they do?" Connor wasn't being sarcastic. It was concern. "Get past you?"

"Yes," he muttered, and went out into the lobby again, looking for twelve-year-olds in the press of spacers in dingy coveralls with non-*Finity* patches.

They were at the vending machines. Linda had a sealed cup in her hands.

"You got to watch them," Connor said at his shoulder.

"I was watching them," he retorted, wanting nothing to do with his help.

He went over to claim the kids.

"You weren't supposed to get up yet," Linda said, spotting him. "We were bringing you hot chocolate."

With cup in hand. He let go a breath. "For what?"

"For breakfast."

He looked at his watch. For the first time. It *was* shift-change. Alterdawn. 1823h. And kid-bodies were justifiably hungry.

"You want breakfast?"

"Yeah," Jeremy said. "Yessir."

He was disreputable, in yesterday's clothes, but he marched them into the restaurant, saw them fed.

A senior came by the table. "Board call, 0100h tomorrow. We're moving faster than we'd hoped."

He thanked the senior, who was stopping at every table. 0100h was in their shift's night. They worked two shifts and then had to scramble to make board-call.

"Tonight?" Vince said, screwing up his face. Linda slumped over her synth eggs on a bridge of joined hands. Jeremy just looked worn thin.

They'd passed out painkillers in the rest-area, and they'd taken them, preventative of the soreness they might otherwise feel, but hands still hurt, feet still stung with the cold, noses were red and chapped, and as for recreation at this port, Fletcher ached for his own bed, his own things; they'd been too tired even to use the tapes when they'd gotten into the room. The vid hadn't even tempted the junior-juniors. Showers had, and hot water produced sleep. They'd just fallen into bed it seemed to him an hour ago.

And they had one more duty to get through, and then undocking.

At a time when they'd have been ready to fall into bed, they'd be boarding.

Twenty hundred hours and they had signatures on the line and scuttlebutt flying through Voyager corridors—as if the whole station had waited, listening, for what had become the worst-kept secret on the station: Voyager was getting an agreement with its local merchanters, with Mariner, with Pell and potentially with Union. News cameras showed up outside the restricted area where they'd held the meetings, and outside the customs zones of *every* starship in dock. Crowds gathered. The vid was live feed whenever the reporters could get anybody on camera to comment: it was the craziest atmosphere JR had ever seen. It *scared* him when he considered it, as—after a hike across the besieged docks, and attended by all the public notice outside— the Voyager stationmaster, three of the captains of *Finity's End*, and three of the scruffiest freighter-captains in civilized space, along with members of Voyager Station's administration and members of the respective crews, showed up in the foyer of the fanciest restaurant on Voyager.

The maître d' hastened them to the reserved dining room.

JR was well aware of their own security, who had been on site inspecting the premises even before they'd confirmed the reservation. They'd gone through the kitchens down to the under-cabinet plumbing and they were standing guard over the foodstuffs allowing absolutely nothing else to be brought in unless *Finity* personnel brought it.

He was linked directly to Francie's Tech 1, who was running security on station.

He was linked to Bucklin, who was shuttling between his

watch over the door and their security's watch on the kitchen.

He was linked to Lyra, who was linked to Wayne and Parton, who were back at the Safe Harbor Inn, literally sitting in the hallway to watch the rooms.

And he was linked to *Finity*'s ops, which told him they were working as hard as humanly possible to clear this port while they still had something to celebrate, and to get them on toward Esperance, where things were far less sure, and where the celebration of an agreement would not be so universal.

Maybe it was an omen, however, that from no prior understanding, the party once seated in the dining room took five minutes to arrive at a completely unified menu choice, to help out the cooks, and *Finity* agreed to pick up the tab.

Besides providing a couple of cases of Scotch and three of Downer wine to the ecstatic restaurant owner, who provided several bottles back again, enough to make the party hazardously rowdy with the restaurant's crystal.

"To peace," was the toast. "And to trade!"

There was unanimous agreement.

"We may see this War finished yet," *Jacobite* said.

"To the new age," *Hannibal* proposed the toast, and they drank together.

"I began my life in peace," the Old Man said then. "I began my life in peace, I helped start the War, and I want to see the War completely done with; I want to see peace again, in my lifetime. *Then* I can let things go."

There was a moment of analysis. Then: "No, no," everyone had hastened to say, the polite, and entirely sincere, wishes that *Finity* would continue in command of the Alliance.

"No one else can do what you've done," the Voyager stationmaster said, and *Hannibal* added:

"Not by a damn sight, *Finity*."

The Old Man shook his head, and remained serious. "That's not the way it should be. It's *time*. I'm *old*. That's not a terrible thing. I never bargained for immortality, and I can tell you relative youngsters there comes a time when you aren't afraid of that final jump. A life has to end, and I'll tell you all, I want mine to end with peace. That's my requirement. All loose ends tied. I want this agreement."

There was lingering unease.

"You've got it, brother," Madison said with a laugh, and got the conversation started again, simply skipping by the statement as a given.

Madison, himself almost as old.

It was a difficult, an unprecedented moment. JR drew a whole breath only after Madison had smoothed things over, and asked himself then why the Old Man had let the mood slip, or why he'd talked about his concerns.

Getting tired, he said to himself. The captain hadn't slept but a couple of hours last night; and even the Old Man was human.

A hard effort, they'd made, to clear this port quickly, before the two ships that had gone ahead of them had had the chance to gossip or disturb the quiet atmosphere they hoped for—

But here at Voyager, thank God, they'd found no attempt to sabotage them, not by low tech or high, not even a glitch-up at the hurried negotiations, where they'd tried to hammer out financial information, and none in refueling. Just getting the signatures on documents wouldn't actually speed specific negotiations at Pell, Mariner, and Esperance, but it certainly put Voyager's vote in as favoring the new system. The Voyager stationmaster, a reserved man courting a heart attack, had looked every way he could think of for a trap or a disadvantage in what they'd almost as a matter of course come to him to offer, and instead had found nothing but good for him in the deal—so much so that they'd not only gotten his agreement and that of his administration, they'd been inundated with information handed to them on Esperance. It even included things they were dismayed to be told, dealings which the Voyager stationmaster had found out, evidently, regarding the stationmaster's affair with his wife's sister—that tidbit of information had come out *yesterday* night at dinner, before

the specifics of their agreement were certain, and come out
with the three merchant captains present—but only one of
them had been surprised.

A stationmaster who routinely had dinner with *every* captain willing to be treated to dinner, at Voyager's best restaurant, certainly found out things.

Two bottles of wine administered in meetings like that, and
the Voyager stationmaster probably found out things the captains didn't even tell their next of kin.

But last night, to them, the Voyager stationmaster had
named names regarding Esperance's near bedfellowship
with Union. Then the captains, at the same table, had outlined the easy operations of Esperance customs, and exactly
what the contacts were by which Esperance obtained luxury
goods.

And those goods shipped right past Voyager, a golden
pipeline from which neither Voyager nor these captains could
derive benefit. Damned right they were annoyed.

The party broke up, *Jacobite*'s captain actually singing on
the way down the dock, the others with their respective crews
headed off, God save their livers, for *more* drinking, probably
with their crews.

They had undock coming: that saved them a breakfast invitation with the station administration. They parted company
with a very delighted and only slightly tipsy stationmaster, and
took their security from the restaurant's kitchen, past a
straggle of determined news cameras, newspeople asking such
questions as: *Can you talk about the agreement? How would
you characterize the agreement?*

No information was the Old Man's order. "Sorry," JR had
to say, to one who tried to catch him; and he hurried to overtake the rest on their walk back to the Safe Harbor.

Madison had said, in privacy after last night's dinner, that
they clearly had a worse problem ahead of them than they'd
imagined, regarding Esperance, and that they might be down

to using the scandal attached to the Esperance administration for outright blackmail value if things were as bad as the Voyager information intimated they were.

It had been a joke. But a thin one, even then. They had everything they wanted at three stations, and they were going to be up against profit motives with a fat, prosperous station which thought it could do whatever it pleased.

"We could turn around," Alan said when the topic came up as they were walking back. "Let Esperance hear about the deal we've made so far with Sol, Pell, Mariner and Voyager, and let them worry for a year whether they'll be included."

"Let them hear that *Sol* is in the deal," the Old Man had said, entirely seriously, as JR, walking behind with Bucklin and their security, listened in absolute quiet. "That's their source of luxury goods, in exactly the same way and through the same connections by which it's been *Mazian's* source of matériel. So Esperance is secretly talking about merchanters long-jumping from Esperance to one of the old Hinder Star ports and getting to the new point from there without Voyager, Mariner *or* Pell . . . becoming Union's direct pipeline to Earth. That's still a long run. And those are *big* ships that have to do that run. That's the tack we'll take with Esperance's local merchanters, and it's a true argument: *we'd* be fine, we have the engines to make it, so we're not talking in our selfish interest when we point out that the majority of merchanters couldn't do it by that route. Small ships would find themselves cut out of the trade with Earth in favor *only* of the likes of *Boreale*, run from Unionside, and I don't think our brothers and sisters of the Trade will like to hear that notion, any more than Esperance will like to hear their little scheme made public."

"If Quen has her way," Madison said, "more of *Boreale's* class will never be built. Not by Union."

"And if I have my way, we won't spend those funds building Quen's super long-haulers ourselves, either. We'll build *enough* ships to keep the stations viable and building. Bigger stations, bigger populations; bigger populations, more trade. Alliance stations will never top a planetary population, but *our* markets are totally dependent on us—unlike Cyteen's. Esperance will never grow grain and she'd get hellishly tired of fishcakes and yeast in six weeks, let alone six years. Which is what she'll be down to if we pull the merchanters together again and threaten to strike if they don't go along. We *have* them, cousins. They may think they're going to doublecross us and go direct with Earth, and they may *think* Union's new warrior-merchanters are going to be their answer, but we, and Quen, have that cut off."

The Old Man, two glasses of wine in him, was *still* sharp and dead-on, JR said to himself. It made self-interested sense even for merchanters like *Hannibal*.

"We don't want to *say* all of that," the Old Man said, "at Esperance. Not until we have Union's agreement on the line, but they're already done for, in any ambition to become the direct Union-Earth pipeline. We just have to get them to sign the document we have. Let them do it in the theory they *can* doublecross us, and get Union ships in. Those ships won't ever materialize because of *Quen's* ship, and because of *our* agreement about the tariffs. And that means Union will define its border as excluding Esperance, because *we* can give Union the security and the trade it needs far better than some backdoor agreement they might make with Esperance. They'll be left out without a tether-line. Just let drift. They don't know that yet." A moment of silence, just their footfalls on the station decking. Then the Old Man added: "In some regards, Mazian is the best friend we've got. As long as Union fears he might come back a popular hero if they push the Alliance too hard, we've got *them*, as well. Mallory wants to finish him. *I* prefer him right where he is, cousins, out in the deep dark, in whatever peace he's found."

What could you say to that? Even Francie and Alan had looked shocked.

About Madison, JR wasn't so sure.

And for himself, he feared it was the truth.

Finity's End eased back from dock with the agility of a light load and a surrounding space totally une..cumbered by traffic, even of maintenance skimmers. And the senior staff on the bridge breathed a sigh of relief to have the tie to Voyager broken.

Francie was the captain sitting, at this hour. The Old Man, Madison and Alan, the captains who'd been nearly forty-eight hours with no sleep during last-minute negotiations and subsequent celebration, were off-duty, presumably to get some rest as soon as they reached momentary stability.

But JR, with hands unblistered, face unburned, had taken Bucklin with him and made his way topside immediately before the takehold, leaving A deck matters, including the assembly area breakdown, to Lyra.

Those of them who'd drawn security and aide duty and stood guard and poured water and provided doughnuts for the on-station conferences, sixteen of the crew in all, had their own aches and had had less sleep than the captains, but they lacked the conspicuous badge of those who, also short of sleep, had done the brunt of the physical work during their two-day stay—the chapped faces and thin and hungry look of those who'd broken their necks being sure the cargo they had in their hold was what they'd bought, without any included gifts from their enemies.

Among bridge staff who'd not been involved in the meetings, Tom T. had slippers on, sitting Com with an ankle bandaged. There had been a few casualties of the slick catwalks. The Old Man had pushed himself to exhaustion, so much so that Madison had had to sub for him at the dockside offices.

JR hadn't even tried to go to sleep in the two hours he had left before he had to report for board-call and get the assembly area rigged.

He and Bucklin had talked for a little while last night about what the Old Man had said. They'd consulted together in the privacy of his room and in lowered voices, before Bucklin had gone to his room, on the subject of their *need* of Mazian, and the captain's pragmatic statement.

"He meant," he'd said to Bucklin, desperate to believe it himself, of the man who was his hero, "that that's until we get the Alliance in order. We need a lever."

"You suppose," Bucklin had said in return, "that Mallory knows what he thinks?"

Good question, that had been. And that, once his head had hit the pillow, hadn't been a thought to sleep on, either.

If Mallory knew the Old Man was less than committed to taking down Mazian, Mallory might well have come to a parting of ways with the Old Man, and sent them off.

And if Mallory didn't know it, and that attitude the Old Man had expressed was what the Old Man had been using as his own policy for years *without* saying so to Mallory, it seemed to a junior's inexpert estimation well beyond pragmatism and next to misrepresenting the truth.

He couldn't, personally, believe it. Mallory didn't believe in any compromise with Mazian, and didn't count the War ended until Mazian was dead.

Neither did he. He saw the future of his command—of all of humankind—compromised by any solution that left a still-potent Fleet lurking out in the dark. And *that* was a view as settled in reality as his short life knew how to settle it.

But they were bidding to make changes.

They'd shown their real manifest to Voyager Station's agents as an earnest of good faith, as they'd insist all other merchanters do.

And, again doing what they hoped to see legislated as mandatory, they backed away from the station, leaving the mail to *Hannibal*, not taking trade away from that small ship, to which the mail contract was an important income; letters wouldn't get there as quickly as if they carried them, but get there they would.

They left now having obeyed laws not yet written, having had put several hundred thousand credits into the local economy . . . done their ordinary business and taken on their commercial load of foodstuffs, with, JR suspected, real nostalgic pleasure on the Old Man's part, an example of the way things ought to work.

It had been five years since they'd last called at Voyager and JR found nothing that much changed from what he remembered, unlike the vast changes at Pell and Mariner. But Esperance, in every rumor yet to hit them, had made changes on Pell's and Mariner's scale: grown wilder, far more luxurious. Esperance had survived the War by keeping on the good side of both warring sides, irritating both, making neither side desperate enough to take action.

And by all the detail the Voyager stationmaster had told them last night and before, Esperance Station had survived the peace the same way, playing Alliance against Union far more than appeared on the surface. Smuggling hardly described the free flow of exotic goods that Esperance had offered brazenly in dockside market, only rarely bothered by customs and not at all by export restrictions: they'd known *that* before they heard the damning gossip from the Voyager stationmaster, regarding the conduct of the stationmaster's office.

Esperance was going to be an interesting ride.

That was what Madison had said last night, when they all parted company. It was what nervous juniors had used to say when the ship went to battle stations. An interesting ride.

And complicating their mission, as Francie had said, among other things in that session last night, Mazian's sympathizers and supporters, including ships like *Champlain*, had to have their chance to back off their pro-Mazian actions without being criminalized. Those ships had to have not just one chance to reform, but time to figure out that the flow really was going to dry up, that it wasn't going to be business as usual, and that things wouldn't ever again rebound back to what they had been—which had tended to be the case just as soon as the Alliance enforcers were out of the solar system.

He understood Francie's observation. Once the small operators knew that there were new economic rules, even the majority of them would reasonably move to comply, but no one expected a ship fighting to keep itself fueled and operating to voluntarily lead the wave of reform.

Hence *Finity*'s extravagant show of compliance . . . and that proof, via the restaurant, what their cargo was, because the persuasion most likely to convince those operators came down to a single intangible: *Finity*'s reputation.

They'd gotten something extraordinary in the enthusiasm of little haulers like *Hannibal*, *Jamaica* and *Jacobite*. And the word would spread fast, among ships the connections between which weren't apparent to authorities on stations.

"We will do a three-hour burn," intercom announced. *"We will do a curtailed schedule to get us up to jump. It's now 0308h. Starting at 0430h and continuing until 0730 we will be in takehold. There will be a curtailed mainday, main meal at 0800h for both shifts, then cycle to maindark at 0930h for a takehold until jump at approximately 0530 hours. We don't want to leave our allies unattended any longer than necessary. We will do a similarly curtailed transit at the point . . ."*

". . . and we will come in long before Esperance expects us. The captains inform us this is the payoff, cousins, this is the place we make or break the entire voyage. This is the place we came to deal with, and if we carry critical negotiations off at this station, we'll take a month at Mariner on the return. Meanwhile we have more of those stylish, straight from the packing box work blues from Voyager's suppliers, and more of the galley's not-so-bad sandwiches, flavor of your choice . . . synth cheese, synth eggs and bacon, and real, Voyager-produced fish. Last in gets no choice. All auxiliary services will be shut down until we clear Esperance."

"Clear *Esperance*?" was the question that went through the line at the laundry, where Fletcher was in line. Toby and Ashley were on duty at the counter ahead, and as bundles came sailing in, three brand new sets of blues came out to all comers.

"He had to mean Voyager," was the come-back to that question, but some of the seniors in line said, "Don't bet on it," and the intercom went on with a further message,

"The senior captain has a message for the crew. Stand by."

"I think he really did mean Esperance," a cousin said glumly.

Fletcher, third from the counter as the frantic pace continued, didn't understand what was encompassed in *no services*, but he had a feeling it meant more inconveniences than they'd yet seen on this voyage.

"This is James Robert," the captain's voice said. *"Congratulations on a job well done. We're about to make up time critical to our mission. There remains the small chance of trouble at the jump-point, if by the time we arrive there has been an action between Boreale and Champlain, or if Champlain should evade Boreale and stay behind to lay an ambush. This is a canny and dangerous opponent with strong motives to prevent us reaching Esperance. Until we have reached Esperance, then, this ship will stay on yellow alert and will observe all security precautions in moving about the corridors. Expected point transit will be two hours inertial for food and systems check. Juniors, please review condition yellow safety precautions. Again, thank you for a job well done at this stopover, and I suggest you lay in supplies of packaged food and medical supplies for your quarters beyond the requirements to accommodate a double jump. We don't anticipate a prolonged and unscheduled push either here or at the jump-point, but the contingency should be covered. Priorities dictate we evade confrontation rather than meet it. Good job and good voyage."*

It was Fletcher's turn at the counter. He picked up clothes for himself and Jeremy as he turned laundry in, and found Jeremy at his elbow when he turned around. "Got the packets," Jeremy said, showing a small plastic bag full, both trank and the unloved nutrient packets, as best he guessed. Jeremy was just back from the medical station.

There were a lot of the packets, of both kinds. Clearly medical had known their schedule before the announcement.

"We're on a yellow," Jeremy said brightly and handed him the bag with the medical supplies. "I'll get to the mess hall, and pick up some soft drinks and some of those ration bars. They'll run out of the fruit ones first. You want the red filling or the black?" Jeremy was already on the move, walking backwards a few steps.

"Red!" It was an unequivocal choice. They'd had them while they were working, along with the hot chocolate. The black ones were far too sweet. Jeremy turned and took off at a faster pace, down the line that was still moving along.

"Hey, Fletcher," Connor said from the laundry line as he walked in the direction Jeremy had gone. Connor and Chad were together. "*Find* it yet?"

Connor didn't need to have said anything. Clearly the truce was over. Fletcher paused a moment and fixed Connor and Chad with a cold look, then walked on around the curve to A26.

He laid the clothes and the bag from medical on Jeremy's bunk, and intended to put the clothes and supplies away.

But, no, he thought. Jeremy might run out of pockets, between fruit bars and soft drinks. He went out and on around to the mess hall, amid the traffic of other calorie-starved cousins, and just inside mess hall entry met Jeremy coming back, with fruit bars stuffed in his pockets and in the front of his coveralls and two sandwiches and four icy-cold drink packets in his arms.

"That should supply the Fleet," Fletcher commented. "You want me to take some of those?"

"I got 'em. It's fine. Well, —you could take the sandwiches."

He eased them out of Jeremy's arm before they flattened. The two of them started back out of the mess hall area, and met Chad and Connor and Sue, inbound.

"There's Fletcher," Sue said. "Tag on to the kid, is it? Who's in charge of whom, hey?"

He could tolerate the remarks. None individually was worth reacting to. But tolerating it meant letting the niggling attacks go on. And on. And if he didn't react to the subtle tries, they'd escalate it. He knew the rules from childhood up. He stopped.

"You're begging for it," he said to them in a low voice, because there were senior crew just inside, picking up their own supplies, and there were more passing them in the corridor. "I'll take you three down to the storage and we'll do some more hunting for what you stole, if that's what you're spoiling for. You two guys going to have Sue do *that*, too?" He'd gotten the picture how it was in that set, and all of a sudden that picture didn't include Chad as the instigator. Not even Connor, who'd hailed him five minutes ago.

Sue was the silent presence. Small, mean, and constantly behind Connor's shelter.

"Fletcher and his three babies," Connor said. "Brat watch suits you fine."

"Sue, are *you* the thief?"

"Fletcher." Jeremy nudged at his arm. "Come on. Don't. We got a takehold coming, we'll get sent for a walk if we start trouble."

Sue hadn't said a thing.

"I'll tell you how it was," Chad said. "You did the stealing and you did the hiding, so you could make trouble. You know damn well where that stick thing is, if there ever was one."

"The hell!"

"The hell you don't."

"Come on," Jeremy said, "come on, Fletcher. Fletcher, we need to get back to quarters. Right now. People can get killed. The ship won't wait."

"You kept the whole ship on its ear all the way to here," Chad said, "you made us five days late getting out of Pell, and now we're running hard to make up. Supposedly you got robbed and you had us looking all on *our* rec time, and hell if you'll do it again, Fletcher."

"It wasn't my choice!"

"Well, it looks that way to me!"

"Fletcher!" Jeremy said, fear in his voice. "Chad, —shut up! Just shut up! Come on, Fletcher."

Jeremy pulled violently at his arm. Seniors were staring.

"Is there trouble here?" a senior cousin asked. The tag on the coveralls said Molly, and he'd met her in cargo, a hard-working, no-nonsense woman with strong hands, a square jaw, and authority.

"No, ma'am," Jeremy said. "Come *on,* Fletcher, you'll get us in the Old Man's office before you know it. Come on!"

Chad and company had shut up, under an equally burning stare from cousin Molly. And Jeremy was right. There was only trouble if they tried to settle it here. He took the decision to regard Jeremy's tug on his arm, and to walk away, with only a backward and warning glance at Chad and Sue.

Tempers were short. They were short of sleep, facing another hard couple of jumps by the sound of the intercom advisements, and Chad had re-declared their war while they'd gotten to that raw and rough-inside feeling of exhaustion, stinging eyes, aching backs, headache and the rest of it. Calm down, he tried to say to himself, no profit to a brawl.

They'd fought. And things hadn't been notably better. Given a chance, he'd have let it quiet down, but Chad had just made him mad. Touched old nerves. It was all the Marshall Willetts, all the jealous sibs, all the school-years snide remarks and school-mate ambushes; and he had it all again on this ship, thanks to Chad.

"What's the matter?" Vince said when he ran into them in the corridor. "Something the matter?"

"Not a thing," Jeremy said, relieving him of any necessity to lie. Vince had gotten to looking to him anxiously at his least frown, and he felt one of those anxious stares at his back as they walked to their cabin. He was all the while trying to reason with himself, telling himself he only lost if he let Chad get to him. He and Chad had had a dozen civil words on dock-side, yesterday, when he'd misplaced the kids and Chad had been concerned. He didn't know how things had suddenly turned around unless Chad was putting on an act.

Or unless somebody had gigged Chad into an action Chad wouldn't have taken on his own.

They shut the door to their quarters behind them, shoved stuff in drawers, put the trank and the nutri-packs into the bed-side slings first, while Jeremy started chattering about vid-games and dinosaurs.

Distraction. Fletcher knew it was. Nervous distraction as they sat down on their respective bunks and opened their sand-wiches and soft drinks.

Jeremy didn't want a fight and was trying to get his mind off the encounter.

But there was going to be a fight, and there'd be one after that, the way he could see it going. He murmured polite answers to Jeremy, swallowed uninspiring mouthfuls of the synth cheese sandwich and washed it down with fruit drink, but his mind was on the three of them back in the mess hall entry, Chad, Connor, and *Sue*.

That encounter, and the chance it *hadn't* been Chad who'd stolen the spirit stick.

Sue was starting a campaign. He could have seen it out there, if he'd ever had his eyes on other than Chad. She meant to make his life a living hell, and Sue was a different kind of problem. Chad and Connor he *could* beat. But he couldn't hit Sue and Sue had every confidence that would be the case. She had the raw nerve, maybe, to take the chance and duck fast if she was wrong and he swung on her, but she was small, she was light, he was big, and he'd be in the wrong of anything physical; damn her, anyway.

Chad and Connor had to have figured what Sue was doing. But if she was the guilty one *they* didn't think so. And might not care. He was the interloper. Sue did the thinking for Connor, and Chad wasn't highly creative, but he was the brightest mental light in that group when he finally stirred himself to take a stand.

He had used to do long reports on downer associations. Intraspecies Dynamics, they called the forms they'd fill out, watching who worked with whom in the fields and who touched whom and didn't touch and who chased and who ran, the experts drawing their conclusions about how all of downer society worked. Now he'd formed the picture on a different species: on how the whole junior crew worked. JR and Bucklin ran things; Lyra and Wayne assisted, and tended to sit on trouble when they found it, just the way JR directed them to do. Toby and Ashley and Nike were a set, Nike being the active force there, but they were thinkers, tech-track, not brawlers.

Sue and Connor were usually the active force in the Sue-Connor-Chad set: Sue dominated Connor and wielded him like a weapon between her and the universe; most of the time Chad just floated free, doing what he liked, generally a loner, even in a group. Chad might not even like Sue much, but she was *in*, and that defined things.

When Chad rose up with a notion of his own, though, Chad got in front of the three of them and used his size to protect them. Connor followed Chad when Chad chose to lead—leaving Sue to try to get control back to herself by picking their fights.

Exactly what she'd been doing. Chad had been fair-minded after their first fight, even civil on the dockside. But something had flared up out there beyond the fact they'd all worked so far past raw-nerved exhaustion they were seeing two of each other.

Sue's *mouth* had been working, was his bet. But Chad *was* the leader in that set, a leader generally in absentia. He looked a little older, acted a little older. In the way of junior crew on *Finity*, he'd probably been in charge of them when they were like Jeremy and Vince and Linda. Connor hadn't grown into his full size yet. But Chad had. Might have done so way early, by the build he had and the way he went at things: Chad didn't fight with blind fury. Chad lumbered in with a confidence things would eventually fall down in front of him—a moment of amazement when they didn't—that came of generally having it happen.

He'd gotten to know Chad in their process of pounding hell out of each other, to the point it had downright stung when Chad turned the accusation of theft back on *him*. He'd actually felt a reversal of signals, after Chad's being a help to him on

dockside, in a way that he hadn't sorted out in the corridor—
he could have lit into Chad on the spot after Chad had said it,
but it wasn't the sting of the attack he'd felt, but that of an
unfair change of direction.

Sue would have had every chance anyone else had had to
get into his room and take the stick, and *Sue*, unlike the others,
might have destroyed it. Now there was trouble, and Sue kept
her two cousins in constant agitation rather than letting anybody think about the theft.

"You listening to me, Fletcher?"

In point of fact, no, he hadn't been. He'd lost what Jeremy
was saying.

"About Esperance," Jeremy said. "And the vid sims."

"Lost it," he confessed.

*"Takehold imminent, time's up, cousins. Get in those bunks
or wherever, tuck down for a three-hour. Don't get caught in the
shower. We're going to put a little way on this happy ship . . ."*

"I said I bet they have some neat sims there, I bet Union
has some we've never seen . . . ."

"Probably they do." Provoke Sue to hit him, grab her and
hold her feet off the deck until she got scared, maybe, but it'd
be a messy, stupid kind of fight and he wasn't anxious to make
himself a target for her to kick and hit and yell. He didn't want
Sue yelling mayhem and getting the whole crew against him.
Chad and Connor were going to side with her. It wasn't damn
worth it.

He had to do something when the takehold quieted down.

He mumbled a "Sure" to Jeremy's request to borrow his
downer tape, and he pulled it out and passed it to him.

By then they were one minute and counting, and he scrambled to get his own music tape set up and snugged down with
him.

He had two choices. Give up, let the situation bully him
into that request to get off the ship—he *had* the excuse he'd
desperately wanted, he'd established with JR that he wanted to
leave and that he was justified, and what was he doing? Now
he was fighting for his place here, not to be run out. He didn't
quite know why, or how he'd come to the decision—the kid he

shared this place with was the reason, he thought, but not all of it.

He'd resolved somewhere, somehow, this side of Mariner, that they couldn't run him out like this, because it wasn't a simple matter, his going or staying. It wasn't even entirely Jeremy, but the complex arrangement that made Jeremy and him partners.

One thing he knew: his going or staying wasn't going to be *their* choice.

He had to talk to Chad. Alone.

He had to find out whether it was Chad's notion to take him on, or whether Chad, like him, was somebody's convenient target.

Chapter

— XXII —

The preparation for a long, double-jump run for Esperance had the feeling of the old New Rules back again. It had the feeling of clandestine meetings in the deep dark and the chance of shots exchanged. It seemed that way to JR, at least, and touched nerves only a few months ago allowed to go quiet. People had a hurried, businesslike look at every turn.

JR sat in the relative comfort of his on-bridge post as the engines cut in and the acceleration pressed him back into the cushion. He watched the numbers tick by, and saw around him a ship in top running order, saw the unusual status on the fire panel, unusual only since they'd declared they were honest merchanters again: the weapons were under test, and the arms-comp computer was up and working on their course, laying down a constantly shifting series of contingencies.

But space was empty around them.

It was that space ahead of them they had to worry about. And in this vacancy, they were running fast getting out of system and on toward what could be ambush of military kind at the next jump-point—or of diplomatic kind at Esperance.

Three hours.

Madelaine reported in to Alan, downtime chatter in the non-privacy of the bridge, that they had the legal papers from Voyager in order. Jake's dry, nonaccusatory report from Lifesupport suggested unanticipated change of plans was going to create havoc in his service schedules and that he was going to request that half of the type one biological waste be vented at the jump-point rather than rely on the disrupted bacteriological systems to convert it.

When the ship being under power forced a long downtime, intraship messages flew through the system—*Hi, how was your stay? Missed you last night, saw a vid you'd like, found this great restaurant* . . .

There wasn't so much of the interpersonal chatter at Voyager. It mostly ran: *I'm dead, I've got frostbite, I'm getting too old for this,* and, *I saw vids I haven't seen in twenty years. You know they've got stuff straight from the last century?* At the same time, and more useful, various department heads, also idle but for the easy reach of a handheld, put their gripe lists through channels. It was a compendium of the ship's small disasters and suggestions, like the suggestion that the long Services shutdown was going to mean no clean towels and people should hang the others carefully and let them dry.

There was one from Molly, down in cargo. *JR: thought you should know. Chad and Fletcher had an argument during burn-prep. Jeremy broke it up, on grounds of ship safety. Chad accused Fletcher in the downer artifact business. Fletcher objected. All involved went to quarters for takehold. For your information.*

There were six others, of similar content, one that cited the specifics of things said and added the information that it was *not* just Jeremy, Fletcher, and Chad, but that Sue and Connor had been there.

That built a larger picture.

There was a note from Lyra that said she'd heard from Jeff about the near-fight, but not containing the detail about Connor and Sue.

There was, significantly, no note from any of the alleged participants, and most significantly, there was none from Jeremy, who was supposed to report any problem with Fletcher directly to him.

The artifact matter was back on his section of the deck. They hadn't time before Esperance to do another search; and the senior staff and particularly the Old Man were going to hear about the encounter, and worry about it. And that made him angry and a little desperate.

He sent back down to Lyra: *The encounter between Chad and Fletcher. Who started it?*

Lyra answered, realtime: *My informant didn't say. It was in the mess hall entry, a lot of witnesses. I could venture a guess.*

Don't guess, he sent back, trying to reason with his own inclination to be mad at Fletcher for pushing it; and mad at his own junior-crew hotheads for pushing Fletcher. He didn't know the facts, Lyra didn't know, and the facts of a specific encounter coming from scattered reports didn't mass enough information on the problems on A deck in general. He wished he could go to voice, for a multiple conference with Bucklin and Lyra, to see whether three heads could make any better sense of the situation with the junior crew; but ops kept jealous monopoly over the audio channels during a yellow alert, and that would be the condition until Esperance.

He keyed a query to Bucklin, instead, fired him the last five minutes' autosave and beeped him. For Lyra:

I want you to tag Fletcher. This says nothing about my estimation of who's in the wrong in the encounter. There're just too many on the other side for any one person to track. He sent the I'm not happy sign, older than the Hinder Stars.

Lyra echoed it. So did Bucklin. He, Lyra, and Bucklin owned handhelds, with all the access into *Finity* systems that went with it; and all the accessibility of senior staff to their transmissions. Nothing in *Finity* command was walled off from anybody at a higher level, and there wasn't *anybody* at a lower level than the juniors were. He couldn't even discuss the theft without the chance of some senior intercepting what was going on—and he didn't want the recurrence of the matter racketing up to the Old Man's attention. That he couldn't find a solution was more than frustrating: it was approaching desperation to get at the truth—and the culprit wasn't talking.

I'm coming down there for mess, he said. It was his option, whether to be on A deck or B, and right now it sounded like a good idea to get down there as soon as the engines shut down and crew began to move about.

We could confine junior crew to quarters, Bucklin sent back.

It was certainly an idea. There was no reason junior crew had to move about during their jump-prep inertial glide. Services were shut down. There was no work to be done.

It would at least let us get clear of system, Lyra sent.

It let them keep status quo with the juniors, as far as the mass-point—where, the Old Man had warned them, senior crew might need their wits about them, with *no* distractions.

Good idea, he said to Lyra's suggestion, and this time did key up the voice function, going onto intercom to every junior-assigned cabin with an official order. "This is JR," he said. "This is a change in instructions . . ."

". . . Junior crew is to stay in quarters until further notice. Junior officers will deliver meals to junior crew at the rest break, and I suggest you spend the time reviewing safety procedures. If you have any special needs due to the change of arrangements please indicate them to junior staff, and we will take care of them."

"I think JR found out," Jeremy said from the upper bunk, the ship continuing under hard push.

"Nothing happened, for God's sake!"

"I told you!" drifted down from the bunk above.

"You told me, hell!" He recalled he was supposed to be the senior in the arrangement, and shut up, glumly so. He wished they'd get rec. Jeremy was hyped and nervous, swinging his foot over the edge with an energy he hadn't complained of yet, but he'd been on the verge.

"You just tell them shut up, is all," Jeremy said.

"Oh, that'd do a lot of good."

"Well, it's better than staring at them. They don't like staring."

"I don't care what they don't like." He had a printout in his lap and he dragged a knee up to prop it against the force that made the page bend. "I'm reading, anyway."

"What are you reading?"

"Physics for the hopeless," he said. It was the manual, the long version, in the section on yellow alert. "What do they mean 'red takeholds'?"

"They're painted red."

"Why?"

"So you can see them. They're all those inset hand-grips up and down the corridors, so you don't splat all over if we move."

"I guessed that. What's this red alarm?"

"The klaxon. If you hear the klaxon you grab hold where you are. If it's just a bell you have time to run to any door and bunk down, two to a bunk, or you get in the shower. If you're carrying anything you throw it in the shower and shut the door."

It was in the print, clearer with Jeremy's condensed version.

"Why the shower?" Then the answer dawned on him, and he said, in unison with Jeremy: "Smaller space."

"So you don't fall as far," Jeremy added cheerfully. "A meter's better than three meters."

"Have you ever done that?"

"Stuck it out in the shower? Yeah. One time JR and Bucklin had six in their quarters, one in each bunk, three in the shower."

"Counting them."

"No. Lyra and Toby snugged up on the bunk base and Toby broke his nose. Everybody was coming back from mess and the take hold sounded, and I bunked down with Angie."

"Who's Angie?"

"She kind of took care of me," Jeremy said. Then added, in a slightly quieter voice: "She died."

He'd walked into it. Damn, he thought. "I'm sorry."

"Lot of people died," Jeremy said. And then added with a shaky sigh: "I'm kind of tired of people dying, you know?"

What did you say? "Maybe that's past," he offered, best hope he could think of. "Maybe if the ship's gone to trading for a living, then things can settle down."

"We're on yellow, right now."

Jeremy's worry was beginning to make him nervous. And he tried not to be. "Hey, we gave the Union-siders a whole bottle of Scotch. They've got to be in a good mood."

"I mean, you know, I didn't think I was going to like this trading business."

"So do you?"

"Yeah. Kind of. I didn't think I would."

"Neither did I. I thought being on this ship was the worst thing that could happen to me."

"Mariner was wild," Jeremy said with what sounded like forced cheerfulness. "Mariner was really wild."

"Yeah," he agreed. "It was."

"Did you *like* it?"

"Yeah," Fletcher said, and realized he actually wasn't lying.

"I did, too," Jeremy said. "I really did. It was the best time I *ever* had."

He couldn't exactly say that about it.

But he didn't somehow think Jeremy was conning him, at least to the limits of Jeremy's intentions. That *ever* touched him, swelled up something in his heart so that he didn't know how to follow that remark, except to say that the time they had wasn't over, and there wasn't any use in their being panicked now.

"The ship doesn't wait," he said quietly. "Isn't that what they said when I was late to board? The ship doesn't wait and nothing's ever stopped her. She's fought Mazian's carriers, for God's sake. She's not going to run scared of some skuz freighter."

"No," Jeremy agreed, with a nervous laugh, and sounding a little more like himself. "No, *Champlain* might be tough, I mean, a lot of the rimrunners are pretty good, but we're way far better."

"Well, then, quit worrying. What are you worried about?"

"Nothing. The takeholds and the lockdowns, this is pretty usual. This is pretty like always." Jeremy was quiet a moment. Then, fiercely, but with the wobble back in his voice: "I'm *not* scared. I never was scared. I'm just kind of disgusted."

"With what?"

"I mean, I liked the liberties we had, I mean, you know, we could go out on docks most always, and Sol Station was pretty wild."

"I imagine it was. You'd rather be back there?"

"No," Jeremy said faintly. "We couldn't ever go outside Blue Sector, ever. They'd just kind of, you know, approve a couple of places we could go to, JR would, or Paul, before him. But always line-of-sight with the ship berth. Even the seniors couldn't. They had this place set aside, we'd stay there, and we could do stuff only in Blue."

"You mean I was conned."

"Not ever. I mean, before Mariner that was the way it was. We got to go out of Blue a little, at Pell. Pell was pretty good. But Mariner was the *best*. It was really the *best*."

"They're talking about us spending a month there."

"If it happens."

"It'll happen. I bet it happens." Fletcher was determined, now, to jolly the kid out of it. "What's your first stop? First off, when we get there, what do you want to do?"

"Dessert bar," Jeremy said.

"For a month?"

"Every day."

"They'll have to rate you as cargo."

Jeremy grinned and flung a pillow over the edge.

He flung it back. It failed to clear the level of Jeremy's bunk. Fletcher retrieved the pillow and made two more tries at throwing it against the push.

"You'll never make it!" Jeremy cried.

"You wait!" He unbelted and carefully, joints protesting, got out of his bunk, standing on the drawers, pillow in hand. Jeremy saw him and tucked up, trying to protect himself.

"No fair, no fair!"

"You started it!" He got his arm up and slammed the pillow at Jeremy's midsection.

"Truce!" Jeremy cried. "You'll break your neck! Cut it out!"

"Truce," he said, and, leaving the pillow with Jeremy, got back down into his bunk without breaking anything, a little out of breath.

"You all right?" Jeremy asked.

"Sure I'm all right. You're the one that cheats on the V-dumps! You're worried?"

"I don't want you to break your neck."

"Good. Suppose you stay in your bunk after jump, why don't you?"

"If you don't get up again."

"Deal."

He thought maybe Jeremy hadn't expected to get snagged into that. There was silence for a while.

"Jeremy?"

"Yeah."

"You all right up there?"

"Yeah, sure."

There was more silence.

An uncomfortable silence. Fletcher couldn't say why he was worried by it. He figured Jeremy was reading or listening to his music.

"So you say Esperance is supposed to be pretty good," he said finally, looking for response out of the upper bunk. "Maybe they'll give us some time there."

"Yeah," Jeremy said. "That'd be better. That'd be a lot better than Voyager. My toes still hurt."

"You put salve on them?"

"Yeah, but they still hurt."

"I don't think I want to work cargo."

"Me, either. Freeze your posterity off."

"Yeah," he said. The atmosphere was better then. "You got that Mariner Aquarium book?"

"I lent it."

He was disappointed. He was in a sudden mood to review station amenities. "Linda and her fish tape."

"Yeah," Jeremy said. There was a sudden shift from the bunk above. An upside down head, hair hanging. "You know she can't eat fish now?"

"You're kidding."

"Says she sees them looking at her. I'm not sure I like fish-cakes, either."

"Downers eat them, with no trouble. Eat them raw."

"Ugh," Jeremy said. "Ugh. You're kidding."

"I thought about trying it."

"Ugh," was Jeremy's judgment. The head popped back out of sight. "That's disgusting."

The engines reached shut-down. Supper arrived fairly shortly. Bucklin brought it, and it was more than sand-wiches.

It was hot. There was fruit pie.

"Shh," Bucklin said. "Bridge crew suppers. Don't tell any-body."

"So why the lockdown?" Jeremy wanted to know.

But Bucklin left without a word, except to ask if they were set. And Fletcher didn't feel inclined to borrow trouble.

They finished the dinners, tucked the containers into their bag into the under-counter pneumatic, and began their prep for the long run up to jump, music, tapes, comfortable clothing, trank, nutri-packs and preservable fruit bars.

"We're supposed to eat lots," Jeremy said, "if we get strung jumps."

"You mean one after another."

"Yessir," Jeremy said, pulling on a fleece shirt. He still seemed nervous. Maybe, Fletcher thought, there was good reason. But they kept each others' spirits up. He didn't want to be scared in front of Jeremy; Jeremy didn't want to act scared in front of him.

They tucked down for the night, let the lights dim.

In time the engines cut in, slowly swinging their bunks toward the horizontal configuration.

"Night," Jeremy said to him.

Fletcher was conscious of night, unequivocal night, all around a ship very small against that scale.

"Behave," he said, the way his mother had used to say it to him. "We'll be fine."

"Yeah," Jeremy said. "You think Esperance'll be like Mariner?"

"Might be. It's pretty rich, what I hear."

"That's good," Jeremy said. "That's real good."

Then Jeremy was quiet, and to his own surprise the strong hand of acceleration was a sleep aid. There was nothing else to do. He waked with the jump warning sounding, and the bunk swinging to the inertial position.

"You got it?" Jeremy asked. "You got it?"

"No problem," he said, reaching for the trank in the dark. Jeremy brightened the lights and he winced against the glare. He found the packet.

Count began. Bridge wanted acknowledgement and Jeremy gave it for both of them.

All accounted for.

On their way to a lonely lump of rock halfway between Voyager and the most remote station in the Alliance.

Almost in Union territory. He'd heard that. . . .

Rain beat on the leaves, ran in small streams off the forested hills. Cylinders were failing, but Fletcher nursed them along to the last before he changed out. Hadn't spoiled any. Hadn't any to spare. He kept a steady pace, tracing Old River by his roar above the storm.

You get lost, he'd heard Melody say, Old River he talk loud, loud. You hear he long, long way.

And it was true. He wouldn't have known his way without remembering that. The Base was upriver, always upriver.

Foot slipped. He went down a slope, got to his knee at the bottom. Suit was torn. He kept walking, listening to River, walking in the dark as well.

Waked lethargic in the morning, realizing he'd slept without changing out; and his fingers were numb and leaden as he tried to feel his way through the procedure. He'd not dropped a cylinder yet, or spoiled one, even with numb fingers. But he was down to combining the almost-spent with the still moderately good, and it took a while of shaking hands and short oxygen and grayed-out vision before he could get back to his feet again and walk.

He changed out three more, much sooner than he'd thought, and knew his decisions weren't as good as before. He sat down without intending to, and took the spirit stick from his suit where he'd stashed it, and held it, looking at it while he caught his breath.

Melody and Patch were on their way by now. Feathers bound to the stick were getting wet in the rain that heralded the hisa spring, and rain was good. Spring was good, they'd go, and have a baby that wouldn't be him.

Terrible burden he'd put on them, a child that stayed a child a lot longer than hisa infants. The child who wouldn't grow.

He'd had to be told, Turn loose, let go, fend for yourself, Melody child.

Satin said, Go. Go walk with Great Sun.

That part he didn't want. He wanted, like a child, his way; and that way was to stay in the world he'd prepared for.

But Satin said go. And among downers Satin was the chief, the foremost, the one who'd been out there and up there and walked with Great Sun, too.

He almost couldn't get his feet under him. He thought, I've been really stupid, and now I've really done it and Melody can't help. I'll die here, on this muddy bank.

And then it seemed there was something he had to do . . .

couldn't remember what it was, but he had to get up. He had to get up, as long as he could keep doing that.

He went down again.

Won't ever find me, he thought, distressed with himself. It must be the twentieth time he'd fallen. This time he'd slid down a bank of wet leaves.

He tried to get up.

But just then a strange sound came to his ears.

A human voice, changed by a breather mask, was saying, "Hey, kid! Kid!"

Not anymore, he thought. Not a kid anymore.

And he held onto the stick in one hand and worked on getting to his feet one more time.

He didn't make it—or did, but the ground gave way. He went reeling down the bank, seeing brown, swirling water ahead of him.

"God!" A body turned up in his path, rocked him back, flung them both down as the impact knocked the breath out of him. But strong hands caught him under the arms, saving him from the water. There was a dark spot in his time-sense, and someone sounded an electric horn, a signal, he thought, like the storm-signal.

Was a worse storm coming? He couldn't imagine.

Hands tugged at the side of his mask. His head was pounding. Then someone had shoved what must be a whole new cylinder in, and air started getting to him.

"It's all right, kid," a woman's voice said. "Just keep that mask on tight. We'll get you back."

The woman got him halfway up the slope. A man showed up and lifted, and he finally got his feet under him.

He walked, his legs hurting. He hung on one and the other of his rescuers for the hard parts, and drew larger and larger breaths, his head throbbing from the strain he'd put on his body.

They got him down to a trail, and then someone had a litter and they carried him. He lay on it feeling alternately that he

was going to tumble off and that he was turning over backwards, while Great Sun was a sullen glow through gray clouds
and the rain that sheeted his mask. It was hard going and his
rescuers didn't talk to him. Breathing was hard enough, and he
figured they'd have nothing pleasant to say.

By evening they'd reached the Base trail and he realized
muzzily he must have been asleep, because he didn't
remember all of the trip or the turn toward the Base.

Somebody waked him up now and again to see that he was
breathing all right, and he had two cylinders, now, both functioning, so breathing was a great deal easier, better than he'd
been able to rely on for the days he'd been out.

Satin didn't want him. Melody didn't want him . . .

The bottom dropped out of the universe. He was
falling. Falling into the water. He fought it.

Second pitch. It was *V*-dump. He wasn't on Old
River's banks. He wasn't suffocating. He was on a ship, a million—
million klicks from any world, even from any respectable star.

His ship was slowing down, way down, to
match up with a target star. They were all right.

No enemies. They'd have heard if there'd been enemies.
Finity's End was solidly back in the universe again, moving
with the stars and their substance.

He opened his eyes. Lay there, fumbled open a nutri-pack
and sucked it down, aware of Jeremy rummaging after one.

"You all right?" he asked Jeremy.

"Yeah, fine."

He saw Jeremy had gotten his own packet open. The
intercom gave an all-clear and told them their schedule. They
had two hours to clean up, eat, and get back underway.

He lay there, thinking of the gray sky spinning slowly
around above the treetops. Of rain on the mask. Of the irre-
producible sound of thunder on the hills.

The room smelled like somebody's old shoes. And two
nutri-packs down, he found the energy to unbelt and sit up.

"Shower," he said to the kid, as Jeremy stirred out of his bunk. "Or I get it."

"You can have it if you want," Jeremy said.

"No, priority to you." His stomach hadn't quite caught up. He had an ache in his shoulders. Another in his heart. "Three hours at this jump-point. We'll both make it."

"Yeah, we're going to make it," Jeremy said, and hauled his skinny body out of the bunk. "No stinking Mazianni at the point, we're going to get to Esperance and the Old Man's going to be happy and we'll be *fine*."

"Sounds good to me," he said, and while Jeremy went to the shower, he got up, self-disgusted, out of a bed that wanted changing, in clothes that wanted washing. He dragged one change of clothes out of the drawer, wished he had a change of sheets. He got out one of the chemical wipes and wiped his face and hands. It smelled sharp, and clean.

He could remember the stale smell of the mask flinging his own breath back at him. He could remember the fever chill of the earth, and the uneven way his legs had worked on the way home.

And Satin's stick in his hand. He'd refused to let go of it. He'd said, "Satin gave it to me," when the rescuers questioned him, and that name had shaken them, as if he'd claimed to have seen God.

He was *here*. He was safe.

He'd clung to the stick during that rescue without the remotest notion what to do with it, or what he was supposed to do.

Satin, in that meeting, had seen further into his future than he could imagine. She'd *been* in space. She knew where she sent him.

But he hadn't known.

He sat on the edge of his bunk, listening to the intercom tell them further details, where they were, how fast they were going, numbers in terms he didn't remotely understand.

But he was safe. He'd come that close to dying, and he sat

here hurtling along in chancy space and telling himself he was very, very lucky; and, yes, beyond a doubt in his mind, now, Satin had sent him here. Satin, who'd known the Old Man.

He wondered if Satin had had the faintest idea he was a Neihart, or why he was on her world, when she'd sent him into space. He'd never from his earliest youth believed that downers were as ignorant as researchers kept trying to say they were. But he'd never attributed mystical powers to them: he was a stationer, too hard-headed for that—most of the time.

But underestimate them? In his mind, the researchers often did.

And in his dream and in his memory Satin had known his name.

Satin had known all about him.

She'd not gotten that from the sky. Sun hadn't whispered it to her. She'd talked to Melody and Patch.

And knowing everything hisa could remotely know about him, she'd sent him . . . not to the station. *To his ship.* Had she known *Finity* was in port? Had she known even that, Satin, sitting among the Watcher-stones, to which all information flowed, on quick downer feet?

Satin, who perhaps this moment was sitting, looking up at a clouded sky, and, in the manner of an old, old downer, dreaming her peace, her new heavens, into being.

She'd known. Yes, she'd known. As the Old Man of *Finity's End* had known—things he'd never imagined as the condition of his universe.

"All right, cousins," the intercom said. *"You can eat what you stowed before jump or you can venture out for a stretch. Both mess halls will be in service in ten minutes, so it's fruit bars and nutri-packs solo or it's one of those hurry-up dinners which your bridge crew will be very grateful to receive. Remember, there is still no laundry."*

Jeremy came out of the shower smelling of soap and bringing a puff of steam with him. It was far better air now. The fans were making a difference.

Downbelow slipped away in the immediacy of clean water and warmth and soap. Fletcher stripped clothes and went, chased through his mind by images of woods and water, the memory of air that wouldn't come, but the shower was safe and clean and Jeremy was his talisman against nightmares and loss.

"Sir?" JR found the Old Man's cabin dimly lighted as he brought the tray in, heard the noise of the shower, in the separate full bath *Finity*'s senior crew enjoyed. He ordered the lights up, set the meal in the dining alcove, and took the moment to make the stripped bed with the sheets set by and waiting.

The Old Man did such things himself. The senior-juniors habitually ran errands, down to laundry, down to the med station, and back, for all the bridge crew, whose time was more valuable to the ship; but the senior crew usually did their own bed-making and food-getting if they were at all free to do so.

In the same way the Old Man rarely ordered a meal in his quarters. He was always fast on the recovery, always in his office before the galley could get that organized.

Not this time. Not with the stress of double-jumping in and short sleep throughout their stay at Voyager. He felt the strain himself, in aches and pains. Mineral depletion. Jeff had probably dumped supplement in the fruit juice, as much as wouldn't hit the gut like a body blow.

The shower cut off. JR poured the coffee.

In a few more moments the bath door opened and the senior captain walked out, barefoot, in trousers and turtleneck sweater, in a gust of moist, soapy air.

"Good morning, sir." JR pulled the chair back as James Robert stepped into the scuffs he wore about his quarters, disreputable, but doubtless comfortable. A click of a remote brought the screen on the wall live, and showed them a selection of screens from the bridge.

They were at the jump-point intermediate between Voyager

and Esperance, a small lump of nothing-much that radiated hardly at all. If there'd been any other mass in two lights distance, the point would have been tricky to use . . . dangerous. But there was nothing else out here, and it drew a ship down like a far larger mass.

Systems showed optimal. They were going to jump out on schedule. JR remarked on nothing that was ordinary: it annoyed the Old Man to listen to chatter in the morning, or after jumps. He simply stood ready to slide the chair in as the Old Man sat down.

He looked up. The captain had stopped. Cold. Staring off into nowhere with a sudden looseness in his body that said this was a man in distress.

JR moved, bumping past the chair, seized the Old Man's flaccid arm, steered him immediately to the seat at the table.

The Old Man got a breath and laid a shaking hand on the table.

"I'll get Charlie," JR began.

"No!" the Old Man said, the voice that had given him orders all his life, and it was hard to disregard it.

"You should have Charlie," JR said. "Just to look—"

"Charlie *has* looked," the Old Man said. "Medicine cabinet, there in the bunk edge. Pill case."

He left the Old Man to get into the medicine compartment, hauled out a small pharmacy worth of pill bottles he'd by no means guessed, and brought them back to the table. The Old Man indicated the bottle he wanted, and JR opened it. The Old Man took the pill and washed it down with fruit juice.

"Rejuv's going," the Old Man said then. "Charlie knows."

It was a death sentence. A long-postponed one. JR sank down into the other chair, feeling it like a blow to the gut.

"Does Madison know?"

"All of them." The Old Man was still having trouble talking, and JR kept his questions quiet, just sat there. The realization hit him so suddenly he'd felt the bottom drop out from under him . . . *this* was what the Old Man had meant at dinner that night back at Voyager. *This* was why it disturbed Madison: that he was *saying* it in public, for others to hear, not the part about the peace, but the part about *finishing*. The captain—*the* captain, among all other captains *Finity* had known, was arranging all his priorities, the disposition of his power, the disposition of his enemy, all those things . . . leading in a specific direction that left his successors no problem *but* Mazian. *That* was why the Old Man had said that peculiar thing about needing Mazian.

No, the Old Man hadn't quarreled with Mallory and then left in some decision to pursue a different direction.

The Old Man had this one, devastatingly important chance to wield the power he'd spent a protracted lifetime building.

Secure the peace. Accomplish it. And look no further into human existence. The final wall was in front of him. The point past which never.

"Shall I call Madison, sir?" he asked the Old Man.

"Why?" the Old Man challenged him sharply. And then directly to him, to his state of mind: "Worried?"

The Old Man never liked soft answers. Least of all now. JR sensed as much and looked him in the eye. "Not for the ship, sir. You'd never risk her. But Charlie's going to be mad as hell if I don't tell him."

The Old Man heard that, added it up—the flick of the eyes said that much—and took a sip of coffee. "I'll thank you to keep Charlie at bay. I've taken to bed for the duration of the voyage. I plan to get to Esperance."

"I'm grateful to know that, sir."

"Precaution," the Old Man said.

"Yes, sir."

"You don't believe it for a minute, do you?"

"I'm concerned."

"And have you been discussing this concern in mess, or what?"

"I haven't. You put one over on me, sir. Completely. I never figured this one."

"Smart lad," the Old Man said. "You always were." He lifted the lid on the breakfast. Eggs and ham. Bridge crew got the attention from the cookstaff on short time schedules. So did the captain. So did the senior-seniors, for their health's sake.

"Yes, sir," he said. "Thank you. I try to be. I suggest you eat all of it and take the vitamins. My shoulders are popping. I'd hate to imagine yours."

"The insufferable smugness of youth." James Robert looked up at him. The parchment character of his skin was more pronounced. When rejuv failed, it failed rapidly, catastrophically. Skin lost its elasticity. The endocrine system began to suffer wild surges, in some cases making the emotions spiral out of control. There might be delusions. Living a heartbeat away from the succession, JR had studied the symptoms, and dreaded them, in a man on whose emotional stability, on whose *sanity*, so very much depended.

"Waiting," the Old Man said, "for me to fall apart."

"No, sir. Sitting here, wondering if you were going to want hot sauce. They didn't put it on the tray."

The Old Man shot him a look. The spark was back in his eye, hard and brilliant.

"You'll do fine," the Old Man said. "You'll do fine, Jamie."

"I hope to, sir, some years from now, if you'll kindly take the vitamins."

"In my good time," the Old Man said in a surly tone. "God. Where's respect?"

"For the living, sir. Take both packets."

"Out. Out! You're worse than Madison."

"I hope so, sir." He saw what reassured him, the vital sparkle in the eyes, the lift in the voice. Adrenaline was up. "I'd suggest you leave the transit to jump to Alan and Francie. Sir."

"Jamie, get your insufferable youth back to work. I'll *be* at Esperance. I'm not turning a hand on this run until I have to."

"Yes, sir," he said, glad of the rally—and heartsick with what he'd learned.

"Out. Tell Madison he's got the entry duty. With first shift."

And not at all happy.

"I'm moving everybody up," the Old Man said with perfect calm. "I'm retiring after this next run. You're to take Francie's post. Madison will take mine."

"Sir . . ."

"I think I'm due a retirement. At a hundred forty-nine or whatever, I'm due that. I'll handle negotiations. Administrative passes to the next in line. Filling out forms, signing orders. That's all going to be Madison's, Jamie-lad. As you'll be juniormost of the captains. And welcome to it. I'm posting you. At Esperance."

The Old Man had surprised him many a time. Never like this.

"I'm not ready for this!"

The Old Man had a sip of coffee. And gave a weak laugh. "Oh, none of us are, Jamie. It's vanity, really, my hanging on, waiting for an arbitrary number, that hundred and fifty. It's silliness. I'm getting tired, I'm not doing my job on all fronts, I'm delegating to Madison as is: he'll do the nasty administrative things and I do what I do best, at the conference table. Senior diplomat. I rather like that title. Don't you think?"

"I'll follow orders, sir."

"Good thing. Fourth captain had damned well better. Meanwhile you've things to clean up before you trade in A deck."

Fletcher. The theft. All of that. And for the first time in their lives he'd be separated from Bucklin, who'd be in charge of the juniors until Madison himself retired. He'd be taking over fourth shift, dealing with seniors who'd seen their competent, life-long captain bumped to third.

He felt as if someone had opened fire on him, and there was nothing to do but absorb the hits.

"Well?" the Old Man said.

"Yes, sir. I'm thinking I've got mop-up to do. A lot of it."

"Better talk to Francie. You'll be going alterday shift, when ops is in question. Better talk to Vickie, too." That was Helm 4. "You've shadowed Francie often enough."

At the slaved command board—at least five hundred hours, specifically with Francie. During ship movement, maybe a hundred. He had no question of his preparation in terms of ship's ops. In terms of his preparation in basic good sense he had serious doubts.

"Yes, sir," he said.

"Jamie," the Old Man said.

"Yes, sir?"

"The plus is . . . I get to see my succession at work. I get to know it *will* do all right. There's no greater gift you can give me than to step in and do well. Fourth shift will do Esperance system entry. You'll sub for Francie on this jump. We'll hold the formalities after we've done our work there. King George can wait for his party. We'll have occasion for our own cele-bration if we pull this off. We'll be posting a new captain."

Breath and movement absolutely failed him for a moment. He had no words, in the moment after that, except, quietly: "Yes, sir."

One hour, thirty-six minutes remaining, when Fletcher stood showered and dressed; and the prospect just of opening the cabin door and taking a fast walk around the corridor was delirious freedom. Jeremy was eager for it; he was; and they joined the general flow of cousins from A deck ops on their way to a hot pick-up meal and just the chance to stretch legs and work the kinks out of backs grown too used to lying in the bunk. They fell in with some of the cousins from cargo and a set from downside ops, all the way around to the almost unimaginably intense smells from the galley.

"I could eat the tables," a cousin said as they joined the fast-moving line. Jeremy had a fruit bar *with* him. He was that desperate. Everyone's eyes were shadowed, faces hollowed, older cousins' skin showed wrinkles it didn't ordinarily show. Everyone smelled of strong soap and had hair still damp.

Two choices, cheese loaf with sauce or souffle. They'd helped make the souffle the other side of Voyager and Fletcher decided to take a chance on that; Jeremy opted for the same, and they settled down in the mess hall for the pure pleasure of sitting in a chair. Vince and Linda joined them, having started from the mess hall door just when they'd sat down, and Jeremy nabbed extra desserts. Seats were at a premium. The mess hall couldn't seat all of A deck at once. They wolfed down the second desserts, picked up, cleaned up, surrendered the seats to incoming cousins, and headed out and down the way they'd come.

"Can I borrow your fish tape?" Jeremy asked Linda as they walked.

"I thought you bought one," Linda said.

"I put it back," Jeremy said, and Fletcher thought that was odd: he thought he recalled Jeremy paying for it at the Aquarium gift shop. Jeremy had bought some tags and a book, and he'd have sworn—

He saw trouble coming. Chad, and Sue, and Connor, from down the curve.

"Don't say anything," he said to his three juniors. "They're out for trouble. Let them say anything they want."

"They're jerks," Vince said.

The group approached, Sue passed, Chad passed—they were going to use their heads, Fletcher thought, and keep their mouths shut.

Then Connor shoved him, and he didn't think. He elbowed back and spun around on his guard, facing Chad.

"You turn us in?" Chad asked. "You get us confined to quarters?"

"Wasn't just you," Fletcher retorted, and reminded himself he didn't want this confrontation, and that Chad might be the leader and the appointed fighter in the group, but he didn't conclude any longer that Chad was entirely the instigator. "We all got the order. You and I need to talk." A cousin with his hands full needed by and they shifted closer together to let her by. Jeremy took the chance to get in the middle and to push at Fletcher's arm.

"Fletcher. Come on. We're still in yellow. They'll lock us down for the next three years if you two fight, come on, cut it out."

"Got your defender, do you?" Connor said, and shoved him a second time.

"Cut it!" Jeremy said, and Fletcher reached out and hauled him aside, firmly, without even feeling the effort or breaking eye contact with Chad.

"You and I," Fletcher said, "have something to talk about."

"I'm not interested in talk," Chad said. "I'll tell you exactly how it was. You came on board late, you didn't like the scut jobs, you didn't like taking orders, and you found a way to make trouble. For all we know, there never *was* any hisa stick."

"Was, too!" Jeremy said. "I saw it."

"All right," Chad said. "There was. Doesn't make any difference. Fletcher knows where it is. Fletcher always knew, because he put it there, and he's going to bring down hell on our heads and be the offended party, and we give up our rec hours running around in the cold while he sits back and laughs."

"That isn't the way it is," Fletcher said. "I don't know who did it. That's your problem. But I didn't choose it." Another couple of cousins wanted by, and then a third, fourth and fifth from the other direction. "We're blocking traffic."

"Yeah, run and hide," Sue said. "Stationer boy's too good to go search the skin, and get out in the cold . . ."

"You shut up!" Vince said, and kicked Connor. Connor lunged and Fletcher intercepted.

"Let him alone," Fletcher said.

And Linda kicked Connor. Hard.

Connor shoved to get free. And Chad shoved Connor aside, effortless as moving a door.

"I say you're a liar," Chad said, and Fletcher swung Jeremy and Linda out of range, mad and getting madder.

"Break it up!" an outside voice said. "You!"

"Fletcher!" Jeremy yelled, and he didn't know why it was up to him to stop it: Chad took a swing at him, he blocked it, and got a blow in that thumped Chad into the far wall. Chad came off it at him, and Linda was yelling, Vince was. He'd stopped hearing what they were saying, until he heard Jeremy yelling at him, and until Jeremy was right in the middle of it, in danger of getting hurt.

"Chad didn't do it!" Jeremy shouted, clinging to him, dragging at his arm with all his weight. "Chad didn't do it, Fletcher! *I* did it!"

He stopped. Jeremy was still pulling at him. Bucklin had Chad backed off. It was only then that he realized it was JR who had pulled him back. And that Jeremy, all but in tears, was trying to tell him what didn't make sense.

"What did you say?" JR asked Jeremy.

"I said *I* did it. *I took it.*"

"That's not the truth," Fletcher said. Jeremy was trying to divert them from a fight. Jeremy was scared of JR, was his immediate conclusion.

"It is the truth!" Jeremy cried, in what was becoming a crowd of cousins, young and old, in the corridor, all gathering around them. "*I* stole it, Fletcher, I'm sorry. I didn't mean it."

"What *did* you mean?" JR asked; and Jeremy stammered out,

"I just took it. I was afraid they were going to do it, so I did it."

"You're serious."

"I was just going to keep it safe, Fletcher. I was. I took it onto Mariner because I thought they were going to mess the cabin and they'd find it and something would happen to it, but somebody broke into my room in the sleepover and they got all my stuff, Fletcher!"

Everything made sense. The aquarium tape Jeremy turned out not to have. The music tapes. The last-minute dash to the dockside stores. The thief had made off with every purchase Jeremy had made at Mariner. Jeremy had broken records getting back to their cabin to *create* the scene he'd walked in on.

But he wasn't sure yet he'd heard all the truth. Fletcher's heart was pounding, from the fight, from Jeremy's confession, from the witness of everyone around them. Silence had fallen in the corridor. And JR's hold on him let up, JR seeming to sense that he had no immediate inclination to go for Chad, who hadn't, after all, been at fault. Not, at least, in the theft.

"God," Vince said, "that was really *stupid*, Jeremy!"

Jeremy didn't say a thing.

"Somebody took it from your room in the Pioneer," JR said.

"Yes, sir," Jeremy said faintly.

"And why didn't you own up to it?"

Jeremy had no answer for that one. He just stood there as if he wished he were anywhere else. And Fletcher believed it finally. The one person he'd trusted implicitly. The one whose word he'd have taken above all others.

Jeremy was a kid, when all was said and done, just a kid. He'd failed like a kid, just not facing what he'd done until it went way too far.

"Let him be," Fletcher said with a bitter lump in his throat. "It's lost. It doesn't matter. Jeremy and I can work it out."

"This ship has a schedule," JR said. "And it's no longer on my hands. Bucklin, *you* call it. It's *your* decision."

"Fletcher," Bucklin said. "Jeremy? You want a change of quarters? Or are you going to work this out? I'm not having you hitting the kid."

Anger said leave. Get out. Be alone. Alone was safe. Alone was always preferable.

But there was jump coming, and the loneliness of a single room, and a kid who'd—aside from a failure to come out with the truth—just failed to be an adult, that was all. The kid was *just* a kid, and expecting more than that, hell, he couldn't expect it of himself.

He just felt lonely, was all. Hard-used, and now in the wrong with Chad and the rest, and cut off from his own age and in with kids who were, after all, just kids, who now were mad at Jeremy.

"I'll keep him," he said to Bucklin. "We'll work it out."

Lay too much on a kid's shoulders? It was his mistake, not Jeremy's, when it came down to it: it was all his mistake, and he was sorry to lose what he'd rather have kept, in the hisa artifact, but the greater loss was his faith in Jeremy.

"You don't hit him," Bucklin said.

"I have no such intention," he said, and meant it, unequivocally. He knew where else things were set upside down, and where he'd gotten in wrong with people: he looked at Chad, said a grudging, "Sorry," because someone once in his half dozen families had pounded basic fairness into his head. The mistake was his, that was all. It wasn't Jeremy who'd picked a fight with Chad.

Chad wasn't mollified. He saw it in Chad's frown, and knew it wasn't that easily over.

"All right, get your minds on business," Bucklin said. "A month the other side of this place maybe you'll have cooled down and we can settle things. Honor of the ship, cousins. We're *family*, before all else, faults, flaws, and stupid moves and all; and we've got jobs to do."

By now the crowd in the corridor was at least twenty onlookers. There were quiet murmurs, people excusing themselves past.

"We have"—Bucklin consulted his watch—"thirty-two minutes to take hold."

JR said nothing. Chad and his company exchanged dark glances. Fletcher ignored the looks and gathered up his own junior company, going on to their cabin, Vince and Linda trailing them. He tried all the while to think what he ought to say, or do, and didn't find any quick fix. None at all.

"Just everybody calm down," was all he could find to say when they reached the door of his and Jeremy's quarters. "It's all right. It'll be all right. We'll talk about it when we get where we're going."

"We didn't know about it!" Vince protested, and so did Linda.

"They didn't," Jeremy said.

"It was a mistake," he found himself saying, past all the bitterness he felt, a too-young bitterness of his own that he spotted rising up ready to fight the world. And that he was determined to sit on hard. "Figure it out. It's not something that can't be fixed. It's just not going to happen in two happy words, here. I'm upset. Damn *right* I'm upset. Chad's upset. Sue and Connor are upset and all the crew who froze their fingers and toes off trying to find what wasn't on this ship in the first place are upset, and in the meantime I look like a fool. A handful of words could have solved this."

"I'm sorry," Jeremy said.

"About time."

"He didn't tell us," Vince said.

"You let him and me settle it. Meanwhile we've got thirty minutes before we've got to be in bunks and safed down. We're going to get to Esperance, we're going to have our liberty if they don't lock us down, and we're all four of us going to go out on dockside and have a good time. We're not going to remember the stick, except as something we're not going to do again, and *if* we make mistakes we're going to own up to them before they compound into a screwup that has us all in a mess. Do we agree on that?"

"Yessir." It was almost in unison, from Jeremy, too.

Earnest kids. Kids trying to agree to what they, being kids, didn't half understand had happened, except that Jeremy was wound tight with hurt and guilt, and if he could have gotten to anyone on the ship right this minute he thought he'd wish for no-nonsense Madelaine.

"To quarters," he said. "Do right. Stay out of trouble. Give me one easy half hour. All right?"

"Yessir," faintly, from Linda and Vince. He took Jeremy inside, and shut the door.

Jeremy got up on his bunk, squatting against the wall, arms tucked tight, staring back at him.

Jeremy stared, and he stared back, seeing in that tight-

clenched jaw a self-protection he'd felt in his own gut, all too
many times.

    Puncture that self-sufficiency? He could. And he declined to.

    "Bad mistake," he said to Jeremy, short and sweet. "That's
all I've got to say right now."

    Jeremy ducked his head against his arms.

    "Don't sulk."

    Back went the head, so fast the hair flew. "I'm not sulking!
I'm upset! You're going at me like I *meant* some skuz to steal it!"

    "Forget the stick! You don't like Chad, right? You wanted
me to beat up Chad, so I could look like a fool, and it'd all just
go away if you kept quiet and you wouldn't be at fault. That
stinks, kid, that behavior *stinks*. You *used* me!"

    "Did not!"

    "Add it up and tell me I'm wrong!"

    Lips were bitten white. "I didn't want you to beat up Chad."

    "So what *did* you want?"

    "I don't know."

    "Well, *do better!* Do better. You know what you were sup-
posed to have done."

    "Yeah."

    "So why didn't you tell me the *truth*, for God's sake?"

    "Because I didn't want you to leave!"

    "How long did you think you were going to keep it up?
Your whole life?"

    "I don't know!" Jeremy cried. "I just thought maybe later
it wouldn't matter."

    He let that thought sit in silence for a moment. "Didn't
work real well," he said. "Did it?"

    "Didn't," Jeremy muttered, head hanging. Jeremy swiped
his hair back with both hands. "I was scared, all right? I
thought you'd beat hell out of me."

    "Did I give you that impression? Did I ever give you that
impression?"

    Jeremy shook his head and didn't look at him.

    "I thought the story was you were having a good time. Best

time in your life. Was that it? Just having such a great time we can't be bothered with telling me the damn *truth*, is that the way things were?"

"I didn't want to spoil it!" Jeremy's voice broke, somewhere between twelve-year-old temper and tears. "I didn't want to lose you, Fletcher. I didn't want it to go bad, and I didn't know how mad you'd be and I didn't know you'd beat up on Chad, and I didn't know they'd search the whole ship for it!"

Fletcher flung himself down to sit on the rumpled bed.

"I didn't know," Jeremy said in a small voice. "I just didn't know."

Fletcher let go a long breath, thinking of what he'd lost, what he'd thought, who it was now that he had to blame. The kid. A kid. A kid who'd latched onto him and who sat there now trying to keep the quiver out of his chin, trying to be tough and take the damage, and not to be, bottom line, destroyed by this, any more than by a dozen other rough knocks. He didn't see the expression; he felt it from inside, he dredged it up from memory, he felt it swell up in his chest so that he didn't know whether he was, himself, the kid that was robbed or the kid on the outs with Vince, and Linda, and him, and just about everyone of his acquaintance.

Jeremy couldn't change families. They couldn't get tired of him and send him back for the new, nicer kid.

Jeremy couldn't run away. *He* shared the same quarters, and Jeremy was always on the ship, always would be.

The history Jeremy piled up on himself wouldn't go away, either. No more than people on this ship forgot the last Fletcher, shutting the airlock, and bleeding on the deck.

Jeremy was in one heavy lot of trouble for a twelve-year-old.

And he, Fletcher, simply Fletcher, was in one hell of a lot of pain of his own. Personal pain, that had more to do with things before this ship than on this ship.

What Jeremy had shaken out of him had nothing to do with Jeremy.

He stared at Jeremy, just stared.

"You said you weren't going to give me hell," Jeremy protested.

"I didn't say I wasn't going to give you hell. I said I wasn't going to throw you out of here."

"It's my cabin!"

"Oh, now we're tough, are we?" If he invited Jeremy to ask him to leave, Jeremy would ask him to leave. Jeremy had to. It was the nature of the kid. It was the stainless steel barricade a kid built when he had to be by himself.

"Jeremy." Fletcher leaned forward on his bunk, opposite, arms on his knees. "Let me tell you. That stick's sacred to the hisa, not because of what it is, but *because* it is. It's like a wish. And what *I* wish, Jeremy, is for you to make things right with JR, and I will with Chad, because *I* was wrong. You may have set it up, but *I* was wrong. And I've got to set it straight, and you have to. That's what you do. You don't have to beat yourself bloody about a mistake. The *real* mistake was in not coming to me when it happened and saying so."

"We were having a good time!" Jeremy said, as if that excused everything.

But it wasn't in any respect that shallow. He remembered Jeremy that last day, when Jeremy had had the upset stomach.

Bet that he had. The kid had been scared sick with what had happened. And trying, because the kid had been trying to please everybody and keep his personal house of cards from caving in, to just get past it and hope the heat would die down.

House of cards, hell. He'd made it a castle. He'd showed up, taken the kids on a fantasy holiday; he'd *cared* about the ship's three precious afterthoughts.

He knew. He knew what kind of desperate compromises with reality a kid would make, to keep things from blowing up, in loud tempers, and shouting, and a situation becoming untenable. That was what knotted up his own gut. Remembering.

"It wouldn't have made me leave," he said to Jeremy.

"Yes, it would," Jeremy said. And he honestly didn't know whether Jeremy had judged right or wrong, because *he* was a kid as capable as Jeremy of inviting down on himself the very solitude he found so painful—the solitude he'd ventured out of finally only for Melody and Patch.

And been tossed out of by Satin. To *save* Melody, Patch and himself.

Maybe the stick had a power about it after all.

He reached across and put his hand on Jeremy's knee. "It'll come right," he said.

"It was that *Champlain* that took it," Jeremy said. "I know it was. That skuz bunch—"

"Well, they're a little more than we can take on. Nothing we can do about it, Jeremy. Just nothing we can do. Forget it."

"I *can't* forget it! I didn't want to lie, but it just got crazier and crazier and everybody was mad, and now everybody's going to be mad at me."

He administered an attention-getting shake to Jeremy's leg. "By now everybody's just glad to know. That's all."

"I hurt the ship! I hurt you! And I was scared." Jeremy began to shiver, arms locked across his middle, and the look was haunted. "I was just scared."

"Of *what*? Of me being mad? Of me knocking you silly?" He knew what Jeremy had been scared of. He looked across the five years that divided them and didn't think Jeremy could see it yet.

Jeremy shook his head to all those things, still white-faced.

Afraid of being hit? No.

Afraid of having everything explode in your face, that was the thing a kid couldn't put words to.

It was the need of somehow knowing you were really, truly at fault, because if you never got that signal then one anger became all anger, and there was no defense against it, and you could never sort it all out again: never know which was justified anger, and which was anger that came at you with no sense in it.

And, finally, at the end of it all, you didn't know which was your own anger, the genie you didn't ever want to let out—*couldn't* let out, if you were a scrawny twelve-year-old who'd been everyone's kid only when you were wrong. You were reliably no one's kid so long as you kept quiet and let nobody detect the pain.

God, he knew this kid. So well.

"That's why you were sick at your stomach the morning we left Mariner. That's why you wanted to go back and look for something. Isn't it?"

"I could get a couple of tapes. So you wouldn't know I got robbed. And I didn't know what to do. . . ." Jeremy's teeth were knocking together. "I didn't want you to leave, Fletcher. I don't ever want you to leave."

"I'll try," he said. "Best I can do." Third shake at Jeremy's ankle. "Adult lesson, kid. Sometimes there's no fix. You just pick up and go on. I'm pretty good at it. You are, too. So let's do it. Forget the stick. But don't entirely forget it, you know what I mean? You learn from it. You don't get caught twice."

And the Old Man's voice came on. *"This is James Robert,"* it began, in the familiar way. And then the Old Man added . . .

". . . This is the last time I'll be speaking as a captain in charge on the bridge."

"God." Color fled Jeremy's face. He looked as if he'd been hit in the stomach a second time. "God. What's he say?"

It didn't seem to need a translation. It was a pillar of Jeremy's life that just, unexpectedly, quit.

It was two blows inside the same hour. And Fletcher sat and listened, knowing that he couldn't half understand what it meant to people who'd spent all their lives on *Finity*.

He knew the Alliance itself was changed by what he was hearing. Irrevocably.

". . . There comes a time, cousins, when the reflexes aren't as sharp, and the energy is best saved for endeavors of purely administrative sort, where I trust I shall carry out my duties

*with your good will. I will, by common consent of the captains
as now constituted, retain rank so far as the outside needs to
know. I make this announcement at this particular time, ahead
of jump rather than after it, because I consider this a rational
decision, one best dealt with the distance we will all feel on
the other side of jump—where, frankly, I plan to think of
myself as retired from active administration.*

*"I reached this personal and public decision as a surprise
even to my fellow captains, on whose shoulders the immediate
decisions now fall. From now on, look to Madison as captain
of first shift, Alan, of second, and Francie, of third. Fourth shift
is henceforth under the capable hand of James Robert, Jr.,
who'll make his first flight in command today, the newest captain of* Finity's End.*"*

The bridge was so still the ventilation fans and, in JR's personal perception, the beat of his own heart, were the only background noise. He watched as the Old Man finished his statement
and handed the mike to Com 1, who rose from his chair.

Others rose. In JR's personal memory there had never been
such a mass diversion of attention—when for a handful of seconds only Helm was minding the ship.

There were handshakes, well-wishes. There were tear-
tracks on no few faces. There was a rare embrace, Madison of
the Old Man.

And the Old Man, among others, came to JR to offer a
hand in official congratulation. The Old Man's grip was dry
and cool in the way of someone so old.

"Bucklin will sit hereafter as first observer," the Old Man
said. "Jamie. You've grown halfway to the name."

"A long way to go, sir," JR said. "I'll pass that word, to
Bucklin, sir. Thank you."

The Old Man quietly turned and began to leave the bridge,
then.

And stopped at the very last, and looked at all of them,
an image that fractured in JR's next, desperately withheld
blink.

"I'll be in my office," the Old Man said gruffly. "Don't expect otherwise."

Then he walked on, and command passed. JR felt his hands cold and his voice unreliable.

"Carry on," Madison said. "Alan?"

Third shift left their posts. Fourth moved to take their places.

His crew, now. Helm 4 was gray-haired Victoria Inez. She'd be there, competent, quiet, steady. Not their best combat pilot: that was Hans, Helm 1. But if you wanted the velvet touch, the finesse to put a leviathan flawlessly into dock, that was Vickie.

The other captains left the bridge. The little confusion of shift change gave way to silence, the congestion in JR's throat cleared with the simple knowledge work had to be done.

JR walked to the command station, reached down and flicked the situation display to number one screen. "Helm," he said as steadily as he had in him. "And Nav. Synch and stand by."

"Yessir," the twin acknowledgements came to him.

He looked at the displays, the assurance of a deep, still space in which the radiation of the point itself was the loudest presence, louder than the constant output of the stars. They could still read the signature of two ships that had passed here on the same track, noisy, making haste.

No shots had been fired. *Champlain* had wasted no time in ambush.

Boreale had wasted no time in pursuit. The action, whatever it was, was at Esperance.

Before now, he'd made his surmises merely second-guessing the captain on the bridge. Now he had to act on them.

"Armscomp."

"Yessir."

"Synch with Nav and Helm, likeliest exit point for *Champlain*. Weapons ready Red."

"Yes, sir."

He authorized what *only* two Alliance ships were entitled

to do: *Finity* and *Norway* alone could legally enter an inhabited system with the arms board enabled.

"Nav, count will proceed at your ready."

"Yessir."

Switches moved, displays changed. *Finity's End* prepared for eventualities.

He did one other thing. He contacted Charlie, in medical, and ordered a standby on the Old Man's office. Charlie, *and* his portable kit, went to camp in the outer office.

It was the captain's discretion, to order such a thing. And he ordered it before he gave the order that launched *Finity's End* for jump, and gave Charlie time to move.

They needed the Old Man, needed him so badly at this one point that he would order medical measures he knew the Old Man would otherwise decline.

One more port. One more jump. One more exit into normal space. The Old Man was pushing it hard with the schedule they'd set. And they had to get him there.

Chapter
— XXIII —

There was silence from the other bunk, in the waiting.

"Kid," Fletcher said after long thought. "You hear me?"

"Yeah." Earplugs were in. They were riding inertial, in this interminable waiting, and they could see each other. Jeremy pulled out the right one.

"I've had time to think. I shouldn't have blamed you about Chad. I picked that fight. Down in the skin. I hit him."

"Yeah," Jeremy said.

"Not your fault. Should have hit Sue."

"You can't hit Sue."

"Yeah, well, Sue knows it, too."

"You want to get her? I can get her."

"I want peace in this crew, is what I want. You copy?"

"Stand by," the word came from the bridge.

"Yessir," was the meek answer. "I copy."

Engines cut in.

Bunks swung.

"He's never done this before!" Jeremy said. "Kind of scary."

He thought so, too, though as he understood the way ships worked, he didn't imagine JR with his hands on the steering. Or whatever it was up there. Around there . . . around the ring from where they were.

"Good luck to us all," came from the bridge. *"Here we go, cousins. Good wishes, new captain, sir. Good wishes, Captain James Robert, Senior. You're forever in our hearts."*

"Amen," Jeremy said fervently.

"Esperance," Fletcher said. He'd looked for it months from now, not in this fervid rush.

But it *was* months on. It was three months going on four, since Mariner. Going on six months, since Pell.

It was autumn on Downbelow. It was coming on the season when he'd come down to the world.

It was harvest, and the females would be heavy with young and the males working hard to lay by food for the winter chill.

Half a year. And he was mere weeks older.

The ship lifted. Spread insubstantial wings . . .

Rain pattered on the ground, into puddles. Pebbles crunched and feet splashed in shallow water as they carried him, as Fletcher stared at a rain-pocked gray sky through the mask.

He knew he was in trouble, despite the people fussing over his health. They'd rescued him, but they wanted him out of their program. They were glad he was alive, but they were angry. Was that a surprise?

They carried him into the domes and took the mask off and his clean-suit off, the safety officer questioning him very closely about whether he'd breached a seal out there.

If he'd had his wits about him he'd have said yes and let them think he'd die, and that alone would prevent him being shipped anywhere, but he stupidly answered the truth and took away his best chance, not realizing it until he'd answered the question.

They'd found the stick, too, and they wanted to take that from him before he got into the domes, but he wouldn't turn it loose. "Satin gave it to me," he said, and when they, like his rescuers, suggested he was crazy and hallucinating, he roused enough to describe where he'd been: that he'd talked to the foremost hisa, and the one, the rumor said, who could get hisa either to work or not to work with humans, plain and simple.

The experts and the administrators, who'd suited to come out and meet them coming in, pulled off a little distance in the heavily falling rain and talked about it, not quite in his hearing. They'd given him some drug. He wasn't sure what. He wasn't even sure when. Four of the rescuers had to hold him on a stretcher while the experts conferred, and he supposed they were frustrated. They shifted grips several times.

But then someone from the medical staff came outside, suited up too, for the purpose; and the doctor encouraged him to get on his feet, so that he could go through decon, with people holding him.

They wanted to put the stick through the irradiation, and that was all right: he took it back, after that, and wobbled out, stick and all, into a warm wrap an officer held waiting for him.

Then they let him sit down and checked him over, pulse, temperature, everything his rescuers had already done; and another set of medics went over those reports.

After that, when he was so faint from hunger his head was spinning, they gave him hot soup to drink, and put him to bed.

Nunn showed up meanwhile and gave him a stern lecture. He was less than attentive, while he had the first food he'd had in days. He gathered that he'd caused Nunn trouble with Quen, and that Nunn now found fault with most everything he'd ever done in classes. He didn't see how one equated with the other, but somehow Quen's directives had overpowered everything but the medical staff. He got sick, couldn't keep the soup down; and Nunn left, that was the one good thing in a bad moment. He had to go to bed, then, and they gave him an IV and let him go to sleep.

But when he waked, the science office sent people with recorders and cameras who kept him talking for hours after that, wanting every detail. He slept a great deal. He'd run off five kilos, the doctor said, and he was dehydrated despite being out in the rain for days. It was an endless succession of medical tests and interviewers.

Last of all Bianca came.

He'd been asleep. And waked up and saw her.

"How are you feeling?" she asked him.

"Oh, pretty good," he said. "They bother you?"

"No. Not really."

"They're shipping me up," he said. "I guess you heard. My *family* wants me back. On *Finity's End*."

"Yes," she said. "They told me."

"You're not in trouble, are you?"

She shook her head.

And she cried.

He was incredibly dizzy. Drugged, he was sure, sedated so his head spun when he lifted his head from the pillow. He fought it. He angrily shoved himself up on one arm and tried to get up, tried to fight the sedative.

And almost fell out of bed as his hand hit the edge.

"Don't," Bianca said. "Don't. I've only got a few minutes. They won't let me stay."

She leaned over and kissed him then, a long, long kiss, first they'd ever shared. Only time they'd ever been together, except in class, without the masks.

"I'll get back down here," he said. "I'll get off that damn ship. Maybe they'll put me in for a psych-over and I won't have to go with them."

"Velasquez." A supervisor had come to the door. "Time's up."

She hugged him close.

"Velasquez. He's in quarantine."

"I'll get back," he said.

"I'll be here," she said. Meanwhile the supervisor had come into the flimsy little compartment to bring her out; and Bianca just moved away, holding his hand as long as she could until their fingers parted.

He fell back and it was a drugged slide into a personal dark in which Bianca's presence was like a dream, one before, not after the deep forest and the downer racing ahead of him.

The plain was next. A golden plain of grass, with the watchers endlessly staring into the heavens . . .

Not there any longer. Never there.

Esperance was where. Esperance.

"Jeremy?" He missed the noise from that quarter. Jeremy was very quiet.

"Yeah," he heard finally. "Yeah. I'm awake."

"We're there. You drink the packets?"

"Trying," Jeremy said. And scrambled out of his bunk and ran for the bathroom.

Jeremy was sick at his stomach. Light body, Fletcher said to himself, and drank a nutri-pack, trying to get his own stomach calmed.

Esperance. Their turn-around point. Midway on their journey.

Chapter
— XXIV —

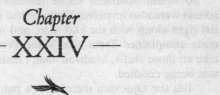

Boreale was a day from docking. *Champlain* was just coming into final approach, an hour from dock.

JR looked at the information while he drank down the nutrient pack and assessed damage. There was *one* piece of information he wanted, and it was delayed, pending. Charlie would check on the Old Man. Meanwhile he knew his two problems were there ahead of him, but not that much ahead, not so far ahead that they could have made extensive arrangements.

He meditated ordering a high-speed run-in that would put them at dock not long after the two ships in question.

It would also focus intense attention on them, at all levels of Esperance structure, and might impinge on negotiations to come. Foul up the Old Man's job and he'd hear about it.

He ordered the first and second *V*-dump, which removed that possibility—and followed approach regulations for a major starstation.

Please God the Old Man was all right. He got down another nutri-pack.

A message from Charlie came through, welcome and feared at once. *"He's complaining,"* Charlie said. *"Says he's getting dressed. Madison says he should stay put."*

He gave a little laugh, he, sitting on the bridge and waiting for Alan to relieve him. Their plans had them saving first and second shift in reserve throughout the run-in. Third and fourth were going to work in that edge-of-waking way bridge crew sat ready during jump, and Vickie was going to be at Helm on dock. That meant long shifts, but it also meant the Old Man was going to get maximum rest during their approach.

So would Madison, whose feelings in this shift of personnel were also involved. Madison had gone on the *protected* list right along with the Old Man, and while Madison hadn't quite complained about Alan's and Francie's ganging up to take all those shifts, Madison hadn't realized officially that he was being coddled.

"Tell the Old Man there's not a pan in the galley out of place, and *Boreale* will be thinking about our presence on her tail as a major Alliance caution flag. She *won't* innovate policy. Isn't that the rule?"

"Don't quote me my own advisements!" the Old Man's voice broke in: that com-panel on his desk reached anything it wanted to. Of *course* the Old Man had been shadowing his decisions.

Then, quietly, *"Not a pan out of place, indeed, Jamie. Good job."*

"Thank you, captain, sir," JR said calmly, then advised Com 2 to activate the intercom, because it was time. The live intercom blinked an advisory Channel 1 in the corner of his screen.

"The ship is stable," he began then, the age-old advisory of things rightfully in their places and the ship on course for a peaceful several days.

Routine settled over the ship. Fletcher would never have credited how comforting that could feel—just the routine of meals in the galley, and himself and the junior-juniors stuck with a modified laundry-duty, a stack they couldn't hope to work their way through in the four days, while senior-juniors drew the draining and cleaning of spoiled tanks in Jake's domain—not an enviable assignment. Meanwhile the flash-clean was going at a steady rate, since they had the senior-seniors' dress uniforms on priority for meetings that meant the future of the Alliance and a diminution of Mazian's options.

He'd never imagined that a button-push on a laundry machine could be important to war and peace in the universe, but it was the personal determination of the junior-junior crew that their captains were going into those all-important station conferences in immaculate, impressive dress.

They had to run up to A deck to collect senior laundry: all of A deck was so busy with clean-up after their run that senior staff had no time for personal jobs. Linda and Vince did most of the errands: Jeremy for his part wanted to stay in the working part of the laundry and not work the counter.

"No," Fletcher said to that idea. "You go out there, you work, you smile, you say hello, you behave as your charming self and you don't flinch."

"They think I'm a jerk!" Jeremy protested.

"We know you're not. You know you're not. Get out there, meet people, and look as if you aren't."

Jeremy *wasn't* happy. Sue and Connor showed up to check in bed linen, the one item they were running for the crew as a whole, and Jeremy ducked the encounter.

Fletcher went out and checked the cousins off their list, and Jeremy showed up after they were gone.

"You can't do that," Fletcher said. "You can't flinch. Yes, you're on the outs. I've been on the outs. They've been on the outs. It happens. People get over it if you don't look like a target."

"They're all talking about me."

"Probably they're talking about their upcoming liberty, if you want the honest truth. *Don't flinch.* They forget, and it *was* an accident, for God's sake. It wasn't like you stole it."

Jeremy moped off to the area with the machines, a maneuver, Fletcher said to himself in some annoyance, to have *him* doing the consoling, when, no, it wasn't a theft, and, no, losing it wasn't entirely Jeremy's fault.

Irreplaceable, in the one sense, that it was from Satin's hand; but entirely replaceable, in another. He'd begun to understand what the stick was worth—which he suspected now was absolutely nothing at all, in Satin's mind: the stick was as replaceable as everything else downers made. You lost it? she would say—*any* downer would say, in a world full of sticks and stones and feathers. I find more, Melody would say.

No downer would have fought over it, that was the truth he finally, belatedly, remembered. Fighting was a human decision, to protect what was a human memory, a human value set on Satin's gift. It was certain Satin herself never would fight over it, nor had ever meant contention and anger to be a part of her gift to him.

In that single thought—he had everything she was. He had everything Melody and Patch were.

And he suddenly had answers, in this strange moment standing in a ship's laundry, for *why* he'd not been able to stay there, forever dreaming dreams with downers. Satin had sent him back to the sky, and into a human heaven where human reasons operated. She might not know why someone in some sleepover would steal her gift, but a downer would be dismayed and bewildered that humans fought over it.

But—but—this was the one downer who'd gone to space, who'd set her stamp on the whole current arrangement of hisa and human affairs. This was the downer who'd dealt with researchers and administrators *and* Elene Quen. She knew the environment she sent him to. She'd seen war, and been appalled.

So maybe she wouldn't be as surprised as he thought that it had come to fighting.

Maybe, he thought, that evening in the mess hall, when he and Jeremy were in line ahead of Chad and Connor, maybe humans had to fight. It might be as human a behavior as a walk in spring was a downer one. It might be human process, to fight until, like Jeremy, like him, like Chad, they just wore out their resentments and found themselves exhausted.

So he'd only done what other humans did. But a human who knew downers never should have fought over Satin's gift. He most of all should have known better—and hadn't refrained. It certainly proved one point Satin had made to him—that he really was a wretched downer, and that he was bound to be the human he was born to be, sooner or later.

And it showed him something else, too. Downers left the spirit sticks at points of remembrance, at Watcher-sites, on graves. Rain washed them, and time destroyed them—and downers, he now remembered, didn't feel a need to renew the old ones. So they weren't ever designed to be permanent. He had the sudden notion if he were bringing one to Satin, he could make one of a metal rod, a handful of gaudy, stupid station-pins, and a little nylon cord. She'd think it represented humans very well, and that it was, indeed, a human memory, persistent as the steel humans used.

In his mind's eye he could imagine her taking it very solemnly at such a meeting, very respecting of his gift. He imagined her setting it in the earth at the foot of Mana-tari-so, and he imagined it enduring the rains as long as a steel rod could stand. Downers would see it, and those who remembered would remember, and as long as some remembered, they would teach. That was all it was. It was a memory. Just a memory.

And no one could ever steal that, or harm it.

No one but him.

He'd been wrong in everything he'd done. He'd waked up knowing the simple truth this time, but he'd still been too blind to see it. He'd *felt* Bianca's kiss, it was so real. And that had been sweet, and sad, and human, so distracting he hadn't been thinking about hisa memories. And that was an answer in itself.

Silly Fetcher, he heard Melody say to him. He knew now what he was too smart to know before, when he'd set all the value on physical wood and stone.

Silly Fetcher, he could hear Melody say to him. Silly you.

He sleepwalked his way through the line, ended up setting his tray beside Vince's, with Jeremy setting his down, too, across from him.

Chad and Connor were just at the hot table at the moment. Maybe it wasn't the smartest thing, remembering keenly that he wasn't a downer and that those he dealt with weren't—but he waited until he saw Chad and Connor sit near Nike and Ashley.

Then, to Jeremy's, "Where are you going, Fletcher?" he got up, left his tray, and went over two rows of tables.

He sat down opposite Chad, next to Connor. "I owe you an apology," he said, "from way before the stick disappeared. I took things wrong. That doesn't require you to say anything, or do anything, but I'm saying in front of Connor here and the rest of the family, I'm sorry, shouldn't have done that, I over-reacted. You were justified and I was wrong. I said it the far side of jump, and I'm still of that opinion. That's all."

Chad stared at him. Chad had a square, unexpressive face. It was easy to take it for sullen. Chad didn't change at all, or encourage any further word. So he got up and left and went back to the table with Vince and Linda and Jeremy.

"What'd you say to him?" Jeremy wanted to know.

It was daunting, to have a pack of twelve-year-olds hanging on your moves. But some things they needed to see happen in order to know they *ought* to happen among reasonable adults. "I apologized," he said.

"What'd he say?" Linda wanted to know.

"He didn't say anything. But he heard me. People who heard me accuse him heard it. That's what counts."

Jeremy had a glum look.

"Chad's an ass," Vince said.

"Well, I was another," Fletcher said. "We can all be asses now and again. Just so we don't make a career of it. —Cheer up. Think about liberty. Think about cheerful things, like going to the local sights. Like going to a tape shop. Getting some more tapes."

"My others got stolen," Jeremy said in a dark tone.

"Well, don't we have money coming?"

"We might," Vince said. "They said we were supposed to have some every liberty. And we didn't get anything at Voyager."

"Ask JR," Linda said. "He's a *captain* now."

"I might do that," Fletcher said.

But Jeremy didn't rise to the mood. He just ate his supper. That evening in rec he lost to Linda at vid-games, twice.

Won one, and then Jeremy decided to go back to the cabin and go to sleep.

That was a problem, Fletcher said to himself. That was a real problem. He was beginning to get mad about it.

• • •

"Am I supposed to entertain you every second, or what?" he asked Jeremy when he trailed him back. He caught him sitting on his bunk, and stood over him, deliberately looming. "I've done my best!"

"I'm not in a good mood, all right?"

"Fine. Fine! First you lose the stick and now I'm supposed to cheer you up about it, and every time I try, you sulk. I don't know what game we're playing here, but I could get tired of it just real soon."

"Why don't you?"

"Why don't I what?"

"Go bunk by yourself. I was by myself before. I can be, again. Screw it!"

"Oh, now it's broken and we don't want it anymore. You're being a spoiled brat, Jeremy. You owe me, but you want me to make it all right for you. Well, screw *that*! I'm staying."

Jeremy had a teary-eyed look worked up—and looked at him as if he'd grown two heads.

"Why?"

"Because, that's why! Because! I live here!"

Jeremy didn't say anything as Fletcher went to his bunk and threw himself down to sit. And stare.

"I didn't mean to do it," Jeremy muttered.

"Yeah, you mentioned that. Fact is, you *didn't* do it, some skuz at Mariner did it. So forget it! I'm *trying* to forget it, the whole ship is trying to forget it and you won't let anybody try another topic. You're being a bore, Jeremy. —Want to play cards?"

"No."

Fletcher got out the deck anyway. "I figure losing the stick is at least a hundred hours. You better win it back."

Resignation: "So I owe you a hundred hours."

"Yeah, and Linda beat you twice tonight, because *you* gave up. Give up *again*? Is this the guy I moved in with? Is this the guy who wants to be Helm 1 someday?"

"No." Jeremy squirmed to the edge of his bunk, in reach of the cards. Fletcher switched bunks, and dealt.

Jeremy beat him. It wasn't quite contrived, but it was extremely convenient that it turned out that way.

Esperance Station—a prosperous station, in its huge size, its traffic of skimmers and tenders about a fair number of ships at dock.

Among which, count *Boreale*, which had sent them no message, and *Champlain*, which had sat at dock for days during their slow approach, and because of which, yesterday during the dog watch of alterday, Esperance Legal Affairs had sent them notification of legal action pending against them.

Champlain was suing them and suing *Boreale*, claiming harassment and threats.

Handling the approach to Esperance docking as the captain of the watch, JR reviewed the list of ships in dock. There were twenty ships, of which three were Union, two smaller ships and *Boreale*; five were Unionside merchanters . . . ships signatory to Union, and registered with Union ports. All were Family ships, still, and four of them, *Gray Lady*, *Chelsea*, *Ming Tien*, and *Scottish Rose*, had chosen to believe Union's promise that their status would never change: they were honest merchanters who'd simply found Union offers of lower tariffs and safe ports attractive and who'd believed Union's promise of continued tolerance of private ownership of their ships. JR personally didn't believe it; nor did most merchanters in space, but some had believed it, and some merchanters had been working across the Line from before the War and considered Union ports their home ports.

Those four ships were no problem. Neither were the three Union ships. They had no vote. Union would dictate to them.

But the fifth of the Unionside merchanters, *Wayfarer*, was a ship working for the Alliance while under Union papers: a spy, no less, no more, and they had to be careful not to betray that fact.

There was, of course, *Champlain*, also a spy, but on Mazian's side—unless it was by remote chance Union's; or even, and least likely, Earth's—that was number eight.

Nine through eighteen were small Alliance traders, limited in scope: *Lightrunner*, *Celestial*, *Royal*, *Queen of Sheba*, and *Cairo*; *Southern Cross*, *St. Joseph*, *Amazonia*, *Brunswick Belle*, and

Gazelle. Nineteen and twenty were *Andromeda* and *Santo Domingo*, long-haulers, plying the run between Pell and Esperance, and on to Earth. *Those* two were natural allies, and a piece of luck, at a station where they already had a charge pending from a hostile ship, not to mention a hostile administration.

Those two had likely been carrying luxury goods, having the reach to have been at ports where they could obtain them; and they would be a little glad, perhaps, that they'd sold *their* cargoes before *Finity*'s cargo hit the market, as that cargo was doing now, electronically. Madison was in charge of market-tracking.

"Final rotation," Helm announced calmly. They were on course toward a mathematically precise touch at a moving station rim.

"Proceed," JR said, committing them to Helm's judgment. They were going in. Lawyers with papers would be waiting on the dockside. Madelaine had papers prepared as well, countersuing *Champlain* for legal harassment.

Welcome, JR thought, to the captaincy and its responsibilities. He hadn't asked the other captains whether to launch a counter-suit. He simply knew they didn't accept such things tamely, he'd called Madelaine, found that she'd already been composing the papers; and the Old Man hadn't stepped in.

He didn't go, this time, to take his place in the rowdy gathering of cousins awaiting the docking touch in the assembly area. Bucklin would be there. Bucklin would be in charge of the assembly area setup before dock and its breakdown after, and Bucklin would be overseeing all the things that he'd overseen.

That meant Bucklin wouldn't be at his ear with commentary, or the usual jokes, or sympathy, even when Bucklin found free time enough to be up here shadowing command. Bucklin wouldn't observe him for instruction, not generally. Bucklin would concentrate his observation on Madison, ideally, and learn from the best.

It was a lonely feeling he had, in Bucklin's assignment elsewhere. It always would be, until Bucklin found his own way to A deck. And the price of that, Madison's retirement, neither of them would want.

He sat, useless, once he'd given Helm the go-ahead. He sat through the advisement of takehold, when crew would be making their way to the assembly area, to stand together, wait together.

He had one critical bit of business, and that was turning up computer-handled and optimum: the passenger ring started its spin-down as the takehold sounded, preparing to lock down just before the touch at the docking cone. It was another chance to rearrange the galley pans if that went short; and to break bones and damage the mag-lev interface if it went long. He saw it, *felt* it, as for a moment they were null-*g* in the ring.

Gliding in under Vickie's steady hand and lightning reflexes. From 10mps to 5, down to .5, .2, .02.

Touch. Bang. Clang.

Machinery the size of a sleepover suite engaged and drew them into synch with the station.

Docking crews would scramble to move in the gantry and match up the lines, to a set of connectors on the probe that were not the same for every ship, last vestige of a scramble of innovation and refitting. Things were changing, but they changed slowly. Always, with machinery that functioned for centuries, it worked till it broke, and change came when it could come.

He sent a *Commend* to Helm. Vickie wouldn't talk for a few minutes. Helm did that to a human being. She wasn't in phase with the universe right now, and Helm 4 would literally walk her and Helm 2 off the ship after Helm 3 shut down the boards.

"Thank you, one and all," he said to the bridge crew, and got up, hearing Com making the routine announcements, sending the heads of sections off to customs.

"First shift captain," he intercommed Madison. "Legal Affairs will meet you at the airlock with appropriate papers." That was reasonably routine, but the papers in question were a countersuit, responding to papers they'd already received electronically. He punched another personal page. "Blue, this is JR. Are we going to have any customs troubles?"

"None yet," the reply came back to him.

Meanwhile the Purser flashed the advisement of a bloc of rooms engaged at the luxury Xanadu, which, the Purser advised him, put them in with *Boreale* and with *Santo Domingo*.

He keyed accept and trusted the Purser to advise Com to advise the crew.

Meanwhile the docking crew was engaging lines and Engineering was watching the connections as thumps came from the bow. The access tube linked on with a clang.

The most of the crew would be getting ready to move, right below them. When he finished here, which would be perhaps another hour if there were no glitches, he would take the lift down to A deck. He would live with his pocket-com, sleep aboard, fill out endless reports. He'd have no chance to hobnob with the juniors in the bar, and he'd ride no more vid-rides in the amusement shops on any station, ever. Chase young spacer-femmes in some bar? Not a captain of *Finity's End*.

He looked forward to the negotiations as the only chance he'd have this so-called liberty to have a little time with Bucklin, maybe coffee and doughnuts in some side conference room, an interlude to meetings the importance of which far outweighed any regrets on the fourth captain's part that he wouldn't sit and talk for hours to his age-mates.

Paul, who'd gone to senior crew before him, was in third shift. Paul had taken two ports and six jumps to quit turning up among the juniors down on A deck, as if he were still for-lornly hoping for something to span the gap from where he was to where he'd been. But it had felt awkward, an under-mining of his authority as new officer over the juniors. He remembered how uncomfortable Paul had made him. He wouldn't do that to Bucklin.

He had access to every message in the ship, if he wanted a sample, ranging from Jeff's query of the schedule for first meal after undock, two weeks from now, to the intercom exchange between Madison and Alan regarding the negotia-tions meeting schedule.

Customs didn't hold them up, as they had feared might

happen for days if Esperance administration wanted to delay the meetings. Crew was exiting on schedule. The lawsuit came in, the lawsuit went out. They'd arrived at 1040h mainday, right near midday, and before judges had gone to lunch. That had proved useful.

They sold their cargo. The voyage was profitable. They'd move the crates out of the cabins next watch. They'd need two cargo shifts, counting that the crates had to be moved by hand on floors that were, by now, stairs, as the pop-up treads enabled industrious A and B deck crew to access areas of the ship that otherwise would go inaccessible when the ring locked.

They'd handle that offloading with regular crew, no extras needed, and the cargo hands would still get their five-day total liberty before they had to load again for Pell.

All such things crossed his attention, as something he had to remember if plans changed without notice. As they well could here.

He received notifications of systems status. No senior captain came to advise him of procedures. Shut-down of systems saved energy and protected equipment, and there was a sequence to the shut-downs. He was a little slower than the more senior captains, because he was looking to the operations list. But he knew that, of the hundred-odd systems that had to go to bed for the next few weeks, they were safed, set, and ready for their wake-up when *Finity* next powered up.

Then he dismissed all but the ops watch, which would rotate by three-day sets. They never left *Finity* without onboard monitoring.

No one said good job. No one frowned. He was relieved no one came running up with an objection of something left undone. He knew things backward and forward, and could have done the shut-down by rote. But he didn't take that risk. And wouldn't, until nerves were no longer a factor.

He walked to the small lift that gave bridge access and took it down to ops, where it let out.

He saw that ops was up and functioning, gave over the ship to the senior cousin in charge—it happened to be Molly—and walked out to the cold, metallic air of Esperance dockside and the expected row of neon lights the other side of the customs checkpoint, among the very last to pick up his baggage—intending to do it himself, though he had regularly done that duty for the Old Man, when they weren't as short of biddable juniors as they were.

"No," Bucklin said, being in charge, now, of the senior-juniors handling crew baggage. "Wayne's already taken it and checked you into your room."

"Understood," he said. Bucklin had handled it. Commenting on it would admit he'd thought about it and not relied on Bucklin's finding a way to double-up someone's duty. So there was no thank-you. What he longed to do was arrange a meeting of the old gang in the sleepover bar in the off-shift, so they could talk over things and get signals straight the way they'd always done. But he couldn't. He couldn't even attend what Bucklin might have set up. "First meeting with the stationmaster," he said, "is in three hours. You'll be there."

"Yes, sir," Bucklin said—as happy, JR said to himself, to have gotten his new job done as he was to have gotten through the shut-down checklist unscathed. "Want a personal escort to the sleepover?"

"Wouldn't turn it down."

"Finish up," Bucklin said to Lyra, *his* lieutenant, now, and the two of them, like before their recent transformation, took a walk through customs and onto docks where the neon signs were bright and elaborate and the sound of music floated out of bars and restaurants.

Esperance in all its prosperous glory. Garish neon warred against the dark in the high reaches of the dockside. Gantries leaned just a little in the curvature of perspectives, and the white lights of spots, like suns floating in darkness, blazed from the gantry tops.

"Fancy place," he said.

"Not quite up to Pell's standard," Bucklin said, and didn't ask what JR figured was the foremost question in Bucklin's thoughts: how it felt to sit the chair for real. But he didn't ask Bucklin how the juniors reacted, either.

Not his business any longer.

The meetings in which the Old Man was going to read the rules to the stationmaster of Esperance, those were his business. That he had a voice in *that* process was a very sobering consideration, and itself a good reason to follow protocols meticulously. Every nuance of their behavior, even now, might be under station observation, what with lawyers and station administrators looking for ways to keep Esperance doing exactly what Esperance had been doing—balancing between Union and Pell.

As some ships might be dubious where their advantage was—or where it might be a month from now.

Someone had urged *Champlain* to sue. It was unlikely that a ship of *Champlain*'s character—a rough and tumble lot—would have organized it on their own. Someone had pulled *Champlain* in on a short tether, and risked exposure of that association. Possibly *Champlain* itself had gotten scared of the enemies she'd gained—and put pressure on someone in this port for protection.

Protect us or we'll talk.

Or, conversely, someone wanted to stall and hinder *Finity*'s approach to the station authorities: sue *Finity* or they'd get no protection from their stationside contacts.

Madelaine was going to shadow the negotiations this time: the ship's chief lawyer, not at the table, but definitely following every move.

"Berth 2," Bucklin said as they walked. "And *Champlain* is 14."

"Not far enough," JR said. "We need a guard on the sleepover, not obtrusive, but we can't risk an incident—and they may try us—maybe to plant something, maybe to start an incident."

"I've put out a caution," Bucklin said.

"No question you would. Damn, I'm missing you guys."

"Feels empty across the corridor."

He gave a breath of a laugh. "I lived through docking. I'm jumpy as hell."

"Don't blame you for that. How's the Old Man?"

Sober question. All-important question. "Last I saw he was

doing all right." He hadn't told Bucklin about the Old Man's rejuv failing. He thought about doing it now. But he'd been told that on a need-to-know, and Bucklin wasn't on a need-to-know. If it had involved a second captain's health, yes. But it didn't.

"Hard voyage," Bucklin said, not knowing that deadly fact. "At his age, it's got to wear on him."

He didn't elaborate. They reached the sleepover frontage. He thought of ways he *could* talk to Bucklin, if Bucklin played sometime aide and orderly. It wasn't the way he'd have preferred it.

It was the way things were going to be.

Walking through Xanadu was like walking through the heart of a jewel, lights constantly changing, most surfaces reflecting. It impressed the junior-juniors no end. It impressed Fletcher.

So did the suite—an arrangement like Voyager with all of the junior-juniors in one, but this time with enough beds. The bed in the central room was as huge as the one at Mariner. The two adjacent bedrooms were almost as elaborate. Colors changed on all the walls constantly. One wall of the main room was bubbles rising through real water, like bubbly wine.

Linda had, of course, to squat down by the base of the wall and try to see where the bubbles came from.

"Let's go on the docks," Jeremy said, and Fletcher was glad to hear the impatience in Jeremy. The kid was getting over it. Liberty was casting its spell over the junior-juniors, luring them with vid parlors and dessert bars and every blandishment ever designed to part a spacer from his cash. Vid-games had become important again, and the universe was back in order.

"There's a vid zoo," Linda said, from her examination of bubble production. "A walk-through. It's educational. There's tigers and dinosaurs and zebras."

"Where'd you hear that?" Vince wanted to know.

"I looked it up while *some* people were lazing around."

"The hell," Vince said.

The bickering was actually pleasant to the ears. "Let's go

downstairs," Fletcher suggested, and instantly there were takers.

It took four hours to set up the initial meeting, that of ship's officers with station officials. Station Legal Affairs said it didn't want the station administrators to meet with a ship under accusation . . . that it would constitute a legal impropriety.

The Old Man suggested the station officials could refuse to meet with a ship under accusation, but they'd damn well better arrange a meeting for an Alliance mission. Immediately.

Sitting aboard the ship, in lower deck ops, along with the other four captains, with the beep and tick of cargo monitoring the only action on the boards, JR watched and listened to that exchange, on which Wayne ran courier. The Old Man was perfectly unflappable, pleasant to every cousin and nephew and niece around him. That was a bad sign for the opposition.

The Old Man dictated a message for *Boreale*, too, one to be hand-carried, a fact which said how much the Old Man relied on the security of station communication systems, even the secured lines, and all prudent officers took note of it. JR wrote the message down and printed it; and Wayne ran that one, too, while Tom B. ran courier for Madelaine's office back and forth in an exchange with Esperance Legal to which JR was not privy.

The message to *Boreale* was simple. *The suit is harassment and will not stand. We will vigorously oppose it and defend you in the same matter. We will hope for your attendance at one of our final meetings with ship captains at a time mutually agreeable, and hope also for your support of the pertinent treaty provisions with your own local offices.*

What came back was:

We cannot of course speak for Union authorities, but we stand with you against the lawsuit. We also hold that, in accordance with both Union immunity and Alliance law, our deck is sovereign territory.

The latter sentence was complete irony. It was James Robert's own hard-won provision in international law and the reason of the War in the first place; and *Boreale* was invoking it to prevent Esperance station personnel from entering their ship to search for records—as *Finity* held to the same right.

But Union held to no such thing within its own territory with ships signatory to Union.

"They stand with us," Madison muttered when he heard the answer. "One could even hope they were on our side when they took out after *Champlain* and started this legal mess."

"But dare we notice that station hasn't charged *Boreale*?" Francie said. "They're very careful of Union feelings at this port."

"Noticed that," Alan said. "Question is, how high does *Boreale*'s captain rank over whoever's in the Union Trade Bureau offices here. I *think* that *Boreale* has the edge in rank, barring special instructions."

"I don't take *Boreale*'s turning up at Mariner total coincidence," James Robert said, breaking a long silence, and JR paid close attention, but as the least informed, he'd kept quiet.

Not coincidence. "So," he ventured, "what *was* the carrier doing at Tripoint?"

"Mallory's business," Madison said. "We think that Mazianni operations have shifted from Sol fringes to a new area the other side of Viking. We thought there'd be something more *Boreale*'s size sitting there observing. We got a carrier *and* then *Boreale*'s presence at Mariner. And a Mazianni ship running for Esperance, the complete opposite direction, when taking out for Tripoint would have thrown it right into the arms of that carrier."

He hadn't thought of *Champlain*'s alternative course. Blind spot. Major blind spot. He was chagrinned.

"So it ran this direction."

"Its chances were better with us. That carrier would have had it, no question. *Boreale* wanted it but couldn't catch it. *Boreale* wanted them alive."

It would be a source of information, one that Union science could probe with no messiness of courts, at least in the autonomy of the Union military operating in what was technically a war zone.

Maybe we should let them, was the unethical thought that

raced next through his mind. *Maybe we play too much by the law and that's why this has dragged on for twenty years.*

No. That wasn't correct. Their playing by the law was exactly what this whole mission was about. Their playing by the law was the only thing that got the cooperation of hundreds of independent merchanters, who otherwise would have supported Mazian with supply at least intermittently and brought him back from the political dead the moment things grew chancy. The result would have been another, far deadlier war, with the whole human future at risk.

Cancel that thought.

"Various interests at Esperance aren't willing to see *Champlain* answering close questions," Francie said. "That's my bet."

"It's mine, too," Madison said. "I think it's a very good bet. *Champlain* was dead if it had gone to Tripoint. *It knew what was waiting there.* It might stay alive if it ran this direction and threatened its own business partners. They're here. On Esperance. At least one strong anchor for the whole Mazianni supply network is right here . . . the contraband, the smuggling, the illicit trade in rejuv, the whole thing. The other leak is probably Viking; but Viking isn't our problem. Esperance is."

It made sense. It finally made sense, how the web was structured. And what the gateway was for the high-priced goods to reach the paying markets, at Cyteen. Cyteen officials didn't like it. But they still drank their Scotch, not looking closely enough at whether it came via a legitimate merchanter or whether it meant rejuv and biologicals were getting to Earth, to the wellspring of all that was human, in trade for supply for Mazian's war machine.

The other captains discussed technical matters. The new one was just filling out the holes in his understanding of what they were doing, and why they were doing it, and why certain Cyteen factions would support them and certain ones wouldn't. Some Cyteeners were defending their world. Others were making money.

Say that also about the position of Esperance in this affair. It had existed by playing Union against Alliance, supporting and not supporting Mazian. It was what the Old Man had said at Voyager: Mazian was essential . . . in this case, to Esperance. Maybe even to them . . . because without him, Union would have had Esperance, and the Alliance would have gone down Union's gullet. As it was, Union would let Esperance slip firmly into the Alliance in return for secure borders—secure from a threat Union itself was helping fund simply because Union had an appetite for what their sole planet didn't produce.

Like lifestuff that wasn't poisonous, or otherwise deadly. Cyteen had made a great matter over its rebellion from what was Earthlike; Cyteen wielded genetics like a weapon; but when it came to creature comforts, Cyteen, just like some this side of the Line, didn't look too closely at the label.

Like Pell, he thought. Like Pell, and its dinosaurs and sugar drinks scantly removed from where thousands had died. People forgot. People were human and didn't look too closely at what didn't look harmful. No single person's little purchase of black-market coffee could affect the universe.

That was the dream people had, that little things were ignorable on a cosmic scale.

Wind blew through virtual foliage. Moist air brushed the skin. It wasn't one of those sims that you wore a suit to experience. You wore ordinary clothes, and just put on disposable contacts. And walked.

And climbed. And walked some more. It might have been Downbelow, but it was too green. They walked over soft ground, and around trees, following a hand-rope.

A tiger was resting in the undergrowth. It stood up, huge, and real, right down to the details of its whiskers and the expression in its eyes.

Vince yelped, and the virtual cat jumped, spat, and retreated, staring at them.

Fletcher had to calm his own nerves and slow his own pulse. "Don't move," he said. "Stand still."

The tiger rumbled with threat. The tail-tip moved, and muscles stayed knotted beneath the striped fur. The place smelled of damp, and rot, and animal.

"It's really real," Linda said.

"Does a pretty good job," Fletcher said. The junior-juniors clustered around him; and his own planet-trained nerves were in an uproar.

They edged past. The tiger followed them with a slow turning of its head.

A strange animal bolted away, brown, four-footed. The tiger bounded across the trail in front of them.

"Damn!" Jeremy said.

Fletcher concurred. They'd had a children's version and a thrills version of the zoo, and he began to know where he classified himself.

Or maybe too much immediacy and too much threat had made them all jumpy.

They walked out of the exhibit with rattled nerves and went through the gift shop, spending money all the way.

Four hours to set up the meeting and then another hour while station officials drifted in from various appointments, in their own good time. Alan and Francie took charge and kept, contrarily, claiming that the senior captain was on his way. On his way . . . for another hour and a half.

"Just sit there," Francie advised JR. "Just sit and be pleasant. Keep them wondering."

So he took *his* place at the table beside Alan, and provoked stares from a long table occupied by grim-faced station authorities and minor Alliance officials.

"Fifth captain," Alan introduced him. "James Robert Neihart, Jr."

JR returned the shocked glances, and suddenly, in possession of the conference table, knew how hard that information had hit. *These* people hadn't known he existed two seconds ago— *another* Captain James Robert, under tutelage of the first.

Now titled with the captaincy, at a time when, just perhaps, they'd been thinking the famous captain couldn't last much longer and that they knew his successors.

Now they knew nothing.

"Gentlemen," JR said. "Ladies. My pleasure."

There was a moment of paralysis. That was the only way to describe it. They didn't know what to do with him. They didn't know what his position was, how much he knew, or *why*. In short, what they thought they knew had changed.

"We," the first-shift stationmaster said, trying to seize hold of what had no handles, "we weren't informed. Is it recent, this fifth captaincy? We hope it doesn't signal a crisis in the captain's health."

Vile man, JR thought. He'd never found a person *snake* so described on sight. And, completely, coldly deadpan, he made his reply as close a copy of the Old Man as he could muster.

"We *aren't* our apparent ages. *Recent* in whose terms, sir?"

Conversation-stopper. Implied offense—within the difference between spacer perceptions and stationer perceptions.

And he'd asked a question. It hung in the charged air waiting for an answer as a dozen faces down the long table hoped not to be asked, themselves, directly.

There was one gesture the senior captain had made his own. JR consciously smiled the Old Man's dead-eyed, perfunctory smile. And at least the two seniormost stationers looked far from comfortable.

"There is a succession," JR dropped into that silence. He'd thought he'd be terrified, sitting at this table. He'd thought he'd conceive not a word to say. Maybe it was folly that took him to the threshold of real negotiations, knowing that the Old Man's arrival might be further delayed. It might be dangerous folly. But the Old Man had taught him. "There always was a succession. It's our way to shadow our seniors, so there's *no* transition. There never *will* be a transition. But Mazian can't say the same. They went on rejuv back during the War—to ensure no births. Those ships *have* no succession." A second, deliberate smile. "We left only one of our children ashore. And at Pell we got him back. Another Fletcher Neihart, as happens. Looks seventeen. Unlike me, he is."

For a moment the air in the room seemed dead still, and heavy. There was no way for them to figure his real age. The face they were looking at was a boy's face. But now they knew he wasn't.

Then a set of steps sounded in the hall outside. A good many of them. The Old Man was arriving with his escort.

He was aware of body language, his own, constantly, another of the Old Man's lessons. He deliberately mirrored calm assurance, to their scarcely restrained consternation, and when Alan and Francie rose in respect to the Old Man and Madison coming into the room, so did he. Four of those at the conference table, in their confusion, rose, too.

"So you've met the younger James Robert," James Robert, Sr. said, and JR would personally lay odds someone's pocket-com had been live and the feed going to the Old Man for the last few minutes. "A pleasure to reach Esperance. I was just in communication with the Union Trade Bureau. Very encouraging." James Robert sat down as they all resumed their seats. "Delighted to be here," James Robert said, opening his folder. He looked good, he looked rested, not a hair out of place and the dark eyes that remained so lively in a sere, enigmatic mask swept over the conspiratory powers of Esperance with not a hint of doubt, not of himself, not of the Alliance, not of the force he represented.

"Welcome to Esperance," the senior stationmaster said.

"Thank you." James Robert let him get not a word further. "Thank you all for rearranging your schedules. You've doubtless received partial reports on the trade situation and the pirate threat. I've just come from the edges of Earth space, and from consultation with our Union allies on matters of security and trade, and on the changing nature of the pirate activity hereabouts." This, to a station that fancied its own private agreements with Union: it suggested Union shifting positions: it suggested things changing; and JR very much suspected the Old Man was going to follow that theme straight as a shot to the heart of Esperance objections.

There were cautions out, in the instructions from Bucklin. *Champlain* being in port. The crew was supposed to confine themselves to Blue Dock, and to go in groups constantly, in civ clothing. Fletcher wore his brown sweater. So did Jeremy, and now Linda said she wanted one.

"We can all have the same sweaters," Linda said.

"The idea," Fletcher objected, "is that civvies look *different*."

"So we look different," Linda said.

He was doubtful that Linda comprehended the idea at all. Linda understood unity, not uniqueness. Linda wanted a sweater. Then Vince did. The notion that they should look like a unit appealed to them, and protests that they might as well put on ship's colors fell on deaf ears. So they shopped. Found *exactly* the right sweaters, which the juniors insisted on putting on in the shop.

Next door to the clothing store was a pin and patch shop, a necessity. Esperance patches and pins were in evidence, along with patches and pins from all over . . . but the ones from Earth and the ones from Cyteen were the rarities, priced accordingly.

It was obligatory to acquire pins or patches, for a first trip to a station, and the junior-juniors, getting into the spirit of the merchanter and trading idea, traded spare pins from Sol for theirs and then bought an extravagant number of extras. The merchant was happy.

Then Vince fished up a Jupiter from his pocket and got a cash sale.

A first-timer to everything, however, had to buy, and Fletcher bought a couple of high-quality Esperance pins. One for luck, Linda urged him, and at least one for trade.

Then he bought another, telling himself he'd . . . maybe . . . give it to Bianca when he got back to Pell. She'd like it, he thought. At least she'd know he'd thought of her, at the very last star of civilized space.

It was a fairly rare pin. Worth a bit, back at Pell.

Hell, he thought, after he'd left the shop . . . after he was walking the dockside with a trio of ebullient juniors . . . well, two, and an unnaturally glum Jeremy, who sulked because nobody wanted to go look for an Esperance snow globe, which Jeremy said he'd seen once, and wanted.

"They had one at the pin shop," Linda said.

"Not the same," Jeremy said sourly. "I know what I want, all right?"

"Tomorrow," Fletcher said. "There's a whole two weeks here, for God's sake."

"Tomorrow morning," Jeremy said.

"Deal." He should have gotten a pin for the Wilsons. He didn't think the Wilsons would know what it was worth, and any pin would do . . . but he could get one before he left, anyway. They'd be bound to drift past another shop, in two weeks confined to Blue Sector.

Bianca, though, might know what a pin like that represented. She knew a lot of odd things. If she didn't know, at least she wanted to know. That was what he'd liked most about her.

And at Esperance, he finally realized he missed her. Missed her, at least, in the way of missing a friend, after all the uproar of almost-love and maybe-love and the feeling of desertion he'd felt, being ripped loose from everything.

So she'd talked to Nunn. He would have, too, in her situation. He'd been angry, he'd been hurt. He hadn't been able to be sure what he felt about her, just specifically about her, until he'd had been this long on *Finity* and into the hurry and hustle of a sprawling family that made him mad, and swept him in, and spun him about, and fought with him and said, like Jeremy beside him, like all the juniors and the seniors, *Fletcher, don't go . . .*

Maybe he'd had an acute attack of hormones on Downbelow. He was in doubt now, after this many temper-cooling jumps, about the reality of all he'd ever felt. He'd been from nowhere in particular. Now he was someone, from somewhere. But all the distance that had intervened and all the change in his own understandings hadn't altered the fact that he'd liked Bianca a lot.

Maybe the hormone part came back if you got close again. Maybe when they met they'd resurrect all of it, and be in love again—

He missed her—he knew that.

But there was less and less they had to tie them together. She hadn't seen the sights he'd seen. She was locked into the circular cycles of a planet and its seasons. She hadn't flung off the ties of a gravity well and skimmed the interface faster than the mind could imagine, living out of time with the rest of the human species. She hadn't stood in an arch of water on Mariner and watched fish the size of human beings swim above her head.

He had so, so much to tell her when they met.

If they ever met.

He'd have to mail her the pin. He couldn't go back to the Program. He'd fractured all the rules. He'd lost that for himself, in the perverse way he had of destroying situations he knew he was about to be ripped out of and taken away from. Especially if you almost loved them, you broke them, so you didn't have them to regret. Sometimes you broke them just in case.

That was what he'd always done. He could see that now, too . . . how he always managed the fight, always provoked the blowup, so he could say he'd left *them*, and not the other way around. He had that definitely in common with Jeremy: the quick flare of anger, the intense passion of total involvement—followed by angry denial, total rejection. Go ahead. Move out. Don't speak to me.

Silly Fetcher. He could hear Melody saying it, when he'd been too kid-like stupid even for her downer patience.

Silly Jeremy, he wished he knew how to say. Silly Jeremy. Be happy. Cheer up.

Change, to a prosperous station, was a frightening prospect.

Change and new information meant that those here who thought they knew how the universe was stacked might not know what was in their own future.

Change in the Alliance and Union relationship might abrogate agreements on which Esperance seemed secure. They stalled. They argued about minutiae. There was a long stall regarding an alleged irregularity in the customs papers. That evaporated. Then they discussed the order of the official agenda for an hour.

Madison was ready to blow. The Old Man smiled benignly, seated at the table, while the Esperance stationmaster absented himself to consult with aides.

And came back after a half hour absence, and finally took his seat.

"The legal problems," the stationmaster said then.

"Third on the agenda," Alan said.

"We cannot talk and discuss matters pertinent to a pending suit . . ."

"Third," Alan said.

"We're vastly disturbed," the Esperance stationmaster insisted, "by what seems high-handed procedure regarding a ship against which no charges have been made, sir. I want the answer to one question. One question, sir."

"Not one question," Madison said. "As agreed in the agenda."

"We can *not* agree to this order. We can't talk beyond a pending suit. We wish to move for a meeting after the court has ruled."

"You can have that, with *Finity*'s trade officer. *In the meantime* . . . you're not meeting with *Finity*'s trade officer."

Madison, at his inflammatory best. JR tucked his chin down and listened to the shots fly.

"I cannot accept Alliance credentials from a ship in violation of Alliance guarantees."

"This is Alliance business, which you may *not* challenge, sir."

"I ask one question. One question. On what authority do you *pursue* a ship into inhabited space?"

"What ship?" James Robert asked, interrupting his idle sketching on the conference notepad—looking for that moment as if he had no clue at all, as if he'd been in total lapse for the last few minutes, and JR's heart plummeted. *Is he ill?* the thought came to him.

Outrage mustered itself instantly on the other side. Outrage perfectly staged. "*Champlain*, captain."

James Robert looked at Madison on one side, and at Francie, Alan, and him, on the other. Blinked. "Wasn't that ship docked when we entered system?"

"Final approach to dock, sir," JR said, and all of a sudden

knew the Old Man had been far from oblivious. "As we came into system. Days ahead of us."

"And what *was* its last port?"

"Mariner."

"While our last port was Voyager." It was dead-on focus the Old Man turned on the Esperance officials. "Hardly hot pursuit. They'd passed Voyager-Esperance before we got to that point. Our black-box feed will have the latest Voyager data. Theirs won't. Ours will have an official caution from Mariner on their behavior. Theirs won't reflect that. They undocked before we or *Boreale* left Mariner. Seems a case of flight where no man pursueth, stationmaster. *Boreale* might have had a dispute with them we know nothing of. We didn't chase them in. And I invite anyone with doubts to examine the black-box record Esperance now has from the instant we docked. It will show *exactly* the facts as I've given them, including a stop at Voyager."

Bravo, JR thought, and watched the expressions of station officials deeply divided, he began to perceive, between pro-Union and pro-Alliance sentiments . . . and those who simply wanted to go on playing both ends against the middle. And unless he missed his guess the stationmaster hadn't accessed their records yet to know where they'd been. Careless, in a man leveling charges.

Careless and impromptu.

"But a military ship can access a black box on its technical level," the stationmaster said. "And your turnaround at Voyager must have set a record, Captain Neihart, if you stopped there."

That man was their problem. William Oser-Hayes. There was the chief source of the venom. JR wanted to rise from the table and wipe the look from the man's face.

The Old Man did no such thing. "Necessarily," the Old Man said calmly. "The military does have read-access. And can delete information. But black boxes . . . and you may check this with your technical experts, do show the effects of military access. Ours wasn't accessed. Check it with your technical experts."

"Experts provided by Pell."

Oh, the political mire was getting deeper and deeper. Now it was all a plot from Pell. And the Old Man was playing cards from a hand they had far rather have reserved for court, for the lawsuit. It gave their legal opposition a forecast of the defense they had against the charges, even if it was a very good defense—an unbreakable defense in a port where the judiciary was honest.

The way in which certain members of the conference looked happier when the Old Man seemed to win a point indicated they were not facing a monolithic administration and that there was sentiment on *Finity*'s side. But the fact that Oser-Hayes did all the talking and that all the ones who looked happy when Oser-Hayes seemed to score sat higher up the table indicated to him that they had a serious problem—one that might well infect the judiciary on this station. That the attack from the opposition had come from the Esperance judiciary and not from, say, the Board of Trade or the other regulatory agencies clearly indicated that the judiciary was their enemies' best shot, the branch most malleable to their hands.

Not a fair court, JR said to himself. The legal deck was stacked, and they might lose the suit even if the other side was a no-show and the evidence was overwhelming. That they'd bullied their way into this meeting indicated Oser-Hayes wasn't absolute in his power, that he regarded some appearances, and had to use some window-dressing with some of his power base to avoid them bolting his camp.

He was learning, hand over fist, that precisely at the moments one wanted to rise out of one's seat and choke the life out of the opposition, one had to focus down tightly and calmly and select arguments the same careful way a surgeon selected instruments. Oser-Hayes was no fool: he meant to provoke the choke-him reaction, which might get the Old Man to make a tactical error—if the Old Man weren't one of the canniest negotiators alive. One time Oser-Hayes had thought he was dealing with a drowsing elder statesman a little out of the current of things: one time the Old Man had let him stumble into it, and start the meeting. They were into the agenda, after balking for hours. A parliamentary turn would see them handle it, and revert back to the top of the list before Oser-Hayes could think how to avert it.

They *were* talking. They had accomplished that much.

But this talk of technical experts provided by Pell as a source of suspicion . . . this talk of deliberate sabotage by agents from the capital of the Alliance—as if the *Alliance government* and *Alliance-certified technicians* would likelier be the source of misinformation and duplicity, not some scruffy freighter running cargo in the shadow market and most probably spying for Mazian—that was a complete reversal of logic. The black boxes on which the network that ran the Alliance depended were of course suspect in Oser-Hayes' followers' minds; the word of *Champlain* against them was of course enough to stall negotiations and tangle them up in the issue of universal conspiracy, which Oser-Hayes insisted on discussing.

Whatever the Old Man's blood pressure was doing at the moment, there was no sign of it on his face. And the Old Man came back with perfect calm.

"Would you prefer those experts provided by Union, sir? I don't think we can access them. But *Boreale* can certainly attest every move we've made. And the next ship arriving in this port from the Mariner vector will most assuredly reflect exactly the same information, as surely the stationmaster of Esperance knows as well as any ship's captain—unless, of course, our technical experts have gotten in and altered the main computers on Mariner, then accomplished the same with seamless perfection on Voyager in ways that would withstand cross-comparison for all future ship-calls at any station in the Alliance—"

"Sufficient time to have gotten signatures on documents is all you need."

"Ah. Is *that* your fear?"

"Apprehension."

"Apprehension. Well, in respect of your prudent apprehensions, we have the precise case number that will pull up previous complaints on *Champlain*, including those that will have different origins and dates than any ship-call we've made. To save your technicians, I'm sure, weeks of painstaking effort . . ."

Weeks only if the technicians meant to stall.

"That *is* something our military status can do somewhat more efficiently: access case numbers. In this case, the last stamp of access on the complaint itself will be the court at Mariner."

Hours of meeting and they hadn't even gotten to the agenda. In that sense, William Oser-Hayes was making all the political capital he could, and JR wagered with himself that behind the scenes Oser-Hayes had people working the records, excavating things with which they could be ambushed, burying them at least beyond access within this port, although the very next ship to call at the station would dump a load of information which would restore the missing files.

The Old Man hadn't mentioned the fact, but a military ship had the means to take a fast access of a *station's* black-box system. JR remembered that suddenly in the light of the local resistance. *Finity* under his command had taken such a snapshot when they'd come in, a draw-down of station records and navigational information exactly as they'd been at the moment of their docking.

It was a convenience, only, in these tamer days. Any ship that had recently left the station for other space contained the same information, regularly uploaded on leaving one station to download at the next. It was the getting of the information immediately on arrival that was the military prerogative . . . because a military ship might be called to action on an emergency basis, in which event it might not have the ten or so minutes it took to receive the total update. They'd drawn a feed when they came in; and they'd draw another any time they liked. Again, military prerogative, useless to ordinary civilian ships, which couldn't read their own black boxes: most people didn't routinely think about it, although he was relatively sure it was no secret from station administrators that military craft did that.

At the next rest break, he passed an order to Bucklin on his own and without consulting the other captains. "Store the on-dock black-box information in the secondary box. Do a simultaneous back-up to safe-cube. Have you got that?"

"Yessir."

"Second step. Take a daily feed from station, at the same time. Run a data comparison. Every day."

They were alone, in the foyer of the meeting area, and Bucklin had with him a piece of electronics very hostile to bugs.

"You think they're going to fix *station records*?" Bucklin asked.

"I think it's remotely possible. Any change in archived files, I want the appropriate section leader notified and given a copy. If they try to change history or wipe a record, I want to know it. This is all a quiet matter. This Oser-Hayes is no fool. He could be doubling from Union—and Union itself has factions that might be counter to *Boreale*'s faction."

"Tangled-er and tangled-er."

"Very much so. *Some* faction or corporation on Cyteen Station might want Esperance to break out of the Alliance; *Boreale* won't act on its own; and it's very likely the Cyteen military will back *us* and the trade agreement with Pell. The result is in their interest. Their trading interests won't universally like it. Their station-folk will. It's far from settled, and my personal guess would be that Cyteen's military would like it to be a done deal before Cyteen's more complex factions find out about it: it wouldn't be the first time they've acted to pre-empt their own legal process. I think Cyteen military, like that carrier back at Tripoint, wants us to get this agreement through. But Oser-Hayes doesn't."

Bucklin nodded. "I'll relay that. I'll sub in Wayne here till I get back."

It was the first decision, JR reflected, as he watched Bucklin go to the door and call Wayne back, the first administrative decision he'd made in his new-made captaincy—one which might duplicate what someone had already ordered, but if it did, the more senior captain's instructions would take precedence. If it conflicted, he would hear an objection. He didn't think he'd hear one over the extravagant expense of one-write safe-cubes, which themselves were admissible in court.

In the meanwhile, if that information wasn't being collected, he wanted it. The facts were vulnerable to technicians, if to no one else, and Oser-Hayes might have cast aspersions on the honesty of the Pell-trained technicians who maintained the black-box system on Esperance, but it didn't mean Oser-Hayes might not subvert *one tech* to do something about damning evidence. Like financial records.

The tone in which Oser-Hayes said *Pell* made it likely that distrust of the central government and of Pell was a driving force in Esperance politics.

Distrust of this place, this station, this administration was becoming his.

They'd been to the vid zoo. They'd seen all the holo-sharks at the Lagoon. That was two major amusements down on the first day.

They went to supper, in the moderately posh Lagoon, which Linda and Jeremy had both wanted, where colored lights made the place look as if they were underwater, and a sign advised that the same disposable contact lenses they'd used in the exhibit would display Wonders of the Mystic Lagoon, purchasable for a day's wages if you hadn't brought your own.

The junior-juniors were tired. Fletcher wanted the bubble-tub back in the sleepover. In his opinion it was time to go back to the Xanadu and settle in for the night. It was well past main-dark and the dockside, which never slept, had gone over to the rougher side of its existence: neon a bit more in evidence, the music louder, the level of alcohol in the passersby just that much higher.

But Jeremy moped along the displays, and wanted to stay on dockside a little longer. "I'm not sleepy," he said.

"Well, *I'm* ready to go back," Vince said.

"We've got two weeks here," Fletcher reminded them. "We agreed. Shopping tomorrow. After breakfast."

"There's this shop—" Jeremy said, and dived off to a curio shop on the row they walked, a crowded little place with curiosities and souvenirs on every shelf.

There were plastic replicas of Cyteen life. There were expensive plastic-encased flowers and insects from Earth. There were packets of seeds done up with pots. Grow them in your cabin and be surprised at the carnivorous flowers.

He didn't think he wanted one of those.

They looked. They looked at truly tasteless things, and walked off the fullness of the supper on a stroll during which Jeremy ran them into every hole-in-the-wall shop on the row.

The kids bought some silly things, finger-traps, a device older than civilization, Fletcher was willing to bet. A plastic shark. Jeremy bought a cheap ball-bearing puzzle, another device that defied time. The kid was cheering up.

Good for that, Fletcher said to himself. It was worth an extra hour walking back to the sleepover if it gave Jeremy something to do besides jitter and fret.

The meeting lurched and stonewalled its way toward an adjournment for the night, the main topic as yet not on the table, and neither side satisfied . . . except in the fact that nothing notably budged. Aides might have carried the details forward during alterday, but there was nothing substantive to work on.

There was, by now, however, a safe-cube or two making sure that if Oser-Hayes had altered data in a record supposed to be sacrosanct, they had a record of before and after. JR was able to get to Madison without witnesses, and under security, after the meeting had broken up and while Francie and a team of discreetly armed security was making sure the Old Man, walking ahead of them, reached the chosen restaurant without crises.

"I've ordered analysis and safe-storage of station feed, then and now," he said. "Daily. Bucklin's gone to Gerald, called back personnel off leave."

"Good," Madison said, and by the thoughtful expression Madison shot him then, no one else had ordered it. And Madison didn't fault his consumption of multi-thousand credit cubes or the holding of the computer security staff off a well-earned liberty. "Good move. Cube?"

"Yessir." The *sirs* still came naturally. "Yes. I know what it costs. But—"

"Run an analysis. I want to know the outcome. It would be stupid of the man. But then—he's not the brightest light in the Alliance. He might think the next passing ship would patch his little problem and no one would be the wiser. Between you and me, the system has safeguards against that kind of thing. A Pell-certified tech, under duress, would alter records quite cheerfully."

"Knowing there'd be traces."

"Knowing that, yes. That's an ears-only, not even for Bucklin. Yet."

"I well imagine."

They walked, he and Madison together, with security hindmost, along with Alan. The restaurant wasn't far, one of those quiet, pricey affairs the Old Man favored, randomly selected from half a dozen near the conference area.

First time in his life, JR thought, he might have gotten up even with the captains he shadowed.

"Dinner," Madison said, "and then no rest for you and Francie and Alan. I have messages I want carried."

The destination made sense. Immediately.

"We can't make headway with this station," Madison said. "So we go to the captains first. This station is begging for confrontation. They won't like it. But I think two ships will go with us without an argument. Don't plan on sleep tonight."

He was supposed to approach another captain? *He* was supposed to carry out this end of the proposition?

It was one thing to talk in conference with the Old Man as certain back-up. It was another to walk onto another deck to persuade an independent merchanter to strong-arm a stationmaster tomorrow. Things could blow up. He could set negotiations back on a single failure to read signals. Or give the wrong captain information that could end up back in Oser-Hayes' hands, or hardening merchanter attitudes against them.

But he couldn't say no. That wasn't why they'd pushed him ahead in rank.

• • •

If they were late-night shopping, Vince wanted a tape store. They visited that, and Vince bought two tapes. Thirty minutes, in that operation, and it was high time, Fletcher decided, to get over-active junior-juniors back to the sleepover before Linda had her way and talked him into another sugared drink that would have them awake till the small hours.

"No," Fletcher said, to that idea.

Then Jeremy took interest in yet another curio shop, not yet sated with plastic snakes and seeds and little mineral curiosities. "Just one more," Jeremy said. "Just one more."

If it made Jeremy happy. If it got them back to the sleepover with everyone in a good mood.

This one was higher class, one of those kind of shops that was open during mainday and every other alterday, alterday traffic tending to lower-priced goods and cheaper amusements. The door opened to a melodious chime, advising the idle shopkeeper of visitors, and a portly man appeared. Justly dubious of junior-juniors in his shop, that was clear.

"Just window-shopping," Fletcher said, and the man continued to watch them; but he seemed a little easier in the realization of an older individual in charge of the rowdy junior traffic.

"Decadent," Linda said, looking around. "Really decadent stuff."

The word almost applied. There were plastic-encased bouquets, and mineral specimens, a pretty lot of crystals, and some truly odd geologic curiosities in a case that drew Fletcher's eye despite his determination to keep ubiquitous junior-junior elbows from knocking into vases and very pricey carvings in the tight quarters.

Out of Viking's mines, the label said, regarding the lot of specimens in the case, and the price said they were probably real—a crystal-encrusted ball, brilliant blue, on the top shelf; a polished specimen of iridescent webby stuff in matrix on the next shelf.

And, extravagantly expensive, and marked *museum quality*, a polished natural specimen on the next shelf, labeled Ammonnite, from Earth, North America. Fletcher's study told him it was probably real.

Real, and disturbing to find it here.

He was looking at that, when he became aware Jeremy was talking to the shopkeeper, wanting something from another cabinet. He didn't know what, in this place, Jeremy could possibly afford.

But he was amazed to see what the shopkeeper took out and laid on the counter at Jeremy's request.

Artifacts. Pieces of pottery.

"Earth," the shopkeeper said. "Tribal art. Three thousand years old. Bet you never saw anything like this."

Fletcher stopped breathing. He wasn't sure spacer kids understood what they were seeing.

But a native cultures specialist did. And a native cultures specialist knew the laws that said these specimens definitely weren't supposed to be here.

"Real, are they?" Fletcher asked, going over to look, but not to touch.

"Certificate of authenticity. Anyone you know a collector?"

He almost remarked, *Mediterranean*. But a spacer wasn't supposed to know that kind of detail.

"Got any downer stuff?" Jeremy piped up.

That got an apprehensive denial, a shake of the head, a wavering of the eyes.

Fletcher understood Jeremy's interest in curio shops the instant he heard the word *downer* in Jeremy's mouth. He bridged the moment's awkwardness with a dismissive wave toward the Old Earth pottery and a flip of his hand toward the rest of the shop. "I always had a curiosity," he said, playing Jeremy's game, knowing suddenly *exactly* what was behind Jeremy's new enthusiasm for curio shops and the other two junior-juniors' uncharacteristic support of his interest in shops where they couldn't afford the merchandise. "I read a lot about the downers. No market for the pottery. But I've got a market for downer stuff."

The shopkeeper shook his head. "That's illegal stuff."

Fletcher drew a slow breath, considered the kids, Jeremy, the situation. "Say I come back later."

"Maybe." The shopkeeper went back to the back of the shop, took a card from the wall, brought it back and wrote a number on it.

"Here."

Fletcher took the card, looked at it, saw a phone number, and a logo. "Is that where?"

"Maybe." The shopkeeper's eyes went to the kids, and back again.

"They're my legs," Fletcher said, the language of the underworld of Pell docks. "You want that market, I can make it, no question. You in?"

"See the man," the shopkeeper said. "Not me. No way."

"Understood." Fletcher slipped the card into his pocket.

"Specialties," the shopkeeper said.

"Loud and clear." Fletcher shoved at Linda's shoulder, and got her and the other two juniors into motion.

Jeremy gave him a sidelong look as they cleared the frontage, walking along a noisy dockside of neon light and small shops and sleepovers.

"Clever kid," Fletcher said. He'd had no idea the track Jeremy had been on, clearly, in his sudden interest in curio shops.

"I said we'd get it back," Jeremy said.

"We?"

"I mean we."

"No."

"What do you mean, *no*? We're on to where there's downer stuff! This is where that guy will sell it off clear to Cyteen!"

"I mean this is illegal stuff. I mean these people will *kill* you. All of you! This is serious, you three. It's not a game."

"We know that," Jeremy said in a tone that chilled his blood. Jeremy, Fletcher suddenly thought, who'd grown up in war. Linda and Vince, who had. All of them knew what risk was. Knew that people died. Knew *how* they died, very vividly.

"*Champlain*'s in port," Vince said. "So's the thief."

"So?" Fletcher said. "They might not sell it here. Not on the open market."

"Bet they do," Linda said. "I bet Jeremy's right."

"I don't care if he's right." He'd been maneuvered all day long by three clever kids. Or by one clever kid, granted Vince and Linda might not have suspected a thing until it was clear to all of them what Jeremy was after. "This isn't like searching the ship. Look, we tell JR. He'll tell the Old Man and the police can give the shop a walk-through." It sounded stupid once he was saying it. The police wouldn't find it. He knew a dozen dodges himself. He knew how shopkeepers who were fencing contraband hid their illegal goods.

"We can just sort of walk in there and find out," Jeremy said. "We're in civvies, right? Who's to know? And then we can know where to point the cops. I mean, hell, we're just kids walking around looking at the stuff. We won't do anything. We can *find out*, Fletcher. Us. Ourselves."

It was tempting—to know what had happened to Satin's gift, and to get justice on the lowlife that had pilfered it. They could even create a trail that could give *Finity* a way to come at *Champlain*, who had the nerve to sue them: *that* word was out even to the junior-juniors. He'd lay odds the crewman's thieving had been personal, pocket-lining habit, nothing *Champlain*'s captain even knew about—just the regular activity of a shipful of bad habits, all lining their pockets at any opportunity. The thief had been after money, ID's, tapes, anything he could filch; and the lowlife by total chance had hit the jackpot of a lifetime in Jeremy's room. Sell the hisa stick, here, in a port a lot looser than Pell, a port where curios were pricey and labeled with *museum quality*?

Jeremy was right. It was a pipeline straight to Cyteen, for pottery that shop wasn't supposed to have—he guessed so, at least. Maybe for plants and biologicals illegal to have. Maybe the trade was going both ways, smuggling rejuv out to Earth, rejuv and no knowing what: Cyteen's expertise in biologicals of all sorts was more than legend—and Cyteen biologicals were anathema in the Downbelow study programs—something they feared more than they did the easy temptation to humans to introduce Earth organisms, which at least had grown up in an ecosystem instead of being engineered for

Cyteen, specifically to replace native Cyteen microbes. He'd become aware how great a fear there'd been, especially among scientists on Pell during the War, that Cyteen, outgunned and outmaneuvered in space by the Fleet, would use biologics as a way of destroying Downbelow. Or Earth. They hadn't; but now they were spreading on the illicit route. Every scientist concerned with planets knew that.

And it immeasurably offended him that Satin's gift might become currency in a trade that, after all the other hazards humans had brought the hisa, posed the deadliest threat of all.

Go walk with Great Sun?

Take a hisa memory into space? What could Satin remember, but a world that trade aimed to destroy for no other reason than profit and convenience?

He looked at the address of the card they'd gotten. It was in Blue. It was in the best part of Blue, right in the five hundreds. They were standing at a shop in the threes. *Finity* was docked at Blue 2, *Boreale* at Blue 5, and *Champlain* at 14. Being in charge of junior-junior security—he'd made it his business to look at the boards and know that information.

"Come on," Jeremy said. "We can at least *know*."

They'd had the entire ship in an uproar, looking for what wasn't aboard; and what Jeremy had known wasn't aboard. Now Jeremy argued for finding out where the hisa stick really was.

And maybe that in itself was a good thing for the whole ship. Maybe *Finity* officers could do something personally to get it back, as the kids could have a part in finding it, and maybe then the whole ship could settle things within itself.

Maybe *he* could settle things in himself, then. Maybe he could find a means not to destroy one more situation for himself, and to get the stick back, so he'd not have to spend a life wondering what Cyteen shop had bought a hisa memory . . . and to whom it might have sold it, a curiosity, to hang on some wall.

"All right," he said, suddenly resolved. "We take a look. Only a look. It's not for us to do anything about it. We can at least look and see whether that guy back there is putting us on. Which he probably is. Do you hear me?"

"Yessir," Jeremy said, the most fervent *yessir* he'd heard out of Jeremy in weeks.

"Yessir," Vince said, and Linda bobbed her head.

"Behave," he said severely, and took the troops toward the five hundreds.

Chapter
—XXV—

Arnason Imports, Ltd. was the name of the shop, not one of those on the front row, which Fletcher had rather expected, but one of those tucked into a nook toward the rear of a maintenance recess between another import company and a jeweler's. It wasn't a bad address. But it wasn't a shop of the quality that the address might have indicated, either, and Fletcher had second thoughts about the junior-juniors, the hour—which meant an area less trafficked than it would have been in mainday. The jeweler's was closed. The other business was open, but it had a sign saying No Retail.

"Not real prosperous," he said, with flashes on the dock-sides of his ill-spent youth. "Just go slow." Jeremy was tending to get ahead of him. "Listen, you. I want it understood. No smart moves here. Believe me."

"Yessir," Jeremy said, bounced on the balls of his feet in that nervous way he had, and charged ahead.

There was no surety the stick was even in the shop. "Calm *down*," Fletcher snapped, and the kids assumed a far quieter disposition. Jeremy was still first through the door, setting off a buzzer, no melodious bell.

A man stood up from behind a desk all but over-whelmed by stacks of oddments, boxes, masks, statuary, shelves with crystal specimens, more of the plastic bou-quets, fiber mats and dried plants, dried fish, one truly large one mounted on a board. There was a whole mounted animal with horns, at which Vince exclaimed, "Wild," and Linda looked appalled.

Jeremy was on to the display cabinets like a junior whirl-wind, looking under counters, into cabinets.

"Wild," Vince said again.

It was impressive. But the man at the counter was on his way to panic.

Fletcher whipped out the card and laid it on the table. "You came recommended," he said. "Man said you had a good stock."

"Best this side of Cyteen," the man said. "Mr. . . ."

"James," he improvised, the fastest name to any Neihart tongue. But then he remembered the Family name problem, and settled fast on what he knew was a Unionside ship. "Off *Boreale.*"

"Union."

"Out of Cyteen. Just doing a little business, here and there, got a few contacts. Man asked me to, you know, pick him up a couple of good items at our turnaround point. He's govern-ment." He'd heard about Cyteen officials on the take. It was rumored, at least, on Pell docks. "I'm looking."

"Got any downer stuff?" Jeremy blurted out.

"The kid's crazy about downers," Fletcher said, at that ner-vous dart of the eyes, and the man darted a glance back. "What I'm interested in is just the unusual. The shop that referred us here, you know, said you might have some back-room stock."

"There's the warehouse." Cagey answers. Saying nothing.

"Not interested in what you can see elsewhere. The man gives me money on account, I'm not bringing him junk, you know what I mean?"

"What price range are you interested in?"

"Say my captain knows. Say that kind of finance. Not interested in running contraband, understand. Just the unique piece. No boxes of stuff. Seen enough woven mats to last me. Stuff's junk. Get those damn bugs in it and it falls apart."

It was a piece of truth, something somebody who was dealing in downer goods would know. If a mat was smuggled and not passed through sterilization, microfauna came in the reeds. Destruction of whole illicit collections had resulted.

"No fools here. We irradiate everything."

"Show me," he said, and shot the kids a be-still look.

The man went to the back door, and left it open while he rummaged just the other side of the door.

He's got something, Jeremy lip-sent, exaggerated enough to read across a station dock, and he lip-sent back, *Shut up.*

The man came back with several bundles. Unrolled mats, weavings, old ones. Fletcher's heart beat fast. He knew which band had produced them.

He managed to brush idle fingertips across the simple pattern and look bored.

Another mat unrolled.

And Satin's stick landed atop it, unfolded out of tissue.

"God." From the back of Fletcher's elbow, Jeremy eeled past Vince and picked it up, held it up to the light.

"Careful!" the man said.

"Jeremy," Fletcher said severely, and willed the boy quiet, his own heart beating hard. He took the artifact from Jeremy's hand. "Looks genuine."

"Riverside culture, maybe Wartime. A lot of stuff got up here then."

When Mazian's forces occupied the planet and took what they damn well pleased.

"I'd believe it," he said easily. He'd dealt in pilfered goods. Never this class of article. *Price* might be the giveaway of an amateur. "What's your valuation?"

"Oh, you've done this before."

"I said."

"You come in here with kids . . . "

"Good cover." He shrugged. "Say I could probably meet this. Customs is my problem."

"I'll arrange which agent. If you meet the price."

This man was going to arrange which customs agent dealt

with *Boreale*. This was no small-time operator. And he'd believed the *Boreale* business.

"So . . . " he said carefully. "What are we talking about in exchange?"

"Sixty thousand."

"Fifty."

"Sixty firm. This isn't Green."

"Fifty-five."

"Fifty-nine and that's the bottom."

"Fifty-nine's fine, but I've got arrangements to make." He was faking it. He had no idea how transactions like this regularly passed, and he dreaded any move, any helpful word from the junior-juniors crowded up against the counter on either side of him.

"Arrangements are easy." The man reached for a paper invoice book. "You arrange your captain does a bulk buy, Earth origin export. I'll give you a certificate. It'll be included." The man scribbled on the paper, tore it off, handed it to him. "That's the total price. It's in there. You see that clears the bank. It'll be in the crate."

He wasn't such a fool as to trust the system. He gave the man a doubting look. "Got to talk to my captain, understand."

"The deal's not done till that payment's in the account. Anybody comes in here, he could buy it if he meets the price."

Oldest sales push in the book. In Babylon, they must have used it. He gave the man the eye.

"You get an offer, you go right ahead," he said. "Takes time to get things set up. Can I reach you mainday?"

"Ask for Laz. My nephew does days. He'll find me."

"Got it." Figure that a place like this had the owner working alterday. Fletcher pocketed the slip of paper, collected the junior-juniors, and left.

They walked out of sight of the door before Jeremy's patience fractured.

"Let's get the cops!"

"Wait a minute!" He grabbed Jeremy's shirt, stopping a

rush to justice. "This isn't a short-change job. This is major."
Jeremy squirmed to be free and he tightened his grip. "You
think this guy doesn't have a deal with the cops?"

Jeremy stopped struggling.

"We're going to do exactly what we told him we'd do.
We're going to go to our ship's captains and see what they
think."

"They're in meetings," Vince said.

"So we find Bucklin or somebody and see if we can get
word to them. You just calm down and let's get back to the
sleepover. They'll show up there. It was a smart idea, looking
in the curio shops. We've got the facts. Let's just use our
heads."

"Yessir," Jeremy said, rubbing his arm.

He'd probably grabbed too hard. He was sorry about that.
He patted Jeremy on the back and the lot of them walked back
toward the twos, toward the gathering-place of *Boreale* crew
and *Finity* crew alike, with their packages and their information.

Found it and found a whole lot else, Fletcher was thinking.
He knew operations like this only by what he'd heard by rumor
and by his study in planetary cultures. If shops like this existed
on Pell, they existed on a far smaller scale.

The warehouse behind the shop, that was likely something
to behold. And his instincts reminded him that no local
authority had done anything about it. Point two, the man
talked confidently about handling customs. About an elaborate system of invoices and cargo packed as what it wasn't.

All of that said the system was well-organized, didn't fear
the law much so long as he put on a good appearance for the
honest officials that might contact the product on its way out,
and that cops on the docks didn't stray into that shop. All his
instincts from his own days on the rough side of the docks said
that the man was doing what he did fairly well out in the open.
There were more curio shops here than anywhere he'd seen,
and he'd bet none of them bore very close inspection.

Ordinary theft didn't shock him. He knew that went on.
This, however, the traffic in planet-produced goods, and the
stripping of planets of irreplaceable artifacts, artwork, human
history and downer faith . . . this was foul.

And dangerous. Slipping goods past the systems designed
to stop it, also happened to slip them past all the safeguards
that detected small lifeforms, and transferred biological materials into places they might, yes, die because they were foreign. But they might not, too.

Satin's gift had come into hands like that. Satin's gift had
found a system like this. Mazian as an enemy . . . yes. He was
in favor of that. But he wanted something done about this
trade, which didn't engage interest on an international level
the way something did that involved guns.

They were worried about Cyteen using genetic warfare . . .
but they smuggled stuff like this.

He brought his small troop into the Xanadu's lobby and
looked for officers.

There was Lyra.

"Got to talk to you," he said. Keeping the junior-juniors
quiet until they could get Lyra to a quiet and private area near
the bar was difficult but he managed it, and Lyra looked at him
with brow furrowed.

"What is this?"

"We found the stick," he said.

Lyra looked blank a moment.

"In a curio shop," Jeremy said, because he wasn't going
fast enough. Jeremy fairly vibrated with nerves. Linda and
Vince were bobbing and restraining themselves with utmost
difficulty. "They're smugglers," Vince said. "They have a
whole back warehouse full of stuff."

"This isn't a joke, right?"

"No joke," Fletcher said. "Each stick is unique as a finger-
print. I know this one. We tracked it down. We're absolutely
sure. They offered me a deal on it, sixty thousand and a fake
cargo invoice, arranged through the captain."

"Through the Old Man?"

"I said I was from *Boreale*."

Lyra looked flummoxed and halfway amused. "This is a good one. —What in hell were you doing out searching with the junior-juniors?"

"It was us tracked it down!" Jeremy said in his defense. "We figured the skuz thief would sell it here, so we just checked the curios, and when we said downer stuff, they sent us to this shop, Blue 512, just right across from *Boreale*! Isn't that a kick?"

"You get to quarters," Lyra said. "You leave this to older crew, junior-junior. —Fletcher, I'll get this information to Bucklin. The captains are at supper. Or were." She checked her watch. "I'll see if I can call Bucklin."

"Yes'm," Fletcher said. "Tell him I can ID the stick, if they need that. Meanwhile we're going to go upstairs."

"Game parlor!" Linda cried.

"Room!" Jeremy voted. "So we can hear when they call."

"Room," Fletcher said, and to forestall protests from Linda and Vince: "The first-run vid, and lunch at the Lagoon tomorrow. Move."

The protocols of which ship to contact first and by what rank officer were sticky in the extreme. It was a case of insult those most disposed to be your allies or flatter those most likely to be your opposition, and the Old Man simply phoned a complete mixed bag from the pricey restaurant and wanted to meet their senior captains for drinks.

They held an impromptu high-level strategy meeting in the tiny banquet room of one of Esperance's fanciest restaurants, next to the bar, and security ranged from *Finity* crew in silver and immaculate *Santo Domingo* crew in dark greens, to the polychrome non-regulation of *Scottish Rose* and *Celestial*, and finally to the tasteful blues of *Chelsea* and the blue-greens of *Boreale*.

They started out the drinking and the meeting with those

captains and solved the protocol problem with each of the captains there calling someone and inviting them for drinks . . . on a massive tab.

JR paced himself with the alcohol, and hobnobbed and good-fellowed his way around the room. The restaurant had planned to close, and a staggering bribe from *Finity* said it didn't. The crowd milled, socialized, Madison and the Old Man holding court at this table and that, and secondary captains began to arrive in numbers that spilled out of the banquet room and into the bar. Then the small restaurant. It was Alliance captains, it was Family ships hauling for Union, it was Union *Boreale*, whose reputation for strait-laced probity and cloned-man humorlessness dissolved in multiple bottles and a wit that had the *Celestial* and *Santo Domingo* captains alike wiping their eyes, red-faced.

Notably, *Champlain*'s captains didn't get an invitation. "I'll bet my next year of liberties *Champlain*'s well aware," JR said to Bucklin, who was part of security. "I wouldn't put it past their station friends to try to slip a ringer onto the wait staff. Certainly they're not getting any sleep this watch."

"I'll see if we can find out from the waiters if anybody's suspect in that department," Bucklin said.

Meanwhile JR brushed up against Madelaine, who'd also shown up. Madelaine and Blue both were having a good time.

"No few legal offices here," Madelaine informed him, among other tidbits. "That chap over there with the mustache, that's *Santo Domingo*. Old friends."

The ships' lawyers were getting together, frightening thought, mixing throughout the bar and restaurant.

Oser-Hayes figured in a number of conversations. So did the infamous lawsuit, as ship captains from both sides of the War wanted to know the progress of the action against Mazian, and as war stories and reminiscences were the bulk of the conversation.

Those, and the information someone had now let slip, that Pell and Mariner had come to terms with Union and that the old Hinder Star routes might see another rebirth via Esperance, which the local stationmaster was resisting.

The party now, with several new arrivals, outgrew the banquet room *and* the bar, and the talk now regarded profits that could be made on a new Earth route using Esperance as well as Mariner-Pell—except for the resistance of the Esperance administration, which was doing everything it could to hang on to a failing status quo.

The entire list of ships docked at Esperance, except *Champlain*, was represented in the restaurant and bar, and JR circulated along with the rest, called on to give the straight story about the lawsuit until he'd lost track of the times he'd told it, asked about the captaincy on *Finity's End* and the Old Man's health until he'd lost track of that subject, too. There was genuine concern about Captain James Robert, genuine interest in a young captain who carried the name.

"*Finity's* best kept secret," a woman said, shaking his hand. "Pleased to meet you." And proceeded to introduce him to half *Celestial's* senior crew. They were no longer just the captains present. In the way of spacer gatherings, it had spread to include several ranks down.

He edged around a group of senior officers and found Wayne, who'd just gotten back from dockside. Wayne gave him a slip of paper, said it was a security matter, and that required a trip over to one of the few lights in the room to read the note.

It was from Lyra.

The item we were searching the skin for has turned up in a shop in Blue. Instructions?

Damn, he thought. He couldn't detach Bucklin. They had a security need here as great as there was possible to have in this end of space.

But he signaled Wayne and took Wayne and the note out to the area where Bucklin and far more senior officers were standing watch.

He showed it to Bucklin, but he went on to show it to Tom R., who was in charge of security. "The hisa artifact that went missing at Mariner," he said quietly. "We've found it here. *Champlain* crew is the juniors' bet. No one's taken any action. I just got this."

"Madelaine should see this. So should the Old Man."

It seemed a good idea. Security rated the matter as above their heads, and he tended to agree. He dismissed Wayne back to Lyra to say they were working on the problem, and wove his way back through the dimly lit room toward Madelaine.

"The artifact," he said, "here, in a shop. *Champlain*, most likely."

"Oh, that's interesting," Madelaine said in a predatory way. "Absolute identification?"

"I don't know," he had to say. "But nothing hisa belongs in any shop here."

"Where's Fletcher?" Madelaine asked.

"I don't know that, either." All of a sudden he very much wanted to know that answer, wished he'd sent Wayne after that information, and it was almost worth chasing Wayne down to make sure. But Wayne had left, almost certainly, the room was crowded, and his mission was to the Old Man himself.

"Sir." He came up at the Old Man's shoulder. "A word. A brief word."

"Back in a moment." The Old Man rose carefully, left the table and the conversation with several old acquaintances, and moved into a dark corner where, by the nature of the party, there was privacy.

"What's the problem?" the Old Man asked.

"The juniors have found the hisa artifact in a shop in Blue. I don't know who found it, I don't know how we know that's the one, but that's the initial information."

"That's very interesting," the Old Man said, exactly as Madelaine had said.

"I thought you'd want to know. That's all."

"Keep it quiet for now. We'll talk. Tell them on no account talk to the police."

"Yessir," he said. "I'll send a courier back." One of the seniors in security, was his intention as he let the Old Man get back to his table and his conversation, but he made it no farther than the next table when Madison snagged him to know what that had been.

He shouldn't have sent Wayne back. He should have held him to serve as a messenger . . . mistake he'd not have made if he'd used his head.

He went to Bucklin, who had a pocket-com. "Call Lyra. Tell her no action. None."

"Yessir," Bucklin said, and made the call on the instant, noise and all.

That was handled, and wouldn't blow up. He went to Tom, the senior security chief present, and ordered a courier back to the Xanadu.

"I want to keep an eye on things," he said. "If somehow someone saw someone and got nervous, I don't want junior-juniors on the docks. It's already a bad idea, just with the meeting here."

"Yessir," Tom said.

He shouldn't have interfered in Bucklin's domain without asking Bucklin what he'd done. It was a kneejerk reaction, to have given that last order, involving junior crew. He wasn't pleased he'd done it; orders from too many levels were a guaranteed way to foul a situation up; and he went back to Bucklin and pulled *him* into a corner.

"I just ordered juniormost crew off the docks," he said. "Shouldn't have. Sorry."

"Beat you to it an hour ago," Bucklin said with the ghost of a smile. "Captain, sir."

They'd watched vid, waiting for a phone call. They'd played cards, waiting for a phone call.

"They've got to do something," Jeremy said. "I bet Lyra didn't even find anybody."

"She'll tell them when she can get hold of them," Fletcher

said, on the last of a bad hand. "They're talking war and peace, here. It's not like they can break off and go chasing after an illegal art dealer."

"Maybe we ought to put in a call to Legal," Vince said. "Madelaine could get a warrant and get that place locked down until they search it."

Vince had a touching faith in the law. Fletcher didn't. But it was late to argue the point. Linda had made two stupid plays, sheer exhaustion, and was still trying. He himself was done for, with the hand he was holding.

Vince calmly did for all of them.

"That's where all the cards were hiding," Linda said in disgust.

"Got you," Vince said. "Want to play again?"

They were playing at the table in the main room of the suite. Fletcher gathered up cards. "I think it's time to turn in. We don't know what we'll be into, tomorrow. We'd better get some sleep."

There were grumbles, the evening ritual, but only half-hearted ones. Jeremy was glum, and hindmost in quitting the table.

"Jeremy," Fletcher said, "it's not the stick that matters. We know. We found it. If something happens, that's bad, but it's not the end of everything. You hear what I'm saying? Cheer up. We'll do what we can tomorrow, and if we get it back we'll celebrate and go to the Lagoon for supper. There's two *weeks* of liberty. We've got time."

"Yessir," Jeremy said faintly, and went off to bed with Vince. Exhausted. They all were. They'd stayed up far later than usual, after a day in which they'd ricocheted all over Blue Sector, to every amusement the rules allowed, and now they were faced with repeats of the notable things to do, leaving him nothing with which to bribe the juniors into good behavior.

It was possible the rules might ease a little and let them spill over into Green, particularly if *Champlain* pulled out—

he thought that if he were the captain of *Champlain*, he'd want to pull out very early, before, say, *Finity's End* and *Boreale* finished their business; and that if he were in that unenviable position, he'd want to take a route that didn't lay along *Finity*'s route. *Champlain* wasn't a big ship, by what he understood, and what it could do was probably limited.

So he could sleep, tonight, secure in the knowledge they'd answered the burning question what had happened to Satin's stick. He didn't want to think what *could* happen to it; and from the early hope that perhaps it would be something the captains could handle expeditiously, now he was looking to the more reasonable hope there would be some kind of legal action. The alterday courts were for drunks and petty disputes. The mainday courts were where you'd start if you had a serious matter.

But even so, he'd told the kids the truth: war and peace was at issue, and artifact smuggling was down on the list somewhere below cargo-loading and refueling and *Champlain*'s next port and current behavior.

He undressed, settled into a truly luxurious bed, ordered the automated lights to dark, and shut his eyes.

Tomorrow, maybe.

Or maybe they'd work quietly, behind the scenes, and come down on that shop with some sort of warrant before they left. It was disappointing to kids, who believed in justice and instant results, two mutually exclusive things, as the Rules of the Universe usually operated, and he didn't want them to lose their natural expectation of justice somehow working . . . but it wasn't a reasonable hope in light of everything else that was going on.

Other *Finity* staff were tired, too. And if they'd hit the pillows the way he had, the deep dark was just too easy to fall into.

Dark and then the gray of hisa cloud.

The view along Old River's shores didn't change. But Old River changed by the instant.

So did he, standing on that bank and watching the wind in the leaves. He and Old River both changed. So did the wind. And leaves fell and leaves grew and trees lived and died. The view wasn't the same. It just looked that way. And the young man who stood there, like the river that flowed past the banks, wasn't the same. He just looked that way.

He wanted Satin to know he'd tried. He wanted to know whether Melody and Patch were having a baby . . . and just wondering that, he saw a darkness in the v of a fallen log and the hill above him, a dark place, a comfortable place, for downers.

He knew who lived there. It was a dream, he knew it was a dream, and he knew that its facts were suspect as the instantaneity of its scene-changes, but he was relatively sure what he saw, and who he knew was there.

In this dream it was months and months since he'd left. Half a year. And in the swift hurtling of worlds around stars and stars around the heart of the galaxy and galaxies through the universe . . . a certain time had passed, in the microcosm of that living world. He had fallen out of time, but Melody and Patch lived to a planet's turning and the more and less of Old River's flowing, and the lights and darks of the clouds above. For them, time moved faster, and a baby was growing, a new baby that wasn't him.

The young man stood on the bank . . . in the curious way of the dream he thought of himself objectively, the visitor from the stars, timeless, skipping forward or backward.

He stood in one blink, this young man, in the shabby cheap apartment of his infancy, seeing the woman dead in the rumpled sheets, and aching because he'd known her so little.

He stood watching a gang of young boys swagger along Pell docks, and was both sorry for them and dismayed. They were such fools, and thought they knew the shape of the universe.

He stood in the deep tunnels of Pell, and watched downers move through that dark, muffled against the cold and carrying lights that made them look like isolate stars.

He stood beside the fields on Downbelow, and looked for Bianca among the workers, but couldn't find her. The young man walked from place to place, and saw others he knew . . . stood in the corner of Nunn's office, and watched the man work . . . visited the mess hall, and watched the young men and women come and go. But the one face eluded him.

He needed to find her. He didn't know quite why, but it was urgent, and he apprehended some danger. He tried to think where to search next, and went from place to place, past people who didn't care, and downers bent on games.

A storm was coming. But that wasn't the danger. The danger was shapeless, and had an urgency he couldn't identify.

"Fletcher!"

He jumped, leaden, and tangled in sheets and dark.

"Fletcher!"

It was Vince's voice. It was Vince's shadow at his bedside, scarcely visible against the faint glow of the ceiling.

He wasn't on Downbelow. Bianca wasn't lost. He was in the dark of a sleepover at the end of the space lanes and a kid he was watching had an emergency.

"Fletcher, Jeremy's gone."

Where would Jeremy go? He was still half asleep, and confused about where he was . . . he'd been jolted out of a vivid dream of loss and searching, and it wasn't Bianca missing, it was Jeremy, and it was real.

Esperance. The Xanadu.

"System. Lights on."

Light began, a soft flare of color in the ceiling.

"When?" he asked Vince.

"I don't know. I just woke up and it's a big bed and he wasn't there."

The light was brighter by the moment, washing down the walls like veils of pink and eye-tricking gold.

Fletcher rolled to the edge of the bed, trying to think, and thinking about Esperance, and game parlors and kids sneaking downstairs in the sleepover for hot chocolate and breakfast . . .

But it was Esperance. And there was more danger here than drunken Belizers.

"If he's gone after breakfast I'll skin him. Is Linda awake?"

"I don't know."

"Wake her. Everybody get dressed. If he's downstairs I'll lock him in quarters when I catch him. God knows how he got past the watch." Docks outside began to form itself in his mind's eye. Jeremy's discontent. Meetings among the captains. Jeremy going out to find an officer who could get something in motion . . .

. . . regarding the hisa stick. The shop, and the man who ran it.

It wasn't just a kid skipping down to get breakfast or play vid games. Jeremy might have gone back to the ship, maybe to contact somebody through ops, to try to talk to an officer high enough to authorize something.

He put on clothes as fast as he could find them in the gathering light. He heard the kids in the next room, heard Linda invite Vince to get out so she could dress. She was hurrying.

Fletcher shoved on his boots. The room lights were up to half, now, in their aurora-like dawn, but the light from the common hall flared bright and white as Vince entered the bath.

Vince came out again. Instantly. "Fletcher, you got to come look!"

To the bathroom? He didn't ask. He went.

In filmy white soap, written across the mirror:
For the honor of the ship.

The Old Man was still drinking coffee, but the captains of *Celestial* and *Rose* were both in agreement about the agreement to cut Mazian's suppliers out and more than a little high on enthusiasm and a new-found friendship. Other captains, more sober, were sitting at tables, arguing the fine details, no few of them clustered about the Old Man.

And the goings on of *Boreale* and *Champlain* were a major interest. Topics like *black market* and *Mazian* always pricked ears up, most of the ships represented in the group quite honestly willing to deal with any paying market, but not in favor of behavior that went across the unspoken codes of conduct. There was debate about *Champlain*'s conduct. There was distrust of *Boreale*'s rigging as a warship conducting trade; there was uneasy, probing converse between ships operating under Union registry and ships operating as Alliance traders, heads together at small tables in the bar. The private dining room had grown too crowded for anyone to sit except the Old Man and his constantly changing, high-rank table companions.

Deals were being cut. The dock safety office had made one visit to be sure the party was orderly: the establishment had exceeded occupancy limits, but nobody wanted to deal with currently good-humored ship's officers.

Deals not only regarding the Alliance treaty. There were deals being done for route-timing, two and three ships agreeing what they'd carry and when, to assure better prices for their goods. There were a couple of younger officers casting looks at each other that said they might end up sleeping-over.

C.J. Cherryh

JR thought by now he'd talked to every individual in the room, and rehearsed his information and answered questions multiple times for each. He'd gone light on the wine. He'd eaten bar crackers that lay like lead in his stomach and taken to soft drinks as the only remedy for the crackers.

He'd wondered about the Old Man's stamina and now he was questioning his own, granted that the Old Man had drunk only coffee and that the Old Man had been sitting down throughout. Madison had joined him, and that table of mostly white-haired seniors had gotten into heavy debate at this late hour.

He was numb. Just numb. Maybe it was because he *hadn't* paced himself, and the old men of the ship knew better, and had known what they were setting up, and had deliberately let this turn into the crush of bodies and hours-long party it had begun to be.

Nobody had gotten rowdily drunk, nobody had been a fool. These were the heads of spacer Families, given a chance to get the lowdown on *Finity*'s business . . . that had been the lure to bring them; then to vent their frustrations with international politics with internationals in their midst; and finally to cut specific deals. These people were high on adrenaline and high-stakes trade. And the fact that *Finity* had supplied a little of the captain's stock to the event, in the merchanter way of hospitality, was a finesse, as *Rose*'s captain had said, that they never got out of the standoffish stationmaster of Esperance.

Oser-Hayes buying a bottle and drinking with merchanter captains? Not damn likely, in JR's opinion, having met the man. It was a new enough experience for the captain of *Boreale*, who, however, was not a stupid man. Captain Jacques, as he became known about the room, was a novelty, one of the faceless Unioners given a human face, a handsome, youngish senior captain with the ramrod bearing of Union military very evident about him, but willing to lift a glass and grin ear to ear in a shocking good humor.

It was possible to *like* the man, and his secondary captains

. . . only three of *Boreale*'s captains present. The unhappy fourth languished on duty, a rule that couldn't be breached.

The captain of *Rose* grew so friendly as to slap the captain of *Boreale* on the shoulder, and that immaculate uniform took a dose of whiskey, all in good humor.

A regular human being, JR heard someone say—before the pocket-com went off.

He went to the hall by the restrooms, which had a little quiet.

"This is JR."

"Lyra here. Jeremy's missing."

"Where's Fletcher?"

"Fletcher was asleep. He's gone after Jeremy, if he hasn't come looking for you—"

"He hasn't. Keep this off the airwaves." Any station could monitor pocket-com traffic. This administration was hostile. And the report should have gone up the chain to Bucklin, before it came to him, but Lyra had been on her own for hours, with a piece of information and a problem and long past time it should have gone to a senior officer. He didn't fault her on that.

"Call the ship."

"I have called the ship. They said—"

"A courier's coming to you. Stay put. Sign off." If she weren't where she was supposed to be she would have said so; and he didn't want details and addresses going to potential eavesdroppers. He went out to the bar and snagged Bucklin. "Get Wayne if you can do it on your way to the door. Get to Lyra at the Xanadu. Get her info and move on it stat-stat-stat. Run!"

"What's—" Bucklin began to ask.

"Fletcher!" he said, and went looking for another *Finity* captain.

Fletcher ran, heart pounding, dodged around the sparse foot traffic of the end of alterday, just before maindawn, the

time when the docks were slowest and most quiet. He'd run all
the way from the two hundreds. The kid had gotten past security—and so had he, just advised Lyra he was going to try to
catch the kid short of his goal and left Linda and Vince on
orders to go explain to Lyra or any senior they could knock out
of bed.

Arnason Imports. The sign wasn't neon. It was painted, in
the way of the better shops, at its end of the nook position next
shops far gaudier. He ran across deck plates washed in neon
green and red from a souvenir shop, dodged a drunk window-
shopper, and walked the last distance, trying to get his
breathing under control.

He'd say the kid had ducked curfew and the captain was
looking.

That was why he'd run. He'd shake the kid till his teeth rattled when he got him out of there.

The inconspicuous sign in the window posted hours as
Mainday & Alterday Service.

The smaller one said: Back in an Hour . . . with no indication how long ago that hour had started.

He tried the latch.

Knocked on the double window . . . quad-layered plastic
that could withstand space itself, if the dock should decom-
press.

The kid had gotten here. There was trouble, and the kid had
found it. He was sure of it. He wasn't quite to panic. But he hit
the window hard enough to bruise his fist.

Hit it again.

It wasn't discreet. It wasn't, probably, smart. He didn't
think he should have done that. But he'd flung down the challenge in a fit of temper, and if he walked off now, they might
have Jeremy, and a notion that questions were about to come
down on them.

If they were in there, the *they* who were dealing in stolen
goods, he'd become a problem to them vastly exceeding the
problem a kid posed.

And if the alterday man was still there, that man knew Jeremy's face, knew Jeremy's business, and knew his face as part of the same sticky problem.

He was in it. He couldn't let them keep that door shut. He couldn't walk off. He could just hope that Lyra got JR or somebody. Fast.

He hit the window again, hard enough he thought he might have broken his hand.

The door opened. He was facing a man he didn't know. "Come inside," the man said, seizing his arm, and pulled. A hard object came against his ribs. He was facing the man he'd met last night, two others—and Jeremy.

That was a weapon up against his side. He didn't know what, and didn't complicate his situation by moving. Jeremy kicked a man to get free, and the man hit him.

"My captain knows where we are," Fletcher said, caught in a time-slowed moment in which he had not the least idea what to do, but his priorities were clear: not to get himself or Jeremy shot or taken elsewhere. "They're on their way. Now what?"

"Son of a bitch!" The man from their first meeting was livid. And scared. "They've got to have a warrant . . ."

"Not our captain," Jeremy said in his higher voice. "You're in deep trouble."

The man slapped Jeremy—far too hard. Dockside years of bullies schooled Fletcher to keep absolutely still. Jeremy wasn't dead. Bleeding, yes. They stood in a shop full of oddments, shelves, specimens, and three guys in a serious lot of trouble with two prisoners and an artifact they didn't want—and with a whole network involved, Fletcher would just about bet.

"Seriously," he said to the man from last evening, "I'd consider making a phone call to your lawyers."

"Shut up!" the guy said, and the one holding him jerked his arm—not steady-nerved, Fletcher guessed; and in the next second the man hit him in the head. Dark exploded into his sight. He went to one knee . . .

"Fletcher!" Jeremy yelled, and he had the make on them, that these were men who *used* guns. He was blind for the moment, and wanted just to get close to Jeremy, get his hands on the kid. There were two ways out of this place. There was that storeroom; and the front door. And they'd think about the front door, but maybe not the other.

"Move!" The guy with the gun jerked him by the collar, and he staggered up and moved toward Jeremy. There were four of them, last-night holding onto Jeremy, short-and-wide between him and Jeremy, man-with-the-gun behind him and skinny-man to the side with another gun . . . he tracked all that, saw the door, and stayed docile while he passed short-and-wide with a gun in his back and last-night holding onto Jeremy, steering him for the back door to this place.

"Captain's going to have your guts!" Jeremy said, and kicked at the man's shins. The man maintained a grip on his arm and shoved him at the door, using one hand to open it; and they were on the verge of going where they'd have a simultaneous accident.

No time. Fletcher spun around and knocked man-with-a-gun into the shelves. Boxes came down; and he didn't wait for skinny-man to close in. He dived at last-night and saw a knife—feinted as if *he* had one and the fool's nerves reacted. The knife went out of line just that far, and he shot an arm past the man's guard, and rammed him aside, trying to get through the door; but a shot ricocheted off it; and last-night was getting up.

He grabbed Jeremy and they ran past a row of stacked shelves, knocking down displays and merchandise on their way to the door.

And man-with-the-gun showed up in their path.

He stopped cold. Kid and all.

The man motioned back toward the storeroom.

The man would shoot. He believed that. But the police had sniffers. Blood anywhere and there was hell denying who'd been where. And now they were thinking; now man-with-the-gun was in charge, last-night being down and nursing a cut on his head.

"In there," man-with-the-gun said; and Fletcher kept a hand on Jeremy's shoulder, stifled one attempt at a revolt, and steered him on through the door.

They'd gotten smart. Skinny-man was waiting inside with a gun on them.

"All right," he said. "You want a deal—"

"Get them out of here!" last-night said. "Use the safety-exit."

The tunnels, Fletcher thought. The maintenance tunnels. The dark network of through which the conduits ran, the air ducts, emergency systems, wiring, everything.

Every station, like every other station. Same blueprint: just the neon signs were different. The whole might be different, but structure, on a modular level, was absolutely identical.

Catwalks, dark. Lose a body in the tunnels and they were lost. Maybe for a hundred years.

The gunman walked them back through the double row of shelves, back to a set of boxes.

"Move those."

"Do it," Fletcher said, afraid Jeremy would try something desperate. The kid was scared. And the kid had reflexes like steel springs. *"Do it, Jeremy."*

"Yessir," Jeremy said, and moved boxes back from the maintenance door.

Shopkeepers weren't supposed to have keys to places that gave access to the maintenance tunnels. The doors should be locked to the outside.

"Open it," the man said, and Jeremy didn't know how to work the latch. Skinny-man had to come close and do it, while Fletcher stood with the gun aimed at him.

"Fletcher," Jeremy said plaintively.

"They don't dare do us harm," Fletcher said, playing the absolute, trusting fool. "They know our ship knows where we are. And they'll search this entire section."

Skinny-man swung the door open. The draft that came out was cold, and the depths echoed as skinny-man, gun in hand, went out onto the catwalk.

"Move," the first man said, and Fletcher said carefully, "Go on, Jeremy."

Jeremy went and Fletcher followed right against him, took firm hold of the kid's sweater and gave a sharp tug when they passed the door and the gun. *Down!*

"Run!" he yelled then, and shoved skinny-man into the rail and slammed the door as he spun around.

Total black. The maintenance doors latched automatically when shut. There was that second of total blindness . . . but skinny-man's gun went off, a deafening sound, a burst of light that burst inches from him. Fletcher shoved him—shocked when he felt resistance fail and heard a body thump and clang down the pitch-black stairs.

"Jeremy, look out!"

He ran, down the steps in the dark, knew by memory where a landing was, where Jeremy's thin body was huddled, clinging to the metal stairs. The man falling must have gone right over him.

And in the same second, light blazed out from the opening door above.

He jerked Jeremy loose from his handhold and dragged him with him—oxygen atmosphere in Esperance tunnels, no need of a mask. He knew the turnings, the pitch of the stairs that turned and that let them go for another catwalk and along Main Maintenance Blue.

Pursuit came down the steps and thundered along the catwalk, shaking the rail in his hand. Somebody yelled—"Get a light, dammit!"

They were in Blue, in the fives. Next door, in the fours . . . they'd be in another recess of shops. They could come out there. Get away. Get help.

"Where are we going?" Jeremy gasped.

"Just stay with me!" He didn't want Jeremy behind him as

a target . . . but a buried bit of knowledge said it didn't matter where Jeremy was: they were shooting bullets, not needles, and a shot could go right through him and hit the kid. It was distance and turns that could save them, and he took them in the dark, in the lead.

The tunnel racketed with echoes, with footsteps of their pursuers trying to find them. "Get someone out there on the docks!" he heard. They had a light. The beam zigged and zagged across the maze of catwalks and girders and conduits, crossed ahead of them, and lent him light to see the webwork of structural support and tension cables and pipes.

He ran behind the beam, raced, lungs burning, toward the exit stairs for the next section of shops. Climbed, towing Jeremy after him. His sides ached. Jeremy's gasps were as loud as his as he reached the door and flipped the emergency latch on a locked door with expert fingers.

The door opened into warmer dark, almost stifling warmth after the cold of the tunnels.

Then light blazed around them. A burglar-light had come on. That meant an alarm had sounded somewhere. He tugged Jeremy through the door into the warehouse of some shipping company, and shut the door. It would latch. Please God it would latch. The other one had been jimmied, surely. They *didn't* know how to open the emergency latch: that was a tricky piece of business.

He got a breath. Two. Slid down the wall, feet braced on the store. "What did you think you were doing?"

Jeremy sank down by him, gasping. "Nobody *else* was going to do anything!"

"Dammit, they hadn't had *time!*"

"*Well, they weren't!* They didn't! I walked in there and I asked to see it again and I just ran—"

"Yeah, and they had a shoplifter lock and they triggered it from under the counter before you ever got to the door!"

"Yeah," Jeremy admitted, with a sheepish glance up. "The door locked."

He didn't want to explain to Jeremy how he'd ever learned about such tricks. The kid was white-faced, sweating.

"Thanks for the help," he said, elbow pressed against ribs aching from the running.

Meanwhile there was a burglar alarm reporting their presence to the police. He wasn't averse to being found by the cops. It was a lot better than where they'd been. But he wanted to get out of it if they could; and he'd caught breath enough. "Come on. Let's see if we can get a door open."

"Fletcher . . ."

He heard the note of fear. Heard the sound of footsteps coming down metal steps, behind the wall.

He grabbed Jeremy's arm, pulled him through the warehoused boxes and barrels toward a door that ought to lead out.

Hoping for a slow-down, for their pursuers to be baffled by the door latch.

Hearing it open behind them.

"Fletcher!" Jeremy had heard it.

He pulled Jeremy with him, ducked over an aisle and spotted a door with Fire Access in red and white letters. That *had* to have a simple turn-toggle latch.

They'd broken through. He heard the footsteps, back among the aisles of boxes. He felt the cold draft. His fingers sought the toggle and twisted. He shoved the door open, shoved, against the air-pressure from the docks. *Fools* had left the door open. He strained, established a crack, and a siren went off as a gale streamed into his face. Jeremy pushed. He braced it wide enough for Jeremy to get by him, and scraped his body out, jerked his leg free last, with a bash on the ankle as it slammed.

"Come on," he said, hurrying Jeremy along. He limped, forced the leg to operate despite the pain and ran for the docks.

Wanting all the witnesses they could get.

The wind began to wail again. They were opening that door behind them. A shot rang out, hitting what, he didn't wait to see.

There was a free-standing block of shops at a right angle to the warehouse frontage. He dragged Jeremy around the corner, in among spacers window-shopping and bar-hopping, ran through, startled outcries in their wake.

Gunshots came from behind them. There were outcries, outrage, panic. He kept running, dodged among passersby diving for cover.

"Stop!" someone yelled, and they didn't stop. Then Jeremy knocked someone down and fell, himself, twisting in Fletcher's grip as Fletcher tried to get him on his feet and keep going.

"What's going on," spacers around them demanded.

"Finity's End!" was all Fletcher could say, trying to hold a winded kid on his feet. "Somebody call our ship!" He tried to run on, but the pain in his side was all but overwhelming. Hands were helping him now, and he pulled Jeremy with him, hearing the sounds of resistance behind him, shouts and curses around the gunfire. There was nothing to say, no wind to say it with. He just took Jeremy the direction open to him, vision too jarred and blurred to know where he was going until he hit someone else and that someone grabbed him.

"Fletcher!"

Chad. Chad and Nike and Toby.

"The whole ship's looking for you!" Chad yelled at him.

"Guys after us," he tried to say, but about that time something sailed past their heads and rebounded off a pressure window, *bang!*

Fletcher ducked into the door-recess of a shop, nearest refuge, got down with arms across Jeremy, and Chad and Nike came in, flung themselves down as a barricade as all hell broke loose outside. Others spotted their shelter, younger crew, not *Finity* juniors, not even all of the same ship, but just at that moment a pressure window exploded right across the aisle of shop fronts.

"They're shooting!" Nike cried.

Chains were out of pockets among the spacers and people

were yelling. Jeremy's head came up and Fletcher shoved it down again. He was shaking. He'd seen riot break out. He saw this one. People with no idea what the fight was were arming themselves, spacers aiming at whatever spacers had at issue.

Like stationers with guns.

"The whole damn *dock*!" Chad said between his teeth. "God, Fletcher. How'd you manage this one?"

"They're trying to kill us!" Jeremy said indignantly.

Then the police showed up, a lot of police, with stunners they were using indiscriminately; and chains swung. Fletcher grabbed an indiscriminate armful of spacer kids and shoved heads down as a flung missile sailed past their refuge.

Nike risked her skull to reach up and try to shove the shop door open. It was locked, people inside with the door barred. She slammed the door with her fist, yelling, "We got *kids*, you damn fools! Open the door!"

Riot spilled past them, police literally stumbling into their shallow shelter, being pushed there by the crowd, driven in retreat by chain-swinging spacers. Someone stepped on Fletcher's leg and a chain cracked against the window over their heads.

Then to a shout of "There they are!" silver-suits showed up.

Bucklin reached them, Bucklin, Wayne, and a handful of *Finity* seniors, creating a barrier between them and the fight.

"Hold it!" Fletcher heard someone shout, then, a voice that hit nerves and stopped bodies in mid-impulse, and he knew that voice . . . he *thought* he knew it. "We've got *kids* here! Hold it, hold it, *stop right there, you*!"

JR. And *Finity* personnel. And when JR used that voice, bodies obeyed while minds were thinking it over. Fletcher's own nerves had jumped. Now he just caught his breath and waited for the missiles to stop.

But in the fading of riot around them, Chad and Nike got up. Toby did. Fletcher let Jeremy and the kids up, then, and hauled himself to his feet, with an ankle swollen tight against his boot.

"Hold it!" a voice yelled. The police advanced on the small collection they made, police, with stunners.

"Hold it!" JR said, interposing himself, and Bucklin and the other *Finity* personnel were right beside him. "Just back off," JR said to the Esperance police, and chains might have disappeared into pockets or trash cans, but the weapons were still there, Fletcher was sure of it. The police were armed, and there were nerve-jolted spacers down from the last encounter.

"Who are you?" The age-old police voice.

"Captain James Neihart, merchanter *Finity's End*, and those are *kids*, here. Nobody's pulling a weapon on our personnel."

"*Rose*'s kids, too," a spacer said, and came in close. "Damned if you wave a weapon near *Rose*'s juniors, mister. Just stow it."

"Get out of there," the lead officer said, and two of the kids who'd run in for shelter scrambled up and walked over to the man who spoke for *Scottish Rose*.

A lot more spacers had gathered, most in civvies, *Finity* personnel among them. The police were increasingly outnumbered, and calling for reinforcements. Fletcher heard the crackle of communications.

"Break it up," the lead cop said, and Jeremy yelled: "Those guys back there's trying to kill us!" And to JR: "This shop had the stick, sir! It's back there in the shop! There's guys chasing us."

"Not now," a spacer said with chilling finality.

"We have a breach in the maintenance system," the chief of the police said. "We have windows broken. We have—"

"They *shot* at us!" Jeremy cried indignantly. "They were firing shots all over!"

"Jeremy found stolen property in a shop," Fletcher said. "I went in to get Jeremy, and they took us both into the tunnels."

"*You're* responsible," the policeman said.

"We ran," Fletcher said. "We weren't the ones with the guns."

"You're under arrest," the cop said.

"No," JR said, and stepped between. So did Bucklin. In two blinks a wall of *Finity* officers and assorted spacers had interposed themselves, blocking the police from action.

"We've had a breach of the tunnels," the police objected.

"We have larceny of *Finity* property and assault against underage crew," JR said.

"Where's your ID?" the policeman asked. "You're not wearing any insignia. How do we know who you are?"

"See the black patch?" a spacer said, not even theirs. "That's *Finity*. He says he's a captain, mister, you get out of his way."

A policeman was using his clip-com. An electronic voice gave orders.

"We've got an impasse here," JR said. "And it's not going to budge. You can try to arrest a handful of kids, which is not going to happen. On the other hand, you can walk back to the five hundreds and take a look at Arnason Imports. And you can start with treaty violation, which is a little out of your territory, but I can guarantee Stationmaster Oser-Hayes will want all the information and evidence he can get. I can add traffic in illicit goods, handling stolen property, and all the way up to attempted murder. *Finity's End* is sovereign territory, gentlemen, and we don't surrender our personnel, but we'll be happy to file complaints and sign affidavits."

There was a muttering among the spacers, silence among the police. Fletcher kept right beside Jeremy. It wasn't a time to say anything. But there was also a human being he'd shoved off a ledge. While they were accounting for things—he might have killed somebody.

"The tunnel passages behind the import shop," Fletcher said very quietly. And the instincts of his younger years wanted to claim the man had slipped on the catwalks and that a shove had had nothing to do with it, but *Finity* had old-fashioned standards. "He was after us and I shoved him. Somebody needs to find him." He added, because he knew damage to those tunnel lines was dangerous. "Somebody needs to search the place. There's got to be lines hit. They were shooting left and right."

"We'll want a statement."

"*Our command* will file a complaint in their name," JR said. "Meanwhile they're complaining of stolen goods at Arnason's and we're filing charges right now. You want a statement, *I'll* give you a statement. We want an immediate search of the premises. I can assure you there'll be a warrant. Our legal office will be contacting your legal office in short order, and I'd suggest the Stationmaster may want answers from inside that shop."

The police were dubious.

"You get in there or we will," a spacer said. "They take *spacer* property in there, we'll go in after it."

And weakening. "We need a complaint and a warrant."

"You've got a complaint. Your warrant should be in progress."

A new group showed up. With a lot of silver hair involved. A lot of flash uniforms.

Ship's officers. A lot of them, Fletcher thought. He saw Captain James Robert at the head of it. Madison.

There was a muttering of amazement among the spacers. The station cops didn't initially, perhaps, know what they were facing.

"I'd say hurry with that warrant," JR said.

Oser-Hayes hadn't wanted a general meeting, involving the ships' captains . . . yet.

He had one.

JR settled at the end of the *Finity* delegation, knowing each and every face at the meeting, this time, every captain that had been at that convocation, every station officer that had been at the court.

There was a notable exception: *Champlain* was in the process of leaving Esperance. The station wouldn't—legally couldn't—prosecute a spacer whose captain chose to defend him, but they wouldn't allow that ship to dock, either.

Wayne poured water. Bucklin was standing watch at the door.

JR sat easily, cheerful in the foreknowledge of the captains' agreement to the terms of the Pell agreement. He sat easily as the Old Man with perfect self-assurance laid the hisa stick on the white table-cloth . . . a weathered, battered stick worth far more than the statuary outside or the furnishings of the room.

In this case it was worth *Champlain*'s reputation, *Finity*'s vindication, and a serious example of the Esperance administration's mounting legal problems. There were rumblings of discontent with Oser-Hayes' administration on a great many fronts, not only among spacers who'd broken up a little of the docks in the general discontent, but among stationers who'd known bribes were being passed to let certain businesses run wide open and in contravention of the law.

And others, who'd known there was something not too savory operating in the courts, the customs offices, the police department, and the tax commission. Name it, and somewhere, somehow, money had opened and shut doors on Esperance.

Nothing had ever united all the offended elements before. Now Oser-Hayes hoped there *wouldn't* be a vote of confidence . . . before they could get the Pell trade agreement finalized.

No, the police had not opposed a unified gathering of ship's captains, officers of the Merchanters' Alliance, and a warrant had fairly *flown* out of the judge's office, enabling a very interesting search of Arnason Imports and a series of arrests of Arnason owners anxious to prove they weren't the only company engaged in illicit trade.

The station news service and the trendy coffee shops were abuzz with official reports and delicious unofficial rumor.

They had an entire smuggling network exposed, not a harmless one, but a conduit for stolen goods reaching all sorts of

places . . . stolen artwork, artifacts, weapons, rejuv and pharmaceuticals including biologicals. Esperance had had something
for everyone—including war surplus arms that were listed as
recyclables. What they'd found in two weeks at Esperance was a
veritable black-market treasure trove . . . and what they'd dis-
mantled *wasn't* going to be back in operation the moment the
current set of merchanters pulled out.

Finity's End had an agreement with its brother merchanters
to pass the word, the total files, the archives on Esperance, and
for one ship to stay in dock until it had gotten agreements from
the next ship to arrive that *it* would linger at Esperance dock—
free of excess charges, of course—to pass the word in turn.

In short, there was a great deal of shakeout in a very short
time, a pace of change that stationers found stunningly fast,
but that spacers, accustomed to arrange their affairs in two-
week bursts of diplomacy, during docking, found completely
reasonable.

Yes, Oser-Hayes would have liked a four-, six-week delay.
Oser-Hayes would have spun things out for months and years
if it had involved station law, with injunctions, stays, post-
ponements, court orders and all manner of tactics.

Not with the Alliance legal system on a two-week push.

And amid all the smooth textures and simple pearl gray
and black of a modern conference room, amid all the modern
flash and glitter of spacers and the smooth, expensive fashion
of the stationmaster and his aides . . . a thing indisputably
organic, hard-used, hand-made of substances mysterious to
space-dwellers. Simple things, Fletcher had said, who'd been
on a world. Wood. Feather. Fiber.

Small, planet-made miracles.

"This," Captain James Robert said, with his hand on the hisa
artifact, "this is the artifact that led us to the problem. Not very
large. Not very elaborate. But important to one of my crew. It
was a gift from Satin . . . *Tam-utsa-pitan* is her name, in her
language. But Satin . . . to us humans. *She* sent it. A wish for
peace. That's what we've come here to find, if you please.

"And in that sense," the Old Man said, "more than humans sit at this table. Understand: we never could explain the War to the hisa, when the one who sent this asked what it all meant. Peace may be an easier concept for them. Hard for *us* to find. But, courtesy of the *Finity* crewman who lent this to our conference, consider this the living witness of the other intelligent species swept up in the events of our time. It'll lie here, while we try to find an answer and sign a simple piece of paper that can clear reputations—"

Oh, *watch* Oser-Hayes' expression when the Old Man held out that possibility: restoration, amnesty. A cleared name and a new chance to be immaculate. Damn sure Oser-Hayes knew the details of all the operations that had ever run. There might be nobody better to clean them up than a newly empowered convert to economic orthodoxy.

"Meanwhile," the Old Man said with a deep, assured calm, that voice that took the tumbling emotions of a situation and settled things to quiet, "meanwhile an old hisa's sitting beneath her sky waiting for that answer. And her peace is that much closer, in this place. I think we'll find it this time—at least among ourselves."

"The whole damn dock, Fletcher. Holes everywhere, a dozen ships emptied out . . ."

Chad exaggerated. Chad had that small tendency. But the court had just met, on the business of inciting a riot. It was vividly in memory.

"Fletcher came charging in there," Jeremy said, perched on the edge of the chair, his whole body aquiver. "They all had guns and Fletcher just lit into them with his bare hands!"

"Mild exaggeration," Fletcher said in an undertone. "You'll make me *ridiculous*. Hear me?"

Henley's Soft-bar was the venue. The station repair crews were patching the last leaks in the station's water and ventilation systems, rendering the name Arnason Imports highly unpopular among two residency blocs of very rich stationers who'd had their water cut off; and the man they'd found with two broken legs and a broken arm in the depths of the tunnels would recover from the fall, but not so easily recover from the charges filed against him.

Jeremy was sitting on Fletcher's right, Linda and Vince on his left. The headlines on the station news above the adjacent liquor bar were full of investigations and charges of which *Finity's End* was officially, today, judged innocent.

In celebration of that fact, the juniors of *Finity's End* owned a large table in Henley's. Bucklin and Wayne were on duty. They'd come in later. But meanwhile it was on JR's tab. So was the rest of the liberty, unlimited ticket to ride, as of this morning.

A round of soft drinks later, Madelaine showed up, in silvers, and patted Fletcher on the shoulder. "Told you how they'd rule," Madelaine said, and pressed a kiss on Fletcher's ear, to the laughter of the table.

But Fletcher didn't flinch. He caught Madelaine's hand and squeezed it, turning in his chair, looking into Madelaine's eyes. Madelaine the dragon. Madelaine, who'd led the effort in court.

"Grandmother," he said, and amended that, stationer-style: "Great-gran. You're a damn good lawyer. Sit down. Have a sip. JR's buying."

"Uniform," Madelaine reminded him. "Even if you're perfectly proper. Later. On the ship. When we undock. Behave. I got you out of this one, you. Don't break up the furniture."

Madelaine was off with a pat on his shoulder. The table was momentarily quieter, everyone eavesdropping.

The hearing today might have been a formality, a foregone conclusion—a verdict against *Finity* would have provoked another chain-swinging riot. But the court had had him scared, on principle. Courts could rule. Things could change. Anything could be taken away. Rule of his life. If it was important to you, and the courts got involved, anything could be taken away.

And he didn't want things taken away right now. He had something to lose—like three junior-juniors, one fairly scuffed-up, all sitting with him sipping soft drinks and figuring out how to spend the wildest liberty of their young dreams.

Like the senior-juniors, who were making tentative, wary approaches to him, under a flag of truce.

Sue hauled out cash chits when the next drinks came. "One round's on me, my tab," Sue said without quite looking at anybody. "Even's even, then. All you guys."

It wasn't the money. It wasn't the drinks. It was the acknowledgement.

"Appreciated," Fletcher said, all that anybody said.

It was a start on repairs. He bought all the senior-juniors a round, in spite of the free tab, because it was the gesture that was important. It dented the finance he had left, but that was the way you did things. It was the gestures that counted. You took a joke, you paid one back. You got as good as you gave. And you owned up when you'd screwed up. Simple rules. Rules that made sense to him in a way things never had.

They ate, they played rounds of vid-games, they had dessert, and they walked back to the sleepover in a group, all the juniors except the ones on duty.

Fletcher lay in bed in the Xanadu that night watching the illusory colors drift across a dark ceiling, thinking he'd talk to Jake about an apprenticeship when he got aboard . . .

Thinking, so easily, of grayed greens, and Old River, and falling rain.

Thinking of a kid growing up, in a cabin alone while the ship rode through combat, a kid who'd written high and wide *ship's honor*, when what he really wanted to save was his own.

He got up and walked back to the kids' rooms, looked in on Linda's; and she was asleep. Jeremy's and Vince's, and they were asleep, too.

They were all right. Jeremy had bruises and scrapes and so did he, but those would all have faded, the other side of jump, and they were leaving in two days.

Some things faded, some things grew stronger. I love you wasn't quite in a twelve-year-old's vocabulary. But it was in that brown sweater the kid almost lived in. It was in the look he got, wanting his approval, his advice, in the couple of fragile years before a kid knew everything there was possibly to know.

He couldn't go back, and sit on that bank for the rest of his life and watch Old River roll by. He couldn't look at a forever-clouded, out-of-reach heaven, knowing the stars were up there, and that all that was human went on in the Upabove.

He couldn't sit on a station for months, waiting for his ship to come back to him, out of a dark that had begun to be more real and more present in his thoughts than sunrises and sunset had once been.

He'd been to the farthest edge of human civilization. And even it wasn't foreign to him. The dark of space was where he lived, where he knew now he would always live. The bright neon of stations, the brief, surreal passage through station lives . . . that was carnival. Life for spacers was something else, out there, within the ships.

He couldn't describe that view to a stationer. Couldn't tell Bianca, when they met, what it was he'd found. He only knew he'd begun to move in a different time than anything that swung around a sun. He could love. He could feel the pangs of loss. It would hurt—there was no guarantee it wouldn't. But there was so much . . . so very much . . . that had snared him in, hurried him along with the ship and kept him moving. For the first time in his life . . . moving, and knowing where he belonged.

Their cargo was Satin's peace. Not a perfect one. Not one without maintenance cost. But the best peace that fallible humans could put together. Overseeing it, making it work . . . that was their job.

"Fletcher?" Jeremy hadn't been asleep. Or picked his presence out of the air currents. Or heard his breathing. The kid was uncanny in such things.

"Just being sure you were here," he said.

"I'm not going anywhere. Won't ever duck out on you again, Fletcher. I promise."

"I'll hold you to that," Fletcher said.

C.J. CHERRYH is the prolific, Hugo Award-winning author of *Downbelow Station*, *Cyteen*, *Rider at the Gate* and almost 50 other books. She lives in Oklahoma.

EXPLORE NEW WORLDS OF WONDER AND EXCITEMENT WITH HUGO AWARD-WINNING AUTHOR C.J. CHERRYH!

"One of the finest writers SF has to offer."
— *Science Fiction Chronicle*

☐ **Cloud's Rider**
   (0-446-60-424-0, $5.99, USA)($6.99 Can.)

☐ **Cyteen**
   (0-446-67-127-4, $14.99, USA)($18.99 Can.)

☐ **Heavy Time**
   (0-446-36-223-9, $4.99, USA)($5.99, Can.)

☐ **Hellburner**
   (0-446-36-451-7, $5.50, USA)($6.99, Can.)

☐ **Tripoint**
   (0-446-60-202-7, $5.99, USA)($6.99, Can.)

☐ **Rider at the Gate**
   (0-446-60-345-7, $5.99, USA)($6.99, Can.)

AVAILABLE AT BOOKSTORES EVERYWHERE FROM

 **WARNER BOOKS**

1035